D0070660

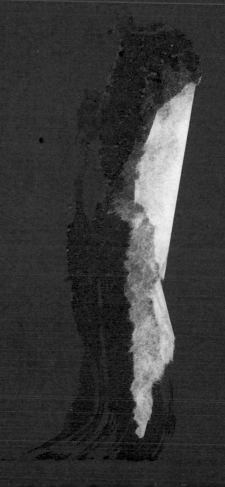

THE HORRORS OF LOVE

Jean Dutourd

The Horrors of Love

Translated from the French
by Robin Chancellor

1967
Doubleday & Company, Inc.
Garden City, New York

All of the characters in this book
are fictitious, and any resemblance
to actual persons, living or dead,
is purely coincidental.

LES HORREURS DE L'AMOUR by Jean Dutourd © 1963, Éditions Gallimard

Library of Congress Catalog Card Number 67–12873
Copyright © 1967 by Doubleday & Company, Inc.
All Rights Reserved
Printed in the United States of America
First Edition

To Camille, dearer to me than any work of creation,
I dedicate this book which filled two years of our life.

J. D.

"And let's get on a bit faster," said Blondet. "You're rambling."

"Isaure," continued Bixiou, looking askance at Blondet, "wore a simple white crêpe dress with green ribbons; she had a camellia in her hair, a camellia at her waist, another camellia at the hem of her skirt and a camellia—"

"Oh, come on! This is like Sancho's three hundred goats!"

"Therein lies all literature, dear boy. *Clarissa* is a masterpiece, there are fourteen volumes of her, and the most woodenheaded playwright would cram the whole of them into a single act. So long as I amuse you, what do you have to complain of?"

Balzac, *La Maison Nucingen*

THE HORRORS OF LOVE

I told him time and again he should write a book: nobody can tell a story the way he can. One day, for instance, he gave me a two-hour account of a cyclone in Guadeloupe he had witnessed when he was about twelve. Not one detail, not one touch of poetry was missing. I saw the earth cower like a frightened beast, the leaden sky, the petrified trees, the stricken people. Then out of his mouth the wind came roaring, he unleashed the tidal wave, the roof tops (if not the very houses) whirled into the sky. He himself, a little boy in this terrestrial shipwreck, had been lashed with ropes to a stout post like a captain to his mast. And so he had remained all through the night, for at least ten hours. Toward the end of the tale, after the cyclone had swept over the island like a gigantic humming top, I could actually see the orange sky of the aftermath. The best touch of all, introduced at exactly the right moment, was a little Negro friend running past the wrecked façade of the house, whistling the gang's usual signal.

I nagged him to such an extent that he promised to set his cyclone down in writing. A week went by and he handed me four sheets of paper with an air at once despondent and triumphant. "I've begun," he said, "but it's damned hard!" I felt very proud of having at last impelled this sluggard to work. So many fine gifts lying fallow! With a smug smile I took up the first page. It began: "As the old saying so truly has it . . ." My endless stupidity then dawned on me and I realized what should have occurred to me a week before, that talking and writing are two different things. Dutifully I read the four pages to the end. It was quite appalling. Like a schoolboy's essay. Who was trapped now? Myself, naturally, the more so as he stood smirking before me, so pleased with his first efforts, with having prised fifteen hundred words from his brain. "I'm glad you made me start writing," he said. "I shall go on. I won't stop till I've done two hundred pages." That didn't worry me. He'd never get beyond ten. But I blamed myself for having sown the seeds of literary ambition in his bosom. Now, because of me, he was going to be unhappy. On top of this he actually wanted my opinion of his scribbling! I could have kicked myself. Because I respect him, I couldn't tell him (as I usually do most convincingly) that it was a masterpiece. Yet I profess a dire mistrust of candor. I know the sensitivity of an artist's heart. One slightly sharp word draws blood; a man needs an absolute faith in his genius to withstand the abuse heaped on him by the critics. I extricated myself with tepid praise and some advice. "Cut every redundant word," I said. "Try to be commonplace, but beware, that doesn't mean common. For example, throw out that 'old saying.' What the hell's an old saying doing in a cyclone in Guadeloupe . . . ?" And so I babbled on for ten minutes, to such effect that there wasn't much left of those four pages by the time I'd finished.

He is extremely good-natured, intelligent, and, I might add, he trusts me. In short we didn't fall out. Two or three months later he spoke laughingly about his abortive venture. I laughed with him and swore to myself that if ever he told me another good story I would try to commit its details, colors, movement and if possible style to memory and then write it myself. This scheme suited me all the better in that invention is my weak point: I paint much more happily from nature. To recapture his turns of phrase, metaphors, characters and settings in the silence of my little study and pin all this down in its proper perspective would suit me to perfection. I thought how he and I could form a two-in-one novelist, and a highly acceptable one at that.

I confess, I bitterly regret that cyclone. But it's too late now to make anything of it. He'll never describe it so lavishly again. The truth is, he's the opposite of a wit who polishes and perfects his stories a little more each time he is asked to tell them. He is capricious: I suppose that, to talk, he needs as much inspiration as I do to write, and how can one ever tell when inspiration will descend? The Lord be praised, it descended on him yesterday. The two of us had been lunching in a cheap dive behind the Jardin des Plantes. We decided to take a stroll. "Did you ever know Roberti?" he asked me.

1: Yes, slightly, seven or eight years ago. I used to run into him here and there, in various people's houses, you know how it is. I can't say I liked him much. There was something subtly unattractive about him. Nice, oh, he was as nice as could be, friendly, forthcoming, even a bit fulsome. It's just that sometimes one takes a dislike to certain faces. Like his, with its fine velvety eyes behind the glasses, its ironic mouth

—you know, the sort that's always on display, the mouth of a man always watching himself, wanting one to say "He has such witty lips" —well, I didn't take to it. And you know me. I need to feel confident before I can make conversation, otherwise it's no go. With your Roberti I used to feel all starched. Stiff and crackling.

HE: You were wrong.

I: Surely. But I just can't force myself. Besides, I tend to be shy. There are certain people I like and admire but still have no wish to meet. Were someone tomorrow to say: Look, I want to introduce you to Balzac, Spinoza or Voltaire, they've been hearing about you and are keen to meet you, come round at such and such a time—I'd be horrified. Horrified. I've read their books, I even know them by heart. But I'm utterly lacking in curiosity about their persons. How do you explain that? I'm only really at ease in the company of idiots like you.

HE: Great men are not entertaining.

I: No, it's not that. Great men are as entertaining as anyone else. But when I'm with them I have the strange feeling I'm getting nothing out of it, learning nothing, that on the contrary I am serving as a meal for them. To me, that's intolerable. I wasn't cut out to be a beefsteak. I'm more of a carnivore than a ruminant myself, and morons are most nourishing. Morons are rich in calories and vitamins. They're beef. I can eat like an ogre.

HE: Roberti should have appealed to you. He was a man on whom one could feast to one's heart's content.

I: Really?

HE: Didn't you respond to his charm?

I: Not at all. I found him detestable. And his provincial outlook got on my nerves. A small-town type playing an old Parisian, no thank you!

HE: Yet he was a genuine Parisian, the son of Parisians.

I: Please, don't raise stupid objections. He was a provincial, I tell you. Look, he was wide-eyed and blasé. That's a sure sign of arrant provincialism. *Things mattered to him.* I've a horror of people to whom things matter. They throw me into a metaphysical panic.

HE: Come on! Roberti wasn't as bad as that. He had taste and a wide understanding.

I: Oh yes, I know. Don't put words into my mouth. Some provincials are the worthiest of men. Roberti was one. I call a man provincial who is blasé about the wrong things and all wide-eyed wonder over idiocies. I once discussed Beethoven with Roberti. He admired him, naturally, but with faint contempt. The ass was blasé about Beethoven. There's a provincial for you. Another time he described to me some little event in his life. It was devoid of interest but he didn't spare me a thing, not the smallest detail. And you should have seen the way he set out those details. He strung them like pearls, caressed them like an old lady at a piano. For instance, at one moment in his story he drank two whiskies straight off and someone laid his hand on his arm. This, I may say, recounted with overtones of mystery and the supernatural! The whole world drinks whisky: nobody makes a saga of it. But Roberti made sagas the whole time. The moment anything touched him personally it became noble, mysterious, significant, sublime. Quite ludicrous. He never admitted as much, of course, but one could feel from everything he said that he regarded himself as one of destiny's elect as it were, that everything that happened to him formed part of a pattern. He talked about himself with respect, with devotion. That sort of thing makes one's head spin—it does mine, at any rate.

HE: There's some truth in that.

I: In love with himself, that's what he was. Dripping with conceit. Ugh! To hell with the breed! They commit the unforgivable sin. The metaphysical sin. Only the most abject humility is permitted to God's creatures.

HE: Roberti was Faust.

I: Faust? For me he was rather Monsieur Bovary.

HE: It's funny you should say so. "Monsieur Bovary." His wife once called him that.

I: How is she, his wife?

HE: So-so. She has aged.

I: Poor woman!

HE: When Roberti went to prison, Agnes behaved marvelously. She never missed a visit. During the trial everyone admired her. Such fantastic dignity and poise! I saw a lot of her at the time. I used to talk with her for hours. "But tell me, Agnes, do you love him?" I asked her. "The question isn't whether I love him," she replied, "but whether or not I am his wife." I'm godfather to one of the boys, you know. Jacques. One day Jacques said: "Father's a dirty bastard!" He's eighteen. As tall as you. She boxed both his ears, wham!

I: Even so, you must have spent some painful evenings.

HE: Yes and no. Far less painful than you might expect. To begin with, as I've told you, Agnes was transformed. I'd always regarded her as a dim sort of person. It was just that she hadn't found her vocation. She was forty-six. Up to then she had barely lived. Then one day tragedy engulfed her family. The night before, she had gone to sleep an ordinary housewife; the next morning she woke a tragic heroine. She passed from squalor to grandeur, from Scribe to Sophocles.

1: Mme. Roberti a heroine from Sophocles? You're out of your mind! Women have a predilection for unhappiness, that's all. Mme. Roberti was no exception to the rule. It's the old notion, how no one really knows himself until he has suffered. One day I mean to write a book about women. I shall show how they are prey to a dual fetishism: that of success and that of suffering. From which I conclude them to be inferior beings.

HE: Fetishist or not, during those truly terrible weeks Agnes was wonderful. She revealed her true self. And like all who find self-revelation she was happy. Weird are the paths to happiness.

1: Did Roberti cause her great suffering?

HE: Oh no. Right to the end he "kept up the fiction."

1: What fiction? I don't understand.

HE: The fiction of marriage, of the happy couple. There are some things he would never have dared do. Thus he took all his meals at home, or nearly all. It was practically unheard of for him not to be there for lunch and dinner. The same went for vacations. For him vacations were sacred. He spent them with Agnes and the children, even if it meant being bored to death for four to six weeks. These were part of his moral obligations. That's how men are: they trample divine and human laws underfoot but consider it sacrilege to break with little habits or play fast and loose with the little conventions.

1: If you ask me, your Roberti was a frightful bourgeois and a hypocrite.

HE: Poor Edouard! Yes, I believe outwardly that's the impression he gave. From any brief summary of him most people would conclude him to be a frightful bourgeois and a hypocrite. But there was a touch of grandeur to his soul. Perhaps he clung to family meals and vacations the way a man falling off a cliff grabs at any bush or tuft of grass. He had nothing else to hand.

1: Did he and Agnes have separate bedrooms?

HE: Far from it. That, too, formed part of the fiction.

1: I wonder how far she was actually taken in by it.

HE: Completely.

1: It would seem she never understood her husband in the least.

HE: Oh yes, she did. She understood one whole side of him perfectly, even though he wasn't easy to understand, especially for a woman. There wasn't a trace of femininity about him. For me, he was the male in all his beauty—or horror, if you like. He was cautious, rather cold,

and he never believed in the impossible, which is a masculine characteristic. He adored the middle way, compromise, making the best of things.
Very patient too: a true Chinese. Time barely seemed to exist for
him. Every now and then I've seen him spend days, weeks, months on
end in a sort of temporal sludge. He was waiting. I never met anyone
who knew how to wait the way he did. His life was an endless waiting.
Whenever, after a thousand little concentric maneuvers, one of his political schemes came off, he would immediately focus his whole attention on another, and so it went on. Sometimes he made me think of a
crocodile digesting with closed eyes just under the water. The years
flowed over his carapace, leaving no trace. He lived only for this waiting,
he found delights in it beyond our powers to imagine.

I: Speak for yourself! I can imagine them very well. I myself am addicted to the crocodile system. Do you suppose, when one is a writer,
that it doesn't require the patience of an angel to kill the time between one book and the next?

HE: Edouard's inertia got on Agnes' nerves. Women love to be occupied, even if the occupation leads nowhere. The inactivity of the
male exasperates them. Of course, Roberti's patience did include a certain measure of laziness. Talking to you about him, I feel as if I were
drawing the ideal portrait of the male, *vir*, as opposed to the female.
To crown everything, he was rational. Reason governed his every move.
He never did anything rash, imaginative, impulsive. Moreover he loved
Reason, was in love with it. He believed in it alone. He had a fine contempt for those who act on impulse regardless of the cost, seeing no
further than the ends of their own noses.

I: It didn't prevent him from acting like a fool, and in a big way.

HE: Oh but that's another matter. I'm speaking of Roberti before the
disaster, Roberti in his normal state, the way everyone knew him, a
Paris deputy, ex-lawyer, Vice-Chairman of the Committee for Art and
Literature. It's not so very long ago. Three, three and a half years. He
was a familiar figure. You'd see him at first nights, meet him at dinner
parties with Agnes, for whom he had even bought a mink coat. He was
friendly with most of the thousand-odd people who make up the Paris
smart set. Then there was the other Roberti, the one who suddenly
blossomed out and lived the story of Faust.

I: I can recognize this Faust's Marguerite but not his Mephisto.

HE: His Mephisto was himself. Everything took place inside him; but
if you look carefully you can see thinly veiled the story of Faust. Roberti
sold his soul rather late in the day, after a fairly respectable life, a
discreet one at any rate, which mightn't perhaps have got him to para-

dise but at least to purgatory. At fifty he could consider his salvation assured, feel he had nothing more to fear either in this world or in the next. Life had never placed him in an awkward situation; he was on the whole honest, generous, benevolent. There are people like that who by-pass tragedy. The sins they commit are of no consequence. For them, these never acquire substance. When they do something dirty they forget it. It leaves little more mark on their souls than their good deeds. It's only skin-deep. Roberti was only skin-deep. I never saw him involve his heart in any of his actions. He held it in reserve. Such people set little store by this earth; it's as if they cared nothing for the world. And so they never carry much weight. I'm sketching all this roughly but you can see the general idea.

Roberti's road, then, had its ups and downs. There were slopes down which he coasted; sometimes it was a fine highroad, straight, wide, well tarred, shaded by tall trees; sometimes it became a stony track, twisting and turning, but there were no crossroads so to speak. It was enough to walk straight ahead. One might reasonably expect this walk to last sixty to eighty years without obstruction; that one day Roberti, very tired and very respectable, would lay himself down peacefully in the ditch and render up his slightly gray soul (only slightly gray, and nearer white than black) to God. But not a bit of it. So long as one isn't dead, nothing is sure. After plodding on for fifty years, my Roberti suddenly came to a crossroads. You may imagine him stopping and scratching his forehead, perplexed as to whether to turn right, left, or keep straight on. You picture him like Hercules between Vice and Virtue. Well, you're wrong. He didn't hesitate for a second. HE NEVER SAW THE CROSSROADS. That's what happens with rationalists. They're shortsighted or lost in their own thoughts. Like an idiot, Roberti kept straight on when he should have turned left or right. I mean he believed there was no problem just when there was one. In short he committed the sin of pride. He had confidence in himself, in his destiny. "Nothing serious can happen to me," he argued. "I am too sensible." Instead of keeping his eyes fixed on the road, instead of scanning the lie of the land, he smugly looked inside himself. He lulled himself with the spectacle of his intellectual or moral success. He lovingly contemplated his untarnished soul.

There's little difference in aspect between the paths of evil and the paths of good. The landscape is much the same. The trees, the houses, the people one meets are the same. Only the meaning changes. Unless one looks out, one never notices. Nothing resembles an angel so much as a demon, and vice versa. Edouard surveyed his surroundings with the same benevolent eye, the same indifference if you like, or the same negligence, as the day before. He believed himself still "protected." He wasn't any longer.

I: All this you're saying has a strong religious flavor. Was Roberti a believer?

HE: No, but with his sort that's not important. Up to the crossroads he never really felt any need of God. He was saved in advance. He was on the right side. He was of the tribe of Abel. Afterward, well, then it was another matter. He'd gone too far. So far that he no longer even knew where he was.

I: D'you think he was damned?

HE: Could be.

I: A heavy price!

HE: Anyway, damned is easily said. We only see things in the rough. There is always a millionth of a fraction of a second which can escape us; that is enough for a soul to slip through. Perhaps Roberti had his millionth of a fraction of a second and is now sitting on the right hand of God.

I: I'm beginning to think that when we get to paradise we're going to meet a crowd of people we've always gone out of our way to avoid in Paris. You wait and see!

HE: I'm afraid so. But they'll have changed.

I: Let's hope so.

HE: Can you imagine Abel suddenly changing his personality and, at fifty, becoming Cain? That's what happened to Roberti. The metamorphosis occurred under my nose. It didn't take long: two years at the outside. Evil finds no difficulty in entering a *vacant* soul. And Roberti's was as vacant as could be. Why did this soul, gray as it was, veer toward black rather than white? Why didn't it even remain its own gray? At first I thought he had damned himself out of indifference, as is often the case. But this was too short a view. It's no more easy to do evil than good. It demands just as much energy. If, like most men, Roberti had followed his own inclination, it wouldn't have led him to hell.

I: So he didn't follow his own inclination?

HE: He followed it in a way. Or rather he didn't: he followed a certain inclination believing it to be his own, but he was wrong. It wasn't. Its slope often struck him as a bit steep, he would slither down unexpected gullies, he would sometimes find himself in strange valleys, but he told himself not to worry. It was impossible that he, Roberti, should ever dwell in such chaotic and inhuman regions; at any moment he chose he believed he could return as if by magic to the gentle hills, pale blue skies and soft climate of the Île-de-France, the serene gardens in which the chosen wander at peace for all eternity. He thought that, with him, nothing was ever lost. By dint of such belief one finds oneself one day at the end of one's tether. Those who, like Roberti, don't watch out but rely on themselves are arrogant at heart; and in the weirdest of ways pride always leads to abasement. One must be vigilant, one must be convinced that nothing is ever gained for certain, one must never cease to tremble. The world weighs heavy. That is its basic quality. Whenever it grows lighter, people breathe again and shout for joy. They are like kites let loose into the sky, they get drunk on space and the empyrean. They think the string has snapped and they will soar up to infinity. Poor wretches! Those are the times when they should be most mistrustful. The string hasn't broken. Abruptly it tightens, just when they least expect it. In a moment everything has come crashing to earth. Fifty years of assiduous—I would even say voluptuous—application of reason led Roberti to madness.

I: You mean to folly.

HE: It's the same thing.

Now is perhaps the time for me to give a brief account of our promenade before continuing with our conversation. It is June. The day is warm. Neither of us wears an overcoat. We are ambling along, pausing every now and then. Not because the sights in the street or the picturesque old houses hold our attention (we are far too absorbed in what we are saying) but because it is difficult to talk without occasionally standing still. Conversation is like music; it lends rhythm to our steps. Moreover our bodies barely exist for us. We are concentrated entirely on our thoughts. To my mind Paris is an ideal place for these long, gossipy walks, especially in spring. Also, since we have lived in it all our lives, it is so familiar that nothing unexpected can occur to distract us.

Anyway, isn't it a sort of novel of Paris life, a contemporary one, my friend is telling me? I am strolling with the writer through the actual setting of his story. Even Sir Walter Scott, so evocative in his historical tales, never offers me as much. Where am I? Since we set out, we have skirted the Jardin des Plantes by way of the Rue Buffon and the Quai Saint-Bernard; we have passed the Halle aux Vins exuding a smell of wine barrels. Here is the Pont Sully leading to the Île Saint-Louis, and the island itself. I glance up at its celebrated line of roof tops against the pale blue sky. What time is it? Twenty-five to three.

I: Supposing we go and have a coffee?

HE: We've only just had one. I'm full for the next two hours. Besides, I'm not thirsty. I just feel like walking and talking. Are you free this afternoon?

I: Absolutely. Free as air. All yours and Roberti's.

HE: What a lad, Roberti, wasn't he? To think that we've known Doctor Faust.

I: You say he had a superstitious awe of Reason. It strikes me old Faust didn't respect Reason that much. He played all sorts of tricks on it. He was on intimate terms with the supernatural. He called up the Devil and ringed him round with magic circles.

HE: In his way Roberti did the same. Of course, with him the supernatural didn't enter into it. He wasn't a character in a play whose actions the author represents in a poetic or symbolic form. But he shared all Faust's emotions, he closely followed his behavior. The difference is that it was invisible. That's how it happens in real life. Things are never allegorical; they never form a picture. Men normally don't have a Goethe at hand to understand for them and depict or synthesize their lives for their instruction. They have to get along as best they can all alone in the dark, find their way through virgin forests, reconnoiter paths that others have already trodden. As a result, they don't get along. Without knowing it, Roberti was more Faust than life.

I: More Faust than life! That's going a little too far!

HE: No, you'll see it isn't. In the story of Faust according to Goethe there are several shocking propositions. In particular that after his metamorphosis the young Faust isn't a bit like the old Faust any more. It's just as if the change of body had engendered a change of soul. Now immortality is memory. What's the use of being immortal if one cannot remember one's previous existences? Directly he's transformed, Faust seems to lose all his memory. He forgets his wisdom, experience, philosophy, all the lumber one can accumulate in ninety years of life. It's a more or less total shipwreck. All he has left are a few tricks of speech and a certain way of going straight to the point that one never has in youth but only acquires with age. This old doctor becomes a young buck.

I: Granted, but . . . ?

HE: But it's always the opposite that really happens. The body doesn't shape the soul; the soul shapes the body. Appearances are reality. The face is the portrait of the heart. I am constantly finding this to be true. I found it so with Roberti. In three years his face had assumed the aspect of his new soul. It began with the eyes. Little wrinkles formed round the lids; his look became dull and hard. Yet hitherto he had had what people call fine eyes, rather velvety and pensive. When he was fifty-two they began to resemble those of a hen. Bit by bit his whole face altered. As if inside him the bones were warping like wood and something akin to a revolution of nature, a geological upheaval, was taking place.

I: Wasn't it quite simply one of those transformations we all periodically undergo? You know the process as well as I do. We don't grow old gradually but every ten or fifteen years we have an "attack of old age" as if nature had forgotten about us and suddenly remembered it was time we caught up. Take me, for instance. When I was about twenty-eight I aged at top speed for three weeks. My hair fell out, my stomach protruded, one morning I woke up with a different mentality; more easygoing and settled. I was appalled. I really thought the angel Azrael had brushed me with the tip of his black wing. And that's what it was, in fact. But the business hasn't only a dark side to it. These earthquakes are fruitful. They ripen the human harvest. When they're over one has ten to fifteen years of tranquillity ahead. Take me: today I look more or less the same as I did at twenty-eight after the metamorphosis. I am now waiting for the next one, which can't be long in coming. When I'm about forty-five I shall know how I'll look when I'm sixty. It will be a painful moment but I've learned to shrug it off. The trouble with the little secrets of nature is that there's only one way of finding them out: by growing old. They never reveal themselves before their time. To return to Roberti, didn't the same thing happen to him at fifty as to me at twenty-eight? That's to say the normal, recurrent metamorphosis?

HE: It's possible that his normal metamorphosis, as you call it, coincided with his moral one and this made things even worse. But I rather had the impression that he was *changing season*. Up to fifty-two, Edouard had been a man of spring: fresh complexion, plump cheeks, rather thin but beautifully wavy hair. And then he abruptly switched from spring to autumn. No mild and mellow autumn, no Indian summer, but an infernal season. His mouth became a curve of disgust. On the other hand he grew a bit thinner; he became younger in bearing. You're going to laugh again at my religious visions, but he seemed to me suddenly inhabited by the Devil! I had the idea he was rotting as he stood, that his blood had changed into a purulent and revolting pus, that everything inside him had become poison. These internal poisons, these brews from a witches' caldron, made fleeting appearances on the surface when his face would look livid, his skin gray, his cheeks flabby, the true decay of autumn. Eaten away, consumed from within, was the impression he gave.

I: All this is highfalutin fiction. And, to make it worse, it's Catholic fiction. For heaven's sake, one doesn't damn oneself because one falls in love at fifty with a girl of twenty-five! You'll never get me to swallow that. It's the purest moonshine. You're making it up! Love's not a sin at fifty. Nor at eighty for that matter.

HE: Of course not. Don't put words into my mouth. Roberti didn't damn himself by falling in love at fifty. He was damned. There's a slight difference. Some people never have to prove whether or not they are generous, courageous, stoical. One may assume they possess these qualities but have somehow never had occasion to put them to the test. Blessed uncertainty! I've known several putative saints of that kind who have never done a single bad deed in their lives because they had the luck never to be placed in a tricky situation.

I: The way I interpret your gibberish, Roberti was at heart simply a sort of Pharisee. So long as his life was simple he behaved more or less decently; but as soon as things grew a bit complicated he showed himself in his true light and everyone could see he was a bastard.

HE: If you like. But there was no reason why things should have become complicated for him. There was every reason for them to remain simple to the end.

I: Anyway, by and large he didn't have much to complain of. Thanks to his bad luck he exchanged a state of mediocrity for one of tragedy. I regard that as advancement. Till he was fifty your Roberti was nothing. He had no soul. And then, at fifty, he found one for himself. Vile, ignoble, whatever you like, but still a soul.

HE: I see we agree.

I: How old was he exactly when he first met the Mignot girl?

HE: Fifty. Their affair lasted three years.

I: Was she pretty? It's hard to tell from the photos. Did you ever see her?

HE: During their affair, not more than two or three times. I still see her occasionally. Pretty? Yes, she was, rather. But love and beauty are two different things. She was unusual. Very attractive, very charming. A superb tawny skin. What was striking were her eyes: huge, brown, gentle, "flecked with gold" as they say in novels. I had always wondered what it meant, eyes flecked with gold, till the day I saw the fair Solange.

I: Of course! She was called Solange. I'd forgotten.

HE: Solange-Antoinette-Louise Mignot, secretary by calling. She was a really nice girl.

I: Why do you refer to her in the past tense?

HE: Probably because in my memory she's bound up with Roberti. Also no doubt because the three years during which she loved Edouard were (and will remain) the only ones she ever really lived. All the rest is padding. She has forty to fifty years of limbo ahead of her. At twenty-five she had the luck to love a man who was in an unusual state and made her suffer splendidly. She was unhappy as hell but she was alive. At times (but they were rare) she was in a seventh heaven; at others (and they were frequent) she was dejected, her heart hibernated. Roberti battered savagely at her soul, he *wore her out,* but I'm willing to bet that during the three years her affair with him lasted she was never bored. In her heart she complained; she kept on telling herself how it was just her luck to fall in with a married man, and middle-aged to boot, who didn't even love her. Yet something deeper still must have whispered that such complaints were only for form's sake. She wore love on her face, and the joy it brings to women. Her little mind was bewildered by it but her instinct (or her heart) reveled in it. The way Roberti loved her was at the opposite pole from the conventional, cliché-ridden idea of love reassuring and habitual. On the face of it he didn't give a hang for her in the accepted sense; never a present, never taking her out, always furtive meetings, a sort of shame and disgust: but love was there all the same, and much more violent than in most of the classical passions.

Poor Solange! From time to time she would nostalgically think how she might have had a "normal" lover instead of this gangster. A young man, kind, a bachelor naturally, who would have sent her flowers, called her in the middle of the night just to hear her voice, just to breathe with her, taken her for weekends to those smart inns around Paris, presented her with handbags or costume jewelry and one day, aided and abetted by time and tenderness, bashfully proposed marriage. . . .

ɪ: Ugh!

ʜᴇ: Wait. She thought all that because it's the normal line of feminine daydreams. But then she would compare this idyllic picture with her actual position and finally decide she preferred being the humiliated mistress of a middle-aged man who made her unhappy. Because he had one priceless quality: she loved him. She had loved him from the moment she saw him. In fact, it was she who seduced him, not he who seduced her.

ɪ: So what? That's how it always happens. The women choose and the men succumb. Probably Mlle. Mignot had a thing about old men. There's a lot of it about. The psychoanalysts call it a father fixation.

ʜᴇ: She was secretary to a friend of Edouard's, whom incidentally you know. Dietz.

ɪ: Abel Dietz? Yes, I remember. But I hardly know Dietz.

ʜᴇ: No matter. Solange, then, was his secretary. She saw Roberti for the first time two years before their affair began. I've rather forgotten the details. Roberti had gone to see Dietz about some question of a grant. Oh yes, I remember: Dietz had bought the Hôtel Boucherat, one of the beautiful old houses in the Marais, a historic monument but hopelessly dilapidated, on the verge of tumbling down, and he was hoping the State would help him to restore it. So Roberti, who specialized in such matters as a deputy, called on Dietz, who was incidentally an old friend. And who should receive him? Who should let him in? Mlle. Mignot. She thought him magnificent, seductive in a rather overripe way but all the more superb for that; she fell for him completely. Into the bargain, he wasn't unknown to her. The newspapers mentioned him now and then in connection with some law that had or hadn't been passed, that he had voted for or against; in the event of some Cabinet reshuffle, the gossip writers would quote his name as a candidate for a ministry. He, Roberti, took no notice of Solange. Or rather, no more than he took of any pretty woman. In other words he gave her the once-over with his dreamy, slightly veiled gaze of a middle-aged charmer and thought vaguely to himself: "My, she's not bad! I wouldn't mind sleeping with that one if I had the chance!" Nothing more. With women Roberti, you know, was always on the *qui vive*, always on the lookout. The Mignot girl crosses his field of vision: why not the Mignot girl?

ɪ: Generally men always on the *qui vive* like Roberti hardly ever make love. They spend their time weaving fantasies and let the fish escape.

HE: That was Roberti's case. He was wildly romantic. Every mildly pretty woman he met plunged him into more or less erotic daydreams. But he didn't often go any further. The explanation is that he didn't belong to the freemasonry of pleasure, the secret society of promiscuous men and women who recognize each other at a glance and have, so to speak, no need of words to arrange their bedding. Roberti would have loved to belong to this Mafia, but it's a gift you either have or haven't. His temperament kept that society's door closed to him. Not to mention the way his life was organized. He was too often seen out with his wife; he was known to work hard at home, taken up with nursing his constituency and his various political activities. Besides, his way with women was far too formal. He respected them in spite of himself. He would make them gallant speeches, flowery compliments, butter them up: *he set out to conquer them.* That's the worst possible approach for someone with seduction in view: they don't take him seriously. Or else he makes them afraid. So on the whole he didn't achieve much success, although women liked him. Those who favored him most were "afraid to love him" and wouldn't give in.

I: Still it seems to me that there floated around him a sort of Don Juanesque halo, a reputation as a seducer. People always referred to him with a knowing smile. "A handsome fellow, Roberti . . . a fast worker, he gets around. . . ." What's the truth in all that?

HE: Very little. As you know, people will say anything. Besides, Edouard wasn't averse to such a reputation, which was vague enough. In fact it was at best a halo. A gilded halo which suited him very well, which enhanced his figure. He contented himself with not denying what he knew to be false but at the same time flattering and harmless. He would even implicitly endorse it by assuming the faintly fatuous air of a conqueror. His real adventures, for he had them, he kept absolutely secret. How to define them? They consisted of obscure passions lasting from a fortnight to six months for women who didn't belong to his class and with whom he didn't get too involved. Secretaries, shopgirls, manicurists, nurses. They all had one thing in common: a certain air of respectability. That's what intrigued him. He liked to think they were above their walk in life, either through character or education; that in their lowly state they were somehow exiles. Each time he took a mistress he would slightly (only slightly—he wasn't even truly aware of it) live the legend of Perseus and Andromeda. So he had to find, or imagine, some purity in these ladies. For nothing in the world would he have sought solace with a professional. He believed in love, or at least in the sentiment. He needed to envelop desire with a hint of rapture. Possessing a body wasn't enough: he wanted a little of the object of his desire's mind and heart thrown in.

I: Rather simple-minded!

HE: Childish, yes, at the beginning. The early stages of his affairs were always delicious. Full of hopes and fears, he would work himself up into a splendid state. He would be drunk on uncertainty. He would employ extravagant stratagems. Should the lady resist for a week or two, all the better. But if after a reasonable period he failed in his objective, he would draw in his horns in a flash. It was the same when he achieved his goal.

I: That's all quite normal. And I'm tired of your endless digressions. We had got to his first meeting with Solange. Did she become his mistress right away?

HE: No, not till two years later.

I: What? He pursued her for two whole years?

HE: Certainly not. He didn't see her more than three times in those two years. She loved him in secret. From the day she showed him into Dietz's office, he filled her thoughts. They were crystallized on him. The idea of Roberti slowly pervaded her. Little by little he became for her a universal yardstick. She endowed him with every perfection. He was a paragon of charm, elegance, intellect, nobility. She automatically compared every man she met with Roberti and only found him pleasing insofar as he resembled Roberti in age, manner, complexion or expression.

I: That's love all right. I know. Skip the development. Solange crystallizes for two years. She arranges to meet Roberti three times. Like an idiot he doesn't realize for a second that she loves him, he's quite uncomprehending. . . . Your story's as old as the world.

HE: True, that's the way it was. Except that the three meetings were accidental. Solange was a fatalist, she put herself in destiny's hands for the rest of the campaign. She more or less made up her mind never to show her love if the opportunity declined to present itself. She, too, was rational. Naturally she found out all about Roberti. She knew he was married, had children and so forth. His life seemed to her something as immutable, untouchable, unshakable, impregnable as the column in the Place Vendôme. One doesn't dream of owning the column in the Place Vendôme. One passes by, looks up at it admiringly and goes on home.

Are women inscrutable or are men simply blind? Solange sees Roberti three times in two years. Each time it's a complete surprise, her heart gives a lurch, she almost faints dead away. Yet not a sign of this appears on her face. She remains as calm as the Mediterranean in mid-August. Her hand is steady. She greets him with every mark of indifference. Roberti hasn't the faintest idea. Even so, he doesn't forget to put on his act: tender smile, long look, lingering handshake. The habitual reaction induced in him by the presence of a beautiful woman. To himself he says: "No point in making a play for that one. She's not for me. She's got too much class. She surely has some young man in tow. Still, one never knows."

I: Was she really all that good?

HE: She wasn't what one would call a classical beauty; she wasn't even specially well built; but everything about her was ravishing and desirable. She was on the slender side, her legs too thin, her bust just a little too big: while it would certainly have prevented her from becoming Miss France, this lack of proportion had great charm. She had pretty, rounded shoulders. Her face was enchanting: a delicate, fresh, well-shaped mouth which she never touched up with lipstick; her nose rather large perhaps, but at once pert and voluptuous (a success in its way); those superb chestnut eyes, so big that one felt one was looking into the depths of her soul, with lashes half an inch long; ears carved by Benvenuto Cellini in person; eyebrows traced by Hokusai; the neck very round, very sensuous, in perfect scale with her bust and shoulders. On top of all this a heavenly skin: pink and gold, verging on golden brown, of an incomparable texture and freshness!

I: Blonde or brunette?

HE: Blonde, pale blonde. Lovely hair, silky but very thick.

I: A dark-eyed blonde? She must have bleached it.

HE: Obviously. But the result was fine. There was nothing in the least doll-like about her and her blondeness didn't look particularly artificial. It was very fresh and becoming. What first attracted Roberti to a woman was her face. His desire was centered on that. He didn't look too closely at the body. A beautiful face made the most misshapen body desirable. Solange's body was very appetizing into the bargain. She dressed with considerable chic.

I: The real little Parisian secretary! There's an amusing character. And up-to-date. What is the twentieth century? Answer: the century of the secretary. One day one ought to write a "Monograph on Secretaries" in which one would survey the various categories: the young, the old, the older-than-she-looks, the sexy, the devoted, the timid, the ugly, the couldn't-care-less, the featherbrained, the ambitious, the dog and the dragon, the Du Barry type, the one whose power goes to her head, the one who bosses the boss, and so on. There could be a chapter on sex and the secretary, another on her family life. The secretary's parents. Her husband, her children when she has any. The secretary lives in the suburbs or outlying districts. She goes home to Courbevoie every evening except Friday, when she goes on the town. Another enthralling chapter: the men who take an interest in secretaries. The kind of charm they find in them. In big offices the battalion of secretaries forms a kind of harem, a tantalizing sort of gynaeceum in which there are always four or five very fair specimens. The gentlemen of the establishment know that every day, from eight-thirty to noon and two to six, they will have at their disposal these obliging, empty-headed, rather idle creatures, always ready for a chat, and that if they set about it the right way they can get to know them quite intimately. Chapter Nine: office idylls. I've left out the young girl of good family who, her parents having fallen on hard times, enlists as a secretary. And the sentimental one who puts flowers on her boss's desk, and the one who packs up at five to six because a dashing accountant is waiting for her downstairs. The world of the secretary still awaits its poet. Tell me, didn't Mlle. Mignot have a crush on Dietz?

HE: Of course. But only a slight one. When he first hired her she was twenty. Dietz is a very brilliant man. It was quite normal for him to arouse her interest. The more so since, from the start, he adopted a very dangerous attitude—that of the indulgent father whom nothing ever surprises and in whom one can confide. I once went to see him about some question of increasing the capital of one of his companies (he wanted me to have the first chance); at some stage Solange came into his office to get some papers signed. He called her "my dear" and I pricked up my ears. There was deep kindliness and affection in the phrase. "Dietz and this young thing are getting together!" I immediately thought, but I was wrong. It was nothing but friendship and sympathy. What had deceived me was that it was said by a mature man to a young woman. In fact Dietz has always had heaps of mistresses— actresses, countesses, society women. He had absolutely no need to number Solange among his trophies. As for her, even if she had a soft spot for him at the start, she never admitted it and he wisely acted as if he had never noticed. On the other hand there was true affection, a true familiarity between them. He appreciated her because she was conscientious, sensitive, frank, and he could trust her. Without being highly intelligent or educated she had an attractive mind, a kind heart and a certain distinction. To this he responded. Rather set himself up as her confidant. Him you know. He's a splendid man, witty, utterly reliable, generous, with the most lofty ideas. He has never forgotten that he started from nothing and, although he's a bit of a snob (that is, he never sees anyone but duchesses, writers and ministers) he never parades it. Equally at ease with Solange or Princess Pignatelli, Darius Milhaud or Anthony Eden. It would never occur to him that Solange was made of a different clay from Marie-Laure de Noailles. Which shows he is doubtless not a true snob. Another detail which describes him well is that he was just as happy with Solange as with his distinguished friends. Happier, even, as she was completely natural and unaffected: she was honesty and goodness unalloyed. By the same token he has had his hair cut for the past thirty years by a little barber down the street who has no talent but chats to him with pleasant familiarity and whom he looks on as a friend. Dietz, you see, is a man with a vocation for friendship and the gift of loyalty. One extraordinary thing about his life is that he has remained friends with every woman he ever slept with, and I promise you there are a lot of them! He's one of those rare men who, so far as I know, has never treated anyone badly. Not even women. The discreet crush Solange had on him lasted for perhaps three months and then changed into friendship and mutual trust. A most calm and restful turn.

ɪ: Tell me, during the two years she waited for Roberti, crystallized on him, did she have lovers?

ʜᴇ: There you're asking too much of me. I don't know. Flirtations perhaps. No more. Solange wasn't the woman to love one man and sleep with another. During those two years, I'd bet my last cent that she remained completely chaste.

ɪ: Keeping herself for the frightful Roberti. Proof that she hoped all along that one day he'd become her lover.

ʜᴇ: Aristotle says that something cannot be true at the same time as its opposite. In affairs of the heart that's rubbish. Solange hoped for nothing but at the same time felt convinced that this man she loved would sooner or later be hers.

ɪ: Brr! It makes one shiver. Just look at us! Toys in women's hands! Even when they're kind, even when they wouldn't hurt a fly, like Solange, who strikes me as a really decent girl.

ʜᴇ: She told herself that all her life she would remain cloistered in dreary waiting for a man who would never come; she was condemned never to find happiness in love, since the only love she wanted was forbidden her. At twenty-three the future hardly extends beyond a few weeks. She viewed these weeks ahead with boredom and disgust. She imagined her whole life as one long winter without a ray of sun: she would marry some nobody, become at best a little suburban housewife, yawn her life away. But at the same time, she felt with a curious insistence that this great love she cherished couldn't be sterile; that in some mysterious way, without her even making any move, she would be rewarded. It was enough to persist, to persevere in her love, to worship without faltering. It was unthinkable for so unswerving a desire to be frustrated. What one really longs for, one always obtains.

I: I seem to remember Plato saying something like "Everything you desire you will have, unhappy wretch!" It's a sinister prediction. It means that all ambition is absurd and one is even more desperate after its fulfillment than before. We never truly perceive the vanity and emptiness of things till we have finally possessed them. There is, in ancient theology, an absolutely terrifying description of hell as being simply the fulfillment for eternity of all the desires which have governed men during their lives.

HE: Well, Solange was an unwitting platonist and theologian. She was heading toward the hell of fulfilled desires believing it to be paradise.

I: One important point: was she a virgin?

HE: No. She had had one or two "experiences" but she wasn't promiscuous. She complied each time out of love or at least attraction. Besides, to my mind these "experiences" rather did her honor. She was the opposite of a flirt. She remained a virgin until she was about twenty. Then one day a boy caught her fancy; she gave herself to him wholeheartedly, judging that this formality was fundamentally of no importance, or else that if one elects to be in love one shouldn't apply too many reservations. But first experiences are never very conclusive. Solange's, as could be foreseen, brought her no revelation. So that when she met Roberti she was no longer a virgin, of course, nor yet a woman either. Besides, her two or three affairs hadn't lasted very long or left much impression on her heart. They were—how shall I put it? —tryouts, the way girls make them nowadays. She was like a little wild animal venturing to the edge of the forest in which it has always lived and then scurrying back to the family burrow. Solange was not unhappy in the family burrow of chastity. That's why I'm almost certain that during the two years she loved Roberti in secret, from twenty-three to twenty-five, she let nobody else touch her. Added to which it's exquisite to be faithful to the man one loves, to sacrifice to him pleasures one doesn't even seek. Also, it wasn't so much to Roberti that she was faithful, since he hardly so to speak knew her, as to the prodigious love she had conceived for him. This love was her work of art, her reason for living, her "ideal." Finally there is the great secret of chastity in women. I maintain that chastity costs them nothing, or at least next to nothing. They can go for months on end without any stirring of the blood. This must stem from their changeable, capricious and sensitive natures and from the difficulty men nearly always find in arousing them. Their bodies slumber. They have no desires. It was all the easier for Solange since what carnal love she had known had proved of little consequence. Nothing beyond the first little surge of excitement. She saw its material fulfillment merely as a rather tedious function, an unavoidable ordeal or else a pledge to be given the man of one's choice.

i: It's not very hard for men to remain chaste either, in spite of what they say. They usually are, much more than they pretend to be. And it's normal. Making love the whole time, changing mistresses every day, turns one into an idiot. You spoke just now of a Mafia of initiates, a secret society of pleasure. I know people who belong to it. They are deadly bores.

HE: Yes. All specialists are bores. Those are the worst. They have no other topic. Stamp collectors, numismatists, globe-trotters, surgeons, engineers are all interested in politics, love, literature. Members of the Mafia have no other interests; they quickly turn into maniacs. Anyway I don't believe they're as happy as all that. Sleeping around is quite amusing for a fortnight or two. After which, like everything else, it must become routine.

i: I should like to get to the first real meeting between Solange and Roberti. These two years of waiting are rather a drag. There was no reason for it ever to end. Why two years? It could have lasted a lifetime. Your story reminds me of the song about a girl who lived at Vincennes and a man who lived at Saint-Cloud. They were made for each other. Unfortunately they never met. Didn't Solange one day get tired of waiting? Didn't she feel like giving fate a little shove, engineering an opening?

HE: Of course she did, and often, but in the way one wants to be suddenly rich or visit Japan. The idea crosses your mind, flits through your heart; for a second you tell yourself it's indispensable, that there alone lie truth and happiness; but since it's impossible, you forget it a moment later. Besides, put yourself in her position. She had built up a whole dream around Roberti. She had functioned like an oyster, that is to say the real Roberti, seen but once, had insinuated himself into her soul like a grain of sand around which she secreted layers of pearl. She had fashioned for herself an imaginary and outsize lover. Perhaps she feared the reality mightn't live up to her dream. A sudden switch from dream to reality isn't difficult; it happens without warning and one adapts oneself instantly. What is difficult is deciding to leave the dream and enter reality. It involves a huge effort of will which becomes all the harder the deeper the dream grows. One is forced to change key, shift from minor to major. It was a vast, vague feeling which possessed her, filled every part of her but did not properly speaking make her unhappy. A very sweet feeling to which she would escape twenty times a day. Whenever she felt cross or upset she would conjure up the image of Roberti. She would evoke the smile he gave her when she opened the door to Dietz's office. She would load this smile with meaning. She was certain she had read tenderness and complicity in it. In which, of course, she wasn't entirely wrong. Roberti would put complicity and tenderness into every smile he gave an attractive woman, on the off-chance. Anyway, as you see, it was all quite bearable. It even had considerable charm. Solange loved thinking about Roberti. It kept her company. It *gave her pleasure*. Sometimes whole days would pass without her expressly doing so, but his presence was nonetheless working within her. He coursed through her veins, he was in the air she breathed.

I: Hell, that's love! If she felt that way, it's impossible she shouldn't have tried to see him, shouldn't have walked round the block where he lived, for instance.

HE: It may be impossible, but so it was. Walking along the street, she would constantly expect him to appear. Whenever she saw a figure resembling his in the distance, her heart would begin to thump. . . . The figure drew nearer; it was someone else; she would tremble for the next ten minutes. Roberti lived in the Rue Oudinot, near the Invalides. Whenever Solange chanced to pass in that direction, down the Avenue de Tourville, Rue de Sèvres or Place Fontenoy, she was filled with a mixture of hope and fear. She would glance furtively to right and left. She regarded these delicious places with awe; they seemed to her the most beautiful in Paris because they were near the house of the man she loved.

I: I find it improbable that she should have carried a torch so long and so faithfully. Torchbearing, whatever you say, necessitates the occasional presence of its object. Normally, Solange's love should have wilted and died of starvation. If you hadn't provided so many details, I would have thought she simply found Roberti to her liking, tucked him away at the back of her mind telling herself, "One day this man and I are going to meet again," and thought no more about it. That's how it usually happens. You meet a woman; she pleases you, you feel you please her; you forget her, she forgets you, and three years later she falls into your arms. For three years the light of love, switched on by that first glance, is dimmed till the right moment arrives.

HE: What is strange is that Solange could easily have loved Roberti all her life without ever seeing him again. She would have embalmed this feeling inside her like a mummy. No, not a mummy, I'm wrong, it's a bad comparison: like a supplementary trait of her character, a *distinguishing mark*. I like to think that, had she not subsequently become Roberti's mistress, the love she bore him would have ended by being as much part of her as an addiction to snails, for instance, or a preference for dressing in blue. One can like snails and never eat them. There are people who live in pink or gray apartments and can never afford to have them redone in blue. One sees dozens of men and women who live with a great unfulfilled ambition and manage none the worse for it.

I: All the same I'm amazed at the girl's placidity. It's unfeminine. When women want something they go all out for it. Fling themselves at it. Sweep aside every obstacle. I am always staggered by their speed and brutality. Even the shiest turns into an Attila or a Genghis Khan. They accept no delay. They can't bear to suffer. The spirit of possession, which they have to the highest degree, presupposes the spirit of conquest. To me, whatever you say, Solange with her two years of torchbearing remains an enigma.

HE: You're overgeneralizing. You say "women." Yes, women are this or that. But there are exceptions. Solange was one, that's all. She was a woman at once ordinary and exceptional. Perhaps also because deep in her heart she heard an obscure voice—what one might call the voice of a guardian angel—whispering in the manner of Victor Hugo that Roberti was "a black sun radiating night" and that she must do nothing to bring him closer. If fate led him to her one day, well and good! But if this meeting never took place, then she must bow her head. The powers above—let us say Providence—had so ordained it. Your weakness, you see, is that you never take the supernatural element in human affairs into account. We don't live in three dimensions but in four. The fourth is more important than the other three. Most of our impulses are controlled by unknown causes, regardless of our passions. In Solange's case there was in addition her own basic character, infinitely calm, infinitely placid. Inclined to dreaminess. Her heart had elected Roberti, certainly, but she was waiting for him to choose her, to light on her of his own accord. If you're fond of feminine characteristics there's an indisputable one for you. In this respect Solange was profoundly feminine. In her long crystallization I see the humble waiting for the male to decide. When their fatal meeting finally took place, she went to him not as a conqueror but as a captive and a supplicant, in utter humility and almost without hope. She only went to get a glimpse of him, to give herself pleasure, to nourish her love a little. He himself hadn't thought of her more than four times in two years, and then only the way one recalls a fine chest or graceful table once admired in the window of an antique shop, so he was a thousand miles from imagining this treasure of love hoarded for him in secret. When, later, he discovered it, it brought him immense happiness; his vanity was enormously flattered; but very soon it horrified him.

I: Don't you feel tired? Aren't you thirsty? We've been talking for at least an hour. At least you've been talking, for I haven't said much. I just listen. Very glad to listen, too. How d'you manage to know all these minute details, all these secret stirrings? I believe you're Asmodeus! You lift the lid of the skull and peer inside. A storyteller is a devil! Tell me honestly, aren't you making it up? With your gift for storytelling, it's impossible that you're not a liar. Mind you, that's no reproach. I've the greatest respect for lies if in the end they lead to truth, and if they are even truer than the truth. One can't be an artist without being a consummate liar.

HE: But no, I'm not lying in the least, I swear. I'm describing things as they happened, as I saw them; at worst as I deduced them. I'm inventing nothing, absolutely nothing.

I: My, you're a real Sherlock Holmes of the human heart. How do you manage it? Give me your recipe.

HE: I haven't one. We're walking along the street and I'm talking. Perhaps it's our walk, the spring, something soft in the air. And then there are your questions, your interruptions. Each time they set me off again. Maybe that's why I can never manage to write. I need someone to talk to. Not a passive companion, not an inert ear into which I can direct my flow of words, but a critical mind, quarrelsome, disagreeable, difficult (although well disposed), in short someone like yourself. Someone who savors the nuances. But not just any nuance; the correct nuance. And who demands it when one's a bit off the mark. When I tried to write up my cyclone in Guadeloupe (remember?) I was unhappy, it went wrong at every sentence because you weren't there to ask questions, to force me to elaborate some detail or other, set the right emphasis, give it the right shape. When I'm alone I lose my memory. As soon as I talk to someone I find it again.

I: With me it's the opposite. I have to be alone in my room in front of my typewriter with four or five hours' peace ahead of me for ideas to stir, memories to return, for the mists of the subconscious to clear. In public I'm as silent as the grave. The first fool I meet strikes me dumb. Sometimes it's painful.

HE: You're a writer and I'm a gossip. You're an ant and I'm a grasshopper. You're the one who's better off. Ants work for their old age while grasshoppers—hell!—they die in penury, and hoarse into the bargain from all their singing.

I: You know, just now I grasped one of your methods.

HE: Did you? Which one? I didn't know I had any.

I: Just now you compared Solange to a chest and a table. Because we were passing an antique shop. You automatically glanced at the furniture in the window. You sought some comparison. The chest and table were there to provide it.

HE: Yes, it's quite possible. But that only confirms what I was saying: I need the outside world to be able to talk. My story always needs pegs to hang on. The more pegs, the more story. Sometimes the peg is you, sometimes a tree, a cloud or a piece of furniture.

I: That doesn't explain the essential: your inexhaustible, inspired ability to talk about people, the way you have of turning them inside out like rabbitskins. Your secret. Give it.

HE: There's no secret. It's just me. My temperament. The temperament of a storyteller, perhaps. I listen, of course, I fill myself with words, record every event that comes my way, but I don't believe that's the essential. I feel that I also hear what isn't said, see what isn't shown. I sense it, as it were, behind the words or actions. Take a connoisseur of painting, for example. He looks at a picture by Rembrandt or Monticelli. He immediately understands how it's done. He sees the painter's work behind the picture surface, the number of brush strokes, the way they've been worked over, the repainting, the daring touches and so on. I'm a bit that way with people. I believe my mind functions like an adding machine. When someone says: "One, two, three . . ." I automatically complete the series: "four, five, six, seven, eight . . ." until I hear a little click telling me I've got to the end. All this sounds a bit obscure, eh? But then things aren't very clear in my own mind either.

I: Yes, yes, it's quite clear. But a bit surprising. I imagined you more like a bee buzzing about collecting honey. The old cliché.

HE: No, not at all. The bee selects. I don't. I take everything. Nothing comes amiss. The smallest, most boring, trivial, humdrum details give me as much pleasure as extravagant emotions or outlandish behavior. In short I'm interested in humanity. I'm an out-and-out altruist.

You now, you're an egoist, or an egotist. You don't give a damn for the outside world. You write people off. You don't descend to details: they bore you. All you like is the philosophy of things, ideas. When someone says: "Give so-and-so my regards," you forget at once and do no more about it. That's revealing. Now *I* faithfully pass them on; that way I can discuss one man with another. Passing on someone's regards doesn't seem much on the face of it but it's already a pathway into men's souls. Little paths lead to big clearings. You yourself told me once how you spend your time eliminating, rejecting. You know too many people, you get too many invitations, you defend your solitude like a lion. I collect everything, throw nothing away. I'm like the old woman who kept a big box in her cupboard labeled "Useless Bits of String." If you prefer a more poetic comparison, I'm like a plant that catches all the pollen on the wind. Not one grain escapes me.

I was hot and beginning to feel tired. On the Quai des Grands-
Augustins the bookstalls were yawning like gap-toothed crocodiles. I
know a rather pleasant café near there. You reach it as you go down
toward the Rue Bonaparte. It's old, unpretentious, shady, welcoming,
rather dirty, with a narrow terrace sheltered from the pavement by
spindly bushes. The art students foregather there to drink pernod and
coffee. The place also sells tobacco, which suited my purpose, as my
pouch was empty and I was longing for a smoke. He let me persuade
him. We went in, sat down, ordered our drinks. "Two coffees!" shouted
the waiter and I lit my pipe with real contentment. My shirt felt de-
lightfully cool on my back; my thighs ached. I should be glad to know
of anything nicer than a soft bench and a shady café interior in spring
with a friend beside one. The waiter brought two filters, which exasperated us as they were too tightly screwed down and the coffee
wouldn't drip through. We burned our fingers loosening them; the
water then shot through in a rush, producing a pallid infusion so hot
that I almost spat out my first mouthful.

I: What a bloody nuisance these filters are! They ought to pass a law
forbidding them throughout the country. Waiter! Waiter!

WAITER: Yes, sir!

I: Have you only got these filters? Haven't you an honest percolator
making an honest *espresso*?

WAITER: No, sir. Just filters. They're the only things that make good
coffee.

I: Prejudice! A myth! The filter's a Gallo-Roman instrument.
Look! My coffee's dishwater. Filters never work. All they're good for
is to drive the customers mad.

WAITER: You should take the lid off and cup it with your hand.

I: Thanks, I know.

HE: Waiter, bring me a rum.

WAITER: One rum!

HE: That's enough about your coffee. Wait till it cools and drink it up. It won't be the first bad coffee you've had, or the last. We have more important things on hand.

I: True. But you must admit the filter's an impossible contraption. Only in France do you find this instrument of torture.

HE: So what? Only in France can one really enjoy life, do the trains arrive on time, painters have talent, workmen work quickly, can one talk with almost anybody, and so on. Wherever you go you'll find pros and cons. After having traveled quite a lot I still vote for France, in spite of coffee-filters.

I: And Roberti? Was he a specifically French product too? I warn you, as far as I'm concerned he's in the same class as the filter.

HE: At any rate he had one specifically French characteristic—a faintly comic one. Just think, even at fifty he still regretted not being a man of letters.

I: I could have sworn it. That makes him perfect. Did he keep a diary like a schoolgirl? Did he write poems?

HE: I don't know. Possibly, but he never showed me any poems or pages from a diary. I said he regretted not being a man of letters. I didn't say he thought of himself as one. It was a pang of nostalgia he had, a little romantic cloud. Can one claim to have really succeeded if one has never produced a novel?

I: Obviously. What an idiotic idea.

HE: Still, that's what he felt in an obscure way. I believe he'd have given ten years of his life to be able to write a fine novel.

I: It would have been a bad bargain. His novel would have flopped.

HE: No doubt. I'm just telling you how things were. Trying to paint Roberti for you in depth. This nostalgia he had for literature may have been absurd but it was rather touching. And for him it held a certain sweetness. Thanks to this unsatisfied ambition he believed his life wasn't completely wasted. As a lawyer, then deputy, he had denied his vocation less than had he become an engineer, doctor, banker or soldier. Speeches for the defense, parliamentary harangues, addresses, even after-dinner speeches can at a pinch be regarded as literature. Had everything he'd written since he was twenty or twenty-five been collected together, it would have filled four or five volumes. Quite a solid output. The wherewithal to get himself elected to the Académie des Sciences Morales et Politiques or even the Académie Française.

I: So he had an eye on the Académie?

HE: Ha ha!

I: Well, why not, after all? The Académie stands for something considerable when one isn't a writer. Even so, a few addresses and speeches for the defense don't add up to much.

HE: Oh, but he had a great project in hand. Well, "in hand" is going a little too far. He had been dreaming of it for a long time. It was a Montesquieu-like work: a monumental *History of Variations in Moral Outlook* to which he intended one day to set aside five years of his life. He hadn't yet written a line, but a little preliminary spadework had been done. In his desk he kept a private card-index labeled "Variations," in which over the years he had amassed about two hundred and fifty cards. This didn't amount to a great deal but it could at a pinch serve as a basis to work from. All the more so since these cards already represented a fair amount of reading and research. For instance, he had one on the customs of the Teutons according to Tacitus and another on those of the Peruvians according to Garcilaso de la Vega. You can see at once the sort of conclusions to be drawn from comparing them. Another example: the Turenne-Grand Condé card and the Moreau-Pichegru card. Two identical cases of treason a hundred and fifty years apart and two entirely different evaluations. Turenne and Condé just as famous and admired after their treason as before it; Moreau and Pichegru the shame of the army and the nation. This type of comparison enchanted Roberti. According to him, Turenne and Pichegru, although of the same country and comparatively close in time, represented two worlds totally different from each other morally speaking. The *History of Variations in Moral Outlook* by Edouard Roberti was, you can see, an ambitious work. He wanted to outdo Montesquieu.

I: Is that all!

HE: Montesquieu's aim was to reveal the wisdom concealed behind the making of laws. Roberti on the other hand sought to prove with ten thousand examples covering the whole history of the world that morality, so imperative and intolerant, is nothing but a succession of arbitrary prejudices, that what is a crime in one age and country is a trivial or even praiseworthy act at other times and in other places. Montesquieu went in search of men's reason, Roberti in search of their folly.

I: I feel sure he would say "their absurdity."

HE: Yes, that was his term.

I: I'm not surprised. It's a fashionable word. The smartest thing in literature today is to explain "with lucid and desperate irony" that the world has no meaning and nothing makes any sense. I note that, even

in his most ambitious schemes, your Roberti didn't display much origi-
nality. I suppose also that when he complacently dreamed of his *History
of Variations* it never entered his head that it mightn't be a useful or
rewarding achievement.

HE: On the contrary, this work of destruction delighted him by its
very nature. It appealed to a sort of deep pessimism of which he himself was possibly unaware.

I: Your Roberti, let me tell you, was a pure product of his time and
country, that is to say the twentieth century and the West.

HE: Yes, I believe he was.

I: How frightful! And that title: a *History of Variations*. He took
himself for Bossuet.

HE: No, but even so he was rather pleased with this Bossuet-ish title,
rather proud of it. He pictured the day when the book would be finished
and published, the articles that would be devoted to it in the papers and
magazines, the luster it would add to his name.

I: Egoism and conceit were not absent from his speculations, I see.

HE: That doesn't prove he lacked talent.

I: Of course not, but since he left no work behind him, since his
History of Variations never passed the embryonic stage, we shall never
know. I don't say a great talent automatically presupposes a great mind.
All the same, Roberti's seems to me too mediocre, too base, too indolent to be creative in however small a way.

HE: No, no, I assure you, you misjudge him. Don't let your dislike
blind you. He was neither base nor mediocre. Just rather lazy. And in
his way (a minor, random way) he *was* creative. Otherwise I'd probably
never have taken any interest in him.

I: How can you talk such rot? You are passionately interested in everybody. You have a swarm of outlandish friends, a gallery of monsters.
You can spend hours on end with a notorious imbecile; you never tire
of questioning him about his life, his love affairs, his moral or intellectual development, his ideas. He fascinates you. Don't deny it. I've
watched you. And I know you.

HE: The only way to like fools is to hang over them and relentlessly
scrutinize them. Their stupidity then becomes clear and logical. Like
any spectacle or landscape. I love every kind of spectacle and landscape.
I really mean it. Even the most arid and desolate piece of land always
conceals a tuft of grass or a buttercup. I like to go out and find them. A
buttercup is a buttercup, whether in a suburban slum or the fairest valley of Provence or Burgundy. To return to Roberti's soul, since that's
what irritates you, I promise you it was strange, profound, full of re-

cesses and dark corners, veins of precious metal and hidden layers. It was a rather rich soul which hadn't followed the road most people's take. At one time in his life (five or six years ago, before his transformation) I truly looked on Roberti as a good friend. I enjoyed his company. We understood each other implicitly. And then one day, you know how it is, the bond loosens. You drift apart for no particular reason. Conversation sags. You meet less and less often. And when you do you are bored. That, for me, is the touchstone. Toward the end, when I found myself with him, I had the feeling I was wasting my time, that instead of listening or playing up to him I might have been somewhere else enjoying myself, learning something, enriching my mind or heart. Passion had turned him into a desert. He was using up all his resources on himself and there was none left for anyone else. He was living on "wartime economy," everything he had was mobilized to one sole end, but he didn't know what that end was. He had become as uncouth and selfish as a nation fighting with its back to the wall. He was stripping himself down to essentials. He was burning his boats. Conquer or die. But conquer what? He'd have been hard put to it to say. He was sinking ever deeper into murky shadows. It's funny, really. Right up to the end victory remained within his grasp. It was close at hand. He never looked in that direction.

I: You're becoming obscure.

HE: On the contrary, it's clear as day. Roberti persisted to the end in one of those passions I call "in-between." That is, too strong for one to muster enough will power to give it up and not strong enough for one to find the courage to give up everything else for its sake. In short the worst situation in which life can land you.

I: The English have a saying for that: "You can't have your cake and eat it."

HE: That's exactly the dilemma in which Roberti was caught. He wanted to eat his cake, that is nourish himself on the soul and body of Solange Mignot, for in his heart of hearts he knew that in her he had "found love." On the other hand he wanted just as doggedly to keep his cake, that is maintain the position in life he had contrived to build up over the years, pursue his manifold ambitions, do nothing to upset the subtle game which by devious means was to lead him to fame and fortune, preserve the sentimental unity of his family and, above all, retain the affection of Agnes, to whom he was deeply attached. He had always been discreet in his escapades (in which, besides, his heart was rarely involved). Thus he lived in the certainty that he and his wife formed an on the whole devoted and united couple with much in common. He was fully aware of the value of this connubial bliss. They had been married for twenty years. I think he had illusions about Agnes' intelligence, but in the long run certain habits of mind had grown up between them which possibly took the place of understanding; also, what is more important, habits of heart. Agnes had learned to read him, she "sensed" him the way a dog gets to know the moods of its master. She always knew exactly the color of the cloud that hung over him or the brightness of the ray of sunlight that lit him up. Roberti was delighted to have such a *witness* at his side. Agnes was his mirror, and a faithful one.

I: He loved looking at himself in mirrors.

HE: Yes. The weights of the scales were roughly balanced. On one side, Solange and love; on the other, Agnes, his position, his family and various rather less heavy weights which nevertheless brought it level. For example, there was his fine apartment in the Rue Oudinot. That didn't count for much but still it counted. He had grown attached to various good pieces of furniture he had bought one by one with taste and discrimination. He wouldn't have willingly parted with them for anything in the world. And of course, had he decided on divorce, so that he could take possession of Solange for good and all, he'd have had to say good-by to that.

I: Victories cannot be won without leaving feathers behind.

HE: So you see what I mean when I say that up to the end victory was within Roberti's grasp. He had only to decide one way or the other. Give up Solange or change his life.

I: And didn't you make him see that?

HE: I tried, but to him everything was indispensable: Solange, Agnes, his furniture, the respect of his constituents and so on. There were too many objectives in the war he was waging, which is tantamount to waging war without an objective, waging a war for contradictory reasons. He was blinded. It was all the more striking in that he would rationalize superbly, never abandoning the beloved Reason which had served him so well since childhood.

I: Whom the gods wish to destroy they first make rational.

HE: In Roberti's case what you've just said is frighteningly apt. Given a little less Reason, he'd have escaped. Had he permitted himself just one impulse, one of those impulses habitual with the thoughtless, he'd have been saved. He who had such a fine contempt for those who see no farther than the ends of their noses, those with their hearts on their sleeves, poor fellow, why didn't he close his ears just once to his vainglorious Reason! All along he believed himself intelligent enough,

44

strong enough, wily enough to keep everything. Only the foolish or
weak are forced back on decisions whereas he, Edouard Roberti, with
his breadth of outlook, his mind so clear and so impervious to wild
fancies, was exempt from such trifles; he could indulge in the lot, he
was big enough to draw on every opposing source of happiness and even
reconcile them. Such are the tortuous ways of pride, and they lead to
the abyss. Beside a man as rational as Roberti, ordinary passions with
their simple violence, their blind transports, seem like modesty itself.
. . . Are you listening? What's on your mind? You've been miles away!

ɪ: I was thinking of all the proverbs he illustrates. "Don't run with
the hare and hunt with the hounds." "Striving to better, oft we mar
what's well." "Fear of one evil often leads us to a worse." Not to mention Buridan's ass, naturally.

ʜᴇ: With regard to Roberti, you know, I'm more reminded of La
Rochefoucauld's maxim: "He who lives without folly is not as wise as
he thinks." He lacked that grain of folly which is like a grain of pepper,
bringing out the savor of wisdom, making plain cooking delicious. I
see him as a baby in his cradle. Several fairies bend over him. One says:
"I give you wisdom"; another: "I give you discretion"; a third: "Good
fortune"; a fourth: "Charm"; and so on. But the wicked Fairy Carabosse says: "I will prevent all these qualities from bearing fruit, for I
will not give you what it is in my power to give—the grain of folly, the
leaven of human dough; I will not give you that crumb of imagination
indispensable for shaping the world and winning salvation. With all
your gifts you will never rise above the mediocre or second-rate. I shall
prevent you from becoming a great man; you will never be Don Juan,
never even Casanova. You will be neither Mozart nor yet Puccini. You
will no more be Auguste Barbier than Victor Hugo, no more Clemenceau than Viviani. Because of my ill will, you will never be steel, only
cast iron."

Besides, all that fits in perfectly with certain details of Roberti's
youth which he told me at odd moments. One thing I find revealing,
and it corroborates my story of the Fairy Carabosse. When he was sixteen or seventeen, after having spent a very placid, earnest youth,
Edouard was taken from time to time with the idea that he was a saint,
or at least that by going to a little trouble he could achieve sanctity.
This disturbed and perplexed him. He saw his friends filled with passions, giving vent to impetuous desires, doing a thousand silly things.
Each in his way was the hero of a little adventure. But search his soul
as he might, he, Edouard, could not find the faintest passion, not the
slightest desire of any kind: it was a dumb soul. In his boyish idiom he

called it "the silence of sanctity." His self-control, which drove him to despair, cost him no effort. For instance, in all his seventeen years he had never managed to lose his temper. He felt this must surely be a terrible failing.

Another thing. He was a frantic bookworm. When still very young he had read all the best authors and, of course, found in them almost all his own ideas. His mind was pretty well equipped, his head very clear. But at seventeen clarity scares one. He would have preferred mysteries, instincts, inclinations. In those rare moments when his arrogance faltered he would sadly think: "I am bookish and an intellectual." That's how one talks to oneself when one is seventeen. Then he would veer to the opposite extreme and go out of his way to admire fools whose only talents were to be brutal, quarrelsome, insolent and chase after every skirt. He would fancy that theirs were the true qualities of leadership. He himself would never be anything but an onlooker.

When a boy is afflicted with such a character it worries him. It is hard to bear. He constantly resents his clumsiness; everything is difficult, everything is twisted. Happily there aren't only bad sides to it. In the first place it inclines him to be extremely frank with himself. Edouard, who was not intrepid in behavior, for he was too young and had no real desires, made up for this by being intrepid in mind. He was never afraid to follow the most daring arguments through to the end nor to face up to frightening ideas. He believed himself well able to understand everything but incapable of feeling. He was so strict in his inner debates that at times his cynicism astounded him. At such moments he regained confidence. Seeing himself so penetrating, so pitiless, he no longer regretted not being stupid.

ɪ: I rather like that character in a child.

ʜᴇ: Yes, it's an attractive quality; it makes for well-behaved children to whom one can talk and who are never dull. They mature late. Up to at least thirty we don't know how they will turn out. Their placidity and equanimity may well sterilize their hearts forever, but equally they can be formidable levers for their passions or enterprises. In the case of Roberti it was the process of sterilization that won the day. He was right to regret the absence of instincts, inclinations, mysteries from his soul, for in truth there were none there. At least not enough, or not ample enough. Those which awakened when he was fifty were abominable and it would have been better had they never made themselves known.

ɪ: One must always go in search of one's soul, even if what one should find is horrible. Only thereafter can one fend for oneself. But damn it, fifty was pretty late. Things had had time to deteriorate.

HE: How very French you are! You have to have everything clear-cut. You bathe everything in a sort of fatalistic light. You want to see everyone in immaculate focus. You believe we are predestined, that of necessity human beings reveal themselves to themselves. But it isn't true! There are some who pass their whole lives without knowing who they are, others who suspect nothing, others who have never troubled to glance at the outside world. The universe is full of the oblivious and the blind. Sometimes they are lucky, sometimes not. That's what destiny is. Had Roberti not gone one day to see Dietz, had Solange not opened the door for him, you have a man who would never have descended into the dark and complex depths of his soul. You would have a life like yours or mine, uneventful, more or less respectable and so forth. He would have remained on the surface of his soul like the vast majority of mankind until he died.

I: Hum! Christian sentiments these, brother! For a mystic like yourself, everything you've just said smacks to me of heresy. And Providence, what do you make of that?

HE: To begin with, I don't believe Providence is that anxious nurse, that fussy governess the priests plague our ears with. It is on a much higher plane, much more vague, much harder to understand. Its movements are on a grand scale, they are natural and invisible.

I: When they aren't earthquakes or tidal waves as in Roberti's case.

HE: No. It wasn't Providence acting in Roberti's case. It was something else. Let's call it the Devil. We may well do that, since we've already spoken of Providence. Providence he never listened to. It was in him, as in all men. But it spoke a foreign idiom which he didn't understand. Or else its voice was too faint. He didn't hear it. He didn't want to listen. Perhaps also the counsels of Providence blended with what he called "the voice of Reason." He never managed to distinguish between the two languages. Both told him to be rational. But there were two Reasons. That of Providence was humble and difficult; Roberti's was arrogant, selfish and apparently easy.

I: If he hadn't met Solange, he would have met someone else who would have led him to exactly the same spot. Solange was only the instrument.

HE: No, far from it. He could easily have never met anyone else. He could easily have never known love. There are masses of people who don't know it and are none the worse off for it. Rather better off, I'd say. Roberti was a very busy man. He had his work, his friends, his social and family life. There wasn't much room left for escapades. Each time he took a mistress he loved her in hasty snatches, so to speak. They were always very brief, almost breathless encounters. You must admit such a life hardly favors Don Juanism or even passion. Love demands leisure. No leisure, no love. In principle love, for Roberti, was out of bounds. He had no reason to venture there. Besides, just think of the conditions that must be fulfilled: he must love and he must be loved.

I: That still only makes two conditions.

HE: Yes, but two major conditions that don't often coincide, that are extremely rare. From which I conclude that the one person capable of sending Roberti to perdition was Solange. With anyone else he'd have been loved but would not himself have loved, or vice versa, and nothing would have happened. Rebuffed, he wouldn't have held out a fortnight, however great his passion. In any case, he wouldn't have felt any passion. He didn't easily become involved. He wasn't the sort of man to be smitten for nothing and eat his heart out in silence. I find it hard to picture him hopelessly worshiping some inaccessible beauty or even falling in love with some indifferent woman who only slept with him out of compliance or lassitude. Before he'd decide to love he must first have some physical pledges, but these weren't enough. At most, compliance inspired in him a superficial gratitude and that pleasant feeling of complicity induced by the sharing of a juicy secret. None of it touched his heart. The love Solange bore him, which was magnificent, boundless, magical, which she had built up twig by twig like a nest in which she could voluptuously lie, was like a sickness which he caught in turn after a rather long period of contagion. I see your objection. You're going to tell me he'd have been contaminated by the love of any other woman, but it isn't true. In the first place, what woman other than Solange—Solange the dreamy, the placid, the resigned, the imaginative, the romantic—would have loved him for two years without so much as a word? What woman wouldn't have wearied after three months and at least put her feelings into cold storage? Second, Roberti's ground, if I may put it that way, was prepared exclusively for the love of Solange. There was perfect suitability, elective affinity, a miracle in fact. What the papers call "the miracle of love." There's no explanation for it. It just is, that's all. One woman in perhaps a hundred million was capable of inspiring love in him, and ill luck had it that he should meet her.

I: Right, I accept that. It's the theory of love by accident. The love that knocks you down like a car, that one might have avoided by going a different way.

HE: Many things that happen to us are accidents, in which we find ourselves trapped through stupidity or want of attention. Or else we have some fleeting urge. For instance, you make some effort (a futile one like lifting a sack of potatoes or shifting a piece of furniture, something somebody else could have done for you) and—wham!—you start a hernia or have a heart attack; whereas had you not made this effort, had you prudently stood aside, you'd have been good for another ten or twenty years free of hernias and heart attacks. The hernia and heart attack were not written in the stars. It's all a question of moderation, prudence, opportunity, proportion, tact, flair, foresight. One must foresee the unforeseen, be on one's guard, that's to say steer clear of danger zones. Apply the "what's in it for me?" system. Have you noticed how the adjective always coupled with "accident" is "stupid," which at first glance is meaningless? An accident is neither stupid nor intelligent. It's a fact, a phenomenon. The stupidity lies not in the accident but in the person who exposes himself to it, because the accident is a fortuitous cause having nothing to do with the personal destiny of the victim. It isn't even Cleopatra's nose, for the nose was still Cleopatra, Cleopatra herself, one of her intimate possessions, bestowed on her at birth and so destined to condition her whole life. No, an accident is an error. It is something which escapes finality, determinism, something which was not present when the problem was set; hence it is inessential, hence it doesn't exist.

I: Stop! You're about to say something outrageous.

HE: People are very sensitive to the stupid, avoidable, unnecessary side of an accident. Imagine someone crushed by a train. They cut off his leg. This amputation fills him with despair. "Oh my leg, my poor leg," he cries. "Only a moment ago I had it, I was intact. If I hadn't stepped forward, if I had only looked up, I should still have my two legs like everyone else. I should possess a happiness I was unaware of and which I perceive in all its glory now it has been taken away from me." To lose a leg in an accident is the ultimate horror. The following instant is especially frightful, when one has a blinding vision of the irreparable: what was, a second before, and what is, now, forever. For a moment one stands on the frontier between the beautiful past and the hideous future. An illness is less agonizing because at least one knows its origins are remote; that it was germinating in one's body; that one is, however little, responsible for it. All at once it enters your head to cross the street because you've seen an amusing shop-window on the other side. You cross. A car you hadn't noticed knocks you down and there you lie with a broken spine, bitterly telling yourself before dying that it's all quite idiotic, that thirty seconds before you were in perfect health, feeling gay and happy, full of hopes and plans and even proposing to waste five minutes looking in a shop-window.

I: I don't see what you're getting at. You say an accident is an error and doesn't exist. After which you explain how a car knocks me down and I am dead. To my way of thinking it must surely exist, this accident which sends me to my forefathers in thirty seconds.

HE: No, it doesn't. It kills you but it doesn't exist. The only part it plays in your life is to put an end to it.

I: That seems a lot to me.

HE: Naturally. But it doesn't affect your soul.

I: Your theory won't stand. Going back to your man with the amputated leg, he isn't the same man when he has one leg as when he had two. The accident affects *his* soul. In denying the accident you're simply denying the outside world. Yet the outside world does exist. Good God, you yourself said as much! And it has a mighty influence on our thoughts and feelings. I grant you Solange was an accident in Roberti's life, but as he didn't die of a stroke the first time he saw her, as he survived this love which flattened his body like a steam roller, everything proceeded as if the accident had been destined for all eternity. The Solange accident, if I understand correctly, quickly merged with his soul and altered it. After a few months it became a sort of "natural adjunct." The flooding of the Nile is an accident too, but it leaves alluvial deposits sufficient to make a whole province fruitful. The Nile flood is at once an accident and a natural phenomenon, just like the meeting between Roberti and Solange. And I'll tell you something else: most people, when they get knocked down by a car, may well think: "How idiotic!" but they nearly always add: "It was meant to be." Accidents are part of fate, destiny, Providence, what you will. Fate is stupid but it is written and, after all, maybe God enjoys writing inanities in His great book.

All things considered, Roberti brings grist to my mill. Solange's love wasn't a train unexpectedly running him down. He saw it coming from afar. He smelled its smoke, heard the rails shudder, the whistle at the level crossing. I suppose in fact that, as soon as she became his mistress, she had an urgent need to describe her love to him in detail, explain how she loved him alone, loved him from the very first moment, and so on. Coward that he was, Roberti would normally have taken to his heels. Such love is frightening. In a flash one foresees all the complications and dramas it can lead to. So one breaks it off, and fast, believe me. Particularly when one is a deputy, Vice-Chairman of the Cats and Dogs Committee, a family man and all the rest. But what does he do, this presumptuous youth? He welcomes this dangerous love, festoons himself with it, drains it to the dregs, wallows in it. For him it's a source of matchless conceit, delirious pride; he tells himself it can never get out of hand—how could it since he doesn't return this love? That it's really too flattering to be loved by such a pretty girl and what a fool he'd be not to take advantage of it. The Solange-Roberti accident was foreseen, old man. All the red lights were on. Whence it was no longer an accident. Roberti was a victim of his vanity or pride. One must always go back to that. He alone did himself in because he was fated to do so.

HE: Certainly one can view it from that angle. Where feelings are concerned, everything's true at the same time. But what I want you to realize is that Roberti was the opposite of the type of man who has accidents. Thanks to his lucidity and love of rationalizing, he had more or less banished all mystery from his life. The world appeared to him as a machine in which there is an explanation for everything, if necessary. From this, as a rationalist, he had evolved one superstition: he believed that to escape death one must be vigilant; that so long as the brain remained clear and on the alert death kept at a distance. "One dies through carelessness," he used to say. In his youth he had got drunk five or six times. The memory of this appalled him. It was carelessness in its full horror. To his mind intoxication, by temporarily depriving him of his reasoning powers, stripped him bare, offered him up naked to the forces of destruction. He felt frail and vulnerable like prehistoric man facing the formidable array of nature and nightmarish beasts. That's why he hardly ever drank. In the same way old age and death take advantage of the slightest moral or physical relaxation to swoop down on one.

I: Sober through pride. That's not bad. That's something out of the ordinary! This man really had pride in his blood. He was sprinting toward damnation.

HE: Would you have had him become a drunkard in order to humiliate his Reason?

I: God, yes, if there was no other way of doing it! There are times when one has to make sacrifices.

HE: And supposing you made one now? What will you have?

I: No thanks, I never drink. But please don't let me stand in your way. Order another rum. The way you're talking, you're burning a lot of fuel. I love the smell of rum; it makes me dream of the Sargasso Sea, the old wooden navy, Guadeloupe where they have such splendid cyclones, the Battle of Trafalgar and the pirates of Treasure Island. It makes a change from the corrupt atmosphere of Roberti's love life. Thanks to your rum I can stick my nose out of the window and get a breath of fresh air.

HE: If you find Roberti's story too painful, let's call it a day.

I: No, no. His story suits me fine. It's just that he isn't my type. Not the sort of hero I'd choose if I were writing a novel.

HE: What sort would you choose?

I: I don't know exactly, but certainly not Roberti. One must have a modicum of sympathy for the character one is portraying. I don't feel any for your friend. Mind you, I wouldn't choose a paragon either. A few years ago I had an idea for a novel. I'd got the title, which was superb: *The Parisians*. It was set during the War of 1870 and the Commune. My hero was a young man endowed with all the virtues; he even had a pretty name—Roland des Charmettes. At the end of a hundred pages I couldn't stand him any longer. Handsome, brave, intelligent, sensitive, having at twenty the mature mind of a man of forty, just rash enough not to appear stuffed, he was practically perfect. But all this perfection made him insipid. Nauseating. I drew a line across the page and there the novel ended. Anyway, I started on the wrong foot. I wanted to write a *beautiful novel* like Balzac or Tolstoy, with all kinds of vicissitudes, war, revolution, disasters, two hundred characters and so on. It was crazy. One should write *ugly novels* which are like nothing else.

HE: Well, I must say Roberti's the perfect hero for an ugly novel. Don't you agree? Prickly, tiresome, hard to fathom, an elusive character, neither black nor white, neither fish nor fowl, complex. None of your fine Roland des Charmettes about him!

I: In *The Parisians* I had a splendid duel. Roland, who was of course a Republican, slapped the face of one Sébastiani, a police commissioner under Napoleon III, who had insulted him. It was his first duel and he didn't come out of it badly. I shall have to read that bit to you one day.

HE: With the greatest pleasure.

I: This duel of Roland's reminds me of something. Was Roberti courageous?

HE: I never had occasion to discover. We never found ourselves in any danger together. But what does courageous mean? There are various kinds of courage.

I: You know perfectly well what I mean. I'm asking you if he was brave. If, for instance, he wouldn't hesitate to punch someone's nose in the street. I mean that superficial form of courage which possibly doesn't carry much weight but which is so attractive. Physical courage. The kind that suddenly bursts out because one gets worked up or has one's heart in the right place.

HE: No, I don't think Roberti had that kind of courage. He was too high-strung. An unexpected onslaught disconcerted him and no doubt his first reaction was to "make himself small" and beat a retreat. Since you mention it, I do remember something. It dates back several years. One day he and I were in a car; he was driving. At a crossroads a man who was in the wrong, that's to say coming from the left, ran into him. Nothing much: a dented fender. The man got out of his car, Roberti likewise, and they started an altercation. The man was in a rage and shouting. Roberti tried to play the same game. Suddenly I felt he took fright. He got back into the car, slammed the door and started off without even demanding the man's address. He was pale. His hand trembled on the wheel. He began to talk rather too fast, the way one does when one wants to conceal an emotion. He told me how this mishap was trivial, after all, and how a police report would have meant his wasting three quarters of an hour and that three quarters of an hour of his "precious life" (those were his words) were worth a lot more than the insurance money.

I shouldn't have told you that. You're going to turn against him even more. But truth comes first. Besides, I'm convinced this anecdote proves nothing save that in certain circumstances Edouard might lose his nerve. The form of courage which consists of punching someone in the street is really a very minor one. It's a reaction brought about by anger, quite natural if one is fiery or irascible by nature. But as I've told you, Roberti wasn't quick-tempered. He was at once high-strung and cold, a curious combination but not such a very rare one. People with really delicate nerves, I've noticed, are often outwardly phlegmatic. Their storms all go on inside; very little of them appears on the surface. And through the constraint it imposes, their outward calm only fosters their nervous condition. Those who are violent, hotheaded, boisterous, tyrannical, disorderly, who don't control themselves but lose their tempers twenty times a day, are never really high-strung: everything evaporates in gestures and words.

I don't believe Roberti was naturally brave. I think, however, that he was not incapable of showing bravery (he had the Military Cross, which, though it may not mean much, isn't usually awarded to complete cowards). I think that in order to show courage he had first to prepare himself for it, make up his mind to it, overcome his sensitivity, after which he no doubt conducted himself as gallantly as anyone else. Besides, one can learn physical courage. Had he been in the ranks in 1914 he'd have learned it after two weeks in the trenches. As to moral courage, there I'm positive: he had a great deal. He was unswerving; he let nothing intimidate him. A bit arrogant, perhaps, during periods of prosperity or good fortune, but always extremely gay and charming, always carefree during bad stretches when nothing he tackled went right.

I: It's as if he were made for adversity!

HE: I often used to think so. He was well used to setbacks. Sometimes it even worried me. Seeing him put up so easily with a rather baleful destiny, I used to think he'd never go very far. Never be a cabinet minister, for example. He had a distinguished mind and personality but with him I could never sniff the intoxicating smell of success, of really high ambition. He never rose above his own nature. He frittered away his time and spirit in pursuit of minor ambitions, second-rate intrigues. Great men are often mediocrities who surpass themselves.

His objectives were small: to be vice-chairman of this or that, sent on a fact-finding mission to China and so on. Whenever these came to nothing (and they often did, for the competition for such trifles is fierce) he would console himself quite philosophically and embark on some other enterprise. In fact, he spent his whole time wanting something. The aspirations of his soul were legion. Thus his life appeared to him a perpetual defeat. He ceaselessly ran up against the world like a goat butting at a wall. Political life, which is a web of intrigues that fail or fizzle out and which numbers a hundred reverses for every success, strengthened him in the by-and-large-mistaken belief that man has practically no power over the world, that is over events. Given sufficient cunning, skill and discretion, one can lightly sway these, divert their course, win them over. But that is the limit of human power. Or so he at heart believed. Ideas of wisdom, the ideas of a rational man. But such ideas would never have entered the heads of Napoleon, Alexander the Great, Julius Caesar or even Louis-Philippe!

I: This Roberti is really not very inspiring.

HE: Well, were I capable of writing, such a man would interest me. I've never met one like him in books. He is unpublished, something quite new. At every turn he has crotchety ideas, weird emotions, the true feelings of a living man and not those of a hero of fiction. He's never stereotyped. He's a human being made up of mind and matter, constantly running into the barriers of the world, making mistakes, all tangled up with his soul, committing blunders in which he gets bogged down or of which he repents, repetitive, hairsplitting, limited in time and space, complex and, above all, heavy. What strikes me is precisely this heaviness of Roberti's. He's not a pure spirit, oh no! He's embedded in the world on which he weighs (a little) and which weighs on him (a lot). So you can see what I mean when I say he deserves to pass into literature. Moreover for him who loved literature so dearly and longed to win fame through it, it would be a strange destiny to enter it through that gate! Most unexpected. One thinks one is an author when in reality one's a character. Not a creator but a creation. Oh little ironies of fate!

I: Such little ironies are common. In the end there aren't many creators. On the other hand there's a mass of subjects, the representation of which can make a picture. Why not Roberti after all? In his way, he's just as good as Manet's lemon or Corot's pond at Ville d'Avray. I'll think about it.

HE: You know, I can give you countless details about him, and not just any details: details about his soul.

I: Those aren't the most important. Those one invents! What's important and always inadequately documented are things like the furniture, the color of the sky, the clothes, the places where one walks, the houses, the state of the weather and so on. At any rate I find your narrative lacking in description. Tell me about Roberti's apartment, the Chamber of Deputies, the way he went from the Rue Oudinot to the Palais-Bourbon. Oh and how, for instance, did he earn his money? That's interesting. That places him at once. One can see who one's dealing with. I presume he wasn't content with his salary as a deputy?

HE: He wasn't grasping over money, but even so his parliamentary salary was meager.

I: Hadn't he managed to get himself onto the boards of two or three companies? That's the great ambition of deputies, so I've heard.

HE: I know he thought of it, mused about it now and then. He even dreamed about it sometimes. But to my knowledge he never brought it off.

I: What, then? He didn't keep up his practice, did he?

HE: Are you crazy? Practice? As if he ever had any! Being a lawyer bored him to death. He had yawned his way through his law exams, combining them for distraction with an arts degree. And then he set up as a lawyer because one has to earn one's living. But it was only a makeshift. He vegetated till he was thirty or thirty-five, getting a brief here and there on minor cases, earning just enough to live on. He contributed to small, unimportant political journals, sent in reports to the *Law Gazette*. Once I questioned him about his early days. I asked why he had chosen the law rather than medicine or literature. With his gifts, his subtle, inquiring, cultivated mind, I saw him better studying to be a professor.

i: And what did he reply?

HE: Well, he was very frank. He told me that at eighteen, after passing his exams, he had pitilessly analyzed himself and drawn an almost mathematical conclusion from this analysis. He had listed his ambitions and potentialities in two columns on a piece of paper. Prime ambition: to become a man of letters. Difficult. He hadn't much talent. He realized his style was elegant and precise but flat. On the other hand he didn't feel in himself that vague but driving inspiration which makes young artists so sure of themselves. He didn't feel he had any "message" to convey. He didn't hear in himself any echo of that little music you sometimes tell me about (I don't hear it myself, either, alas!), that indomitable, unique little music which is the sign that one has "something to say."

i: Did he know of this little music's existence?

HE: Naturally not. I didn't know of it myself until the day you described it to me and explained what it meant. In short he had concocted poems (very bad ones, like everyone else) but try as he would he could see no great work stirring in his depths. So he crossed out literature, that's to say art in general. He argued as follows: "The highest human activity is art. That activity is closed to me because I lack the mysterious spark which makes one Mozart, Van Gogh or Baudelaire. . . ." (Note the three names in passing: they were his three great idols at eighteen; his taste wasn't bad, though inclined to follow the fashion.) "I can never be anything more than a gifted amateur. What comes after art in my scale of values? Politics, which is also a kind of art but much more accessible, demanding no special gift save a degree of intelligence and character. So be it, then, I shall go in for politics. One day I shall be the master of France. I shall accomplish great things. I shall emancipate the workers, I shall be an unrivaled negotiator in world affairs and perhaps in my old age, like Clemenceau, I shall win a war."

i: I say, that's not at all bad. I like Roberti better at eighteen than at fifty. Ah, the lofty and compelling ideas one has at eighteen! Great men are those who at fifty have accomplished what they dreamed at eighteen.

HE: Doesn't it form a rather charming picture, young Edouard on his iron bed in his student's room, deciding on his future gravely, earnestly, without illusions? It's not without grandeur.

1: What lacks grandeur is Roberti at fifty, a minor deputy, having capitulated on every front and become a mere caricature of his youthful dreams. By the way, you still haven't told me what he lived on.

HE: Wait for it! The whole pleasure of storytelling lies in digressions. Not to mention the fact that Roberti's "years of apprenticeship" are important. I want you to have a complete panorama of him, his whole destiny, Roberti white, gray and black, Abel and Cain, Tiberius Gracchus and Faust.

1: All right. At eighteen, then, he opts for politics.

HE: He pursues his argument. "What is the short cut to politics in France since 1879?" he asks himself. "The law. The great revolutionaries were nearly all lawyers. Gambetta was a lawyer, Poincaré a lawyer, and so on." In this way he ran through about fifty politicians who came from law school.

1: Clemenceau was a doctor and Jaurès came from the teaching profession. So did Herriot.

HE: Yes, I know there are exceptions, but after all the vast majority of politicians in France came from the law faculty. Consequently Edouard told himself: "I shall be a lawyer," and there he showed undeniable courage, for the law bored him to tears. It was at the opposite pole from his tastes and interests. But he thought it was an ordeal to which it was essential to submit, that he would emerge from it fortified, that it would give him the intellectual armor he needed. On several occasions he told me the three years he spent studying law were the worst in his life and how he often thought dejectedly that he had chosen the worst possible course. But he never gave up. He trudged through the arid wastes of the law with a perseverance deserving admiration. After which he set up as a lawyer and began to dabble in politics.

1: And naturally joined the Radical Party.

HE: Naturally. It was a prudent and deliberate decision. The Radical Party is hardly a party at all. It has a policy because it has to have one. It is above all a school for government, a nursery for ministers. At least it was before the war, when Roberti first started in politics. You can imagine the circumstances (which I'll spare you): the advantages of the Radical Party for a young man who thinks he's ambitious and at the same time public-spirited. At least that's how Edouard saw himself. He qualified as ambition the dilettantism which had led him to choose politics as a sort of lesser art, a substitute for painting, music and above all writing. As for public-spiritedness, he was genuinely imbued with it. For him it was (and always would be) a vague and moving aspiration. He thought a life worth living if it furthered a nation's happiness; that it was almost as fine to foster the institutions of the state, give bread to the poor and freedom to all, as it was to write masterpieces. After five or six years he had become municipal councilor for his district (he lived at the time near the Gare Montparnasse, in the Fifteenth Arrondissement). Then, when he was about twenty-eight, he married Agnes, who was twenty-three. She was the daughter of a wine merchant from the Gironde; she brought with her a small dowry on which the couple set themselves up in a smart apartment in the Rue Oudinot, way beyond their means. But Roberti believed they must challenge fate. In short they now went through twelve difficult years. He had thought he would slide into politics like a knife into butter, but politics put up a stout resistance. He had imagined himself a minister at twenty-five, instead of which he was forced to climb the ladder step by step, to struggle in obscurity, address "Young Radicals" on Wednesday evenings, take on the secretaryship of the Fifteenth Arrondissement and expend more genius in petty intrigues than was required to rule the Spanish Empire. I think these twelve lean years, when he wore himself out in frantic and ludicrous struggles, were very detrimental to his mind and heart. They accustomed him to minor objectives, minor activities, patience, mediocrity, pettifogging detail—things toward which he was all too readily inclined. They sustained and fostered the petty and timorous side of his nature. In this sense one can say he had no luck. Who knows? Had he had a rapid and brilliant career, had he swiftly been faced with major problems, his life might have been quite different. Applied to vast projects or weighty responsibilities, his discretion and meticulousness would have proved valuable assets. Moderators, useful counterweights. Whereas in fact they merely became cannon balls chained to his ankles.

It was not till after the war that Roberti was elected a deputy. During the war he had behaved rather well, though without heroism. I mean, he didn't join any Resistance movement. But he kept in secret touch with the militant radicals of his district. He was "on the right side," that is to say he was a Gaullist; he corresponded with the few personalities of his party who were persecuted by the Germans or the Vichy government. This honorable conduct earned him the Radical candidature for one or another of the Paris electoral districts at the general election of 1945, and he just managed to sneak in. It was a great day. He could finally give up being a lawyer. I shall skip the details, the new deputy's thrill as he took his seat in the Chamber for the first time, the respect shown by the ushers, the splendor of the setting, that semicircle which is indeed very fine and imposing with all its memories of Parliament's great hours, its lobbies, its library, its superb ceiling by Delacroix. Roberti took giddy possession of it all. He responded instantly to the clublike atmosphere that prevails in the Chamber of Deputies and, being a good mixer, quickly learned to adopt that air of familiarity and complicity which is more or less essential. But at heart, you see, he was less thrilled than he appeared to be (above all to please Agnes, who had waited for this moment with at least as great impatience as he). The fact is, he had desired it too long: his desire had gone stale. To become a deputy at twenty-five would have been truly extraordinary, a joy he would have relished to the full in a wild burst of happiness. At thirty-nine it still had its savor, no doubt, but this was less pungent. He had worked too hard for it. It wasn't a gift but something earned, and earnings bring far less pleasure than gifts. It wasn't a springboard but a finishing post, the fruit of fifteen years of obscure and dreary labor. When he finally bore off the prize, I think Roberti realized that success isn't *picturesque*, isn't an unknown and enchanted land to which one miraculously comes, a Canaan or a Tahiti where one instantly forgets all one's past trials to live in unalloyed happiness. Success doesn't touch you like a magic wand; on the contrary, one chases after it a long time and only catches it at the end of a hard run. One is tired, worn out, broken, breathless; one can only clasp it limply. Roberti, after his election, collapsed like the runner of Marathon at the end of his course. The goal was reached and he must have felt it was high time and that he would have been incapable of running another yard, which was untrue: one can always run another yard or mile, or even a thousand miles, however worn out one is, so long as one hasn't got there. But arrival breaks the muscles, puts an end to one's efforts, switches one from the active to the passive state. So long as Roberti was flinging himself into the fray, so long as he was fighting, he didn't suffer. He was in the heat of battle. But directly he took his seat in the Palais-Bourbon he ached all over. He never wanted to get up again. This helped to strengthen his belief that success never comes quickly but can be achieved only by means of countless patient maneuvers and that when one arrives it is through seniority, after an infinity of tedious and even exhausting toil. Those, I believe, are the roots of his character, the reasons why he turned into someone so patient, so resigned, so stoical when necessary. It also explains his tenacity and persistence, particularly over everything concerned with the preservation of his seat in the Chamber of Deputies.

He was grimly attached to this seat he had been to such trouble to win; he was determined not to sink back into the poverty of the past. He overlooked nothing which could ensure his re-election, strengthen his position in the Radical Party, earn him the gratitude and affection of his constituents by performing every little service he could for them, avoid giving substance to any unpleasant hint in the satirical press. I could list the various precautions he took for hours. The inevitable result of a life and experience of this kind was finally to mitigate considerably the disinterested ambitions of his youth. Concern for his personal position always guided his political activities. Since he was honest and well-intentioned, he strove to reconcile the public good with the good of Roberti. Hence his attitude was never absolutely clear; on the contrary he appeared in French political life as an ambiguous, complex character, tortuous and subterranean, who would never truly take wing (although morally above suspicion) precisely because of his caution, his hatred of committing himself too far, his horror of taking a frank and open stand over anything. His distrust of all romanticism and extremism, his sense of proportion, often prevented him from voicing lofty ideas, though this would have given him pleasure.

I come now to your earlier question: what did he live on? I've told you he wasn't greedy about money. Even so, he didn't want to have to chew his nails toward the end of each month: that struck him as absurd for a man of his worth, and even faintly degrading. After his first election he soon found two or three companies to take him on as legal adviser. Big concerns love having a deputy to work for them and the deputy is delighted with such an arrangement, which brings in a comfortable income without demanding much effort. In this way, Roberti doubled his parliamentary earnings.

I: I don't much care for that. It smacks of trading on influence.

HE: Oh, that's going too far. He would never have done anything for his employers that went against his principles or his conscience. For instance, had he been legal adviser to a firm doing government work he would rather have quit than procure his client a contract he didn't deserve. Besides, I'm convinced the term "trading on influence" never occurred to him; it would never have entered his head, when he went after these little sources of extra income, that they could ever influence his political activities.

I: So in the end he was pretty well provided for, if I'm any judge.

HE: Oh come now, no. He lived way beyond his means. The secret of this lies in the fact that he never denied himself anything. He coveted objects. Now a piece of furniture seen in some antique shop, now a pair of shoes. He had a "shoe fixation" and owned over twenty pairs of every description, from sealskin after-ski boots to patent-leather slippers. It was odd, this passion for shoes. It harked back to his years of poverty. Like many men he loved fine, supple, rich-smelling leather and he had suffered in the old days from being unable to indulge in the luxury of it. He had promised himself that if ever he became rich he would have shoes by the cupboardful. Purchasing a pair of shoes never lost its thrill. For him it was the ideal buy, the one that provides unmitigated joy, almost a sense of power.

Objects held a fascination for him. Like a sudden desire sweeping over him, he would quite simply fall in love with a Louis-Philippe armchair, a silk dressing gown or a crocodile wallet. He must own it. Besides, he loved to indulge his whims. Possibly this acted as a safety valve for his Reason, which at times he surely found wearisome or irksome. It was also a revenge on the days when he was forced to deny himself everything for lack of money. That makes you smile? Well, it *is* rather comic.

To round it off, I'll throw in one amusing detail. He used to put by special funds for what he alluded to (with a touch of irony) as his "pleasures." He had set up a special secret account from which he could draw the wherewithal to buy small gifts for his conquests, take them to semi-smart restaurants and pay for hotel rooms. It didn't amount to much, for these young ladies came, as you know, from humble origins: it cost little to treat them to an illusion of high life. Roberti's generosity stopped short at that, for he was a bit of an ass over his amours. He wanted to be loved for himself and would never have stood for paying a woman in cold blood or giving her presents which might be construed as rewards for her compliance. At fifty he loved and was loved like a young man. That's not so bad for an amateur, for a man taken up with other interests, is it?

I: You paint with vitriol! Those last touches to his portrait are really damning. I suppose that, not content with being selfish, lavish toward himself and stingy toward others, he also rationed the housekeeping money?

HE: He was rather selfish but not stingy. He gave Agnes all she needed to run the house and even more. The result was an honest middle-class way of life. Without living like young princes, the boys cut a good figure in the world and at school. So far as Agnes went, he made it his duty never to deny her anything. Had she been extravagant or vain, she could have been dressed by the leading couturiers without his taking the least exception. But she never troubled much about her appearance. She was content with the services of a little dressmaker who, incidentally, turned her out quite smartly. She was less elegant than her husband (in spite of the mink). Seeing Roberti with his family one was put in mind of the male animal, a pheasant or lion superb in dazzling plumage or majestic mane, flaunting all the beauty of the species beside the comparatively drab female and young.

The apartment in the Rue Oudinot was very pleasant. It contained a cook and a maid. On evenings when Roberti entertained they hired a man in a white jacket, always the same one with whom they had developed a certain familiarity, ostentatiously calling him "Albert," and whose easy manner led guests to assume him to be the resident butler.

Living beyond one's means is a habit which is not without charm and has its good sides. But a time comes (around the fifties, in fact) when one develops bouts of giddiness. One is no longer so young or so fit, one tells oneself. Roberti had agonizing qualms which would wake him at four A.M. He would then conjure up all sorts of melodramas: outvoted at the next elections; dismissed by the firms that employed him; reduced to the meager parliamentary pension; arrears of tax dating from his years of carefree splendor catching up with him; having to quit the fine apartment in the Rue Oudinot, where they were so well off, for a three-room hole at Saint-Mandé, and worse. What dismayed him most was the thought of having to sell his smart car and take to buses. For him that was the ultimate downfall. To shake off these nightmares he would tell himself erotic stories which were quite good at bringing back sleep.

I: Listen, I've an idea. Let's get out of this bistro. I've had enough of sitting here. It's a lovely day. Besides, there's something I want to hear you say.

HE: What's that?

I: Something like: "Then came a day when Solange rang the bell of Roberti's apartment."

HE: Why all the rush? Going too fast takes all the pleasure out of the story.

I: Even so, one shouldn't go too slowly either. Let's get down to the plot.

HE: What is the plot?

I: The loves of Roberti and Solange, of course.

HE: That strikes me as very thin. Not exactly ambitious. I wanted to tell you about a man's destiny, about joy and sorrow, good and evil, the world bearing down on mankind like a lid, the countless wills interweaving or colliding with each other: the kind of huge uncertainty of life, in which nothing is entirely true or entirely false, in which all is compromise, approximation, groping, expediency, in which nothing ever wholly succeeds or irrevocably fails. In short I wanted to do in words what novelists never do with their pens. To be for once the mirror moving down a road, and so faithful a one that at first sight you think there is no mirror, that what you see is nature itself.

I: So . . . ?

HE: So you pose limitations, you confine me within the tiny framework of a love story. To hell with love stories! We've seen enough. We don't want any more. What price yet another love story after *La Nouvelle Héloïse, Le Lys dans la Vallée, Adolphe, Manon* and the rest of them? We know everything about love, everything. There's nothing left to learn. It's all been said, all been written. Love is the Bois de Boulogne on a Sunday, the Place de la Concorde at six P.M., the Métro in the rush hour. I want to take you up the Cordillera of the Andes, make you freeze on the pack ice, die of thirst in the Gobi desert; I want to show you the view from the top of Everest. I want to be your Virgil and take you for an unforgettable tour of the fortieth subterranean floor of hell, where one can see Lucifer embedded in ice and darkness, his great bat's wings all stiff with rime, as in Gustave Doré's engraving. That's the trip I offer you and all you can find to reply is: "Let's go and get some air along the river."

I: Tell me, are you by any chance related to Baron Munchausen? Aren't you ashamed of going on like that? All right, let's climb the Himalayas, let's descend to the fortieth subterranean floor. But first let's get out of here. Let us in fact walk along the river. Waiter!

WAITER: Yes, sir!

I: What do I owe you?

WAITER: Two filters and two Negritas. That makes four-fifty.

HE: Put it away. It's my treat.

I: No, it's on me. You're doing the talking. You're reciting a novel I may copy. At least I can treat you to a coffee and two rums.

WAITER: Four-fifty from ten. There's your change. Thank you, sir. Service is *not* included.

The sun was superb on the Quai Malaquais. In spring the hottest hour of the day is still quite acceptable. We had recovered our breaths in the bistro. My shirt was no longer sticking to my shoulderblades. As for him, the rum and coffee had brought color to his cheeks. There's nothing like the spring sun to bring the dark gray stones of Paris to life. It flecks them with color, penetrates and transforms them into agate or opaline. As if it were amusing itself by imitating the Impressionists. It has a wild time with their shimmering tints. At three-thirty on a spring afternoon, Paris seen from the quays has the air of a city built of sards or cat's-eyes, translucent round the edges, traversed by mysterious flashes of light; it is a fairy-tale city such as was viewed on the horizon by the knights of fable as they rode in quest of adventure, or by the urchin Arabs of the glorious days of Islam, who knew so well how to drive Shaitan crazy.

On the threshold of the café we blinked our eyes. There was a delicious tang in the air in spite of the traffic, the passers-by leafing through the books on the stalls and a long, gleaming carapace of silver which the sun had cast over the Seine. In the blue sky three or four white clouds, motionless, like tiny sailing boats, shaped like little Iceland on the map of Europe, faintly swollen, awaited a gust of wind to send them gliding over Normandy. It was a marvelous moment, brimming with charm, one of those moments when one becomes aware for a dazzling second that life is good since it can now and then and without warning distill such poetry. That's what one needs to recall in chill old age, when reckoning up the account of one's griefs and joys: how at such a moment in my life I strolled along the quays on a spring afternoon and for a second or two grasped all the secrets of creation; nature poured over my soul like a fabulous honey. Life is a long, prodigiously dull poem in eighty cantos, full of repetition, padding, gibberish, bad jokes and horrible circumlocutions, but it deserves to be read with care because of the occasional sublime line provided by the gods on which one now and then stumbles, unforeseen and quite unconnected with what has gone before or is to come. Perhaps, thirty or forty years on, the memory of my long stroll through Paris while a friend regaled me with Roberti's story will return one evening to illumine my sad thoughts of old age. Perhaps this memory will form part of my secret and foolish treasure of little unexpected joys. Every man knows such "privileged moments" which nothing outwardly betrays; they spring from a mysterious and fleeting harmony between spirit and body, weather and landscape, which all at once envelops you. The beginnings of a storm in the country are particularly conducive to such raptures, when the earth exudes its deep smell like a woman waiting to be made fecund.

HE: Finally a day came when Solange rang the bell of Roberti's apartment.

I: Who answered it? I feel sure it was Agnes.

HE: No, Agnes was out. The maid opened the door. She was an elderly, rather overfamiliar maid called Germaine. When waiting at table she would add her mite to the conversation; she would proffer advice, grumble, scold Monsieur; she would protect Madame, whom she sometimes called "my pigeon," and domineer the children. For a while I thought Germaine was a genuine "natural"; then I realized she was creating a character for herself. She had built up an image of the elderly servant—forthright, outwardly difficult but kind at heart, touchy, quarrelsome, standing on her dignity, having her "moods" but devoted unto death. When disaster fell on Roberti she didn't wait a second to give a week's notice. She claimed that she didn't dare look the tradesmen in the face. The baker made her blush, the milkman paralyzed her, mere sight of the butcher made her wish the earth would swallow her up, and as for the wine merchant, he flatly turned his back on her. How could she put up with such insults, a respectable person like her with a lifetime of hard work and integrity behind her? She hadn't "deserved as much." Roberti hadn't been in prison a week when the excellent Germaine left her pigeon flat after having first staged a terrible scene. As if Agnes had been responsible for everything, planned it all with the sole aim of injuring her reputation.

I: Charming!

HE: The more so since Germaine had also accurately smelled a future shortage of cash in that house. The rat leaving the ship.

I: I presume this Germaine had been with the family right from the start, when Agnes was a little girl. Did she bring her from Bordeaux?

HE: Far from it. Germaine had been with the Robertis only nine or ten years. They got her through an employment agency like anyone else. But she quickly assumed her ways of an old and trusty servant. No doubt it was part of her nature to be familiar, complaining and so on. She had a vocation for conducting herself like a domestic in a Molière play. Unfortunately times have changed. Germaine was born a century or more too late. In the days of Napoleon III or the Ancien Régime she would have spent her whole life with some big family of the nobility or bourgeoisie, one of those stable, eternal families you find in Saint-Simon or the Comtesse de Ségur. She would very likely have left behind a stainless reputation for domestic probity and fidelity. Like Roberti, she had no luck either. To return to the point, the Robertis were not averse to their maid's familiar attitude. In a way they played up to it. They were not above letting their friends gather that Germaine had practically been Agnes' nursemaid, that she was a piece of family furniture, inherited just like the piano or the bookcase.

In addition to these qualities, Germaine had further armored herself with a knowledge of men and a prophetic soul. The moment she saw Solange she detested her. This charming, attractive, modest, rather shy, elegant young thing framed in the doorway filled her with a relentless antipathy, merely because she was pretty and charming and some people take grace in others as a personal insult. But what is so remarkable is that such sudden, violent and instinctive reactions, which cause little more than a touch of irritation at the time, assume a terrible significance later on in the light of events. One feels that all in a flash one has had a glimpse of the future. When the Commendatore knocks on Don Giovanni's door, thump, thump, thump, thump (four times), Leporello is seized in the grip of intense fear, for he knows that no good can come of a phantom. Don Giovanni, on the other hand, though far more knowledgeable and with a much wider outlook on the matter, is unafraid. Yet Leporello does well to tremble. It is he who is in the right. It's not uncommon to arrive at the truth by a wrong path. Prophets are simple souls who accurately deduce the future from facts they interpret in the wrong way.

Germaine had opened the door to other pretty women before Solange without experiencing any particular displeasure. Sometimes she would even chaff Monsieur about these fair visitors, who were family friends and, as she knew perfectly well, no harbingers of sin. But by a gratuitous twist of her mind, out of pure ill-humor at the sight of Solange, whose existence she hadn't so much as suspected a moment before, she now conjured up visions of a gaudy popular romance, a scandalous and forbidden passion. Circe was standing before her. Germaine had a simple mind through which meandered a procession of highly colored popular engravings. She was convinced that the same causes always produced the same effects; that a stepmother, for instance, always bullied her stepchildren, ruin irrevocably drove bankers to suicide, marriage for love unfailingly brought happiness. Insatiable consumption of women's magazines and popular novels had firmly anchored these simple notions in her mind, giving them the sanction of print. Faced with Solange, Roberti would fall an instant prey to the devil in the flesh. This respectable, middle-aged man would founder within three months like the legendary Professor Unrath in *The Blue Angel*. At all events, she assumed a forbidding stare and said almost rudely to Solange: "Wait here. I'll ask if Monsieur can see you." And there in the hall she left her without even inviting her to take a seat. Solange had merely asked to see M. Roberti, she hadn't said who she was, but Germaine had guessed that, despite her allure, she was no society girl. She had sensed that she was only an underling, for whom there was no call to put herself out. D'you get the way the spirit of prophecy works? From false premises one arrives at correct conclusions. Germaine had a stupidly romantic imagination, a head thick with idiotic ideas, and it was just these which gave her a general insight into the future. It is easy to understand why prophets are detested. Their certainty infuriates intelligent people who see only its arbitrary side and won't admit that truth can emerge from such narrow and stupid arguments. When I read the Bible I always think of the Robertis' Germaine. I picture the old Hebrew prophets as looking exactly like her. They were surely old fools, their minds stuffed with catchwords and clichés, stubborn as mules and making melodramas out of everything. Melodramas are popular with the public, which loves traditionally pregnant situations. But in the long run few people are candid enough to dare compose them. David and Solomon and the Roman proconsuls, who were shrewd and subtle men, must have seethed when the prophets started spouting their nonsense. Yet it was the prophets who were right. The things they foretold came about by other ways than those they had foreseen, but they came about just the same. Whence the belief that they possessed supernatural powers, that they were in communication with Jehovah.

ı: You could add that there is a kind of wisdom underlying clichés and popular superstitions, something resembling the spirit of proverbs. Everyone laughs at proverbs, delights in inverting them or making one contradict another; nevertheless they certainly represent a universal experience: they are the conclusions drawn by humanity from events observed millions of times over with hardly any variation. I myself used to laugh at proverbs but finally I ended by respecting them, seeing in them a treasure, an heirloom, a collection of recipes handed down from century to century as protection against some of the world's abuses, a breviary for the common run of mortals, a guide through the daily ambushes of life. Of course they are often petty, down to earth, circumspect, unfit for such men as Goethe, Baudelaire, Napoleon or Don Quixote, but they work well for those without ambition, philosophy or knowledge of men. Most people go through life equipped with nothing but a hundred or so proverbs. They would go to the stake rather than admit it, they aren't always even aware of it, but these hundred proverbs enable them to get through sixty or eighty years without any major catastrophe just as well as if they based their conduct on the principles of Kant or Plato. As for your Germaine, it's quite simple, I can see her as clearly as if I'd known her: wherever she went she took the bundle of proverbs her parents had wrapped up for her in her childhood, dipping into it whenever the need made itself felt.

HE: So Germaine abruptly left Solange standing in the hall, as if the latter were delivering something from a shop or a nun begging for money. She trailed her slippers toward Roberti's study, where he was working.

I: What at?

HE: Ah, there you have it! Here's where destiny steps in. Roberti was working on a legal problem for Dietz.

I: Was he also Dietz's adviser? You didn't mention that.

HE: No, he wasn't. But from time to time, when Dietz had some tricky and confidential business on hand, touching on the fringe of politics, he trusted the legal side of it to Roberti in return, as you can imagine, for a sumptuous remuneration. Roberti liked these little windfalls, which augmented his regular income. He never turned them down. It was money which could be spent shamelessly and without compunction, allowing him with complete peace of mind to buy an unnecessary pair of shoes, a suit or a fine edition of the complete works of Stendhal.

Roberti worked like a gifted slacker, that is to say about five minutes in every hour; but he would do as much during those five minutes as ordinary people do in sixty. The rest of the time he would roam round his study, inspecting the backs of the books in his bookcase, rereading for the thousandth time the cards in his *Variations* index, looking at himself in the mirror. Dietz's business had cost him two days' work to this rhythm, that is to say about two hours of actual thought and drafting. Now Germaine stumped into his study and declared: "There's a floozy asking to see you. What shall I say? One of them fancy pieces who treat you like dirt just because you're a servant. Germaine doesn't like that. It's best Monsieur should know it right away." Pure calumny. Solange hadn't looked down on Germaine at all. On the contrary she had given her a sweet smile. But contempt for servants was part of Germaine's popular imagery. Note in passing that she referred to herself in the third person, like Caesar in his *Commentaries*. It's not uncommon with elderly maids; at least so I've noticed. Roberti, his attention aroused by the word "floozy" said: "Show the lady in, I was expecting her." In fact he was only expecting a messenger, a faceless office boy.

I: This is where I interrupt. You must give me, and in detail, the reason for Solange's visit. Look, here's someone who goes two years without showing her face and now all at once, on some bogus excuse, she's ringing at the door of her heart's elect. It's not good enough. I'm listening.

HE: It's not hard to explain. A week before, Dietz had invited Roberti to lunch at Maxim's. A business lunch of no interest. He had brought the documents with him. He handed them over to Edouard for study and said: "They're too important for you to return by post. How long do you think it will take? A week? Right. On such a day at such a time I will send someone to collect the papers and your proposals." That's all.

I: That's all, that's all. . . . It won't do. I want to see behind the scenes. To begin with, why did Dietz send Solange instead of an office boy?

HE: For the excellent reason that his office boy was sick.

I: Well, well! Sick! On that very day!

HE: Yes. Sick. Destiny, as you can see. Sooner or later destiny was summoned to take a hand in this affair. Mind you, it could just as well not have taken a hand, or at least not at this precise moment. But things generally happen as if the mind were exerting an influence on events. I wouldn't go so far as to say that Solange's love for Roberti, her powerful concentration of feeling, emitted waves which gave Dietz's office boy a cold and forced him to take to his bed for two days, but neither would I venture to say that this played no part in it whatsoever. In any event Dietz told Solange one evening: "On your way home I want you to collect an urgent and important packet from M. Roberti, Rue Oudinot. Don't bother to come back here. You can bring it in with you tomorrow morning, my dear."

I: And how did she take that?

HE: You know how women never betray anything. She merely replied:

"All right, sir," but she was overcome by wild excitement. A storm at the bottom of the ocean with not a ripple on the surface. Nothing could have been further from her thoughts than such an errand. Roberti's name, unexpectedly uttered, reverberated within her like a salvo of cannon fire. The idea that in half an hour's time she was to see this man, speak with him, touch his hand, took undisputed possession of her with the implacable force of reality when it rises up and banishes one's dreams. The shock was all the more violent in that not only was she not thinking of Roberti at that moment but moreover she had barely thought of him for the past week, to the extent that in a very vague, fleeting way the idea had more than once brushed her mind that her love was fading, that she was perhaps beginning to get over it. (This by the way gave her no joy; on the contrary she feared the loss of her love as one does the loss of a cherished habit.) Destiny steps in when one least expects it, when one has finally despaired of it; it comes at the last minute, at the last second. Who knows? Solange had perhaps begun the process of "decrystallization." Her love was about to die of starvation. Three more months would perhaps have been enough for it to wither away and the meeting between her and Roberti would then have been without consequence. Once again, Roberti would have had a close shave. But Dietz needed a legal opinion, the office boy fell sick and a man was lost.

Even so this chance, this pebble dropped in the pond, deserves a moment's reflection!

1: No, it deserves none. One doesn't reflect over fools. I've just been wondering where the flaw was in your argument, trying to put my finger on your sophism. I've found it. It's the lukewarm, the flabby, the uncertain, the weak who are subject to chance, those sluggish and empty souls who after a disaster cry: "Oh, if only I'd known!" I don't say the stouthearted are entirely safe from the ambushes of fate or that they escape love when this descends on them in all its splendor, but at any rate they are better armed. They defend themselves more staunchly and have a chance of winning. There are some souls that loiter idly just below the surface like those fish known as loach, which are stupid, greedy and swallow every hook. Roberti's soul was a loach. As for your theory of chance, it's a pretty one, I admit; it's enticing and it threw me off balance. But you're forgetting one thing, namely that in whatever happens to men, even the utterly fortuitous, quite unconnected, preposterous, purely coincidental things are just as important as those provoked by their most persistent and deep desires. Why? Because they're irrevocable. A second before it happens an accident is chance, I agree. It could still be avoided. But a second after, it's destiny. One can no longer escape it. Q.E.D.

HE: You know, I am not difficult. If you want to call chance destiny, let's play it that way.

I: Solange is still standing in Roberti's hall, by the way. Don't you think she's beginning to wilt? Get on with it, will you?

HE: She's doing fine in the hall. Before going after her, I've two or three more things to add. This in particular: I don't believe that when she called on Roberti between six and six-thirty that evening, Solange had any forebodings whatsoever. Deep inside she was in a state of violent agitation, complete upheaval, but this didn't *speak* to her. It was a great stirring of mute masses, like a silent movie about the beginnings of the world, in which you might see whole continents engulfed by the sea and the chain of the Alps rise up from the plain without hearing the faintest sound. Solange heard nothing inside her. She only felt vaguely uneasy. Her heart was beating strangely, in a minor key so to speak. She had no more idea about her state than someone afflicted with a tumor of the brain the first time he has a dizzy spell. At most she told herself: "I am upset, I feel scared. How silly! Come on, my girl, courage! He doesn't even know you're alive. He will never know you love him. Our meeting will be confined to Good evening and Good-by. That's nothing to tremble over!" For in fact she was shaking. As in books, her knees "felt like giving way," that's to say she felt that delicious weakness in her legs which accompanies a pounding heart when one is seized with an emotion involving happiness.

On the Boulevard des Invalides, Solange still felt that as yet everything was uncertain, since she was waiting for a man of whom she knew nothing to reach a decision about her, to which she would submit accordingly. At heart she never imagined her life would change. Although it filled her whole being, her love had no reality. She shared it with no one. Her solitary brooding over Roberti had made an almost unreal character of him. She could barely picture how he looked. She had even forgotten his features, which isn't surprising: one can love someone madly without remembering the shape of his nose. She couldn't even have said if she was happy. The fatalism to which she was prone further clouded her thoughts. The mind (or heart) is never prepared for solemn meetings or historic events. One approaches them in a complete silence of the imagination.

I: How the devil do you know that?

HE: I invented it, so it's true.

I: Bravo! It certainly sounds true.

HE: Things couldn't have happened otherwise. Solange making for the Rue Oudinot must have had the thoughts and feelings I have outlined. Try and give her other ones: they wouldn't stand up. You know the mathematical method of *reductio ad absurdum*. One could apply it here. For instance, picture her bubbling with joy, dancing down the street, or else imagine that her sense of virtue had swept over her and she was promising herself to appear cold and indifferent. You know quite well both conceptions ring false. There are ten or fifteen other equally absurd possibilities. So I reject them. Only one admissible attitude remains. The one I've described. Of course, when I want to deduce someone's thoughts or feelings in a given situation I don't go through all this process of elimination. I go straight to the plausible solution. It's a matter of instinct. There's a sort of arithmetic of the soul. I merely need to know the subject's general character and the emotion that collides with it. Given these simple data, I can deduce the most complex developments. One just needs a certain gift. I have one for the mathematics of the emotions.

I: A true novelist. What a tragedy it is you can't write!

HE: When Germaine told Roberti that a "floozy" wanted to see him, he wondered for a moment who the devil it could be, then concluded that it must be one of Dietz's secretaries. He had just completed his report. But in spite of his normal calm and imperturbability, he had a shock of surprise when Solange walked into his study. She was what they call a "ravishing sight." Her grace and beauty were essentially those of the day. The cover in color of a women's magazine! No man is capable of resisting that. A woman who looks like a fashion model is part of our mythology. She is the nymph, the dryad of our time, the ideal naiad. The supreme object of our dreams and desires. Even the most earnest or uncouth of men cannot prevent her from occupying his thoughts now and then.

Roberti wasn't in the least expecting to see Solange. She had completely faded from his mind. However, he never forgot a pretty woman. He never forgot a once-felt desire. His previous meetings with her, particularly the first, rose up in his memory. He immediately recollected the lingering handclasp he had given her, her air of mystery, that mystery of pretty women which alas means nothing at all but into which one can read promises if one wishes. Yes, all this flowed back into his soul, where it seethed for a few seconds. Then it simmered down. It was just one of those gusts of romance to which he was prone. He always gazed earnestly at beautiful women, dreaming of the pleasures he might derive from them. But something protected Solange. Roberti felt intim-

idated by her. He found her too beautiful. Beauty is often an obstacle
to love. It discourages advances. "It's impossible," one tells oneself, "for
so perfect an object to find the slightest attraction in so imperfect a
creature as I." Such was the first conclusion Roberti drew when confronted by Solange. Humility is a virtue more widespread than we think,
for it can easily go hand in hand with pride. Second conclusion (but is
it a conclusion? Let's rather say a vague and melancholy reflection):
"Here's an extremely pretty woman who would probably bring me great
happiness. But she's not for me. She'll never be for me. There are treasures in her I shall never possess." In such matters Roberti's imagination
was of the liveliest. In an instant he felt himself bursting with love, desire and melancholy, although fundamentally it meant nothing at all.

I want you to see him clearly at this moment, face to face with
Solange at last. It was the crucial moment in his life and nobody knew
it, he least of all. I find this notion rather moving. It makes me think of
those carefree country outings that end in tragedy. You know: you go
for a picnic on the banks of the Loire. The weather's fine. Not too hot,
not too cool, but scintillating like a Vouvray. You eat well, drink well,
take a nap, then all at once decide in the late afternoon to go for a
swim. The Loire is such a beautiful river! Next morning you wake up
with a headache, a roaring temperature, pains in your back and a numb-
ness in your legs. The doctor calls: it's polio. You only just pull
through and are left a cripple to the end of your days. And all because
the air and the Vouvray had the same tang and you decided to bathe at
five in the afternoon! Can you imagine the memory that picnic on the
banks of the Loire must leave in the mind of the victim (or in the
minds of those who love him)? That beautiful Loire which watered the
Renaissance in France, watched the loveliest castles in the world rise up
on its banks and numbers among its sons and poets men like Rabelais,
Du Bellay and Balzac, that gallic Loire from which Gargantua's mare
drank and in which the gentle gables of Clochegourde are reflected for
eternity—for a wretch so accursed it is the Styx.

I must confess I was very fond of Roberti. I always found him most
cordial and he even displayed a rather touching confidence in me.
Sometimes, which is more remarkable still, he not only asked my advice
but *actually followed it!* That just shows you! Anyway I never think
without a twinge of the moment when his destiny appeared before
him, when in fifteen minutes his life was gambled and lost without
anyone being able to help him, just as if he had caught polio.

Earlier I told you of the crossroads Roberti never saw. Well, here it
is. We've reached it. Roberti's study at the moment when Solange en-

ters and sits down is the study of Doctor Faust. Mephisto is floating in the room. You can't see him, you can't hear him, you can't smell him (though apparently he stinks). But he's there and he doesn't miss a trick. The cards for the *History of Variations* slumber in their file like homunculus in his bottle. And Roberti doesn't realize that he holds in his right hand a pen dipped in his own blood. He moves to sign . . . no, not yet. Five minutes' reprieve!

ɪ: In God's name out with it! What happened? Did he fling himself at her? Did he rape her? All these stylistic effects over less than nothing! My word, you're a true man of letters!

ʜᴇ: He never stirred. He sat like a fat insect behind his nice Louis XVI desk on which stood a lamp casting a reddish glow, the "subdued light" of seducers and scholars. Solange sat facing him; most of the time she kept her eyes lowered but when she raised them they were very grave and one might have sensed a sort of beseeching look in them. He spoke. She replied. They made small talk. She explained why she had come. He didn't listen. Just so, he didn't listen. Solange's fresh young voice, slightly husky, imperceptibly breathless, fell on his ears but he heard nothing. Her appearance had so to speak made him withdraw into his shell. This was a reaction he often had when he found himself alone with a pretty woman; he would think of other things as if his mind were troubled by desire. What were his actual thoughts? He was waiting for the small talk to come to an end. He refused to listen to this meaningless prelude. He was filled with boredom and desire. Solange's remarks bored him (he had to force himself to reply, the effort it cost him being reflected in his face) because they prevented him from hearing the sweet music of desire echoing in the depths of his being.

ɪ: What exactly is "the sweet music of desire"? I warn you, with me fine phrases carry no weight. Could you reproduce it on the piano? No. So cut it out, will you?

ʜᴇ: But of course I could reproduce it on the piano. And I don't even need to seek very far for it. Any of Mozart's gentler sonatas would do. Or Don Giovanni's serenade—*La ci darem la mano*. That's taken the wind out of your sails, eh?

ɪ: Mozart's music in Roberti's knees or entrails? It's ludicrous.

ʜᴇ: No, it's not ludicrous, it's true. Roberti's body was filled with music. I grant you Mozart is a bad choice. It was more of an adagio, something slow and rather dull, in a minor key, played on muted cellos and basses. Something by Albinoni or Corelli. Charming music, elegant but at the same time second-rate. Or what about this? Have you ever been for a cruise on a sailing vessel? A three-master, for example? Well, when you're on the high seas and there's a stiff breeze blowing you can hear the boat sing. It's the hull, the shrouds, the halyards, the rigging, all vibrating. Such music's a wonderful thing to hear, combined with the good smell of tar. It sends sailors into ecstasies. That's roughly what I had in mind when I spoke of the sweet music of desire in the depths of Roberti.

For good measure, I can even give you the words of the song he was singing to himself to the music in his knees, his lungs, his nerves and muscles.

I: To my mind he's loitering badly at his crossroads.

HE: Yes, yes, he is loitering. He is making the most of what's left to him. Making good use of his reprieve. And he's quite right. If only he knew what lay ahead of him! He would be appalled if he only knew the deep significance for him, and him alone, of the tender, grave, good, comely face of Solange. But of course he only sees the side issues of the adventure. How can he guess that this is love in person seated before him? That he has been passionately loved for the past two years? Solange, for him, is an unknown quantity, a newcomer. All he can discern is the chance of a harmless and pleasant affair with a secretary, like many others he has begun and ended in the past. I promised you Roberti's secret song, his *Vieni alla finestra o mio tesoro*. Here it is. He thought Solange was "really ravishing." One of those tender notions beautiful strangers were apt to inspire in him sprang to his mind: that the features of this girl before him were modeled in his heart for all eternity. But the spirit of criticism awakened: this little explosion of romanticism made him laugh to himself. If that were really so, his heart was the mold of many women! A veritable casting foundry! But I'll cut the metaphors. Roberti was humming to himself: "This girl is the type of woman I have always dreamed of. My type. Which means I shall never possess her, for one never gets the women who would bring one true pleasure. It's a contrary world: one is never their type, and as it's they who decide in the last resort. . . . I am a blind man. Anyway the world is nothing but shadows, phantoms and illusion. Here is a woman gazing at me with every appearance of tenderness and it doesn't mean a thing. She's probably reminding herself that she's used up her book of Métro tickets or planning to fry herself an egg this evening. If I got up without further ado, took her in my arms and kissed her, she'd think she had been struck by lightning."

I: That's not a song, it's a recitative.

HE: It is even a whole opera, for there is also the Roberti-Solange duet, the ballet of looks passing between them, Solange's own secret melody and so on. All of it blending, meeting and parting, with counterpoint. I have often thought that a serious writer, were he prepared to take the trouble, could produce a book of a thousand pages merely by studying a man's life for five minutes through a magnifying glass.

Roberti's thoughts were quite coherent but he was saying the first thing to enter his head. He wanted to detain Solange as long as possible. For instance, in a panic of embarrassment she said: "I'm taking up your time, Monsieur. I must be going." Whereupon he cried: "No, no, not at all, on the contrary. Here I was, fed up with poring over these papers and a charming young woman comes to offer me some diversion! Do stay for a few minutes. I'm delighted to have the chance to talk to you." He asked her insipid questions about her office hours, her interests and so on, solely to keep her with him for a moment. Suddenly his heart started to beat violently: why shouldn't he get up and kiss his visitor? He only had to make up his mind to it. It all depended on him. Inside him the little song of desire quickened. His age. Fifty. The horror of it. A dirty old man. Gray hair. Glasses, round shoulders, a pallid skin. But no. Let's not exaggerate. On the contrary a rather fresh complexion and a certain charm. A man doesn't have to be young or handsome to appeal. Not to mention the fact that there was a look of really urgent tenderness in Mlle. Mignot's eyes. Roberti summoned the memory of several past experiences to the rescue. He had gazed like this before into the eyes of unknown women, women who had then become his mistresses, after which he had recalled his first questioning looks, his initial uncertainties. In a fortnight's time Mlle. Mignot might quite possibly be his alone and he would remind himself of this moment. Such emotion, which seems intolerable while it lasts, becomes part of the past and takes on exquisite meaning after the event.

Roberti's mind may have been governed by cheap fiction but he also had no illusions. The romances he wove were realistic, that is to say his imagination was as wild as a shopgirl's, but he furnished these dreams with true-to-life details which mitigated their silliness and destroyed their charm. Mlle. Mignot was assuredly a little fool. She was falling for him. Right. The first stirrings of love are often delicious: he would thrill to the discovery of all this new creature's secrets; greedily would he learn her private vocabulary, her habits, her caresses. How wonderful her eyes must look in certain circumstances! To take possession of this heart, this mind, which only yesterday were still quite unknown to him, to occupy them like conquered territory, live intensely in this person, invade her, become for her the one and only object in the world, those are pleasures which never grow stale. But no! "Pleasure" is a poor word. One should say passion. Roberti, who was no Don Juan, had one Don Juanesque quality to the highest possible degree: for him the enjoyment of women was not enough; it even meant comparatively little. What he wanted was to subjugate, overwhelm, annihilate. While he took the body he coveted the soul, which moreover he obtained in the same moment. In love, the spirit wears out faster than the body. He had experienced this many times. Two weeks are usually enough to exhaust it. Mlle. Mignot's would doubtless last no longer. Even so, these two weeks still lay ahead. For the moment he stood on the threshold of discovery. And this moment was all the more precious in that as yet nothing was certain. Perhaps the discovery would never be made. Solange was sitting stiff-backed in her chair, yet her pose couldn't have been more graceful. Her eyes were so opaque as to appear fathomless.

"She's surely a little fool," Roberti delightedly sang to himself, for realistic details formed the most succulent items in his romancing. "She has a lover as foolish as she, a 'boy friend' whom she'll marry one of these days. What does he do, I wonder. He must be an honest, serious young man who saves money. They will make a nice little French couple steeped in mediocrity. Maybe they will vote for me at the next election. They will have a smart modern kitchen bought on the installment plan, two children, and they'll be very unhappy. So much for them. After six months of marriage one will see them on Sunday evenings sitting side by side in the restaurant, dumb, silent, bored to death with each other. Two empty shells. And like that for the rest of their lives! I'm sure she has a lover. It's impossible for such a pretty woman to be free. It's unthinkable that something which appeals so strongly to me hasn't already appealed just as strongly to someone else. Someone younger, more appetizing and above all less tied than I am."

All this is long in the telling. But what is long is not so much the song as my translation of it into words. In reality all these thoughts passed in a flash through Roberti's mind. They followed one on another without logic. For instance, immediately after thinking what I've just told you, he imagined without any transition that he'd already had Solange. He had conquered her (he didn't know how, he skipped the difficult part!). He was thrilled by this conquest. In a twinkling he raced through two weeks of pride and joy. But what then? He knew himself well. Thirty similar adventures had taught him how exacting his heart was or, rather, how quick it was to develop contempt and disgust. There was nothing he didn't know about the fantasies evoked by desire, and this he always took into account. Even while the rapture seized him, he would think ahead to the time when this same rapture would have subsided and the being who aroused it would no longer be shrouded in mystery. What is a woman whom one has possessed and doesn't love? A sexless creature devoid of interest, as dull as a relative. Nothing but a tiny mind, limited in every respect, a face grown hateful since it recalls a weakness now incomprehensible to the very person who succumbed to it. These sad reflections often held Roberti back from lechery, proving that he wasn't very sensual by nature. But they didn't always.

ɪ: Listen, there's no reason why this memorable interview shouldn't last for a century. Does Roberti make his mind up, yes or no?

ʜᴇ: Lord, you're impatient! No, he doesn't make up his mind yet. He always found it excessively hard to come out of his shell and force himself onto other beings. A woman had to have a really exceptional appeal for him to set about seducing her.

ɪ: You contradict yourself the whole time. First you present me with Roberti as a womanizer, then as bashful. Let's get this straight.

ʜᴇ: I am not contradicting myself. He was exactly that: a bashful womanizer. They do exist, you know. They're even not at all uncommon. Roberti went to love as a coward goes to war, filled with a panic so painful that sometimes the most dangerous act of folly cost him nothing to allay it. Arrant cowards have sometimes become heroes that way. True conquerors are perhaps those least equipped to conquer, and conquest is the reward of weak men who dare to make superhuman efforts.

Since earliest childhood Roberti had never been out of love. When he was small his romantic heart was on fire over little girls who ignored him. As an adolescent he ate his heart out over teen-agers from whom he obtained at best a few furtive kisses. When he grew up things went a bit better because he had acquired authority and a bold eye, but even so they were never very brilliant. The reason for this is that he never showed enough determination. Nothing puts women off so much as lack of determination. Their instinct whispers to them that here is no burning desire. That is why, in love, the truly wise are the bold, those who tell themselves a moment's happiness is well worth a hundred rebuffs, those who never weary of trying, who cast their "dignity" to the winds and charge head down into every adventure. Even if they resist, most women certainly prefer an aggressive man who shows them scant respect to a timid (or sensitive) man who weighs the pros and cons and, even if the pros win the day, always acts at the wrong moment. About ten times in his life Roberti had been *blinded by desire* and found it most rewarding. His other bits of good luck had been due mainly to the determination of his partners.

He found it difficult to find the first words to say to a woman. His normally inventive and nimble mind failed to produce that sweet and beguiling small talk with which seducers instinctively know how to start a conversation with a strange woman and set the right bantering tone. It's a misfortune to think too much. These myriad whirling thoughts paralyze action, since they reveal its consequences before even the first step is taken. Now Roberti practically never forgot himself. Whenever he sought for something to say, his whole being instantly set itself in motion and the words he found never seemed to him strong enough to carry the enormous weight of his moral and physical image.

I: Even so he has really got to take some step, move some pawn. Because Mlle. Mignot is about to depart. Highly disappointed, I imagine. By the way, you talk all the time about him and never about her. What was she up to while Roberti thought things over? What was in her mind? After all, here she was in front of the man she had loved for two years. That's really something!

HE: She was amazed not to be beside herself with joy. She could see Roberti was affected, that he was studying her with interest. But she thought perhaps she was mistaken. Perhaps everything he said was true: how he was bored, how he was glad of a diversion. She was filled with humility before this wise and majestic figure. A twofold shyness had come over her. First, the shyness natural to a modest young woman confronted with an imposing middle-aged man; second, that of a woman in love before the object of her adoration. I haven't said much about Solange during this encounter because she's infinitely less interesting, here, than Roberti. Far less subtle, far more naïve, far greener. She's like a little animal, a cat with a silent and expectant soul. A female waiting for the male to notice her. In her innermost thoughts and feelings she must have had a sense of disappointment. A disappointment due less to Roberti than to herself. She blamed herself for not feeling overwhelmingly happy.

I: You'll never get me to believe that with her antennae of an amorous female she didn't sense Roberti's agitation. She must have felt how things were but she was just a little deceiver.

HE: Solange a little deceiver? That's rich! She was candor itself. So much so that one might have thought her devoid of imagination. It's unnatural to be so trusting and naïve! It denotes a purity and nobility you won't often meet and which anyway generally pass unnoticed. Those who possess them are too modest (and, to be frank, too limited) to realize they have souls more beautiful than those around them. And certainly the latter will never perceive it for themselves. Similarly there are several beautiful flowers in the world that bloom unseen amid forests of thistles and bracken, a number of precious stones which have found their way into bags of glass beads, their brilliant and delicate fires burning only for themselves. In addition to which Solange was by nature rather resigned, inclined to fatalism. Allowed at last to behold the man who for two years had been the object of her dreams, alone in a room with him, she suddenly became aware of the gulf separating her dreams from the reality. Dreams are puffs of smoke which we shape for our pleasure; we twist them as we will, we are all-powerful. But reality is stubborn, exhausting, impossible to mold. We break our nails and our heads against it. The Roberti she loved was a ballad hero, a disembodied figure without weight, a puppet which she made dance according to her fancy. The real Roberti was a being firmly rooted in the world, a sort of Gulliver enchained by the thousand bonds formed by the Lilliputian occupations of a man of our time. And so, instinctively, Solange stiffened against herself. She was afraid of giving way to tenderness and emotion, though this didn't prevent her from feeling tender and moved. She drew comparisons between the real Roberti and the Roberti of her dreams, the way a painter might compare a picture painted from memory with the model. But she was a modest painter, a Sunday painter. She found the real thing far more beautiful than her creation. Roberti's gray—let's say pepper-and-salt—hair touched her, as did his face which, though still smooth skinned, plainly betrayed signs of fifty years' wear and tear. He had rings round his eyes and rather heavy lids. All these marks of weakness (or age) overwhelmed her. They were the wounds of a lion. She tried to make an inventory of everything that was not perfect in him, everything denoting frailty or decline, because she felt, unworthy creature, miserable insect, that these were the only ways by which she could approach him. What do you say to such humility? Isn't it sublime of its kind? When you think that Solange was worth a hundred Robertis, at least as regards her heart if not her mind, and then see her knocking discreetly like this at the back door, making herself so small and abject, you feel like weeping at the blindness of humankind.

Solange had no particular fancy for elderly gentlemen. She hadn't the slightest "father fixation," as you call it. But by one of those sentimental paradoxes one so often comes across, it was on account of his age that she had fallen in love with Roberti. His fifty years had not been an obstacle but, rather, an encouragement, a help. As if in her eyes the fact of being fifty was a physical blemish, an imperfection by means of which the god descended into the world of humans, became accessible, could be loved with some hope of return.

It never occurred to her that her youth, beauty and freshness were riches at least as precious as Roberti's intellect or social standing. That they were on a par, he and she, with perhaps an advantage in her favor. Youth never pauses to reflect that it is young, that this is a great possession, a beautiful thing to offer, something of great worth to give in exchange. Love makes one blind, not toward the person one loves but toward oneself. Loving, one can no longer see one's self; it is lost to sight and forgotten. No longer knowing whether one is handsome or ugly, hateful or charming, one is merely convinced of being the most disinherited creature in the world. Believing one no longer has a right to anything, all one expects is alms.

I must now describe something Solange used to feel whenever she was faced with some distinguished man exuding a strong personality. With a blend of earnestness and amusement she would ask herself what she would do if this gentleman suddenly took it into his head to fling her down on the divan. Ordinarily she thought she would lack the courage to resist. Not that this perturbed her in the least, but she felt she would probably submit out of a mixture of shyness, sympathy and awe; that while it would doubtless give her no pleasure, it would also cause her no disgust. I believe women often indulge in such fantasies at moments when they are regarding you with the utmost gravity. In short Solange didn't attach a tremendous price to her favors. She remained pure by instinct rather than moral conviction. Her purity was physiological and spiritual, in the same way as one has brown hair or is prone to melancholia. It was a quality and not a principle.

Faced with Roberti she was far too deeply stirred and too preoccupied battling with her heart to elaborate on any such eventuality. Moreover that evening, contrary to what was usual, no air of authority emanated from Roberti. Solange felt him to be agitated, uncertain, and she took heart from it. His hesitation gave her time to summon up her strength and wisdom, and if she made up any story to herself it was beyond doubt one of those moral and rather silly tales in which one offers oneself up as a sacrifice, as a martyr, the sort of thing women often invent when they're weighing up a situation. Scraps of clichés flitted through her head: "What would be the use? . . . Where would it lead us? . . . It would be madness. . . . No, I couldn't . . ." and so on. But watch out, I am giving all this a kind of order. Her thoughts were in fact very nebulous. I simply want to make you hear the slow, confused, vaguely modulated twelve-tone music echoing in Solange at the same time as a clear melody rang out in Roberti. I am playing you the theme of refusal in counterpoint to the theme of desire, or rather the theme of half refusal blending with the theme of hesitant desire. As you can see, we are still at the opera! But it's a modern opera in the style of Alban Berg, long, slow and sad with intermittent gleams like shafts of moonlight reflected at the bottom of a well. Solange was also thinking that in ten minutes she would politely say good-by and leave without anything having happened. She was thinking how one waits two years for a momentous meeting, pins all one's hopes on it, longs for it as for the earthly paradise, and that when it finally comes it is just a moment like any other, a meaningless incident without any future. She was thinking how Roberti might well be attracted to her but that he, too, had common sense, that consideration for his life, home, wife and children would unquestionably prevail and he wouldn't even venture so far as to kiss her hand. She was already taking steps to destroy her love once and for all, so impossible of fulfillment did it seem at this moment.

You're going to tell me again that I am taking my story at a snail's pace. But listen. One simply has to pause here for a minute. For we've reached one of those privileged moments when destiny is caught red-handed and its meaninglessness becomes apparent. It is not an implacable clock, a meticulously adjusted time bomb; it is a fat, blind spider which gives you a lethal bite if you stumble on its hiding place, a huge and deadly beetle zooming heavily round the dim lamps of mankind. One must learn how to put one's lamp out every now and then, to give the insect time to wing its way elsewhere. No, my friend, destiny has nothing in common with classical tragedy, in which the lines of verse bite into each other like the oiled cogs of a machine and lead you in five twists of the mechanism to the fatal outcome. Take Roberti and Solange, tragic figures if ever there were. A mere nothing could save them from tragedy forever. They have five minutes left to decide their fate and they don't know it. They are both unsure of each other. Granted, this perfect doubt is the mark of love. But one can sometimes pass great love without seeing it, because at a given moment one has doubted just a little too much and hasn't dared make some gesture. Even a second before making his fatal gesture, Roberti was still questioning himself anxiously as to whether he should make it at all and had almost decided not to. He had so much work on hand, he had just ended a rather bitter little affair, he needed a rest! But Solange had pretty hands. She had removed a glove. As he talked he enjoyed studying this little hand. It was trembling slightly. He wondered what this could signify. I spare you the comparison of the trembling hand with the fluttering bird, but it did in fact occur to Roberti, who wasn't averse to facile poetry. All at once the fatal notion struck him. With a sort of double-take, as in a comic movie, he suddenly wondered: "Can she be excited too? Is she trembling because of me? Then she must like me. All right, I'll try my luck. We'll see." The abrupt taking of such a decision is a stimulant. His heart began to beat very fast. He carefully eyed Solange's bosom to see if it was heaving under the pressure of a similar agitation. Emotions fill a room the way a storm fills the sky. The atmosphere of the study became electric. Solange rose to leave. "It's now or never," thought Roberti. She held out her hand. He raised it to his lips, then kissed its palm, which is always regarded as a declaration. Solange made feeble efforts to withdraw her hand. Emboldened by her lack of purpose, Roberti took her in his arms. She barely struggled. Both were utterly overcome. She by love, he by his precipitate decision and the prideful and pleasurable prospects he glimpsed ahead. They murmured idiotically to each other. She said: "No, no . . . let me go. Think of your children!" Roberti lied with complete sincerity: "You're adorable, I loved you the first time I saw you. We simply had to meet again one day." Isn't it odd? Solange's feelings were being expressed by him. He tried to kiss her on the mouth, thinking that thus the main thing would be achieved, that the rest would automatically follow from this kiss. She gathered up all her strength and turned her head away. That evening the best he could manage was a peck on her cheek. Gradually his emotion subsided. What is such agony is the uncertainty and waiting. Immediately one goes into action the brain becomes cool again. "Think of your children!" she had said. How amusing! Gently he teased her about it, unaware of the confusion such a remark laid bare.

ɪ: Hold it! Stop there. The scene is over. Cut the transitions. One can always tell bad novels from the fact that they are full of transitions, and good ones from the fact that they are not.

ʜᴇ: Right, I'll stop. But I must say it's a pity. I still had masses of little emotions, fascinating little bits of behavior to show you.

ɪ: Don't. I can guess them. That's enough. It's even better. One must be like Rembrandt, that is to say paint in the depths of a cellar pictures devoured by shadows. Here and there one can pick out a nose or the ray of light from an oil lamp falling on a finger, a piece of gold braid or the plume of a hat, and it's sublime, the supreme height of painting. Shakespeare proceeded in exactly the same way.

HE: Oh, but I'm not Rembrandt or Shakespeare. I'm just a sort of organ-grinder. A fellow like Rutebeuf with his endless stories . . . At best Chrétien de Troyes or Guillaume de Lorris. My only quality is to be prolific. So if you're after damming me up, pruning me, trimming me into a celebrity, you are in for a disappointment. Do you know those big long-haired dogs? Old English sheepdogs, I think they are. Their hair hangs down over their eyes, they have hindquarters like a cart horse and feet like an elephant. You clip them and nothing is left but a wretched little beast, skinny as a rabbit, shivering in a dirty pink skin.

I: It's not a question of clipping but of combing you.

HE: I must tell you all the same that Solange and Roberti, after they parted, were each filled with an uncontrollable joy.

I: I might have guessed.

HE: Yes, but their joys differed. With Roberti it was the joy of flattered vanity and desire in anticipation of his victory. The conquest of someone like Solange does a man honor. Out of superstition he forced himself to think that she was going to "come to her senses," that their clumsy embrace meant nothing, that once she set foot in the street the sort of enchantment with which she had been smitten would fall away and she would laugh at his effrontery. But something persuaded him this wasn't so. He had an inner conviction of his triumph. And it was a triumph so unexpected, so astonishing that it still left him breathless. He told himself he would savor it to the full later on, when his excitement had abated. He was like a man who has just come into an unlooked-for inheritance, who finds himself suddenly rich and dreams of all this wealth; it is still out of reach, he hasn't yet enjoyed it but from now on it is part of him, of his personality, increasing his stature and changing him for the better.

I: Pretty shabby as a reaction.

HE: Shabby or not, that's how it was. I am not Ariosto. I don't sing *Orlando furioso* but *Eduardo placido, Robertino miserabile.* I'll go on if I may. Roberti, then, was filled with joy. I would slander him if I said he was also filled with conceit. It was better than that: it was pride. Possibly he didn't feel the joy of Napoleon at Marengo, but at least the keen delight of an infantry lieutenant who has brought off a daring and well-organized surprise attack by taking intelligent advantage of the lie of the land and the distraction of the enemy.

I: The enemy? Don't be funny!

HE: Yes, quite so, the enemy. Woman is the enemy of man, isn't she?

I: Agreed, agreed!

HE: Besides, Roberti had unwittingly just declared a war which was going to lead him to capitulation, betrayal, subversion and revolution. His War of 1870. He was beginning with the capture of Saarbrücken. He never guessed that it would end with the flames and massacres of the Commune, in sheets of petroleum and blood.

I: Relax. What a lot of highfalutin comparisons! His War of 1870, hell!

HE: Well, what then? What happened to Roberti as an individual can perfectly well be compared to what happened to France as a nation in 1870. It was worse even, for France recovered. She survived, then rallied and became a great power again. Whereas Roberti was cleaned out, gone to blazes, annihilated, thrown on the rubbish heap. The lives of men are more tragic than the lives of nations. A nation lives for one or two thousand years. It has resources. Nothing is ever completely lost. But a man? If once he puts a foot wrong he is done for.

In short this stupid kiss on the cheek, given in panic and confusion and received with equal panic, nevertheless marked for Roberti the beginnings of a great love, the only one he ever knew. The love of his life. That same evening he was full of the joys of spring. Twenty years younger, gay as a lark, with moments in between when he would fall into an incomparably delightful reverie. He thought of how he would call Solange the next morning, of the meeting he would fix with her, of the more or less brief defense she would put up against him. He had to dine out that evening. He was enchanted by the idea that he was going to take with him a secret happiness, a brand-new diamond hidden in the depths of his soul. "People will see me as I usually am," he thought, "and they will never know I am someone else. That I am like a man who has dug up a treasure at the bottom of his garden and told nobody." Take careful note of this: it's an important trait of Roberti's character. The delight in secrecy. The joy in dissimulation. The taste for occult power. He had always been tempted by the idea of a double life. This was all the more remarkable in that he was neither furtive nor a mystery-monger. No, with him it was a deep-seated inclination, nurtured and given roots by his position as a public figure who is constantly under observation and must never give grounds for malice. You see, he was more proud than conceited, or at least his conceit, under the pressure of circumstances which prevented him from naïvely displaying it, had turned in on itself and become pride. Similarly he had a deep affection and respect for Agnes; to deceive her was nothing, but he would have been deeply upset had she known of it or should it reach her ears. Not to mention that she came from Bordeaux and so was fairly hot-tempered, being quite capable of venting her fury, even of acting on a wild impulse such as packing her bags, leaving the house and demanding a divorce.

I: Well! That's a new one! And here was I picturing Agnes as a gentle, long-suffering, resigned sort of person. . . .

HE: Yes, she was gentle, long-suffering and resigned, but she also had her occasional fits of temper and it was thanks to these little outbursts from Bordeaux that she kept some power over her husband.

I: You're not going to tell me he was afraid of her?

HE: No, of course he wasn't, but these marks of her character showed him how far he could take liberties or, if you prefer it, the limits to which he could be free and easy; they showed him the point at which he should lay down his smokescreen.

I: But why? Did he want peace or did he love Agnes?

HE: Both. Men have a horror of scenes. They would do anything, commit any act of cowardice, tell any lie to avoid a drama. Besides, Roberti loved Agnes very sincerely and deeply. He didn't want to cause her the slightest pain. He told himself the unhappiness she would endure if she discovered his infidelities would be out of all proportion with the pleasure these escapades brought him. These rather empty, rather scandalous, even I would say furtive pleasures to which he clung (but the way one clings to a trinket, a book or a suit) were totally unqualified to plunge Agnes into despair. Nothing is more shocking to the mind than to see great results stem from trivial causes. By being secret as the grave, Roberti suppressed every cause. There was an added advantage in this, namely that while he shared many things with Agnes —tastes, thoughts, ideas, feelings—this sharing sometimes bored him. He would then feel a need to withdraw into himself, retire in solitude, retreat into his shell. Little secrets were ideal for this purpose. He thereby had a private world to which no one, not even Agnes who was so close to him, had access. Still less his friends and acquaintances. He was secretly very proud of these dark recesses he had arranged within himself. They were his Gyges' ring, his method of acting the invisible man. Whenever he was upset, harassed, preoccupied, he would dive into his remote and unknown little lake, withdraw into his secrets as into a private chapel which can only be entered by pressing an invisible button in the paneling and where one can dream in seclusion, hidden from the world.

I: I'm astonished at what you say about Agnes. It doesn't fit in at all with the magnanimous attitude she displayed after the catastrophe.

HE: On the contrary, it fits very well. To Agnes a Roberti running around night spots would have been shameful and ridiculous. She would have left him in rage and disgust. But Roberti an adulterer, Roberti a murderer, Roberti unhappy, Roberti heading for damnation was quite another matter. It put everything on a different plane where her little outbursts from Bordeaux had no place. It called for understanding, loyalty, blindness, love. In short, magnanimity. Agnes was, as you so rightly say, magnanimous. Her little soul became great. She rose to the occasion. Perhaps it needed such an occasion for her finally to become herself. In the Roberti family at that time a reversal of strength or a shift of interest took place. While Roberti was sinking into the abyss, Agnes was rising up to the heavens. He who had always been taken for a brilliant man showed himself to be nothing but a miserable wretch, while the little self-effacing woman whom everyone more or less patronized and treated with contempt, only putting up with her because she was her husband's wife, became a kind of saint.

1: You referred just now to a "rather bitter little affair" from which Roberti had barely emerged. What was that?

HE: Oh, that dated from four or five months earlier. An affair which had lasted eight to ten weeks with a girl called Odile. For once Roberti had got himself rather involved. This Odile appealed to him greatly. She was a striking, well-built girl with beautiful pale blue eyes, rather Flemish in type. Marmoreal but sensual. Blonde too, like Solange, but her complete opposite. Just the type to whom Roberti never appealed. This made him all the more intrigued, all the more attached to her. He saw her almost every day. They used to meet in a room in the Rue de Vaugirard which Odile borrowed from one of her friends. This additional secret further increased Roberti's happiness. She was very demanding, apparently, and I think he managed on the whole to satisfy her demands, which gave him cause for great pride. But she was a baffling creature, both in mind and body. Baffling at least to Roberti. She didn't even share his political views and in her company he felt faintly embarrassed at belonging to the Radical Party and being one of its more prominent figures. When he talked to her, when he held her in his arms, he had a sense of fundamental incompatibility at the same time as of great good fortune. She liked none of the writers, poets or artists he admired, which provides a good measure of the gulf between them, for literary tastes are unerring. This woman's mind subscribed to standards as different from his as a Tibetan's might be from a German's. Even when desire united them in lovemaking, he felt no closer to her. Sensual pleasure flowed in her down strange channels and at quite unexpected moments.

ı: Oh, what pretty euphemisms! And what happened? Did Odile the mysterious drop Edouard the complicated?

HE: Yes, and to my mind in a rather comic way. One day she announced that she was going to get married.

ı: I hope he took it gallantly and gave her a handsome wedding present?

HE: No, far from it. You're way off the mark. He was horror-struck; filled with an extraordinary despair. He valued his Odile for two reasons: first, because for him she represented a rarity, a unique piece in his collection. With her he was on strange ground. He was a traveler exploring exotic lands. He had the illusion of entering forbidden territory without a passport. He had completely lost all critical faculty. For instance, he didn't tell himself she was a fool because she despised Mozart and admired Tchaikowsky and Bartók, because she looked down on Renoir and praised abstract painting to the skies. No, he listened to her expounding her ludicrous tastes as he would have listened to a woman from India or Iceland telling him about the customs of her people, its civilization and legends. The second reason for his attachment was this very way Odile had of eluding him on every level. Even when he had thoroughly satisfied her and she showed her gratitude by talking affectionate nonsense, the prattling of a little girl which came over her in such moments, he still felt millions of light-years away. You can imagine how all that greatly stimulated his heart and senses. We always relentlessly pursue those who are never so far from us as when they seem to be ours alone.

On the other hand I don't know what young Odile's feelings were for Roberti. She had found him attractive, of course, and I suppose she must have felt some harmony between their two skins. But she must also have felt that an unscalable wall divided them, which a great love might have demolished but not a mere fancy. She was, I believe, easy enough in her ways, taking lovers as a boy takes mistresses. One of these, more permanent, of longer standing perhaps than the rest, must one day have proposed marriage. She accepted and gave Roberti the brush-off in fifteen minutes of considerable brutality. Like a rude awakening from a dream. She banished him from her life. When she announced it he could hardly believe his ears. Deep inside him nothing was really hurt. It wasn't love he felt for her but rather a passionate curiosity, and sexual attraction, of course. Yet he had a hideous feeling of being uprooted. He hadn't bargained for this. During the eight to ten weeks their affair had lasted, he had constantly interpreted curiosity as love and had almost persuaded himself that he was in fact in love.

Something odd now happened which is typical of Roberti's rational, logical way of behaving. He hesitated momentarily between which of two attitudes to adopt: that of the rake, the libertine, the red-heeled marquis who extricates himself from painful situations with a pirouette and a mocking smile (the situation, one must admit, was piquant and offered material for some fine jokes!); or the romantic attitude of the flouted swain who watches the murder of his love with a breaking heart. Roberti had a moment's hesitation, as I say. Then he told himself the second attitude was truer to what he believed his real feelings to be. He staged a ridiculous scene, one of the savage and bitter kind with wounding, cruel words protesting devotion, passion, incurable grief and so on. In short humbug in earnest, in which he instantly developed a cast-iron belief and which in turn led him to suffer in reality. Being a woman and consequently having a weakness for drama and rhetoric, Odile cannot have been displeased. All in all, this scene wasn't such a bad wedding present! In conclusion Roberti had a brain wave: "I wish you every possible misfortune," he announced. I think the suffering he thus artificially engendered for himself was considerably mitigated by the satisfaction he felt at holding forth in the tragic mode and polishing several gems of spite. "Good-by," said he to the young lady in a voice of doom. "Good-by," replied she in the same tones and they parted forever. Which didn't prevent Roberti, a week later, from sending Mlle. Odile a mocking note in which he ironically apologized for his intemperate language. A note he had written under the sway of several emotions; partly because he felt faintly ridiculous, partly to provide a small literary compensation for his woes, partly to appear in a better light and lastly in the hope of throwing a new bridge between her and himself. The note remained unanswered. A pity. It was well turned.

ɪ: That's a splendid Robertian anecdote! And a rather touching one. He really was an ass. How can one possibly lack judgment to that extent? At fifty! Love and politics are the most dangerous things for the mind because they constantly place a man in situations where he is obliged to talk nonsense.

ʜᴇ: How's that?

ɪ: Oh, it's quite simple. When you go in for politics you make propaganda for your party or your ideas. When you go in for love, you make propaganda for your heart, your face, yourself. In both cases you are bound to lie, hence to talk rubbish. To an impartial observer nothing appears more stupid than the lies of amorous or political propaganda in their various forms: indignation, exaggeration, polemics, enforced optimism, emotionalism and so on. One can see the play-acting or the puppet show all too clearly. It's at once shocking and absurd. I wonder which is the worst, the cynical politician who thinks black and talks white, or the fool taken in by his own lies. Your Roberti with his little tricks was really way out! To heap love on top of politics is too much for one man. He would have needed a superhuman genius to save his soul. By the way, what was this Odile who listened to Bartók's music and slept with a middle-aged gentleman? Surely not a manicurist or a student.

HE: No, this one worked in a library. Extremely well turned out. Immaculate hands and glossy hair. She must have been about twenty-eight or thirty. Semi-intellectual, very taken up with the things it was smart to admire. A progressive, as should be. Which didn't prevent her from being flattered by the attentions of a Radical deputy. For her, too, Roberti was a rarity. Her collection consisted mainly of painters without talent, journalists and (fitfully) university students.

I: Was Roberti unhappy for a long time after she jilted him?

HE: Oh yes, extremely unhappy for three or four days, and depressed for another two weeks. By the end of three months it was all forgotten.

I: *"Chagrin d'amour dure toute la v-i-i-i-i-e!"*

HE: I find three months, two weeks and four days a most honorable time to mourn a lost love. All the more since it wasn't the first. Roberti had had three or four others before. Now here's an interesting detail. It was almost never he who took the initiative in breaking with his mistresses. And do you know why? Because he didn't love them. For him they were simply objects of convenience he didn't want to part with. But they, after a while, had had enough. They guessed (in spite of all his consideration and kindness) that they didn't mean very much to him, that they were giving him a great deal while he was giving nothing, that he was arid, at least in that facet of himself which he showed them. They divined in him an organic inability to love. So they dropped him. Generally this hurt them more than it did him, but they had the courage to do it. As a rule it suited him to be got rid of in this way. It spared him from having to make up his own mind and provoke tiresome scenes. Besides, it left him the injured party. He would bow out gracefully; these dismissals caused him a twinge, let us say a prick, of pain, but it didn't last long and served to heighten his sense of regained freedom. On three or four occasions, however, the prick had been sharper and he had taken it for genuine regret. These imagined regrets lasted about three months. Each time they recurred, he tasted again their special savor. It wasn't wholly without charm.

One day, I remember, we were talking of this kind of thing and he said to me: "Being unhappy in love is very enjoyable, whatever they say. It's like a gust of youth. I have always kept the tenderest memories of such times." It's true, there is something so personal about sorrow, it is so closely bound up with our souls as to be part of our very selves, so to speak. It's a poetic sorrow, even when it isn't very deep. It makes one at once morose and benevolent. One feels at once alone and in company. For Roberti, for this aging man, suffering of this kind was like a fountain of youth. The reaction of a man of thirty. As he never mentioned it to a living soul except me, who am nobody, it quickly healed. It's the confiding of them that keeps the wounds in one's heart open. The man who out of inclination or necessity keeps silent about his pain sees it diminish almost while he watches.

I: Regarding this Odile, you said "a type of woman." Fair enough, but I like things to be precise. Did this apply to her moral or physical appearance?

HE: Both. Anyway, moral and physical appearances are the same thing. The form and content complement each other. There were those women who scared Roberti and those who didn't. Behind the oval face, the more or less silky skin, the candid or piercing eyes, the proud or sagging bust, he could quickly recognize what kind of soul lay hidden: welcoming or mocking, demanding or passive, ardent or placid. Obviously Roberti's "type" was not the Amazon-type Odile, the tarty, the pleasure-loving or the boyish. Besides, all those women have a forthright manner, a sort of decisiveness which disconcerted him. Perhaps he didn't feel big or strong enough to master such high-spirited mounts, who must themselves equally have felt that here was not the rider for them. No. Roberti's type was the languid, rather Creole beauty, a woman more soft and resigned, with slender limbs, a full bosom, delicate and yearning features and the smooth skin of an odalisque nourished on sweetmeats. All things considered, Solange came close to fulfilling these requirements. Think back to the sketch I drew of her. I don't know if Roberti became aware of it the moment she walked into his study, but he must have had some confused inkling. She was the complete opposite of Odile. She represented tranquillity, the norm, the renewal of a treasured experience, above all understanding, that much talked-of understanding. What in fact is a woman who "understands" you? She's not only a woman whose mind has affinities with yours and who recognizes your least thought or feeling: she is also and above all a woman whose body responds to the obscure and capricious demands of your own body. The more Roberti came to know Solange, the more he had the illusion that she "understood" him since he discovered that the more he possessed her the more she adapted herself exactly to his desires.

1: Did she really understand him?

HE: Certainly. For the same reasons. Of course, I'm not saying she followed all the countless twists of his subtle mind but she could read him, she could sense him. By and large she had a fair (although exaggerated) idea of her lover. After all, she was in love; and it was complete love, recto and verso, body and soul.

1: We got to the day after the first kiss, if my memory serves! You'd never have made a historian, you know, with your slowness and attention to detail.

HE: Why not? History is something that has always tempted me. I should love to recount the life of Guizot, for instance, or Cardinal Dubois. Or else the disputes of the wars of religion. I should treat my subjects like Proust or Joyce. It would be tremendous!

1: It would be catastrophic, as you would include everything. You would resurrect history in its totality, recording every slightest movement of the soul. Can you imagine where that would get you?

HE: I don't know. The Académie, perhaps?

1: Don't be an ass, that's not what I mean at all. It would lead you completely to superimpose history on reality. If you carry it to its logical conclusion, reproducing the life of a man who perhaps lived for thirty-two years, let's say from 1730 to 1762, reconstructing this from beginning to end, omitting nothing, explaining everything, would take at least thirty-two years. I say "at least," for this would mean discussing only the man in question, omitting all his friends, enemies and relatives, assuming that all the events which had either a close or remote influence on his behavior were already known. Multiply your fellow by the number of people who lived at the same time as he did. Multiply him by all the men who have existed since the beginning of the world. Multiply mankind by its actions, reactions, its individual and collective doings, draw up the balance sheet of causes and effects. . . .

HE: Stop! You're making my head spin. Conclusion?

1: Conclusion: compress. I don't deny that Roberti's story is absorbing, but the way you're recounting it, it's set to last as long as his actual life.

HE: Don't exaggerate. I imagine we shall have more or less said everything in a week. On condition, of course, that we stick to the amours of Roberti and Solange, that is to say limit ourselves to three years by and large.

I: Well, I'm damned—now you take yourself for God!

HE: *I take myself for God?*

I: Yes, for God alone can be a historian in your sense of the word. He alone knows the story of mankind in its entirety, with every single detail. It is inscribed in His great book as it takes place. It is constantly spread out before His eyes like a planisphere. There are billions and billions of pages in this great book. God's advantage is that He can read it all in a flash whenever the desire takes Him, as if it wasn't a sequence of facts but one single, gigantic panorama. That's what it is to be eternal and infinite. But we are neither one nor the other. We are hemmed in by time and space. So we must abandon hope of being historians. One can at most aspire to be a moralist or a philosopher, that is to distill information or romantic distractions from the past, of which, incidentally, we merely possess snatches and distressingly terse summaries. Do you appreciate the conceit of the man who calls himself a historian? Quite simply he seeks to resuscitate the dead. In other words to compete with God. The supreme sin. Heading straight for hell. It's amazing how no theologian has thought of this and reserved a few jolly posthumous torments for Herodotus, Tacitus, Saint-Simon, Michelet, not to mention Theodor Mommsen, of course.

HE: Don't try to be funny!

I: All right, I agree. Tacitus and Saint-Simon didn't take themselves for God. But they were more modest than you are. They contented themselves with being polemists or novelists. Which is the most a historian can lay claim to. Something you'll never achieve owing to excessive conceit.

HE: Stop indulging in metaphysics. I am a gossip. I gossip. No more and no less.

I: You appall me! You a gossip? Oh come! Gossips are those who talk without saying anything. And you say plenty! You remind me of Hugo's Gwymplaine: "What are you laughing at, sycophant?—I do not laugh.—Then you are terrifying."

I remember clearly that at this stage in our conversation we were languidly walking up the Rue des Saints-Pères, which had been warmed by the morning sun but nevertheless preserved an age-old coolness. We must have crossed the Boulevard Saint-Germain, which is as tumultuous as the River Rhône and almost as wide. The Rue des Saints-Pères flows into it like a busy tributary. They have recently put up traffic lights where the two meet. This floodgate, opening every ninety seconds and closing again almost at once, is a great boon, for the Rue des Saints-Pères—an eminently navigable thoroughfare whose current streams in a southwesterly direction—transports hundreds of vessels. The new Faculty of Medicine which has been built there attracts a swarm of bicycles, scooters and antique little cars which are the students' customary means of locomotion. This Faculty of Medicine, set squarely at the corner of the Rue Jacob, resembles some ignoble factory erected by tasteless industrialists in the middle of a charming landscape. Bars for the young sawbones have insinuated themselves between the antique dealers and bookshops, to such effect that for about three hundred yards the street round there has lost every kind of amenity. Before it reaches the traffic lights the street narrows and the buses loom large like barges. The dusty sunlight of Paris in June is one of the most endearing things in the world. The hubbub of cities has a charm not entirely unlike that to be found in the harmonious, muted, distant sounds of the countryside.

Past the confluence of the Boulevard Saint-Germain the Rue des Saints-Pères becomes quite dark, that is to say it grows so narrow and the houses there appear so tall that the sun can barely reach into it, which for me is no grounds for complaint. I have always thought that cities are nothing but vast caverns in which men must first and foremost find shelter from nature, including the sun. To my mind our ancestors were very well advised when they took as rigid precautions against that planet as they did against rain or hail. I was vaguely thinking, as I strolled through this welcome coolness, that old streets like this may have something in common with certain peaks of the Alps where the snow never melts. On the top of Mont Cervin there are still patches of snow contemporary with Louis XIV. Why shouldn't the dear old Rue des Saints-Pères have preserved in one of its shady corners some pocket of air dating from the time of Cardinal Fleury, or some puff of wind from the year 1750? There are mysterious hormones in this air breathed by the stout Parisians, so obliging and well mannered, of the Ancien Régime. There is something soothing and gay about old streets, which isn't due to their architecture alone.

HE: I am not as terrifying as that. And to prove it I am going to tell you the rest of Roberti's and Solange's story. I shall treat the subject like a competent novelist working in the suburbs of Paris, a Cartesian with classical leanings and a great admirer of *The Princess of Cleves*, that wicked stepmother of French literature. Does that satisfy you?

I: Wait a minute! I don't like *The Princess of Cleves* any more than you do. I even once wrote a poem about the lady. Would you like to hear it?

HE: Of course.

I:

> *The Princess of Cleves,*
> *Oh how I hate her!*
> *When faced with her imitator*
> *My stomach heaves.*

HE: It's a bit thin.

I: But it's uncompromising. It cuts short any argument. *The Princess of Cleves* has bedeviled and emasculated us for three hundred years. I've buried her. Do you know why *The Princess of Cleves* appeals so strongly to second-rate minds? Because it's a bad novel, crude, stodgy, suggesting nothing, arousing no emotion, false throughout. For my part I can see no genius in it; merely the labored product of a lady fortunate enough to have received the excellent education of the seventeenth century and to know the language well. *The Princess of Cleves* is hollow and genteel. The opposite of the people we like. The opposite of Saint-Simon, Balzac, Proust, Victor Hugo, even Mérimée and Stendhal. It's as nauseating as *Paul et Virginie*.

HE: Now it's you who seem to be getting off the subject.

I: Admit all the same how amazing it is that *The Princess of Cleves* should have survived for three hundred years, that the trollop's head wasn't chopped off during the Revolution. But no! She's still with us. Stuffed. Holding her pose uncramped for three centuries. She's the chief adornment of the waxworks museum of French literature. She always finds some housemaid to brush the cobwebs off her farthingale. There is always some ass at the Sorbonne ready to explain how she embodies "that subtle French balance between stylistic grace and correct proportion." Which, between ourselves, is monstrously untrue. She is the least graceful and least balanced character one could possibly find. Stiff as a broomstick, a dragon of virtue, exaggerating chastity to the point of absurdity. The sort of church flea that would drive a saint to perdition. I would also be interested to know why there are always several writers in every generation who feel impelled to rewrite *The Princess of Cleves*, in other words to produce a dry, finicky, trivial, "typically French" novel in which nobility of sentiment vies with earnestness of style. Who on earth do they take themselves for? I detest that type of folklore.

HE: You've turned very violent all of a sudden. Writers are like wolves: they sleep with one eye open. Is literature your one and only passion? I've never seen you so worked up before!

I: What do you expect? Literature is my profession. I know it well and practice it honestly. Quite understandably, therefore, I take matters connected with it to heart. Only discuss defective plumbing with a conscientious plumber, badly cut clothes with a good tailor, stringy meat with a high-class butcher or ill-fitting dentures with a scrupulous dentist, and you will arouse the same indignation. Nothing provokes a good craftsman so much as to see the triumph of the third-rate. Trash that has sold well for three hundred years is quite enough to drive one wild.

HE: Look, I absolutely agree with you about *The Princess of Cleves*. But even so, if this trash has survived for three hundred years the basic material can't have been so bad!

I: There, my friend, you put your finger on the advantage, for artists, of living in great times. The artistic current in seventeenth-century France was so strong that it carried everything along with it, preserved everything, even the little droppings of old Mother Lafayette. Nowadays, even if one has a hundred times more talent, one can't be sure of surviving. Because we live in an age of decline, when three quarters of civilization has been forgotten and people no longer even know how to speak French, still less write it. People have "ideas." Masses, whole slabs of them, by the ton. But as they write them badly, these poor ideas shrivel up within three months. Having ideas is putting the cart before the horse. Any artist will tell you so or, rather, would have told you so a hundred years ago. What one really needs is a sense of form. The feeling of being a huge matrix, a fabulous mold in which one merely needs to pour molten bronze, gold or silver. Given a sense of form, you can relax: ideas always come to fill it. Given your built-in music box, the world provides all the melodies you require. The rest is mere journalism. Old Corneille must have felt like that when he redis-covered tragedy. He must have heard it echoing majestically within him. The words then followed on their own, like iron filings attracted by a mighty magnet. And that is why this nitwit, this old concierge of a *Princess of Cleves* still exists. She had the luck to see the light of day at the same time as *Phèdre*, the *Discourse on Universal History*, the *Memoirs* of Cardinal de Retz and the *Thoughts on the Comet*.

HE: One comforting thought is that there is nothing, positively noth-ing, of M. de Nemours about Roberti.

I: I apologize for letting myself go like that.

HE: Not at all. It was most entertaining. Monsieur J. D. gesticulating in the Rue des Saints-Pères over *The Princess of Cleves*. It was a sight worth seeing. Most endearing. Artists have to be aggressive and un-pleasant. Indulgence is the lot of us poor amateurs who create nothing, or of critics whose prime duty is to be fair. You others need excess. You need to admire immoderately and reject furiously. I suppose that for you it's a matter of life or death. Some works act as a tonic and others as poison on your delicate organisms. When you vomit up the Princess, you do it thoroughly. You spit her out whole. I envy such reactions. I, alas, can digest everything!

I: Please, let's not get emotional. I've been unforgivable. I reproach you for digressing and here am I doing the same thing myself. We sim-ply must follow some proper plan. We've been discussing Roberti's story any old how. We must tackle it seriously or my novel will never get written. Supposing I were to transcribe our conversation word for word, just as it has been taking place up to this moment. Do you realize what the result would be? We've been talking for over three hours and al-most nothing has happened. Roberti has merely stolen one little kiss from Solange, and only on her cheek at that. I have asked you several times to tell me about Agnes and the children: nothing doing. And Solange's family, what were they like? And what has become of Dietz, whom we have hardly seen? You've told me several times that Roberti was a good husband and father, but that's just a gratuitous statement. You've done nothing to demonstrate it. In a novel it's not enough just to state something. The reader has to see, be convinced by an unequivocal and pressing reality. At the risk of upsetting you I solemnly declare that Agnes doesn't exist, Roberti's sons are ectoplasms and Solange has so to speak no objective life of her own. I don't feel the world surrounding your heroes. I should like to feel it. Measure its weight, too heavy here, too light there. I should like to hear the creaking of daily life. To have an occasional glimpse down one of those avenues which unexpectedly open up for men to plunge into at a gallop. It's true, you know. Life may be cramped and narrow, but every now and then openings, moments of freedom appear; one leaps at them with an elation which lasts sometimes for a day, sometimes for a whole week. What's your answer to that?

HE: I have several answers. In the first place you're not going to sit down and transcribe our conversation word for word. That would be appalling. I am just providing the raw material; you will organize it and make a proper chronological story out of it. That's your business, not mine. I'm not concerned with literary composition. Second, I like to take my time and describe things as they occur to me. Third, Roberti and Solange are still under a glass dome. The beginnings of love are always far outside the everyday world. When two people first discover each other, there are always several days during which they live in a kind of vacuum, a lonely paradise where nothing can disturb them. It is later, after the first awakenings, when love moves in with its train of complications such as dates and outings, secret rendezvous, dissimulation, adjustments to one's timetable and so on, that the world begins to weigh heavy again. Be patient. You're going to see Roberti anxiously looking at his watch, inventing excuses for being late, raking up all sorts of lies to cover himself, getting irritated with Solange for complicating his life like this and feeling affectionate and remorseful toward Agnes. But we haven't got there yet. We are still under the glass dome of budding love. Fourth, Dietz. What do you want me to say? Maybe he'll come back into my story, maybe he won't. I don't know yet. It all depends. Roberti's story is not yet fully written in my head. I am remembering things piecemeal. One detail evokes another; an argument stems from some anecdote as it occurs to me, and so on. I am spinning the thread as I go along. You can see the thread I produce, but I may say the raw wool is very thick and matted. I am going to shock you now. If Roberti's story were fully written in my head, I wouldn't be telling it to you. It would bore me. I should yawn my head off. Naturally I know it. But—how can I explain this?—it seems to me that by telling it I reinvent it, rediscover it and thereby discover my-self. So you must forgive me if it's a bit disorganized.

I: I hope you will have some more to say about Dietz. I like him. And also Germaine and her prophetic soul, which I find delightful.

HE: We'll see. Probably I shall. One final thing. Agnes and the chil-dren. Everything comes to those who know how to wait. Now I shall tell you about them. This is where they come in, where they start to impinge, to exist, that is to say breathe, interfere, complicate and poison everything with their innocence and thus play their part in the damna-tion of Faust. Here goes!

I: At last!

HE: I say "Here goes!" but I don't quite know at which end to begin.

I: What does that matter? Begin anywhere you like. A good draughts-man approaches the paper with his pencil and doesn't lift it again until the drawing is finished. Whether he starts with the feet, the hair or the stomach is of no importance. Everything's in the finished drawing. Proceed.

HE: I've told you Agnes was forty-six at the time of the disaster. Therefore, when the affair began, she wasn't quite forty-four. That's not old. Nowadays one is still almost a young woman at that age. Be-sides, Agnes looked young because she hadn't lived much during those forty-four years. An untroubled life leaves no marks on the skin. To keep your girlish complexion, keep a girlish heart! Nor had she tasted any of those heady joys which etch wrinkles and leave signs of fatigue as effectively as sorrow. In short she was unimpaired. Time and her three pregnancies had passed lightly over her. Her cheeks, while no longer blooming, were still smooth. What aged her was her hair of faded chestnut flecked with white, which she had set in ringlets. I can't think why she was so fond of this horrible hairdo. I suppose she must have thought it looked sober and in good taste. In any event it undeniably lent her a certain style which was not without distinction. A number of countesses of the Faubourg Saint-Germain around 1825 must have cultivated similar ringlets out of a sort of pride in their no-bility, in protest against the current fashions, the pretty women, the new rich, and out of nostalgia for the Ancien Régime. She is a small woman, as you know, with a rather good, well-proportioned figure and beautiful legs. Her face isn't what you would call pretty, but certainly attractive. On social occasions she had a charming smile, subtle, wel-coming, faintly ironic, which showed that here was someone to reckon with. A rather deceptive smile, actually. Not stupid, you could even call her intelligent, but short on ideas. She only talked well about things close to her heart: her husband, her children, her home. For instance, I never heard her say anything of interest about a book she had read or a play she had seen. In spite of this I am never bored in her company. And I like her trim little shape and her ringlets. She's a familiar and likable figure who forms part of my "picture of the world"; she features up to a point in my album of family photographs. Dear Agnes.

I: You seem very fond of her.

HE: Yes, I am indeed. She commands both my affection and my respect. Besides, I can say I more or less discovered her when things took a bad turn. Not only did calamity fail to undermine her pride, but it gave her a new pride which I, for all my sharp eyes, had never suspected. People sometimes surprise us that way. And make us feel faintly ashamed. I was ashamed of having failed to appreciate Agnes.

I: After his peck on Solange's cheek, did she notice any subtle change in her dear Edouard's attitude?

HE: Good God, no, not in the least! Edouard was exactly the same before the peck as after it. Identical. It wasn't his first by a long shot! Besides, Agnes was trusting by nature and not a bit jealous; as she had very little imagination it never entered her head that Roberti might employ the time when he was not at home in adulterous carryings-on. She quite simply believed what he told her. She also had great tact and was impeccable in her conduct toward him. She never demanded explanations and would never have dreamed of hunting for evidence in her husband's pockets.

I: Now that's most important! Not jealous. How odd! Are there any women who aren't jealous?

HE: Agnes.

I: And do you think I'm going to be satisfied with that? It's part of a woman's nature to be jealous and possessive, especially when she's a married woman who has purchased her husband, who is duly and contractually his owner. No, no, you must find something else.

HE: I didn't say Agnes wasn't possessive; I said she wasn't jealous.

I: Don't quibble. Possessiveness in women expresses itself through jealousy. A woman who isn't jealous is a woman who doesn't love her husband or has ceased to love him. Lack of jealousy simply implies lethargy, inertia, indifference. That wasn't the case with Agnes. And so?

HE: So what? She wasn't jealous, full stop. She simply didn't have a suspicious, fussy, prying, meddlesome mind.

I: Did it never occur to her that in twenty years of marriage there must have been a few occasions when Roberti kicked over the traces?

HE: I don't believe she was often troubled by ideas of that kind.

Roberti was very good to her; he led a well-regulated home life. He had been quite content to let himself be caught up in the family web; he had formed various habits and more particularly had made his family adopt them. Agnes had long known that her husband was first and foremost a rational man who never did anything impetuous. He went off soberly to sessions at the Assembly and his various other occupations. He returned home at the times when he said he would. In short he was very equable, not living for the day (that is to say moody and temperamental) but on the contrary very much the same from one day to the next, so much so that all the members of his family thought they knew him well, had recognized all his quirks and fads and adapted themselves to his timetable. I am skating rapidly over all this; it helps to fill in the picture but would be tedious to elaborate. Naturally it was all based on a misunderstanding. Roberti secretly regretted having established such a well-regulated family life that it left him only a tiny margin of independence, while his family grumbled to itself over father's despotism, his punctual and watchful presence. And so Agnes' mind worked as follows: seeing Edouard so settled, so attentive, even exacting a home-lover, she was sure she was loved as much as she loved herself. And after all she wasn't mistaken. Roberti was fickle in his mind, in his conversation, but not in his conduct, and Agnes, however she stretched her imagination, could never have contrived to picture him murmuring sweet nothings to a dumb little blonde. Such a lascivious picture in the manner of Fragonard or Saint-Aubin couldn't possibly have been further from her thoughts. When Roberti's character darkened she was quite astonished. When she finally learned that her husband had a mistress it made her deeply unhappy, naturally, but her grief was not that of a jealous woman. It was that of a woman bowed down by fate, the grief you feel when someone dear falls gravely ill and you watch him slowly dying with no hope of saving him. Such was her character. I can say no more than that. It is all I know.

ɪ: Did she subsequently get wind of Edouard's infidelities?

ʜᴇ: You mean his previous little adventures? No. Roberti had buried all that in utter secrecy. They had passed into oblivion. Anyway, you must beware of optical illusions. I told you at some length about Odile, but she was an exception in his secret life. You would be wrong to think of him skipping from one mistress to another. His secret life was intermittent. He never had more than one or two mistresses a year, and often they were mere passing fancies, affairs of a night. He would drop any woman he had just slept with like a hot potato if either she had disappointed him or on the contrary he had disappointed her. You see what I mean?

I: Oh perfectly! Always that pride. He couldn't bear to see anyone who had witnessed his inadequacy a second time.

HE: Exactly. He had had several mortifying experiences, poor man! Being high-strung, this wasn't perhaps surprising. With him the sympathetic predominated over the vagotonic. Any strong emotion, such as overeager anticipation of a pleasure or else its opposite, namely incomplete desire, or again the discovery of some flaw in the object desired, would completely paralyze him. He extricated himself from these ludicrous situations or half defeats by laughing and joking his way out of them. But his heart was at the same time filled with bitter resentment and he would feel such a distaste for the woman who had provoked the fiasco that for nothing in the world would he have seen her again. Nowadays, you know, love is becoming very difficult! We haven't enough time or places to go. We lack the requisite leisure to allow desire to grow within us, soak it up the way a sponge soaks up water, come to the act of possession in that state of ecstasy which is only attained after a long bout of cooing and endless preparations. Gone is that process of slow and intoxicating discovery, gone that slow and skillful ascent to paradise! You take to each other, say so and rush to the nearest hotel to prove it. Fifteen minutes later you find yourself back where you began. How can one help one's style getting cramped? Love considered as a lesson in Swedish gymnastics. Personally I find it appalling. Love reduced to the mere act, with nothing before or after, seems to me the acme of boredom. To my mind love without words, without its tender avowals, setbacks, delays and disappointments, is of no value whatsoever.

I: Tell me, do you really have ideas about love? It's funny, but I never manage to think of you as having emotions and a sex life like everyone else.

HE: Really? Why not?

I: Oh, I don't know. Perhaps because you're so keen on observing the lives of other people. One gets the impression you have no time left to devote to yourself.

HE: Don't worry, I do have a little.

I: There's something rather monstrous about your faculty for recording everything to do with the people you meet. There's something slightly inhuman about you, I must say; your eye is a camera and your heart a darkroom.

HE: Oh come on! I'm not as black as all that!

I: For me, you are a sort of priest. Someone with a heart too big to be employed for personal ends. Your heart was made to be a receptacle for the joys and sorrows of mankind.

HE: Are you trying to pay me a compliment?

I: Lord yes, it could be taken as a compliment.

HE: One of these days I'll tell you about my love life. It is even more secret than Roberti's, which is to my credit, since on the one hand I am nothing and on the other I have nothing to hide from anyone.

I: Bravo! I like that. To return to Roberti, it's strange all the same that Agnes never learned about his secret pastimes, especially when the Solange affair broke. Scandals generally raise an almighty wind which blows open every door. A mass of filth wells up out of the past. It is seen in a false light, what's more. The glow of scandal makes everything, even the most innocent behavior, look suspicious and sordid.

HE: Well, no. Agnes is still convinced that Roberti was smitten in middle age by a sort of love sickness, that he was laid low by a quaternary fever. He had always displayed the cunning of a serpent and this had borne its fruit. He left not a trace, he never put a thing in writing. When one of his adventures ended, it really did so. There wasn't a scrap of material evidence to be found. Nothing but a twofold memory, in the minds of Roberti and his partner, and it was in the interests of both to keep quiet about it.

I: Women are never so discreet.

HE: We must assume that Roberti's girl friends were. And then there was another thing: the difference in their backgrounds, an additional guarantee against being found out. In France society is almost as rigidly divided up as in India. The different worlds never intermingle. It is inconceivable for a manicurist or stenographer ever to cross the path of a deputy's wife or turn up in the same circles as the deputy normally frequents. Moreover Roberti reduced to a minimum the chances of being seen by anyone who might recognize him. He arranged his dates by telephone; he went to them in his car, opened the door, in got the damsel and away he drove with his prey. He then raced off to conceal his happiness in discreet hotels in remote corners of the city. He even wore dark glasses! Far from boring him, I believe all these precautions amused him. There was a conspiratorial side to his nature which they satisfied. He liked playing the eel that slips through everyone's fingers.

From all this you can see there wasn't the slightest reason why Agnes should be jolted out of her serenity. Poor woman, the best explanation she found after the event for the sudden and unexpected affair between Roberti and Solange was her husband's twenty years of fidelity.

She told herself it was inevitable that this sober man should one day suffer an emotional and physical explosion. And she absolved him from it. She reproached herself for having been dull, drab, and failing to preserve her youth, failing to hold his interest. Humbly she examined herself in the mirror and found herself old and dowdy (which in any case was untrue). The way people err when interpreting the actions and feelings of others is something that continually fascinates me. In the case of Agnes it would have been cruel to undeceive her. I think in fact that the formula she invented was less painful than a revelation of the truth would have been, namely Roberti's deceit, his furtive amours, his unknown soul. She believed in all good faith that she had been Edouard's sole possessor for twenty years. She had had twenty years' enjoyment of him. I use this word in the real-estate agent's sense, the way one says "the enjoyment of a property."

I: Are you sure you did the right thing in this instance?

HE: Does one ever know whether one has done the right thing? The right thing is the least one can do: it merely requires a little courage. What is difficult is to decide where one's duty lies. Duty is seldom clear, simple, straightforward, obvious: that would make it too easy. It is nearly always ambiguous and one has to adjust one's sights the whole time. Duty can never be based on principles, for example, except in the case of those fools who are incapable of judging a situation and blindly rely on the maxims dinned into their heads in their youth. Duty is volatile, fluctuating, as changeable as life itself. For me, a man who does his duty is like a tightrope walker. In short, so far as the right attitude to adopt with Agnes goes, I hesitated for a long time. I asked myself exactly where my duty lay: should I tell her all, everything I knew about Edouard, so as to turn her against him, convert her sorrow into resentment, or should I take the opposite line and conceal everything? A tricky decision for a man of duty to take! All the trickier in that obviously it would have been infinitely harder to say: "My poor Agnes, you have been deceived right from the start. Edouard was in reality a mysterious character addicted to furtive little love affairs and he fooled you for twenty years." In trying to find where one's duty lies, the more difficult course is a temptation extremely hard to resist. I would have had to compel myself, force myself to talk to Agnes along these lines; it would have been a frightful effort and a dirty trick into the bargain. All the appearances of duty, as you can see! I think it is to my credit that I resisted it. I told myself that, far from proving a substitute for Agnes' unhappiness, rage and resentment would only increase it and that I shouldn't place this added burden on her shoulders. I also told myself that in telling the truth about Edouard I ran the risk of maligning him. In fact his flirtations, his little affairs, his intrigues with cheap shopgirls hardly counted. Taking one of them to an hotel meant no more than treating himself to a good lunch in a restaurant. But how could I explain that? You yourself must realize it wasn't possible. As soon as one betrays somebody's secrets one is up to a point guilty of slander, a policeman making his report in whose words everything appears in a bad light. In trying to convey truth we are like a clumsy painter trying to convey nature: the drawing is crude, the colors false, the composition top-heavy. There are certain pictures which are slanders, resembling the soul of the painter who made them much more than the model he aimed to reproduce. Even photography is deceptive. So I let Agnes preserve her illusions. All things considered, by interpreting events in her own way she came closer to the actual truth than if she had known the thousand little surface truths which would have blinded her to its real essence.

What did Agnes mean to Roberti? I shall try to show you. Up to now I have depicted him apart from her, living on his own account, with no mention of the countless bonds by which he was attached to her. I have stuck too closely to my subject and only shown you the side of Edouard concerned with his love life. But overworking one's subject leads to painting *trompe l'oeil*. In fact I have been the reverse of a traditional novelist. I should have begun by drawing you a complete picture of Roberti's social and family life. Showing you the respectable citizen, the husband, the father. I should have described him returning home with presents for the whole family: a silk scarf for Agnes, Vigny's poems bound in vellum for Jacques (hideous, but a nice thought!), a box of watercolors for Pierre, the second son, and for Jean, the youngest, six beautiful lead soldiers chosen with special care. Roberti at family lunch would also have made an amusing picture: holding forth, inventing comic paradoxes for his children, coining maxims, seeing himself as a patriarch who could be a wit as well. The children loved listening to him and would play up to him. Agnes admired this husband of hers who somehow contrived to be as witty at home as he was in public. Following which I would have skillfully analyzed the slow deterioration of this fine character, the hidden passion flooding through his nervous system, the loss and damnation of my hero. Had I a gift for composition, that is for chronological order, I think I would have painted a much truer picture than I have done by laying all the emphasis on Edouard's secret thoughts and actions.

I: I'm not so sure. It's arguable. Roberti the honest deputy, the good husband and father, with fifty years of respectability and the Legion of Honor, couldn't matter less. He's devoid of interest. He's the stuff for a middle-class American novel. But Roberti the secretive, the wayward, the complex is intriguing. You would never have embarked on his story at all if he hadn't turned into a murderer. What is so fascinating is the hidden paths which led to his crime. You haven't done so badly for a beginner!

HE: Really?

I: Yes, yes, I promise you. You mention the Abel side of Roberti in passing. Well and good. But that's enough. What matters is the Cain side, everything in Abel that eventually paved the way for Cain, the remotest origins of Cain, the budding monster.

HE: That's very nice of you, but you mustn't exaggerate. We all have a bit of Cain in us, some potential cancer of the spirit, but most often it never shows. It lies dormant and we die healthy. I only saw the Cain in Roberti after the event, when the spotlights had shifted; given the way he ended, I then went back to the beginning and began to look for causes.

I: Here, don't start all over again! This philosophy of chance, of nothing being inevitable, is getting on my nerves. Directly things happen it means they had to happen. Full stop, paragraph. Napoleon had every chance of winning the battle of Waterloo. Wellington had made every possible mistake. But Grouchy was a fathead and Blücher won the battle. Bang! The face of the world was changed. I can't see why you, who believe so strongly in necessities, in invisible forces at work, in powers underlying nature, should cling to this idiotic theory of chance the May bug which one can thwart by extinguishing one's lamp. I'd rather you told me some more about Agnes, the children and Roberti in the family circle. You needn't go into it too deeply but you must draw the contrast all the same.

HE: Well, it's just as I've told you. A good father and a good husband. Nothing to reproach him with there. With Agnes he had of course shared over twenty years of intellectual and sentimental partnership. He didn't feel love for her so much as tenderness. An immense tenderness. How can one give a name to one's feelings? I must confess I never venture to do so without misgivings. Wasn't this tenderness love? A love woven out of habit, affectionate understanding, mutual consideration, companionship, a united front? One estimable characteristic of Roberti's was that he never discussed Agnes with his mistresses. Not for anything in the world would he have fallen back in his opening gambits on the old argument "My wife doesn't understand me, we have nothing in common, I no longer love her." He would have regarded that as a vile betrayal, as sacrilege. He never even mentioned her name. It was his way of remaining faithful to her in the midst of his infidelities. Put another way, his escapades were never acts of revenge or reprisal. They had nothing to do with Agnes, they took place in another world, in that part of him exclusively devoted to his own ego. I cannot stress too often that this was a small, even minute part of him. I should like to give you an exact idea of its importance in relation to his life. Take a desk, for instance, one of those pretty eighteenth-century desks of inlaid rosewood. It is about five feet high, three feet wide and eighteen inches deep. It has eight or ten visible drawers and a secret one concealed under the flap. What does such a drawer represent in terms of size, of capacity, compared with the whole desk? Practically nothing. When the dealer sells you an eighteenth-century desk of inlaid rosewood he doesn't refer to the secret drawer or, if he does, it is only as an afterthought, after extolling the marquetry and woodwork, its quality and craftsmanship. Well, I have done the reverse for Roberti. I've talked almost all the time about the secret drawer, as if the craftsmanship, marquetry work, quality of the wood and style of the maker were unimportant. So now I'm seizing the chance to put things in their proper perspective.

I: As a rule, it's one's most precious possessions that one locks away in secret drawers.

HE: No, it isn't! Not the most precious. Simply the things one doesn't want to leave lying around. For precious things there are safes in the underground strong rooms of banks. Secret drawers have served, since time immemorial, to hide love letters.

Roberti, then, shared with Agnes a deep community of interests. "Their hearts beat as one," as the saying goes. He had more or less molded her in his own image. On her wedding day she was just a young girl from the provinces, pleasant enough but totally inexperienced, with the mental outlook of all girls, that is to say vapid, rather silly and full of prejudices. At least that's how girls were before the war. I gather they have changed since.

I: Not very much. They take lovers instead of confining themselves to flirting. But at bottom they're the same. They have become easy and willing, but none the more attractive for that.

HE: My! What is this sudden "parthenophobia"?

I: Oh, there's nothing sudden about it. I share Baudelaire's ideas about girls. I never appealed to them even when I was eighteen, and they didn't appeal much to me either. Besides, generally speaking I'm

not mad about the young. They bore me with their bad taste in literature and their romanticism. I have horrible memories of my own youth.
I only began to feel more or less at home with myself when I was
about twenty-eight, after my metamorphosis.

HE: Well, Agnes at any rate was a very nice girl of the thirties.

I: Was Roberti in love with her?

HE: Yes, I believe he was. The way one is with a girl one contemplates
marrying. It's a fresh, innocent, unimpatient and serene kind of love.
You take your time because you know you have the rest of your lives
in which to find out about each other. You linger over the preliminaries, you revel in a mass of foolish and sweet nothings. Roberti had met
Agnes on a holiday at Arcachon and she had aroused a strange new
feeling in him which did not fit in at all with his way of life. He was
twenty-seven or -eight; a lawyer, as I've told you; he also dabbled in
local politics, sat on committees and addressed Young Radicals on
Wednesday evenings. He lived without ties in a bachelor's semisqualor;
his little apartment behind the Gare Montparnasse had at least one
advantage: he could take his mistresses back there. But everything palls
in the long run. No doubt he wasn't cut out for a carefree life. The
ease of it all depressed him. I believe he yearned for some yoke. It was
just like him to go and fall for a young girl from the provinces, pure as
a flower, ignorant as a fish and lively as a swallow. A perfect girl! The
ideal girl! Agnes gave him a nostalgia for an orderly life. In the first
place he was charmed by her pretty face, beautiful legs and trim little
body; second, she embodied for him centuries of provincial tradition
and cautious wisdom, hosts of copper saucepans, family furniture polished for three hundred years, ten or twelve generations of middle-
class Gascons, industrious, frugal, prudent and cunning, who had lived
with dignity amid their gardens and vineyards. It went to his head.
Have you noticed how Parisians, those children of asphalt, generally
prefer to marry into provincial families? It gives them a feeling of putting out fresh roots, of being replanted in the soil.

Round about thirty is a critical age for a man, the age when one
makes serious blunders or, rather, when the blunders one makes begin
to be irreparable. Perhaps Roberti had undergone the same transformation as you and had realized that youth, the time when things don't
matter, the time of harmless muddle, was over. That he must settle
down if he wanted to leave some mark on the world. At any rate, Agnes
fascinated him. This lighthearted, conventional, lovable girl, probably
made beautiful by the prospect of marriage, represented for him an attractive experiment to be tried and brought off. He suddenly discovered

eternal France, ageless humanity, common sense, in short salvation according to man's ancient precepts. He thought heaven had sent him Agnes in the nick of time as the crowning point, the final goal and masterpiece of his twenty-eight years of life. He told himself that after having let his spirit roam free, after having experienced most things and guessed at the rest, he had returned to "true values"; likewise that it isn't through force of intellect that one grasps the profound truth of commonplaces. To revert to banality, you know, is a great temptation for lofty minds. The greatest, probably, because it represents the highest ambition, the one which succeeds and cancels all the others. Only mighty geniuses can yield to it and draw fresh strength from it.

After Roberti had married he was extremely happy. Marriage suited him perfectly, with all it meant in terms of orderliness, timesaving and economy; it answered all kinds of secret longings in his heart. Agnes had been admirably brought up by her mother, who had taught her what housewives knew in 1760 or 1880, namely a mass of priceless knowledge which today is forgotten. From this point of view she was a luxury and an anachronism, in the same way that a beautiful eighteenth-century house built of stone, with carved ornaments, sculptures, vast and spacious rooms, speaks of a way of life and philosophy utterly different from the hideous roughcast buildings of the suburbs. Roberti was enchanted by this creature from another century and another world. Besides, nothing is so enjoyable as to find oneself married to someone one doesn't know, whom at best one can only guess at, only glimpse, but to whom one knows oneself to be superior in almost every respect! Nothing is so enjoyable as to think how one is going to instruct a pretty disciple in life, taste and knowledge. How one is going to lead her from discovery to rapture; how everything she learns will have first been selected for her by oneself. You can imagine how Roberti, as we know him, set about the education of his wife. It took him five or six years, all of them delightful. He was enchanted. What a godsend, this girl who had read nothing but cheap novels and brought him a mind as virginal as her body! He filled her up, crammed her with everything he knew. He saw to her literary, musical, artistic and even political education. He made her read all the writers he admired in the mid-thirties, that is to say Giraudoux, Aldous Huxley, Jules Romain, Gide. Especially Gide.

ɪ: Hmm!

ʜᴇ: Well, what do you expect? Roberti was an intellectual snob. He wanted to be avant-garde in his tastes and sensibilities. He followed the fashion while sincerely believing he had good taste.

I: Even so, the things he admired were pretty second-rate. How could he have fallen for all that junk?

HE: You must remember they were great men in 1935. People used to talk about "Giraudoux the magician." Jules Romain and Huxley were profundity and intellect personified. As for Gide, he was Goethe.

I: Incredible but true. Go on.

HE: Let's be fair. Roberti also introduced Agnes to fine writers like Proust, Chesterton, Meredith, Fogazzaro, Whitman and so on. He took her round the museums of France and Italy, made her listen to Moussorgsky, Borodin, De Falla and Albéniz to the saturation point. Spanish and Russian music were all the rage in Paris before the war. Purcell and Handel were also being rediscovered. I know all this represented just a fashionable craze, but at least it was good quality. Better than Marcel Prévost, Massenet or Leoncavallo. Similarly he took her to exhibitions of Utrillo, Marquet, Bonnard and Miró, which was all the more laudable in that he also showed her Fra Angelico, Zurbarán and the Impressionists. I call that a good intellectual average, though it never rose to quite the highest level. One final detail in conclusion: Roberti didn't like Hugo.

I: But hell, that's a sacred touchstone! Not to like Hugo is the badge of idiocy.

HE: You see, I'm keeping nothing back. He didn't like Hugo because it was fashionable at that time to run old Hugo down, sling mud at him, poke fun at him and proclaim him to be stupid. So Roberti fell into line. He very properly ran old Hugo down. He smugly repeated his beloved Gide's *mot* of "Hugo, alas!"

I: The monster! The bastard! The louse!

HE: It's a real pleasure to tell you a story. You take such a lively part in it! One could never call you a dull audience.

I: Some things are sacred. Father Hugo is one of them. When I see some fool trying to be smart about the chain of the Alps, it makes me mad.

HE: All right, but calm down. Roberti, then, spent five or six years acting as Agnes' tutor. Things like that forge bonds. How could one help loving someone whom one has so to speak created? Pygmalion must always love Galatea, he can't help it; and Galatea must equally love Pygmalion. They make an ideal couple. I would almost go so far as to say, like Diderot, that incest between father and daughter must be the most satisfactory form of union.

Agnes was ignorant but no fool. She was Molière's Henriette in *Les Femmes Savantes;* she had read nothing but she had plenty of good sense. In making her read good (and less good) authors, Roberti brought off a tour de force of which few husbands are capable; he lifted his wife out of the world in which she had grown up, which was the only one she knew and loved, and made her part of a different world. He detached her from her childhood, her parents, her previous thoughts and feelings, in sum from everything which as a rule poisons family life; he made her a naturalized Robertian.

i: How sad! Henriette in love with Trissotin and spoiled by him.

he: Not at all. You exaggerate and distort everything. Roberti wasn't Trissotin. He was a "man of good will," of the type one meets in his favorite novel.

i: I almost prefer Trissotin.

he: Come on! You're letting your feelings run away with you. There was nothing really bad about Roberti in spite of his little absurdities, his little snobberies. I must apologize for mentioning Victor Hugo; it was a touch of malice I couldn't resist. I knew it would get a rise out of you.

But have I made the bonds between Roberti and his wife clear? They formed a close web of affection. She had need of him in order to think; he was in a sense her father confessor. He needed her as a support, as someone to love and admire him, comprehend even his slightest quirks and fads. He was never so pleased to see her as when he had just been deceiving her: it was like a return from exile. Agnes was his homeland. Hence his infinite precautions and appearance of strict fidelity. There was no common yardstick between his love for Agnes and his chance encounters. The latter meant so little to him that, given the slenderness of his emotional involvement, they were almost without reality. So it was inconceivable that such peccadilloes should disturb the harmony of his married life in any way. This may be the attitude of a crook and a cheat but not of a complete bastard. On the contrary it reveals a certain scrupulousness. I would even call it humane, for nothing is easier than candor. Seen close to, the precautions he took to bury his adventures in inviolable secrecy—the precautions of a dissolute or shamefaced husband, niggling to the point of absurdity—were so many proofs of his love for Agnes. I should like to find a comparison to make you understand this particular state of mind.

i: There's no need. I get it. The Lord Chief Justice furtively removes his Legion of Honor rosette before entering the brothel.

he: That's it. As a gesture it's comic but also, up to a point, touching. It isn't just hypocrisy. To me there's something symbolical about it. The man who enters the brothel isn't the same as the man who received the decoration. They are two segments of his life totally divorced from each other. The brothel answers to obscure and short-lived needs, it's a concession to the animal side of him. The rosette represents the rest, that is almost everything: the honest judge, the legal authority, the man dedicated to a worthy and serious cause. What does the brothel represent in the judge's life? Two hours a month. Virtually nothing. Conclusion, he's absolutely right to pass this little weakness over in silence.

I: Well, there you are! By this token Roberti is absolved. White as snow.

HE: No, not absolved but put in perspective. If we're going in for judging and moralizing, let's try at least to take every element of the problem into consideration and weigh all the motives carefully. What is the sense in condemning people on summary evidence, by virtue of rigid principles? Novelists and poets have to be far more cautious than policemen or judges, for when they condemn it's not just to prison or pain of death but to everlasting damnation.

I: Oh, my God! Clearly you're no novelist or poet or you wouldn't be so categorical. "Everlasting damnation," if you please! Possibly, if one is Balzac or Dickens or Shakespeare. Richard III, Major Bagstock, Camusot and Macbeth are in hell. So far as I am concerned, I want none of that responsibility. I want to remain free to indulge my whims. I want to be able to sling mud or praise people to the skies without feeling that this is affecting them. I want to have my likes and dislikes, even if they are unfair. And whatever you do, you'll never manage to make me like your Roberti. There's something shoddy about the fellow, and when I say that I'm not passing judgment, it's just the way I feel. I sense in him a basic, essential shoddiness. His was not a noble soul.

HE: Nor was it ignoble.

I: Perhaps not. It was second-rate. A second-rate soul with streaks of meanness set in a rather brilliant mind. And again, one could argue as to whether his mind was brilliant, given his taste in literature and other predilections.

HE: Oh, allow him something!

I: What strikes me as most to his credit is that he was your friend, and one of long standing. Which must mean that he had a few good points, however intangible.

HE: Yes, yes, he had. One could feel him radiating warmth and intelligence. Haven't I managed to make you sense this by now?

I: To be absolutely fair, yes, a little.

HE: But you're stubborn, eh? You refuse to give in.

I: Yes, it's odd. Something inside me resists Roberti and even rejects him. I'm not doing it on purpose, I swear. I just find him incompatible. I've never felt very drawn to Doctor Faust. His is a soul I find quite incomprehensible, a whole range of passions and desires I simply cannot imagine, a revolt against the human condition, an ambition which fills me with horror. No doubt because I detest dupes and because pacts with the Devil, whether conscious or not, whether signed or implicit, are always bad bargains. Do you know whom I find the one really sympathetic character in your story, who captures my imagination, who has strength and substance, who is even outstanding in his way?

HE: Well, I don't think it can be Germaine. Or Dietz. It must be Solange, it can't be anyone else.

I: No, it's yourself. You, the narrator, with your monstrous faculty for X-raying people, revealing everything, sparing no detail and yet being indulgent, never judging, never condemning, always finding extenuating circumstances. You may not realize it but you're the hell of a character yourself! You are huge, you are an oak tree spreading your vast shadow over Roberti, Agnes, Solange and the rest. An oak which can talk, telling the story of the men who have dwelt beneath its branches. And not only that: you also know the seasons, the wind, the birds and caterpillars; your roots gossip with the worms and moles. Will you tell *my* story like this one day?

HE: But you have no story. You're utterly uninteresting. You don't live, you create. The story of creation is beyond telling. Your life is as dull and flat as that of a country grocer wholly wrapped up in his business. And if ever you happen to have feelings (I won't go so far as to say passions!) you need no one to sing them in your stead. You rush to write it all down. What can one say about a man to whom nothing is without interest, who feeds everything into his work? I enjoy talking to you, you are even my favorite person to talk to because no one so appreciates oddities, quaint truths, improbabilities; but about you I have nothing to say that you haven't already said yourself or don't already know. Right. We have flattered each other quite enough. Let's get back to Roberti.

I: I'd like to hear something about the children. I still can't quite picture them, in spite of the lead soldiers and watercolors.

HE: Very well. In 1955 they were fourteen, thirteen and ten.

I: Was Roberti fond of them? Was he a good father?

HE: Excellent. Very kind. Even a bit too kind. As with literature and music, he followed the fashionable ideas on upbringing. Now, for the past thirty years it has been the fashion to be gentle and tolerant, which isn't always good for children. Parents give them free rein; they go in for moral persuasion, argue with them and make allowances for their quaint ideas, worry about giving them complexes or traumatic anxieties. In other words, the little Robertis were not what one might call well brought up. Their school record was poor; they were sometimes insolent. They could have done with a few good spankings. When I pointed this out to Edouard he retorted that they were fine boys, which was true, and that he wanted them above all to trust him. He wanted to be loved, not feared.

I: Did he by any chance say he wanted them to look on him as their friend?

HE: Naturally.

I: Coming from him that doesn't surprise me. He certainly never missed a cliché.

HE: He also said: "I am a democrat in the Assembly. There's no reason why I shouldn't also be one at home."

I: How idiotic! Democracy should stop short at the front door. A democratic father who puts his decision to the vote only messes things up and succeeds in making everyone unhappy.

HE: It didn't go quite as far as that. In spite of his "thing" about companionship, his children on the whole respected him and he more or less made up for his lack of authority with kindness. When he was angry with them he told them so in a pained tone of voice which I found rather silly and comic but which apparently had its effect. He would stop bringing them presents for two or three weeks. The boys no doubt knew they had a rather weak father, but this weakness also served as a sort of defense. They humored him, and so enabled him to take pride in this deplorable method of upbringing. In any event, things are as they are. Nothing is perfect but everything comes right in the end. In its muddled way the Roberti family was not unhappy, there was a lot of laughter, and Agnes, who had preserved her instinct and whose good old ancestral principles Roberti had not completely killed off, knew more or less how to keep order. She was an excellent mother who loved without any regard for being loved in return; in other words she lost her temper, distributed a few well-aimed blows now and then, shouted at them and forbade them the movies or other outings when they deserved it. So the boys felt much more respect and affection for her than for their father. Naturally they didn't realize this. But I could tell from a thousand imperceptible little signs. And then Agnes had a way of sheltering her brood with her wings which was admirable. One could feel her stout heart generating maternal love the way an atomic pile generates power. So you see, the weakness of the one was offset by the character of the other and everything was fairly satisfactory in the end. The Roberti family was a microcosm of the world, where everything creaks, nothing fits properly and power is seldom in the hands of those most worthy of it, but in which destinies nevertheless work themselves out without major catastrophes.

I: Without major catastrophes! And what about wars and epidemics, dams which burst because they have been built by incompetents, industries which die because they're run by fools . . . ?

HE: Yes, there are catastrophes but they are rare. There was also one in the Roberti family. But all in all, one gets by. That's what I meant. And one snatches little joys out of each day. One lives to the end of one's term; and when one draws up the balance sheet one sees that life has been better than one had feared and less good than one had hoped. As if there were a giant pendulum in the world, some all-powerful moderating factor which generally prevents excess.

I: This *Weltanschauung* is highly questionable. I could just as well maintain the opposite: that violence and excess are our daily bread, that war is the normal state of man, disaster his routine and so on. But never mind.

HE: That doesn't contradict my philosophy. My pendulum is within us. As a rule, even in the midst of the worst calamities, people usually manage to fall on their feet. In even the blackest seas of grief there are little islands of gaiety, or at least of comparative calm, long intervals during which one doesn't suffer, during which the organism, the heart and mind resume their regular ticking, during which biology hums its old immemorial song. I can't remember if I told you the Roberti boys' names.

I: I know the eldest was called Jacques.

HE: The other two were called Pierre and Jean.

I: He didn't take much trouble!

HE: Don't you believe it. It is just because there was a purpose behind these names that I brought them up. They are even very typical of Roberti's ideas. Whereas his friends pretentiously christened their children Thierry, Alain, Régis, Paul-Charles, Chantal-Claude or Patrick, he thought it an excellent thing to give his own sons traditional names. This touch of ostentatious simplicity, this refusal to be like everyone else, seemed to him the hallmark of a superior man.

Do you begin now to sense the pressure of the family on Roberti? Can you see the sentimental web it wove? For Edouard his wife and sons were his very existence, extensions of himself, as much part of him as his arms or legs. They were his past and future, his horizon, his foreground and background. They were at once the far distance and the immediate proximity. But one doesn't think the whole time about one's limbs, except when they give one pain. Now Agnes and the boys never caused Roberti any pain. At the most, occasional slight irritation. That is the negative shape paternal and marital love assumes most of the time. One simply doesn't see it. Yet it exists and is even very strong. I wonder to what extent he knew how devoted he was to his family. Emotions which slumber in the depths, which nothing ever stings into wakefulness, pass almost as unrecognized by those who feel them as by those who inspire them. Roberti had long since acquired the habit of looking on himself as a rather detached character with a heart I wouldn't call exactly cold so much as impervious, detached, unconcerned. He didn't feel himself capable of boundless love. It seemed to him that, throughout his whole life, he had generally taken more than he had given where sentiments were concerned, whether it was a question of friendship or of love. So he sometimes thought in his moments of idle fancy that should he one day find himself left alone, Agnes and the boys having flown for some reason or other, he wouldn't take so badly to this new state, by God; indeed it might even hold certain charms. But that was mere idle dreaming. In reality his family was the wall that sheltered him from the world and marked the permanent boundary of his field, just as it was the farthest point beyond which he could not see. That's very French, isn't it? The family as a social cell. Roberti the broadminded, the fearless thinker, had ended by becoming superstitious about this home he had created and whose cornerstone he was, that is to say its founder, provider, mainstay and philosopher. It is odd and rather comic, although touching; he regarded this creation of his with deep respect, even a little shyly, as if he had built up something too big for him, something sacred and untouchable.

i: Might I suggest a slight pause here? This last analysis of yours was particularly exhausting and demanded such concentration that I can't take any more. It was a miracle of subtlety and detail! Like fine needlework, like miniature-painting! But one thing in all that you have said puzzles me. I didn't interrupt at the time because you were going full steam, pushing with some difficulty through your cactus forest. What are emotions which slumber in the depths? What are feelings unrecognized by those who inspire them and those who feel them? A sentiment exists only insofar as it reveals itself and makes itself felt; it has no life of its own like a tree or an animal. It is a link. Some of your remarks are a bit steep, I must say, when you let inspiration carry you away! Irma doesn't know she loves Jules. Jules doesn't know he loves Irma. Moral: Irma and Jules don't love each other.

HE: That's an impressive argument but it's I who am in the right all the same. Sentiments most certainly do slumber like hibernating animals, bears or badgers. They do have a life of their own; they work in the depths, in secret and in silence, like metals. So that sentiments unrecognized by those who feel them and those who inspire them can very well exist, *be there*, exerting an invisible, incomprehensible but powerful influence. They are hidden lumps of radium. Their mysterious radiations can kill, atrophy or save. That's the way it goes, I promise you.

I: Listen: I'm in no condition to argue. I'm worn out. I can't walk another step. I need a break.

HE: But certainly. Let's go and have a beer. Why not here, at the Lutétia Bar?

I: I'm not so much thirsty as longing to sit down. Let's go instead and watch the kids playing in the Square Boucicaut. I have always had a weakness for the place and since it's just opposite . . .

Sure enough, we were at the Sèvres-Babylone crossroads which stretches like a fertile plain between the two mountain groups of the Hôtel Lutétia to the east and the Bon Marché stores to the west. The little Boucicaut garden is a triangle in spite of its name of "Square." It projects like a spit of land, an island, between the Rue de Sèvres and the Rue de Babylone, which meet there in a vast apotheosis of buses, taxis and pedestrians. It is enclosed by an iron railing. By a strange trick of acoustics, as soon as one has passed through the gate the tumult of the crossroads seems to fade into the distance. One moves into another world, a quiet and ancient world, a museum of greenery where the little boys and girls of our own day suddenly grow fifty years younger. Lightheartedness, cast-iron lampposts and composition statues flourish here under the tutelary eyes of a forester—very smart in his green uniform and cap adorned with a silver hunting horn—and the tenant of the public convenience clad, like a waitress in a Swiss pastry shop, in a pale blue blouse with white facings stiff with starch. This comely lady of uncertain age stands beaming at the door of her establishment, which may be old and blackened with soot but is always welcoming. It was in just such a chalet that Proust's grandmother had that famous "little attack" which moves us so to sadness when we read about it in *Le Côté de Guermantes*. The chalet in the Square Boucicaut is all seamed with pitch, calked like an ancient bumboat, the pitch itself old and turning gray. Yet it still bears a joyous poster dating from 1910 and extolling the merits of Lion Beer. This depicts a fat, red-faced, jovial man, a sort of ogre or Gargantua, winking broadly as he buries his beard in a frothing tankard. I believe he is wearing a boater. In front of him, twentieth-century civilization asserts itself in the shape of an apparatus labeled "I Tell Your Weight."

At the eastern end of the Square the visitor can see the patroness of the place: Mme. Boucicaut herself, proprietress of the Bon Marché stores, friend of the poor, professional benefactress who lived from 1816 to 1887 as the monument's inscription testifies. This monument is at once majestic and mean. Mme. Boucicaut, larger than life in gray stone dismally streaked by the weather, stands erect at the top of some steps. She is rigged out like Queen Victoria. In her left hand she holds a muff; with her right she receives the homage of an ecstatic little urchin, cap in hand, his neck wound round with a comforter. Behind Mme. Boucicaut, leaning forward in admiration, the Baroness Hirsch, another lady of good works but lesser reputation, veiled like a widow or a nurse. To the front of the monument one of the poor, a haggard and desperate woman with her baby at her breast, waits for the good lady to notice her existence and bring it some relief. Unless she is the mother of the little urchin with the cap. In which case she is either too shy or too ashamed to step forward and say thank you. She sends her son instead, a nicety which will not pass unnoticed. The pigeons, which respect nothing and no one and descend in clouds into the Square every ten minutes, have added their own blemishes to those of time, so that Mme. Boucicaut is extremely dirty. I don't know why this monument has such a horrible effect on me. It exudes all the self-satisfied and patronizing vanity of the nineteenth-century middle class, its insolent prosperity, its offensive charity. I don't know very much about Mme. Boucicaut. Perhaps she was a really good woman. In which case this group of statues maligns her.

In the middle of the lawn has been set another statue, equally gray with age and totally inexplicable. It represents a naked woman, muscular and buxom, with an infant in her arms. She is leaning back in her chair with her legs crossed and appears to be winking roguishly. Over her head and shoulders is thrown the veil of a lascivious dancer, like those worn before the war in an Edwardian brothel.

Finally, at the western extremity of the garden, the City of Paris, concerned to provide amusement for the young, has permitted the erection of several swings. It is naturally in this corner that the children gather with their shrill squeals. On a June evening this makes a very pleasant sound, especially in the heart of Paris. It is, after all, a natural noise.

We sat down on a bench and I immediately became conscious of my calves and thighs. We had been walking and talking ever since the Jardin des Plantes!

HE: You were right, it's good to sit down. And this is a very pleasant spot, particularly in June and at this time of day, when the worst of the heat is over. I didn't realize it while I was talking, but I needed a little peace and greenery.

I: Wouldn't it be strange, and in a way moving, if Roberti had brought Solange here, to the Square Boucicaut, on their first outing? Just imagine: the two of us following in their footsteps, sitting on the same bench, trying to reconstruct their words, listening across the years to the feeble echo of their heartbeats. . . . What a pretty romantic scene! Like something by Victor Hugo only better, more harrowing, because it doesn't concern us, because one of the characters is no longer alive. All the sadness of memory, of feelings which were and are no more, of people who love, desire, are happy, suffer and pass on. Come, make an effort! Give me this scene and I'll write the novel. I'll write it for this alone, for the pleasure of fitting it in between pages 150 and 200, of spinning it, decking it with pearls, polishing it bright, making it a masterpiece of tenderness and melancholy. You can't refuse me this after I've listened to you all the way from the Jardin des Plantes.

HE: Yes, it wouldn't be at all bad. The two of us sitting on the same bench where, four years before, Roberti and Solange exchanged their first confidences, their first real kiss, where these two beings hailed each other, recognized and ran to meet. . . . I can see how it would appeal to you. Unfortunately things didn't happen that way at all.

I: I knew it!

HE: On the evening of the peck, as I told you, Roberti had to dine out. A rather classy dinner including one or two ministers, a painter, a millionaire, a prince and fashionable women. The kind of dinner which, contrary to what people think, is never boring because each guest always has a measure of wit and a few stories to tell about his walk in life. The kind of dinner, too, which Roberti loved to attend, for he saw it as the symbol of his social success. The crowning of almost every ambition is to be allowed to make empty conversation with well-bred people. It's a fine thing when you come to think of it; it restores confidence in the human race, civilization and so forth.

When he and Agnes arrived at this party round about nine, Roberti was still glowing from his peck on Solange's cheek. He was full of dreams and so happy that his gaiety spread to others. He was thinking deeply of the bright adventure awaiting him tomorrow or next week. He was thinking of Solange as Christopher Columbus must have thought of America the day he finally set foot on its soil, when he still did not possess it but could see it stretched out in splendor before him, unhoped for, immense, awaiting his discovery, beautiful as nature the morning after creation. The peck had filled Roberti with an absolutely delicious secret; it had filled him to the brim with nectar.

I: Glory! Love at last!

HE: Wait! It's not as simple as that. He indulged in this dream because he knew its precise worth. He knew perfectly well it wasn't love. Love would have sickened him, he would have resisted it with all his might. No, no, it was egoism. The complacency of a lion after devouring a gazelle, digesting it in a state of euphoria. Throughout the dinner sudden gusts of pride swept through him. For instance, whenever he and his neighbor fell silent he would speed down to his innermost self to contemplate his new secret for a moment. He thought how he possessed a happiness unknown to all those around him. He evoked Solange, trying to recollect her face or figure the way one struggles to remember a poem one hasn't had sufficient time to learn. Certain lines, seemingly so obvious when one rereads them, stubbornly elude one and nothing, no effort of memory, can bring them back. Nature's forms are as difficult to recall as those of human genius, doubtless due to the mere fact that they exist, that they are unique, inevitable, indisputable. These dives into his inner self enchanted Edouard. His secret glittered there like a fabulous treasure. He was a miser gloating over his gold and taking a pride in its possession all the greater in that no one suspected its existence. Such is the way of those who love secrets. Quite the reverse of conceit, as you can see, but not unconnected with it either. I would call it a private conceit, a conceit for himself alone, since at the same time Roberti was voluptuously thinking: "If only all these people knew the pleasures awaiting me, which I, a man of fifty, have earned by my charm alone, they would be flabbergasted!" On several occasions I discussed with him this love of secrecy in which he took such keen delight. He confided a curious thing, namely that brooding over secrets is never so enjoyable as when one is sitting at a dinner table surrounded by innocently eating people who see you as just an ordinary guest, all of a piece, as simple and animal as they are. His leanings toward betrayal found irresistible encouragement in this pointed contrast.

All the same, if there is one thing that effectively contends with private secrets and vanities, it is snobbery. After about half an hour the magic of the meal, the ministers, the prince and above all the pretty women won Roberti round and eclipsed the fresh and simple Solange. What a miserable conquest compared with the two women sitting on either side of him! These were indeed what are customarily known as beauties. Their glitter, their impact, their assurance, their distinction, their splendor dazzled him. The *"femme du monde"* hasn't yet vanished. Our society has them just as Molière's, Marivaux's, Balzac's and Proust's did. At any smart dinner you will meet the Marquise Dorimène, the Countess Araminte, Madame d'Espard and the beautiful Oriane. The only difference is that today they receive anybody and everybody and have fewer servants. But the conversation is the same, full of Christian names and innuendoes; the same breeding, the same poise, skillful coiffures, makeup, jewelry and sumptuous gowns. They wear "corrupted, rich and triumphant" perfumes which go to the heads of the poor fools of artists, doctors, businessmen or deputies. They don't even have to be beautiful or graceful. Their proud bearing is enough to make them desirable. Men covet them the way they covet thoroughbreds or Rolls-Royces, because they represent the ultimate achievement.

So Roberti sat eating his filets of sole between two of the latest-model Rollses and admiring them besottedly. He admired himself too, by the same token. He admired himself for knowing how to eat, for not fumbling with the knives and forks. He admired himself for being there, for having "arrived." This dinner party was being held in the Faubourg Saint-Germain, just as in 1825. What a way he had come, from the Gare Montparnasse to the Rue de Grenelle! A way almost as long today as a hundred years ago, despite the advances in methods of transport. Twenty-five years ago Roberti was giving pitiful little talks to the League of the Rights of Man and now here he was chatting familiarly with Araminte and Dorimène, and in their own language what's more. He spoke their language without any accent, as if it were his mother tongue. He had acquired even its subtlest nuances. You see, today the self-made gentleman has one satisfaction his forebears never knew: that of being able to remember his difficult start in life. In the old days he had to act as if he were born in the silk, on pain of being chaffed by genuine noblemen. Today it's no longer worth it. A penurious childhood, an obscure youth and a few years of lean kine look very well in the biography of a successful man. He is said to have displayed intelligence and courage. The decline of societies can be measured by these changes of perspective. If the upper crust itself is becoming human, where shall we wind up? The end of civilization is nigh.

I: Don't worry. The upper crust doesn't give a damn for the intelligence and courage of self-made men. It only accepts them because of their names or their power, their fame or their usefulness. There's nothing human about it.

HE: Let's hope so. Where was I?

I: Roberti sitting between two smart women in an ecstasy of snobbery.

HE: Yes, that's it. An ecstasy of snobbery. Drunk with worldly success. When Solange floated to the surface of his thoughts, he felt ashamed of her. What was this poor girl beside Dorimène and Araminte? Toinette or Marton. At very best Suzanne. An attendant, a chambermaid. A charming creature, certainly, but a negligible quantity, unfit to occupy the mind of a person of rank like the Marquis de Roberti. How does one treat the Martons and Toinettes? One seduces them, of course. Almaviva wasn't indifferent to Suzanne's charms. But one would never consider falling in love with them. That would be too absurd.

Don't retort that Roberti was a bastard with a petty mind, that would explain nothing. I'm just showing you the corrosive action of snobbery (especially when reinforced by novelty) on even the strongest feelings, that's all. When one mixes in society everything else appears negligible, remote, minute, ridiculous, grotesque, inconceivable and slightly shoddy. Nothing exists but the delightful and futile people who have admitted you into their gilded company, so amusing and so innocuous. I can understand it perfectly, for at one time I shared a similar feeling. Have you been to many operettas?

I: Certainly not!

HE: Well, I've seen dozens. I think I must know them all. *Sidonie Panache, Rose Marie, La Fille de Madame Angot, La Mascotte, Ciboulette, Véronique* and the rest. In fact, whenever I had good marks at school my parents used to take me as a reward to the Châtelet or Mogador theaters, which in those days were the two temples of operetta in Paris. There was also the Gaîeté-Lyrique. At what age was this? Between seven and twelve. Five years of my life were dedicated to operettas! That's how one becomes a scholar. Hum any tune and I'll tell you at once whether it comes from *Les Brigands, Le Postillon de Longjumeau, L'Étoile, Les Deux Pigeons, Le Coup de Roulis, No, No, Nanette* or the *Mousquetaires au Couvent.*

Operettas are always the same. Childish plots, actors who, when they aren't singing, speak their lines in an artificial falsetto, pretty dancing girls with powdered thighs who come on every now and then to skip about in a ballet. I used to adore it, I was simply crazy about it. All the crazier, I realize today, in that I was always slightly bored and, child though I was, found it all rather silly. But operettas transported me into a world of chocolate cake, rivers of lemonade, fountains of golden syrup, and made me pity my everyday life. I couldn't understand why life wasn't some long, joyous and sentimental operetta, full of smiles, low comedy, powdered thighs and jolly music. I despised myself for having tiresome and real sensations, for being subject to stomach upsets and measles, for going to school to learn the multiplication table, for doting foolishly on my papa and mama, for being so unpicturesque, for understanding so little of the way of the world, since I hadn't contrived to live like Count Obligado or the jolly Maître Florès in *The White Horse Inn.*

I: But what an entrancing picture! You in short pants at the Mogador theater . . .

HE: Yes, isn't it? The nostalgia these operettas gave me lasted several hours. Sadness at being so different from their characters, at failing to hear any gay and inexhaustible melody welling up inside me, vied with the joy I derived from the entertainment. Then gradually I came back to life; all this dwindled and faded away until it was reborn with the next operetta.

I believe that society affects snobs in the same way. But there are two kinds of snob. The diligent, hardened ones who go out into society every evening, who never so to speak leave it, who are the permanent actors in the great operetta of society; and the occasional ones who go into society about once a fortnight, the way I used to go to the Mogador theater, and for whom it offers diversion and a change of surroundings. Roberti belonged to the latter category. Dinner parties, galas, receptions, cocktail parties were the rewards earned by his good marks, his place at the top of the class in the public school of Radical politics, his success as a good pupil at the Palais-Bourbon. There was nothing about him of the professional snob who ends by becoming a perfectly pleasant character in an operetta but stereotyped, without soul or substance, the embodiment of futility. It follows that Roberti's organism needed no more than a few hours to shake off his intoxication with society and the wild notions it inspires. These faded away in his sleep; he would wake up the next morning with a faint moral headache, that is to say a twinge of regret. The feeling, to be precise, left by a wasted evening spent without profit to mind or heart, an evening when one has merely paraded oneself, talked nonsense and enjoyed the pleasures of vanity which are so keen at the time but so meaningless to look back on. As meaningless as old newspaper articles, old theater programs, old outmoded dresses, as meaningless as everything which has its brief moment of being topical or smart.

I: Society life regarded as an operetta. You must be right.

HE: Obviously I'm right. The day after the dinner, then, there was not a trace of snobbery left in Roberti. It had vanished. He was sober again. He had returned to his life without music. Solange was reinstated in his heart (or mind, whichever you prefer). But this first betrayal of his in favor of Araminte and Dorimène had slightly blurred her image.

I: Shifting and erratic, this man!

HE: Yes. And even more shifting and erratic than you think. My God, how hard painting a soul can be! Much harder than a landscape, because in a soul everything coexists: sunshine and rain, storm and drought, day and night, sun and moon, cold and heat. One needs brushes of every shape and size and millions of tubes of color. At the same time as Roberti was contemplating a rather tarnished statuette of Solange, another part of his mind was telling him that this young woman suited him ideally, that she fitted into his real life, that she fulfilled all the requirements of a mistress after his own heart, that she was an amazing piece of luck. Beside her, the two women at dinner were quite unreal. Almost sexless. They were two pictures in a museum, two Largillières that one admires in passing and would like to have in one's drawing room but knows one will never possess. Society women were no game for Roberti. He probably never had one. To make a career with society women one has to start pretty early, around eighteen or twenty. But until he was thirty-five Roberti had remained in the backwaters of local politics, in the shadows of an in-between world where he met only members of the middle or lower classes. So he had grown used to a certain type of mistress, the type I described earlier. If a society woman had taken it into her head to seduce him I dare say he'd have been scared out of his wits. He would probably have pretended not to understand, in spite of the fillip it would have given his vanity. He would have felt afraid of being intimidated, of failing to rise to the occasion. Not to mention that one can't treat a banker's wife like a manicurist. She requires caution, time, expense, consideration and courtesy. With her one can't play the cad with impunity, and it is difficult to drop her when the fleeting desire she inspired has gone. Finally, affairs with society women are always common knowledge and Edouard didn't want Agnes to suffer or, if not that, appear ridiculous.

I: May I take a short cut, since you haven't the courage to do so? *He calls Solange and makes a date.*

HE: Don't rush me. This telephone call is a whole story in itself. To begin with, Roberti cogitated for three quarters of an hour before making it. He hesitated, he was afraid, his heart thumped, he told himself he was about to do something foolish. He wondered if it wouldn't be better to lie low, abandon the whole venture before embarking on it. He was going to make endless complications for himself, he was too old and so on. Was it worth starting again on the old game he had played so often during the past thirty years? The words of love, the ready-made phrases, the furtive meetings, the telephone calls, the obligations, the presents, the letters, the affair itself when it began to wear thin, the exhausting maneuvers required to bring about a peaceful break —he was suddenly overwhelmed by the prospect of it all. It almost made him feel sick. Love rose up before him in all its horror. It was the child of a night of Edom, black, featherless, with pale and bleeding wings. It was love according to Gavarni and Baudelaire, with its infinite tedium, its stale and loathsome smell, its cowed prostitute's eyes and pasty complexion of the morning after. Why the devil should one go to such trouble for something so revolting? The fact remains that some people get intoxicated on love the way others do on tobacco or sedatives, and Roberti was doubtless one of these despite the rarity and insignificance of his adventures. Note, I said tobacco and sedatives, not morphine or opium. They are minor intoxicants of the kind indulged in by sensible people. There doesn't seem much harm in heavy smoking or taking a sleeping pill every night. One doesn't feel one is endangering one's body or soul. Yet they are habits that can rapidly become dominant, turning into obsessions which it is the very devil to get rid of. Roberti wasn't a love addict, obsessed by lechery, wallowing in vile orgies, brothel-haunting, skilled in Oriental fantasies, avid for new sensations at any price. No. He was just one of those smokers who have to have forty cigarettes a day, who go to bed with an aching head and a bitter taste in the mouth, for whom tobacco has almost lost its taste but who still can't do without it. They hate this shoddy little vice which enslaves them; *they can never refuse a cigarette*. In the same way Roberti could never refuse a woman, even if he wasn't very attracted to her, even if she barely attracted him at all. It was beyond his power to do so.

ı: You told me not three minutes ago that he would almost certainly have refused a society woman.

HE: Well, it's a contradiction, that's all. You aren't going to quibble over a contradiction, are you? Life consists of nothing else. Besides, I'm not responsible for the contradiction; in this case it's Roberti's. He couldn't refuse a woman but he would have refused a society woman. Sort it out as best you can. It's the truth, and truth disregards logic.

ı: Well, does he telephone or not?

HE: Yes, he telephones, he finally makes up his mind.

ı: As one might have expected.

HE: He called her at Dietz's office. He didn't know where else to reach her. In the excitement of their kiss the day before he hadn't thought to ask for her home address. "Abel will think it rather odd of me to phone," he told himself. "Anyway, if he answers, I can always ask what he thought of my memorandum. But it's awkward. It's not like me to call up this way. He'll wonder what's behind it all. It won't take him long to figure that I'm after his secretary. I'll look like a regular fool." Dietz had other employees besides Solange. Solange herself shared her room with a "colleague" called Mlle. Angioletti if I remember rightly, Catherine Angioletti. "Who's going to answer?" Roberti wondered while the telephone rang. "I'm going to ask for Mlle. Mignot; they will inquire who's speaking; I shall give my name which everybody there knows. It'll look fishy, very fishy. They'll make fun of me. I shall be the laughingstock of Dietz & Co., the dirty old man, the senile sex maniac. Charming!" In fact, as soon as Roberti took an interest in a woman he became the victim of an optical illusion. He believed that his desire was written on his face for all the world to read like an open book, that the smallest, even the most innocent of his actions betrayed him. According to him, people were always on the lookout for this kind of thing, always quick to spot love even when it only showed the tip of its nose. They would see it even where it didn't exist. As soon as Roberti was in love he was filled with acute anxiety over "being found out." This didn't derive solely from his secretive habits and liking for undercover maneuvers. It was linked with another trait of his character: fear of ridicule. Being in love is ridiculous. It provokes mockery, pity, malicious gossip and finally contempt. Roberti couldn't stand contempt. "A Frenchman can stomach anything but contempt."

I: Only the weak and vain are unable to endure contempt. Great men love to be despised. They find it amusing.

HE: Yes, in this respect Edouard was not a great man. When a woman attracted him he would wait till he was quite sure she felt the same way before declaring himself, so mortified would he have been by a rebuff. What could be more ridiculous than revealing your flame to someone utterly indifferent, giving her such a hold over you, offering her such an advantage on a plate?

I: God bless my soul!

HE: Yes. And once the affair was under way, there followed the crazy precautions of a spy, of a secret agent working in enemy country, a conspirator or a burglar, combined with feigned indifference; these naturally didn't preclude a few indiscretions, for we can't always think of everything or prevent our attention from wandering now and then. Not to mention untimely mishaps. Whenever Roberti walked down a street with one of his ladyloves, he would constantly turn and glance anxiously around him. Were the lady sitting beside him in his car, he was always terrified lest someone might see them together.

I: May I remind you, in case you've forgotten, that the telephone is ringing in Dietz's office?

HE: I haven't forgotten. I'm just coming to it. Thank God, it was Solange who answered. She was more or less waiting for this call and keeping an eye on the telephone. Inwardly she was in a state of violent agitation, of wild uncertainty; rather the state of mind of a novice about to take her vows. Her period of probation had abruptly ended. But there was a dominant note of happiness in her apprehension. She recognized his voice the moment Roberti said "Hello." Their two hearts were beating madly, although for different reasons. Roberti was rather stiff and awkward. He was afraid that at any minute someone—wife, son or servant—might enter his study. He was vexed with himself for having succumbed to the telephone's temptation. Solange's voice was cold and impersonal because of Mlle. Angioletti sitting beside her. This irritated Roberti. Stupidly, so as to force a tender or even equivocal remark out of her at all costs, he kept asking embarrassing questions such as: "You're not too cross about the way I kissed you yesterday evening?" "No, Monsieur, of course not," replied Solange. He told her how pretty she was, how he had acted like a fool but didn't regret it a bit, how "marvelous" it had been. He had quite simply lost his head (which was true anyway but in saying so, using it as a lover's argument, he almost believed it was a lie). "Imagine," he added with a short laugh, "losing one's head at my age! Still, that's what happened. And how lucky I did! I shall never be able to show my gratitude for the thrill you gave me."

I: Not bad! And how did she react?

HE: You can picture her delight. "How charming he is!" she thought. "He really liked me. Can he love me?" But she couldn't say anything, she didn't want the Angioletti girl to realize she was talking to an admirer. To warn Roberti she thought up lines like: "I'll give M. Dietz your message without fail, Monsieur." She spoke these words in such a way that no one could mistake their hidden meaning, which was: "I can't say any more at the moment because I'm not alone." There was even a hint of anguish in her voice which enchanted Roberti: it betrayed that he already had a certain hold over her. He was compromising her, forcing her into a kind of complicity. There was already a secret between them, since she didn't want it made known that he was telephoning her. He tormented her with indiscreet questions, partly to reassure himself, partly to test his new power. He could sense Solange sitting paralyzed at the other end of the line, spellbound at a distance, unable to move, unable not to reply, unable to hang up. He knew he was putting her in an awkward position but it gave him such intense satisfaction that, but for the fear of being interrupted by one of his family, he would have spun this game out much longer. He had been keenly aware of Solange's vulnerability on his account and he flung himself, as you can see, on this poor little trembling, terrified, unprepared, almost defenseless adversary. There are people like this who show no consideration in love, who wage it like a war as soon as they have the upper hand; in other words they love less than they are loved. Roberti had joined battle brilliantly. His first skirmish couldn't have been more encouraging.

I: And the meeting?

HE: Well, the meeting was fixed for the next day, as Solange wasn't free that evening. Apparently her brother was coming with one of his friends to fetch her from the office.

I: Ha! The Mignot family enters the scene. And none too soon. What was the brother's name, by the way?

HE: Oh come now! Valentin!

I: Oh yes, of course, Valentin! How could I have forgotten? It's not such a common name.

HE: The friend he was bringing along was Jacques Legay; you remember he came up at the trial. He even gave evidence.

I: There's one thing you haven't told me. Where was Dietz's office?

HE: You might say, "Where is it?" It's still there. Dietz isn't dead and, so far as I know, he hasn't moved. Avenue de l'Opéra, almost at the corner of the Rue Louis-le-Grand.

I: That's splendid. An excellent touch for my novel. The Avenue de l'Opéra at six-thirty P.M., at closing time, will make a charming picture. Vivid and picturesque. Why? Because at that hour it is swarming with people who normally have no place there, like Florence in the tourist season. A population of shopgirls, clerks and secretaries hurrying back to their remote districts and outer suburbs or lingering to chat on the sidewalk, or strolling idly off in pursuit of entertainment along the Boulevard des Italiens. The Avenue de l'Opéra, I repeat, is Florence. More foreigners than natives and a site famous the world over. Anyway, you see what I mean.

HE: But that's not possible, old man! If ever you take it into your head to write Roberti's story, you simply can't place Dietz's office in the Avenue de l'Opéra. Don't you see? That's where it really is!

I: What has that got to do with it? I'll change Dietz's name, that's all. Call him Bouchard or Goyenetche. Whatever happens, I shall keep the Avenue de l'Opéra. It's too good to lose. Besides, I can see it, I can feel it. It's extraordinary, the magic of names. You only have to say "Avenue de l'Opéra" for me suddenly to be there. At this moment I am not sitting in the Square Boucicaut but standing in the Avenue de l'Opéra at six-thirty P.M. watching the girls in their flowered frocks with their imitation-crocodile plastic bags; the pretty typists just released from their cages, chattering like birds of paradise; the shopgirls from the luxury boutiques who are smarter than their customers; the assistants from the ticket agencies; the bank clerks in their badly cut suits; the congested traffic. No, no, you can't refuse me the Avenue de l'Opéra. It's vital, it's indispensable. The fair Solange needs the Avenue de l'Opéra. It's her natural setting. Can you picture Atala anywhere but on the banks of the Meschacebé? I, now, can't picture Solange anywhere but on the Avenue de l'Opéra, sometimes alone, sometimes with her friend Angioletti, her brother and Legay. She belongs to this migratory population of six to seven P.M. When she's alone she loves to go window-shopping, unenviously, before catching her train. Incidentally, where did she live?

HE: With her parents. Miles away, Avenue Daumesnil, almost at Vincennes.

I: Good. Excellent. Still with her parents at twenty-five? She must have been undemanding!

HE: What do you expect? The housing crisis. Rather slender means. Anyway not enough to pay for a decent apartment. Add to that

Solange's indolence. Her life was arranged in a certain way, organized, settled. She was by nature easygoing, gentle, obliging; she was fond of her parents and, like most people, she certainly had no imagination. It never occurred to her that her life might be other than what it was, that she only had to reach a decision for everything to change. Fate had set her down in the Avenue Daumesnil; she had grown up there; it was her native land. Since nothing compelling beckoned her elsewhere, there she remained. She had her own room, which still bore traces of her childhood: a doll or two, a Teddy bear and a mass of little objects, the kind of things life accumulates in people's rooms the way the surf piles up shells, pebbles and flotsam on a beach. The rather fragile, pretty-pretty, cheap, sometimes faded objects which appeal to young girls. This room was adorned with a set of varnished pinewood with flowers stenciled on it and was always kept very tidy, very bright and girlish. There Solange felt protected from the world. She would withdraw to it to brood over her joys and sorrows, which had never hitherto been very violent. When she became Roberti's mistress and he began to exert an influence over her, the room took on a different aspect. Framed color reproductions appeared on the walls, of paintings by Picasso, Van Gogh and Braque, looking utterly absurd, one must admit, in this model room setting for a young girl. Similarly the shelf beside her bed was seen to burgeon with books by Sartre, Graham Greene, Simone de Beauvoir, etc., in short the smart literature of the day, the writers who, for Roberti, had replaced those he admired in 1935.

1: It's true what you say about people's lack of imagination. I'm always baffled by it. They live in holes like rabbits. They never realize that the world is vast, full of variety and resources. It never occurs to them to put a foot forward, go out and explore a little. Rabbits? What am I saying! They are woodlice under the floor boards. They put up with everything: the mediocrity of their state, the cantankerousness of those around them, the endless boredom of the daily round, the sickening familiarity of the landscape, the insipidity of their lives, anything rather than budge. It isn't even fear of the unknown. It's purely and simply laziness. The inability to conceive of any life other than the obvious one confronting them. So obvious that it masks the universe. They tell themselves that life is what one has, what one is, and not what one might have, what one might be if only one troubled to bestir oneself. How sad it is! So Solange was like that, was she? After all, why not? Ninety-nine per cent of human beings are devoid of imagination. Perhaps that is why humanity continues to exist. This is the heavy weight, the anchor that holds it down. If all men were imaginative, fanciful, inquisitive, daring, things would probably have taken a very bad turn and there wouldn't be a single human being left on earth.

All the same I think that Solange, at twenty-five, might well have rented herself a little room somewhere, broken away from her life in the family womb.

HE: I'm sorry, but things are as they are. Solange's family life suited her purity. It may well have preserved her from several squalid adventures, several easy temptations. This doesn't mean she felt particularly vulnerable as regards the snares of the flesh. Far from it. I simply mean that deep within her was a sort of organic wisdom. It is weak people who expose themselves to temptation, flirt with it and are sometimes amazed when they yield to it. We all of us instinctively choose what we desire. Those who erect a barrier between themselves and sin are by nature the least disposed to sin; they even feel a certain aversion for it and do everything they can to put it further out of reach. So all is for the best and nothing happens which shouldn't.

An instinct for self-preservation had therefore done just as much as a lack of imagination to ensconce Solange in her parents' humble apartment on the Avenue Daumesnil, where her brother lived too, incidentally. They were a very united family, who bored each other without admitting it. Everyone was taken in by everyone else, which is the foundation for a solid home life.

I: My God! This picture of the Mignot family is horrifying. Asphyxiating! It turns one's thoughts to suicide.

HE: Horrifying and asphyxiating to you and when seen from the outside. But for the Mignots it was all very nice and cozy. They loved each other with that family devotion compounded of habits, prejudices, traditions, moral outlook, constraints, mutual allowances, blindness and a host of indiscretions. For instance, Father Mignot, whose first name was Jules, was an old fool but nobody suspected it. Members of a family regard each other like those bits of furniture whose shapes and sharp edges are so familiar we no longer notice them and can no longer say whether they are beautiful or ugly, so used to them have we become. If a man tells you: "I know my wife's or my son's character inside out," don't you believe him. It's almost never true. It means he knows how to use his wife or son the way he uses a cupboard or armchair, knows how to prevent the cupboard door from creaking when he opens it, and that his body has adapted itself so well to the uncomfortable armchair that he prefers it to any other. No more than that. But he has long since lost sight of his wife's and son's souls, if he ever so much as glanced at them in the first place. This is proved by the fact that we are continually seeing husbands staggered at being deceived by their wives, fathers thunderstruck on learning that their sons have been imprisoned for theft, and so on.

Let's leave Father and Mother Mignot out of it for the moment, if you don't mind. We'll return to them presently. I should prefer now to talk about Valentin. He was a sober young man, of a character which always struck me as incongruous and I would even say against nature. He was rather fat, lymphatic by temperament and his hair was thinning although he was only twenty-six. Big brown eyes and a nice smile. He longed with all his might for a well-ordered existence. His one idea was to offer his loving heart to some girl, have four children and lead to the end of his days that tidy and commonplace life which the weeklies define as "happiness." You must admit these are surprising tendencies in a young man.

I: No, they are more widespread than people think. It must reflect a certain fear of life, of loneliness, of adventure. Young men of this type dig themselves in with their parents like your Valentin. They need a nest in which they can curl up at night. They want a protective shell around them. So they pass without transition from the parental home to the conjugal home. Do you know my theory about having children?

HE: No?

I: Well, I maintain that people produce children to keep them company, to surround them with noise and movement, fill time, kill time, in short avoid boredom. How can one otherwise explain this frantic desire for self-reproduction, leading as it does to so many disappointments and financial headaches? When the children grow up they become an audience you can annihilate with your chatter, while they repay you in kind. Aren't you always astonished by the resistance parents put up if their children want to leave them in order to travel or get married, when they really ought to be entranced by the idea? It's because they are terrified to see their diversion vanishing.

HE: Well, it's a convincing argument but a damning one. It certainly provides a sound explanation for poor Valentin. What was so comical in his case was that he never had any luck. His little affairs nearly always turned sour. In fact, when they saw his intentions were serious, his sighs honorable, the girls took fright and ran. That's just like women! They all dream of marriage, they force poor wretches who are dead against it into proposing, but the moment anyone seems disposed to lead them to the altar they turn pernickety. Because the little trollops want to do the conquering! It must also be said that Valentin didn't have a happy touch. There is no greater Jonah than a man anxious to marry at all costs: it was his misfortune to meet only girls set on enjoying themselves. Valentin didn't make a very beguiling lover, I imagine, and the prospect of passing the rest of one's life with him was quite enough to dampen any enthusiasm. He didn't offer his "fiancées" anything new: he talked too much like their fathers. He was too sensible, too provident, too respectful, too correct. Instead of setting their imaginations on fire, he cooled them down. At all events these irksome setbacks hadn't cooled *him*. His obsession about marriage had withstood ten rebuffs. He was sure that one day he would find a pearl, the perfect, devoted girl who would replace his father and mother and with whom he could prolong his childishness until he breathed his last.

Valentin didn't confine his ambitions to himself. He wanted to ensure the happiness of those he loved as well. His *matrimonomania* extended to those around him. Consequently he had taken it into his head to arrange a match between Solange and young Legay, his lifelong friend and boon companion, and he felt confident of success. What joy to be able to call Legay his brother-in-law one day! By then he himself would be married as well. The two couples would see a lot of each other, often go out together, rent the same cottage at Royan for the summer. Then there would be children, swarms of devoted cousins. Such were Valentin's dreams. He schemed enthusiastically and apparently not too clumsily to bring his best friend and pretty sister together. Anyway, Legay was keenly aware of the latter's charm and even a little in love with her. But Solange had a friendly and familiar way with him which deprived him of almost any hope. So he didn't think of her too much. Each time Valentin proposed that the three of them should go out together, Legay would nevertheless feel a little stab of pleasure which strengthened his affection for his friend.

ɪ: Exactly what type of person was this Legay?

ʜᴇ: A fine boy. One of those young men who belong to an utterly different generation from ours: the class of 1950. It's amazing how the face of a country can change in ten or twenty years. I can no longer recognize France. Do you remember, when we were twenty, how our friends thought it smart to act blasé; they had withdrawn from the world. They were quite indifferent as to their fate, like the young marquesses of 1793 who joked as they were led to the guillotine.

ɪ: Yes, I remember. I felt very ill at ease with most of my generation.

ʜᴇ: The class of 1950 is quite different. Today I see around me young men like those of 1848 or 1914, eager to influence the world, shape it, achieve success while remaining mindful of the community. It's interesting. These boys are rather austere, brave, stubborn, well mannered, totally lacking in irony and conscientious. To me, that's good. Legay was like that. He had one or two minor technical diplomas. Only minor ones. I don't think they entitled him to call himself an engineer. But he was certainly more than a craftsman. Let's say a superior craftsman. He was an electrician. Have you noticed how the old French spirit of craftsmanship has taken refuge in electrical work and motorcars? The old qualities of the French craftsman of the past are now to be found in garage hands and television repairmen. They enjoy their work; they do it skillfully, diligently, intelligently and devotedly. Young Legay worked in a television shop. Thanks to his knowledge of electricity he understood the business inside out and was keen to better himself. Not just to be a shopkeeper with a nice shop of his own, full of modern objects in varnished wood finished with chromium or copper. He aimed higher.

I: Oh yes? Tell me more.

HE: Well, for a start he had made an invention.

I: An invention? Legay? But that's splendid! It's pure Balzac. This changes everything. What was it?

HE: Obviously it was connected with television. I wonder if I can describe it to you because after all I know next to nothing about television. Anyway I'll try. If I talk nonsense, I don't suppose you for one will notice.

I: Never you mind.

HE: All right. You know that the dream of television manufacturers is to make increasingly thin sets. Legay had managed to do this. It had taken him a year and a half but he had succeeded where real engineers had failed. He had studied the problem deeply and tackled it with considerable perseverance and empiricism. The empiricism of a technician, of someone who hasn't sacrificed too much of his manual skill to book learning. Engineers, now, make swift calculations, draw up plans and grasp only the symbolic side of things. No doubt they have forgotten how to be patient. On paper nothing resists them. Whereas craftsmen, artisans, accustomed to wrestling with materials, ceaselessly groping their way, pursuing perfection from one approximation to another with their hands (instead of going straight to it with their brains), artisans, I say, take no account of their time or labor. The brain is proud, the hand is humble. I don't think an engineer would ever have stood for devoting eighteen months of his precious life to something so inessential to the progress of science as the paring of a few inches from the thickness of a television set. For Legay, a year and a half were nothing. He didn't regard his life as precious and this little objective of an extra-thin television set seemed to him well worth the mobilization of all his faculties.

ɪ: I like that a lot. The persistent handyman with a fixed idea.

ʜᴇ: Of course there's always something rather absurd about the home inventor, the man who perfects an unburstable inner tube or an instant coffeepot and takes himself for Edison or the Lumière brothers. The same can be said for Legay, I know. But among every hundred thousand self-taught nitwits there is always one who is genuinely scrupulous, determined, not stupid, and who discovers something. Well, Legay had discovered something.

He had first taken the screen, the thickness of which he had reduced to half an inch. That was his Problem Number One, the whole novelty of the undertaking. Do you happen to know how a television screen is normally made?

ɪ: I haven't the faintest idea.

ʜᴇ: It is shaped like an enormous glass tube, rather like a blunderbuss, which takes up a lot of room. Ten to fifteen inches long. In place of this, Legay built a screen made of a sheet of fluorescent plastic, the sides of which were covered horizontally and vertically with thin copper wires set parallel. The image is normally formed by a spark at each intersection of the wires. The sheet of plastic obstructed the spark which it transformed, so to speak, into permanent light. I believe the problem of the wires preoccupied Legay for a long time. They had to be so tremendously fine, almost invisible. In the end he was forced to replace his copper wires with platinum ones, which sent the bill sky-high and ran him into debt.

ɪ: You're amazing! How do you know all this?

ʜᴇ: Well, one day Solange offered to introduce Legay to Dietz, so that he could tell him of his invention and seek his advice as to how to exploit it. I chanced to see Dietz the next day and he told me all about it.

ɪ: And you understood and remembered it all? What a man!

ʜᴇ: I'm surprised at it myself, considering that it rather bored me at the time. At least, it didn't interest me. But I have an odd memory which must register things regardless, since I look at nothing and remember everything.

ɪ: The perfect novelist! How tragic you can't write! Go on.

ʜᴇ: After having made his screen, Legay had a setback. In fact, he had built his television set like all the others, with wires and valves, and he realized it was just as thick as the rest. He tried stacking the valves in tiers, reducing the wiring as much as possible, but it was no good. The set was ten inches thick. A monster. Poor Legay went through several bad weeks. He told himself he had slaved in vain. That is when one realizes the disadvantages of insufficient education. One retains a very narrow, down-to-earth outlook. The idea that his flat screen was already a most important discovery never crossed his mind. For him it was a useless improvement. Time and again he was on the point of breaking it up with a hammer in his fury.

There's something rather fine and touching about this, something in the great tradition of artists. Legay was close to the solution and couldn't see it. His setback obscured the view. And then one day, or rather night, for it came during a bout of sleeplessness, inspiration descended.

1: Marvelous!

HE: He reasoned as follows . . . wait while I get the details right . . . yes: "The big glass tube of ordinary sets leaves a lot of room for the valves. My screen leaves none. So we must get rid of the valves. But how? By replacing them with transistors, by heaven! Since they make low-volume wireless sets by using transistors, why not do the same for television?" A valve is as big as your thumb. A transistor is a little bit of metal less than half the size of your fingernail. The conclusion leaps to the eye. Legay the inventor of transistor television. Here is where his lack of education becomes apparent: he hadn't thought things out logically. A true engineer would have first thought of the transistors, then told himself: "Transistorization"—I'm sorry but that is the word —"is of no interest unless one can first do away with the tube, which would leave a lot of free space." Legay followed the opposite course, that of intuition, which leads one straight to the worst difficulty. The path followed by men of genius, in other words. So that an imagined difficulty caused him more worry and despair than a genuine obstacle.

1: I find Legay enchanting. And this is the man Solange didn't love! God, how stupid women are!

HE: Wait, I haven't yet finished. Legay, then, assembles his extra-thin set, which he manages to reduce to a thickness of two and a half inches, less than a dictionary. He is thrilled, wild with joy. He hangs his set like a picture on the wall facing his bed. Then another idea occurs to him. A typical handyman's idea. A lazy man's idea, he called it. How to switch the set on and off without having to get up? Remote control already existed in the United States. "I will do better," he thinks. He attaches to his set a tiny microphone, sensitive only to ultra-sonic sounds, with a little circuit. From his bed he blows an ultrasonic whistle which turns the set on or off according to whether it is already off or on. Isn't that rather splendid, a television set obeying a whistle like a dog?

All these triumphs went to his head. Nothing seemed too much for him. To complete his achievement, crown it with glory, he decided to tackle a major problem, one to which all the television experts have applied themselves without ever finding a solution: how to abolish the aerial. But here he was less fortunate, being only half successful. He managed to fit the aerial inside the set but it worked satisfactorily only in Paris, and then only in certain districts. Not everywhere.

I: Bravo, bravo! Long live Legay! It's even finer to end with a slight setback. Why didn't he live under Louis-Philippe instead of today! He'd have been a minister and peer of the realm, like Popinot.

HE: Maybe. But the world is far more difficult today than it was in 1835. Far more unstable. The paths to success are shorter but less sure. It seems to me that nowadays publicity and know-how carry much more weight than actual merit, compared with a hundred and twenty years ago.

I: Do you think so? I on the other hand believe the world doesn't change and that it's always the same men who scale the social ladder: the strong, clever and forceful, whether they are gangsters or honest men.

HE: Democracy does a lot to corrupt morals, you know. It accustoms the public to words, that is to say boasting and slander. Add to this the political press, the advertisements for household goods, foodstuffs, motorcars and so on, and you have a world dominated almost exclusively by lies, very hard to understand for a simple honest-minded man who believes in the virtues of hard work, frankness, talent and perseverance. Under Louis-Philippe there was no doubt just as much hypocrisy and callousness as today, even more; but fewer risks. The social game wasn't yet debased. Society was slippery but not treacherous. Nowadays everyone is out to get you, particularly the undeserving. In France in the second half of the twentieth century, the chances of being unlucky are greater than ever before. All this by way of telling you that Legay, once his invention was completed, was thoroughly perplexed. He didn't know how to sell it.

I: But you told me Dietz had advised him.

HE: Yes, Dietz advised him, and extremely well. But just then Legay had rather lost his head. Success had filled him with all sorts of proud and foolish ideas. He had taken a dislike to the man Dietz sent him to because he didn't flatter him with compliments. That wasn't his way.

Yet in spite of his brusqueness the man was honest and able. Legay never noticed this. He was conscious only of the lack of compliments, which upset him, so he missed a fine chance to make his fortune. In the end he stupidly sold his invention for ten million francs (that is to say a hundred thousand francs today) to a shyster who made a quick profit of twenty or thirty million out of it. The shyster was far from short on compliments. He knew what sort of currency talented young men need to be paid with. Besides, he laid the ten million francs on the table. Legay couldn't resist them. But this is looking ahead. We haven't got that far. We are still in the Avenue de l'Opéra at six-thirty. Legay hadn't yet constructed his flat screen. He was still taken up with research. He was making discouraging experiments with his copper wires. As a result, he was charming. He had the gaiety of explorers who feel themselves on the track of a great discovery, the peace of mind and amiability of people who are employing all their faculties to the hilt. He was full of optimism, full of energy; he was an unknown genius. He poked friendly fun at Valentin while they waited for Solange.

I: Don't forget the big scene.

HE: What scene?

I: The outing. Legay, Solange and Valentin on the spree. Don't do me out of that if you can help it.

HE: Oh, I'm not much good at bravura pieces. I'm just describing things as I knew them. Life doesn't go in for bravura pieces. It waters down events, emotions and behavior. It's the worst possible cook. It transforms them into hash, stewed fruit, mashed potatoes and broth. Sometimes it produces something so insipid it makes you sick; sometimes it adds so much pepper that it blows your head off. *You* want caviar and *foie gras* for every meal! I hope you don't imagine that I, who have no imagination, no creative talent, can do better than life? It's quite enough that I manage to reconstruct things as they were.

I: Life sometimes does present one with bravura pieces.

HE: Well, all I can say is that Solange, Legay and Valentin strolling down the Avenue de l'Opéra and the Boulevard des Italiens wasn't one of them. Solange brought along her friend Angioletti, they all shook hands, Valentin insisted that they go somewhere for a drink. Cogitation. Where? Finally they settled on the Café Napolitain. "All right," cried Mlle. Angioletti, "but not longer than fifteen minutes. I must get home to wash and set my hair." Valentin ordered a Suze, Legay a tomato juice and the young ladies Cinzano. Valentin wondered what sort of a wife Mlle. Angioletti would make. She was a brunette with a milky skin, good-natured, very voluble and gay, a nice and pretty girl. He found her so pleasant that he proposed another outing for the four of them the next evening.

ı: But the next evening Solange had arranged to meet Roberti, hadn't she?

HE: Yes. Valentin's suggestion was most inopportune. She was seeking some escape, some honest excuse for refusing, when Mlle. Angioletti thoughtlessly cried: "But tomorrow evening's not possible! Solange already has a date. I heard her just now fixing it up on the phone." She wasn't being malicious, just tactless. A thoughtless girl heated by the Cinzano and the conversation, blurting it out because she couldn't hold her tongue, because she hadn't been taught manners. But the effect on the brother and sister was considerable. Solange blushed. What rotten luck! Roberti and she had barely met before a little fool was trumpeting it to all and sundry. She interpreted this indiscretion of Mlle. Angioletti's as a bad omen. At the same time she felt a secret thrill of joy: this was the first trial her love had brought her. Nothing really unpleasant, of course, just a faint embarrassment. At any rate, it could be counted among the tribulations of love. This was the insignificant beginning of a long series of cherished bruises, the harsh note which would perhaps set the key for the future music of her life.

Valentin, who was intuitive about such things, immediately realized this must be a lovers' assignation and was extremely put out. Solange could read him like a book. She followed the progress of his increasing annoyance step by step. The fact is that Valentin, a scrupulous, moral young man obsessed by his ideas of marriage, was like a Corsican brother. He kept careful watch over his sister's virtue, which did the family such honor, adding luster to the name of Mignot. He didn't like Solange to have flirtations. He held himself more or less responsible for her.

ı: I rather admire that. It's a highly respectable form of brotherly love.

HE: Highly respectable, certainly, but also very wearing for whoever is its victim. Valentin was almost as tyrannical as a jealous husband. He all but used to ask Solange whom she had been out with and open her letters. So you can imagine how, when he learned later of Roberti's existence and his sister's relations with him, it drove him out of his mind. A man of fifty, married and a father! What an indelible stain! He told himself Solange had gone mad and he must save her. Not only did he want her to marry but he had got it firmly into his head that the husband would be Legay and none other. Like all narrow-minded people, he was stubborn. When he had an idea he clung to it, even if the idea was absurd, utterly impracticable, bearing no relation to the facts of the case. The trouble was that the poor man hardly ever had any ideas, and when by chance one occurred to him he found it quite marvelous. As if he had unexpectedly won a lottery. It's by no means unusual for fools like Valentin to leave their mark on the world. They hammer their rare ideas into it with the same force as we hammer a nail into a wall. No matter where. In the most unheard-of, absurd places—but the holes are there. These alter situations, give rise to fresh combinations, new causal sequences. There was no sense in wanting Legay and Solange to marry. It was a perfectly preposterous idea, a figment of his brain. And what a brain!

ɪ: Why? Legay was a very good choice.

ʜᴇ: Yes, but Valentin didn't look at it that way. He liked Legay quite by chance, just as he might have liked an imbecile.

ɪ: May I say you give chance too much scope in your conception of the world? Chance is neither so diverse nor above all so pure. It is always blended with something else. I believe chance only accounted for sixty or sixty-five per cent of Valentin's friendship with Legay. The remaining thirty-five or forty per cent was made up of esteem, of instinct. He must have realized Legay was a fine fellow. And perhaps he even sensed unusual ability in his friend, for which he admired him. What I like in Valentin is his sort of primitiveness. He wasn't spoiled by the inanities of our day. He was stupid, yes, but as people were two hundred years ago. To my mind it is almost better to be stupid in the manner of two hundred years ago than to be intelligent in the manner of today. There's a touch of grandeur about Valentin opening his family portals to a man he respects, Valentin honored by the admission of a man of worth into his clan. But let's get back to the Café Napolitain. How did Legay react after the girl friend's gaffe?

ʜᴇ: He didn't. He never noticed it. He was thinking more about his extra-thin screen than about love. The one who was really upset was Mlle. Angioletti. She realized instantly that she had cast a chill over the company. So she soon made herself scarce. The atmosphere was blighted. The evening took on an air of drudgery. Conversation was stilted. Even dinner in a good little restaurant in the Rue Villedo failed to break the ice. Following which Legay, Solange and Valentin went to a movie and became engrossed in an idiotic American murder story; they then went their separate ways. Legay was rather depressed but on getting home the sight of his copper wires made him happy again. There's your bravura piece!

ɪ: I must admit it was a sinister spree.

HE: I can't help it, that's the way things go. You arrange a little party and it's all ruined by an unfortunate remark. Instead of having a good time, you spend an evening steeped in gloom. Such is life.

I: That Angioletti girl! What a fool!

HE: No, she was a good girl. The next day she apologized profusely to Solange, who anyway bore her no grudge. Angioletti had a well-earned reputation for thoughtlessness and putting her foot in it.

I: What did Valentin do for a living? Nowadays people's professions form part of their personality.

HE: What do you think he was?

I: I would say a salesman.

HE: Really? Why?

I: I don't know. I just see this tall, quick-tempered slob with his big eyes and thinning hair as a salesman. A good talker. That is, repeating twenty times a day with the same conviction the same old claptrap extolling his firm's goods. Inventing new arguments. Bringing back full order books every evening. Knowing all the ins and outs of Thingumbob's electric cookers. Why they are better than any other and why every retail shop should stock at least half a dozen of them. I can equally see him as a shopwalker in the Magasin du Printemps or the Galeries Lafayette.

HE: You're way off the mark. He was just a bank clerk. He was a sedentary type, was Valentin. Not a nomad. He spent his life behind a pay desk and hoped to end up as manager.

I: A bank clerk? How disappointing! What a lack of imagination! How colorless! Who isn't a bank clerk nowadays?

HE: Exactly. Why should Valentin have differed from anyone else? Supposing he'd been a Corsican, he'd have worked in the Customs or the penitentiary administration. In Paris, the heroine's brother worked in a bank. It's quite in order.

I: When Solange and Valentin said good-by to Legay after the movie and set off homeward to the Avenue Daumesnil, what did they say to each other?

HE: Well, Valentin wanted to find out whom Solange had a date with the next day. He asked her point blank. But she retorted like a petulant little girl squabbling with her brother: "It's no business of yours. I shall go out with whoever I want to." She was infuriated by the idea that he might raise obstacles to her love. Valentin had no right to try and control her feelings and relationships. She was astonished at the extent of her vexation. As a rule she readily submitted to her brother's questioning. But as often happens in such cases, his tactless inquiry merely strengthened her desire to give Roberti everything it was in her power to give: her heart, her body, her mind, her thoughts, even her full time if he required it. That is how women are. Love turns even the gentlest into a wildcat, red in tooth and claw, the moment anyone appears to be eying her prey. I am certain that, during the journey from the Boulevard des Invalides to the Avenue Daumesnil, Solange hated Valentin with all her might. This determination of his confronting hers seemed all the more detestable in that it was based merely on convention and not on any right. She felt very frail and at the same time indomitable in the face of this idiot's blind obstinacy. "Anyway, don't do anything foolish," he added sententiously. This stung her to fury. Anything foolish! She, Solange, the most serious-minded among her circle of friends and acquaintances! Valentin had really gone too far! Yet he had unwittingly put his finger on the truth. She was indeed preparing to do something foolish, she was fully aware of it. But this foolishness seemed to her something admirable, highly original and anyway inevitable. Nothing is got for nothing. For her, Roberti represented Happiness, and Happiness is beyond price. One has to bleed oneself white, beggar oneself, in order to purchase a mere morsel of it. "One must know what one wants from life," thought Solange as she walked at midnight along the Avenue Daumesnil a few paces behind Valentin. "I want Edouard Roberti. I love him. He likes me. We will be happy. And to hell with conventions, prejudice and what people will think; to hell with my virtue. And to hell with Valentin! He'll just have to put up with it. My life is my affair, not his. After all, *he* wouldn't have to sleep with Jacques Legay if I married him. *I* would. Ugh! How ghastly! Every man except Edouard Roberti revolts me. He is my love. I want to merge with him, merge into him, love him to the point of self-oblivion. Live only through him. I don't mind his age. On the contrary, I like mature men. I don't mind about his children, his wife, his position. If necessary I'll make do with *Back Street* to the end of my days. I am meeting Edouard tomorrow evening. How shall I live through the hours between? They will seem a century. I shan't sleep a wink tonight. I'm far too worked up. I'm fond of Valentin, but if he comes between Edouard and me, if he should dare try to separate me from the one man in my life, I'll see him in hell first."

ı: My word, what a to-do! I don't think much of Solange's thoughts, though. They seem rather childish and commonplace.

HE: Women in love don't have thirty-six thousand ways of soliloquizing. Placed in a similar situation to Solange, the Duchesse de Maufrigneuse would have said much the same to herself, I assure you. Possibly she might have expressed her feelings rather differently, if that! The amusing thing about it all is that Solange's protestations completely reassured Valentin! He was sorry he had been so suspicious. He "came to his senses." Obviously she wouldn't do anything foolish! That wouldn't be like her. She could be relied on. He even felt ashamed of having been so unpleasant. Solange, little Solange, with her beautiful candid eyes, her peach complexion, her staunch and pure heart, could never behave badly in any circumstances. The angels were watching over her. He, Valentin, had no need to torment himself. His sister's anger, her eyes blazing defiance, restored his good humor. Such indignation was unmistakable: it was innocence itself!

I: Perfect, splendid, very funny!

HE: Funnier than you think, for Valentin, through his clumsy questioning, had driven Solange a long way down a path which hitherto she had only followed hesitantly and shyly. He had been a decisive factor. He had suddenly made her acutely aware of her love, led her to define it and give it intellectual shape. You know as well as I do the immense power of words and how frequently things which never really existed before because they had never been formulated suddenly spring to blazing life when they are put into words. Well, that's what happened that night to Solange. Two chance occurrences—Mlle. Angioletti's tactlessness and Valentin's anger—went far to consolidate a love which, though very powerful already, was still somewhat vague and poetically unreal. Solange felt this love must undeniably exist since it was running into so many obstacles, since it had to be fought for. She learned how violent it was from the force with which she found herself defending it. She measured the extent of her passion and discovered that it occupied a boundless territory within her, that it had pushed its frontiers far out of sight. The slightest skirmish on its periphery found her fully mobilized against the enemy.

People's blindness and incomprehension always fascinate me. Doesn't it make an extraordinary picture, Valentin regaining confidence in Solange at the very moment when, through his own stupidity, he had succeeded in crystallizing everything for her and committing her to the "foolishness" he so greatly feared? It's the perfect image of the way of the world, a symbol of all human relations. The history of man is nothing but a chain of errors and misunderstandings, and in spite of this it has been carrying on since time began with every appearance of logic, every semblance of sense! It really calls for a moment's admiration.

The midnight episode in the Avenue Daumesnil is a crucial point in the chronicle of the loves of Roberti and Solange Mignot. Once again the May bug I call destiny hurls itself at the lamp. What little things disasters hang on! A friend's gaffe and a brother's bad temper. Whatever you say, I shall continue to believe that almost nothing in life is inevitable, that there are always endless possibilities, that history is never written in advance. We only recognize destiny once it has passed. We call chance destiny after the cards have been played. Whence I conclude that, given much wisdom, nobility and resignation as practiced by the old Stoics like Epictetus, one can easily avoid the May bug. One has to begin by stifling all the passions in one's heart. It is our passions that light the lamp.

I: In other words you deny tragedy.

HE: Absolutely. Tragedy is necessity. Within or without. But necessity doesn't exist. It is a fabrication of the poets, who enjoy collecting causes and effects and finding links between them. This makes an impressive effect, I don't deny. But you won't find anything like it in life, where I can see nothing but confusion and meaninglessness. The causes are scattered, the effects preposterous. Tragedy offers us beautiful avenues leading inexorably to the Tarpeian rock, down which we advance with measured tread, never pausing to look where we are going; whereas life is a labyrinth of alleys, steps, belvederes, twisting streets and dead ends. Especially dead ends. It is really fantastic the number of blind alleys and "no outlet" roads one ends up in after endless trudging. I am still awaiting the great poet who will apprehend this fact and embody it in his epics. The poet of things as they are, that is of things which at any moment might cease to be, which misfire, which pass unseen by us all because they are too vast for the human gaze to take in. I am awaiting the poet whose eyes will at last perceive the ultraviolet rays of reality, as unfathomable as God. We shall then see the birth of true tragedy, and all the poetry which delighted our fathers will seem mere mumbling or nursery tales. Mankind will at last have found its mirror, which a mighty hand will hold over all the paths down which the descendants of Adam and Eve pass.

I: That's all very fine but you're not the first person to have thought of it. In the best cases it produces someone like James Joyce, who is three quarters unreadable, the remaining quarter being full of Irish flummery. I'm sorry, but until your literary theories find a genius to give them expression I shall stick to Shakespeare, Corneille, Cervantes and a few other rudimentary ancients of that ilk. I've a weakness for Shakespeare, you know. I really admire his work. It's not at all bad, as mumbling and nursery tales go.

HE: You always like to have the last word. Yet what I am saying is true. There is a "school of truth" in art and literature still waiting to be founded. Something which has nothing to do with realism or naturalism but which will express our life as it is, in all its sublime muddle, its endless complications, its chain of misunderstandings, its dark clouds. Don't you agree?

I: No. I think poetry is fine as it is and that Homer discovered everything from the start. I think music is fine as it is. You will never improve on Beethoven. I think painting is fine as it is and that Rembrandt is the supreme genius of all time. Or else man will have to change, become a different creature with twelve arms and an eye at the back of his head. The conception of art as the "mirror of life" is absurd and utterly false. And do you want to know why?

HE: Yes, I should like to hear your reasons.

I: Because art forms part of life, in the first place; it is a department of it by the same token as love, politics, freemasonry and bridge. An artist is a man with feelings, fads, pleasures and pains. He is neither a camera nor a tape-recorder. He functions according to the age-old laws of nature. Naturally an artist's work is a representation of the world, but not just any representation: his own personal one. In other words something peculiar to him, unique in coloring, bent and warped, distorted and magnified by his own feelings. Before it resembles nature, a work of art first resembles the artist. If the mirror you hold up over men's paths is not a distorting mirror, then it's a bad one.

Second, life is full of things that don't matter, full of perishable goods. Why on earth do you want to preserve them like bits of bodies bottled in formalin? Literature is not a medical museum. It's a shop full of illusions run by a weird and slightly mad character who, for the delectation of his customers, constructs silhouettes which he uses to tell stories like the love of Tristan and Isolde or Napoleon's Russian campaign. It is not the artist's business to retrace life in all it meanderings but to give an apt summary of it in which the details are distilled into poetry and the invisible springs to the eye without need of expression. Examples: Homer, Beethoven, Rembrandt. The artist's quest is like the extraction of a diamond: he has to chip away the matrix, scrape it clean and throw out the dross, excavate huge piles of earth to find at long last one tiny piece of pure crystallized carbon. But this carbon is the hardest, most brilliant, most transparent of all minerals. It can scratch anything and nothing can scratch it. I apologize for this cascade of metaphors but I want to make you see that there exists a sort of connective tissue of life which is valueless and therefore doesn't deserve to be preserved by art. Or rather that the mission of art is to render the most complex things with the utmost simplicity, to shed light by means of a daring synthesis on the hopeless tangle of human relations, with all their misunderstandings and lies. The rest is just bunk. The idle speculation of pedants and ignoramuses. That is how I feel about *this important question*. And now I'd be very glad if you would tackle that part of Roberti's story dealing with this worthy parliamentarian's first outing with Mlle. Mignot. Your practical work is better than your theory and your poetry rates higher than your ideas on poetic art. That is the sign of all true creators. They do their work and subsequently invent grandiose principles to explain it. But we who know the ropes also know the proper worth of systems. They are concocted after the event for the use of nincompoops, to make them take us seriously. And now get on with it. Roberti comes in his car to fetch Solange the next evening as she leaves her office on the Avenue de l'Opéra. He has the jitters. "I hope to God she's quick," he thinks. "Everyone will see me and wonder what I'm doing here." Or doesn't he?

HE: He does.

I: It wasn't hard to guess. And then . . . ? What has come over you? Only five minutes ago you were talking your head off.

HE: My literary theory isn't really so absurd.

I: So that's it, is it?

HE: I assure you I have never found this idea of mine about life in any book, yet I'd bet my last penny it's a sound one. I wish someone would one day write a great book, something as fine as Balzac or Dickens but in which there was fog, if you get my meaning.

I: I get it perfectly. Look, perhaps I'll write your foggy book for you if you tell me Roberti's story to the end. Does that cheer you up?

HE: Do you think you could put in all the fog it calls for? Do you think you could sound the foghorns now and then? Besides, you mustn't forget there are moments when the fog lifts completely and things become as clear as when a shortsighted person puts on his spectacles.

I: I won't.

HE: It will be difficult, you know.

I: I only enjoy things which present difficulties. I must say I feel rather tempted to write a dreadful novel, like nothing anyone else has done, full of fog, foghorns and spectacles. In art the only things that matter are those which bear no resemblance to anything already done or said. But don't build yourself illusions. Even if our novel, remarkable and original as it may be, is a success, it won't basically say any more than the oldest chronicles of mankind. We shan't be doing anything different from what Plutarch, Ariosto, Tolstoy and the rest of them have already done. Those are the limitations of our condition. If we want to abandon the human condition we descend into gibberish and end up in a void. But don't worry. The human condition is always the same and endlessly renews itself. Eternally old and eternally new. In short one can always get some fun out of it. Not to mention that with our novel we may invent a new rhetoric. And in that case, victory! We should have one or two hundred years of peace ahead of us, until through the efforts of our disciples we in turn become hackneyed. Do you realize we could kill off the novel for a century? What a triumph! There are only two ways of achieving fame when it comes to the grand manner: either by inventing it or killing it off. Corneille and Racine.

HE: Bravo! We will treat the novel to a first-class funeral such as they gave the return of Napoleon's ashes, with an almighty hearse, twelve hacks with all the trappings, pompoms and flowers all over the place, the band of the Imperial Guard, the whole works! Millions of people of every race and color will follow the coffin. You will be coachman and I'll be pallbearer. We'll play all those wretched readers such a requiem that they'll never be able to hear a thing again. We'll remodel their ears, din our new music into them, blast them with a fabulous, unheard-of literature! Death and Transfiguration of the Novel!

He was in a simply ridiculous state of excitement. He got up and skipped a few *entrechats* to the astonishment of an outraged little boy and girl who burst into shrieks of laughter. I rose as well. I begged him to calm down. After all, writing a novel isn't such a mighty exploit that one must needs call out the Prince de Joinville and the Old Guard as they did for Napoleon's ashes. But in France anything connected with literature arouses an extreme, I would even say disproportionate, interest in those who have least to do with it. As we were on our feet we decided to leave the Square Boucicaut by the gate giving onto the Rue Velpeau. We both felt refreshed and relaxed. The sun shone down on the Rue de Sèvres with rays incarnadine, daubing the houses with pink and ocher just as if we were in Italy. The sounds of the city lapped round us once again, but this was not unpleasant after the peace of the Square. The sunlight was caught in veils of gilded dust, overlapping like gauze curtains in a theater. We heard the rumble of the traffic, the voices of the pedestrians; behind us, at the Sèvres-Babylone crossroads, a policeman was blowing his whistle fit to burst.

At this end the Rue de Sèvres is not attractive. The huge Bon Marché stores give it a commercial aspect which, while not wholly incompatible with the traditional high tone of the Faubourg Saint-Germain, makes one cruelly aware of the march of time and the vicissitudes of civilization. Here the Faubourg Saint-Germain resembles an aristocrat who, after being ruined by successive revolutions, has gone into trade. Opposite the Bon Marché, shops with loud signs and gaudy paintwork have taken over the ground floors of the ramshackle old buildings. There is something artificial and depressing about all this glitter overlying all this decrepitude. As if a traveling fair had settled there permanently. The shoeshop evokes a shooting alley and the grocer a coconut shy. A little lower down toward the Boulevard Montparnasse is a movie house whose huge voracious jaws, all glass and aluminum, multicolored posters and giant lettering, recall the gaudily painted canvas booths where lovers of the grotesque flock to see the Siamese Twins, the Bearded Lady and *Androuida* Daughter of Mars, who has a neck four feet long, six tits and voluminous thighs.

In this part of the Rue de Sèvres, on the north side, the only trace of nobler days is the blackened porch of the Hôpital Laennec; but this is the sole survivor of its kind, saved, God knows why, from the shipwreck in which the beautiful Parisian architecture of former centuries has been slowly foundering for the past hundred years. This porch gives onto a shameful cluster of brick hospital buildings whose ugliness and funereal air of despair are likely to worsen the condition of the sick who are taken there.

The Hôpital Laennec, of course, stands at the corner of the Rue de Sèvres and the Rue Vaneau, which is crossed two hundred yards farther down by the Rue Oudinot. We weren't far from the place where our hero had lived so long.

ı: I've an idea. Supposing we make a detour? I'd very much like to see where Roberti lived.

HE: Really? Why?

ı: Oh, no special reason. Just for fun. As a sort of sentimental pilgrimage. Besides, it would get us out of this dreary Rue de Sèvres. We could go by the Rue Vaneau, which is as green and shady as a lime walk. Wouldn't it be rather nice to go and say hello to Agnes while we're about it? It would give me a chance to look over the apartment. And also refresh my memories of her, which are dim, to put it mildly.

HE: Out of the question. We can't just drop in on Agnes unannounced. I never visit people without first giving due warning. To my mind it's the height of bad manners. And what would we say once we got there? "We were just passing. My friend here wanted to see what sort of a woman Roberti's wife was, so up we came." No, we really can't. You go if you like; at any rate I won't go with you. You must just make out on your own. Say you're selling vacuum cleaners or collecting for blind children.

ı: Don't be so unkind. I can't for the life of me see what's to prevent us calling on Agnes. You're passing her block; what could be more natural than to look in for a moment on an old friend? Why not take her a present while we're about it? A box of sweets or a bunch of flowers. I'm with you. I won't say a word. I'll act shy and tongue-tied. I'll pretend to be rather self-conscious: "A lovely day, Madame, don't you agree?" is all I'll say. And after ten minutes I'll discreetly tug at your sleeve to remind you we have to keep an appointment and off we go. It wouldn't look suspicious in the least, I swear.

HE: Perhaps you're right.

ı: Let's go, then.

HE: No. I'm sorry, but I just don't feel it. It doesn't fit in with my story. It might easily block my flow of inspiration. Were I suddenly to see Agnes in the flesh with her trim little figure, her quick movements, her charming smile, hear her faint Bordeaux accent, it would throw me badly. It would have the same effect as if Roberti's ghost were suddenly to rise up before me cloaked in fire and brimstone.

I: How odd you are!

HE: Well, *you* ought to understand. Here I've been for the past four hours telling you Roberti's story, with which Agnes is so closely involved. I need to stand back from the characters; feel something of the novelist's detachment. The real Agnes, with the texture of her skin, her ringlets, the blue veins on her hands, her whiff of eau de cologne, would embarrass me beyond words. Her portrait as I've drawn it would instantly strike me as crude, clumsy, divorced from reality. It would throw me off balance. Not to mention the thousand different emotions that would swoop down on me at the mere sight of her. I'd cease to be the impassive, stonyhearted storyteller I've been so far. Beware—I too can be sensitive. I can become human at any moment. In which case, good-by to your novel.

I: But you saw her only last week; and you'll be seeing her next week. What harm can it do you to see her now?

HE: Please, just let's leave it at that.

I: Very well, I won't insist. But I warn you, we're missing a lot by not calling. We should have had two different views of her, yours and mine. With a little luck she might have talked about Roberti and I could have then heard for myself not only how her voice sounds and her tricks of speech, but also her arguments to justify her husband. Because she must have some. I'll bet my last penny she has absolved him. And we're losing all that through your moodiness. Let me add that a novelist, while he writes his novel from memory, from the requisite distance, never scorns to go every now and then to check up on some visual detail, question some witness, listen to the talk of one of his models. That doesn't upset him. It helps him, it enables him to correct mistakes, to stick more closely to the truth.

HE: Look, let's split the difference. We'll go round by the Rue Oudinot. I'll show you Roberti's house but we won't take it any farther. I don't want to call on Agnes. I don't want to see her today. The building alone will convey quite a lot. A whole way of life, an atmosphere of its own.

I: Right, I'll settle for the house. That will be something at least.

HE: I prefer it so. Let me arrange things my own way. I know what's good for me and what isn't.

I: A real prima donna, you are! You don't make my job easy.

HE: What do you mean? I'm telling you everything. You just have to transcribe it. I'm switching on all the lights for you. All you have to do is copy everything down, set it to music.

I: Set it to music, yes. Copy it down, no. It's impossible, beyond my power, just to copy. You must leave me a few things to invent, otherwise I'd be fed up with the book after the second page. That's why I wanted to see Agnes. I wanted a little firsthand material to transform by my own means. But let's forget it.

HE: Agreed. Let's push on with the story. We have reached the point where Roberti is sitting sulking in the Avenue de l'Opéra because Solange is five minutes late. He is in a combination of bad temper and anxiety. In his usual way he is imagining all kinds of wild possibilities: that Solange has had second thoughts and, regretting her promise, has decided never to see him again; that she has taken such a dislike to him that she has told her office she's sick, so as to avoid meeting him. She has spent the day with her boy friend, to whom she has poured out the whole story, and they've had a good laugh over her middle-aged would-be lover. "I'll give her till a quarter to seven," thinks Roberti. "At a quarter to on the dot, I'm off. If she turns up at ten to, it'll be her loss. She won't see me, and she'll never hear from me again either. I'm not the sort to be kept waiting." What else? He keeps glancing in every direction. Ten people he knows will pass just as the fair Solange is climbing into his car, jubilantly take note of this and spread it all over Paris. He almost reaches the point of hoping the girl will stand him up. All his desire has evaporated. He feels nothing but unmitigated boredom at the prospect of his forthcoming date. At best, Solange will gently offer him her "friendship." This last thought puts Roberti in a rage. Really, he never has any luck! Nothing but endless letdowns! However used to disappointment one may be, it is no less bitter each time. Of course, one ends by becoming imbued with a spirit of resignation, but perhaps that is sadder still. Roberti mitigated his defeats by anticipating them in advance, even superstitiously forcing himself to believe more in defeat than in any other possibility. To anticipate the success of an enterprise was, in his view, tempting the Devil. Whence a warping of his intellect, an inner pessimism which by dint of being assumed had become genuine. He had made himself failure-prone. I point this out in connection with the thoughts provoked in him by Solange's delay, to show how it wasn't confined to his political activities but applied to everything, even his emotions. He felt as if he were walking down a straight, dreary road, flanked on either side by a high wall which not only shut off the landscape but also denied him access to heavenly estates, fabulous parks, those enchanted gardens through which human beings now and then have the good fortune to stroll. Very rarely for him was there ever a gap in these walls through which he could surreptitiously slip, secretly to enjoy a few stolen pleasures.

i: That's really funny—Roberti in his car, having a fit of the blues and bewailing his fate because his girl friend is taking some time to repowder her nose.

he: Yes, it's comic but at the same time pitiful because it illustrates how impossible it is for human beings to communicate. While Roberti was brooding on this gloomy note, Solange was in such a state of turmoil that she was shaking all over. She had waited for this hour of their meeting with an impatience I shall define as permanent, since it hadn't relaxed at any moment throughout the day. Her heart had been beating the whole time in a different way from other days, as if it had dropped through her chest and were thumping in her stomach. Since early morning all her gestures had been rather too jerky, not fully under control. The previous night's scene in the Avenue Daumesnil had led her to take a decisive step in her own mind. She was Iphigenia bent on sacrifice. But what sacrifice? Can one call a sacrifice something one longs for body and soul, a joy which promises to be overwhelming? Yes, I suppose one can. When all is said and done, one never sacrifices oneself in despair but always in exaltation. One never imagines a sacrifice bringing sorrow and nothingness, but on the contrary a happiness greater than any everyday life has to offer.

The appointment was for six-thirty. At six-thirty Solange was ready. But when the half hour struck she was seized with a typically feminine notion. She told herself she looked perfectly hideous and *must* go and tidy herself then and there, run a comb through her hair, allow herself five minutes' grace to calm her heart.

i: Even so it's odd, this great love kept alive on daydreams for two years, in no way diminished by its object's absence, and now all at once bursting into a fierce blaze. Yes, it's odd. It doesn't often happen that way.

he: It's probably more usual than you think but no one ever mentions it. It has a name, what's more: they call it love at first sight. Why shouldn't Solange have fallen in love at first sight with Roberti? You know as well as I that love has nothing to do with youth or beauty. Roberti's appearance, the charm of his personality, the look in his eyes immediately struck echoes in Solange of the deepest and most mysterious kind. He was the wind that played on the strings of this Aeolian harp for two years. There is no explaining love: all we can do is determine its existence. I couldn't tell you why Solange fell in love with Roberti any more than she herself could, come to that. There are some loves whose progress can be traced step by step, loves compounded of admiration, esteem, habits, slowly deepening and spreading desire. But there are others which spring up fully armed out of nothing, which are quite self-sufficient and descend on you like grace or misfortune. Roberti's drama lies in his contamination by this love he had unwittingly aroused. He caught it the way one catches the plague or cholera. His organism was no doubt less resistant to this disease than Solange's; he had never been vaccinated. It caused his death.

I: There's something inhuman about Solange.

HE: I don't quite follow you.

I: To be so utterly the prey of a single emotion one has created for oneself and nurtured for two whole years without any external sustenance—I find that inhuman. Next to the helpless and unsuspecting Roberti, who would be appalled if he knew the truth, she seems to me as terrifying as doom itself.

HE: Everyone in love is inhuman, I suppose. But as you will see, Solange was rather less so than most. I compared her just now with Iphigenia, not with Hermione. She was offering her neck to the knife. She wasn't handing Orestes a sword so that he might go and kill Pyrrhus. The doom lay in her loving Roberti, who was so ill suited to her, when she was equally ill suited to him. Obviously, viewed from a different angle, you can also say they were made for each other since their consuming and disastrous love—almost always painful for her, almost always exhausting, fraught with tedium and lassitude for him—was in its way an exceptional success. In short, there is the moral viewpoint and the esthetic one.

I: There is also the viewpoint of probability, if I may say so. Two things in your story bother me. First, the Avenue de l'Opéra at six-thirty P.M. It's an impracticable spot. There's a monster traffic congestion. How was Roberti able to park his car?

HE: Exactly. He couldn't. He was in a traffic lane; the problem this posed contributed to his bad temper. He was expecting a policeman to appear at any moment to move him on. The idea of displaying his deputy's card so as to avoid this contingency, of being discovered even by an anonymous cop, crucified him. Yet were he to drive slowly round the block he ran the risk of missing Solange.

I: Right. That's most important. It needed clarifying. Traffic jams and the delays they cause are an essential element of modern love.

Many's the time I've happened that way on a man and woman I know who had no business together in the same car. If you want to paint love in 1955, you mustn't pass such matters over in silence or you'll forfeit an essential part of the picture. Our age is one of snatch-and-grab adultery. Everything conspires against love. People not only work too hard but don't even know where to park their cars.

Second, I'm not convinced by the reason you give for Solange's delay. She knows one cannot park in the Avenue de l'Opéra. She is awaiting Roberti as if he were the Messiah. She is ready ten minutes early, and now she returns to the washroom to titivate, to give her little heart time to calm down. No, I can't accept that.

HE: Yet that's how it was, I promise. I could easily have said that Dietz had kept her back to finish some urgent work and you'd have raised no objection. But I didn't. When a great and long-desired happiness finally comes within one's grasp, it happens that we sometimes don't reach out for it straightaway but raise some little barrier, invent one last delay. We must sense that the period of waiting and longing is the happiest time and therefore try to spin it out a little further, since the fulfillment, however delicious, will never quite live up to it. That is what happened with Solange and it seems perfectly plausible to me. Besides, perhaps she was also feeling a bit scared.

When she finally turned up, eight or ten minutes late, Roberti's smile of welcome verged on a grimace. He kissed her hand pointedly and perfunctorily. But she smiled so tenderly that all at once he reverted to his romantic mood. He began to recover faith in his star.

I: Are you going to ruin this first meeting the way you did the Valentin-Legay-Solange party?

HE: Probably. Anyway I shall do my best to ruin it for you since it turned out to be totally dismal and idiotic. True to form, Roberti was in a hurry. Secretly he cursed the traffic jams. He drove down side streets, both to save time and to avoid being seen. His idea was to get to the Bois de Boulogne, pull off the road and "strengthen his position." But time was getting on. He was expected home for dinner. He talked polite and slightly forced trivialities. He was impatient to give Solange a real kiss, a contractual kiss so to speak, which would be a guarantee for the future. "We won't go anywhere for a drink," he said, "it's such a bore. Supposing we drove round the Bois? It's very romantic at this time of day. Let's go and breathe some chlorophyll." Once in the Bois it was a different story. No place was good enough to stop. After driving round several times he finally picked the most unsuitable, most conspicuous corner. There, fresh uncertainties. Happily Solange freed him from these by laying her hand on the wheel. It was an opportunity not to be missed. Roberti placed his large hand over her small one and raised it to his lips, while summoning into his eyes all the charm he could muster. The paralyzing spell was broken. There was no further need for talk. The time had come for deeds. Gently he caressed Solange's cheek and neck, to which she showed no objection. Then he took her chin, turned her face toward him and gazed soulfully into her eyes. She didn't resist. She was utterly yielding. And now she was no longer smiling. Her lovely eyes seemed so moist that he wondered if they weren't full of tears. There ensued a moment wholly exquisite for both of them. Even Roberti, though not in love, though merely a hunter on the point of ensnaring his prey, was not insensible to its charm. They were no longer in a car in the Bois de Boulogne in the twentieth century but lost in some wildly romantic mountain valley. The contractual kiss was a huge success, followed by several more given and received with all the requisite ardor. Solange was completely relaxed in Roberti's arms while he caressed her violently, intimately, in a state of high excitement.

i: Oho! So this outing in the Bois wasn't so dismal or idiotic after all. What then?

HE: Then they talked. After all that kissing and fondling it wasn't at all hard to find things to say. Roberti, who rather liked to enjoy undisputed sway over women's hearts, found a clever formula for asking whether she hadn't a boy friend or fiancé in the background. As you can imagine, this was vigorously denied, which pleasantly tickled his possessive instinct. In fifteen minutes Solange had become closer to him than to any other person. She described to him her outing the previous evening with Legay and Valentin, Mlle. Angioletti's gaffe and her own revolt in the Avenue Daumesnil. She flung all this at his feet in homage. She even took a kind of pleasure in thus betraying those close to her to a man who only three days before was a total stranger. Roberti appreciated the full value of this betrayal; he reveled in it. He even treated himself to the luxury of asking a few questions, indulgently poking fun at Valentin and guying Mlle. Angioletti. Their kisses, his victory, had already put him in high spirits and this final tribute from his captive, her confiding these intimate details, made him sparkle. Solange was charmed by such gaiety and youth in so serious-minded a man. Her love grew in geometrical progression. "How sweet and amusing he is," she told herself. "Oh God, make him love me!" Two or three times she spluttered with laughter like a little girl. Every now and then Roberti glanced at his watch. At a quarter to eight he announced to his conquest that they must part. This was a blow. She had counted on spending the whole evening with him. He apologized profusely for being unable to take her home and left her at a Métro station near Montparnasse.

I: Unspeakable. He is utterly unspeakable. So he dropped her off at the Métro?

HE: Yes, and drove off at top speed so as not to be late for dinner.

I: It's staggering! What a light it sheds on his soul! What a vile character! He deserved everything he had coming to him. One doesn't behave like that. He was obviously a complete boor. What did Solange think of such behavior?

HE: I don't believe she thought anything at all. You know, the spirit of criticism isn't exactly widespread. People generally take things as they come. They seldom tell themselves they might have been different. Always that lack of imagination. Due as much to the circumstances in which she was born and had lived as to her natural modesty, Solange was not accustomed to much consideration or attention. In the Avenue Daumesnil she hadn't received a very elaborate upbringing, not one of those solid bourgeois or aristocratic upbringings which make one particular as to one's due and conscious of one's dignity. She didn't know what is "done"; nobody had told her. She never suspected that a man who claims to be in love with you and pursues you is supposed to put up a certain show; that little attentions, some outlay—bunches of flowers, gifts and letters—are the indispensable ingredients of love; that since love is the most priceless thing in the world, a man can only buy it with the most precious currency—his life, which is to say his time. She knew nothing. She was ignorant. She was twenty-five and unused to the ways of the world. Her only guides were her pure heart and true instinct, to whose weak protests she refused out of modesty to listen. Since Roberti had set her down at the Métro at eight-fifteen things could not have been otherwise.

I: Didn't she even feel disheartened?

HE: Yes, she did, but it was a physical rather than a spiritual reaction. Roberti had stirred her blood in the Bois and hadn't fully quenched the flame he had lit. She had in fact been quite ready to give herself to him that evening. In the corridors of the Métro, in the half-empty train, through the monotonous clatter of wheels and rails interrupted by brief halts in dimly lit stations, her frustration irked her cruelly. But I wouldn't swear she was actually conscious of it. Of course she had dreamed of something quite different from the drive in the Bois and this lonely return home in the Métro. Even so, she felt not the slightest resentment. It was quite natural for such a busy man to give her no more than an hour and a half of his time. It was she who was at fault with her crazy romantic ideas.

God knows what she had imagined! How he would be waiting for her in some beautiful long white car, open naturally, an Alfa-Romeo or Ferrari; how he would bear her off into the gloaming amid a roar of exhaust; how she would say: "My hair's going to get in a mess! Don't go so fast!" to which he would reply: "I am taking you to the end of the world." They would have gone to dine in the country. After dinner they would have danced to slow blues; pressing him to her, to the rhythm of the music he would have whispered in her ear those meaningless phrases halfway between a kiss and a murmur and gradually, imperceptibly, she would have found herself alone with him in a pretty hotel room hung with toile de Jouy and smelling faintly damp. There would have been a big fire in the grate whose light would have flicked red shadows over her amber skin. The next morning they would have woken in charming disarray, very early, so that he should have time to take her back to the office. Wrapped in the sheet, with tousled hair, her body aching with an exquisite languor, she would have thrown open the shutters; sun and birdsong would have filled the room. . . . She knew this was mere foolishness, a fairy tale, and that there wasn't the faintest chance of things turning out that way; all the same, in the Métro her disappointment overshadowed her happiness. Shyly she thought Roberti might at least have dined with her. Notice I say "shyly." She bore him no grudge. She was a hundred miles from reflecting that he might have behaved badly or selfishly. In short she underestimated herself.

ɪ: Yes, because after all Roberti, during this first meeting, treated her as an object. He used her the way one uses a tart whom one hires by the hour. And at least the tart gets paid for it. He paid nothing. Not even a bunch of violets. Not even a drink.

ʜᴇ: True, but he doesn't deserve to be condemned outright, even so. He was worked up, he was pressed for time, he was hamstrung in every possible way. He'd have been thunderstruck to be told he had behaved like a cad. He had squeezed his meeting with Solange in among the countless occupations which absorbed his day. He hadn't anticipated anything but a rather brief encounter in order to "make contact," to "spy out the land." He had treated her to a very pleasant hour and a half. He had talked brilliantly, kissed skillfully. He wasn't displeased with himself, he felt he had cut quite a good figure, that things had by and large turned out well. Once again love was offering its miracle, that is to say a young and pretty woman who came to him, desired him, felt in her heart and flesh the need to merge with him. He had been chosen; he had been elected. Such matters provide delightful food for thought. He drove home feeling deeply satisfied. He wondered whether Solange had left any trace of her perfume on him, in which case he'd better light a cigarette to get rid of it. Agnes and the children greeted him with their usual warmth, so that by half past eight his happiness was complete.

I: I should like Roberti and Solange to sleep together. When will this happy event take place?

HE: Soon, soon. Don't be impatient. We are coming to it.

I: I wonder what's holding us back. The two interested parties are agreed.

HE: What holds us back is always the same thing: the problem of time. Poor Roberti, a public figure, hadn't a moment to call his own. Besides which he was punctilious. He regularly attended the Assembly. In those days the Assembly worked very hard, it was always sitting. Committees met frequently. Members were earning every penny of their salaries. Besides which Roberti also had his professional sidelines, to which he devoted set periods during the week. Not to mention the hours when he received his constituents, which were sacred, and the countless other things a deputy has to do to maintain his credit in his district; regular meetings, reports, publication of the local bulletin and so on. All of which leaves little room for fun and games. Maybe the parliamentarians in 1955 were not equal to the occasion, maybe they governed the country badly; at any rate, one cannot say they were in-active. And in the evening there were dinner parties, first nights at the Opéra or some theater from which Roberti could not afford to absent himself on account of being Vice-Chairman of the Arts and Letters Committee.

I: What a life!

HE: Yes, I suppose that to a man like you, who loves solitude, such an existence must seem the acme of futility and boredom. But one shouldn't judge by one's own standards. Certain men give of their best when surrounded by noise and bustle. Roberti belonged to that category. He needed to hear the world around him humming like a gigantic factory and demanding his full attention. This gave him his bearings; only thus was he able to assume the true shape of his soul. Such is no doubt the mark of the man of action as opposed to the man of thought. Thought and action are the two means by which men try to find themselves. Solitude dilutes the man of action and silence rots him. He has no use for them. He gets nothing out of them. For him their climate brings death. He needs something to be going on all the time; this has the same effect on him as the instruments of an orchestra on a tenor, whose voice soars up and dominates the melody being played around him.

I: That, by the way, provides an explanation of the term "a political tenor"!

HE: It's my own explanation. In fact, I believe that what is known as a political tenor is simply a man who has a beautiful voice and gives full vent to it on the rostrum, besides knowing how to get himself talked about on every possible occasion. Anyway it is true that it's the tenor who is on the stage, in the glow of the footlights, it's the tenor at whom the public looks, whereas the musicians playing the score are in darkness down in the orchestra pit.

Roberti, without taking leading roles, belonged to that category of singer. It was part of his nature to pay meticulous attention to every manifestation of the outside world, either to turn it to his advantage or to organize it, direct it, bring it to bear on some distant project. His mind was not creative in your sense of the word, that is to say he was incapable of prising a complete work out of himself as a painter or writer does. But he could well have achieved that other sort of work which consists of organizing the world out of whatever elements it offers. This kind of work is in essence quite different from that of artists; it belongs strictly to politicians, whereby they sometimes change the fate of mankind, and it can only ever be achieved amid tumult.

I: Ugh! How horrible! I loathe the world of action.

HE: Loathe it, really?

I: When you write a book or paint a picture, you enjoy a feeling of extraordinary power. Your will has no bounds save that of your talent. You alone are master on board the vessel of your creation. You are Robinson Crusoe on his desert island. You are Adam telling God: I want a lion, a giraffe, a grasshopper, a diplodocus, and immediately obtaining them. There is no one to thwart your decisions, no one comes to give you advice, no one is in a position to plague you. Whereas with actions it is just the reverse. One has thousands of other wills to reckon with, come to terms with, divert, circumvent or overcome. One has to adjust one's work the whole time. It is like clay to which one has given a general shape but which is constantly being distorted by thousands of ignorant or callous thumbs. The politician spends his whole life remodeling. The labor of it! The waste of time! Action leaves you only a tiny margin; the margin of what is *possible*. Art or, if you prefer it, contemplation leaves an infinite margin. Nothing prevents you from aiming at the impossible and even achieving it. The older I get, the more the possible bores me and the impossible attracts me. It seems to me that in the long run the man of action must become completely impotent and sink into despair. Just look how statesmen die: worn away to the bone, no longer believing in anything and in action least of all. They die in total pessimism, because forty or fifty years of ceaseless activity have taught them that man has no will of his own, which incidentally is untrue.

HE: Your clay metaphor is a pretty one but it has no connection with reality, for the politician's raw material is in fact men's wills. A great statesman has as much power over them as a great painter has over colors or a great writer over words. Words and colors are intractable too, I believe, and pull in many different directions unless one has a dazzling gift for manipulating them. Cavour, Bismarck and Clemenceau drew the society of their day with the same virtuosity, the same firmness of line, I would even say the same freedom as Delacroix, Ingres and Manet drew their pictures. They encountered no greater obstacles (at least none other than those inherent in their art); they mastered their materials.

I: Cavour, Bismarck . . . We've come rather a long way from Roberti.

HE: Wait. We're getting back to him. We are agreed on this, aren't we, that the best and probably only path by which to descend into the depths of one's soul, and so be happy, is that of difficulty, of overcoming difficulties?

I: Yes, we are. When my writing goes well, I never feel tired. An artist's daily work draws on his strength and regenerates it at the same time. A patent phoenix system. The actor is never ill when he walks onto the stage, even if he has a raging temperature.

HE: Well, a man of action finds his work an identical source of fatigue and repose. Take a minister, no matter who, no need for him to be a genius, just a common-garden minister; he works fourteen hours at a stretch; he is worn out, of course, but he feels just as fresh, just as gay as a poet who has flogged himself to death writing an ode. He enjoys the special happiness of those at peace with their consciences. You can arrive at the same result whether in tumult or in silence. So that action, with its diversity, its mobilization of all one's senses, its antennae perpetually probing the outer world, leads to the same result as thought, with its concentration and withdrawal.

Can you now see that Roberti's life wasn't futile? That it answered to the demands of his nature? His aptitudes were not perhaps innate but they had in fact become an essential part of him. When we say "a man of action" we immediately think of fiery Achilles, Sir Walter Raleigh, the Chevalier d'Éon, Saint-Exupéry and so on. But we are wrong. Those were sportsmen. The men of action were Ulysses, Cardinal Fleury, Guizot, Herriot; no doubt they varied in quality but they all had in common prudence and a taste for compromise solutions, long-term planning and a sense of achievement, whether great or small. They loved the profession of action because they knew that thereby runs the road which must lead them to their innermost beings. Even if they didn't know this, they sensed it intuitively.

Roberti, a Radical deputy, loved his job and performed it scrupulously. He found no detail of it irksome. Everything about it seemed to him necessary in that it contributed, however little, to the public welfare and his future promotion. Note in passing that these two factors, through an illusion widespread (and quite natural) among politicians, were linked together in his mind, the first being a function of the second. He reckoned that the post of minister would bring him new insight into his soul and abilities by reason of the power it would confer on him. Meanwhile he neglected none of the petty obligations of his office. He gladly answered every letter from his constituents; he took the various steps they asked him to take; he read the newspapers carefully. Likewise he would often muse affectionately over the parliamentary rules and customs. They governed his life, his habits, his preferences. He was sentimentally attached to the minutiae of protocol or legislative procedure, in the same way a painter loves the smell of paint or the manual side of his art—stretching canvases, priming them, laying out his palette and so on. In his eyes all this formed part of a higher purpose, which was the greatness of the State and the country. We have harped enough on his pettiness. It is only fair to stress other qualities of his which I find rather admirable. He considered that representing the people was a sort of priesthood and that it was dishonorable not to perform all one's duties meticulously. He even liked his deadly committee meetings. He liked the sort of trance into which they would lapse after an hour or so, the monotonous voices of the members making their reports, the cigarette and pipe smoke. When one enjoys one's job one does it well. Roberti was a model deputy and accordingly very taken up with it.

I: When did he find time to sleep with Solange, then? When did he see her again?

HE: He saw her again the next day. He devoted an hour to her when she left the office. The day after that he arranged to have lunch with her. For the following week he saw her almost daily. These were charming escapades in which they both delighted. Once they went to lunch at Suresnes. On another occasion he found time to drive her home to the Porte Dorée.

I: So he was in no hurry to reap the fruits of his victory.

HE: Well no, as you see. There were several reasons for his holding back. In the first place, he never had more than an hour or an hour and a half to spare for Solange. But anyway he wanted to prolong this preliminary stage. He wanted to be certain, when he took her to the hotel, that he had exhausted all its charms. He was enchanted by his gradual discovery of Solange in the car and on their strolls through the Bois de Vincennes, by the caresses he stole from her almost under the noses of the passers-by, by these hasty and always threatened meetings. Also he was letting his desire grow, spread through him until it filled his whole being to the very marrow. He was carefully preparing his own sympathetic magic. He was controlling his passion. Solange appealed to him hugely; he set great store by her youth and beauty. Possibly he feared the moment when it would become all his.

I: I don't get it. Was he afraid of failing her?

HE: He wanted to feel sure of himself, so that everything should prove the utmost success. He was charging himself with desire the way one charges a battery. He told himself he needed at least a week of desire, fascination, hypnotism, in order to attain love in all its perfection. He was letting Solange's body take possession of his mind and gradually set it on fire. At night, as he went to bed, his thoughts of her drove him to frenzy; he would enjoy in anticipation every conceivable pleasure of the senses, he would recount them, describe them to himself to his inexhaustible satisfaction. The moments when he met Solange formed the one bright spot of each day.

I: That's quite subtle.

HE: Yes. He knew perfectly well she was his for the asking, that he only had to reach out to take her. But by this almost painful period of waiting he was preparing himself for a joy beyond bounds. He told himself how, once he had had her, he would never again experience such a thrill from breathing the scent of her neck, which in its sweetness reminded him of jasmine. How the thrill he got from feeling her flesh beneath her dress, from slowly running his hand over her nylon stockings, would never again be so overwhelming. Hitherto his adventures had always come to an abrupt fruition. For once he decided to linger over these first stirrings of love and savor their charm to the full.

I: And Solange? What did she think of this delay? Did she agree to it?

HE: Oh yes. Absolutely. She looked on it as an engagement period.

She lived in a state of exceptional love and exaltation. This was clearly visible, moreover. She was already so pretty that she could hardly become any more so; but love had brought a new light into her face and a sort of pensive glow into her eyes. At the office she was so gay that Mlle. Angioletti told her ten times a day: "You're in love, my girl!" She never tired of hearing this, as it consecrated her happiness. For her the brief hours she spent each day with Roberti were moments of celestial joy which left her so overcome that she desired nothing more than what he gave her. She would look forward to these lunchtime or evening meetings the way one looks forward to a vacation, the sea and sun. She was familiarizing herself with Roberti and grateful to him for allowing her time to get used to him. Not so that she could lose her shyness—that was impossible: with him she felt too humble, too young and foolish—but in order to rid herself of her gaucheness, to learn to know his gestures, his warmth, the smell of his clean and well-tended body, to respond to his kisses in the way he liked and so on. She told herself how he had sensed that between them there was a slow acquaintance to be built up with a long association in view, and that before they were united their bodies must take full measure of each other.

At any rate it wasn't for her to decide. Such decisions were being taken for her and that always strengthens a woman's love. Women like to be disposed of. Nothing appeals to a woman so much as having to place her will in a lover's hands.

i: I know all about that. It's nothing new.

he: What, you know all about it?

i: Certainly. It's traditional psychology. The man who spins out the preliminaries is as old as the hills. It has been described over and over again.

he: If I'm boring you, you've only to say so. I'll stop right now and we will finish our afternoon at a movie.

i: Oho, now he's angry! Wherever will literary vanity turn up next?

he: No, nothing can make me angry. But the last thing I want is to bore you.

i: Don't be so put out. You've no idea how funny you sound! And it's just silly. If you want wide-eyed admiration you've chosen the wrong audience. What are you complaining of? We agreed that I should argue and goad you now and then. Anyway, who is writing this novel? You or me? Me. So let me direct the proceedings a little. I know what I need and what is irrelevant. If I let you start spouting your head off, you'll be treating me to another cyclone in Guadeloupe in a few minutes and then God knows where we'll land ourselves.

HE: All the same, your remark about traditional psychology was pretty tough. I didn't deserve that.

I: Yes you did, entirely. What is the good of rehashing what has already been done, and done well? When it comes to studying the emotions of a man who knowingly postpones his moment of happiness, we shall never improve on our illustrious forebears. We shall never surpass Stendhal for delicacy of touch, Balzac for power, Dickens for deliberation, Proust for details. So . . .

HE: Still, it's a fact that Roberti waited eight days before he went to bed with Solange. That's how it was. I have to say so at the risk of duplicating Stendhal. How would you set about that in the novel? Would you put: "With regard to the analysis of our hero's emotions in this particular instance, the reader is requested to refer to Stendhal, who has said the last word about it"?

I: Do you know, you've just made a discovery.

HE: What?

I: And a far reaching one. Without meaning to, you have had a stroke of genius. The idea of using novels as if they were scientific reference books. This would bring about a gigantic step forward in our knowledge of the human heart. Imagine a novelist working out a plot. He sees that most of the situations, emotions, characters and developments have already been exploited in *War and Peace, Sodom and Gomorrah, Little Dorrit, Splendors and Miseries, Adolphe, The Egoist* and so on. What does he do? He first writes his story, then he inserts various passages from the great masters where they naturally fit in, just as a mathematician bases his arguments on Fermat's or Pythagoras' theorems.

HE: How perfectly idiotic.

I: It would be idiotic if the great novelists wrote just anything. But they don't. They depict life and men with as much insight and precision as Newton, Poincaré or Einstein put into their calculations. My system has a further advantage in that it would spare us a great deal of bad writing. If, instead of slaving with their limited means to rewrite what has already been written in immortal words for all time, the four thousand novelists who proliferate in France at this moment would content themselves with reproducing this as it stands, the public would end by having better taste. But to do so they must needs be modest and drop their conviction that they have more wit than Voltaire. Or quite simply be well read, which is seldom the case.

HE: Stop! You make me dizzy with your paradoxes. I've caught you red-handed in the act of contradicting your principles. You've told me a hundred times that knowledge of men always starts afresh from zero. That we haven't advanced one step since Plato. That our experience cannot be passed on. That art can evolve but never improve since every great artist attains perfection and so forth. Let's get this straight. I suppose it's the same with literature. Every writer must rediscover the world on his own account, starting with himself. He must experience for himself the feelings of a man who postpones sleeping with his fair Dulcinea for a week and express them in his own way, even if it's crude and clumsy. It's just too bad if it has already been dazzlingly well done a dozen times before. Perhaps he will find in his heart or mind some detail, some word Stendhal overlooked, which will make its small contribution to the problem.

I: You are confusing experience and ignorance. There are some things one has to take for granted. Otherwise the flimsiest novel would run to ten thousand pages. Most saga novels are unreadable because the author spins everything out and spends three paragraphs describing how one opens a door. Hardly useful information! Roberti's waiting for eight days is worth a mention, a sentence, no more, certainly not all this turgid development. Since you've got me with my back to the wall I shall add this: that in burbling on with your subtle psychology you were way off the subject.

HE: Well I like that! On the contrary, I was plumb in the middle of it. I was thinking as much just now, while I was talking. "At least," I told myself, "he won't be able to say I'm rambling or going off at a tangent in this instance!"

I: You were. For you've told me everything except the one essential.

HE: And what in your view was that?

I: To show me how this adventure of Roberti's with Solange differed from his previous ones; next, to analyze the difficulties he encountered, make me feel the resistance, the opposition of the outer world. Take these luncheons. What about them? You explain at some length that Roberti's time is completely absorbed by his work and social obligations and here he is suddenly guzzling at Suresnes like a Victorian masher on a spree, and driving his girl home in the evenings to the Porte Dorée like a respectful and bashful lover. Don't you feel this calls for a few words of explanation? It's a far cry from the Paris of 1955, with its traffic jams, the fine-meshed net of modern life, this sort of overcrowded bus of a world in which we live, where at the slightest movement we bump into three other people, where everybody's eyes are upon us, where love is almost impossible for anyone who doesn't wish to be seen.

We are in the rarefied atmosphere of bad novels where everything takes place in the desert, in the ether, where no material obstacle is ever encountered, where the heroes move about like disembodied spirits, where sacrosanct psychology has a high old time, where man only fights against himself. You might as well know that this type of literature makes me yawn, sends me to sleep, strikes me as the height of futility and ineptitude. I want you to build up around your characters a complex, tangled world, heavy to handle and eternally frustrating. And in this I am only serving up your own theories.

HE: I get it. I have shown you this week's "engagement" from the outside, on the surface. You want the inner workings.

I: Exactly. I want the real reasons. Not the states of mind. I couldn't care less about the states of mind. They are as tedious in novels as in life.

HE: Right. I'll do my best. Let's begin with the luncheons. There were only two. The celebrated one at Suresnes and another in a bar behind Notre Dame, a dingy and discreet place where Roberti was sure not to meet anyone he knew.

I: For such a man, I find two clandestine lunches in the space of a week quite good going. It verges on the improbable.

HE: Maybe, but one must assume that love, curiosity, the spice of the situation lent him wings—or imagination. A man who lives a secret life has antennae. He knows just how far he can go without arousing suspicion. With Agnes, Roberti had not exhausted his credit of lies, if you see what I mean. The apparent regularity of his life enabled him in certain circumstances to indulge in a little delinquency. He was a model prisoner, one of those sly ones who inspire such trust in their guards that the cell door is never bolted. Roberti, whose assets included a countless number of lunches at home, pleaded two important meetings, with the Budget Assessor or the Minister of Fine Arts, and Agnes swallowed these excuses whole. The more so since he had a quite admirable way of lying: he never gave details, which is the height of subtlety so far as lying goes. It is only achieved after long practice.

I: Well now, I would have thought on the contrary that good lies were the ones backed up by a lot of small truths.

HE: An error. A fatal error. You don't know the first thing about it. Bad liars produce a mass of explanations. Gifted liars lie coldly, economically, as if they were telling the truth. Everything they say seems unquestionable because they don't make the slightest attempt to appear plausible. As their lies are generally enormous and thus far less surprising than the truth, they are believed every time. They appear truer than the truth.

ɪ: Tell me about the lunch at Suresnes. Why Suresnes? That puzzles me.

ʜᴇ: For heaven's sake! Suresnes is very quiet. Nobody goes to lunch there during the week and one can get there in twenty minutes. Anyway Suresnes was poetic. A lunch at Suresnes looks well in a chronicle of love. Roberti told himself that perhaps this lunch would be followed by a stroll through the woods, which would not be without its charm. But he was out of luck: that day it rained buckets. They had lunch in a huge empty room; mournfully they ate the *pâté maison* and the creamed chicken, dreamily they drank the Alsatian wine traditional among lovers! But it was most agreeable all the same. Solange was full of gratitude. Although his plans were thwarted by the rain, Roberti was not bored. He talked a great deal and was pleasantly surprised to find Solange playing up to him. She was gay; happiness made her animated. She felt as if she were traveling far away from Paris and her daily life. After lunch they got back into the car but didn't set off straightaway. They spent nearly an hour in each other's arms, amply screened by the rain which drummed on the roof. This rain had certain advantages after all! So much for the lunch at Suresnes.

Just now we were talking of the glass dome of budding love. So long as he hadn't become Solange's lover, I believe Roberti superstitiously told himself he was running no risk. The outside world was not yet bearing down on him. Or rather, his longing to see her was so great that it gave him the strength to fend the world off. He was "coping" —meaning that his appetite for Solange was keen enough to inspire various lies, find the necessary time and so on. Besides, it would seem that in such circumstances the world, through some odd complicity, shuts its eyes, relaxes its grip, recedes, becomes soft and flabby. The mesh of the net widens; one can slip through it at will. Although I wonder how, it is a fact that the beginnings of love affairs are always easy, that everything then is light, everything, to quote your expression, takes place in the desert or the ether. Probably the reason is that in the eyes of a man in love everything apart from his love loses its importance and appears trivial. The discovery of the object he loves monopolizes all his attention and purpose. A lover abolishes the world. But this doesn't last. As soon as the object is possessed, the world comes racing up behind him and his troubles begin again.

ɪ: You see, I was right to ask you for an explanation. Now you're really on the mark. This is excellent.

HE: Then again, Roberti knew women. He knew that the first thing to be done is to block off the horizon of those one loves or wants to possess, stand between them and the world, obsess them. This is the gift which appeals to them most. It springs from their nature. Anyone who assiduously, shamelessly pursues them, pesters them with endless letters, telephone calls, unexpected visits, is always sure of being well received. They even give a warm welcome to men who don't attract them. This is how they betray their horror of loneliness. As Roberti could never see Solange for very long at a time, he arranged to see her at least once a day. These meetings were so to speak his initial investment. When one really wants something, one spares no expense to get it. During the first week of their affair he elected to see her every day and managed this without difficulty.

I: Men also require the physical presence. At the outset of a love affair the attraction between the man and woman is equal and reciprocal. Anyway, who takes all the first steps, who constantly displays himself? The man. It isn't just a question of tactics. He also needs to see, to touch, to hear. Were the roles reversed, were it the woman who did the chasing, can you see any man still holding out after a week of being pursued?

HE: I can assure you women are far more sensitive than men to the reality of love, that is to say to physical presence.

I: I don't believe it for a moment. And you can't use the example of Mlle. Solange Mignot eating her lonely heart out for two years to contradict me.

HE: But that was quite exceptional; besides, Roberti was unaware of it. Tactics played a great part, believe me, in the daily meetings he arranged with her. Obviously I couldn't measure exactly how much of it was tactics and how much actual desire, since nothing in love is clearcut or precise, nothing is absolutely pure, and some calculation always enters into every emotion. What is certain, however, is that he didn't need her presence to sustain his desire. You will see this for yourself presently. When they finally become lover and mistress, normal relations will be established between them. Roberti will give her much less of his time and poor Solange will begin to suffer from his absence. All I am really trying to say, and in this you will agree, is that the force of imagination is stronger in men than in women. When he is away from his mistress a man has a great capacity for evoking her, almost seeing her with his mind's eye. This is not to say it satisfies all his desires but it does mitigate some of them. I don't believe women possess this faculty. In their lover's absence, their imagination slumbers and they feel their loneliness in all its horror, abandoned and without resources. That is why the infidelities of women are far more serious than those of men. The unfaithful man never forgets the woman he is deceiving. The unfaithful woman only deceives once she has forgotten; when a new and persistent presence has superseded a presence in eclipse.

1: By the way, when Roberti took Mlle. Mignot home to the Avenue Daumesnil in the evening, it must have made him late for dinner. God, how complicated it all is.

HE: While he was kissing her in his car, he would glance furtively at his wristwatch from time to time.

1: Horrible detail!

HE: He always had some little lie in reserve to cover himself.

1: As far as I can see, his little lies were already going strong.

HE: Yes, but they were slight, impromptu lies run up at the last minute; he didn't attach much importance to them as yet, since they weren't concealing anything very serious. So long as things hadn't got beyond the stage of kisses, caresses, walks and talks, he didn't feel really guilty, that is to say really vulnerable. So he rather neglected his lies. He didn't apply himself to them wholeheartedly, as he had done in the past. He didn't yet need an alibi.

1: I must say, what makes man irrevocably, innately, essentially ridiculous is the lack of proportion between him and the universe.

HE: Well! So now you're getting onto metaphysics, are you?

1: Oh, I'm never completely off it; and I must say Roberti makes me more metaphysics-minded the whole time. What a spectacle he provides —this poor man on the brink of eternity, on the frontier between the two worlds, wriggling like a little worm, furtively glancing at his watch, taking care not to be late for dinner, concocting his absurd lies! What a lesson! Bossuet, where art thou? Alas, neither you nor I are up to portraying Roberti. He needs a Pascal to depict him vainly squirming amid the silence of infinite space.

HE: Pascal didn't write novels. He wasn't even a historian. He only spoke of God. History, the novel were things too imperceptible. They verged on godlessness.

1: Admit all the same that it's both frightening and absurd, as Pascalian as could be, to watch this poor Roberti, shortly to appear before his Creator although he doesn't know it and keeping an eye on his watch because of dinner. It's a staggering picture. It gives me the shivers. No one has the right to think so little of death.

HE: If you look at it that way, every human action is ridiculous and lamentable, untenable and senseless.

ɪ: So I sometimes tell myself when I can't get to sleep.

HE: Well, you're wrong, since on the one hand human actions are closely adapted to our condition and mean nothing other than what they express. It is no more ridiculous to keep an eye on one's watch so as not to be late for dinner than it is to put on a coat when it's cold or eat when one is hungry. On the other hand there are noble or heroic actions which are not futile in your sense of the word and which I dare say encroach upon the other world, stem from God. Charity is never ridiculous; on the contrary it is always sublime. The same is true of pity, provided of course it isn't given with any eye to self-improvement but practiced in all humility. If, when I describe Roberti's precautions, you summon up the silence of infinite space, you are cheating. I would further add that you're arrogant. You mustn't look down on men from the summit of Mount Olympus or from up in paradise, not even from the height of Pascal's *Pensées*. You are only a man yourself, and what is to prevent you from bringing down the same ridicule on your own head as you hand out so generously to others? So long as we are in this world, what could be more absurd than seating oneself on God's right hand, gazing down at one's own kind through a telescope and dismissing them as green fly?

ɪ: Your humble pardon. I am not seating myself on God's right hand. I am simply claiming the quality of a *thinking* green fly. I am a green fly with a sense of the absurd and possibly a little more attentive than the rest. I am being no harder on Roberti than I would be on myself. Besides, one should set infinite space alongside man every now and then. It gives a sense of scale. A rather cool breeze blows down from infinite space which clears the brain.

HE: My God, we don't need infinite space to measure the littleness of Roberti. You're going too far.

ɪ: True. He's little even in men's eyes. Why are you telling me about him at such length? I have wondered about this several times since lunch. What has the wretch to teach us? His whole story is so sordid, so depressing! It's not a tragedy, it's a squalid drama in which nothing much happens. The longer you talk, the less I care for him.

HE: Who knows? Maybe that's what I'm after.

ɪ: But in that case you're destroying the novel. You're destroying my interest. Roberti's a man I would certainly have avoided like the plague. It's no pleasure for me to meet him again in a book. Not to mention that characters in books are far closer to us than the people we know in real life. Thanks to you, I know Roberti far better than if I had met him every Tuesday for two years. The same thing often occurs to me in the movies. Watching dreary people going through dreary adventures on the screen, I ask myself: Why the hell am I here? Why am I forcing myself to listen to this rubbish and stare at these idiots to whom, if they were real and alive, I wouldn't give a second thought or even a glance?

HE: But that's a horribly bourgeois argument! You're talking like the people who run down Buffet and treat him like a criminal for painting ugly women. How odd you are! How often have you told me that the subject is nothing and that all that counts is the way it's treated?

I: Lord, I'm beginning to think I was wrong. That ever since the Jardin des Plantes you've been showing me I was mistaken. The subject forms part of art as well. A beautiful woman is more beautiful than an ugly one, even in painting.

HE: Even when it's Bouguereau who paints the beauty and Rembrandt who paints the ugly one?

I: You're beginning to get on my nerves. Are you determined to make me sound silly? Of course not! Beauty is worth more than ugliness, *given equal talent.*

HE: Forgive me, but I'm going to serve up one of your own maxims: One doesn't choose one's subjects; they choose you. I already warned you. I haven't played any dirty trick on you. I told you at the start that Roberti was Faust. The story of Faust is colossal but it isn't beautiful. There is no greatness about Faust, at least not after Mephisto has signed the pact with him. You're a romantic. I proclaim a man's damnation and you expect an apotheosis. You believe we descend to hell the same way as we ascend to paradise. I am taking you on a visit to Satan's abode. We are still on the threshold. We have barely ventured two or three steps inside and you are already holding your nose. For heaven's sake don't be so finicky! You want a hell made to order, corresponding to your literary or artistic prejudices. You want a hell like a hall of mirrors with reflections, dim lighting and gilt all over the place, a well-bred sort of hell where they play good music and the inmates affect a refined melancholy when they're not enduring a bout of indescribable agony. A hell like Dante's, Michelangelo's, Mozart's.

I: Yes.

HE: Well, permit me to tell you that you have the ideas of a shopgirl. Mozart and Dante were too gentle. They let their natural goodness get the better of them. They created underground palaces for distinguished guests. I go further. Or rather my instinct whispers to me that while they painted with bitumen and sulphur, they forgot the one essential, the most vital thing of all.

ı: What is that?

HE: Mediocrity. For mediocrity is the very mark of evil, its absolute seal, the form in which it is endlessly reborn. Evil is never splendid. Hell may be all red and gold, it may look like the Opéra but it's made of plaster. The red is turning black, the gilt is tarnished, the plaster is flaking. It is full of draughts and the windows are broken. It's a desolate landscape, a region strewn and stinking with excrement. Damnation is wholly horrible. No splendor redeems it. I see nothing but tarnished tinsel, leprous decorations, streaks of damp and mildew. Faust is a miserable wretch and once the pact is signed with the Devil his soul assumes the very semblance of the hell he has chosen. In other words it becomes dirty, ramshackle, rotten, it exudes a sweetish smell of carrion and filth, it is visibly crawling with maggots. After selling his soul Faust is nothing, nothing, nothing. Even Goethe himself, for all that he was Goethe, was caught out by this fact. In order to give his work a certain richness he was forced to invent witches' Sabbaths, cavalcades, fifteenth-century doublets. For me, with Roberti, there can be no indulging in flashing swordplay, no indulging in Beelzebub, no indulging in Barbary steeds or naked women. I can only show you damnation itself, shorn of its demoniac pomp. As a result of which you are acting squeamish. But I tell you I knew Roberti, knew him very well. I knew the Brocken was not far off, that I had Faust before me and that Mephisto, albeit invisible, silent, odorless, was clinging to him like his own shadow, like his skin, constantly seeing to it that he honored his signature.

ı: In one respect Goethe is better than you. He doesn't go into all these hideous realistic details. His Faust never took Marguerite to lunch at Suresnes, thank God, and we aren't regaled with that young lady's stupid daydreams.

HE: So what? Do you suppose Marguerite was made of better stuff than Solange? They are virtually one and the same person. If she strikes you as less silly, it is only because she lived in better times. There are far more opportunities for being stupid today than there were five centuries ago. Have a little courage. Hear Roberti's story through to the end. Then write it. If you record my words exactly, you will have set before men's eyes a hell more true and loathsome than any ever imagined before. A hell in keeping with this wretched and overpopulated century of ours. With my own eyes, with my own soul, I have seen a man pass into the eternal flames the way men always pass into them (although nobody knows it), that is to say like a shivering bather who dares not take the plunge but timorously dips in his toe, then his foot, then his leg and finally his whole body. I watched Roberti entering the stream of fire this way. After that, what does anything else matter? It is a fantastic exploit. Not that it's rare, of course. On the contrary it happens very frequently, but as if by some deliberate arrangement there is never anyone there to serve as a witness and bring back the horrific tale. I am inviting you to carve the porch of a cathedral. I am your Pope Julius II. I am offering you the Sistine Chapel before Michelangelo painted his *Last Judgment*. I am providing the subject. All you have to do is work it up. That is the easiest part. And here you are already feeling sickened. Already you've had enough. No! Get out your smelling salts. Sip some aqua vitae. Show a bold front, soldier. There are other things besides fairy tales and epic poetry. It is sometimes necessary to descend into the shadows, explore the caverns underground. Men like Fabrizio or Pierre Bezukhov are not the only heroes of novels, Hamlet and Bérénice are not the only great figures of tragedy. It is up to you to clothe this poor fool like an emperor, with sublime poetry.

1: Roberti clad in imperial purple would look like a comedian or a scarecrow.

HE: Just as most emperors do.

1: But for heaven's sake, men like Nero, Richard III, Oedipus, Agamemnon or King John were of a different stamp from Roberti. Their souls were different too. They were great in their evil. And they were kings. They were born to rule or else they seized power, which is no small matter; it presupposes a grandeur of purpose, mighty concepts, impatience and daring.

HE: Are you going to let official titles impress you? All those men were utter bastards. They only made use of power to commit hideous crimes. Whereas had Roberti been an emperor he would have been Titus or Marcus Aurelius compared with them! I can see no greatness of soul in Richard III or Agamemnon. Nothing but fine raiment. Their soul cowers in a dark corner like an evil little beast, a ferret or a weasel, and it stinks. All these great men you have quoted carry a different smell about them: the nauseating smell of blood. For in the end these gentlemen took a hand in it themselves, *did their own dirty work*. You can say what you like, murder is not very savory. Split skulls, gouged eyes, gaping stomachs with the entrails hanging out, little boys strangled in the Tower of London all require a pretty thick skin, wouldn't you say?

1: But don't you understand anything at all about tragedy? What makes the greatness and horror of Macbeth is precisely the fact that he isn't a butcher. His crimes are superhuman ordeals from which he himself emerges half dead. Take the scene in which we see him after Duncan's murder. He is appalled at himself, he can hardly bear it, he's already in hell. There's evil in all its deadly splendor. Roberti is the flawed product of a worthless century. I don't want to be the poet of chlorosis.

HE: Get along with you, you won't be the poet of chlorosis. Write, with Roberti, the tragedy of our time. He too had his fits of revulsion. You will show him with the knife in his hand, with blood on his shirt and trousers, hating the whole world including himself. I only ask you to listen. Violence, you see, is never far removed from our lives and yet God knows Roberti detested violence. You talk of Macbeth and Richard III but you've forgotten someone else. You've forgotten Hitler. There's a man burdened with crimes and also a tragic figure. You don't see any greatness in him, I imagine, any more than I do. What remains of him after the holocaust? A coarse, debauched-looking face, a stupid book and, to judge from the photographs, a few enigmatic smiles verging on the obsequious. The face of a man who has kissed the Devil's arse and preserved from this contact the stamp of an indelible vulgarity. At the age of fifty Roberti too kissed the Devil's arse. I've told you how it transformed him.

I: Yes, and I was expecting to see a soul led astray and destroyed, a few horrible but mighty deeds. Instead of which, what do you ask me to do? Contemplate a slug, a frightful bourgeois who is constantly afraid and behaves like a skunk. You are describing the loves of a fool and a bastard. It is like watching ants, insects, there's not a trace of humanity about any of it. Even Dietz has disappeared, and I was rather counting on him since he promised to be an engaging character. It's all getting smaller and smaller, we are sinking into nothingness.

HE: You're so impatient!

I: How, impatient? I've been listening to you since lunch. It will soon be dinnertime. Earlier I was hungry, but Roberti has taken away my appetite. What sort of novel do you expect me to get out of his peck on Solange's cheek, his first drive in the Bois, his lunch at Suresnes? There's nothing to it. It's totally null and void. All I could produce is a parody of a novel.

HE: There is sometimes more pith and poetry in parodies than in serious works. Look at Don Quixote, a paragon of a parody, or Tristram Shandy, which has no story at all.

I: Oh, to hell with your comparisons.

HE: Besides, isn't self-parody one of the usual practices of life itself? Life never stops repeating and caricaturing itself. We switch from parody to tragedy without transition. One moment we are Don Quixote, the next we are Orestes or Oedipus. At this point in our story Roberti is still at the parody stage. The average deputy's activities are doubtless a mere string of clichés, of words uttered a hundred thousand times before, of actions and plans made and remade a hundred thousand times by his colleagues and predecessors. Politicians have all been alike since the beginning of time, even if circumstances vary and events never repeat themselves in quite the same way. Similarly nothing is more of a parody, more absurd, than the beginnings of a love affair, when one of the lovers makes plans, arranges dates and believes all he desires from life are the "favors" (meaning carnal enjoyment) of the other. In love the stage of parody stops much later, when the soul has been made captive, when it is flayed and heavy with suffering, when on waking one morning one views within oneself a foreign land, what I shall call if you'll permit me the virgin forest, the savannah of passionate love. One is then like a traveler lost in an unknown continent. Like a being fallen from his rightful place, seeking in the shadows and unable to find it. This is what Roberti will come to. And when this happens I guarantee he will no longer be a parody. Or else he will be one in such a way as to give no more cause for laughter. His parody of love is leading him to real love. It won't be a parody of murder that he commits. And if he is already damned, it is not a parody of damnation.

At the moment you find everything null and void because he is in the no man's land before things really begin. He is filling the empty space lying between the frontiers of the land of Abel and the land of Cain. Or, if you prefer, he is going through one of those dead or half-dead periods with which all our lives are filled, to which we pay no heed and which are the daily bread of existence. He is going through a time which might well hold no significance at all, a time similar to countless others in his life. For him nothing has changed. Solange represents just another mistress; she intrigues and attracts him, certainly, but no differently from thirty previous adventures of his. You may say I'm driveling but here lies the lesson, it is here that in the light of subsequent events we can observe the passing of the Devil. Roberti offers us proof that, in its beginnings and throughout a long part of its progress, a man's damnation resembles his general tenor of life and the man himself. The slope down to hell is so gentle, so imperceptible that one fails to appreciate one is going downhill. Hell nearly always begins in a familiar guise and the Devil first appears to us as the image of our own face in the mirror.

If you write the novel, I believe it is over these early stages that you will have to take the greatest care. It will be difficult to convey this impression of emptiness and nothingness, this poverty of feeling, this aridity of soul, this parody of life. You will have to go out of your way to be neither heartless nor despairing nor, above all, trivial. I suppose the great pitfall of parody is banality, and nothing is harder than caricature. One must prevent oneself from getting carried away by enthusiasm and adding a line too many. I wish you joy of it. Will you be able to show Roberti open to all the winds that blow like a shed in the middle of a plain? Will you be able to show the utter absurdity of it all without falling into platitudes? This particular kind of absurdity will be terribly hard to describe since it isn't the kind that men like Monnier or Flaubert loved and re-created. It's an almost etymological absurdity. The paralysis of a hypnotized animal. The bewildered and terrified feeling of an animal which glimpses its own destruction. It is not for nothing that we say "the mark of the beast" when we talk of the Devil. And now here's something to please you. The preliminaries are over. Look where our walk has brought us! Here is the house where Roberti used to live.

The setting sun shining down the Rue Oudinot made us screw up our eyes, for the gray cliffs of the Rue Vaneau had accustomed us to a gentler light. The building didn't exactly stir my imagination. It was one of those tall, somber, heavy and solid houses such as were beloved of the Baron Haussmann, who scattered them all over Paris, thereby turning it, alas, into a Second Empire city. Roberti's apartment was on the second or principal floor, adorned with a long balcony running all along it. There decidedly wasn't much to be got from this sooty but majestic façade, behind which six or seven generations of rich Parisians had dwelt and which was already beginning to look faintly historic. Who could have lived there? People leaving no trace, no achievements behind them, whose hearts had not been big enough nor minds keen enough to ensnare fame, bourgeois families which had possessed nothing but money and passions now forever extinct. I am always acutely conscious of the ludicrous quality of the past. Evidence of the futility of the dead, when not offset by art or beauty, makes me sad. Seen through our eyes, the second half of the nineteenth century is the most sinister period of all, for those with power were devoid of taste. All that remains is the squalor of their ostentation.

I glanced through the open entrance. There were columns and marble in the vestibule, treated in the grandiose-bourgeois style, and it smelled of stone like a cathedral. I was overcome by a deep feeling of tedium. In any case the Rue Oudinot is not beautiful. Here and there it seems to have come down in the world: ugly houses built of cheap materials have recently been erected. It was a long time since I had passed that way; I had forgotten how it looked. The one pleasing thing about it was its calm, which is unusual: indeed the street isn't long and soon merges with the Boulevard des Invalides, which evokes the sea, so wide and bright does it appear.

Contrary to my expectations I felt no desire to linger there. I had thought that, in default of seeing and talking with Mme. Roberti, the building would at least arouse some emotion in me, react on my heart, serve as an intermediary between what had actually happened and what I could make of it from my friend's tale. Even the thought that one of our characters was still living behind those walls was no help. I regretted the detour we had made on my foolish insistence. Roberti had clearly picked this building purely for its respectability. But these surroundings he had known so well and to which he had grown attached out of habit, these places he had ceased to see by dint of living in them, told me no more than might any other corner of Paris. The intermediary had failed. Such disappointments are frequent.

I have curious reactions. Sometimes, with me, boredom turns into despair. To be honest, this despair isn't very deep. But it can happen that, instead of the pleasure or instruction I was expecting from some encounter, a wave of hopeless boredom suddenly breaks over me and since it is I as a rule who have got myself into these situations I don't know how to get out of them. So I subside into gloom and despondency; I am like a rabbit caught in a snare. This is how I felt in the Rue Oudinot. Perhaps also our reflections on hell had disposed me to find nothing to my liking, least of all this building in which a man had watched his soul gradually go to perdition. However that may be, I wanted to get away from it as quickly as possible. We had been silent for two or three minutes.

HE: Well?

I: I've seen enough, learned enough. Let's go.

HE: Do you still want to go up and see Agnes?

I: No. Funny, isn't it?

HE: Not really. I didn't think you would.

I: You didn't think I would? Tell me why. I'm intrigued. I had no such idea myself.

HE: Oh, I know you. You're a sort of hermit. You suffer from any contact with the outside world. You fear it. Everything flays your sensibility. You prefer inventing to looking. It gives you more trouble but does you less harm.

I: What's this you're saying?

HE: The naked truth.

I: You really think so?

HE: I don't think, I know it.

I: So, according to you, I'm a bookworm, a philosopher in an ivory tower, a frog, a cold-blooded animal afraid of everything and fleeing to the bottom of its pond at the slightest disturbance? You think I am the perfect example of a sensitive plant, an owl whose eyes are hurt by the daylight and who cares for nothing but the disused and empty barn it has made its home? I live in lonely silence, ever preferring boredom to distraction, long hours of cloudy dreaming to rich and rewarding talk with friends? I wallow in gloom and the dull monotony of overfamiliar surroundings, while waiting for inspiration to well up out of all these moral or emotional fetters, watching the drop of ink as it oozes from the tip of my pen to spread in a shower of words across the paper? Is that how you see me?

HE: Well . . .

I: And what do I do when I have laid my daily clutch of written pages? Throw myself into other routines, repeat each day the same trivial comments to the nine people who normally form my circle. I know these nine people will always be exactly the same, that nothing can ever occur to upset them, that they think more or less as I do, that they are calm and tranquil, hating violence and exaggeration, that they stand like a bulwark between myself and the world at large. I am so acutely sensitive that the sounds of the world have to be muted, filtered, exquisitely refined before they reach my ears, or else I might easily go mad. I wrest from the world around me only a millionth, a thousand millionth part, an infinitely minute grain of matter; yet this tiny drop of fuel is enough to start off my little music box. Enough? Even too much. I am a ship in full sail. The faintest, flimsiest breath of wind sets me in motion. Have I interpreted correctly?

HE: Yes, yes, that's it.

I: That is really your idea of me?

HE: Lord, yes, more or less.

I: Well, you're not wrong.

HE: I also think your sensitivity doesn't prevent you from being insensitive. I think that, like most artists, you have a heart of stone, that few things really affect you deeply and that you are consoled as easily as you are upset.

I: Wait, there you're going a bit too far!

HE: In short I see you as having a sensitive soul under the hide of a rhinoceros.

I: Or the opposite: the soul of a rhinoceros under a sensitive skin.

HE: Possibly.

I: Are we discussing me or Roberti?

HE: Which interests you most, him or yourself?

I: Myself, of course. Even so we must take things in order. Let's get done with Roberti first. Then, if you like, we'll fix a date and I'll spend the next two years talking about myself. It's a subject on which I am exceptionally well informed. You said that the preliminaries were over. Is this another empty boast or are we at last going to get down to the horrors of love? I warn you, if Roberti and Solange don't go to bed together within the next five minutes, I'm off and you won't see me again for a year.

HE: Very well. They go to bed. So there! Does *that* please you?

I: No. You're not going to skip over this event in one sentence. You're going to tell me everything. How it took place and whether it was a success or a flop.

HE: It was a flop, obviously. Sinister, creaking, painful, ludicrous, pitiful.

ɪ: How discouraging this Roberti is. Well . . . ?

ʜᴇ: He had arranged everything for this great day. As I've told you, he had been waiting till his imagination was completely inflamed and his desire had become almost intolerable. He had picked a Saturday afternoon, when Solange didn't have to work. He had proposed fetching her in his car and they had agreed to meet at two-thirty at a corner of the Avenue Daumesnil a hundred yards from the Mignot house. Roberti drove up at two-twenty-five, his heart beating fit to burst, not on account of Solange but because of the decision he had taken and the revelation this afternoon was to bring him. His pounding heart worried him. He listened carefully to his whole being, rather perturbed by such agitation. He knew how excessively impressionable he was and mistrusted himself. The idea of a fiasco which had been lurking ever since breakfast gradually began to take hold of him. His chest felt tight. He was faintly trembling. Viewed objectively all this is rather attractive, don't you think? So much excitement when one is fifty and a success in life, with thirty similar experiences behind one! With every fresh adventure Roberti had of course had fears, palpitations, violent stirrings of the emotions, but this time they were really excessive. It never crossed his mind that the explanation for such unwonted excitement might possibly be love with a capital L, the love he had never really known despite several fair or flattering successes. No, he never told himself that this forthcoming encounter represented something unique and extraordinary in his life and that was why he was so worked up. He was a hundred miles from imagining that his heart might be at stake in this affair. He tried to recall the agitation he had felt while waiting for other women, Odile for example, and took comfort from evoking these old thrills. But can one trust the memory of one's feelings? It is just as unreliable as the memories of the body. Have you noticed how the body remembers its pleasures far more clearly than its pains? This is no doubt because the former are much less varied. There is an infinite wealth of possible pains between the toes and the hair, whereas I can count hardly more than three or four pleasures in the world: love, food, sport, relaxation. It is further curious to note that in memory pleasures are enhanced while pains diminish.

ɪ: Yes, yes, that's true. When I was seven I ate *pâté de foie gras* for the first time in my life. I remember it today as a most stupendous event. *Foie gras* today never tastes like the *foie gras* of my childhood and yet they're the same.

ʜᴇ: You must have gone in for some kind of sport as well. Remember the marvelous lassitude of one's limbs, the feelings that one's skin was breathing. They were unforgettable sensations. Not only unforgettable but also they become magnified the further they recede in time. I won't enlarge on memories of physical love; they speak for themselves.

I: What's the connection between all this and Roberti on tenterhooks in the Avenue Daumesnil?

HE: This: that his memory deceived him as to his reactions in similar circumstances in the past; it enhanced them, augmented them. He told himself he had been overwhelmed in the same way by Odile, Jacqueline, Hélène, Irène, Monique and the rest, and that all things considered Solange didn't excite him as much as these ghosts had done in their time. Now this was an error, an optical illusion. If there existed a Geiger counter to locate love, it would no doubt have remained silent with Odile, Jacqueline or Irène, but it would certainly have been ticking on the day Roberti waited for Solange in the Avenue Daumesnil.

He was completely deluded as to the causes of his excitement. He persuaded himself that he was building it up merely for his own pleasure (or pain), that it was a purely physical manifestation. He accused his body, and his body alone, of being responsible for his agitation and the thoughts spinning round in his head. This body, with its sensitive and constantly twitching nerves, had its own laws and they were always mysterious.

"It's my body that's in love," he thought, "not my heart. I know myself. It always happens like this. As soon as I've had the girl, my one idea will be how to get rid of her. I am a seasoned trooper, a veteran who has gone over the top thirty times, who can boast the military cross and ten mentions in dispatches but who is just as afraid the thirty-first time as the first." He was in fact gripped by desire and apprehension, just as a soldier or an animal is gripped by fear or the desire to flee. What part does the soul play in these impulses? None, or very little. It accepts them, that's all.

I: Or doesn't accept. There lies the whole problem. There are cowardly bodies with courageous hearts and vice versa.

HE: How do you mean? Your objection is valid in an absolute sense but totally inadequate in this instance. Love isn't war. In love one runs no risk in following the panics of the body with one's soul. They are short-lived and of little consequence. Resisting fear and resisting the turmoil of desire are two analogous activities but they have nothing in common so far as the results are concerned. A soldier who lets his fear get the better of him courts disgrace and often death. A man who allows himself to be deliciously thrown out of control by his beating heart risks nothing. Since he aimed at making Solange his mistress, Roberti had no reason to try and control himself. Nor was it within his power. And he positively reveled in his turmoil. There was even a twinge of pain in his pleasure which made it exquisite. Alone in his car he oscillated between joy and despair. Just as his prey was within his grasp he began having second thoughts about the whole business. He told himself that if for some reason Solange stood him up, he would feel at once bitterly disappointed and acutely relieved. Edouard was like that: always prepared to give something up just as he was about to attain it. Success and all the obligations it would entail terrified him. This was a deep-rooted and little-known trait of his character—one which he hardly acknowledged even to himself—yet it often made itself apparent in many spheres of his life and perhaps explains why he never enjoyed a more brilliant career in politics. But I'm digressing, I fear.

I: Yes, in your usual way you are. I know that fiction is the art of digression, but carried to the point you do it becomes inhuman. So Solange keeps the date.

HE: She does. At two-thirty on the dot. She had guessed that Roberti liked punctuality and didn't want to miss one second of his company, which to her was so rare and precious. She had walked out on her parents and Valentin, who had pulled long faces: indeed they were in the habit of spending Saturday afternoons all together, devoting themselves to useful, agreeable and unimportant activities. Between the house and the appointed corner she had glanced back a number of times to make sure Valentin wasn't following her. He was quite capable of it.

When she got into the car, Roberti's palpitations didn't subside. On the contrary the sight of this woman he so greatly coveted and whose arrival made it impossible to go back on his program only served to increase his agitation. He always found intense difficulty in suggesting taking a woman to an hotel. He never knew quite how to set about it. An hotel is a formidable object. It leaves no room for ambiguities, whereas love in its beginnings, while you are still feeling your way, finding out about each other, has such a need of ambiguities, clouds, misty backgrounds and twilight. The hotel casts a crude and immodest light on love. It reduces it to desire, to the basic function; it makes it offensive. Impossible to pretend one is going there in all innocence, as one might go anywhere for a bit of quiet, to avoid prying eyes and enjoy a little privacy and necking undisturbed. No. One goes to the hotel for the "act." No more and no less. This revolted Roberti's sense of delicacy. He loathed the idea of passing for a cynical and practical man (which at heart, of course, he was). He would have far preferred to play the romantic and ethereal lover, to lead his conquest imperceptibly to the final consummation without a word being said about it. He envied bachelors. If only he had had one of those convenient and reassuring bachelor apartments where one can take ladies on the plausible pretext of a quiet drink or a heart-to-heart talk! Without counting that the hotel puts a man on his mettle. When he has gone to such lengths to get there he has to go into action or forfeit his honor, even if he has lost all his nerve en route.

1: How absurd! At his age! The more so as women know perfectly well what's what; they aren't in the least shocked at the suggestion of spending a couple of hours in a quiet corner; as a rule they are impatient for the gentleman to make up his mind to this important step. Women are just as cynical in their thoughts as men. This is a detail one always forgets if one is a man. The word "hotel" doesn't scare them a bit.

HE: At any rate it didn't scare Solange, who had naturally had time during the past week to wonder just how Roberti was going to set about organizing their lovemaking. She had more than once pictured the hotel. Remember what I said earlier on about her previous little adventures. For her the hotel was no alarming novelty, no terrible and mysterious place where girls have frantically to resist being dragged. She regarded it merely as a convenience, the inevitable refuge for illicit couples. Moreover she lacked imagination. For her the word did not evoke a fate worse than death. At the most a clandestine act, rather daring and not without allure, like going in secret to see a risqué movie. She also told herself, of course, that it would be an extraordinary and intoxicating experience and that she would preserve an undying memory of it in which the chosen surroundings would play an important part. She too felt deeply stirred as she got into the car. Her instinct whispered that the moment had come when the seal would be set on her love forever.

1: How did the jovial Edouard set about telling her that this wasn't going to be like all the other times, that they were now going to get down to essentials?

HE: Well, the jovial Edouard allowed himself a few minutes to recover his breath and his wits. Solange said: "Don't let's stay here; my brother or parents might walk by at any moment. What shall we do today?" He rather irritably started the car and asked with some embarrassment: "Haven't you had enough, my angel, of going for drives?

Wherever we stop, whether in a street or a wood, there are always twenty-five people watching us. It's horrible. I thought today we might possibly go and *hide our happiness somewhere.*" He was taking the plunge, as you can see. "Hide our happiness somewhere" was an inspiration. He said it very well, with just the right tone of serious banter. Besides, the phrase was cleverly chosen. It left it open for him to go smartly into reverse if he saw Solange taking fright.

ɪ: But she didn't take fright. On the contrary she said to herself "At last!"

ʜᴇ: I don't know what she said to herself but I do know what she said to him. It was so unexpected, so surprising, that Roberti was dumbfounded; he felt all the initiative being taken out of his hands and another fear asserted itself: that he might fail to rise to the occasion! He had been expecting a meek and timid little lamb and now he suddenly discovered his lamb was a bacchante.

ɪ: Oh come on, you're getting me all on edge! What did she say that was so sexy?

ʜᴇ: Don't worry, it was nothing sexy. Just a brief remark, quite insignificant when taken out of its context; but in the circumstances it implied that its speaker was not, as had hitherto been supposed, a little bird paralyzed by love, an ecstatic and cooing female who had completely abdicated her free will; she was—oh wonder!—a woman with a heart, with ideas and conscious hopes. Roberti had never suspected this. He had gone along with the notion of having an impersonal mistress thinking and acting only through him. He had anticipated defenses to be stormed, a feeble resistance which he would have overcome without much ado, affronted modesty, in short "carrying on." He had imagined a terrified victim to be coerced. He hadn't foreseen the new Solange who revealed herself with this remark.

ɪ: Are you going to tell me what it was, yes or no? What a bastard you are!

ʜᴇ: "Aha, so the great day has arrived!"

ɪ: What great day?

ʜᴇ: That's what she said.

ɪ: No! How disconcerting women are!

ʜᴇ: Aren't they? And Solange said it with a knowing and satisfied smile which even held a hint of mockery. I must tell you that she immediately added: "It makes me very happy, darling." Whereupon she tucked her arm inside Roberti's. By now he was completely bewildered, wondering if he hadn't been mistaken all along about this girl and trying to adjust his values at top speed, struggling to adapt himself to this lighthearted creature sitting beside him, this creature capable of joking at so solemn a moment, carefree and ironic and laughing, even faintly mocking.

"Where are you taking me, my dear sir?" she continued, still smiling. She could hardly have been more accommodating, more willing. But such equanimity didn't at all suit Roberti, who was fearfully thinking how he would now have to reckon with this unsuspected personality who was going to be demanding, draw comparisons and expect more than he might be able to give her. To his horror he saw Solange *coming to life*. The notion of a possible failure thereby gained in substance, if I may so put it. Only a few moments before it had been just a vague apprehension; now it was almost an obsession. However, "I'm taking you to a quiet and shady spot," he replied, "far from the madding crowd, where there will be just you and me."

ı: What an extraordinary way of expressing oneself!

HE: It was his own way. That's how he talked. It was at once natural and mannered. He never said anything quite simply. He gave even the most banal remarks a precious or literary twist, not so much to impress his listeners as to please himself, as a sort of private luxury. People who read a lot are often like that. In their talk they constantly quote well-known authors with an undertone of parody and without naming their sources, as if the whole of life were already described in books and every event were just an excuse for referring to them. I've noticed you do it yourself now and then, without being aware of it.

ı: *I* talk like Roberti? But that's dreadful!

HE: No, you don't talk like him but you sometimes display that trick of people whose brains are stuffed with countless snatches of quotations and which consists of describing feelings, acts or observations more or less in the same words as writers have used, as if life were just an endless and faintly comic repetition of what has been said in books, as if nothing really mattered since it has already taken place and so been recorded.

ı: I promise I'll be careful in future.

HE: But no, why should you? It's often amusing and stimulating for those in the know. I love it when for instance you say: "A sight easier to imagine than to describe," or "Here's a little work of my own making."

ı: You appall me. You're the Devil incarnate!

HE: There you are! That's just the kind of thing Roberti would have said.

ı: Oh God! I'll be afraid to open my mouth.

HE: That's all right by me. Fine! I'll get on with my story. Edouard was at the wheel with Solange's arm tucked into his. She laid her head on his shoulder in a pretty little show of affection which put the lid on his embarrassment. It was at once a gesture of abandon and possession. He felt trapped, at the mercy of an unknown adversary who, by some incomprehensible sleight of hand, had snatched control of the proceedings from him. It had needed but a word, a smile! That is the way of sensitive and impressionable natures. Solange, for her part, didn't appear in the least excited. She was the image of confidence and happiness. She snuggled up against Roberti but her warmth and perfume stirred him so little that he began to feel anxious and wonder if his imagination, which was subsiding so rapidly, wasn't going to play a dirty trick on him and lead to his humiliation.

He had arranged to take her to a house in the Rue d'Argenson where they knew his ways. It was a discreet and unobtrusive establishment situated in a street which, as Roberti knew, hardly any of his acquaintances ever visited. Since he was driving fairly fast and it was a Saturday, when there is less traffic about, they soon arrived.

I: Wait, wait. Even on Saturdays it's quite a trek from the Avenue Daumesnil to the Rue d'Argenson. I can't imagine Mlle. Solange keeping the same position the whole way. And I can't see Roberti, so concerned about his good name, putting up with a blonde head on his shoulder for very long.

HE: You let nothing escape you. Do we really have to descend to such petty details?

I: We do. Otherwise you produce a novel for anaemics. We don't want that, do we? We don't want to be like Marcel Prévost. We are writing for red-blooded, robust readers who demand a literature stuffed with proteins. So go on, I'm listening.

HE: Well, while Roberti navigated the *terrae incognitae* of the Avenue Daumesnil, the Place de la Bastille and the Boulevard des Filles-du-Calvaire, he wasn't unduly disturbed by Solange's pretty head on his right shoulder. But he told himself that when they reached a more civilized part of the city he would have to find some decent way of making her revert to a more seemly pose. Near the Place de la République he had an inspiration. He began to shift about and feel in his pockets, and finally asked her to light him a cigarette, giving her the pack.

I: A nice touch. Bravo!

HE: It is a charming moment full of intimacy and complicity when a young woman lights you a cigarette in a car. Solange took one or two puffs and then gracefully placed the cigarette in Edouard's mouth, which gave him a satisfying sense of possession. This ravishing creature sitting beside him was looking after him like a beautiful Arab slave girl ministering to her lord's wishes. Cigarettes play their part in love; this shouldn't be overlooked!

I: But we aren't overlooking it!

HE: At the end of the Rue d'Argenson Roberti carefully parked his car quite a way from the hotel but not too far, so as not to be exposed overlong on open ground to the fire of looks from passers-by. His legs felt like putty and he was desperately wondering if this adventure wasn't turning into a grisly chore. He carefully glanced all round, in case any familiar figure should loom up. Suddenly his heart lurched. Who was it walking thirty yards ahead of him, easily recognizable from behind?

I: I'm asking *you*.

HE: Gallardin.

I: Who is that?

HE: One of his parliamentary colleagues. A supporter of the extreme right wing, vicious as the itch and malicious as only members of extremist minorities know how to be since, having never enjoyed power or responsibilities, they don't know the force of words, say anything that comes into their heads and play at being *enfants terribles*. These sort of people are to be feared. Always ready to use the vilest methods to discredit their political rivals. Caught out with a girl by Gallardin in the Rue d'Argenson, what a disaster! If Gallardin were to turn round, you could be sure that all Paris would know the next day that Roberti, that irreproachable figure, was just a dirty old man. Not to mention the weekly for which he wrote editorials in what is known as a "truculent" style.

I: What weekly?

HE: Don't you read the papers?

I: Not much.

HE: I must admit the one in question is more of a private and confidential kind, but it is quoted in the press reviews and widely read in Parliament and at editorial desks. It is called *The Firing Squad*. Rather a good title, don't you think? In short, Roberti instantly anticipated the worst. He told himself that *The Squad*'s gossip column would reverberate with this every week until he died. He remembered poor Salengro, the Popular Front minister driven to suicide by a press campaign of the extreme right. "M. Roberti, whom I sometimes run across in the Rue d'Argenson . . ." Gallardin would repeat twenty times a day with biting irony, on the floor of the Chamber or in the lobbies. And that is the way careers are ruined, that is how reputations are lost. Roberti, always so prudent and timorous, hadn't deserved such rotten luck. In his shock and vexation he let go of Solange's arm.

I: So he was holding it? It's scarcely believable, it's out of character.

HE: He had probably taken it automatically, or else felt that he couldn't do otherwise, that it was a ritual gesture, that a man and woman going to make love for the first time can't just walk down the street as if they hardly knew each other. At any rate he was holding this pretty arm leaning on his own, and he dropped it. What to do? He didn't want to hurt Solange by appearing to take cover. There were still about twelve yards to go before the hotel entrance. Fervently he hoped Gallardin wouldn't turn round, at the same time reproaching himself for putting too much longing into this hope. Thoughts as intense as his at this moment, an apprehension so acute, couldn't fail to be emitting waves in front of him. Roberti believed in psychic influences, in telepathy; he was almost certain that with his ill-considered fears he had already alerted the malignant mind of his colleague. He could find nothing better to do than lower his head, cover his eyes with his hand and hurry on. It was like running the gauntlet. Twenty seconds to go before he was safely home. I assure you those twenty seconds seemed interminable. Luckily Gallardin continued to walk indifferently ahead. Even so, as he dived into the hotel entrance Roberti couldn't resist the temptation to glance up. It was just then that Gallardin turned. Roberti had time to get a clear glimpse of his preoccupied air. The expression of someone deep in thought, who sees things without registering them. This relieved him but didn't altogether appease his anxiety. Later Gallardin might recall the incident, be suddenly flooded with light and cry: "Why, that was Roberti!" However, the damage was less grave than might have been feared. Solange completely misinterpreted this sudden panic. When Roberti pressed forward she thought desire was lending him wings and felt most flattered by this brutal tribute to her charms.

I: Do you think Gallardin turned round because Roberti was thinking about him too intensely?

HE: Surely. But I also think it was because Roberti had spotted him that Gallardin didn't see him.

I: All very subtle and contradictory.

HE: Subtle perhaps, but not contradictory. I think, in fact, that in this instance Roberti's thoughts did him a disservice and at the same time protected him. That is to say they alerted Gallardin by their violence but also, for a few seconds, forbade him to turn round. There was a sort of séance of hypnotism. I am also convinced that Roberti's frantic longing not to be recognized prevented Gallardin from really seeing him. Anyway, everything passed off as if Gallardin had noticed nothing. He never made the faintest allusion to the Rue d'Argenson: *The Squad* never published the remotest item about it. And after all, there's nothing so very extraordinary in that. We constantly have occasion to observe the power of thought. It bursts from the brain like a cannon shell. It is a third arm, a gigantic arm with which we can tap the shoulders of people a hundred yards or miles away. Sometimes it is also a smokescreen which makes us invisible. Thoughts concentrated solely on one desire sometimes by their very existence fulfill this desire. I know hundreds of tales of fugitives who have eluded their pursuers when they were literally trapped and at bay. At such moments their thoughts were so intense that they acted like Gyges' ring. They cloaked them the way its ink cloaks an octopus.

I: Your worst enemy, you know, is your passion for images. You pile up fifteen metaphors to illustrate the smallest argument. Of course there's truth in what you say, but couldn't you express it more economically? I needed no smokescreens or octopus ink to get your meaning. These comparisons are threadbare. You ought to reread good writers like Mérimée, Voltaire or Jules Renard. At heart you suffer from verbosity. I never noticed it so much as today.

HE: I know perfectly well you needed no ink or smoke, but I did. I pursue ideas with words or images. That's how my mind works. I can't help being long-winded and involved, bristling with metaphors (new or old). As for verbosity, I don't pretend to anything else. I'm not the writer. You are. Why should I force myself to be brief? *I* don't have to please the public. I confine myself to providing you with the raw material in bulk. It's for you to sort it out, like a historian extracting his story from a mass of tedious old documents.

I: Another comparison!

HE: Really, I admire my patience! You spend your whole time insulting me yet I go on telling you your story, building up your novel for you, doing all your work. Such ingratitude and malice are disgusting!

I: Come off it, you're delighted! You won't often find a listener like me, attentive, tireless, ready to listen without flinching for ten to twelve hours on end! For it strikes me this is going to last till midnight.

HE: A least.

I: Instead of taking offense, you'd do better to get on with our visit to hell. Try to give me facts if you want to be helpful. Events. Give me the material for a novel.

HE: In everything I've already told you there's enough for a whole saga, a mighty river.

I: No. A lake. A wide expanse of foul and stagnant water, sluggish, black and viscous, covered with slime, pulsating with hordes of revolting aquatic creatures down below, a slow and mysterious life of protozoa, tadpoles and sticklebacks.

HE: Ah! That's not such a bad result! Our novel will be a deep and poetic lake like the Lake of Carucedo, below which lies the old town of Luiserne which the geographers do not know. That suits me fine, a lake into which the reader descends like a deep-sea diver. . . . The Paris of 1955 lies intact, untouched, at the bottom of our lake, entangled in the weeds of memory, petrified, overgrown with limestone deposits, phantomish, pallid, ghostly; in its streets drive phantom cars which hoot in silence at spectral passers-by. Roberti is a specter, Solange is a specter, Gallardin is a specter. We lean over the lake and see them deep down below the water. How beautiful! Do you realize we are about to discover unknown literary territory? We are inventing submarine literature!

I: Oh please! Submarine literature! You're raving. Just stick to modestly telling your story instead of posing as the founder of a new school. There's nothing more ridiculous than the founder of a school, unless it's his pupils. Look around you: we have in France today about half a dozen founders of schools. Aren't they too comic for words?

HE: I must confess . . .

I: If you have time one day, go and leaf through the 1930 collection of the *Nouvelles Littéraires* in the National Library. You will see who were the master thinkers then and what is left of them today. In 1990 the master thinkers of 1960 will seem as ludicrous as those of 1930 appear to us now. The new novel will have become the old novel, a baroque antique object like Gallé vases or Lalique glass. Something for collectors of curios. What is fashionable becomes unfashionable. Your submarine literature, let me tell you, is a good joke. All literature is submarine insofar as it is written in the past or imperfect tense. Proust, for instance, seems to me a submarine writer of greater stuff than you. He explored oceans. Your lake is the one in the Bois de Boulogne, which they dredge every twenty years and bring up pianos.

HE: You make me laugh. You're a wolf of letters. When some poor lamb of a "new novel" writer passes your door, you fling yourself on him with a howl and bury your fangs in his neck. Why? He's done you no harm. Everyone's got to live.

1: Why must everyone live? I don't see the necessity, as Diderot said.

HE: Ten years ago you couldn't be sarcastic enough about Sartre's novels.

1: Because they were bad and badly written. Don't you agree?

HE: That still doesn't prevent Sartre from doing very well today and being more widely read than you are.

1: Now that's an intelligent and high-minded remark. My compliments. By that token Sartre will never achieve such big runs as Dumas. You're beginning to get me down. We're way off the subject once again.

HE: Yes, yes, that's just what I was saying: you only get excited about questions of literature. You shout and wave your arms and flash your eyes. It's really very comic! A literary wolf, that's what you are. A lone, wicked, hungry wolf who doesn't play the wolf's game for, not content with crunching up sheep and attacking shepherds, you even bite your fellow wolves. Even old three-hundred-years-dead she-wolves like Mme. de La Fayette don't escape your wrath.

1: I don't look on the four or five women writers of our day as she-wolves. They are fat lambs with tender flesh. They rouse my appetite whenever I see them. Similarly Sartre is a fat sheep. A big black sheep who has begotten dozens of little black sheep which frighten the white lambs, but that still doesn't make wolves of them.

HE: You agree, then, that you're a wolf.

1: Certainly, and it's to my credit. I loathe the literary dogs who have their dinners guaranteed to the end of their days because they perform the tricks their public expects of them or do the degrading work demanded by their masters. I have no chain, no kennel and no friends. When I go out hunting each morning, I never know whether I shall bring back a pittance for my family that evening. But I prefer this life to any other. I have chosen it and it suits me. I like the risks, the freedom, the discredit, the bad reputation. I'm not tied to anyone or anything. Everything I have has been gained at swordpoint. Long live wolves, by God! There are six or seven wolves in Paris and I take it as high praise to be numbered among them. We wolves live to be old and gaunt with gleaming eyes and mangy fur. On summer evenings we sit on our backsides on the river banks, pensively watching the dead dogs float by on the current, while nature sings melodies which we alone can hear.

HE: You don't appear to have done so badly for a wolf! One of these days you'll be elected to the Académie and we shall have the pleasure

196

of seeing a wolf in a green coat with gold braid down to the navel and a cocked hat between his velvety ears.

ɪ: And why not? One of my ancestors disguised himself as a grandmother.

ʜᴇ: You're an artful devil! You've an infernal gift for turning everything to your advantage.

ɪ: There's always some truth in what people say, even in their jokes and lies. Especially when the jokes have a touch of poetry. Where there is poetry, there is truth. And I think that, without meaning to, I put a touch of poetry into my description of a wolf's life. I exaggerated, of course, but it wasn't wholly fanciful. Besides, it was you who began this talk about wolves. Ideas like that never come to me spontaneously.

ʜᴇ: Like hell they don't!

ɪ: I should like to make a modest suggestion. Something that will surprise you.

ʜᴇ: What?

ɪ: Let's get back to Solange and Roberti. I trust you haven't entirely forgotten those two? You know, the middle-aged deputy and the typist? We were discussing them just now. You rather felt like telling me their story. We had muddled along as far as the Rue d'Argenson. We were even, if my memory serves, entering an hotel. I'd rather like to know what we are doing there.

ʜᴇ: Supposing we skip that episode? It isn't very interesting. Roberti was too worked up. His performance was worse than bad, although not quite hopeless.

ɪ: Oh no! None of these changes of policy. I'm not going to let you start choosing what to tell and what not to. You've kept me walking ever since the Jardin des Plantes. You owe me some compensation. You're going to sketch me a pretty picture in the style of Crébillon *fils* or the novels of the fifties, when this sort of scene was described down to the last detail. I regard that as my just reward. I've been listening to you so long and with such patience that I've a right to some recreation.

ʜᴇ: Do you want obscenities?

ɪ: Oh, "obscenities" is a big word. No, but I'd like some data, a few sighs, a small dose of sex.

ʜᴇ: But that's of no interest at all.

ɪ: No psychological or artistic interest, but entertaining.

ʜᴇ: I've a horror of smut. Besides, the subject hardly lends itself. This first embrace was very dismal, without the slightest thrill, at least on Roberti's side.

ɪ: I'm not asking you to be smutty but to paint me an erotic scene.

Something sad and moist and heavy. Something you will fill with the heartrending poetry of ill-matched love. I'm not preventing you from being solemn about it. That would make it all the more moving.

HE: It's no good. Solemn pornography is detestable. And as a literary method it strikes me as highly dishonest. It seems to me a novelist has simply the right to say of his characters: "They made love." I'll allow him to add "well" or "badly." Everything else is pandering to the public, sensationalism and dirt. The reader is perfectly familiar with the details. There's absolutely no need to remind him of them. He hasn't forgotten them, you may be sure.

I: As far as literature goes, I agree. But just now we are talking man to man. We must enjoy ourselves occasionally. You've been stuffing me with psychology, I'm choked up with it. I need to relax. I swear I won't put one detail in the book.

HE: What I find interesting to describe in a love scene is not the movements of the bodies but the movement of the souls. Damn it, we're not naturalists! Nor doctors. We are students of the human heart. Everything that goes on outside the heart is boring and unimportant. Hardly worth mentioning. I'll gladly tell you what went on in Roberti's soul as he made love to Solange for the first time, because that is curious and instructive, because it sheds light on Man. But don't ask anything else of me. If it's diversion you're after, read *The Hazards of the Hearth*, *The Love Life of a Hospodar*, *Fanny Hill*, *Felicia* or *Philosophy in the Boudoir*. They are fairly detailed and thorough works, I believe. I would never dare try to compete with them. When I happen on some rather elaborate description in a modern novel, I yawn. It does nothing to stir my imagination. Far from it. I feel as if I was being treated to a lecture on the sexual habits of lobsters or locusts, a deadly topic if ever there was one. Besides, it has become hackneyed.

I: For God's sake!

HE: When Roberti entered the fateful room, he felt ice-cold. He had fallen into a bored and cloudy reverie. He told himself the ceremonial indispensable to a first occasion would set the seal on his humiliation. Solange, on the other hand, was gay as a lark, languorous and not the least abashed. Her beauty and glamor were for Roberti a cause for added despondency. She looked at him in a way which implied how she was expecting great things of him. He tried to warm himself up by declaring how much he loved her, desired her, had longed for this moment, was overwhelmed. But it was little help. The fire was quite dead and nothing could be done to reignite it. Ideas remote from the business on hand floated through his head. He could distinctly see his study, his colleagues on the Arts and Letters Committee; he thought up ingenious arguments for the passing of a law which was dear to his heart and so on. In short his soul was eluding him just when he would have liked to keep it concentrated and attentive. He tried to call it back and pin it down but this was even more disastrous, for then he could only think of the wretched figure he was about to cut. His wherewithal now seemed the most ridiculous thing in the world, both awful and lamentable. What about Solange's beauty? you will ask. But beauty is of little avail when one is subject to these violent lapses of the imagination. Beauty is nothing. On the contrary I believe some imperfection would do more to revive desire in that it would restore confidence by depreciating the partner.

Roberti tried desperately to play for time and postpone a consummation he was beginning to dread. He put on an admirable show of passion which merely made the girl more ardent than ever. She had, I repeat, no imagination. She was excited of course, but her emotions followed a normal pattern. She wasn't sidetracked or undermined by hypersensitive nerves. Added to which she was by nature of a highly amorous disposition and had no need of extensive preliminaries to arouse her. Roberti, who was well aware of this, grew increasingly cold and detached. He was taking part in something from which he felt completely divorced. He was an outsider. "His heart was no longer in it." Where was his heart? Miles away! He thought nostalgically of what he was missing at this moment. Instead of being with this dreary doll, he might have been with his dear Agnes, who understood him so well, or with his fine boys or at the opening of the Courbevoie Museum, making a speech, shaking hands and *enjoying himself,* instead of which here he was stupidly saddled with a mistress he would have to get rid of. What a bore! We think we are grabbing some pleasure only to find it turn into an ordeal. A wave of discouragement swept over him. An infinite lethargy. No trick seemed worth the trying. With dazzling speed Solange was turning into a complete stranger who meant less than nothing, an object evoking at best a chilly admiration. She had no more effect on him than a Madonna by Botticelli or a statue by Houdon. He found her sighs, the tremors running through her body, the fond or intimate gestures she ventured as embarrassing as the tactless or stupid questions of some fool to which one is obliged by good manners to reply. At the same time he raged against himself and, so to speak, castigated his body for landing him in such a mess.

1: Well, you haven't done too badly for someone who despises earthy details! How brilliantly suggestive you can be! Poor Roberti, what rotten luck!

HE: What else could one expect? People governed by their nerves, sensitive and high-strung people whose souls change color every other minute, are liable to this kind of mishap. Anyway it's never very serious. Just a bit humiliating at the time, owing to that absurd sense of sexual honor with which men are afflicted. If men prone to fiascoes would only admit it with a good grace they would be far less unhappy, as they would discover there are a great many others like them. But they are fools. They wait for the women they have let down to betray them instead of philosophically admitting it first.

I: Even so, if I've understood rightly, Roberti wasn't a total flop.

HE: No, not total. He was experienced, and experience helps to get one out of tricky situations without too much loss of face. By dint of simulating the gestures of passion, feigning ecstasy, doing all he could to rise to the occasion, in short enacting a dismal and degrading parody and feeling very sorry for himself, nature restored a dim hope which he exploited to the best of his ability. There!

I: My God! Your story gets sadder and sadder. I can't think of a more desolate love scene in the whole of literature. It is worse than Madame Bovary in her cab.

HE: It was hell, in fact. Indeed I am convinced there are countless people who have been through similar experiences and who, the first time they held the object of their most violent desires in their arms, felt like dying of cold and boredom. And then again, what I enjoy is ferreting out the truth. The real truth, the truth which is never spoken but is entered in invisible writing in the Great Book of God, where it remains for all eternity. That self-truth we are due to discover intact and complete when we die and pass into eternal life. I am sure Roberti, in hell, is eternally reliving this miserable love scene with Solange and that the boredom and disgust of it will pursue him to the end of time, to Doomsday.

I: Eternity is a long stretch for expiating the little things of life. God must now and then take pity on the damned and in His mercy grant them forgetfulness of their crimes, don't you think? It seems to me that in ten or fifteen thousand years Hitler should in the normal course of events be granted an amnesty. The more so Roberti, who has fewer deaths on his conscience after all. But tell me how the visit to the hotel in the Rue d'Argenson ended.

HE: Oh, you know how men are after a flop or a semifailure. They feel an urge to be funny, to show they don't take it to heart; they crack jokes and epigrams about their shortcomings and laugh at themselves. Roberti took this line. He even took it with the heaviness and insistence of someone at heart deeply vexed and anxious to conceal it at all costs. Solange listened to it all without understanding a word. Watching him, her wide eyes clouded with sadness. She was filled with a vague but deep sorrow which stemmed from her body, whose desires were far from fulfilled, and came to gnaw at her heart. By a strange emotional paradox, all her shyness had returned. In spite of what had happened she had no feeling of superiority. It would never have occurred to this good and gentle creature to take advantage in any way of someone she loved. In her fashion she was even more unhappy than Roberti. He at least had no enemy but himself. He was feeling the refined pain of an affronted fop. For her it was different. The pain was more pressing, not unlike that of a penurious clerk who has been fired. Can you see this? There are two worlds here, two ways of suffering. The second is perhaps less noble than the first but it is far more acute. Solange was incapable of saying a word. Roberti's bitter jokes were as utterly lost on her as if he had been talking to a dog. They even struck her as out of place. Doubtless she wouldn't have minded her lover's inadequacy at all if, instead of trying to cover it up by showing off, he had made up for it by sincerity and gentleness. He was giving his semifailure an importance she would never have accorded it. But his obsessive determination to appear in a good light came first; he must at all costs raise himself in his own esteem and buy back with wit what his body had lost.

I: I should like an example of Roberti's jokes. They must have been weird.

HE: In a tone of smug jocularity he said: "It must be rather pleasant in certain circumstances to have the heart of a butcher boy." Or: "It is always with those one would most like to impress that one appears at one's worst." Or again: "That's the trouble with desiring something too much: it leaves one too exhausted to take it when it comes. My way of paying tribute to your charms may be a trifle odd, my love, but I assure you it has its points. From one angle it is even rather complimentary." And more such twaddle.

I: And what did Solange reply?

HE: Nothing. All she said, which was sublime insofar as anything to do with this affair could be sublime, was: "Edouard, I love you."

I: Not bad, I agree. But everything's simple when one is in love. One suffers, forgives and goes on loving.

HE: Roberti was embarrassed and furious. He hated Solange for the low opinion he thought he had given her of himself. Now he only wanted one thing—to get this witness of his inadequacy out of his sight. This Saturday he had planned to stay with her till dinnertime, but around five o'clock he invented an appointment and took her back to the Avenue Daumesnil. It was more than he could stand to spend another three hours in her company. Tenderly she kissed him good-by, for she could see he was at odds with himself and felt sorry for him. With perfect tact she refrained from asking when he intended to see her again. But once in her room she fell on her bed and wept bitterly, sobbing her heart out, not like a little girl in trouble but like an unhappy woman. Her sobs were so loud that Valentin heard them in the next room. They gladdened his heart. He told himself his sister must have been given the brush-off by some young man and now at last he would be able to marry her to Legay, who was so kind, who would amply console her and also make a delightful brother-in-law. People often marry on the rebound and congratulate themselves for it later. Had anyone asked Solange why she was crying so hard, she would probably have found it difficult to say. She had no very clear idea. Just a deep sense of desolation in her heart. Roberti had purely and simply driven her to despair. She could now see how love is something horrible that scorches, that hypnotizes like a snake; how it is a malady of which we refuse to be cured. She wept so copiously that the Teddy bear she kept on her bed was soaked. In spite of his contentment, Valentin was touched: this sobbing was going on too long. He loved Solange and her grief upset him. He shared it without knowing its cause, which is the touchstone of love (brotherly or otherwise). His spirit was, I believe, so close to that of his sister that it took on the same hue. Presently, when he could bear it no longer, he knocked on the wall and shouted: "What is it, Sol? Can I help?" He called her Sol. It was her family nickname. "Go away," replied Solange between sobs. "Just leave me alone!" —"All right, all right," shouted Valentin. "I won't interfere. Have a good cry then. It's your age!" But he thought furiously to himself: "If I could just lay my hands on the bastard, I'd love to break his jaw. I'd know how to make him marry her—poor little Solange." This notion, sacrificing his dear Legay as it did, clearly testified to a deep brotherly love.

ɪ: What is most clear to me is that Valentin had a wide misunderstanding of the causes, effects and circumstances.

ʜᴇ: That's quite normal. Like most people, he was the dupe of his own emotions. Instead of looking at the world, he looked inside himself. He had formed a certain idea of Solange which was very far from the truth and he based his deductions on these false premises. For instance, without ever having dared to ask her right out, he believed she was still a virgin. This naturally led to a whole series of totally erroneous feelings, reactions, attitudes and judgments. Besides, you know as well as I that wrong interpretations are the daily bread of human relations. It has been the same for thirty or forty thousand years. I see no reason why it should change.

I: What, in your opinion, did Valentin love in Solange? She herself or his idea of her?

HE: I don't quite see what you mean. To Valentin they were one and the same. For him, what he imagined was real.

I: Of course. It was a stupid question. People build up arbitrary images of their friends and relations. After which, when the behavior of the person concerned doesn't live up to their preconceived ideas, they cry: "How you have changed! I no longer know you!"

HE: That is exactly what Valentin bitterly said of Solange on several future occasions.

I: I'm sorry, but we haven't got that far yet. What were Roberti's thoughts while Solange was sobbing over her Teddy bear? Was he thinking about her? Did he feel at all sorry for her? Did he tell himself he had behaved like a heel?

HE: No, no, nothing of the kind. He was far too busy erecting barriers against her in his mind. He was concentrating all his thoughts on himself and the present moment. After depositing Solange in the Avenue Daumesnil, he started by taking a deep breath, heaving a profound sigh of relief which came from the heart. "Well that's over and done with, dead and buried," he told himself. "Farewell, Mlle. Mignot!" He was coming out of a painful and humiliating dream. He was at once displeased and relieved. Displeased with what had happened, with himself and above all Solange. Relieved to find himself once again alone, with no immediate or future obligations. Balancing up the events of this ruined day, he concluded that the two hours spent in the Rue d'Argenson barely existed, didn't count. Not a total waste of time since at least this episode had rid his body and mind of a desire. He had held in his arms a woman whose possession had once seemed the most precious thing in the world, and now she had lost all her appeal and mystery for him. The mere thought of her filled him with agonized boredom. He would never see her again so long as he lived. He never wanted to hear of her again. He cut her right out of his life. Consigned her to oblivion. She would vanish into the teeming and meaningless swarms of human beings who people the earth's surface. Gradually a sort of good humor returned, of the kind he always felt after breaking with a mistress as if, together with freedom and innocence, he was re-discovering the immense and infinite richness of life. He was one of those who cannot bear the weight of other people for long. He felt as sick of Solange as if she had been his mistress for six months and had smothered him with uncalled-for and possessive devotion. All in all, this semifailure had its good points; it had nipped in the bud an affair which might have become long, tricky, dangerous, complicated at any rate and very quickly a nuisance like all affairs. Roberti didn't want to be in love. This apparent defeat was at bottom a victory. He had lost an amorous battle but had once again won the old war of love, in which success consists of killing one's own feelings. His recent torpor and indifference were things of the past. On leaving Solange he had, as if by magic, recovered his usual liveliness. He thought with amusement and con-tempt how if, at that very moment, heaven were to send him some houri, he certainly wouldn't disappoint her. He cursed these lapses of his, these "intermittences of the body," as he called them, parodying Proust. I believe he began to whistle.

What was he to do about Solange? You asked whether he thought of her. Not only did he not think of her, but he did not want to think of her at any price. I mean, he made absolutely no attempt to picture what she might be feeling in her heart, he took no account of her as a living and suffering being but only as a cumbersome object he must get rid of on the best possible terms. He couldn't stand the thought of having caused anyone disappointment or distress. Such an idea filled him with horror. But instead of trying to make amends, mitigate the disappointment or distress by redoubled affection, he preferred to run away. To my mind this is an interesting trait peculiar to the man of action who refuses to let setbacks get the better of him, preferring to brush aside a failure and move on to something else rather than struggle to retrieve the situation. Roberti was the same in politics, although here he was more persevering and only abandoned a project when it was patently doomed beyond recall. His misadventure with Solange was not the first of its kind. Each time he had behaved in the same way; gone to earth, played possum. Each time he had been the victim of the same collapse of the imagination. Each time desire had turned into repugnance.

    I: Careful, your motor's idling.

    HE: How do you mean, my motor's idling?

    I: Marking time, if you prefer it. You're getting bogged down in subtleties. Padding. You have no sense of moderation. Let's get on to the next episode.

HE: Well, after having more or less written off Solange, Roberti felt like a little recompense. You'll never guess what he did. He went to the Assembly. That day they had been debating something quite unimportant. It was over. Still, a few members lingered on in the lobbies. He joined them. Having failed in his duty of marital fidelity, he felt an urge to perform some minor social or civic duty. He joined three or four Radical deputies in a discussion on a proposed new law on education which had been several weeks on the agenda and in which he wasn't very interested anyway. But this discussion had a wonderfully tonic effect on him. One final point worth mentioning: Gallardin was there. On seeing him Roberti had a youthful impulse. He went up to him and shook him by the hand, which was hardly his wont with this dangerous and dubious colleague. It was a rash challenge to fate but it was exhilarating. Gallardin was surprised. "Shall I tell him" Roberti asked himself, "that I saw him this afternoon in the Rue d'Argenson?" The Devil tempted him sorely; the remark trembled on the tip of his tongue; but at the last moment he hit on something far more subtle which at the same time furnished him by implication with a sort of alibi. "It seems to me," he said, "that you are attending debates very assiduously these days, my dear Gallardin. You almost seem to sleep here. Just now, during old Schumann's speech, I saw you drinking in his words, although the constitution of Little Europe's a rather arid topic, don't you think? Besides, it can hardly be designed to please you." This was risky, for after all Gallardin might easily have been absent during the speech in question. But luck was with Edouard. "I've a weakness," replied Gallardin with a snigger, "for Schumann concertos. They inspire sweet dreams. Anyway you are wrong: I wasn't listening, I was composing letters. You didn't listen much yourself, I take it?"—"We Radicals," said Roberti stifling a surge of joy, "are not very Europeminded, you know." Whereupon he went home and spent a delightful evening with his family. Germaine, the maid, greeted him in the best tradition of her character. "And how has Monsieur enjoyed sucking the people's blood today? Or p'raps Monsieur has at last brought down the government, just for fun!" This was of course the wildest flattery which secretly enchanted Roberti, who was not so powerful a figure as to be in a position to overthrow governments or be accused of sucking the people's blood. Germaine knew exactly what she was up to, believe me, when she gave vent to such remarks. Roberti loved this familiarity and naïvely believed it was her way of demonstrating her affection and admiration through her own special brand of humor. To Agnes he described at some length Schumann's speech, which he hadn't heard, and also his exchange with Gallardin. Agnes laughed several times. This greatly touched Edouard and raised his marital love to a high point of combustion that night. Solange was buried for good and all. Dinner was very gay. Over the dessert Papa announced: "Who's for the movies?" at which the boys acclaimed him with enthusiasm. They rushed off at once to get ready and, as they say in novels, fifteen minutes later an observer standing at the corner of the Rue Monsieur and the Rue de Babylone might have seen this happy family chatting gaily as it entered the movie house known as the Pagoda, a bizarre edifice in the Chinese style where students and cognoscenti can see rare films.

ı: The story of Roberti and Solange might easily end here, you know. And I for one wouldn't regret it. We could go and have a nice quiet dinner followed by a movie. The Pagoda, for instance, where they show rare movies for cognoscenti like us!

HE: It's quite true that the affair could have ended here. Several of Edouard's previous adventures had concluded, petered out like this, with a family visit to the movies. And he thought it would be the same on this occasion. All in all, his day had been not so much exceptional as rather ordinary, marked only by a fleeting disappointment, one of those countless disappointments of which all our lives are woven. He had had others; there was no risk of a blunder, a pointless mistake of this nature bringing down the solid structure of his life. In the darkness he could feel beside him the warm presence of his wife and sons, who so to speak were one with himself, tied to him by so many bonds. This was where truth and permanence lay. Solange was just a butterfly he had tried to catch but which had eluded him. One of the commonest kinds of butterfly, such as are to be found in Paris by the thousand.

Absently he followed the events unfurling on the screen. He found more entertainment in the pleasant and melancholy thoughts preoccupying him, not to mention the difficulty of taking an interest in a movie when one is oneself an actor in a real-life adventure. He reflected with wry pleasure how he was no longer so young, how he would doubtless enjoy further adventures, but that these would grow increasingly unimportant. He gazed ahead into the future. He contemplated his old age and found it not without charm. He would have accumulated various honors, he would become a minister, possibly premier, and he would hold this office for a long time, since the country would finally learn to value his prudence and sagacity. He settled down to dream of a sort of future glory, not dazzling but not without substance, with a white-haired Roberti risen by seniority and without fuss to be the Father of the Nation, an essential ingredient of the French scene, of the nation's history, as familiar to all and sundry as the obelisk in the Place de la Concorde or the Luxembourg Gardens. Compared with such dreams, poor Solange obviously faded right out of sight.

He descended from these heights to tender thoughts of Agnes, who was his partner, who had been traveling the same road at his side and at the same pace for so long. She too had known the lean years, the hopes, the setbacks, the success. *She had shared twenty-two years of his life story.* He felt for her that kind of affection, so close and so deep, that soldiers have for their brothers-in-arms. She had never doubted him. Given such devotion, such faith, marriage was plainly not an empty sacrament.

I: Decidedly, there is nothing more effective than a rebuff to bring people back to honest thinking.

HE: Yes, it's a well-known fact. It isn't the offense that engenders remorse but the punishment. Whence the utility, not only social but also metaphysical, of having laws. When I was young I was always astonished to see murderers or swindlers on trial breaking down in the witness box and repenting of their crimes. I took it for hypocrisy. I thought it impossible to repent so swiftly of something carefully planned and executed in full knowledge of what was at stake and which had procured great benefits. Had those men not been caught they would have continued to enjoy the fruits of their crimes in perfect peace of mind and even felt rather proud of themselves. I told myself it was all put on to impress the judge. But I was wrong. In fact their arrest and the trouble in which they had landed themselves had opened their eyes. Their tears were sincere. But don't misunderstand me and conclude that I'm preaching. On the contrary I am convinced that as a rule an unpunished crime doesn't weigh heavily on the criminal's conscience. I have an idea that, in his *Confessions,* Rousseau says something like: "Remorse slumbers in times of prosperity and reawakens in adversity." This is a very true observation. It isn't always hyprocrisy when men see disgrace in the scandal rather than the offense; because it is the scandal which makes the offense futile, taking away the advantages the offense had procured and only leaving the stain. Had Roberti given a brilliant performance with Solange he would have had quite different dreams at the movie. The offense would have been the same but it would have seemed to him enjoyable, since no unpleasant memories were attached to it. Although the motives may be identical, a successful crime is greater, in absolute value, than an unsuccessful one; but by a common illusion it appears smaller to the man who commits it: it is just a stroke of luck, a good trick played on destiny for once looking the other way, something one can "take with one." In the Pagoda, Roberti was going through the inverse process. He was exaggerating his offense because it had proved a failure. He was angry with himself, he was "loathing his crime." In common parlance, he was turning over a new leaf. He made high-minded resolutions. So benevolent did he now feel that he reproached himself for having so brutally abandoned Solange. He made up his mind to telephone her in two or three days' time, ask her out to lunch and explain to her, gently and paternally like an indulgent and understanding adult, that they must break it off, that he wasn't the right man for her, that she should marry a nice boy as soon as she could and so on.

This return to common sense gave him a kind of satisfaction which he took pleasure in prolonging. But he was also intelligent enough to suspect that the source of his satisfaction was not altogether pure, that it in fact derived from his semifailure in the Rue d'Argenson. He was always able to stand outside himself; nothing was easier for him than to observe his own thoughts and pass them through the sieve of irony. At one moment he gave himself a mocking smile in the darkness and shrugged his shoulders.

ı: Aha, at last a likable trait.

HE: Forgive me if I repeat myself but it is really amazing to catch destiny red-handed so often. It was endlessly running up and down like the ferret in the song. As if heaven were constantly watching over this poor wretch and opening its gates for him. Nothing was ever irrevocably lost. There was always a chance to save the situation. And Roberti never saw the open gates. Or rather, he approached them but then changed direction. Some inner force was implacably heading him toward hell. Not a huge steel hand but a soft, shapeless and protoplasmic stream, a warm and limpid current. Deceptively limpid. Irresistible. The Gulf Stream of pride. Nothing is more deadly than the pride of a man sure of his common sense, since it is invisible, since it assumes the guise of perfect humility. We never illustrate the more extreme forms of diabolic temptation; as if artists dared not face up to them or were powerless to depict them. Artists tell us of excess, rebellion, magnificent sin, a thirst for knowledge, power, crime. None of which gets us much further. What is really horrifying and before which all but scoundrels or great men flinch is naked, crude temptation. But who make up the troops, the rank and file of Erebus? What about the millions suffering in Gehenna? The obscure and undistinguished, who roast none the less for that? Where do all the inadvertently damned come from, those accursed through carelessness, who for hundreds or thousands of years have been weeping tears which never extinguish the flames in which they burn? This is what we are never told, though this is what it would be so instructive to know. Satan is less stupid than we think. When his traditional means fail him, he has this crowning resource of mediocrity, of habit, routine, reasonableness. I feel certain that hell is full of rational men who have gone down to it slowly but surely, taking every precaution on the way and so complacent over their temperance that they never suspected for a moment that this was straight where they were heading.

1: Look, what do you mean exactly by destiny running up and down like a ferret? At every, or nearly every moment in life we are the masters of our fate. It is an old notion called free will. You don't have to be very enlightened to earn your salvation. All you need is a soul that refuses to subscribe to certain acts and dismisses certain thoughts as being too vile. All you need is a little determination and a few principles. There's nothing very hard about it. I don't say it is enough to bring you happiness, fame or fortune in this world, but I guarantee it will win you salvation in the next. And in the long run that is what matters. It is a question of dying in peace.

HE: But don't you understand anything at all about men like Roberti? His reason was working the whole time; it was his one and only guiding light. This means that he always wanted to do better, that through reasoning he corrected the impulses of his heart. The heart is not arrogant by nature; but the head which thinks, and thinks frantically, is arrogant. It ends by believing itself to be infallible. A man who lets his reason guide his emotions cannot fail to be arrogant. Consequently he is a prey for the Devil, who (it is his prime concern) prevents him from seeing destiny however often, even daily, the latter appears on the scene. Strangely enough a proud man mistrusts himself far more than a humble man. He mistrusts his heart, he never heeds it. Whereas it is with the heart and the heart alone, which is a mysterious and reliable compass, that we manage to traverse the world without losing ourselves in its virgin jungles. There are some Christians who coldly maintain that "reason is the Devil." This tenet, which used to appall me twenty years ago, now shocks me less and less. I have grasped its truth, or at least what truth lies hidden in its elliptical and disconcerting form.

However robust one's constitution, there comes a moment when one's strength deserts one. Still talking, we had by now reached the Place Cambronne and as my friend spoke these last words I suddenly felt ready to drop. I was worn out. As for him, he was as fresh as could be and ready to talk for another ten hours. I am rather fond of the Place Cambronne, spanned as it is by the elevated Métro whose bulky iron superstructure provides cool and shade. Before plunging beneath it, the Avenue de Lowendal spreads out into a sort of delta of greenery which forms two squares. One is dedicated to Garibaldi, in whose honor they have erected a statue so high that his stone beard is level with the treetops. He clenches his right fist with the utmost vigor; on his head he wears a mitre like a pope's or an archimandrite's. The other square is inhabited by a ferocious bronze lion crouched on a rock, its tail outstretched, its lips drawn back in a terrifying snarl, ready to spring. Below the rock a naked Arab clutching a dagger is doing his best to hide. He doesn't look too happy about it. Impossible to tell whether he's a hunter who has got into a tight corner or just someone who has rashly gone for a walk in the desert. This group could well be the work of the animal sculptor Barye. At least it seems to me to bear the stamp of that artist but there is no signature visible on the plinth.

Set around the Place Cambronne are six cafés, which goes to show the attraction of the place. One of these, on the corner of the Rue Frémicourt and the Rue de la Croix-Nivert, has a strange sign: it is called the Royal-Cambronne. Such a combination of words would hardly have pleased the hero of Waterloo, whom Louis XVIII outlawed and kept prisoner for six months in the Abbaye prison. Another dispenser of drinks is more simply entitled Le Métro, which is not a bad idea since the Métro undeniably gives the square its particular character with its metal stairs and cast-iron archways with their daring ornamental scrollwork whose languid swirls are typical of the taste of 1900. I know few spots as profoundly Parisian as the Place Cambronne, which is neither beautiful nor picturesque. This is not the Paris of the tourists, archaeologists, journalists and esthetes, nor even of the poets. It is the real and intimate Paris of the lower and middle classes, the inveterate Parisians; charmless and graceless but with all the poignancy of a native land. I even took pleasure in the din of the Métro thundering over its girders every two minutes. The Métro is more poetic than the bus; it dives into Paris the way the Blue Train dives into Provence. At night, as its lights thread their way level with the first stories of the Boulevard de Grenelle, it seems to me as beautiful, as mysterious and mighty as the great express trains of Europe. I thought fleetingly (and not without nostalgia) of its benches, the sound of its wheels on the rails, its smell, its gentle rocking. My fatigue swept over me. I was drunk with words and walking. Talkers are inhuman. They probably think it less tiring to listen than to talk, but that is not true. Listening is killing even if, like me, one puts up a passable defense.

"I'm utterly done in," I said. "I can't walk another step. My eyes are smarting, my throat is dry, my nostrils are on fire. I shall have a headache in five minutes. I could sleep nonstop for twenty-four hours. I feel as if I had just crossed the Sahara on foot or been through a lecture at the Sorbonne. I've got the 'museum ache,' as if I had spent the whole day in the Louvre. And I'm hungry. Let's go and dine. After that, things will be better. God, what an ordeal! It's the last time I shall let you tell me a story."

"That's it," he replied. "Let's go and dine. But where? Have you any ideas?"

I hadn't, apart from wanting a really huge meal, as I could foresee that at the rate we were going we were unlikely to get to bed before two A.M. and even that was being optimistic. I urgently needed to get my strength back.

"What would you say to the Pavillon Royal?" he went on. "It's rather pleasant at this time of year, when it's hot. We could dine outside under the lights. I'm going to treat you this evening. I owe you that much. What shall we do? Take a taxi?"

We stopped one which came prowling down the Avenue de Lowendal. The driver, a forbidding character in a cap and a dirty mustache, eyed us with hostility and peevishly asked:

"Where are you going? Me, I'm off to my garage at Levallois. So if it's the République or Pigalle you want, I'm not taking you. I'm late as it is."

"We want the lake in the Bois de Boulogne," said I as dryly as I could.

"Very well. Get in," said the driver in a voice full of regret.

We got in and as I sat down on the caved-in seat I felt a happiness such as I had forgotten existed. The taxi, which had seen younger days, stank like the bedroom of a shady hotel. A sweetish smell of dirty linen and dried sweat blended with the reek of gas. It was revolting but I was past caring. Happily the owner of the vehicle had installed behind his seat a sliding glass panel so that his passengers could be shut off from him. I closed this, although I normally enjoy chatting with taxi drivers, who as a rule conduct a colorful conversation; this one, however, struck me as being too unprepossessing a character.

We drove down the Boulevard de Grenelle and then crossed the Pont de Bir-Hakeim. Dusk had not yet fallen but the light was turning blue, verging on violet. Suddenly all the lampposts sprang alight, which is a charming moment in the Parisian evening. The taxi swung round the gardens of the Trocadéro, which seemed to me unnecessary, but taxi drivers follow weird routes. A few minutes later we were bowling down the Avenue Henri Martin, dismal and opulent, where it is almost as dark as the alleys of the Marais on account of the trees.

I: French taxis are the most uncomfortable in the world.

HE: I never thought about it. Yes, it's possible.

I: And I'll tell you why. Because as a rule they are private cars fixed up with a taxi meter. In private cars the back seats are sacrificed for the sake of the front, so the driver lolls at his ease while his passengers sit folded like concertinas with their chins on their knees. Oh for the old red and black G7s of yore! Some firm of French car manufacturers really ought to decide to build special taxis. The ones in London are admirable, like square boxes, which enables them to turn on their own axis. Beside the driver there's a place reserved for the passengers' luggage as well. That's what I call a taxi.

HE: With all your ideas you ought to be a municipal councilor. After the reform of coffee-filters, the reform of taxis. Haven't you got in your files some little plan for lighting the streets by making the buildings phosphorescent or extending the Métro as far as Saint-Nazaire?

I: At least admit that Paris taxis are absurd. What is the point of having long pointed cars made to cruise at eighty in a city as choked up as this one? It's idiotic. To my mind it illustrates one of the countless harmful results of individualism. I presume most taxi drivers are self-employed and don't work for a company. So they buy the same cars as the bourgeoisie, to use them on Sundays for family outings to Robinson or Nogent.

HE: That's rather nice for them, isn't it?

I: It's very nice for them to take the wife and kids out for an airing, but it could be done just as well with a square taxi. Ah me, vanity, vanity!

HE: I think the car manufacturers must figure that a special production line for turning out five thousand taxis would cost too much and they'd never get their money back.

I: Oh come! Lend me a few billions and I'll set up taxi companies in every big city in France, in every capital of Europe and America. That would absorb a hundred thousand taxis within a week. After which I'd take a squint at Africa and India. I'd invade Calcutta, Bombay, the Cape, Abidjan, Dakar and New Delhi. Nor would that stop me from extending still farther. I'd sign contracts with Bangkok and Saigon. I'd sweep the whole American market. I'd break Wall Street. I'd spread square, comfortable, sensible, maneuverable French taxis over the whole surface of the globe. I'd become a benefactor of all the citizens in the world. Ah, how splendid a business life must be if one invests it with a little daring and poetry! Our big businessmen are cowards. They wail because capitalism is dying. But it is dying through their own fault, because they are pusillanimous, because they no longer know the meaning of poetry. Poetry is the lifeblood of all businesses. Sometimes I tell myself that perhaps I was wrong to become an artist, that is to choose the most difficult calling in the world. With my gifts I could have enjoyed undreamed-of success in the army, diplomacy, banking, espionage or politics. And in business, oh ho! I should be a billionaire right now if I had applied to it a quarter of the faculties I draw on merely to write a little book of fifty pages.

HE: So you think.

I: What do you mean, so I think? I'm telling you, I'm sure of it.

HE: You're not the first to take that line. Balzac, among others, and Chateaubriand followed it before you. You will allow that they were just as gifted as you, I trust. Well, poor Balzac proved a pretty woeful businessman. Instead of making money he squandered all his royalties. As for Chateaubriand, he just managed to be an ambassador and a minister, but not for very long.

I: You don't understand me. What I had in mind was not *taking an interest* in business or politics while continuing to write (of course that's heading straight for disaster) but changing one's weapons. Applying to business or politics the reasoning, energy, perseverance, zeal and method indispensable to creating any work of art. Applying oneself to them with seriousness. The same seriousness. This seriousness, even. It is a question of saying to oneself: "For twenty years I have spent five or six hours a day writing, that is to say toiling at a superhuman task such as no normal person would have the courage to tackle. So that morally and physically I'm *as strong as an ox*. From today on I'm determined to apply all this strength I have built up to moving an object infinitely less heavy and infinitely less fragile." Conclude for yourself. Were I to give up writing to devote myself to industry or the Stock

Exchange, I would be like an athlete capable of lifting six-hundred-pound weights but content to lift nothing heavier than a book. I am always astonished at the lack of seriousness in businessmen and politicians. They don't know what it is to meditate, to evolve schemes which preclude chance. They don't know how to make an idea work, in other words study it from its eight or ten different angles, foresee its potential development and the scope it offers for combination with other ideas. Their reasonings are always very brief, their flashes of insight briefer still, and all done in a haphazard atmosphere of confusion, improvisation and groping in the dark. Another thing: unlike artists, businessmen and politicians don't have to create a world out of nothing each morning. When they sit down at their desks, the world is already there waiting for them. Their work is confined to sorting, cutting and arranging. Not to producing something out of nothing. Artists are architects who provide not only the stones for their buildings but also the site! They conjure this up by the wave of a magic wand. And I'd have you know that the magic wand technique is exhausting. It demands intensive training. Imagine a drum major juggling with his baton or a tightrope walker throwing clubs fifteen feet up in the air and catching them again while he spins plates on the tip of his nose as he walks along a high wire. But the baton is solid silver, the clubs are of iron, the plates are made of tungsten. Naturally every movement must be graceful and powerful and perfect. If the fellow makes one slip he breaks his neck, the clubs fall on his head and kill him. A magic wand is not made of elderwood or bamboo. It is the broadsword of the Teutonic knights, the oak tree uprooted by Roland in order to smite Oliver. To wield it one needs colossal biceps, believe me! Biceps kept in careful trim. What are you sniggering at?

HE: I was thinking how sarcastic you were just now about my taste for metaphors. You don't seem to be short of them yourself on occasion, if the topic inspires you enough.

I: How right you are! Well, it means we are both of us poets. I take back everything I said. Or apply it to myself. Whichever you like.

HE: Will you allow me one objection?

I: What is it?

HE: Can you explain why there are so few writers who chuck literature in order to become millionaires in heavy industry or through government contracts? After all, it's rather nice being a millionaire. Whereas it's a risky business being a writer; how can one know whether one has genius and will go down to posterity?

I: Pardon me! We know that kind of thing perfectly well. As for your question, my answer is this: when one has acquired the habit of tackling difficult things, one no longer has any inclination for easy ones. That is why artists don't become deputies or go into commerce. That is why they mostly prefer to scrape along on their royalties. Mind you, I'm not talking of just anybody. There are three or four thousand writers in France today who would do far better to take up honest toil in the hosiery trade than continue to write rubbish into which they haven't put the slightest thought or effort. On the other hand they would succeed just as little in the hosiery trade as in literature. If you see what I mean.

HE: I see above all that you are prepared to use any means to justify yourself. God, what infatuation!

I: I do have a kind of modesty, even humility, I assure you. It's just that I like to make my position clear.

HE: Look, let's take a recent example; Barrès. You agree that he was a great writer?

I: I do. And I can see what you're getting at.

HE: Let me go on. He takes it into his head to stand for election. He is elected.

I: And he proves an average deputy, in no way outstanding, who doesn't even rise to be a minister. You see? I'm not following you, I am one jump ahead.

HE: Well?

I: It's quite simple. Barrès didn't apply his writer's faculties to politics. He went on writing books at the same time as he attended the Chamber of Deputies. He only applied part of his faculties to the latter. After this had lost its initial entertainment value, he came to the conclusion that it was far harder and thus far more entertaining to make literature than it was to make politics. So he made politics offhandedly, indifferently, in his spare time. Naturally this is not the way to become a leader of men.

HE: You don't convince me at all. These are sophistries born of your insane presumption. Some people have a gift for writing, others for politics, others for trade and so on. It's not enough to be intelligent. One needs to have a certain disposition, a certain turn of mind. However great your faith in the universality of your gifts, I am certain you haven't the faintest idea of the particular brand of soul necessary to make a statesman. A statesman is born with the virtues and vices peculiar to his position. High office merely accentuates them.

I: What vices? What virtues?

HE: I believe a statesman must of necessity possess an innate malice or, if you prefer, a certain form of insensitivity. Are you like that? No. So don't become a politician. His nature comprises cruelty, spitefulness, selfishness and a high-mindedness that will stoop to any baseness. He despises men while aspiring to their happiness. He is disagreeable on principle. Everyone knows this. Look at Richelieu or Napoleon: the opposite of an artist's soul.

I: Were I to apply myself, it seems to me I could easily become selfish, disagreeable, a hypocrite in public and a cynic in private, spiteful and all the rest of it.

HE: No, you couldn't. Each man must stick to his trade.

I: You're infuriating. It's impossible to discuss anything with you. You keep having to raise objections.

HE: My present one is excellent.

I: Exactly. Objections kill conversation. The minute there's an objection, no one wants to listen. Anyway, if anyone contradicts me I shut up. I only talk to people about things to which I have given some thought. If they don't or won't understand, it's their loss. I have no gift for repartee; the best arguments always come to me when I get home. Only nitwits and gossips, who can't think unless they talk, like to argue. That is how they go in pursuit of their ideas. You can count me out.

HE: You can't complain on my account, really. I almost always share your views.

I: That is why I often talk to you. I've already been talking to you for six or seven hours, which is more than I do for anyone else.

HE: Well, for your pains I shall treat you to dinner.

I: I warn you, I'm famished. I shall choose the most expensive things on the menu.

HE: All the better.

I: But no champagne, eh? I loathe the stuff.

HE: No champagne.

I: Here we are. I'll pay for the taxi.

HE: No, leave it to me.

I: Nothing doing. I am going to have caviar and *foie gras*.

And I did. They were delicious and cheered me up a lot. We washed them down with an excellent claret with a bouquet of sandalwood and spices evoking the port of Bordeaux in its more prosperous days. I could happily dash off forty pages about this dinner, but that would be carrying things a bit far, especially since in aiming to convey real life in all its variety this narrative, as some readers may have noticed already, can hardly boast of unity or compression. The Pavillon Royal, also known as Drouant du Bois, is one of the nicest possible places on a warm spring evening. It faces the lower lake of the Bois de Boulogne, at the corner of the road to Suresnes and the road from Neuilly to La Muette. One dines in the garden, which is lit by lampposts each surmounted by a number of globes. These shed a most cheerful light such as must have shone down on the open-air dance halls of the old days. A few yards from the diners, strollers pass chatting on the pavement just as they did a hundred years ago, and the sound of their talk mingles with the Viennese waltzes played by the restaurant orchestra. All that is lacking is the horses' hoofs clopping along the road, but for which one might be back in the age of Louis-Philippe. As we got out of the taxi I was struck by a good smell of trees and verdure, intensified by the warmth and the evening air. Cars were passing softly and silently along the road to Suresnes. Some had switched on their headlights although darkness had not quite fallen, and these modern fireflies added greatly to the charm of the place, to this sort of urban-cum-rustic fairyland to which for a minute or two I was strangely susceptible.

From the manner in which my friend was greeted by the waiters and the maître d'hôtel, I gathered he was a regular customer. They addressed him by name, made a great fuss of him and asked for his news. A little of this glory reflected onto me. Since I was in the company of someone so famous, I must be of some importance myself. The maître d'hôtel treated me with a deferential familiarity which I found delightful. The whole attitude of this majestic figure implied: "Our friends' friends are our friends." It is extremely flattering to be given such a reception, especially at so august an establishment as the Pavillon Royal. Finally they led us to a table which they guaranteed as the best. It was circular, covered with an immaculate cloth and groaning with glasses and cutlery. After our grueling walk, our lunch in the dive behind the Jardin des Plantes, our two halts in the bistro on the Quai Malaquais and the Square Boucicaut, such comfort and attention took me out of myself and put me in the best of humors as if, after a long and exhausting journey, I had come to stay in a palace. I even enjoyed the Viennese waltzes, although the orchestra was playing them in rather too muted a fashion for my taste. I wondered how Roberti would have withstood this sudden invasion of the good things of life and the pleasures of this earth. There are times when famous restaurants are reminiscent of hell, when the diners in evening dress evoke for the philosopher a herd of swine guzzling in their trough. But that wasn't the case this evening, or else I wasn't feeling philosophically inclined. On the contrary, the Pavillon Royal struck me as one of the most innocent of places, a boon from heaven like those oases where the traveler can rest in the shade and quench his thirst with pure water.

I: Roberti smiled in the dark at the Pagoda.

HE: Yes, yes. Don't fuss, I haven't forgotten.

I: Well, what finally happened? Did he call Solange or did she call him?

HE: No, she didn't call him. After that sinister episode in the Rue d'Argenson, her return home and her outburst of despair on her bed, she determined not to be the first to telephone but to wait till he felt like seeing her again. She was sure he would.

I: I just don't understand a single thing about this character.

HE: That's because you have a habit of putting yourself in other people's skins. When you speculate about somebody's thoughts or feelings you imagine you are that person. You mentally put yourself in his place and study your reactions, your own reactions.

I: You're right. That's exactly what I do. In this instance I am putting myself in the skin of the thwarted, jilted, sobbing Solange and I feel wild with rage, humiliated to the core of my being, filled with disgust for myself and for Roberti. I feel positively murderous. At any rate I am irreconcilable.

HE: Those are laudable sentiments but they show how one should never put oneself in other people's skins if one wants to understand them, for Solange didn't feel like that at all. In the first place she wasn't humiliated. At least her humiliation (if humiliation there was) didn't impinge on her consciousness. Moreover generally speaking she wasn't given to feeling humiliated. I would even call her "unhumiliatable" because she was by nature very humble, convinced that she had no claim on anyone's respect, and because her parents had never given her any guidance as to the finer points on this score. Of course, I don't say she wasn't capable on occasion of feeling vexed, nor did she tolerate rudeness, but you must understand that this is not at all the same thing. It only goes to show, alas, how gaps in one's education can have the most deleterious consequences. When wise parents teach their children manners they inculcate them at the same time with a whole moral system and code of honor. Solange's natural delicacy made up in many respects for her ignorance, but for want of experience her soul was vulnerable in places. Out of this good soul no one had troubled to make a proud one.

Another characteristic of hers which I have already mentioned has to be taken into account here: her fatalism. As she wept over her Teddy bear she felt utterly bowed down by destiny. She made no resolves for the future. That is no doubt why she was sobbing so hard; she was accepting her fate, not struggling against it. "I am too miserable," she told herself; not, "I shall do this or that to avenge myself," which would doubtless have comforted her.

Finally, there was love. With people like Solange, love is something sacred, priceless; for its sake no tortures are too great, it justifies every act of cowardice, everything else must defer to it.

I: The typical ravages of heart-throb magazines.

HE: Maybe, but that's how it is. In the depths of her despair she was still hypnotized and enthralled by her love. If this didn't appear to be heading for happiness it was nevertheless love of the most fiery kind, love of the highest quality. Consequently it took precedence over every other consideration. When inhabited by a god one does not begrudge the mortifications the god demands.

I: Is this sort of superstition of love, in your view, a modern phenomenon caused by overindulgence in cheap fiction and the movies, or has it always existed?

HE: There you're asking too much of me. I am not a historian or a sociologist. All I am doing is depicting Solange Mignot in a given situation. Even so, I believe people are more sloppily romantic today than they were one or two hundred years ago. Overindulgence in cheap fiction and the movies has no doubt helped to make fools out of people who were formerly only ignorant. Cheap fiction and the movies have certainly created new manners, new prejudices. One shudders to think of the third-rate hacks, the nauseating scriptwriters who form the outlook of the general public.

I: "Form the outlook"! Don't exaggerate. I'd like to stand up for the general public. When they go to the movies or read their serials, they don't believe it all. They know perfectly well just how seriously such diversions deserve to be taken.

HE: Yes, but they end by creating a climate of stupidity. Look at

Solange. She had an honest mind and a simple heart, she hardly ever read trash and on the whole the movies she saw were good ones. Yet she was contaminated. She had the form of an eighteenth-century Frenchwoman, a pretty head sculpted by Houdon, a charming figure in the style of Falconet, but she had the prejudices of the twentieth century. A Frenchwoman at the time of Louis XV would never have believed in love the way she did, not even a young wench nurtured on *Grandison* or *The Memoirs of a Man of Quality.*

ı: That is a fascinating aspect of modern sensibility.

HE: Fiction has always exerted an influence on manners, you know, especially love stories.

ı: Yes, but in the old days fewer people knew how to read, there were fewer novels and they weren't reinforced by the movies. It is interesting to note how in this age of technics, industry, trips to the stars, atomic fission, population explosions, rabid nationalism, the cold war between socialism and capitalism and all the other horrors which I shall refrain from naming, the rights of the little human heart are proclaimed with just as much persistence and diversity.

HE: I have my own ideas about that.

ı: Tell me.

HE: I believe heart-throb magazines and sentimental movies are patent medicines.

ı: Go on.

HE: The air of twentieth-century cities is unhealthy. Children are sickly. So every day or two at school they are given vitamin pills. That helps them to keep going till their vacation. It enables them to inhale the gasoline fumes and soot without too much harm. It helps to build up their little bones, gives body to their thin blood, resilience to their nerve cells. In short we try with vitamins to replace the sea air, the chlorophyll of the trees, the evening croaking of the frogs in the ponds, the homemade bread, the milk still warm from the cow and the eggs brought in fresh from the hen house.

Heart-throb magazines and sentimental movies are spiritual vitamins for adults. The industrial world in which we live is unhealthy, lethal; it is so contrary to human nature that we cannot endure it without medicines. To avoid being asphyxiated by factories, electronics, organized labor, journeys into space and East-West power-bloc politics, men stuff themselves with silly rubbish, old melodramas rehashed to suit the taste of the day, canned idylls and pop music. These act as a counterweight. They form a barrier against the despair which would grip the human race were it suddenly to realize what it has done with the world God gave it. Whence it follows that the more science progresses, the more bad movies, idiotic novels and trite love songs will be produced. Anyway, none of this I am saying is new. It is an old natural law that the more savage the age, the more mawkish we are. Conversely, sentimentalism recedes as times grow easier. During golden ages men are admirably direct.

One more thing. We are only at the beginning of the scientific era, which means that the manufacturers of spiritual vitamins are clumsy, feeling their way, still far from running a fully developed industry. They are at the same stage as chemists were fifty years ago, when they were timidly inventing patent tonics like Eau de Mélisse and Boldoflorine. Have a little patience! In twenty years' time you'll see!

I: Stop. Stop. You're taking away my appetite. To think that there has been only one scientific civilization in the history of man and that bad luck had it that I should be born just then! Me, a man of the thirteenth century; me, a contemporary of Plato or Balzac! Really it's too bad! I wasn't made to live in a permanent state of revolt and exasperation. It's wearing me out.

HE: You are fortunate in your misfortune. Scientific civilization is only just beginning. There are still ample remains of bygone days with which one can build oneself a reasonably impregnable and comfortable bastion.

I: I know. My trouble is that I don't particularly desire to build myself this bastion. When one is an artist, one can't cut oneself off from the world and take refuge in the past, however bewitching it is. I am not an antique dealer. For instance, I have never been able to bring myself to write a historical novel. I am only interested in the world as it is today. I am reduced to looking at it with horrified eyes and describing it with repugnance. What a fate!

HE: I'm glad to know you're unhappy!

I: Shut up, will you? I can see what's at the back of your mind and it's a frightful cliché. Also it is immensely silly. The best epochs for artists are those in which their individuality can blossom out in a civilization which suits them. They have a name, what's more; they are known as classical epochs. I should so much like to have been a classical man! A classical man without political, human, esthetic or moral problems. A simple classical man, happy in his genius and in the genius of his time. Someone rather like Boileau. I could weep with regret and self-pity. But all this is a far cry from Solange.

HE: No. Not really. Because Solange is a woman of today, a heroine of our time, and one can only fully understand her by placing her in an over-all picture of the twentieth century, in the warped perspective of our particular sensibility, our idiosyncratic absurdities. I don't say her thoughts or feelings would have been incomprehensible in the age of Voltaire, but they would have seemed very exaggerated, very exotic, whereas today they don't surprise us at all; up to a point we even find them touching. We are less intelligent or, if you prefer, less pure than Voltaire's contemporaries. We too have been contaminated by the general climate of stupidity. It has penetrated our defenses. Your sensibility is closer to that of Solange Mignot than to that of Voltaire. You enjoy a sort of complicity with her which you don't share with him.

I: Yes, but I also enjoy a complicity with Voltaire that I don't share with Mlle. Mignot and her kind, not to mention a certain number of my contemporaries of both sexes.

HE: Your case proves nothing. You are a writer. You constantly reread the old authors. Your head is stuffed with their feelings and ideas and cadences. You even use their own words and expressions. You are like the Roman masons at the time of the Renaissance who used to pinch the ancient stones of the Colosseum or the columns in the Forum to build their new houses.

I: That didn't produce bad results. Rome is very beautiful! Besides, art always consists of making something new out of old material. Chénier said so in a famous poem.

HE: Anyway, all I mean is that you can put up a better defense than most people, because by constantly reading and rereading good authors who write well and have a healthy outlook, you absorb large quantities of an antidote to the poison of modern stupidity. But that isn't so with most people, even intelligent ones, who read nothing at all, who are exposed defenseless to the contagion, who are porous, as it were, and have been hideously corrupted by contemporary sentimentalism. To return to Solange, I maintain that her way of being in love was typical of our age which is not, as certain irresponsible people claim, an age of immorality, libertinism, excess and "lust for life" but on the contrary very sanctimonious, very tearful and very verbose. An outdated age in spite of airplanes, bombs and all the rest.

I: It would be interesting to dissect what was genuine from what was artificial in Solange's love, don't you think?

HE: Frankly no, I don't. Love is a sort of chemical precipitate and you will shed no new light on it if you play about at breaking the precipitate down into its original elements. Come to that, it is not a precipitate. It is a mayonnaise. Sometimes it takes, sometimes it doesn't. Mayonnaise cannot be explained by yolk of egg and olive oil.

Nor by the hand which stirs it, for that matter. Anyway, what is love?

I: A great question!

HE: You know as well as I do that love is not a spontaneous and natural feeling introduced by the Creator into the human heart, but a product of civilization. It is the result of a thousand things acquired by mankind since it first existed. Love is a question of manners, conventions, traditions, sensibility, the organization of society, literature and so on. One day, forty or fifty thousand years ago, love was invented like the wheel and marked a stage in the evolution of mankind. It follows that everything about it is artificial if you view it from a certain angle. But from a different angle, everything about it is natural. Solange loved Roberti absolutely and everything about her love which derived from cheap novels, bad movies, the intellectual and sentimental debasement of the world today was so inseparably mixed up with the age-old sediment of humanity that it formed one solid slab of homogeneous feeling. It had inspired every particle of her, it had taken such possession of her mind that no room was left there for anything else. You don't suppose, I trust, that she rationalized this love, tried to disentangle what was true from what was false in it? On the contrary, she welcomed it as if it were a descending angel, a ray of grace which cannot be gainsaid, so dazzling that one dares not examine it too closely.

In the cheap novels we mentioned I always burst out laughing when I come across such a phrase as: "She was suffering like an animal"! Yet there is some truth in this cliché. Love does on occasion make women suffer like animals, that is to say when it is unhappy love they endure it the way an animal endures pain, without seeking a cure, incapable of doing anything but moan and lick themselves. Solange weeping over her Teddy bear "suffered like an animal." She never thought of suppressing the causes of her suffering, in other words the causes of love. She never thought of subjecting herself to the radical treatment of expunging Roberti from her heart. She simply told herself, poor thing, with that unflagging good will of the uneducated masses: "I've had no luck. We've had no luck. But I shall see him again; I shall be whatever he wants me to be. I shall ask for nothing. One day I shall be truly, completely his mistress and we shall know a happiness beyond bounds." She was licking herself, you see. Licking herself but nothing more. The most impressive thing about it is that she was right. In the midst of her undefined grief she was foretelling the future. Our wishes always come true. I am constantly amazed by this fact. The soul controls events and matter lies down before the mind like a dog. How can we continue to doubt the existence of God in the face of such phenomena? If the mind of such an insignificant creature as Solange Mignot can alter the world solely by willing it, what can the mind of God be like? God thinks, and the chain of the Alps becomes as flat as my hand, cedar trees sprout up in the middle of the ocean, ice covers the whole world, the sun catches fire, the dinosaur says "Cuckoo" and Man says "Why?"

i: Pretty. Oh very pretty, this cosmogony! Bravo.

HE: For me the proof of God's existence lies in this docility of matter, this way it has of sooner or later obeying every behest that comes from man. We live in the constant miracle of our thought and speech, which move buildings without our even noticing. Man does not see himself. Even less therefore does he see God, whose presence nevertheless stares us in the face at every crossroads. This experience of God which I shall qualify as a daily occurrence seems to me far more convincing than the arguments of the philosophers, which are so profound and subtle but which I can never manage to remember. I have read the proofs of God's existence expounded by Descartes twenty times over and I would still be quite incapable of repeating them were you to ask me. Whereas the proof of God's existence according to Solange Mignot is borne in on me the whole time, it never leaves me. Proof according to Solange and according to me, for I too have experienced the omnipotence of human desire over the world, just as you and all men have done, even the weakest and most deprived of them.

i: I might point out in passing that I am not taken in by your lyrical flights. I too have read the philosophers. They have one advantage over you—their precision. I know two or three who, were they to hear your poetico-mystical speculations, would bring you up short with some little principle of causality from which you would find it very hard to extricate yourself.

HE: But I am not a philosopher. I express what I feel, that is all. Never mind if it is all fantasy. It is truth to me. As I have arrived honestly at this truth, making no concessions and trying always to see it clearly with an unbiased eye, this truth has for me a general value. It has become a sort of faith. And if it pleases God to appear to me in the absurd and sacrilegious form of Mlle. Mignot's longing for happiness, why should I seek elsewhere? God nearly always manifests Himself in an unexpected and equivocal manner. He likes the absurd best of all. That is how He deflates our pride and solemnity. God is disconcerting and facetious. It is the Devil who is solemn. It is the Devil who is logical; he lulls our suspicions to sleep with the glamor of reason. I would refer you to St. Philip Neri, whose edifying life consisted of eighty years of helpless laughter, so comic did God seem to him. For him sorrow was the mark of the Devil, from whom everything sad derives. And the story of Roberti, so sad and so dark, is a strictly diabolical one set under the sign of the fundamental curse.

ı: I was, in fact, just about to ask you to come down from these theological heights and return to ourselves, Solange and the good Roberti.

HE: Well so I have, as you can see. But I hadn't strayed very far since Roberti's story, like that of every other man, was enacted simultaneously on earth and in heaven.

ı: If you dare compare man to a puppet moved by invisible wires, I shall stick you in the stomach with the butterknife!

HE: Never fear. I was thinking more of an inverted pyramid. Its base is infinitely huge. I imagine an eternal eye gazing down the length of one of its ridges, a look emanating from the melodious darkness of paradise, a look which nothing escapes and which travels faster than light. It descends to the point of the pyramid where it sees something infinitely small, namely a man. It sees Roberti. Roberti exists in the sight of this awe-inspiring eye. There is my comparison. That is what I mean when I say that men's stories always take place on two levels. They are constantly being weighed, judged and transfigured, these stories. And ever subject to revision as well, modifiable down to the last split second. They are at once eternal and transient. They exist, and everything can take place as if they had never existed.

ı: I say, the *foie gras* is really inspiring you. How are you going to get down from these heights and tell me the rest of Roberti's sordid tale? In spite of what Victor Hugo said, it isn't easy to mix styles. I really admire you. I myself could never switch, the way you do, in a flash and without any transition from God to the hotel in the Rue d'Argenson. I'm not so nimble. I need time to turn round.

HE: One only has to tell oneself that nothing is insignificant, that a whole life, a complete destiny can be contained in an embryonic thought, in the mere outline of an impulse. God is up in heaven and at the same time down on earth. Besides, a man's mind functions on the system of a scenic railway. Take for instance a priest reading his breviary as he walks along in shoes that are too tight. At every moment his thoughts swing between God and his corns, climbing up to heaven, descending to his toes, praising the holy angels and cursing the cobbler. A scenic railway, sure enough. The poor priest is borne along on a little train of thought running up and down hill at top speed. That is how our life is. We are torn between the Almighty and sore feet. So don't suppose I am going to waste time hunting for transitions. You have embarked with me in the front coach of the scenic railway; we have hung motionless for one or two minutes on one of its summits. A slight push and *brrooomm,* we are down at the bottom again.

ı: You are making me feel sick.

ııɛ: And down at the bottom what do I find? Roberti, soberly waiting for us, existing, looking ahead, making plans, thinking of the future, feeling satisfied or anxious, skipping from one moment to the next like a child playing hopscotch.

ı: Do something for me, will you? Drop this solemn Biblical tone. Put a brake on your metaphors. Tell me things simply.

ʜɛ: The day following his escapade at the Rue d'Argenson and his evening at the Pagoda, Roberti didn't think much about Solange. He had dismissed her, expelled her. Now and then she would flit through his mind like a wan fleeting ghost, an unpleasant but unimportant memory. He had settled back once more into his family and professional life, where he was very much at ease. Even so, as a man of the world, he felt a certain remorse. He told himself how he must at least telephone Solange *out of politeness,* the way one telephones one's hostess after a dinner party. He told himself he had behaved like a cad. But the thought of speaking to her filled him with inconceivable boredom. Besides, where should he call her? At her home? Out of the question. Had she even a telephone? It would be easy to check that from the directory. Easy, of course, but beyond Roberti's power; moreover he had no idea how she spent her time. Did she go home for lunch or did she just have a snack in some bar on the Avenue de l'Opéra? As for calling Dietz's office, asking for Mlle. Mignot, saying he was one of her friends ("It's personal") and having a rather stilted conversation with her broken by moments of heavy silence, what an ordeal! There remained the expedient of sending her flowers, a beautiful bunch of roses accompanied by an ironic note, but this raised difficulties as well. He couldn't remember Solange's exact address; the Mignot family would be astonished and plague her with awkward questions. In short the day was frittered away in such petty tergiversations and in the end he did nothing at all. Oddly enough, as the hours went by his heart hardened. That evening he told himself his laziness and lack of decision had on the whole been a good thing, that one is always right to put things off till tomorrow. He had gained a day, he would gain a week this way, he would bury himself in silence, dive out of sight, and when he reemerged this adventure would be completely obliterated. Let Solange for her part get over her disappointment, just as he would get over his.

That's life. Everyone must bear his own pain. One cannot take on all the troubles of the world singlehanded, even those one has caused.

I: The perfect gentleman! What, not even a bunch of flowers?

HE: Not even that. Nothing. *Niente. Nada.* Silence. Oblivion. Roberti was tiptoeing out of Solange's life without even troubling to close the door behind him. But he was not a man to go very far. As I said, he became more selfish and ill-natured as the evening wore on, but conversely he woke up the next morning feeling much more kindly, more indulgent, as if sleep and the sort of innocence it can bring had softened his mood. That afternoon he thought of Solange with a hint of affection. He even caught himself feeling sorry for her and reproaching himself. But none of this came from that inner core of the spirit where pure love resides. It remained skin-deep, a surface emotion. He wasn't feeling very pleased with himself, that's all. He determined to do something, if only for decency's sake. But what? Roses. That was it. He would send her a dozen superb roses and to hell with what anyone might say. With these twelve roses he would absolve himself beautifully. He would show he was a man of the world. He might even write a letter as well. A rather peevish, melancholy letter. A letter? Wait! That could lead to trouble. The day ended without his having done anything.

I: How long did he hold out?

HE: Five days. Little by little he began to think differently of Solange. By the third day the image of this charming girl had started to haunt him and he had embarked on another process of capitulation. The inverse process, as it happens.

I: Give me details, please.

HE: The details would be rather dreary. A man who falls in love, falls out of it and then into it again is an everyday phenomenon. I find it more interesting to enumerate the series of shifting emotions Roberti went through during these five days, because in this way you get a development, a rainbow, a sort of progression; you can see how a man's heart functions in such a given situation. First, he consigned Solange to the Devil; he never wanted to see her again. A purely animal reaction. Next, he felt what I have called "a man of the world's remorse," but inertia and disgust got the better of him. He cared so little about Solange that he hadn't the strength to order a bunch of flowers from the florist, nor even to look up her address in the telephone directory. He read himself a moral lecture: glorification of the family, hard work, etc. Third, resentment over his partial failure began to wane. "After all," he told himself, "she's a very sweet and pretty girl. I believe she really loves me. I've been a bit of a bastard. I must have a talk with her and make the break decently." Another day went by, but this new state of mind became more pronounced. Fourth, the prospect of seeing Solange again, of renewing relations with her, appeared in a different light. What would it be like? She would almost certainly be as meek as a lamb and melt into his arms. This would prove a great temptation to which Roberti (who knew himself and his inability to resist any feminine appeal) would surely succumb. Do you see the graph of his emotions and how it swung from one capitulation to the other?

ɪ: Thanks. It is admirably clear. A bit terse perhaps, but we can see about filling it out later on, if necessary.

HE: Fifth, he made up his mind. He would see her again. He must. There were limits to bad behavior. These four days of lying low had seemed very long. Like four centuries in fact. What must Solange be thinking? He found the low opinion she must have formed of him very depressing. He sought reassurance by telling himself that love feeds on silence, on unspoken words and riddles, that she must intuitively know he had gone to earth for noble and loving reasons.

ɪ: Very funny and very true!

HE: Sixth: "I can't rest on my tarnished laurels at the Rue d'Argenson. My honor is at stake in this affair." At which point, of course, all was gambled and lost. Roberti was once again filled with dreams. Details other than those of the past few days returned to him. He remembered the lunch at Suresnes; the hopes and desires he had on that occasion, how willingly Solange had yielded to him, the tenderness he read in her beautiful eyes, her firm silken skin, her caresses. He felt he might be selling a treasure cheap. He would call her, fix a date, win her forgiveness for his five days of desertion by inventing a few flattering lies (you can imagine how it never occurred to such an old parliamentary fox that he might not be believed). How mysterious our bodies are; desire now welled up again! Roberti, who had every reason to believe he could on occasion give a brilliant performance, no longer doubted that victory would be his. He drew up a plan. He would take Solange back to the Rue d'Argenson, show her magnificently what he was capable of and, following this, break with her with all the honors of war. Finally visions of the Rue d'Argenson itself, hitherto banished by his rage, rose up before him. He saw Solange again in the half darkness, breathed the delicious scent of her body, heard her saying "Edouard, I love you." Never for a moment did he suspect that "My honor is at stake" was just a sophism dictated by this love returning so violently after five days of eclipse. Yet such a sudden wave of happiness should have given him pause. But we never notice the things that stare us in the face. Once again we see that love is blind, and in a sense quite different from what people generally think.

During this last stage in his reflections, one of the visions that touched Roberti most was that of Solange in the Avenue Daumesnil, after getting out of the car, leaning down to say good-by. She had given him such a sad and tender smile; her way of bending down to the window betrayed such a wealth of love that he could not now understand how at the time he had been unaware of it. Even her mocking "So the great day has come," which had so terrified him then, now seemed full of charm. In a word, he began to "crystallize" again at top speed and I for my part find this second crystallization of great interest in that it is something rare, seldom described and seldom appreciated; thanks to it we can grasp part of the complex and little-understood mechanism of love, that subterranean river whose pure stream carries along every imaginable kind of scum.

I: The mechanism of a river—hmm! Once you get going you say anything that comes into your head. But let it be. It's just poetic license and the pitfalls of inspiration. Go on.

HE: Well, after all that Roberti was in a ripe state to call Solange. On the fifth day he did.

I: Where did he call her? At home or at the office?

HE: At the office. He couldn't wait a day longer. He was consumed with impatience. He was prepared to overcome any obstacle in order to see his dear precious Solange again then and there. He gripped the telephone like a gun. When it was answered he cried in stentorian tones: "Mlle. Mignot, if you please." A clear, soft voice trembling with joy, the voice of a nightingale hidden in a leafy tree on the other side of a river, replied: "Speaking, dear M. Roberti." Edouard was at once stunned and thrilled. This greeting came as a dual surprise. He wasn't expecting Solange to reply and even less that, when he finally got through to her, she would be so cordial from the start. He had prepared ingratiating and persuasive speeches to overcome her coldness and justifiable rancor. And lo, no coldness, no rancor; on the contrary he was being greeted as if nothing had happened, as if they had only parted the night before, as if he were an impulsive and ardent lover who inspired not only love but also gratitude. This abrupt reversal of the situation took him unawares. He had a stroke of genius. Instead of getting involved in a series of wretched lies, he cried without further ado: "Solange, do you love me?"

I: Bravo!

HE: Admittedly, such a point-blank question was rather dashing in the circumstances.

I: And what did she reply?

HE: For a few moments, nothing. There was a pause as if the line had gone dead. "That's wrecked it," he thought, "I've made a complete ass of myself. She's just a little fool and here am I talking to her as if she were a duchess!" Finally, with a sort of quiet passion Solange said: "More than life itself." Roberti felt deeply abashed; at the same time he was enchanted. This was even better than forgiveness. It was an amnesty for the past and for the future, the solemn declaration of a love which nothing he might do could destroy, an assurance that this love he had inspired was immune to his own behavior. All at once Solange appeared to him as the ideal woman: a heart radiating goodness, a supreme haven, a sea of balm for all his self-inflicted wounds now and to come. He was suddenly so moved that a lump formed in his throat and his eyes filled with tears. Tremulously he asked her if she would dine with him that evening. No price was too high. He was ready to do anything! Yes, she would, she was free, what a good idea! She didn't hesitate for a second. She was simplicity itself.

I: I wish you would show me her state of mind as readily as you do Roberti's. What was she feeling during all this? What was going on in the wings?

HE: Oh, with Solange it was much more elementary. An unshakable conviction gave her strength. She *knew* that sooner or later Roberti would get in touch with her. She was waiting for him. She hadn't of course grasped all the reasons which had driven him into hiding for five days, but she had a vague and general idea of how he must have been feeling. She felt sorry for him, like a mother. She regretted not being in a position to comfort him, to smooth away with maternal tenderness the chagrin which, as a lover, she had involuntarily caused him. She attributed to this mature man the emotional torments of a boy and here, after all, she wasn't so far from the truth. I am rationalizing and simplifying it all, while in her it was merely a sort of gaseous or nebulous cloud. These weren't ideas forming in her mind, propositions following each other in logical sequence, so much as powerful but amorphous feelings. They troubled her deeply. They compelled her attention in the same way that Wagner's music compels a musical but ignorant ear hearing it for the first time. One doesn't follow this music with the mind as one does that of Mozart or Beethoven, who have something captivating to tell which mobilizes one's thoughts like Voltaire's prose or Hugo's poetry; rather does one submit to it and let it flow over one;

slowly it makes your soul change color, it generates within you two or three vast but imprecise emotions. Such was the case with Solange. Wagnerian music was echoing within her, which she couldn't understand but to the magic of which she responded. Besides, is not beautiful music merely the transposition of our more elusive feelings? Like most people, Solange didn't know how to translate feelings into words either for her own or for other people's benefit but this inner music, this private music of her own she knew well and, even if certain modulations were too difficult for her to grasp, she was nevertheless unmistaken as to the general meaning of the melody.

ɪ: It is true that most people think in music and not in words. Still, that's not a sufficient reason for novelists to twiddle their thumbs. They are given the music but it is up to them to find the words. They write the libretto after the event, after the opera has been completed.

ʜᴇ: And what else have I been doing since noon, if you please, but translating thousands of human melodies into words for you, recounting in detail an opera which has everything in it, even the final catastrophe with chorus of demons and angels? I am singing you the full-length version of *Faust* and even adding a wealth of fresh details. You might at least acknowledge this. Not to mention that it takes quite a lot of nerve to compose a *Faust* after Marlowe, Goethe, Berlioz and even old Gounod.

ɪ: Don't make me laugh! Go on with the duet between Faust and Marguerite. You were singing it superbly, since you're fishing for compliments.

ʜᴇ: Well, they met that same evening as arranged. He opened the door of his car, she gracefully climbed in, settled beside him like a bird and gave him an adorable smile; he kissed her passionately; everything was fresh, everything was fine. Their lives, so sad the day before, had suddenly become wildly happy. Love is as capricious as meteorology. Roberti took Solange to a secluded restaurant on the top of Montmartre where they enjoyed a delightful dinner. All his desire had returned, and this sharpened his wit and made him a most attentive companion. This time the "intermittences of the body" worked in his favor. Gone were all his misgivings. On the contrary that evening Solange reassured him as if he had known her for a long time. He felt she was his for the taking and knew that this time he wouldn't disappoint her. Perhaps his semifailure of the previous week and the bitterness to which it had given rise were necessary trials through which he had to pass before attaining the bliss that was written in the stars for this night. Solange, moreover, was revealing herself in a different light from usual. Was she feeling particularly sure of herself or did the joy of her refound love give her wings? She prattled away with all the verve of a schoolgirl, pressed tenderly up against her lover, her beautiful eyes filled with trust and adoration. Here was neither the little animal of the first days nor the young bacchante of the Rue d'Argenson, but a woman with whom one shares a delicious experience of long standing. There was nothing to which Roberti responded so readily as familiarity and now Solange, without his quite knowing how, had become familiar to him. Familiar and at the same time a stranger—that was the miracle. Desire (and love, since we must give it its correct name) suited him. He too had very beautiful eyes. Although slightly coarsened by age, his face was still fresh and healthy; his fine silvery hair was extremely alluring. He no longer had the slim waist and broad shoulders of a man of thirty, but his suits were so well cut that they made up for lack of youthfulness. Finally, he exuded a pleasant smell of shaving lotion and Virginia tobacco, a blend which apparently never fails to turn girls' heads. In short he was still a most desirable man, objectively speaking. He radiated great charm, of which he was well aware and knew exactly how to use it for his own ends. He had that slightly superficial type of wit consisting of apt remarks, amusing comments on other people's absurdities, slight but unexpected ideas and original turns of phrase, which has an immediate appeal. I need hardly tell you he shone at his best that evening, exalted as he was and bent on recapturing a treasure he had rather hastily and unwisely renounced. After dinner, finding himself in the street with Solange, he murmured: "I'm not leaving you. Let's go to the Rue d'Argenson. Would you like that?"—"Do you really want to?" she asked. "More than anything in the world," he replied. For once this came from the heart, though it didn't prevent him from reflecting that he had spoken his lines well, putting just the right amount of passion into them. This shows, incidentally, how a lack of illusions, skepticism and a mania for belittling things lead to errors of judgment just as grave as do an excess of illusions, enthusiasm and faith. By dint of refusing to believe himself in love, refusing to believe in deeper feelings, refusing to see them, persuading himself that he was incapable of sharing them, Roberti found himself one day completely beset by passion. It was then too late to fight against it, to maintain it within reasonable bounds.

ɪ: And what about the Rue d'Argenson?

ʜᴇ: Fortunately life has its privileged moments from time to time. That evening was one for Roberti and Solange. Besides, everything conspired to the success of this encounter. The darkness, the mild evening air, the poetry of Paris at night. Even their furtive entry into the hotel only added to the poetry and romance of it all. Roberti was upborne on wings of love and, so I believe, put up a truly brilliant performance.

I: Excellent. I'm glad to hear it! The poor man doesn't give us many grounds for satisfaction. For once we won't grudge him our compliments. Solange must have been delighted, poor thing.

HE: Her cup, as they say in novels, was full. And for his part Roberti was aglow with pride and joy, for his vigor backed up by past experience was such that he had made his mistress beg for mercy. He had even shown a measure of brutality which had been received with all the requisite submissiveness. This dazzling victory, carried off with flying colors, canceled out his previous defeat. Edouard, moreover, now evolved an argument—highly typical of him—that having displayed such superiority he was no longer in danger of falling in love with Solange. When you have ensured that a woman depends on you for her pleasure you can neglect her, ignore her with impunity. She cares far more for you than you do for her. By winning the second round he had gained a distinct advantage over his adversary. Already he was adopting a protective and condescending manner. Within an hour he had conquered a slave who would henceforth be his to command; he had purchased a pretty ornament with which he could do as he pleased. *His spirit would be free.*

In this he was once again grossly mistaken, for he reckoned without his overweening conceit which always led him to feel affection for those whom he sensed admired him. He never foresaw that Solange's adoration, her boundless submission were going to bind him far more effectively than any coquettish, unsatisfied and capricious woman would have done. Finally he was underestimating a physical harmony by and large rare and even exceptional. For the moment his desires were exhausted; it never occurred to him that they might revive the next day or the day after and that, enriched with memories, they would be painfully acute. He never reflected that, if Solange from now on depended on him, he would no less depend on her. He had in fact only triumphed over the young bacchante—had subdued her, tamed her—and that was a dangerous triumph. When one is fifty, one doesn't with impunity possess a young bacchante who is utterly devoted and on whom one plays like a great virtuoso.

Everything is delicious in armorous combat. It unrolls like a symphony with adagios, allegros and heroic marches. Together these two, if you will allow the metaphor (which is possibly not in the best of taste), succeeded in interpreting Beethoven's Seventh or Eighth without a single false note. It was as fine as Toscanini! But perhaps the best moment comes after the final chords have died away, when the protagonists lie exhausted, *disjecta membra,* and after a brief pause begin to murmur confidences. It is then that their hearts, which have too long been silent, take revenge and they try through words to bestow on each other the delights of tenderness. I think that men, at any rate, seek to curtail these moments, whereas women would like them to last forever. The one idea of the male, after the act of love, is to break away from his companion and go out and seek society. Having found release, he once again recovers his enterprising and heroic spirit. Roberti never failed to react in this way. But that evening he was pleased with himself, which made him talkative. He cracked jokes, told funny stories and had the added satisfaction of hearing his dear little dove break into giggles several times. He was victorious on every count, as you can see, including that of conversation. Finally he lit a cigarette and, as Stendhal says, felt as happy as Napoleon at Marengo. Who can sing the triumphant hymn of joy which rises with the smoke of the cigarette men puff after having proved their vigor?

I: You can. It's just the sort of poetico-burlesque flight you love.

HE: Even so, Roberti rather forced the pace and toward eleven-thirty deposited Solange in the Avenue Daumesnil. Since it was dark, he let her snuggle up against him in the car the whole way. She was happy; every now and then she raised her big eyes and gave him a heavenly smile. He thought she had grown much more beautiful since seven o'clock and attributed this transformation to himself. Her eyes were more sparkling, more alive, and she had an exquisite pallor. What a tribute to her lover's powers!

They parted amid kisses and bursts of laughter. Tenderly Roberti watched Solange ring the front-door bell. Since she couldn't bring herself to go inside but stood there on the doorstep gazing at him, he finally moved off. Sweetness has its limits. Nonetheless, as he drove back like a whirlwind to the Rue Oudinot he was very gay and whistled like a blackbird. At the other end of Paris Solange responded with a similar gaiety. She went to bed humming a song of the moment. Valentin heard her and was extremely annoyed. He wondered what his sister could have been doing out so late. Or rather he didn't, since he dared not contemplate the worst, namely that she had a lover, and a lover what's more who led her to sing songs by Edith Piaf. As she undressed, Solange breathed in the scent of Roberti's toilet lotion, the scent of

Roberti himself on her body and underclothes, and thought she would faint for joy.

Roberti too was permeated with the smell and perfume of Solange. He lit a cigarette and carefully blew smoke over his clothes in order to dissipate the clinging scent of jasmine. What he whistled was not a popular song but snatches of a Vivaldi concerto.

I: Obviously. Given the man, he couldn't whistle anything else. Vivaldi was in fashion.

HE: Don't think I am trying to impress you with his musical culture. I merely mentioned Vivaldi because it provides an amusing sidelight. One sings *La Vie en Rose* while the other whistles *The Seasons*. Two worlds, two social classes.

I: No, far from it. One world. One and the same social class. The one and only class (and there is no end to it) of people who get their ideas from the papers and form their taste from the radio. In 1955 Vivaldi and Piaf were the same thing.

HE: How do you mean? Vivaldi was a great composer.

I: You know perfectly well what I mean. Don't play the fool. Of course Vivaldi was a great composer but no greater than Handel, Schumann, Verdi and fifteen others. Now Roberti only knew Vivaldi because it was smart to know him, because he was the great discovery of modern musicologists. You see where this leads? He didn't give a fig for music but with Vivaldi he could appear up-to-date. As far as I am concerned, I shall start liking Vivaldi again when his records are no longer sold in the big stores; in other words in about ten years' time.

HE: Why shouldn't one share the crazes of one's day when they are respectable?

I: Because, whatever its object, any craze on a national or international scale is intolerable. Nauseating. It becomes pure conformism, established and consolidated for the worst possible reasons. I don't want to join in the universal chorus of helots. I don't want to chant the fashionable catch phrases, even if they bear Vivaldi's signature. To me this century is hateful because everyone says or sings the same thing. People can no longer quote anything but the newspapers. There's no quiet corner left in the West, it's done for. Everywhere you find the same mixture: a smattering of culture and a hell of a lot of stupidity. Roberti whistling Vivaldi in his car at midnight in 1955 after committing the sin of adultery in a hotel in the Rue d'Argenson makes a real genre picture, a period engraving. In a hundred years time it will appear as picturesque and out of date as Fragonard's and Messager's *The Swing*. Roberti is most definitely *a man of our time!* He has all the hallmarks, even the most abject. Ugh! Are you still surprised at my sighing for the age of Louis XIV or life in Athens under Pericles? The conformism of my time, the imbecilities of this budding scientific age turn my stomach. One day, if I have enough talent, I'll write *The Modern Misanthrope*, the tragi-comedy of a poor man like me, besotted with the stupidity around him, driven mad by having to hear the same thing endlessly repeated by millions of mouths and seeking a desert in which to end his days, for silence is better not only than stupidity but also than unanimity. We no longer live in a world of wolves, alas! We live in a world of parrots, which is far worse!

HE: All this in connection with the wretched Edouard whistling Vivaldi rather than *The Blue Danube!* You exaggerate, I assure you.

I: No, I don't, you know it perfectly well. If it was you whistling Vivaldi, for example, it wouldn't matter because you really care for music and could just as easily be whistling Schubert or Pergolesi. But in Roberti's case it provides us with a major sociological landmark. We are focusing our spotlight on a corner of contemporary sensibility. We are catching it in the act. And it is shocking to behold. There. Now I'll be quiet and listen while you describe his return to the fold after playing truant.

HE: Well, every time he had an adventure he found a special joy in returning home, as if he had been gambling with this precious home of his and it was an unhoped-for stroke of luck to see it again. He would open the door with a beating heart. How would Agnes receive him? Would she be her usual equable and friendly self, or would he find the tragic features of "one who knows"? Instead of staying at home with the children, she might have gone out; an unhappy coincidence might have led her steps to the Rue d'Argenson just as he, Roberti, was diving into the hotel with his mistress. How appalling! He arrives home with a sanctimonious smile on his lips to find Agnes standing stiffly in the drawing room waiting for him. She is white as a sheet, her eyes are blazing. With a trembling voice she asks: "Where have you been this evening?" He falters, stammers, lies. She crushes him with contempt and announces that she is leaving, that she won't stay a minute longer with someone so vile . . .

I: A hideous picture!

HE: Hideous but uncalled for and above all very conventional. However, such were the visions provoked in Roberti by a guilty conscience, and it was an ever-renewed delight for him to find Agnes awaiting his return in blissful ignorance. Her smile of welcome when he came in overwhelmed him with joy and gratitude. At such moments he truly loved her.

1: How very vulgar!

HE: It's the reaction of a lucky gambler. He told himself that once again he had won on both counts, that once again he could take it with him.

1: One thing about your Roberti is beyond me. Why did he take all these precautions? Why did he struggle in this way to maintain the fiction of marital fidelity? It isn't clear to me. I don't see the basic reasons for it. Cowardice is no real explanation, nor is respectability, nor the fear of gossip. Such a man, always on the lookout for women, full of eager desire, imagination and romantic leanings, doesn't go to so much trouble. He gets carried away by his temperament and his wife just has to put up with it. As a rule she patiently nurses her wounds and waits for her erring spouse to come back to her, which he never fails to do after about thirty years. I tell you frankly, I simply don't understand Roberti. Putting things at their worst, Agnes stages a scene and demands a divorce. Where is the tragedy in that? Divorced and free, he is all the happier. No more need to hide, to indulge in all those degrading pretenses and lies. You can't really claim it's possible to care for a woman whom one deceives at every turn, whose existence is a permanent irritation and forces one into crazy contortions.

HE: And why not? Roberti loved Agnes with all his heart. On the other hand he needed sexual distraction. There is nothing magic about it and I'm surprised you don't understand something so elementary, so common. At the same time, you are right in saying that cowardice and fear of gossip are not enough to explain his precautions and anxieties. His attitude was governed by a more subtle exigency. The root of the matter is that he felt a deep respect and admiration for the particular kind of love enjoyed by faithful couples. A man and woman who spend all their lives together, who end by merging into one and the same soul, one and the same being, seemed to him one of the most beautiful of human achievements. He wanted to have experienced it himself. But he also wanted the thrills of adultery.

1: Good Lord, that seems pretty difficult to reconcile.

HE: Difficult but not impossible. By dint of all his precautions and secrecy he managed to deprive his adventures of almost any reality. He forgot them, he constantly purged his heart of them so that it could savor the pure delights of conjugal bliss. In this the trust of his wife, who saw him as a model of the faithful husband, was a great help.

1: There is a name for that. It's called hypocrisy. It is even the worst kind of hypocrisy, since Roberti started by being hypocritical with himself.

HE: "Hypocrisy" is going too far, but it's true that it was as much for himself as for Agnes that he played this comedy, spending so much time at home, going through all his lies and contortions. He wanted his union with Agnes always to remain as it had been during the first three or four years of their marriage. He wanted to preserve what had once been, and was, *so beautiful* for all time. Moreover he had a fondness for complications. He felt at ease with them. They added spice and glamor to his life. He would have missed all this had he divorced. After returning Solange to the Avenue Daumesnil, he loved his anguish as he turned the key in his apartment door at midnight with his heart pounding fit to burst. He loved it all the more in that he was almost certain it bore no relation to reality.

His children were asleep. His wife was reading in bed. It was a picture of peace and innocence, the respectable family man joyfully returning home after the day's toil. A piquant, touching contrast after his recent debauchery! Two contradictory emotions (or rather discordant ones, just as there are deliberate and often delectable discords in music) usually dominated him at such times. On the one hand he succumbed to the friendly charm of the atmosphere and features of his home, as if he were seeing them again after a long absence; he felt faintly embarrassed, even ashamed, to have been indulging in excesses which accorded so ill with his family's simple and transparent life. On the other hand he would think with perverse satisfaction of the secret act he had just performed, of that world of rapturous violence, youth, sentimental entanglements and sexual license which he had just quitted, of that "double life" he kept so jealously secret and which gave him such a sense of superiority. He had several faces which he masked or unmasked in turn to suit the occasion and this gave him an intoxicating sensation of power. Who would have guessed that this same man could be within the space of an hour the impetuous lover of a pretty girl he had enslaved, whom he was capable of treating as roughly as a gigolo, and the respectable fifty-year-old returning to his well-run apartment? They were two totally different characters and he must have had a strangely capacious mind to harbor both of them.

He went to sleep sniffing the scent of Solange on his hands, in which he could discern a hint of jasmine. These scents were a whole book in themselves! Proudly he recalled how he had worn her out. He pictured her graceful, abandoned pose; he evoked her in the darkness, his eyes wide open, waiting for sleep with a smile. He was certain she was think-ing of him with love and *gratitude*.

ɪ: Oh, oh! Dangerous reflections for a vain man.

ʜᴇ: Not only for a vain man. Dangerous for any man whatever.

ɪ: Do you think so? There are some brutes who don't give a damn what the woman who has granted them her favors thinks of them. There are cynics too, who know just how much such gratitude is worth and take care not to let it tickle their vanity.

ʜᴇ: No, no, you are too indulgent. You give human beings too much credit. No brute is so thick-skinned, no cynic is so inveterate as to re-main indifferent to the good opinion of his abilities a woman may have. M. Perrichon slumbers in every lover.

ɪ: Glory be! M. Perrichon? Are men as ridiculous as that?

ʜᴇ: You remember the story: M. Perrichon is climbing in the Alps; he slips and almost falls over a precipice but Armand saves his life. Later it's Daniel's turn nearly to kill himself. M. Perrichon saves Dan-iel. The end of the comedy shows him making up to Daniel while he treats Armand more and more coldly. The lesson emerging from this is that good turns earn the gratitude of those who perform them and not of those to whom they are done. I believe that here Labiche glimpsed a great human truth. One might claim the existence of a "Perrichon's law." Daniel bestowed a priceless gift on his benefactor; he enabled him to feel proud of himself. He endowed him with a quality he did not possess—courage. Perrichon's law similarly applies to love. A lover who sends his mistress into ecstasy grows fond of her by reason of all the pleasure he gives her, which she derives from him, with which he alone (so he thinks, sometimes with truth) is able to provide her. I can en-visage a sequel to M. *Perrichon's Trip* in the shape of M. *Perrichon and Love*. It would make a pretty comedy, in which M. Perrichon, con-vinced that nature has endowed him with very poor capacities, dis-covers thanks to the cooperation of a young lady that he is on the contrary a mighty stallion and lets himself be led by the nose in the daytime by a woman over whom he triumphs superbly every night. It would be comic, don't you think? And original?

ɪ: I don't find it so original. It's normal to grow fond of those one makes happy. Besides, love is quite different from mountaineering. There is no connection. How can you draw such weird analogies? Anyway you're forgetting one vital point: in M. *Perrichon's Trip*, Dan-iel *pretends* to slip on the edge of a crevasse and contrives the whole episode so that M. Perrichon should believe he has really saved him. If you transpose this into the sphere of love you fall into the familiar situation of the whore who deludes her simple-minded customer by simulating rapture. In love the pleasure received forges a bond just as strong as the pleasure given, if not more so. Look at all the plays about jealousy; every one of them confirms this. The jealous man cannot bear the idea of a rival enjoying the same happiness as he.

HE: Forgive me, but I can think of another example against that: the man so confident of his power over a woman that he wants this woman to give herself to another who is sure to disappoint her. She will then draw comparisons which will be all in his favor, so that she will admire and love him even more. This happens more frequently than we think and to my mind represents the height of conceit in love. M. Perrichon could also go to such extremes if need be. He could even provoke them, fling the object of his passion into the arms of a friend and hold the candle. It would make a bit of cuckoldry worthy of Molière. I can foresee several rather painful, gritty, farcical scenes which would make excellent theater, a tragi-comic figure like Arnolphe or Georges Dandin who would—why not?—even express himself in alexandrines. Just think!

I: I'll think about it next year, when I've finished a novel describing the loves of a deputy and a typist, providing you ever reach the end of Roberti's story. Was this digression on love and M. Perrichon really necessary?

HE: Yes it was, because it enables you to grasp another aspect of Roberti's nature. Every time he performed brilliantly with a woman and so felt certain of his power over her, he almost wished she would deceive him and thus form by comparison a proper idea of his capacities. There was no sacrifice he wouldn't gladly have made in order to be appreciated and admired for his true value. Even that.

I: That seems to me typical of a petty soul who needs reassuring as to his own worth.

HE: Needs reassuring—yes, that's it. Where doesn't the need for reassurance lead us! It's rather pathetic, don't you think?

I: I'm sorry but it doesn't arouse any pity in *me*. On the contrary it strikes me as highly dangerous. Petty souls in need of reassuring end by committing the most hideous crimes. In extreme cases it creates appalling characters like the Marquis de Sade and Hitler. It produces "the blackest villains," as they used to say in the days of Louis XIV. In spite of his being so indulgent, such a good husband and father, and having so soft, so eroded a character, your Roberti belonged to that race. The race of little souls who are noxious because they are afraid of seeming inferior. I know it's a very popular type nowadays but I can't put up with it. I don't share this warped romanticism. I go on liking people who have no need for reassurance, who make the best of their fears and live with them in dignity. I shall always prefer Epictetus or Pascal to Gilles de Rais. And if one must feel pity, it is to these brave souls that mine goes. I offer it to them with my admiration and friendship. I feel a profound antipathy for Roberti. He and I are incompatible. You told me earlier that he began by belonging to the tribe of Abel and then opted in middle age for the tribe of Cain, but I don't agree. He was always of the tribe of Cain without knowing it. It was written in the stars at his birth that he should shed the blood of a fellow man. I believe he always had in the depths of his soul this creeping uncertainty which, like his constant fear of failing to rise to the occasion, is the mark of Cain. But he was a modern Cain well concealed even from his own eyes. For the soul of Cain is like an ancient rock. The wind, rain, sun, sea and the mill of time have rounded it, ground it flat and made it almost invisible. Outwardly they have given it almost the same gentle shape as the soul of Abel.

HE: Don't you think that's going a little too far?

I: It was Roberti who went a little too far. What is Cain? A man who denies original sin. A man who rebels against the human condition, in other words wastes his time. He holds others responsible for his woes. He won't admit that it's possible to endure misfortune. He is a son whose father has squandered the family fortunes and who makes the whole world responsible for his bad luck instead of accepting his poverty and rising above it through his own efforts. The opposite of courage. I didn't pay much attention to Roberti's trial but I can remember the gist of it fairly well and what I am saying seems to tally with what I understood of it.

HE: All the same, it's pretty vague and allegorical.

I: But true. You can't deny it.

HE: I don't know. We could argue about that forever and a day. You and I don't see things in the same light. You have a "tragic view of life," that is to say you always contrive to see necessity in whatever happens. I don't. This leads to a fundamental divergence in philosophy, so in my opinion we'd do better to leave it alone. We can get along very well together with different philosophies. We agree on enough topics not to squabble over major abstract principles which anyway serve no useful purpose.

I like the ballet danced in smart restaurants by the tailcoated maître d'hôtel and white-jacketed waiters. When we had settled the account of the caviar and *foie gras* there was a swirl of movement around us. The waiters beamed, the maître d'hôtel stepped forward with his folio-sized menu; affably he bent over my friend and murmured in tenderly confidential tones: "We have a superb *aiguillette de boeuf mode en gelée* tonight. I can warmly recommend it. It is quite excellent. Unless you feel like *poulet à l'estragon*, which is also first-rate.

HE: All that is too fattening. I'd rather have some fish.

MAÎTRE D'HÔTEL: Poached turbot? *Sole au champagne? Truite aux amandes?* We also have *loup grillé au fenouil* but it takes twenty minutes.

HE: Poached turbot would be perfect.

MAÎTRE D'HÔTEL: And for the gentleman?

I: I'm not sure. Reading a menu always fills me with indecision. I still feel very hungry. But I should like something out of the way. I'm bored by *poulet à l'estragon* and *boeuf mode* is rather dreary. Would you by chance have any *anguille au vert?*

MAÎTRE D'HÔTEL: Alas, no, Monsieur.

I: Then some venison, a *filet de chevreuil à la sauce grand veneur.*

HE: Are you crazy? You'll make yourself sick.

MAÎTRE D'HÔTEL: It's not available. It's the close season. What would Monsieur say to a *tournedos Rossini?*

I: No.

HE: That's typical of you. You only want what isn't on the menu. Why not try a *caneton aux olives?*

MAÎTRE D'HÔTEL: Or a small *croustade de langouste?*

I: Mmmmm . . .

HE: Have the *boeuf mode* and stop fussing. It will buck you up, since you seem to need it. And bring us another bottle of claret.

I: Very well, a *boeuf mode*.

MAÎTRE D'HÔTEL: You needn't worry, Monsieur, we serve liberal help-ings. You won't feel hungry after that.

I: I see you have *girolles à la provençale*. Are they done with garlic?

MAÎTRE D'HÔTEL: A pinch of garlic, yes, Monsieur.

I: Then I'll have *girolles à la provençale* to follow.

MAÎTRE D'HÔTEL: I can see exactly where Monsieur's tastes lie. Per-haps you would prefer some *cèpes à la bordelaise* instead? They are also done with garlic.

I: No thanks. When it comes to mushrooms I prefer *girolles*. They are gayer. *Cèpes* are tired and flabby. *Girolles* are dry, springy, crisp and tender.

MAÎTRE D'HÔTEL: *Cèpes* are an acquired taste. You either like them or you don't. So that will be a poached turbot, an *aiguillette de boeuf*, a *girolle*. Shall I serve steamed potatoes with the turbot?

HE: Yes, please.

MAÎTRE D'HÔTEL: And a little melted butter?

HE: With a slice of lemon.

MAÎTRE D'HÔTEL: Naturally.

I: Wait! Cancel the *boeuf mode*. I don't feel like it. Bring me duck instead.

MAÎTRE D'HÔTEL: Very well, Monsieur.

HE: Go and place the order quickly before my friend changes his mind again.

I: I claim the sacred right to waver.

MAÎTRE D'HÔTEL: Monsieur is quite correct. He must have exactly what he likes best.

HE: You don't know him the way I do. Give him enough rope and he'd fill a whole order book for you with his gastronomic tergiversa-tions.

MAÎTRE D'HÔTEL: But that's what we're here for. If Monsieur can't make up his mind, it's because he likes the look of everything. It's a great compliment to the house.

I: Here at last is someone who understands me! Well, I'll stick to the duck. That's final.

This paralysis of the will which grips me in restaurants is strange. As if a magician had cast a spell over me, I become like Buridan's ass which can never decide between the water bucket and the hay bag. There must be some explanation but I have never troubled to find out what. Thus I preserve within me a number of failings of which I could easily rid myself and a number of obscurities, the way one clings to some hideous ornament, some useless object, purely out of habit or laziness—possibly out of superstition. One likes to find oneself invariably the same, even over trivial matters. As a rule I dwell cozily enough in my heart and mind as they are. They make an apartment full of discomforts to which I have nonetheless grown accustomed and which are dear to me. I have dug my little hole there. Nothing ever gets lost in spite of the untidiness and bric-a-brac. I have evolved a beautiful theory about discomfort which I shall one day put in writing if I have the time. Discomfort is an excellent thing for man; it makes him modest and industrious, keeps him in touch with the real world. I have almost come to believe that the indecision I display in restaurants adds to the pleasure to be had from such places.

HE: I didn't know of this foible of yours.

I: Which one?

HE: This inability to decide what you want.

I: I'm only like this in restaurants.

HE: Did you know it's a characteristic you share with Roberti? He was like that over everything. Not only in restaurants. Because he always wanted everything and having to choose means having to eliminate. When you choose a woman, you eliminate all the others. Every time Roberti was faced with a choice he would conjure up a vivid picture of what he would lose by making it and this made him writhe in torment. By ordering duck you deprive yourself of lobster. The capacity of our stomachs isn't infinite. By taking Solange you deprive yourself of Juliette, Simone, Janine, Sylvie and Beatrice. You have a horrible feeling of renouncing the world, its joys, its glorious surprises. You are locking yourself up in a cell which appears no less gloomy and bare because you are entering it of your own free will and bolting the door yourself.

I: You really have the oddest conception of love.

HE: It isn't my own conception I'm giving you now. I'm simply trying to explain a certain way of feeling Roberti had. Besides, it was your hesitating between the duck and the lobster that made me think of it. I suddenly remembered this characteristic of Edouard's: indecision, the desire to have everything. Seeing him so greedy, watching his struggles to hoard up the most contradictory sensations, I sometimes used to compare him with a delivery man from a big store, tottering beneath a huge pile of parcels and boxes because he wants to make only one round. Packages constantly keep falling off the pile; he stoops to pick them up but as he does so he lets another fall, and so on interminably.

I: Like the story of Sisyphus.

HE: Yes. Roberti was the Sisyphus of hatboxes. If I had to paint a symbolic portrait of him I would depict him staggering through life overloaded with parcels. One is labeled "Adultery," another "Marital Fidelity," a third "Politics," a fourth "Literary Ambition," a fifth "Indifference to Worldly Goods," a sixth "Love of Material Objects" and so on. There are too many for me to be able to list them all: with every step Roberti took, the pile of boxes shifted dangerously, yawned apart and miraculously re-formed, but this state of affairs couldn't go on forever. A moment came when all the parcels fell. Badaboommmm! Poor Sisyphus was dragged down in the general collapse. He lost his balance, that precarious balance he had maintained with such skill for fifty-two years. To add to his woe, this occurred at the most inconvenient spot and at the worst possible moment, just as he was walking along the edge of the cliff overhanging the infernal regions.

1: Oh these metaphors, these metaphors! When will you drop this horrible mania of yours? There are few things I hate so much as forced metaphors. This last one is really monstrous. Besides, it proves nothing. To go back to the beginning of your argument, I see a fundamental difference between Solange and my lobster. I am eating duck today but I can eat lobster tomorrow if I feel like it. The one doesn't preclude the other except at this given moment. Solange precludes other women, certainly, but when she takes possession of your heart and your senses a well-known phenomenon occurs which you haven't taken into account: she replaces all other women. She is the epitome and synthesis of them all. She sends Sylvie, Janine and Beatrice into oblivion. With Solange you can trace the whole history of love without skipping a single chapter. You don't in any sense enter a cell. On the contrary she opens up for you the great portals of life, opens them onto an endless and infinitely varied landscape. As for your hatbox idea, do you mind if we drop it?

HE: Forgive me, but my hatbox idea is not so farfetched and I shall take the liberty of rounding it off with the help of what you've just said. Roberti thought he could without harm add the "Solange" parcel to all the others with which his arms were already full. But he failed to notice that this parcel was far heavier and more cumbersome than the rest, a parcel which called for every ounce of a man's strength. To hold it firmly, he should have unburdened himself of all the others. This he didn't do out of a mixture of conceit, avarice and blindness or, if you prefer and as I have already said twenty times, because he was rational. All myths meet in Roberti. He was Sisyphus, but he was also Oedipus offending the gods and Polycrates hesitating to cast his ring into the sea. And I could easily find a dozen other figures from antiquity who foregathered in his complex soul. Not to mention Faust, of course.

ı: Don't bother. I can find them for myself. Get back to the point, for heaven's sake, in other words to the story. And if possible tell it without metaphors. It is the story I need; the story is what I shall never be able to invent.

HE: Have you noticed how, in a love story, the words which crop up most frequently are "the day after"?

ı: Those words crop up most frequently in any kind of story, because stories follow the time sequence and time is divided into days, you goon.

HE: Yes, but "the day after" plays a particularly important part in love stories. The day after or the day before. Hardly ever the present moment. This is specially striking in cases of adultery. Love takes place much more in the mind than in bed. We hope and desire and remember and regret; we relive our moments of rapture far more than we actually experience them. We make plans which in the event always have to be altered, we lose ourselves in dreams through which we try to revive transient pleasures. Except for a privileged few, love is solitude. But a "magnetized" solitude, if I may put it that way, a teeming solitude which scarcely oppresses us at all, so strong are the emotions with which we fill it. Rarely, in fact, does one have the right (or inclination) to live permanently with the woman one loves, never leaving her side, drawing inexhaustible refreshment from her company. Most often love is inopportune; it comes too late, when our lives are set and nothing can be changed without causing disaster. So lovers think a great deal about each other. Their obsession compensates for the lack of the other's presence. That is why frustrated love is as a rule so enduring. We substitute poetry for all that we miss by not seeing our beloved. She appears to us like a beautiful figure by Rembrandt or Caravaggio, that is to say three quarters hidden in sublime shadows. All we can see are a few brush strokes of exquisite light which we never weary of admiring. In his solitude the lover recalls these patches of light and sets his imagination to filling out the shadows. There is no end to this pursuit; it procures moments of sweetness and ecstasy far surpassing those of reality. I have often wondered why people in love take pride in their love and implicitly regard themselves as superior to those who are not in love. It is due to this ability to dream with which their love endows them. They recognize it as a creative gift. They build up their love, just as an artist pursues his work, in solitude.

ı: I should like to know why you inflict all these commonplaces on me. They are completely out of place here.

HE: Don't worry, it's not for the pleasure of treating you to traditional psychology. It's to let you know that, as an old hand at love, Roberti knew this process well and mistrusted it. But here again his rationalism and overconfidence played a dirty trick on him. If you will allow me to adopt Stendhal's phrase, he believed himself to be a devotee of *love inclination*, which is merely a pleasant and stimulating diversion, but completely immune to *love passion*. He was convinced that for Solange he would feel nothing but the love inclination he had so often felt for other women throughout his life. He told himself there was no harm in dreaming, desiring, hoping and remembering, so long as this remained within the confines of love inclination. It was just a meaningless game, a diversion, something to make one feel gay or, rather, lively and which it would be wrong to forego. And so, the day after his exploit, he put no curb on his happy memories and thoughts of delights to come. As a crowning lack of caution he argued as follows: "Here is a girl I fancy, whose senses respond to mine; a very sweet girl. I mustn't use her up too quickly. If I see her every day I'll be sick of her in a fortnight. But if I stagger our meetings, if I only see her every third or fourth day, our affair may last two, six months, possibly a year."

I: The typical reasoning of middle age, of a man who wants to husband his resources.

HE: You think so?

I: Obviously. Roberti's true argument was not what you maintain at all. It was this: "I am over fifty, while she is only twenty-five and moreover very ardent. If I set myself to give her daily proof of my love I won't last two months. So I will only see her once or twice a week at the most, in order to give her an exaggerated idea of my capacities." This was barely conscious reasoning, of course. The body gives its advice in its own way, in its sibylline language. The conscience translates this into its own tongue, in other words gives it moral motives and colors it with pretexts. One hardly ever says to oneself point-blank: "I haven't the strength I had when I was twenty," especially when it comes to love and one is still only middle-aged.

HE: I'm sorry but you're wrong. Roberti's reasoning was exactly as I have told you and not as you have interpreted it. It wasn't the typical reasoning of a man of fifty but typical of him, Roberti, and those like him. He had already followed it thirty times, at every stage in his life. It was the reasoning of a thrifty, provident, rational man, a man who had never been afraid to love but on the contrary had been afraid of not loving enough and of being loved too much. With Roberti, love was like a fire which is hard to light and constantly threatens to go out.

If you pile on logs you smother it; you can only make it last by occasionally adding a few twigs.

1: A shallow character!

HE: Yes, if you like. A shallow character, but accepting its shallowness, exploiting it and turning it to his best advantage. Anyway make no mistake, this applies to the moral Roberti, not the physical Roberti who, even at fifty, was in no way diminished but just as brilliant as he had been at twenty or thirty. In fact, he had never experienced any decline in his vigor.

1: You will never convince me that, when he embarks on an affair with a girl just half his age, any man of fifty doesn't take a few precautions, if only to avoid failing to live up to her idea of him.

HE: I promise you that in this case such considerations never came into it at all. Roberti never even saw what would have been obvious to the most shortsighted: that around fifty is a critical age—an age when one runs a severe risk of falling in love, especially if one has never been in love before, and when a pretty girl is a mortal danger. All he saw in his affair with Solange was a routine adventure and he made his usual dispositions. He clung to the cynical reasoning of a blasé man who gets the most out of life and makes his pleasures last. Behind him he had forty-nine years of cramped emotions, cautious behavior, skimpy liaisons; his life was a pendulum which had never swung very wide; besides, one doesn't change at fifty! Great love doesn't descend on one at fifty. No, no. Gently he would grow old by Agnes' side; his boys would make careers for themselves; he would help them; he would go on till his dotage, from one re-election to the next. That is how he saw his future and in no other way. Solange was just an episode.

How infinitely preferable a little true folly would have been to all this wisdom! How much more rewarding a little naïveté would have been than this fallacy about love. But how can one act against reason? How can one go against experience? One must let them proceed, with their train of disasters.

1: Well, we are as we are. You can't make a man of a given character behave as if he had a different one. You can't make a man of experience behave as if he had none. It is like asking a banker to get rid of his money because it only causes him headaches or because he misuses it, and go and beg in the streets instead, on the grounds that being a beggar would suit him better and make him happy. Don't worry, your banker will always prefer his stomach ulcers and insomnia (apparently the usual consequences of financial operations) to the carefree life and cast-iron health of the beggars in the Place Maubert. Contrary to the old adage, I have observed that the man capable of doing the most can rarely do the least. A rational man finds it as hard to commit an act of folly as a lunatic does to behave sensibly. I am surprised that you, who so often evoke destiny, cannot see as much in this particular aspect of character, though it is here and nowhere else that destiny resides. Destiny consists, in fact, of all those secret temptations, distortions, divagations of the soul, those habits of thinking or feeling we unwittingly contract; it is the experience we have accumulated one way or another, it is a series of good or bad strokes of fortune which have molded the mind so that it has developed a certain concept of the way of the world, a certain philosophy to which it more or less conforms and which leads it to success or disaster. That is how I myself conceive of destiny, if the word has any meaning at all, if it isn't just an invention of poets or an old wives' tale. Roberti seems to me the perfect illustration of this approach. In him as you have described him and shown him in action, I find all the elements of his own perdition. The situations a man finds himself in are meaningless as such. Everything depends on the courage with which he faces them, on his capacity for resistance, in other words his strength of spirit. Otherwise how can you explain why some people with tragic lives are full of confidence and gaiety, while others who have every reason to be happy sink into the blackest gloom?

HE: You produced a pretty proposition just now when you said that "one can only argue if one is in agreement."

I: My exact words were that "in order to argue one has to be of the same opinion." I call it Ballanche's Theory, for it was Ballanche who made this extraordinary discovery. Genius turns up in the oddest of places!

HE: Well, by virtue of Ballanche's Theory I solemnly declare as follows: I believe that my conception of destiny and yours are, each in its way, correct and that it would take little, a trifling argument, to reconcile them. Listening to you, I find it impossible to say you are wrong; but I also find it impossible to deny that I am right. It follows that our attitudes are not contradictory but complementary. That is why we each find so many arguments to defend them, but for which we'd have dropped the subject long ago. We disagree on the surface but we agree at heart. I have taken one step in your direction. Now you take one in mine. Admit that the outside world with its accidents accounts for half of a man's destiny. Half, I say. No more. Fifty per cent. That is the margin of good or bad luck which results in one's making out or not.

I: Fifty per cent . . . That seems to me a pretty wide margin.

HE: Don't haggle. The world always has one chance in two against us, however stout the heart that resists it.

I: The world can certainly make us very happy or unhappy, it can leave us alive or kill us. But it can exert no influence on our futures. It can do nothing for our salvation or damnation. A noble soul remains noble amid the worst of difficulties. A petty one finds a way to betray its pettiness in the midst of the most persistent successes. That is my creed.

HE: A noble soul, a petty soul! Extremes! But there are very few extremes. On the other hand there are masses of average souls. What do you do about the average saved or the average damned? It is they who people paradise and hell, just as nations are peopled by average citizens and not by geniuses. It is they who interest me, those whose damnation or salvation hangs by a thread all their lives. I'm not talking about St. Vincent de Paul or Judas. I am talking about Tom, Dick and Harry, for whom good or bad luck are not just empty words but formidable realities, whom a mere nothing, a coincidence, a happy encounter or a spiteful remark can tip into good or evil. Roberti, since it is to him we are devoting this evening, might equally well have reached harbor in his dinghy, sailing close to the wind and avoiding shoals and reefs as he had done for forty-nine years. But he happened on Solange, on this Nausicaä who proved far more fatal to him than any Circe, and he went down. At the point our story has reached, he had already crossed this fifty-per-cent margin, this margin of the world's good or bad luck. Destiny was now contained within himself, and this was the worst thing that could possibly have happened since his soul was incapable of extricating itself singlehanded, without the external support of chance. He was driven back on his own resources and suddenly we see that he was a man without resources. We can also see that this upright man had evil latent within him. For him to be saved now, Solange would have had to die, be run over by a car or drown herself in the Seine.

I: Rather a drastic solution.

HE: But the only one, and as it didn't happen . . .

I: Before I forget, let me point out that purgatory was invented for average souls. I imagine paradise and hell must be pretty empty. One cannot bump into many people there. But purgatory, ah, what a crowd! Think of all the billions of people crammed together like sardines in a tin! And now perhaps we can come down to earth again, because these brave theological disputes aren't getting us very far. We shall find out all about hell, purgatory and paradise in due course, and anyway we're not asked for our opinions on them.

HE: How can you say that? We are asked every hour, every minute of our lives.

I: I wish you would tell me one thing. Do you intend to describe every episode of this affair in detail as you've done so far?

HE: There's still a lot to come, you know.

I: Admittedly you're a good storyteller but even so you're not Scheherazade. I don't want to get to bed too late. I am afraid a day-by-day diary of Roberti and Solange's affair might become a bit of a bore.

HE: It would have been rather tempting. Something a writer ought to tackle. The complete diary of a great love affair which should at the same time be a mediocre one, as great loves usually are. Everything. You would have put everything into it. All the greatness and all the mediocrity. And the passing of time, now slow, now racing ahead, with its acres of boredom, the wounds and humiliations it inflicts. Showing love in all its splendor and all its horror, living a life of its own, with its own features, like the scourges or blessings of heaven, as terrifying as cholera or the seven plagues of Egypt, as beautiful as the harvest or the world's first vision of a rose in bloom. Reproducing life as it is and as no one ever knows how to convey it. Ten thousand pages. Twenty fat volumes. A monument of literature. Doesn't that tempt you?

I: No. I'll tell you why artists never show life as it is: because it would be insufferably tedious. It isn't very hard to portray reality. I don't pretend it is within the reach of the first fool you meet but at least it is not a superhuman task. All one needs are eyes and ears and a gift for photographic reproduction. Copying reality is the first step in art, or the first step in a revival after art has been bogged down a long time in mannerisms. That is the least one can do. What one has to produce is something truer than the truth and believe me, that is tough. Out of one cubic meter of life, after employing the indispensible alchemy, you get one cubic millimeter of art. And even that is reckoning generously, just to show you the amount of reality which enters into the *truer than the truth*. You have to multiply truth by at least a thousand, that is to say dehydrate it, reduce it, increase its density to fantastic proportions. There are certain stars, I believe, whose matter is so dense that were you to fill a matchbox with it this would weigh as much as a locomotive. Well, art is the same. The problem is not to construct a locomotive. Anyone who applies himself can do that, given a plan and the necessary parts. The problem is to construct a matchbox which weighs as heavy as a locomotive. Doubtless that is why there aren't many artists. When you ask me to mirror the daily events of a great mediocre love, you are offering me the locomotive. I've no need of that machine. It's the matchbox I want, the precious matchbox weighing a hundred tons.

HE: Done! A hundred tons is a lot. But I'll try to run you up a matchbox weighing fifty pounds. It will be something to go on with. Anyway that's none of my business. It's yours, rather.

I: Listen, set your sights at a matchbox and not at a locomotive. That's all I ask. I'll work at it too. Between us we may achieve a hundred pounds and then, as they say, bingo!

HE: All the same, do please keep the details I've given you about the beginnings of Roberti and Solange's affair. The beginnings are always so exciting, so fascinating, even if the affair is a dingy one! There's a sublime light in the first stirrings of love, of every love. Each time one feels the same amazement as at the creation of the world.

I: True. The discovery of a new being to whom one is drawn by desire and curiosity is always wonderful. It brings the same rapture every time. Even if one hasn't a single illusion left about humanity, one lets oneself get caught up by it all over again. The wiles of women are not exactly varied or subtle, God knows, yet they are enough to ensnare the most hardened philosophers. A tender gesture, a smile, a veiled look and they are hooked. They know perfectly well what lies behind the smile and gesture and look: an undistinguished soul, a limited mind, narrow prejudices and almost no conversation but never mind, they are dazzled. I should like to know why.

HE: You needn't expect *me* to tell you. I never look for the why of things; I confine myself to observing and, if possible, understanding them. It is a modest approach which to my mind conforms with our humble human condition. When people ask me "Why?" I always like to reply: "I don't know *why* but I do know *how*." Besides, *why* is generally of no importance. It is *how* which is worth the telling. You, being an artist, ought to understand that. Artists are specialists in *how*, philosophers in *why*. If you ask me why the beginnings of love are the best part, I could at a pinch offer surmises, list various possibilities and give you my ideas on the matter, which are without interest. But if you ask me how, I'd be in my element. I'd show you the beginnings of love in all their beauty, I'd furnish all the details. And my reply would have answered both questions, for many *hows* end by equaling a *why*, many descriptions add up to one explanation.

I: If you want my opinion, what you really excel at is in reversing your views, hedging, bluffing and confusing the issue. Right. Let's push on. Life wouldn't be long enough to answer all your propositions point by point.

HE: I must be an utter nitwit since I am continually amazed when you level this type of reproach at me.

I: You a nitwit? To my mind you're the complete artful dodger.

HE: I promise you I'm not. I just say what I think in all innocence. I promise you I believe implicitly in this "how-why" business. You ought to know me well enough by now! You ought to know I don't go in for poses, that I hate poses, that I say things as they enter my head, that I always try to find my own truth, after which I speak it without further ado.

I: You're very subtle for someone who claims to be ingenuous and you explain yourself with too much perspicacity.

HE: But none of that precludes ingenuousness, believe me.

I: Perhaps, after all, you are right.

HE: I always do my utmost, that is to say I push my observations and deductions as far as I can. After which I have no strength left to change my views or confuse the issue. Such changes of view as I appear to make stem quite naturally from what I have been saying. They are the shiftings of truth. Truth also shifts its view and why not?

I: Oh, oh! Truth! There's a rash word. So you hold the truth, do you?

HE: No, of course not. But I believe I have succeeded in tracing, marking out and pinning down my own truth. I have put its complex system into order. I have applied this system and it works. It works! Its movement spreads outward and has repercussions. It may be that sometimes it ends in an about-face. A cunning and skillful man is a man who spares himself; who keeps well within his powers so that he has enough left to dissemble or contradict himself. A simple unsophisticated man is a man who goes to the extreme limit of his power and sometimes even beyond it, even at the risk of putting himself in the wrong or making a fool of himself; he is a man who throws everything he has into what he says or does and burns his boats behind him, so sure is he of his heart. When he reaches the goal he set for himself he has as little breath left as the warrior of Marathon at the end of his race. Can you see the warrior of Marathon amiably smiling and handing out autographs after having covered twenty-five miles at the double? Poor wretch! He flung himself down, his heart burst in his chest and he died within the hour. When I am talking I always try to imitate the warrior of Marathon, who to my mind represents the height of ingenuousness.

I: I surrender. You are ingenuous. Since lunch you have been running a marathon of ingenuousness. But after having lauded the exploits of the marathon runner, who will have a word to say about the sufferings of his teammate? Let's get on to the matchbox.

HE: How are we going to tackle this box?

I: Through something you haven't told me, which seems to me far more important than any of our moral considerations: by giving such a brilliant performance on his second visit to the Rue d'Argenson, did Roberti bring Solange any revelation of the senses? It's an important point on which the rest of the story depends.

HE: Ah, it isn't as simple as that! Revelations of this kind are not immediate, staggering, dazzling. They are progressive. They are like a sort of education. Although she was sensuous, Solange was very ignorant about this type of thing. Nobody had as yet awakened her. Like most women, she only knew of love by hearsay. I believe she was surprised. Pleasantly surprised. But she didn't immediately appreciate this initiation through which Roberti was taking her. She didn't grasp its extent. She failed to appreciate its significance. She didn't see how heavily this chain would weigh her down in the future. Do you remember how I described her, how Roberti pictured her as he fell asleep? She was broken, worn out and very happy. She felt "wonderful." In spite of all the evidence, she remained in the dark as to the real reasons for this completely new and delicious sense of well-being. She thought how extraordinary, how utterly *different* it was to be united with a man one really loves, how matchless was the joy it brought. But her ideas stopped short at these vague considerations. She was still unaware of any physical transformation. Realization of this only came later. Three weeks or a month later. She then told Roberti: "You have made a woman of me; before I knew you I was still a little girl." Such words must ring pleasantly in a man's ears.

From that moment Solange's love took on an entirely new shape; it was transformed. I mean it lost all its abstract quality and became a complete and ruthless passion feeding on motives which had the powerful support of reality. By the same token it became more selfish. Roberti, who hitherto had been a goal to be achieved, was promoted to the (higher) rank of an instrument. She began to need him. Her body added its desires to those of her mind and this combination, this multiplication of desires produced love in its completest form.

I: So here we are!

HE: Yes, here we are. We are about to leave one Solange and find another. Hitherto we have been considering a young girl, but her spirit now changes under the influence of her body. All at once she grows up. It's a moving transformation, all the more so in that there was nothing dramatic about it, it produced no striking change in her. As a girl she had never been vain and hard, uncompromising and insensitive, like so many girls, but on the contrary affectionate and devoted, taking no pride in her purity and youth. To draw a rather high-flown comparison, she was not Mathilde de La Mole but rather Mme. de Rênal before her marriage, before she met Julien Sorel. And then Julien arrived on the scene and Mme. de Rênal became a woman who loved to distraction, suffered and committed acts of folly unthinkable a month before.

I: There is something damned funny about Roberti in the role of Julien Sorel!

HE: Naturally. I am not comparing these two characters, only the kind of love they each inspired and the women who loved them. Roberti was loved with a veritably Stendhalian, in other words immoderate and tremulous love whose chief characteristic was complete and utter devotion. As you may suppose, he never suspected it for a moment. Or rather, yes, he did: now and then the suspicion flitted through his mind that he had engendered an exceptional passion but he preferred not to dwell on it. Such an idea upset him, it filled him with revulsion. Excessive love, or a love on too high a plane, becomes a burden; it creates obligations. There was a basic selfishness and vulgarity in his soul which always led him to despise his mistresses and, despite his outward show of respect, treat them fundamentally as whores.

At about this time I chanced to call on Dietz twice within four weeks. Thus I had occasion to confirm Solange's physical transformation with my own eyes. To the practiced observer this was surprising. Within four or five weeks her face had assumed an incredible look of relaxed calm, like a beautiful statue over which time had gently passed, which has been polished, mellowed and humanized by two or three hundred years of existence. There were no special signs to indicate this, since nothing in her face had altered, but everything about it was subtly different. The curve of the nose seemed purer, the eyes looked larger. The texture of the skin was more delicate and the complexion even smoother. Her body, too, had blossomed out. There was a new grace about her waist and hips. These were no longer the waist and hips of a girl. Even her neck struck me as different, although on each occasion she was wearing the same dress. It is astonishing how a woman in love can become desirable overnight, despite her air of deep preoccupation and the singleminded fidelity to be read in her face.

Another result of this metamorphosis was that Solange looked at life with new eyes. The last traces of her childhood had vanished. She staged an *auto-da-fé* of her dolls and "Souvenir de Dieppe" shell-encrusted boxes. The tear-stained Teddy bear was consigned to the dustbin. At the same time her heart changed in texture, so to speak. It learned more seriously how to conceal its feelings, and how these can bruise or inflame. Up till then nothing had really mattered. Her youth had been as vigorous as the jungle, where lush vegetation springs up almost at once to smother even the most violent geological upheaval. It had remained unimpaired, for she had a child's unconcern and gift of forgetfulness. But with Roberti everything was different. A frown would worry her for two whole days. She spent her time in a continual state of alarm which seemed to her frightful. Her very life hung on a kind or unkind word. After parting with her lover she would go to bed feeling the luckiest of women, in a state of indescribable felicity, but the next day her anxieties would return. Roberti did not telephone. Two, three, four days would go by without any sign of life from him. Slowly she would sink into a despair all the more terrible in that she couldn't share it with anyone but must continue to display her usual cheerfulness. Then at last he would telephone and she was filled once again with tumultuous joy.

These ups and downs age one quickly. I mean, they age the soul; for as to her physical appearance, it became more heavenly each day. Due to the emotional experience she was acquiring and the gravity reflected in her face she had lost the look of a young girl, but this face was as smooth and downy, its flesh as fresh and luminous as ever. There weren't even any dark rings under her eyes. In short she was entering that sober period of life when things begin to *leave their mark*. When one ceases to be marble and becomes flesh. Venus touches the statue of Galatea and it becomes a woman with a normal body temperature and a womb to bear children, a tongue to speak words of love, a heart to be gay or sad. The old myth is constantly reborn at every stage in our lives, at every turn in our biology. Let us pause for a moment with Solange at the crossroads of youth and maturity. These are the important events of our lives. They mean far more than wars, migrations, the partitioning of provinces. They are the great adventure through which every one of us must pass.

One person who was struck by this transformation was Legay, but naturally he was a hundred miles from guessing its cause.

I: Why "naturally"?

HE: Because men rarely think things out. They note appearances but leave it at that. They don't seek for an explanation of what they see. Legay admired Solange with all his heart, he found her ravishing, but the suspicion never entered his head that this new beauty might be the fruit of love. True, he was influenced by Valentin, who had inordinately sung his sister's praises and successfully persuaded him that she was still a child as far as her heart was concerned. For Legay, Solange was "the perfect girl." In his more lucid moments he told himself that after all she was twenty-five—nearly twenty-six—and that at that age she couldn't have such a very girlish heart. But he soon banished such sacrilegious thoughts. From his talks with Valentin, his daydreams and cloudy plans for the future, a sort of hope had crept into his heart that one day her friendship would turn to love and she would wish to "share her life" with him. In short he was in love. This was by no means a consuming passion but a tender and protective love, a love of the shiest kind which he was careful to hold in check since he had never been shown the faintest encouragement. He dreamed, but only up to a certain point. He dreamed conditionally, if I may so express it, and kept watch to see that love should not invade him completely. Besides, at this time he was deep in his researches into extra-thin television sets, which preoccupied him a great deal and proved an excellent defense against the invasions of love.

I am no more than outlining all this because it only forms the background to our story, but I dare say you can see the general picture clearly enough. Right. From time to time, once or twice a week, Valentin would arrange an outing with Solange and Legay to which he sometimes invited Mlle. Angioletti—you remember, Solange's colleague at Dietz's office—and they would have good times together.

i: I remember perfectly. You already described one outing with the four of them, the day after Roberti kissed Solange for the first time.

he: Correct. What I am going to tell you now came six weeks later, in other words the great event in Solange's life had meanwhile taken place. Valentin, then, had arranged another outing. It was a Saturday evening. Solange had spent the afternoon with Roberti and they had naturally gone to the Rue d'Argenson. There she had acquired an even greater radiance than usual, which made her particularly alluring.

Love often makes us benevolent. On the other hand it is contagious. Solange's mind was entirely taken up with Roberti, who had raised her to seventh heaven; she was full of gratitude and ready to find everything beautiful. She was imbued with a faintly weary tenderness; her face betrayed such fulfillment, such inner joy, that Legay was deeply impressed. "Here is a girl," he thought, "it would be marvelous to love." Such reflections are only preludes; they lead straight to action. This is where love is contagious. Solange's love for Roberti, which found such violent expression in her features, her looks, the inflections of her voice, pounced so to speak on Legay, who failed to identify its nature. In other words, he felt in a confused way that she was imbued with love and this fascinated him, like a fish eying a baited hook. All this love bestowed on another appeared to him like an unknown treasure (unknown even to Solange), possibly destined for him and of which he might at least try to possess himself. "Solange"—so ran his thoughts—"is ripe to fall in love with someone and that someone may well be me." It was almost as if he could read expectation in her eyes and invitation in her pensive smiles.

This contagiousness of love is rather odd, don't you think? We catch love exactly like a disease. Not content with contaminating Roberti, Solange also contaminated Legay. Her love was infectious, like tuberculosis or leprosy. For you will have noticed that it was not with her, her beauty or her charm, that they fell in love; rather was it as if the love with which she was infected spread and propagated itself. She was a germ bearer.

I: Ugh! What a horrible comparison!

HE: Horrible but accurate. Legay experienced it that evening. He contracted the disease. The microbe jumped on to him.

I: *The Microbes of the Heart*. A nice title for a novel of love.

HE: They are very noxious microbes and they spare no one. Even Valentin didn't escape.

I: What's that? Don't tell me he fell in love with his own sister!

HE: Good God no, poor fellow! The germs worked their way into his organism but had a quite different effect. He began to hate Solange's love and fight against it. He saw her as the victim of a powerful and enthralling emotion of which he himself knew nothing. He was disgusted by the idea that she was enjoying a happiness in which he played no part. At this time, mind you, he still hadn't found anything out. He was still at the stage of conjecture. But Solange's radiance didn't leave him much hope. She was in love for sure, and her love was returned. It was time he butted in. So he attempted to force the situation. He took Legay aside and said: "How do you find my sister tonight?"—"Sensational!" replied Legay enthusiastically. "Yes, she's really looking her best," said Valentin. "I have an idea. It's too silly, the three of us going about the way we do. I am going to leave you together." Legay was delighted at this suggestion. "That's swell of you," he said. "Thanks a lot." But it mustn't have the appearance of a trap. Valentin's plan was this: they would all three of them go to the restaurant and then he would pretend to have an attack of indigestion. This wouldn't be difficult as he was a bit of a glutton and always overate. "I'm not feeling too well" he would declare. "I think I'll go home to bed. You two go and enjoy yourselves. You can tell me all about it."

The plan worked splendidly. Indeed, Valentin threw himself into it wholeheartedly. To make it appear more plausible he consumed twice as much food as usual and made himself really sick for two days. After his departure Legay proposed that he and Solange take a walk down the street. The old tactics of shy lovers. Walking seems to lend them courage and maybe they think it puts the object of their passion in the same tender, dreamy frame of mind as themselves. In any event, after ten minutes Legay, who was neither a Machiavelli nor a Talleyrand and had racked his brains in vain for some subtle approach, blurted out with a thudding heart: "Solange, for some months I have been trying to find a clever way of telling you I love you but I haven't been able to. I can't go on forever like this, so I've decided you had better know about it for better or worse. Now I've said it and I feel much better." Solange walked along staring at the ground. She was not surprised at this outburst; she knew Legay found her attractive and she had seen through Valentin's little conspiracy. Even so, she had hoped that—at least for some months—she wouldn't have to face a declaration. She made no reply. She was very put out. Now that Legay had done it, had taken the plunge, he was going to make her a formal proposal. Which he did. "I sometimes try to imagine my future without you," he went on. "It is dreary and hopeless. With you, on the other hand, it is wonderful. Whenever something makes me happy, I tell myself: 'How marvelous it would be to share this happiness with Solange, with the girl I love.' And when things go badly I say to myself: 'Oh, if only Solange were here I wouldn't give a damn!' I know it's difficult to say such things without seeming silly but it's true. That's how I feel. And, silly or not, I'm glad I've told you."

I: How nice he is, Legay! Of course Solange was so dumb she didn't understand a word.

HE: Make no mistake, she understood perfectly. But what would you have her do? One can't begin to love someone just because he has a fine character. That would be too easy. Once launched, Legay drew fresh courage from every word he spoke and told her a great deal more. He even waxed eloquent. In fact, he would have persuaded anybody save a woman in love. Actually, if only he had made this declaration two months earlier instead of that evening, he would have won her over. And once again destiny would have been changed. But two months earlier he was not yet ready and Solange was not yet carrying the virulent germs of love.

Turning down a proposal is always embarrassing unless one's a bitch. Solange would have defended her love for Roberti like a tigress but, faced with poor Legay who was close to trembling, who was so harmless and so touching in his appeal to her, she was filled with a deep wave of pity and affection. Besides, no girl ever lends an indifferent ear to a proposal of marriage. Even if her heart is otherwise engaged, it stirs emotions too deep and atavistic for her merely to feel annoyed. I believe Solange fleetingly regretted not being free and therefore unable to consent to becoming Mme. Legay. But her love for Roberti, her determination to live this love through to the end, was an imperative law she was powerless to break. Many women are like that: they regard their feelings as sacred and irrevocable. They obey them blindly, like the catechism. Sometimes it's exasperating.

I: And how did she get out of it?

HE: Admirably. At once with candor and tact. She had no experience of the world, as I have told you, but a good and delicate instinct. Gently and kindly, in a way which left no room for misunderstanding, she told Legay that she was very fond of him, that there was no one for whom she had a greater respect, but that she didn't love him. This was followed by the usual speech, but delivered in tones of genuine regret. So much so that the poor fellow was not really hurt and managed to preserve a faint optimism in the midst of his disappointment. He did, however, venture to ask whether by chance she loved someone else. Yes, she said, and this ought normally to have closed the subject. But, moved by some strange confidence which nothing justified, he replied: "One day you will stop loving this man and I shall be there. I'll be waiting."

I: I don't care for that so much. It sounds silly and melodramatic. I'm surprised at it, coming from Legay. I thought he had more self-respect.

HE: Silly and melodramatic maybe, but logical in the circumstances; as for self-respect, that has nothing to do with it. Legay needed to say something of this nature to cheer himself up. Not to mention that, without seeming to, such promises prepare the future, adapt it in advance. As often happens in such cases, his love for Solange had been considerably strengthened by the declaration he had just made: it had taken shape; it had begun to exist objectively. An hour before, he could easily have given her up; but once he had brought his love into the open, once he had taken cognizance of it by giving it expression, such a sacrifice seemed beyond his power and he must at all costs have some hope to cling to.

I: Whatever explanation *you* may find, the fact remains that in saying

"I'll be waiting" he showed a lack of self-respect. There's a vast difference between Solange the pure young girl and Solange the secondhand mistress. There was only one thing for Legay to do and that was to say "I wish you joy of him" and walk off.

HE: You always have to put yourself in other people's skins. But Legay's skin is not yours. His moral outlook, his heart and feelings were quite different from yours. He had a working-class background. A naïve young man, he had no prejudices and no sense of honor. He didn't look on himself as *ridiculous* because the woman he loved did not love him. It was all one to him whether Solange was a virgin or not. For him the problem didn't present itself in this light: he didn't love this girl for her face or body alone; there was no vanity or possessiveness about his love; he loved her for herself, for her gentleness, her goodness, her soul. He loved her because he believed her to be an exceptional woman, not by intellect but by *nature*. For him she had a rare and precious nature worth making sacrifices for, worth waiting for. Legay was a humble man, he had no sense of superiority, least of all toward the woman he loved, whatever her shortcomings. She was in love with someone else. Very well. So what? It wasn't her fault, poor girl. It was neither a crime nor a vice. It was far less serious than if she had been a liar or a thief.

I: What rubbish! Do you want to know what I think? Your Legay was a socialist.

HE: Ah, I hadn't thought of that! Well then, long live socialism if it roots out bourgeois prejudices where love is concerned.

I: Only to substitute even sillier ones.

HE: Let's leave politics out of it. I simply wanted to show how he differed from you.

I: And you've spoiled him for me.

HE: Oh come, face facts. People are what they are. I never said Legay was a genius or a hero. Yet, such as he was, with all his strength and weakness, his moral outlook and his naïveté, he wasn't so bad. To return to Solange, she was not in the least put out by his love, in spite of its being so inopportune. In a way she was even grateful to him for loving her and this to my mind does her credit, since the natural inclination of a woman in love is to laugh at any other man who rashly ventures to pursue her. Finally, she asked him to keep their conversation secret. Valentin, when he had got over his indigestion, made it his most urgent business to rush for news, but he was sadly disappointed. Legay remained as close as an oyster. He confined himself to saying that nothing important had emerged from his heart-to-heart with Solange.

"I suppose she hasn't by chance fallen for anyone else?" Valentin inquired. Legay replied that he had no idea. The plot had failed and Valentin was furious. In spite of his question, he had a pretty clear idea of what was going on. What slob could Solange have got herself involved with? He gave himself a week to find out. Following which he would take steps to break up this infuriating idyll. Legay was the one man on earth who could make Solange happy; he was as certain of it as if he had had a revelation. Leaving his friend, he said, "Don't worry, I'll fix everything," in a tone so determined, so full of conviction that the other took strange comfort from it.

ɪ: Valentin is wonderful. He's a character out of antiquity. I realize you despise him, find him absurd with his fixed idea and his gluttony, but I must say I like him hugely. I find him enormously appealing. Here, now, is someone with a sense of honor! He was made to live in Rome at the time of Pope Sixtus IV, clad in a black doublet with a dagger at his side, feuding with the Orsinis and Colonnas. Then he would have fought the Commendatore Roberti, he would have laid him flat with one blow of his rapier and that would have been that. Instead of which he was a bank clerk in Paris, took the Métro and went to the movies on Saturday nights with a socialist electrician. What an age!

ʜᴇ: Yes, it's true that Valentin was not a man of our time. It's interesting how such ancient human souls—simple, upright, violent and limited—can lie concealed beneath the ready-made suits from the Belle Jardinière! Valentin didn't wear the clothes for which he was fitted, nor cut the figure for that matter. He had a right to a doublet and dagger, he didn't deserve the plump body and chubby cheeks of a Parisian pen-pusher; he was a character out of Marlowe or Otway. You'll never guess what he did after his emergency measures fell through.

ɪ: I can guess quite easily: he laid an ambush.

ʜᴇ: Correct. Three or four days later Solange carelessly announced that she wouldn't be home for dinner. From ten o'clock onward Valentin patrolled the pavement of the Avenue Daumesnil. He was determined to catch her in the act, that is to say watch her return to the fold and study the face of the friend who would certainly escort her. He lay in wait for an hour and a half; finally a black Peugeot drew up outside the house. Valentin was on the doorstep. The car remained there a good five minutes. The windows were closed but, thanks to the light from the street lamp, he could clearly see his sister chatting to a man who looked rather past his prime. The latter had one arm round her shoulders. She gazed at him with a tenderness which sorely vexed Valentin. The man was behaving in the most possessive way. With his free hand he was stroking her knee. Valentin could see this knee where the nylon stocking gleamed in the light. The man then bent down and kissed Solange in a most indecent manner, as if he had every right to do so. Valentin seethed with rage. The car door opened and Solange got out. At that moment the man's face was caught in a beam from the lamppost and Valentin had a clear view of him. "But he's an old man!" he cried to himself. "His hair is quite gray!"—"Good night darling," he heard Solange say: "Sweet dreams and don't forget me!"—"Disgusting!" thought Valentin. "He's got a potbelly!"—"Good night, my angel," said the man. "I'll give you angel, you old bastard!" thought Valentin. "He must be at least sixty." This was an exaggerated assessment, for Roberti hardly looked more than forty.

As Solange reached the entrance to the house, Valentin rose up out of the shadows. "Ah, so it's you? You made me jump," she said. "What are you doing here? Have you just come home?"—"I was waiting for you," said Valentin in a sepulchral voice. Solange felt herself blush at once for shame and fury. "Ah, I get it," she cried. "So now you're spying on me! Congratulations! My brother's playing detectives."—"Go on up," said Valentin, "we'll talk about this in your room."—"I've no intention of talking," retorted Solange. "This man you've seen is married and has children. He's my lover and I adore him. I wouldn't give him up for anything in the world, not even you." Valentin was flabbergasted. Stunned at her words, all his rage turned to grief. "But Solange, my dear," he said in a trembling voice, "he's an old man. You can't love him, it's not possible. You're going out with him because he's offered you a good job or something. But he's fooling you."

I: Poor Valentin!

HE: Poor Valentin perhaps, but it would have been better left unsaid. This grossly unfair accusation that she was behaving like a tart wounded Solange more than she could say. She didn't understand that her brother was trying to find extenuating circumstances for her. All she saw was the insult. She gave him a look of such hatred and contempt that the wretched young man felt quite desperate. "Let me pass," she said icily.

I: What a tigress! And such a gentle character! To think that only a month back she was sobbing over her Teddy bear!

HE: That is how women in love are. Valentin, however, wasn't one to wallow in despair for long. By the next morning he had himself in hand. At least he knew what he had to reckon with and, however appalling the damage, he had measured its full extent. He began to reflect and, for once, forced his quick temper under control. It wasn't going to be easy to demolish a man of whom Solange had spoken so ecstatically. It would take six months, possibly a year. He would have to work underground, dissimulate, patiently mine away, create a hateful atmosphere and so on. But nothing would deter him from this holy crusade. Then he thought fondly of his dear Legay, to whom he had more or less given his word. This happiness Solange found with her "fellow," for so he defined Roberti in his thoughts, not knowing his name—this happiness revolted him. It made her sin even worse so to speak. Have you noticed how families hate to see one of their members being happy on his own or even, at a pinch, being quite simply happy? All happiness found outside the family circle, without its advice or help, is a prime insult to the social cell it forms. This powerful emotion was added to the others filling Valentin's soul. It all produced a great upheaval in this soul, which was unused to chewing over such complex problems. Before going into action he had allowed himself a few extra days to reflect. Such wisdom shows that he cherished no illusions as to the seriousness of what was going on. Narrow-minded and hot-tempered as he was, he saw clearly that he would have to dissemble, like a primitive warrior who learns on the battlefield that a strong arm is not the only answer and there are certain circumstances in which strategy, ruses and bluff are necessary to ensure victory.

Naturally there could be no question of considering Solange's heart. By falling in love with a married man, an old man, she had created an intolerable situation. Valentin, who had a quite exaggerated sense of responsibility, considered that fate had struck at him personally. But his small mind reasoned according to his resources, his traditions, if I may so put it. Twenty times an hour he would ask himself: "But what has happened to Solange, what has come over her?" In fact, simple people search for answers by ceaselessly repeating the questions that perplex them. It doesn't seem a very effective method, since incessant self-questioning on lines too vague or too general to lead anywhere ends by completely clouding the mind. Valentin was naturally brought up short by this riddle; but he took a sort of pleasure in vainly repeating it over and over. It worked like an incantation; like the keening of mourners, it lulled his sorrow to sleep. "What has come over Solange?" The only explanation he could find was: "She has gone mad." An answer barely more adequate than the question. Once again we find ourselves faced with the inner music. Valentin believed he was thinking; really he was just singing a lament to himself. Even so, the trouble with fools is that they tend to accept the conclusions to which their groping leads them as articles of faith. For Valentin, Solange's madness became a firm tenet. She had gone out of her mind. No other supposition was possible in the face of behavior as insane as hers. Unfortunately, where the cure of madness was concerned, he didn't share the theories of modern psychiatrists. In this respect he was not much more advanced than the men of the Middle Ages who held that lunatics must be locked up, beaten or burned in order to root out the devil within them.

Viewed from outside, love stories, even the most beautiful, the most rapturous in the world, always appear sordid. Why? Because outsiders only perceive the external details and incidental consequences. They see an unhappy wife, a husband driven to despair, cascades of lies and deceit, cruelty which seems futile, suffering and waiting and plotting and degrading duplicity. They don't sense what lies behind all this: the secret and ineffable joy lovers give each other and which is a motive powerful enough to turn a hitherto gentle and candid woman into a consummate liar, an implacable enemy, or a likable and considerate man into a brutish lout. So they ask themselves with their cool and lucid minds how love can withstand for even two days all the discomforts, all the discredit, all the muck it stirs up. Valentin was like this over Solange's love. He couldn't conceive how his sister's fits of depression, her outbursts of tears, her haggard or morose expression, her long despairing hours of waiting, her hastily snatched meetings, could fail to open her eyes within a week or two. It was really too silly for such a pretty girl, leading such a simple and pleasant life, to make herself ill over an old goat! She was Titania in love with an ass because Oberon had cast a spell on her. What aberration could have led her to fall in love with a monster, to choose this shameful life "beyond the pale"? What diabolical twist of her heart had led her to fling herself into a world of shame and secrecy when it was so good to live out in the open with one's head held high in respectability and innocence?

What particularly vexed Valentin in this contingency was that he couldn't seek the advice of Legay, whom he had imperceptibly formed the habit of consulting on almost every score. Legay was full of common sense and simplicity, with what in the old days used to be called "an upright mind." This didn't always furnish very profound judgments but it endowed him with a fair to middling wisdom which astounded the quick-tempered and impulsive Valentin, who tried hard to emulate it. An added reason for wanting Legay for his brother-in-law. In the event, the only persons to whom he could unburden himself were his parents. He decided on this after a few days of his own special brand of pounding about in circles which is peculiar to men of his character.

1: Describe this pounding about please.

HE: It's quite simple. Take a rudimentary mind like Valentin's, most of the time sterile. An idea drops into it. This is an event. Valentin looks at his idea with surprise, like a hen that has laid a duck's egg. Besides, the idea resembles an egg. It is spherical or, rather, ovoid and perfectly smooth. Impossible to penetrate it. What chick, what duckling can it enclose? A fathomless abyss of questioning. He must wait. Nothing can be learned until the egg has hatched.

I: The hostility you display toward poor Valentin pains me. Anyway, where does the pounding about come in?

HE: Wait. We are only at the first stage. The idea, then, dropped into Valentin's empty mind. It took shape as follows: "Solange is sleeping with an old man. Shall I tell our parents or not?"

I: An elementary train of thought.

HE: Elementary for you but not for Valentin. Two days elapsed between the first proposition and the second, between the statement of the fact and the dilemma it posed. Here is where the pounding about begins. Valentin pounded in circles, stamping on the egg as if he wanted to break it. "If I talk to the parents, they'll be horrified, poor things. They've always been so respectable. . . . They didn't deserve this. . . . Their daughter, their own daughter . . . A married man . . . Yes, but on the other hand, they'll have to know. . . . Mama will talk to Solange. . . . Papa will put her to shame. . . . There'll be the three of us against her. . . ." and so on and so forth.

I: I don't call that pounding about. Valentin was weighing the pros and cons like anyone else.

HE: Then I apologize. I must have explained myself badly. In summing up his thoughts I made them too clear, too articulate. In actual fact he flung himself with his whole weight on the dilemma. He trampled it flat. People who weigh the pros and cons list the various arguments and finally subtract one from the other. For Valentin the process was different; he pulverized the arguments, he turned them into porridge. Having once obtained this porridge, he was no further ahead than before and his final decision was a matter of hit or miss. Let me make another comparison. Everything went on as if his thoughts were drowned by a sort of tom-tom inside him whose rhythm grew more and more obsessive day by day. "Solange and her old man, *boom boom boom boom boom!* Solange and Legay, *boom boom boom boom boom!* Tell the parents, *boom boom boom boom boom!* Deal with it by myself, *boom boom boom boom boom!*" That is pounding about. It consists of interminably repeating to oneself a few contradictory but coexistent ideas. It's not a question of reconciling these or taking a stand after due consideration, but of shaking all these ideas up together like knuckle-bones in a bag, rubbing one against the other until they have lost all shape. After a few hours or days of such mashing one is worn out but ripe to take a decision. This is the way people who don't know how to reason warm up their instincts, for in the end it is the instinct that decides, just as it could have done right from the start.

So Valentin, after three or four days of pounding about, stifled his conscience. Some people are prevented by a misconceived solidarity from bringing help to dear ones who are heading for ruin. He was the opposite. Solange was in danger: he must do everything he could to save her, even if this meant betraying her, for it would be a betrayal to tell their parents and involve them in any action against her. He arranged the family conclave with a certain dramatic flair which considerably alarmed the poor Mignots. They were good people, simple and easygoing. It must be something very grave for Valentin to have resolved to shake them out of their torpor. Father Mignot was retired from the post office, where he had ended his career as a postmaster; he was a tall, thin, dreamy man who said little, thus concealing the fact of his stupidity. Mother was a pleasant, equable character, kindly in a negative way, that is to say weak, accommodating, rather indifferent.

I: A fine pair of counselors!

HE: Nonsense! The Mignot parents were like most human beings. People who had never read a book in their lives. So it isn't surprising they were fools. They had to make do with what little experience their dim and on the whole contented lives had taught them. Forty years' experience is wholly inadequate. One needs two thousand. The two thousand years' experience to be had from the works of good authors. As a guide to life one must have some idea of the major novels, epics and tragedies written since Homer. Here's a little picture of the scene: Mama was in her apron; Papa had his waistcoat unbuttoned and his tie off. In a sepulchral voice Valentin declared: "Solange is up to no good," and went on to explain the position. There was one really idiotic comment to be made and inevitably Father Mignot made it. "This had to happen," he announced sententiously. It is the phrase fools always fall back on to express their amazement at anything unexpected, unpredictable or unusual. The other two nodded their approval. Although there was no special reason why *this* should happen (that is, why Solange should become the mistress of a middle-aged, married family man) they paused to admire Father for his perspicacity and knowledge of the world.

When Valentin had finished his story, the elder Mignots gave vent to such forceful comments as: "Well, here's a pretty kettle of fish. It just goes to show. If this isn't the limit. And to think I had absolutely no idea. I was only telling myself yesterday she's been looking out of sorts. One can't trust anyone these days. The little hypocrite! Oh my goodness, whatever shall we do? The disgrace of it! I'd never have believed it. A man old enough to be her father! Why can't she stick to boys of her own age? . . ."

ɪ: Stop it! You're making me sick. I can just hear them.

ʜᴇ: Coward! I only have to "switch the sound on" for thirty seconds and you immediately turn it off. Reproducing the Mignots' clichés is rather like my describing their furniture. This was the kind of thing Solange heard every day, much as she saw the cherry-wood dining-room suite and the four imitation Louis XVI armchairs in the sitting room. The miracle is that she was in no way affected by it. She passed unseeing and unheeding through these horrors, like a Christian saint in the Colosseum at whose feet the lions lie down meekly like dogs.

To return to the family conclave, a whole hour was taken up with remarks of the kind I have quoted. The Mignots were sorely put out and I believe would have much preferred Valentin to have held his tongue. They found themselves in fact in the throes of a conflict which seemed to them extremely involved and which I shall try to unravel for you. On the one hand their popular traditions inclined them toward severity; they had a patriarchal concept of the family, in which the parents hold undisputed sway while the children have no choice but to obey. On the other hand they were twentieth-century parents: I mean, they had more or less abdicated their authority. Valentin had long since taken their place when it came to decisions regarding Solange. Under any circumstances he had always stood by his sister. He was her ally and natural protector. For instance, when she reached seventeen Father had wanted her to go into the post office, while she had hankered to be a private secretary. Thanks to Valentin's intervention the private secretary won the day. This initial victory dispossessed the elder Mignots of their parental power. But what was happening now? Valentin found himself in the position of an absolute monarch forced by tragic events to convene the states-general and invoke their help in subduing the populace or imposing exceptional sacrifices on it. This unusual attitude disconcerted and embarrassed them. "Careful," they told themselves, "we'd better watch our step. Otherwise we'll get all the blame, as sooner or later these two are bound to join forces again." Notwithstanding Father Mignot, who from serving in the Great War had preserved the habit of getting worked up about anything and everything, cried: "When I was young, things like this didn't go on. I can't keep up with young people nowadays. But I for one am not going to beat about the bush. If Solange doesn't give her fellow up in forty-eight hours, by God I'll throw her out!" This ill-considered declaration had a curious effect: it sobered them all down and destroyed the budding coalition.

I: None of this is very serious. Did these poor people at least decide what attitude to adopt, what action to take?

HE: Decide what? What action? Solange was over twenty-one. Father's threatened ultimatum showed them the absurdity of adopting an uncompromising attitude. Their sole weapons were moral considerations, appeals to decency and common sense, and these carry little weight against love. In the end they agreed it would be wisest to "wait and see," meanwhile registering their disapproval by studied frigidity.

I: Was sulking all they could really find to do? It's not credible!

HE: Sulking is the last resort of fools. When they don't know how to get out of a situation, they fall back on shocked dignity.

I: How grotesque! Scowling at a twenty-five-year-old girl because she has taken a lover not to the family's taste.

HE: Believe it or not, the Mignots thought this project quite remarkable. Besides, they believed they were still dealing with the Solange they knew, their obedient little Solange whom they stubbornly persisted in regarding as a perpetual adolescent. Such a docile child would never withstand two weeks' hostility. Besides, anyone could tell her affair with her "fellow" wouldn't last. He would seize the first opportunity to drop her. Then they would see her return to the fold, filled with remorse and shame. They would push through her marriage to Legay and all would be for the best in the best of all possible worlds. The Mignots felt so sure of their victory that they paraded an air of anxiety from which they derived considerable pleasure. Valentin alone was really unhappy. Whatever the respect he professed for his parents' experience, the future seemed to him less simple and certain. This discussion had greatly disappointed him, but what else could he have expected? His parents clearly knew nothing about life. He also realized he had failed to find the right words to jerk them out of their harmless dreams, the striking images and poisonous colors needed to fire their imaginations. The poor young man had too limited a vocabulary. God, how difficult it is to communicate with one's fellow beings, even one's own parents! We think we speak a certain language and they interpret it quite differently. Valentin would have liked to describe the kiss he had watched Solange give her lover, convey the tone of her voice when she said "Let me pass," color his story with all the passion and hatred he himself had witnessed, but it was impossible. There are no means to express such subtle nuances. This kind of dilemma is a very general one. Most people don't know how to talk. They give such garbled, uninspiring accounts of their experiences that they nearly always mislead their listeners. Helplessly they watch misunderstandings grow before their very eyes. For all their cries of alarm, nobody cares what they, the actual witnesses, felt. People only judge by the documentary evidence, failing to appreciate that this is only half the picture, only its outward aspects. We find the same phenomenon with historians, especially when they are earnest and humble, when they abide by men's deeds as testified by ancient documents and dare not advance theories as to the feelings which must have underlain and inspired them. Factual truth is only half the truth. One needs to be a poet or at least a philosopher to make oneself understood. With Valentin, of course, this was far from the case.

Round the dinner table that evening Solange met tight-lipped faces and icy looks. Even her mother did her best to appear harsh despite her easygoing nature. She realized immediately that Valentin had been talking and this galvanized her. When someone is inspired by a cause he believes just and proper, nothing deters him. Faced with these sullen scowls, she assumed a provocative air. If this was the beginning of a "cold war," she thought, it was beneath her notice; if it grew too unpleasant, it was always open to her to quit the parental home and set herself up in a rented room where she would live as most of her friends did. Two months earlier such a move would have seemed to her the height of sacrilege. The Mignots, for their part, seethed with rage. Their obtuse minds sensed an infuriating determination in Solange. It would have been beyond their power to feign cheerfulness or affection. Sulking suited them admirably; it enabled them at once to register their disapproval and conceal the fact that they were frightened.

I: Frightened? Really?

HE: Yes, frightened. Solange suddenly frightened them. They were thoroughly disconcerted by this girl who wore her love like armor. There comes a time when parents feel afraid of their children, perceiving that these have ceased to be the transparent, familiar little creatures who loved them more than anything in the world, and become men or women with secrets and passions and absorbing interests in which they play no part. Such a time had come for the Mignots. It saddened them and added fuel to their rage. All at once Solange was a woman to whom they no longer dared *tell everything*. This "child" (as they were in the

habit of calling her) had without asking their leave crossed the river
of life and was now standing on the other side.

Into what regions was she heading, which they would never know?
Solange was expecting to be brought to trial after the meal and prepared to defend herself tooth and nail. But nothing of the kind happened. They confined themselves to drily wishing her good night.

I: When she next met Roberti, I suppose she made a pretty tale of
all this? Women know how men like them to suffer on their account.

HE: Yes, her first impulse was naturally just that. But a little thought,
or more precisely her instinct, dissuaded her. She was beginning to
know Roberti and was afraid that Valentin's scheming and her parents'
antagonism might scare him off. In the past four to six weeks she had
sensed (I say sensed, not understood) what sort of man she had to
reckon with—how evasive, shrinking, obsessed by fear of scandal, tortuous, emotional and, if necessary, cruel he could be. Not that Roberti
had in any way revealed himself to her but she was already taking her
bearings on him with the sensitive perception of a blind man. No, no,
Solange said not a word to Roberti and, since he never inquired, he only
found out much later on what an ordeal she had been through for love
of him. She merely displayed a redoubled devotion which he welcomed
with the indifference of an idol accustomed to the worship of the faithful or, rather, accepted as a tribute to his performance as a lover and to
his charm. She saw her new position in a light at once tragic and
gratifying. "My family is against me," she thought. "I am going to have
to fight them. Even Valentin is deserting me. But never mind. I have
found something far more precious which amply makes up for what I
am losing." I believe that to be a very feminine reaction. Indeed, with
women love supplants every other emotion. The minute they are en-
snared by it, they overstep all bounds. They will ecstatically ruin themselves for love; they never hesitate to burn their boats even when they
don't have to. This is a reflection of their capricious, ardent, uncompromising natures. They make immense sacrifices for their lovers which
cost them next to nothing and expect equal sacrifices in return which
they don't get, for men are cautious, timid and slow to react, more
often given to compromise. For women, love is a god whose decrees are
not to be questioned; for men it is a political problem to be solved.

I: What idiotic things you can say! What do you mean by a political
problem? That in your view men covet women in the same way as they
covet a seat on the town council or in the Chamber of Deputies,
and put the same kind of energy into obtaining them? Don't be so absurd!

HE: No. That isn't exactly what I meant, although some such ambition does play a part in men's desire. To my mind masculine love is characterized by its practicality. Men organize their love in terms of their lives, whereas women organize their lives in terms of love. So that for women love poses no problems. They enthusiastically sacrifice everything for it. Whereas for men it sets constant problems. They have to adjust it, apportion it, prevent it from eating too much into their jobs, their livelihood, their social position. All the more so when they are public figures like Roberti, married and absorbed in sometimes important work. That is what I mean by a political problem. Love forces its way as best it can into the cluttered souls of men, whereas it takes sovereign possession of women, who divest themselves of everything else on its approach. Solange was an exemplary lover in that, while having sacrificed or being ready to sacrifice everything for love, she asked for no sacrifice in return. She "understood," that is to say resigned herself to being merely an accidental feature in Roberti's day or week, to loving him more than he loved her, to thinking of him more than he thought of her, to organizing her life in terms of the moments when he condescended to see her. She was like a fighter pilot who may be ordered into the air at any moment, dancing attendance beside his plane. She even loved this waiting. It was an *adjunct*, so to speak, one of the conditions of love, and anything which had a bearing on love, even suffering, was divine. This typically feminine approach was certainly due in part to her youth, her generosity and naïveté, but it also corresponded with her character, which you must by now be beginning to know. Like most women she lacked the creative spirit or, if you like, a certain form of initiative; she needed a guiding peg on which to hang her fatalistic mind, her passivity, her docility, her obedience. Hitherto this peg had been her parents and Valentin, who took decisions for her, lived in her stead, organized her life, inspired her with a filial and sisterly devotion strong enough for her to place her destiny in their hands. But then Roberti appeared and love, physical love with all its effects on the heart, completely altered her bearings. It was to him that she now looked. It was through him that she began to live. The Mignots and Valentin immediately ceased to be her mentors. From one moment to the next they became strangers.

She saw Roberti again three days after the family scene I have just described. They went to the Rue d'Argenson, where Roberti surpassed himself. He had lost every trace of physical shyness with her and was beginning to learn the mysterious paths which led her to ecstasy. This amused him and strengthened his attachment, not to mention the

superior man would have scorned and considered degrading. He had
been moved by Solange's words. His emotion was—how shall I say?—
more artistic than sentimental. Hearing them or, more precisely, contemplating the picture Solange conjured up as she spoke, he was filled
with the joy of an artist who has at last achieved the perfect curve
he was striving for. She was telling him that he was young and handsome. We readily believe declarations of this kind, especially when they
are reinforced by burning looks and sinuous gestures and when, moreover, one has only fifteen minutes earlier been granted unequivocal
proof of their speaker's feelings. So Roberti believed Solange, but believed her in the same way that an artist believes his work when it
tells him he has talent. That is to say, whereas he knew perfectly well
he was neither handsome nor so very young, he believed he still had
enough appeal and amorous skill to implant the all-powerful illusion
of good looks and youth in a woman's heart. Just as an artist loves his
work when he sees it fulfill his aims, so Roberti, listening to Solange,
became aware of a fresh reason for loving his mistress, over whose
senses and heart he ruled as absolutely as a poet over his poem or a
composer over his symphony. You know better than I the depth of intimacy that exists between the creator and his creation, and how grateful the former feels to the latter for reflecting him like a mirror. Well,
Roberti had an analogous feeling which instantly took hold of him and,
so to speak, fixed his love the way a vitamin fixes the calcium in the
body, the way a fixative fixes a light charcoal sketch on paper. There
was clearly no barrier, either sensual or mental, between him and Solange. They were on the same level; in her he found the exact imprint
of his body and feelings. Such ideas advance love with giant strides.
They weave bonds which may long remain invisible but which are very
strong, so that one day one wakes to find oneself bound hand and foot.

God, how fascinating the study of misunderstandings can be! The
intelligent get at cross-purposes just as much as the stupid. What Roberti principally took in of all that Solange said was her closing remark
of "It's you who will no longer want me." This struck him as a most
satisfactory response to his veiled threats, a most reassuring gesture of
submission. Since she envisaged the possibility of his one day abandoning her, he need no longer worry on that score. She was accepting her
status as a concubine who might be set aside at any moment. What a
relief!

I: It's a common phenomenon; people see only what they want to
see and take figures of speech for promises.

HE: Taking figures of speech for promises is one of the mainsprings

278

of misunderstanding. There are others. Masses of them. I have reached the point of no longer seeing anything in human relations but a monumental and all-embracing misunderstanding. Nobody understands anybody. Everyone is enclosed within himself as in a sealed bottle. He only hears his own inner sounds which drown out all the other sounds of the world.

I: It can't always have been like that. The way I see it, the lack of understanding increases and decreases according to the ups and downs of civilization. During primitive epochs it proliferates, it is all-pervasive; then it dwindles as civilization develops, customs become less rude and language grows purer. In classical times, that is times when there is a flowering of grammar, it is almost nonexistent. How long does a classical age last? One or two hundred years. After which the language becomes debased, literature becomes more complex and grammar collapses in ruins. Then misunderstanding enters once more into men's relations. It is one of my old hobbyhorses that few problems can withstand serious grammatical analysis. A little research would reveal that wars have been declared because of a misplaced relative pronoun. We live in an age of decadence in grammar, hence in an age when misunderstanding flourishes once more. During the Middle Ages misunderstandings sometimes led to the stake. We haven't got quite that far but we're heading that way. Those are the revenges of grammar. We have at our disposal a huge vocabulary with only a poor quality cement to bind it. We have lost the secret of the grammatical cement of the seventeenth century. The future looks black to me! Your Roberti is a striking example of all this. Just suppose that, instead of being a deputy in 1955, he had been a presiding judge at Aix or Dijon under Louis XV. What a difference! He would have been far less foolish. Above all, he would have spoken better French, which presupposes sentiments of a higher quality, a firmer judgment, a simpler philosophy and a less neurotic character. To me it is clear that a mind formed by Corneille and Bossuet must be constitutionally more robust than a mind formed by Gide and Giraudoux. There is nothing to equal Patru's speeches for teaching one how to talk and listen without excessive fear of misunderstanding.

HE: But here I completely agree with you. When I say "Roberti was a man of our time," I don't attach any weight to it, I assure you; I am not claiming a great discovery. No, no, far from it. I say "Roberti was a man of our time" in the flattest and most noncommittal fashion. It is just an objective statement, neither sad nor gay. Roberti the man of our time is not the same as Roberti a Councilor in the Parliament pleasure he himself derived from the surprising conformity of their bodies. That day Solange was at once so sad and so happy, she felt so abandoned by everyone and so close to her lover, that suddenly she exclaimed: "What is going to become of us?" It was through this sigh, this sibylline utterance, that she betrayed her confusion. Roughly translated, her meaning was: "I have broken with my brother and parents. You for your part find in me a woman who fulfills all the needs of your body. Will you have the courage to leave everything for me as I have left everything for you?" Roberti didn't dare face up to such an implacable translation but even so he was badly scared. His immediate reaction was: "God damn it, I've made her too fond of me and she's suggesting that I marry her. Why the hell did this have to happen?" He parried at once, for he was never short of repartee when it came to amorous dialectics. "What is going to become of us?" he said. "Upon my soul, I don't rightly know [gaining time]. I think we are going to be wildly happy [concession, politeness]. I am incapable of looking further than a week ahead [that's my philosophy and I can't change it]. For you I feel a strange attraction, an insatiable appetite [added politeness but this time rather offhand]. How long will it last? Maybe six months, maybe twenty years [with me nothing is certain, I never make promises I can't be sure of keeping, I am a free man, not a hope of putting a rope round my neck]. But in twenty years' time I shall be seventy; a bit old for a gigolo, don't you think? [a joke to end up with, to minimize the affair, reduce it to tiny proportions in comparison with life and the world in general]." A pretty speech, what? A little masterpiece of evasion. He delivered it lightly but in his mind it served as a sharp warning. After this, Solange must understand how things stood. She wasn't dealing with just another lover but with a man who claimed the permanent right to change his mind and who could never be caught off his guard. Oddly enough, this speech had far more effect on its maker than on its audience. It completely reassured him. He had the common failing of intellectuals, who believe it is enough to say something for it to be so, for it to imprint itself forever on another's mind. While he spoke, he hid from himself the abyss Solange had opened up before him. As for her, it left her saddened and touched. More than anything else she realized that in twenty years' time Roberti would be seventy and she felt immensely sorry for him. He must be very unhappy to say things like that! She threw her beautiful arms round his neck, kissed him passionately and murmured: "Be quiet. What are you trying to do? Make me cry? You are handsome, you are young. For me you are handsomer than anyone else. You are younger than I am. I have found myself in you. You have changed me into a woman. I am madly in love with you. I want you. I think of no one but you. When you are seventy I shall be forty-five, old and wrinkled, and it's you who will no longer want me."

I: It's difficult to imagine being loved like that! How stupid women are! Always it's the idiots and bastards who inspire the greatest passion. Can you picture a woman talking like that to a really superior man, a Beethoven or a Rousseau? Never! They keep such transports for mediocrities.

HE: It's normal. Superior men have no need of such things. They find consolation in their superiority. Besides, they are hardly ever *lovable*. Artists are vampires who take everything and give nothing; they devote all they have to their work, it's all they ever think of. You quote Rousseau and Beethoven but they must have been impossible to live with! Entirely wrapped up in their work, lost in their creative activity! And beastly characters into the bargain, bawling at everyone when their work went badly, sickeningly jovial when it went well. The same with statesmen: Napoleon slept with France. One can't go to bed with everybody. One has to choose. If you sleep with France, with painting, music or poetry, then France, music and poetry reward you by being in love with you, they murmur bewitching words worth anything Solange said to Roberti and embrace you more passionately than ever Donna Elvira did Don Giovanni. For women to love you they have to feel you belong wholly to them, that you have no other passion which might lead you to forget them for a week, a month or a year. That is why superior men are as a rule rarely pursued by members of the opposite sex. Besides, they have a peculiar kind of intensity which strikes a chill. To them, nothing is anodyne. They have a strict mental discipline, a rigid system of thought which renders them incapable of that fantasy and inconsequentiality which makes life seem fun. Their logic prevents them from talking nonsense and sweet nothings. This is unforgivable.

I believe, to talk like Sainte-Beuve, that Roberti was "in parts a superior man." But his superiority was incomplete. He slept neither with France, nor with art, nor with a high ideal. He slept only with women, and even those weren't out of the top drawer. So he was completely at liberty, there was no reason why he shouldn't be loved and loved passionately. Everything that was not superior about him conspired toward this by concealing such superiority as there was. Do you see what I mean? He was quite capable of clowning, talking foolish nonsense, even behaving as extravagantly as a young buck in the rutting season in order to adapt himself to his conquest. All affectations which a truly of Provence in 1660 or a member of the Convention in 1793. He has his own characteristics, his own peculiar savor. He represents a particular moment of sensibility. I don't claim this to be a privileged moment or more valuable than any other. Like you, I believe the sensibility of the French in 1660 was preferable to that of 1960. But we happen to be living now, not in 1660, and we have to choose. Either I am an archaeologist nostalgically reviving ways of being and feeling three hundred years old for his private pleasure and amusement, or I am a living person breathing the living scents around him. That is the question. I don't have to hold my nose because the smell of today is less fragrant than that of the seventeenth century. It interests me because it is the smell of our time. This in no way prevents me from regretting, like you, that I wasn't born into the world in a better age. What I am really getting at is that, to me, my attitude is more sensible than yours. Or let us say more pragmatic. I adapt myself to the world into which I have been cast, I try to get to know it and, if not like it, at least enjoy it. I don't despise it the way you do. I neither exaggerate its worthlessness nor my own distaste for it.

1: Thanks for the lecture!

HE: I'm sorry, but *you* read me lectures the whole time. So don't go getting annoyed because just for once I take the liberty of disagreeing with you. When you are alone and thinking back over this, you'll see that I'm right. You'll see it all the more clearly in that you admitted only just now that you don't know how to live in the past either.

1: Yes, I said that, but not in that way; I meant it slightly differently.

HE: Oh come! You're getting lost in nuances. There are some distinctions so fine that they are mirages and meaningless. This is one of them. Aren't you an artist? An artist is never a historian, nor an archaeologist, nor an antiquarian. You said as much yourself. It's just too bad if you were born under Romulus Augustulus rather than Octavius Augustus. Be sensible and sing your song on your electric lute with frequency modulations. Never mind if it's not up to the clavecin or the viola da gamba. One must do one's best with the means to hand. Roberti was not the Président de Brosses and his *History of Variations in Moral Outlook* was a far cry, alas, from the *Letters on Italy*. But such as he was, I find him more interesting than the Président de Brosses even so, just as a mathematician is more interested in the theorem to which his own researches have led him and of which he will be the discoverer than in the theorem propounded by Newton two hundred years ago. In the history of mathematics Newton's theorem is more important than that of M. Libellule, professor at the College of

Nancy; poor M. Libellule represents only a tiny link in the chain of mathematicians and his name will not survive; but this doesn't alter the fact that mathematics today cannot dispense with M. Libellule's modest toil and that in one specific respect this humble seeker in the provinces is more important today than the great Newton.

I don't say I feel closer to the Roberti I knew than to the Président de Brosses I never knew (that wouldn't be altogether true) but there is between him and me that inexplicable brotherhood, that foolish but irrefutable brotherhood between contemporaries which means that whatever happens to him concerns me directly and strikes endless echoes within me. Even though we are at opposite poles as regards sentiments, character and even taste, I feel an understanding and affection for him which enable me to recognize the faintest stirrings of his soul.

I: God, what gibberish! You talk like a "new novelist." In another five minutes you'll be brandishing "human values" at me. How dare you talk such drivel? How dare you compare the excellent Président de Brosses with that lout Roberti?

HE: I am not comparing them. I am simply saying that we know everything about the Président de Brosses. We have turned him inside out, he is transparent. He has passed into the heritage of mankind with his arms, baggage, writing desk, wig, malice, irony and critical mind. There is nothing left for him to teach us about himself, ourselves, Italy, the French spirit, the intellectual pleasures of good company and so on. Whereas we know nothing about Roberti at all. He is opaque, mysterious. And his mystery is our mystery. The mystery of the second half of the twentieth century. This mystery may possibly not interest anyone in fifty years' time, but right now and to me, a man of the second half of the twentieth century, it is fascinating and I am making every effort in my power to penetrate it.

I: What will no longer be of interest in fifty years' time doesn't interest me today. It is mere journalism and I hate journalism. Besides, you have forgotten one thing in all your fine arguments: that there are a host of mysteries in every age which simply don't deserve to be explained. I call all these trivial thoughts and tiny sentiments, this seething of stray impulses, decisions, hesitations and habits "the connective tissue of life." At the root of this lies my belief that men's hearts do not change. I am convinced that these mysteries of the second half of the twentieth century which so arouse your curiosity are similar in every respect to the mysteries of the thirteenth century or the Fronde. The human conscience pursues a wealth of minor activities which are the same in every age and correspond to our bodily activities. They are of no importance, of no interest whatsoever. No trace of them survives because they don't deserve to leave any.

HE: I hope you realize all this supports my case? If no one has ever described the minor activities of the human conscience, all the more reason for doing so now. We have a very false idea of earlier centuries. We imagine them peopled with heroes and saints because writers have only left us portraits of outstanding people. I think it is time we democratized literature, filled it with these "proletarian" sentiments which the proud writers of the past considered beneath their dignity. Let us leave our great-nephews a complete portrait of man; in this way they will be spared from doing it for themselves.

I: Oh, you get on my nerves. Your theories are a bore and not even new. Our conversation is getting swamped by commonplaces. Drink some claret; it is quite excellent, I must say, with a strong "stem," as they say in Bordeaux. How was your turbot?

HE: Not bad. And your duck?

I: Sublime. Melting. Look, I haven't left a scrap.

HE: And did you like the *girolles?*

I: *Girolles à la provençale,* my friend, are one of the joys of life.

HE: So you feel a bit better?

I: Well, I wouldn't say no to a little something . . .

HE: What an appetite!

I: I am gathering strength in view of the fat book I am going to write about Roberti. Besides, it's a fine evening and we have walked and talked a great deal. My little brain has been ticking away like mad. That makes me hungry. In fact, I'm going to say something nice for a change. In spite of my cantankerousness, I am completely happy. All this—our discussion, the good food, the weather, the claret and this smart restaurant—have made me completely happy. I am very grateful. We have spent a good day.

HE: It's not over yet.

I: All the better; most things end too soon.

HE: Would some cheese add to your happiness?

I: It certainly would.

HE: Maître d'hôtel! M. Sébastien! May we have the cheese board, please!

M. SÉBASTIEN: Certainly! Gaston, Henri, remove these gentlemen's plates. Philidor, the cheese!

HE: I didn't introduce M. Sébastien to you before because you were like a ravenous beast. Now perhaps you will be able to pay us a little attention.

I: M. Sébastien, I am delighted to make your acquaintance. I have eaten an excellent dinner.

M. SÉBASTIEN: Maître, the honor is all mine.

HE: You see? He calls you "maître." That doesn't happen every day. M. Sébastien is a man who knows his way around. I whispered to him who you were just now.

I: When people address me as "maître" it is always to make fun of me, but I can't find the slightest trace of irony in M. Sébastien. I am more touched than I can say. I have always dreamed of being old, and this "maître" gives me an exquisite foretaste of my old age.

M. SÉBASTIEN: I know Monsieur's name well, of course, but I've never read any book of his.

I: You're not the only one, alas. But patience!

HE: And how is the family, M. Sébastien?

M. SÉBASTIEN: Oh, we mustn't grumble, apart from Mme. Sébastien. Her sciatica, you know.

HE: And your son? Doing as well as ever?

M. SÉBASTIEN: He's in his second year at the Polytechnique.

I: But that's splendid.

HE: Just wait and see, it'll be a pushover. He'll come out top. He'll be running the Tobacco Monopoly in no time. M. Sébastien is a happy man. His is a real success story. Of course, he has always shown great determination and perseverance.

M. SÉBASTIEN: If I told Monsieur my life story he'd surely make a novel of it.

HE: Well tell it him then, M. Sébastien. It's a fine life, one to be proud of. Even if my friend doesn't make a novel of it, I know he'd be interested to hear it.

I: That's very good of you both. Do you think a novel consists simply of copying out a story someone has told you?

HE: Pooh, more or less. One only needs to be Balzac.

I: If it came to that, I could have had fifty old girls telling me their life stories on the grounds that they would make a marvelous novel.

HE: Don't listen to him, M. Sébastien, he's joking. He's one of the dry kind.

M. SÉBASTIEN: I was born near Aubagne. My father was a farmer. I was a difficult kid and not much good at school. I used to come home with torn pants and black eyes. Always fighting and brawling with my friends. Running wild, as you might say. As a result, when I left school my father set me to herding goats. That was no fun at all. Every evening when I got home I would start to argue and get my ears boxed. I slept in the attic on a straw mattress. One day I'd had enough and ran away. My sisters, who had jobs in Marseilles, were in the secret; between the two of them they gave me a hundred-franc note. That was a lot of money in those days. I came up to Paris, I who so to speak had never left my hole before. I had a southern accent you could cut with a knife. Everyone laughed at me. My father used to tell me I was a fire-eater. Indeed, I thought I would conquer Paris in six months. Instead of which, poverty and a rough time. The only job I could find was as a dishwasher at the Petit Marguery. And I had reckoned without my temperament. I was a hot-blooded young devil. At Aubagne they used to call me "a fine boy." At eighteen I had become a fine lad with hair plastered down after the fashion of those days. I met Yvonne. She was seventeen. She was a workman's daughter. But a workman's daughter in 1925 was like a peasant's daughter. Strictly brought up, serious, sensible and all that. There was no television or anything of that kind like in America. "Sébastien," she told me "we'll get married when you've become nice." Yet I was always nice to her. I used to take her to the silent movies, and we used to go canoeing on the lake in the Bois de Boulogne. I still feel sentimental when I think of it. But I was only nice to Yvonne. A proper devil with everyone else. A quick tongue and all too free with my fists. No one was going to turn his nose up at *me* in the street. This couldn't go on. I was more and more in love with Yvonne and more and more difficult to put up with. The days when I washed dishes at the Petit Marguery were a long way behind. I had got on in the profession. I was a second waiter, but not a very permanent one. If a customer spoke to me in a certain tone it was all I could do not to empty the sauceboat over his head. I hardly ever kept a place more than three months. You know, there's an iron discipline in our profession, and the head maître d'hôtel has to be obeyed like a general. I couldn't put up with that. I used to answer back and get slung out.

Yvonne was in despair. "Sébastien," she said, "you'll never settle down and I shall die of misery because I can't marry you." After a while remarks like that begin to worry you. I didn't know how to set about improving my character. It was as if I had a wild beast inside me. I tried to keep it chained up but it was always breaking loose. One day I said to myself: "I've got to kill this beast, it's the only way to be rid of it; it's the only way to sober down. But how to kill it? By getting it eaten up by other, even fiercer wild beasts." So you'll never guess what I did. I signed up for five years in the Foreign Legion. Yvonne backed me up. "I'll wait," she said. It was tough but I left the beast behind there. I was in the Riff War. Military Medal and nine mentions in dispatches. I killed four men with my own hands. When I got home, after my release, I was a different man. The beast was dead. I felt much stronger, much more sure of myself and I never lost my temper any more. Killing four men had left its mark, so to speak, because I had killed all of them in anger and this (although it was war and my duty) had soiled me.

Yvonne had waited. Her parents found me changed for the better. Before, they couldn't stand me. "Good riddance," they had said when I signed up. But Yvonne's constancy and the way I had turned as meek as a lamb made them change their minds. Yvonne and I got married and I began to know what happiness means. Everything went my way because I had had the courage to do five years in the Legion and because those five years had transformed me. I always maintain our biggest enemy is in ourselves and before we undertake anything we have to kill this enemy.

I: That's a very fine story. Thank you for having told it to me, M. Sébastien. I am very glad to have heard it.

HE: But wait! It isn't over. The best is still to come. M. Sébastien began by conquering himself, as he has told you; but that was only the beginning of it, only a first campaign. After that he conquered the world. Wait and see.

M. SÉBASTIEN: Monsieur is right in saying that was just the beginning, for when I was fifteen it had cost me nothing to run away from home. I wasn't happy there, I was bored and I was too hot-blooded. By running away I was just following my fancy. But I only understood this later on. At the time I was very proud of myself and on coming to Paris I thought "Long live freedom"; I was as merry as a grig. It goes without saying, a lad of fifteen who runs away from home thinks he's a bit of hero. Whereas when I signed up with the Legion I had death in my heart. I thought of my little Yvonne who perhaps wouldn't have the patience to wait for me and of those five years of forced labor I was condemning myself to as a punishment for my lack of discipline.

After my marriage we moved into two rooms in the Rue Ganneron in Montmartre. We had a bit of money. I had my savings because, during my five years in the Legion, I had tightened my belt and hardly spent a penny so to speak. Yvonne had her trousseau and twelve thousand francs her grandmother had left her. This gave us time to look round. In fact, we had a six months' honeymoon in Montmartre. She played at housekeeping. Did all her shopping in the Rue Lepic, where everyone knew and liked her. On Sundays we went out on our bikes, had lunch at Nogent, went canoeing on the Marne and ended the day dancing at the Coliseum. All my past life seemed far, far away! I told myself happiness had been a long time coming and that I had paid dearly for it, but it was worth every sacrifice. The bad times and poverty were over. I had left them behind once and for all. Deep inside me I had the conviction that I had paid my tribute to fate and would never be unhappy again; a bit like a debtor who rushes to settle his debts and gets a rake-off because he's paid them back before they were due.

I looked round quietly for a job. At twenty-three, even if one's been in the Riff War, one doesn't worry too much and fear of the future doesn't keep one awake at night. Yvonne and I lived comfortably enough but we didn't do anything foolish and what we had put by would have kept us going for several months more. At any rate I had sworn to myself she would never have to work. I wanted her to give me children and be able to spend all her time looking after them, seeing to it that they became as quick and dainty as she was. I had a peculiar kind of foresight. I was young but I knew what life was like and I told myself that love, if it's to last, must change its face a few times. For the moment me and my little wife were lovers, with nothing in our heads but the joy and selfishness of having each other. I could see her changing before my eyes from a girl into a woman. In two or three years she would need to be a mother, because the girl's love for her bridegroom would have subsided and this would have to be replaced by the calmer but deeper love of a mother for the head of the family, the breadwinner and protector.

Fate had decidedly changed for me. After scowling at me so long, it was now beginning to smile. While I was job-hunting my lucky star had led me to M. André, who happened to need someone just like me, young but keen, presentable, not shy and ready to work twelve hours a day in order to better himself. My military decorations inspired confidence and this pleased me, because they were things I had won all on my own and I could see that in the long run my efforts were bearing fruit. Thanks to M. André I got to know the hotel business inside out; I've always made a good living and Yvonne has never been obliged to do anything but look after the house and bring up the children. M. André had such confidence in me that in 1938, for three weeks at the height of the season, he entrusted me with the running of all his establishments at Deauville. I was the boss. When I handed over the books he said to me: "I couldn't have done better myself." Coming from him, that really meant something.

The only dark spot in this rosy picture was the matter of children. Yvonne couldn't have any. They said she would have to have a little operation and I loved her so much that year after year I refused to let her have it. I couldn't stomach the thought of her stretched out on the table. It gave me nightmares. I told myself the surgeon might make a slip, she might start a hemorrhage, her heart might stop beating—all the crazy ideas one gets when one loves someone and is always terrified by their frailty. However, in the end we were so sad at having no one but ourselves to think of, however fond we were of each other, that we made up our minds. But I took every possible precaution. I picked the best surgeon in Paris, a university professor, and the most expensive clinic in Neuilly. A queen couldn't have been better looked after. The operation went very well. I had an idea for her convalescence. I had secretly bought a nice house at Cassis. In those days houses didn't cost what they do today and I had been able to save some money thanks to M. André. I took Yvonne there and told her: "This is ours!" She couldn't believe her eyes. It was beautifully furnished, it had a big garden and the Mediterranean a few yards away. A dream. And at last we were going to have children. Then in September came the war and I was called up.

I am not a coward. Ten years of happiness hadn't made me soft. All the same, I had a fit of terrible despair. I was sure, when I left, that I would be killed. Yvonne was pregnant. This great joy we had wanted for so long was getting to look more like a catastrophe. What would become of her if I wasn't there any more, with her little orphan? Ah, I didn't go off to war singing, I can tell you. When the Germans attacked in May 1940, I was in Alsace and thought my last hour had come. They had posted me at the corner of a wood with a machine gun and strict orders to hold out till someone came to relieve me. I had several belts of cartridges and some grenades. They were shelling me with a mortar. I don't know how I managed to stick it. With my machine gun I killed sixteen of the enemy. I watched them go down like ninepins and was full of disgust and horror for what I was doing. In spite of Yvonne, at moments I wished I could be killed myself so as not to have to carry on with the butchery. Between gun bursts I talked to God and asked Him to forgive me the crimes I was committing for the sake of France. I was completely mad. When I came to the end of my last belt of cartridges, I retreated about thirty yards and threw a grenade at my machine gun so that the Germans shouldn't get it. I was bleeding all over. I had a bullet in my shoulder and another in my chest. I was black with powder and my hands stank of death. I was unconscious when the

Germans picked me up. When I came to, on a stretcher, there was a crowd of jerries and an officer standing round me. I wondered what was going on. The officer explained in French that they were paying me military honors.

I was filled with a deep joy. For me the war was over, and over honorably. My wounds hurt like hell, I couldn't move, but I knew I would not die. And it did me good to find those Germans treating me with respect. When I had recovered they sent me to a prisoner of war camp from which I escaped after two months. They caught me and put me in a fortress, but I managed to escape once again. This time it worked. In 1941 I rejoined Yvonne at Cassis. I had a baby daughter. She is twenty-one now. She's called Catherine. It was an amazing moment, finding my wife again, my house and the child I didn't know. I wouldn't have missed it for the world. Yvonne was as proud of me as if she were my mother! She had cut articles out of the papers the year before describing my adventure with the machine gun, which had earned me the Legion of Honor for military valor, just like in Napoleon's time!

I was fated never to see my children born. In fact, in November 1942, when the Germans occupied the free zone, I had to flee. I was an escaped prisoner; they would have arrested me in twenty-four hours. Yvonne was pregnant for the second time. We had gone over our accounts. There was enough money left to live for about two years provided she was sensible. I left it all with her except for a thousand-franc note and five gold sovereigns which she sewed in the lining of my jacket. I had friends who knew all about the movements of certain allied ships in the Mediterranean. At midnight I was put in a motorboat which took me out to sea, where we found a submarine that had just surfaced. The next evening I was in Algiers and the day after I had put on a uniform again.

In the submarine I had a terrible fit of depression. I looked back over my life; I had had ten good years, ten years of happiness, and then luck had turned again. I was going back into the dark which I thought I had left behind me forever. I was being thrown back into that life of violence from which I had already suffered so much and from which I thought I had redeemed myself forever by my five years in the Legion. We are always having to start afresh; nothing in life is ever gained for sure. I was very surprised by the reception they gave me at Algiers. Apparently the story of my adventure in May 1940 had spread through the army and I had become quite a figure. Although I was only a warrant officer they treated me kindly and even with respect. They told me I was a fine soldier. I couldn't get over it. The war filled me with such horror that if any chap had dared to tell me I was a hero I'd have cracked his jaw. I had left Yvonne and my little Catherine with death in my heart. Still, I must admit the consideration shown by the officers and my comrades in Algiers did a lot to make my exile easier. I no longer felt a complete stranger. The conditions were tough but my good conduct in the past had gone ahead of me. Vanity's a funny thing!

I took part in the landings in Sicily and our fine Italian campaign. I crossed the Rhine and the Danube in the little boats of Marshal de Lattre. This war wasn't a rest cure but it was far less nasty than the ones I'd known before. We had the feeling victory was pushing us forward from behind like a big hand. Everything went well and quickly. We were stronger, more intelligent, braver, gayer than the enemy. Each one of us felt a bit like a knight in armor. This was especially true of the French army; it may not have been big but it was magnificent, a sort of epitome of the great French armies of the past. What we liked best was seeing our generals disobeying the Allied Command and winning successes to which they had no right. They went round poaching victory under the others' noses. You can imagine how that went down with the troops! All in all, I'm not sorry to have been through it. I don't say it reconciled me to war, but it did to some extent wipe out my sense of shame. It left me with a good impression, as they say.

You know, gentlemen, I believe the only thing worth telling about a man's life is his youth. For even if he's living in poverty, everything then has a brilliance and charm we don't find any longer when we get our gray hairs. My youth ended with the war, in 1945. War is a young people's affair. When it doesn't kill you, it preserves you. How can I explain? War ages the spirit incredibly fast and at the same time preserves inside you a kind of innocence. In one way the years of fighting count double; but in another they only count for half. I can see what I'm saying is obscure, yet it's the truth. I reckon that, owing to the war, its ordeals and inhuman obligations, my youth lasted until I was thirty-eight. That's how old I was when they finally sent me home. Just think: thirty-eight years of youth! I shouldn't complain!

Anything I could tell you about my present life wouldn't be of much interest. In 1945, having got home for good and all to Cassis, I felt like a farmer after the harvest, when the hay is in, the corn is sold and he prepares to make himself snug for the winter. I told myself that the time for tragedies was over, but that the time for difficulties was about to begin. You can see for yourselves, this wasn't the attitude of a young man. It was the misgivings of a mature man who knows life is a chain of worries which eats you away like water dripping on a stone. Thank

God, Yvonne still loved me as much as ever and I had two beautiful cherubs of kids. The second was a boy and I'd only seen him once for two days when I was on a bit of leave. He's called Guillaume. He's the one who's at the Polytechnique now. Catherine is engaged to a nice lad who will be a full-fledged architect next year. When one hasn't got very far in life oneself, it's a great joy to think your kids will be better than you are and may even come to feel a bit ashamed of you.

HE: M. Sébastien, nobody could ever feel ashamed of a man like you, least of all your children who love and respect you in a way that few of your customers here are shown by their offspring. But tell me, how are things with you today?

M. SÉBASTIEN: Why pretty well, Monsieur. I am fifty-four. Besides my place at Cassis, I have bought a boardinghouse at Avignon where I've installed a manager, and I have an interest in a chain of hotels going up in Spain. I've been offered the job of running the Ritz Hotels in Europe, but that seems rather a lot to take on. I don't think I shall accept. I'm toying with the idea of retiring to Cassis next year with Yvonne. She's kept all her looks. Perhaps we shall be grandparents, for Catherine's set on marrying her architect soon. I shall have a boat and be free at last to read all the books I've never had time for in my life. I'm not sure if you know, but my house has two guest rooms. One of them looks over the sea and you'll be very welcome at any time if you'd care to honor us with a visit.

I: I want to thank you particularly for having told us your story, M. Sébastien. I won't be able to make a novel out of it; it's too fine. It would take more talent than I possess. It might possibly call for genius. And I'll tell you something in confidence: listening to you has made me very happy. I needed something like this. You have led a good life, M. Sébastien. You accepted all its risks and trials with your heart in the right place. My friend and I have been spending the afternoon talking about a man who was the exact opposite of you and it almost made me sick. When one is sunk in a morass of ugly and cheap behavior, one comes to feel the world is nothing but a foul swamp. Then you appeared, M. Sébastien, and I was transported as you might say to the top of the Alps, where the air is pure and everything is bright and clear. In fifteen minutes you have lifted me out of a sewer full of dirty and contemptible passions through which my friend here has been having a fine time dragging me for eight or nine hours with a hurricane lamp. I can't tell you how grateful I am. Thank you, M. Sébastien, for having lived such a good life and for having described it with such modesty. May God keep you to the end of your days in the hollow of His hand, may He watch paternally over you, who do him such honor and prove that His creatures are worthy of respect. Your children will never feel ashamed of you because you are not "a man of our time." And I for one am proud to have met a man such as I would like all the men in our country to be.

M. SÉBASTIEN: You make me blush, maître. I can't take all the credit for it, you know. At bottom I was just lucky when I was eighteen to meet Yvonne, who was beautiful, sweet and true, and whom I felt I should love all my life. And I *have* loved her too, I love her more than my children even though I'd let myself be hacked into pieces for them. She has been my star. Wherever I was, at Sidi-bel-Abbès, Marrakesh, in Alsace, in my fortress in Pomerania, at Cassino or by Lake Constance, I kept my eyes fixed on her. Everything I did I did for her, to make myself fully deserving of her, because I knew it wasn't only me she loved but also my honor; because she is not one of those women who can give their full love to someone they despise. I've told you into the bargain how I wasn't a coward. It wasn't so much all the fighting which took it out of me, in spite of my disgust for it; it was being separated from my wife and kids. Oh well, that's the way life is. If I were to tell you what Yvonne and I have done, you would never believe it. I've bought a plot in the cemetery at Cassis, so that we can be buried there side by side, and I've written in my will that I want our two coffins to be tied together with chains. A woman like Yvonne is a treasure and if I have done anything at all worth doing it is because I have always referred everything to her. Whenever I stop to think of everything that has happened to me, like today when you have been good enough to listen to me, I tell myself heaven sent me Yvonne when I was eighteen to save me from myself. For someone as good as her to fall in love with the young hooligan I was then means that she saw qualities and a gentleness in me I didn't see for myself, which left to myself I would doubtless never have seen and therefore never have tried to bring out. Well, that's all, gentlemen. But I have wasted enough of your time.

I: Don't you believe it, M. Sébastien. I could spend hours listening to you.

M. SÉBASTIEN: Excuse me, I am wanted. I'll see you again shortly. Maître, I recommend the Gorgonzola.

I: Thank you, M. Sébastien, that's exactly what I was feeling like.

HE: See you soon, M. Sébastien. We won't leave without saying good-by.

I: M. Sébastien's quite a hero. A character from Plutarch. What a contrast with poor Roberti. I wouldn't mind spending three weeks with him and Yvonne at Cassis myself. Is it true she's as beautiful as ever?

HE: I only saw her once. A fine figure of a woman. She has good features, a grave and gentle expression and a superb smile. They are excellent people.

I: I must say, M. Sébastien's story coming in the middle of Roberti's has had a tremendous effect on me. It has brought me back to life. Like coming out of a tunnel. It was life as opposed to death. Good as opposed to evil. And so completely, so undeniably good that I'm wondering if it wasn't Providence which led the worthy M. Sébastien to cross our path today.

HE: No, it wasn't Providence, it was me. I brought you to the Pavillon Royal because I knew we should find him here and I was sure you would take to him.

I: Even so, it's odd for a man like that to be content to be a maître d'hôtel.

HE: In the first place, he isn't a maître d'hôtel. He doesn't wear tails, as you can see for yourself. He's a sort of host, major-domo, factotum. And then, he's not ashamed of his profession. He's not vain. I'm not like you: I find the fact that he has remained quietly in the catering business, because that's what he really knows about, only adds to his stature.

I: But how can one tip a man like that?

HE: It's perfectly simple. One doesn't.

I: All the same, he must receive tips from people who don't know who he is?

HE: Well, those he accepts. It's all part of the job. They don't imply any insult. It is no more difficult to accept a tip than it is to recommend Gorgonzola to gluttons like you. No more difficult than sloshing paint over a wall if one's a house painter.

I glanced furtively at my watch. It wasn't yet ten o'clock. At M. Sébastien's behest the waiter called Philidor had placed an enormous slice of Gorgonzola on my plate, together with some good crisp bread and curly little pats of butter. It was all very appetizing and, in spite of everything I had already consumed, I tackled this fresh supply with gusto. The Gorgonzola was as creamy as could be desired. My companion thoughtfully watched me munching. For my part, I reflected that Philidor was a weird name. By an elementary association of ideas I thought of Diderot, the Café de la Régence and the famous chess players of the eighteenth century. My thoughts then reverted to M. Sébastien, whom I could see bustling round a few tables off. He had a way of attending to the diners which was at once elegant and full of simplicity. He was not very tall. He had the palest of blue eyes, was rather young-looking for his fifty-four years and his face wore a faintly noble expression, at once attentive and detached. The expression of a man who has acquired a philosophy with his heart and not with his mind, which is a roundabout way of doing it but leads to the same heights. The last word of this philosophy is to know that in life all is vanity but that one must nevertheless meticulously perform all its duties as if on the contrary nothing was vain, as if the smallest things were fraught with significance. I could almost read this in the gestures of M. Sébastien, who didn't consider it beneath his dignity, after having lived like a patriarch and an ancient warrior, to take orders and attend to the comforts of a few well-to-do people having a night out.

The orchestra had switched from Viennese waltzes to the light music of 1900, which appealed to me equally well. The violinist had stepped down from his platform to plant himself in front of a most unprepossessing couple in their sixties and was playing *Destiny* with great intensity and feeling. From there he passed on to another table at which a pretty blonde with a snub nose and glistening teeth was brightening the lives of three elderly gentlemen. For this endearing creature he selected from his repertoire Monti's *Csárdás,* which the orchestra accompanied with such verve that for the next five minutes it was almost impossible to talk. I devoted these five minutes to cult of the Gorgonzola. Our second bottle of claret was dangerously empty. One of the three elderly gentlemen (was it the lover, the husband or the protector of the young blonde?) slipped the violinist a fifty-franc note, which seemed to me excessive. The whole scene, the music, the happy impression M. Sébastien's story had made on me, the softness of the air, the rich enticing smells of the restaurant, all turned this moment into an unlooked-for interlude of happiness, such as I had already enjoyed twice before that day: once on the Quai Malaquais, as we left the bistro where we drank our coffee and rum; and again here, at this same Drouant du Bois, when we had arrived earlier on after our savage walk across Paris under the burning sun. To have three moments of happiness in one day certainly deserves a mention. The more so in that it is a kind of happiness one never refers to since one never knows exactly what causes it. It is born of a subtle and fleeting combination of tiny circumstances, a brief harmony between one's spirit and the world. It is "made out of nothing" like a model run up in haste by a great dressmaker. I think M. Sébastien and his fine story played a considerable part in the joy with which I was suddenly filled. We are never so happy as when men give us reasons for liking them. At least, that is how it is with me. The spectacle of noble deeds gladdens my heart like beautiful music. It is as if my soul had left my body and was deliriously riding astride the melody being played.

HE: M. Sébastien has led us rather astray from Roberti and I'm not quite sure how to get back to him. Especially as we are now about to enter the dark and terrible regions of satiated love, of love persisting while hating itself, love growing like a tumor. I feel as if I had already told you two novels and was now embarking on a third.

I: Two novels, three novels? I hadn't noticed. Where are they?

HE: By and large I see things like this: the first novel ends at the moment when Roberti was preparing to sleep with Solange for the first time. It covers about eight days. It is the novel of incipient love. The second lasts from six to eight weeks. It is the novel of love at its zenith.

I: At its zenith! You're not hard to please.

HE: Yes, yes, at its zenith. This whole period in Roberti and Solange's lives may at first sight seem squalid and deplorable, but only because words are inadequate. It was illuminated from within by the dazzling flame of pure love.

I: If you say so.

HE: I say so because it's true. You mustn't be deceived by appearances. Solange was enraptured despite her unhappiness; Roberti was enraptured despite his blindness and pusillanimity. They were both enraptured unwittingly.

I: I don't get it. Happiness is inseparable from the awareness of happiness. If one doesn't know one is happy, one isn't.

HE: Forgive me, but it is possible not to know one is happy and yet to feel it. If I may hark back to one of my old metaphors, happiness is like a master painting. One doesn't take it all in right away. One requires time. One needs some artistic education. The first time you look at a Rembrandt, you are filled with a strange feeling of peace or joy. It is only on your fourth or fifth examination of it that you begin to know what it is about. Besides, almost everything in the world is invisible. Happiness can descend on you yet entirely escape your notice. Two or ten years later, the veil is rent and you tell yourself: "Good heavens! At such and such a time in my life I knew happiness! And I failed to identify it when I had it! How stupid, how blind I was!" Basically, things only become real once they have ceased to exist. Every man is the novelist of his own life; he only rediscovers time after it has been irretrievably lost in the past; he only truly lives his pleasures and his days after they have flown. We often marvel at people who live through historic events—social upheavals, the death of Joan of Arc, Caesar's crossing of the Rubicon, the murder of Henry IV, the proclamation of the Republic in 1792—without noticing a thing, continuing to live as usual. On the other hand we never hear of anyone going through a great love affair with equal impassivity. Yet people do, and they form by far the greatest number. People don't perceive history in the making, even when it is staring them in the face. Well, I maintain that love passes just as unnoticed as history. I say that Venus is just as transparent as Clio and that is why one must have a singularly piercing eye if one wants to depict love for, most of the time, one's task consists of depicting the invisible, giving it shape and substance, lifting it out of the world of abstract ideas into that of visible appearances. It means looking ten years ahead to a future when everything is at last understood and assessed, when everything is marked at its true value. This, in my humble opinion, is one of the missions of the poet: to grasp the truth of beings who lie to themselves, to be always a few years older than they or, if you prefer, to live in their future, observe them with the eyes they will themselves have when they have lived a little longer. Do I make myself clear?

ı: Oh yes, completely. And a bit of a bore, too. Instead of philosophizing, you'd do better to fix Roberti's bearings. That would at least be to the point. And anyway I need them. I'm rather lost.

ʜᴇ: That's easy. We are in Paris in the spring of 1955. Everything I have told you occurred roughly between the fifteenth of May and the fifteenth of July.

ı: That makes two months.

ʜᴇ: Yes, two months more or less. I can't give you the exact dates. I didn't keep a diary of this affair. I never anticipated that I should one day be describing it to you. At any rate, I can promise you these events are not telescoped in my memory. If I say two months, it was in fact about two months, within a week or so. Anyway, I don't suppose your love of precision demands absolutely exact dates. Besides, the Roberti-Solange story doesn't belong to history, that is to say it didn't alter the course of human events. It is a "scene from private life," one of those ripples visible on the surface of every society but without any far-reaching effects. It is only interesting to the extent that it enables us to grasp a few little-known aspects of the hearts of men and women. Now the heart is ageless, or rather timeless. So it is of no importance to establish whether Roberti slept for the first time with Solange on the twenty-seventh of May or the third of June.

Something more interesting to know, or at least recall, is that the spring of 1955 was a very fine one. It was hot. There were storms. Roberti and Solange's early lovemaking was marked by this heat which added something extra, it would seem, to their passion. They would meet under a burning sun or on stifling evenings. Solange wore dresses of muslin or printed cotton which thrilled Roberti as they brushed against him, so light that they were scarcely more than a veil, a cloud masking the ravishing, ever-desirable nakedness of Mlle. Mignot. The end of June 1955 was particularly scorching. All this heat went far to foster love. It intensified everyone's mood, I think; that is to say it sapped all our energies where work was concerned, but filled the flesh with expectations and desires and violent longings. We were no longer in France, no longer in Paris, but in some indolent, sun-scorched land; we were in Naples or Africa. There are times like this when nature assumes an unreal air; when, although we are awake, we feel we are living through an at once gentle and oppressive dream. Our behavior is barely influenced by moral considerations. Strange, this poetic power of the barometer, isn't it? No, I am wrong: it is love penetrating everything around it and imbuing it with poetry. For Roberti and Solange, the dog days of late June and early July 1955 were made fabulously poetic by love. When they entered the rooms of the Rue d'Argenson with their half-closed shutters, with only thin shafts of sunlight cutting across the shadows, they would fall exhausted with heat into each other's arms. Slowly they would be refreshed by love. Love was a river into which they would plunge their sweating bodies like travelers exhausted by the sun and a long journey. They would emerge from it with a new vigor and a physical contentment so deep that their souls rejoiced.

Nothing was lacking from this happiness, not even the fact that it was precarious (which only increased the frenzy with which they clutched at it) since the summer vacations, that is to say the separation of the two lovers, were drawing near.

I can't say that a separation of six to eight weeks caused Roberti undue alarm. Six to eight weeks don't loom very large, alas; they pass rapidly when one is in one's fifties. Actually, he was not displeased at the idea of this separation; it would give him a chance to regain control of himself. In fact, where Solange was concerned he was a prey to two opposing feelings. On the one hand he realized that the pleasures he enjoyed with her were becoming necessary to him; on the other she was an encumbrance, he couldn't conceal from himself the fact that she was rather dumb. This, moreover, was a contradiction with which he was already familiar and it reassured him: it proved that only his body, not his heart, was involved in this affair. In the past he had known similar contradictions with other women whom he had dropped without hesitation or regret. Such contradictions were even rather consoling. They gave rise to a slight pang which was not without charm. Given a certain amount of experience one knows that, although one doesn't by any means often meet women who are sensually one's perfect match, this is not so very rare either. Do you follow the man's logic? He reasoned like this: "A purely physical attraction doesn't provide adequate grounds for being in love. Sexual pleasure is interchangeable. All the women's bodies I shall possess in the future may not bring me as much delight as Solange's, but there will be a few of them whose desires will accord well enough with mine. What is unique and above all precious is a woman who loves you and whom you love in return, whose soul resembles yours. Solange, then, is in no way precious to me and if our temporary separation ends in a final break, it will be annoying just as losing one's keys or breaking a fine Sèvres vase is annoying, but it will be no great loss."

At other times Roberti thought how these vacations he would spend with his family would make a delectable contrast with the exquisite scenes of adultery that absorbed his thoughts. He considered how agreeable it would be to contemplate them from a distance.

This man of action, who doubtless shouldn't have spent too much time in thought, had preserved from his false vocation of a man of letters a taste for reverie and the habit of scrupulously reliving in memory his more privileged moments. He got only a rough sketch of the good things which came his way during the day and would develop these at leisure later on, when he would then expand and quietly savor them. There were times when he would even abruptly leave a gathering where he was enjoying himself so as to go and make the most of it unhindered in solitude. In short he had a small heart, a heart of small capacity which would fill up very rapidly, which needed leisure and tranquillity to absorb its sensations. He felt just as happy, sometimes even more so, when he parted from people as when he met them.

For all of this, he looked ahead: he made a point of arranging a last meeting with Solange on the eve of his departure, in order to give himself indigestion, as it were, so far as she was concerned. I hardly like to employ so vulgar an image but indigestion was exactly what it was, a deliberately induced indigestion. He was anxious not to take away with him the slightest regret, the slightest desire. He thought that possibly, this last time, he might exhaust all the desire he still felt for her or that, putting things at their worst, this final orgy would at least procure him two weeks of peace, would for two weeks lull his body (and by the same token his mind).

I: I see you're determined to spare me no horror.

HE: And why should I? Such details illustrate certain truths. Roberti's calculations as I have defined them were neither peculiar to this particular man nor to the particular kind of love he felt. Who in his heart of hearts doesn't make similar calculations? They exist none the less for being only half-conscious or because one dares not admit them to oneself. Anyway, everything always depends on the point of view we adopt or the words we employ. You are using my very words as a stick to beat Roberti. But if, for instance, I had said: "Before leaving Solange, he wanted to be merged once more with the woman he loved, wanted to draw strength from her, commune with her in the flesh, tra-la-lee, tra-la-la," how would you have reacted?

I: I'd have burst out laughing.

HE: Yes, you might well have burst out laughing because of the clichés, the idiotic phraseology. But the thing itself wouldn't have caused you any revulsion. On the contrary. You would have been touched; you'd have found it contained a hint of melancholy, a certain nobility. Roberti would have struck you as a romantic and sincere lover, faintly ridiculous but not at all ignoble. Yet it would have been exactly the same. His calculating doesn't affect the position in any way. Here again, moreover, we are putting our fingers on his dream world. One should never trust people's thoughts, even the most secret, even the most seemingly cynical. Thoughts can lie as well as words. They even lie more, since by being and remaining private their aim is to deceive the thinker himself, who *knows*. Who can say in this instance that Roberti's actual thoughts express his truth? Who can say that this truth is not really to be found in the noble, romantic, faintly ridiculous sentiment that no one, least of all he himself, suspected? Roberti was a man with a preconceived idea or, if you prefer, a system, to the effect that he did not love Solange, that all he felt for her was a sensual bond. Consequently he adapted all his thoughts to this system, twisting them to fit in with his preconceived idea. Worse still: his thoughts

adapted themselves to his system of their own accord; he only acknowledged them once they had shown their credentials. So, like all men
with a system, he could not help lying to himself, and lying incessantly.
His system misdirected all his thoughts, suggested specious and naturally ignoble explanations for all his acts. Only complete sincerity (that
is to say complete simplicity, the humble and immediate recognition of
our true feelings) enables us to live without inner baseness. There are
some men who are never honest with themselves, whose whole inner
life consists of proving to themselves a thesis which they have arbitrar-
ily concocted and who, parodying Descartes, might take for their device: "I think, therefore I lie."

i: Objection.

he: What do you mean? There can be no objection. Everything I've
said about the way thoughts can lie is incontestable.

i: My objection has no bearing on that. It refers to Roberti giving
himself indigestion with Solange.

he: Well?

i: Well, I don't quite see it. How can one store a person up like that?
It's more the opposite which occurs. The more frequently one has a
woman one loves, the more one desires her. Love is like the sun or
morphine. You catch sunstroke but you can't store up sunshine for the
winter. Once the sun goes in, you are cold. Similarly, if you are a morphine addict, it won't help in the least to give yourself a double dose
of the drug as a precaution. Once it has worn off you'll suffer the torments of hell. You'll feel its lack twice as strongly.

he: That's a strange objection, coming from you. It's not like you.
It's a woman's objection. I'll go even further and say it's the objection
of a woman in love who constantly needs proof that she is loved in
return.

i: Hell! Do you really think so? Yet you could hardly say I'm a feminine type!

he: Oh, don't worry. It does your delicacy honor. It shows you have
a pure mind and a simple heart.

i: That's encouraging!

he: Look, in your objection you make no allowance for two factors.
First, the Robertian system. In Roberti's eyes Solange was not a woman
to be loved; she was an object created for the satisfaction of his body.
Second, it was just a question of desire. He told himself that if he
could suppress his desire by satiating it he would at the same time suppress Solange. God knows none of this is very hard to understand. Take,
for instance, a soldier on leave. What is the first thing he does? He

300

rushes to the brothel and has his fill, in anticipation of the next six
weeks when he will be confined to barracks.

1: Poor Solange!

HE: Why poor Solange? She had no inkling of this. All she saw at
their last meeting was an impetuous and passionate lover who gave an
even more brilliant performance than usual.

1: I say poor Solange because she was pouring a priceless wealth of
love over Roberti and this frightful character was using her like a whore.
It makes an ugly contrast.

HE: He thought he was using her like a whore, but it wasn't true.
That is what makes the beauty of this story. Roberti was a man walking
through shadows. A sort of Oedipus, in his way. The things he did, the
feelings he felt, had two faces. Or rather they appeared harmless on the
surface but had a hidden meaning which was terrible. The gods were
deceiving him. The gods were mocking him. He was even more tragic
than Oedipus in that he based his behavior on pettiness and meanness;
for him this was a familiar spiritual landscape which inspired him with
complete confidence. But this landscape was just a setting, a façade behind which lay true love, "love passion," that is to say a destiny as terrible as that of Oedipus, who murdered his father and married his mother
unawares.

Reverting to the objection you raised just now, it is worthless so far
as Roberti is concerned, but perfectly valid for Solange, who was a
woman and did not lie to herself with regard to love. She felt that no
excess could ever assuage the longing for Roberti in her heart and that
the vacation to which she normally looked forward with such excitement were this year going to be a severe trial. In the Rue d'Argenson
she dared not cry, although she longed to do so, for fear of antagonizing
her lover. She knew that tomorrow the sun would be overcast and she
would be cold, that the morphine would be used up and that she would
suffer the torments of hell, as you so rightly said.

Grief makes shy people dumb, especially when they have sensitive
hearts and simple minds. Solange clung speechless to Roberti, gazing
up at him with a fierce intensity. Occasionally she heaved a deep sigh.
It was the unmistakable grief of a dog about to be abandoned by its
master. But Roberti was bent purely on enjoying himself. The selfishness of sex combined with his own natural selfishness prevented him
from noticing anything wrong. At length, however, it did flit through
his mind that Solange might be unhappy. This both surprised, flattered
and annoyed him. It was splendid to think she might be sad at parting
from him, but she oughtn't to betray it; good manners demanded

that she show a bit of life. All his caution was once again alerted. On his return he would be more vigilant and circumspect than hitherto; he would discourage her more assiduously, see even less of her. What did she mean by this soulful carrying-on, these sighs, this mute grief whose extent he dared not measure? It was such bad form for her to spoil his last meeting like this! He sought to relieve the situation by joking. Like a good parliamentarian he was trying, you see, to alter events with words, but Solange heard none of it. She was too busy listening to her own heart, which felt so full that she fancied she was nothing but one huge aching heart. She couldn't even force a smile. Finally, almost inaudibly and with an effort, as if it were a painful concession, she murmured: "Will you think of me a little during all this time?"—"Here it comes," thought Roberti. "She's going to ask me to write to her." But she didn't ask for anything, which so disconcerted him that he found himself promising to do so. This trait illustrates Edouard perfectly; thus it happened that sometimes he would overreach himself, give something he wasn't being asked for and which, only a moment before, he had been determined to refuse. Such impulses are hard to explain. I for one have come to believe they stemmed from his constant wish to appear in a good light, to seem generous and magnanimous—a wish that was strongly developed and always urged him to prove to himself what a "fine fellow" he was. On top of this he suddenly warmed to the idea that Solange would anxiously await his letters, would keep them like a secret treasure in her handbag, lovingly read and reread them, learn them by heart; he glowed at the thought that he would continue from afar to bring this creature happiness, to live in her heart and mind. How much is such a sentiment compounded of love and how much of vanity? At any rate, her joy at his announcement gave him a pleasure which wasn't just flattered vanity. In gratitude and smiling for the first time, she cried . . .

ɪ: I don't give a damn what Solange cried in gratitude and smiling for the first time. I'm sure it was something like: "Oh, you're so good to me! You'll never know how much I love you." All women talk the same rot. In their eyes carrying on a relationship *by letter* represents the supreme happiness. It is the consecration of love. I'd rather you furnished me with some practical details. Where, for example, Roberti went for his vacation and what Solange had arranged for hers. And the dates. When Roberti left, when he came back and so on. And how they organized their correspondence.

ʜᴇ: But that's of no interest at all. He went one way, she another. He had rented a house at Antibes from the fifteenth of July to the fifteenth of September. As for her, she had arranged to spend three weeks in Spain during August with Mlle. Angioletti.

I: Oh yes, I had forgotten about her. But it's rather amusing, this trip through Spain. I like the idea of these two typists going abroad like two ladies of fashion. I'd have been annoyed not to have heard about that. It provides another period detail. I'm astonished that you, who are so fond of this sort of touch, never thought to tell me about it. Can you imagine the equivalents of Mlles. Mignot and Angioletti visiting Spain in 1830? When I write our novel I shall make this a two-page digression. I shall explain the blend of curiosity, pleasure and pretension which prompted these girls' visit to Spain. It will be marvelous.

HE: You will also have to add this, at least as far as Solange is concerned: that she had elected to go to Spain because she refused to spend her vacation at Bandol with Valentin and Legay. I am afraid this detail may rub some of the gloss off your digression.

Right. And now, with your permission, we shall return to the Rue d'Argenson, since I haven't quite done with that episode. Before you interrupted me, I was on the point of telling you something important, something Solange said which will most certainly merit a two-page digression, if not more.

I: Let's have it.

HE: I told you how she was filled with gratitude. The promise of receiving letters had in a sense unknotted her soul. Roberti's letters would be a precious draught of water enabling her to cross the endless desert of her vacation. Things were working out all right; the reality was less frightful than she had feared. She felt a surge of tenderness toward this generous man who, without loving her (for she was sure he didn't really love her, so convincing had he been on this score), was condescending to waste an occasional half hour scribbling love letters to her. When the heart eases up in this way, we tend to divulge deeply hidden desires to which we would doubtless never admit in normal circumstances. We feel a need to expand, a need—how shall I put it? —to unburden our souls, immolate ourselves, burn our boats, reveal our innermost selves. And this is what happened to Solange, this artless girl capable of stubborn silence, certainly, but incapable of guile, incapable of skillfully presenting a secret ambition without causing alarm.

I: What a lot of beating about the bush! What did she actually say?

HE: She said: "I should like you to give me a child!"

I: Is that all?

HE: It's pretty sensational, don't you think?

I: Yes and no. At bottom it was to be expected. There always comes a moment when women want one to make them pregnant. But it does seem to me that with the Mignot girl this moment came pretty quickly. I feel sorry for Roberti. It must have knocked him back a bit.

HE: I don't believe he really understood the significance of this wish. In any case, he failed to perceive that it came from very deep within Solange. And above all he never for a moment contemplated that this desire of hers for motherhood might in any way affect the shape of things to come. It's odd to see how inattentive an experienced man can sometimes be. At crucial moments poor Roberti was always looking the other way, almost as if on purpose. In the first place, as I have said, he didn't take the matter seriously. He thought it was just one of those things people say in the heat of the moment, one of those lover's exaggerations of no consequence or importance. The urge for motherhood is completely beyond men; they can't conceive how anyone could wish to carry a child in his belly, suffer in giving it birth, love this unknown being issued from one's own flesh. Their minds are too full of too many other interests, when it isn't with their love lives or their careers. And yet Solange's intensity, her imploring look, to some extent undeceived Roberti. She wasn't speaking lightly; she was expressing an atavistic desire of her flesh and heart. Strange as it may seem, even the realization of this fact was not enough to alarm him. Believe it or not, he even had a weird feeling of contentment. This man, normally so quick to take fright, to beat a retreat at the first sign of even the most illusory threats against his liberty, was foolishly charmed by the idea that a young and pretty girl would be glad to give him a child, to contract with him this mysterious and immemorial union. Solange wanted to be his woman in the fullest sense and he found this very touching. These are the typical reactions of a mature man. For a young man, putting his mistress in the family way is just rotten luck, but for a middle-aged man who doesn't have to worry about money, who hasn't to feel concerned about the future, who needs to prove to himself that he is still not old, it is a renewal of youth, an exhilarating source of happiness. The pleasures of youth only truly become pleasures in our old age; they are then mere pleasures with no painful reverse side to them and, what's more, they take us deliciously out of ourselves. "Why, it's true," thought Roberti, to whom it had never occurred before. "I might easily treat myself to a natural child. My position in life makes it quite feasible!" Solange's proposal had been made in total and plainly visible disinterestedness, and he knew his mistress well enough to feel certain she was setting no trap for him. He felt a sort of gratitude before such a sacrifice. She was offering him a secret marriage. So much did she love him that she was volunteering to wreck her life; she was demanding no guarantee; all she wanted was this child, this survival of her lover within her. For love of him she was aspiring to self-ruin.

ɪ: But that's sublime in its way.

ʜᴇ: Oh, sublime! Don't let's exaggerate. Solange was a woman of twenty-five and in her prime. She had just discovered physical love and it had left her stupefied and dazed. What she was feeling above all was the physiological need to have a child, which is the habitual outcome of a violent awakening of the flesh. Before such an urge, all other considerations pale. Everything else is brushed aside: future, reputation, society. It is like a fit of dementia, and anyway women frequently commit every kind of folly in order to have children. This is something men can never understand, since it is totally alien to their natures. Have you ever chanced to wonder at the zoo what the appetites or urges of a panther, flamingo or crocodile can be, tried to imagine them to yourself and of course failed? It is the same with women. They are as remote from men as swans or gazelles. The male and female bodies know nothing of each other, meet gropingly and unite most of the time in mutual ignorance. This, to my mind, is the true drama of the sexes. Between men and women stands a barrier like the one between two species of animal; and that is why we talk of "the miracle of love," thanks to which this barrier occasionally crumbles. It is a miracle indeed, for it occurs but rarely and then only in total darkness.

Roberti clearly failed to realize that Solange was even more preoccupied by the reproductive instinct of the species than by love of him. It is only fair to say that she hardly realized it any better herself. She believed (in the clear zones of her consciousness) that he was the only man in the world capable of arousing her; she wanted a child by him to serve as a brand on her shoulder, so that the world might know she belonged to someone and that this belonging made her prouder and happier than freedom. Roberti was deeply touched; he hesitated to tell her that this idea of a child was impracticable and outlandish, and finally said nothing. As always, he gave himself an *ignoble* explanation for his attitude: how he couldn't in all decency exclaim that Solange was crazy; how in proposing to make him a father she was paying him a great compliment, a great courtesy, to which he must reply with equal compliments and courtesy, that is say by at least pretending to be pleased.

ɪ: What a ham!

ʜᴇ: A false ham. He thought he was hamming when he was in fact sincere. His lies re-established the truth. Aren't these twists and turns of truth odd and interesting? Anyway, it is probably quite normal for a man who lies to himself to tell others the truth by saying the opposite of what he is thinking. This is how things involuntarily right themselves for the greater glory of the truth. In proof of which, after having wished her a pleasant holiday and shown a reasonable amount of regret at leaving her, Roberti began to dream with a touch of complacency. He had driven her back and there had been no end of kisses in which he had taken more pleasure than usual. For once he had been in no hurry to cut them short. He had then proceeded slowly homeward, his mind full of thoughts and images which would have alarmed anyone less conceited. But he wasn't afraid of his dreams; they would never turn into passions since his rationalism would always hold them in check. In other words he relied on mediocrity; he was depending on it to serve him as a guardrail. He never imagined that this rail might one day not be there. I trust you note the contradiction in passing: outwardly Roberti was always trying to appear in the best possible light; inwardly he always strove to find the most ignominious explanation for his actions. This was his style as a man of the twentieth century. The twentieth-century man says: "Lucidity above all." It is his device. Whereby he deceives himself just as much as the men of other centuries ever did. He has a low opinion of himself, so to speak; he is convinced of the littleness of his soul and when this soul one day leads him into the age-old, fantastic forests of humanity, where lurk Merlin, Melusine, the Five Hundred Demons, the Dragon and all the rest of them, he is utterly bewildered.

Roberti in his car drove pensively, as one might say. He reflected that after all it would be most romantic to have a bastard. The boy would be brought up in secret and one would go to see him on the sly; he would take one for his uncle or guardian; as one didn't live with him and would only see him occasionally, one would inspire great friendship and confidence in him. He would be a love child, or at least the child of desire, a child who would be closer to Roberti than his legitimate children. If having a secret mistress is already enthralling, what can it be like to have a natural son? To lead a double life is to live doubly, to be one man multiplied by two. Edouard knew his three legitimate children—his three sons with whom he spent every day—inside out, he could clearly distinguish in them what they had inherited from Agnes, from himself and from their forebears. What would his genes produce with a woman who was not Agnes? That was fascinating food for thought and he gave himself up to it wholeheartedly. He sketched a portrait of himself as a "young father of fifty" which he found charming. It was all the more piquant in that there was a hint of sacrilege in imagining any woman other than Agnes being the mother of his children. There was also one beguiling side to this reverie, in that the fact of having a bastard must always impart a delicious feeling of revenge on the family. Every father nurtures in a remote corner of his heart a vague resentment against his wife and children, who consume his substance and grate on him a hundred times a day with the rough edges of their characters.

ı: Good. I see. He was playing a game. Romancing.

HE: Yes, he was playing a game. But there is always a lot of seriousness in games. I find it most odd and noteworthy that at the idea of having a bastard, Roberti didn't immediately hide his face in horror but on the contrary gave it careful consideration and made it an object for daydreaming. Considerations of prudence naturally prevailed in the long run. "I have quite enough *occupations* as it is without landing myself with a bastard. And I always want to be a free agent. If Solange had a child it would mean being tied to the little goose forever. She'd have a permanent claim on my time, attention and money. Brrr . . . ! Out of the question!" He pictured her giving birth in the clinic and this picture somewhat cooled him down. He saw himself sending flowers, imagined himself sitting at her bedside in the maternity ward, heard the wailing of the baby. It was at once so horrifying and so absurd that he simultaneously began to shiver, smile and press down hard on the accelerator. He must get back quickly to the Rue Oudinot to dispel these fancies! Momentarily, even so, this cynic had well and truly toyed with a highly dangerous notion, and not without pleasure.

ı: Forgive me, but I don't quite follow you. Why are you making so much of this business of a natural child? After all, Roberti never had one by Solange. There's enough reality in this world, enough that is real in his story, without cluttering it up with might-have-beens.

HE: Oh, oh! Careful! Your logic is failing. In reporting Roberti's dreams of paternity, I am dealing not with possibilities but with realities. I am reporting a fact, for it is a fact that he brooded complacently and at length over the notion of having a child by Solange. I will even add that, although he never put it into execution, this idea never completely deserted him either. Every now and then it would flit through his mind and, depending on his mood at the time, he would either contemptuously reject it or else toy with it. Little impulses, suppressed desires and daydreams play as great a part in any assessment of a man's character as his actions, especially when, as here, it is a question of a persistent, recurrent and insoluble dilemma.

In the second place this abortive reverie, which ended as one might have expected in cynical and rational resolves, forms the first glaring sign of love given by Roberti. Naturally, had anyone told him so, he would have protested with genuine indignation, he would have retorted (in all good faith) that he was "having fun," that it was an "idle fancy," but he would have been wrong, he would once again have been deceiving himself. In the light of subsequent events I can tell you that his dream about the possibility of having a natural child was one of the indirect ways whereby love wormed its way into him. Given the *fact* of this dream, outside observers like you and me, who do not occupy his soul but watch it changing from above, the outside observer, I say, can see that the terrain has altered, that the conditions are no longer the same as they were at the start, that the balance of power has begun to shift. Within six weeks Roberti had become porous. A sort of tenderness had seeped into him. Solange's proposal had altered their relations. By saying "I would like you to give me a child" she had breached his defenses. She had unwittingly put her hand on a hidden catch which opened for her a door into her lover's soul. Henceforward he would always regard Solange as different from an ordinary mistress, that is to say a now convenient, now inconvenient object; she was a woman who had wanted to have with him the closest union, which is given substance in the form of a child.

That is why I have been into this at such length. I think it was worth it. I have reforged before your eyes the first big link in the chain which bound Roberti, this man of fifty, so tightly to Solange, this woman half his age. And if you permit me I shall expatiate a little further, because there is also her view of the problem, on which I have barely touched and which is just as important, if not more so. Pay particular attention to it when you write the novel; forget not a single detail. For thanks to this, for the first time in the history of literature, a writer, you yourself, will show the true mainsprings which lead to the waxing or waning of a passion, the fundamental and hidden reasons for which love either lives or dies. In fact, what had begun to attach Roberti had, by the same process, begun to detach Solange. She wanted a child, she asked the man she loved to give her one, nothing could be simpler. But he refused. She suffered. Time passed. The urge for motherhood became more and more pressing. It destroyed love. Supplanted it. Conclusion?

ɪ: I hardly dare think!

ʜᴇ: Go on! You're very warm!

ɪ: Conclusion, she had a child by someone else.

ʜᴇ: Exactly!

ɪ: You certainly have an odd way of tracing events. You crawl along like a snail for eight to ten hours and then, all of a sudden, you give me the end of the story in a flash. That's not playing fair. It's intolerable. So Solange got herself pregnant. By whom?

ʜᴇ: Wait. You'll find out. I'm not giving away the ending. I am simply allowing you a glimpse into the future. I am letting you momentarily see what hasn't yet happened, what is still very far from happening. I want you to get a clear idea of the Solange "equation." Between love and motherhood she finally chose (or rather her body chose) motherhood. I would go so far as to say that all her inclinations, thoughts, feelings, joys and sorrows led her by mathematical progression from love to motherhood. She sacrificed the man she loved in order to have a child by another whom she didn't love and who wasted no time giving her this child, not without generosity but not without calculation either, because he knew that this was a good opportunity to get her wholly to himself.

Some sentiments are like human beings. Their fate is decided from childhood. You asked me to give you your "bearings." I have done so, although rather differently from the way you wanted. I have given their souls' bearings. Had I to define the love of Roberti and Solange, qualify it, summarize it, I would say more or less that this love was molded and dominated by two profound convictions; on the one hand Solange wanted a child, that is to say she aimed to develop her love, fulfill it by transforming it; on the other hand Roberti wanted most earnestly to believe (and did) that he wasn't in love. The final outcome of these two attitudes was inevitable. Solange's love would slowly decline without her realizing it and above all without her wishing to admit it, until the day came when it would be so debased and disfigured that she would be forced to draw the logical conclusion. Conversely, with Roberti the lie would gradually flake away, so to speak, under the pressure of the truth. He would come to believe less and less profoundly that he was not in love. He would maintain this fiction in his own eyes as long as he could; he would maintain it almost to the end, and this would prevent him from seeing disaster in time to avoid it. Only after disaster had fallen, too late from every point of view, would he realize the full extent of his error and the mess he was in, which was of course irremediable. Such is the normal spectacle of life. To my mind Roberti, relying alone on his heart and intelligence, cultivating mirages right up to the catastrophe, provides a fairly good illustration of the man who fails to appreciate the tragic side of life until after the event, when nothing more can be done. The history of mankind is a series of wasted opportunities because of men's lack of foresight and the eternal self-deception which is their lot. Here we catch the sin of pride redhanded and can observe the havoc it creates. It is indeed a very familiar and insufficiently exposed form of pride, to refuse to see the world as it is and prefer the arbitrary conception of it one has forged for oneself. But the world is impossible to shatter; preconceived ideas can never prevail over reality. They are pulverized by reality, so awe-inspiring and indifferent, and the disproportion in strength between the two is so great as to become laughable. There is nothing more ludicrous than a man stubbornly persisting in his private lie in the belief that this tiny piece of grit will halt the monstrous cogs of the universe or make them turn in the opposite direction.

I: Stop! I know that philosophy. It is more or less my own. So don't waste your breath on it. Anyway, don't you think you are getting a bit off the beam when, with regard to poor Roberti bogged down in his private contradictions, you mobilize the "monstrous cogs of the universe"?

HE: No, I don't agree. Every man, even the most mediocre, deserves to have the monstrous cogs of the universe mobilized on his account, since he is capable of conceiving these cogs, since he can, or at least could, see them if only he would trouble to open his eyes; since, finally, human life is a reduced version of the great life of the universe.

I: We say "a microcosm," it's shorter.

HE: I am not short and what is more I don't like microcosms.

I: Why, it's true, you *have* given me my bearings. Thank you. At last I know where I am with Roberti and his lady love. But I should also like to be enlightened as to my own fate.

HE: Your own fate?

I: Yes, my immediate fate. How long do you expect to go on talking? Have I a hope of getting to bed before dawn?

HE: Lord, to do the thing full justice, to give all the details and philosophy of it, you would have to grant me seven or eight more hours.

I: That would roughly take us to six A.M. Pretty late for an early riser like myself.

HE: Provided I cut things as short as possible and on condition also that you don't interrupt too often, I could possibly give you the general idea in three hours.

I: I shall interrupt as often as I need to.

HE: Then don't complain if you get to bed late. Personally, I'm easy. I get up whenever I want. At teatime if I feel like it.

I: It is just because I don't want to get to bed too late that I shall interrupt as often as seems necessary. Were I to let you ramble on to your heart's content, we'd still be here next month.

HE: Do you feel tired?

I: I did before dinner, but eating always bucks me up.

HE: Would you like some coffee?

I: No thanks, not at night. Roberti's story is a long one and you have been dragging it out unreasonably, but even so it fills me with a sort of excitement. I am kind of impatient to hear it to the end, merely because it seems to me a possible subject. A cup of coffee on top of this and I wouldn't sleep for the next two nights. Besides, it's very good of you but I haven't yet finished my dinner. I don't intend to stop short at the Gorgonzola.

HE: Oh, I beg your pardon. What would you like now? Maître d'hôtel!

MAÎTRE D'HÔTEL: Yes gentlemen? Would you like a sweet?

I: Have you any strawberries?

MAÎTRE D'HÔTEL: Certainly, Monsieur. Or perhaps you would prefer crêpes Suzette or a soufflé au Grand Marnier?

I: No. Strawberries. They are my favorite dish and this evening I only want what I like best.

MAÎTRE D'HÔTEL: With cream?

I: Exactly, with cream.

MAÎTRE D'HÔTEL: Very good. And for Monsieur?

HE: Some fresh fruit salad.

MAÎTRE D'HÔTEL: And coffee to follow?

HE: For me, yes please, but not for my guest.

I: Wait, I'll have some after all. To hell with economy.

HE: Bravo! And bring us your plum brandy as well.

I: Don't you find something indecent about stuffing ourselves the way we are doing while at the same time studying the damnation of Faust-Roberti through a magnifying glass?

HE: Good Lord, it never struck me that way.

I: Anyway, what the hell! Roberti is one thing, our dinner's another. Artists have to sustain themselves, put some fuel in their machine so as to be able to make music.

HE: But no one's accusing you! Who are you defending yourself against?

I: Myself. Every time I catch myself according undue importance to the good things of life, I feel a sort of guilt. At this moment, for instance, I picture myself standing on the edge of a cliff in storm and darkness, holding my plate of strawberries and cream in my left hand and my spoon in my right. At the foot of the cliff laps the Styx, at which I curiously glance between mouthfuls. This contrast gets on my nerves. Dante didn't munch chocolates while he visited hell. He was thin and hollow-eyed. I feel ridiculous.

HE: Calm yourself. You are not Dante. Nor am I Virgil. We are just two bright lads of the positivist era having a good time while we tell each other stories. Eat up your strawberries without remorse. Your appetite delights me. I wish I had your way with a fork. Besides Dante, too, was a bright lad of the thirteenth century and he can't have turned up his nose at a salmi of guinea fowl on occasion. There is no one more voracious than a thin man. They are all insatiable. Tell yourself you are on a campaign and that the troops have to be fed if they are to show courage and endurance. Tonight, through my agency, the Lord has sent you *foie gras*, caviar, duck, Gorgonzola and strawberries, just as he formerly sent seven years of feast to Egypt. You have eaten of the *foie gras* and caviar of the Lord. Render thanks unto Him and don't look for trouble where it doesn't exist. Just because poor Roberti was damned (or so we suppose) is no reason why you shouldn't eat. Your fasting won't prevent what has been from having been.

I: Typical Jesuitical arguments.

HE: Why no, they are Biblical arguments. The arguments of a simple man who aims no higher than he should and refuses to give himself airs. Victor Hugo understood this perfectly, in his extravagant and comic way, when he said that as one grows old one becomes "a bourgeois of the Helicon," passing "from the tripod to the pulpit" and finally "renting a cottage with a balcony on the edge of the abyss." That's good, don't you think? Well, it was we two he was thinking of, we two this evening. We are familiarizing ourselves with horror. We are subduing it. It comes to eat from our hand. Presently we shall go and smoke our cigars (Havanas, of course) on the balcony of our cottage and contemplate the abyss without turning a hair. So eat up your strawberries. Look, here they come. They are superb.

WAITER: Monsieur will tell me how much cream . . .

I: Stop, that's just right. Thank you.

HE: I hope at least they are good?

I: Divine.

HE: There, you see, you said it yourself. The opposite of diabolic. All is for the best. Perhaps I may take advantage of the fact that your mouth is full to return to Roberti.

I: It's not so full that I can let you off describing their vacation.

HE: Do you think that's really necessary?

I: Absolutely. Vacations are like the hellish life of Paris. They set the scene. They are one of the great institutions, I would even say one of the great myths of the modern world. I absolutely insist on hearing all the silly things Mlles. Mignot and Angioletti said to each other, guidebook in hand, before Burgos Cathedral. I want to see Roberti on the Côte d'Azur, counting the days separating him from his dear delightful work and his dear and even more delightful love life, Roberti a victim of the convention of the vacations, wasting thirty or forty days of his life relaxing when he is not a bit tired, bored stiff with having nothing to do sandwiched between his wife and sons.

HE: My friend, you have just about said all that was needed: the vacations as a modern myth, Solange and Mlle. Angioletti discovering Spain with all the requisite artlessness, Roberti dying of boredom tethered to his beach. If you want to develop this theme when you write the book, you can do it on your own. I advise against it, however, since you would risk lapsing into an archly humorous description of modern customs and nothing could be more sinister than that. The petty bourgeoisie of the twentieth century, whose life is just a series of comic mishaps, is a subject which has always struck me as being of annihilating banality. It's too trivial to be truly comic. It is merely laughable, that is to say it leads to the worst kind of literature. I hope that isn't what you're after?

I: Just listen to him! Now he's insulting me. What I am after is to write a novel of modern love, in other words as complete an inventory as possible of love in the second half of the twentieth century. Accordingly vacations, a modern institution which didn't exist under Louis XV, Theodoric or Pericles, occupy a place which one mustn't exaggerate, naturally, but which one shouldn't overlook either. So tell me about these vacations. Describe them. They are not in the least beside the point; on the contrary, they *are* more or less the point, or at least a part of it. You have to bring them in. Otherwise we might as well be writing Perrault's fairy tales.

HE: Roberti discovered one thing at least during this vacation: Solange's soul, thanks to the letters she wrote him. These came as a revelation.

I: Here is where I stop you at once. Where did he receive these letters? Surely not at his house? So it must have been at the post office. I want a sketch of him going on the sly every two or three days to fetch his love letters.

HE: How tiresome you are with your passion for detail! Obviously he had his letters sent to the post office; it goes without saying.

ɪ: It goes even better by being said. Was he afraid Agnes might find out?

ʜᴇ: Agnes was a discreet woman. She would never have opened any letter addressed to her husband. She was neither inquisitive nor suspicious. Besides, Roberti gave her the most convincing proof of his fidelity and affection two or three times a week. However, one never knows. She might well open one of Solange's letters by mistake. If one is going to take precautions one might as well be thorough and anticipate the least likely eventualities. Imagine the scene had Agnes chanced on a letter beginning "My darling precious" or "Beloved angel . . ."!

ɪ: How absurd these perpetual palpitations are.

ʜᴇ: It serves no purpose to crow over him. We have to take people as they are and, *starting from that*, try to see them clearly. Following which you can moralize if you still feel like it. Roberti valued the image Agnes had built up of him. Through her, he could contemplate a picture of himself which he found pleasing.

ɪ: A false image.

ʜᴇ: Not entirely.

ɪ: What? An old dog who chases girls and acts the devoted spouse. I call that the height of deceit.

ʜᴇ: It was a deception which included himself, which took him in as well.

ɪ: That's even worse.

ʜᴇ: It's neither better nor worse, it's something quite different. The fact that in Agnes' view he preserved the glamor of an ideal husband gave him a high opinion of himself. It was—how shall I put it?—as if he were seeing himself through Agnes' eyes. Moreover it tallied with something real, for he cared deeply for his wife. He was afraid of causing her sorrow, he knew he would share in this sorrow as if it were his own. What I am now saying is a bit obscure but I promise you it's true. As I think you have already remarked several times, Roberti was not a man of one sole and unique truth but of three or four truths existing side by side. It may have been his truth to be the fiery lover of Solange Mignot, but it was just as much to be the sober husband of Agnes; it may have been to lead a life of disorder and sexual excess, but it was also to be a reliable, peaceable, transparent man. Roberti the faithful spouse was, if I may so put it, a possibility which was almost real. Potentially he had all the qualities and inclinations of a faithful husband.

ɪ: I don't think you can be aware of the comic side of what you are saying.

HE: I am never very aware of the comic side, generally speaking, because I always try to see the reasons behind things. And once one has explained something, once one has broken it down into its various components, it ceases to be comic. A clown's face makes you laugh, but if you consider one by one the natural features of the man who disguises himself as a clown followed by his makeup, paint, powder, wig and so on, you no longer feel like laughing.

I: A specious argument. A false analogy. A clown, in his way, is a work of art. It's as if you were saying that from the moment you see how a picture is put together, how Rembrandt or Goya applied the paint or solved some problem of perspective, you cease to admire the picture.

HE: You are right. I withdraw the clown. But what I said about being aware or unaware of the comic side remains true.

I: Hmm! That too is debatable but I'll let it pass. We shall never get done otherwise. Let's go back to the post office. Did our two turtledoves write a lot to each other?

HE: Once or twice a week. I told you how, thanks to these letters, Roberti discovered Solange's soul. They were charming letters written with a certain style. People reveal themselves far better in their letters than in their words or gestures. I believe that here, in a condensed form, we find a phenomenon akin to the one we were discussing earlier on with regard to artists and what you call their "little music." The little music Solange put into her letters was altogether light and airy, delicate and witty.

I: What did she have to say?

HE: It matters less what she said than the way she said it. They were eight-page letters in which everything flowed spontaneously, as if each time inspiration had descended on her. In them she spoke the best French language of love without its appearing to have caused her the slightest difficulty. One could sense in them a soul at once naïve and subtle, unsophisticated and faintly mocking, which was most surprising. And all this borne along on what one might call "a great surge of love," with occasional lines of such sincerity that they appeared profound. Roberti, for his part, wrote pedantic and artificial epistles which cost him some effort and which Solange greatly admired.

I: Women have a gift for letter writing. They are well known for it. And love is a subject which inspires them. It inspires men far less. They always rack their brains when writing to their mistresses. I would point out that you haven't yet given me a sketch of Roberti going to the post office.

HE: I'll give you a sketch of him leaving the post office if you like: after having read the latest letter he would tear it up, and the envelope too, and scatter them to the winds. But he couldn't stop his heart from beating as he entered the post office; nor could he prevent himself from feeling gay after reading these genuine tokens of Solange's love. She was gaining substance for him in a curious way. He was so astonished that she should write so well that he felt a new kind of respect for her. Following on which he marveled at how subtle his instinct had been in leading him to choose her for a mistress. He thought how his little Solange most certainly did him no discredit and how, had he been capable of feeling love for a woman, she would have been fully deserving of such love. It was very pleasant to discover in this way, and from a distance, someone about whom he thought he already knew everything, to learn that she had a fine spirit. Very pleasant and very flattering. From time to time he felt gusts of acute longing to see her again.

I: How long did his "indigestion" last?

HE: Eight or ten days. Possibly a fortnight. For about two weeks he hardly thought of Solange or at least didn't think of her with desire. And then, at the end of two weeks, this desire naturally revived, but only intermittently; memories of the Rue d'Argenson returned; he began to dream again. What is odd is that he never thought of hastening his return to Paris. He was bored, he was counting the days, but he also felt a certain contentment at the idea that this exile was self-imposed. He had a vague feeling that it would be counted in his favor.

I: Counted by whom? And why?

HE: Oh you know, that sort of thing is inexplicable. It's just a *vague feeling*, nothing more. When one is unhappy, or even merely bored, one tends to think it isn't entirely futile, that one will somehow be recompensed for it. Perhaps this is an aftereffect of Christian morality. It is in the same category as the adage that every good deed has its reward. We are here, so to speak, in the "soft regions" of Roberti's soul, those endless indeterminate plains which he sometimes thought he saw when he looked inside himself.

I: God, how I hate this type of meaningless metaphor! Soft regions, indeterminate plains of the soul! You must think you're Chateaubriand. It's grotesque!

HE: I believe that in most souls there are regions which are not so much dark as misty, where shapes are ill defined and the emotions, like weary and myopic travelers, grope their way and are a prey to mirages and hallucinations. Is that a little more intelligible?

1: Barely. Now it's like Sainte-Beuve. However, I get a vague idea. To do you justice, you talk gibberish but once one gets used to it one begins to see a sort of meaning behind it all.

HE: Thanks. Of course, you'll be able to put it all into short and simple sentences. Roberti's boredom, then, appeased his conscience. He told himself that he and he alone was still the arbiter of what was happening to him, and this thought was on the whole rather gratifying.

1: It seems to me that here we have a psychological point worth investigating. Roberti was free as air. He only needed the smallest excuse to return to Paris and wallow in debauchery. Nevertheless he dug himself in at Antibes, where he was bored. What was this strange curb he was applying to himself? It's not the first time we've seen it happen. What was the motive behind it?

HE: It probably stemmed from the *rational* conception he had of life, from his profound, almost instinctive belief that one must never hurry destiny on, that things come about in their own good time and never sooner, that any impatience is a form of violence which is always punished. And then there was also that mysterious scale of compensations which operated permanently in his mind, as I mentioned a few moments ago. Finally we must never forget that, in his way, Roberti had a strong sense of duty. The family vacation was a sacred duty and by no means a painful one either. Nothing came amiss to him; he knew how to get pleasure out of innocent vacations and family fun. He enjoyed them all the more in that his secret added a certain spice to them. He probably needed this long period of solitude. It enabled him not only to relive the past but also to live the future in advance. I pointed out just now that every man is the novelist of his own life with regard to the use he makes of his memories and the way he gathers them into a fine, lucid and meaningful tale. But the novel can also develop in the opposite direction when one has enough material to sketch out the future, arrange the emotional or practical setting in which it will take place, savor in advance all the pleasures with which one guesses it to be pregnant. One sets out one's soul like a finely laid dining-room table: destiny has but to bring in its wines and dishes; one is all prepared to tackle them with the heartiest of appetites. I have another image, if you don't like this one. Roberti was preparing himself to see Solange again like a music lover who, before going to an opera, carefully studies the libretto and score so as not to miss a single note, a single inflection of the voices or the music. It was a very long libretto, an interminable score. He needed no less than six or eight weeks to unearth all its riches.

ɪ: And all this complacency, all these daydreams about his absent Solange never aroused his suspicions? They never led him to suspect he might be suffering from love with a capital L? You'll never get me to swallow that.

ʜᴇ: As a matter of fact all this daydreaming and complacency reassured him, so true is it that when one has established a system for oneself one subordinates everything to it. "Were I in love," he told himself, "I should stop myself from thinking about Solange. I would apply my mind to other things. There is no lack of things to occupy my mind and the poor poppet would soon be forgotten. What proves I'm not in love is that I think of her with pleasure, without that touch of bitterness which is the sign of love. Thinking of Solange doesn't harm me. So there is no love in me. Only desire. One day this desire will die. All too soon, alas! I know myself! Let me profit from it while it lasts, enjoy myself, dream, run through my little movie." His illusion was all the greater in that it was never Solange's soul (despite her sweet letters) which he evoked in his reveries but her body, whose charms he took stock of with detailed precision.

ɪ: Wasn't he jealous? Didn't he tell himself she might easily fall in with some swain on her travels?

ʜᴇ: Not in the least. He hadn't that kind of imagination. Just as he never managed to conceive how hurt she might be by his coldness, so he was incapable of imagining his mistress in another's arms. Through her ardor she had given him a pledge of fidelity, so to speak. There are some demonstrations which can reassure for two whole months. So, you see, this lack of jealousy contributed further to his peace of mind. Love necessarily implies jealousy; conversely, no jealousy, no love. In sum, Roberti was convinced that he thought of Solange in exactly the same way as he thought of any other of life's pleasant prospects where no passion is involved and which are just as enjoyable to desire as to attain. He thought of her as he would think of a handsome Régence armchair seen in an antique shop, which it would be fun to buy; it would really look very well in the drawing room. Can you see the general trend of his sentiments, or rather the trend he thought his sentiments had?

ɪ: Yes, I can. I see this poor man embedded in his falsehood. And for once I will even pay you a compliment: I find you have admirably illustrated how an intelligent man can act like a fool. There is something rather splendid about Roberti's failure to see what would have blinded anyone else with its obviousness. It is extraordinary to watch him acting like a fool through an excess of rationalism; I find it fascinating. Few novelists, I think, have ever paid attention to this particular kind of stupidity. One might even give it a name. What would you say to "emotional pedantry"?

HE: Yes, that's a good term; but does it altogether apply to Roberti?

I: Indeed it does. A pedant is a man whose mind is stuffed with a mass of opinions, arguments and knowledge, and who nearly always applies them the wrong way. He's a man who adjusts the world to his mind and not his mind to the world, who has a system of *a priori* references. There is one category of emotional pedants I know well, and who in their way function like Roberti—the literary critics, beginning with their prophet and messiah, Sainte-Beuve.

HE: Oh, oh! The wolf of letters awakes! He sleeps with one eye open.

I: The literary critic is a man who, through excess of intelligence, excess of knowledge and references, understands practically nothing. And even here I am only referring to the superior kind of critic. Most of them are ignoramuses who have set themselves up as critics because that is less difficult than being a pork butcher or a lawyer, because it requires neither apprenticeship nor a diploma.

HE: Well, well! I trust you won't put these fine ideas into our novel. I want it to sell. If you trounce the critics they'll crucify you, or else they won't mention you at all, which would be worse.

I: Rest assured, I am not completely crazy. I am past the age of tilting at windmills.

HE: You? Why, hardly a week goes by without your galloping off to cleave a windmill. As soon as you spot one on the horizon you see red, dig your spurs into Rosinante and charge! The number of times I've seen you, after one of your fine outbursts, dangling in the air from one of the sails! I must confess, at such moments it's you who looks foolish, not the windmill.

I: Maybe.

HE: Don't say anything about literary critics in the novel, I beg you. It would be empty provocation. What purpose would it serve? Besides, it's way off the subject. You are beyond the age of gratuitously making enemies. It would be childish.

I: Don't be tiresome. If I feel like saying Roberti had the intelligence of a literary critic, I will do so. It is an interesting point which carries us a step—just a little step (but it is always little)—forward in our knowledge of the human heart. Why should I put myself out? At my age I am not going to start shivering and shaking at the idea of offending M. Dugrumeau, literary correspondent of the *Corrèze Courier*. That would be absurd. From the moment I put pen to paper, I have always felt absolutely free to speak my mind and to hell with everybody. It's a point of honor with me. As soon as I get an idea I write it, even if I should be proved wrong. Thanks to which I am neither very rich nor very famous, I am reviled by a host of fools, but I have a few readers who like me, trust me and know that I never lie when I write.

HE: Tara, tara, tara-ta-ta! Beethoven wrote his Eroica Symphony with Bonaparte in mind; you write with yourself in mind. That is certainly an advance no one will overlook.

I: Having lost the argument, the gentleman falls back on "caustic" irony. But I'll have you know it leaves me quite cold. It would take more than irony to make me renounce an opinion I believe to be right. In my way I am a martyr to the truth. For love of it I never hesitate to make myself ridiculous. Ridiculous and obnoxious. It pays in the long run. I'd even say it is the price of salvation. You'll see how a hundred years from now I'll be poisoning the lives of school children!

HE: I will or I won't see. In literature one never knows who will live and who will die.

I: Begging your pardon, one knows perfectly well. Just say the word and I'll list for you the four thousand living dead of contemporary French literature, those whose books are dead the moment they are published, the moment they are written. I could also enumerate the half dozen who won't die after they have been buried.

HE: I certainly won't say the word. Above all I won't have you naming names. You're quite capable of printing them later on in the novel. That would be a fine state of affairs! Not content with antagonizing the critics, you now set about almost all your fellow authors. Carry on like that and you'll end up in the gutter.

I: Why not? It's a fine thing to end up in the gutter like Cervantes or Christopher Columbus. Chateaubriand himself, at eighty, was on the verge of penury.

HE: Aha, so it's Christopher Columbus now. Oddly enough, you haven't yet compared yourself to Napoleon.

I: There are two necessary and sufficient conditions for survival in literature. I say two. To fulfill only one of them is not enough. If you don't tell the truth and if you don't tell it in music, you die. That's categorical, mathematical, immutable.

HE: So, according to you, among all the fat books being published today, so full of ingenious ideas and discoveries, written by honest and sober-minded men with the sweat of their brows, none will live on? That's pretty rough.

I: I can't help it, art is not democratic. In art it isn't necessarily the good student who wins the prize. It is the elect, the man born with that little music inside him and the ability to perceive the truth of the world. Art is pre-eminently aristocratic. Artists are privileged beings, as hateful as the nobility of the Ancien Régime but far more secure. What they have can't be taken away from them. There can be no night of August the fourth. Prince Aragon cannot cede his privileges, even if he wished to with all his heart, to Citizen . . .

HE: No names!

I: Very well. Let's say Prince Proust and Citizen Bourget, if you prefer it.

HE: Yes, I do. If you must at all costs quote names, choose your examples from the dead. They, at least, are not dangerous.

I: You would have me tilt at windmills, but on condition that they have lost their sails and are falling into ruin. Now you're sniggering.

HE: I'm sniggering at the thought of what you said a short while ago: how you reserved the right to interrupt as often as you found necessary in order to proceed more quickly! And here you are wasting five good minutes riding your literary hobbyhorse, painting yourself in the guise of a fire-eater, as good M. Sébastien would say. Where does it lead us? It's not your novel we are writing, but Roberti's.

I: Physician, heal thyself! Now I've heard just about everything. Well then, let's push on, since you take it that way. Describe Roberti at Antibes. That's where we were, isn't it? And while you're about it, describe as well the two girls charging headlong through the Prado, with Mlle. Angioletti whispering to her friend: "I say, isn't Velasquez lovely? They really knew how to paint in those days, it's not like this modern art." And Toledo? They didn't much care for Toledo, it's too depressing. Actually, the whole of Spain is depressing. Beautiful but depressing. Austere's the word. There's a lot of poverty and the roads are very bad. They are putting up splendid buildings in Madrid. The population looks as if it had resigned itself to the regime. Franco's definitely got the upper hand. They say he's thinking of retiring and placing the crown on the head of the Prince of Asturias. In one way that might be a good thing, but in another it could lead to trouble. However, they had a pretty good time all the same. It was very hot. One should never go to Spain in August. The climate is famous for its extremes. You either die of heat or perish of cold. Never go for a walk in the Sierra Morena without an overcoat, especially in the evening. The French climate, which is temperate, is much to be preferred. But you must see the Alhambra at Granada, it's like being in Morocco. You meet a lot of French people in Spain. It always sounds too funny to hear French being spoken abroad. At El Escorial there's a room known as the Rotting Room: it's where they used to put the corpses of the kings of Spain. You only have to wander a bit off the main road to see it's a poor country: everything is peeling. The sun, of course.

HE: Marvelous! You deserve to be prosecuted for defamation of character!

I: I forgot the *carabineros* with their cocked hats. They're so picturesque!

HE: You ought to write a supplement to the *Dictionary of Received Ideas*. Silliness has surely annexed fresh territory (even if it's only foreign travel) since Flaubert's day. Save in one or two minor details, I think Solange and Mlle. Angioletti's trip must have been just as you have described it, or at least that they described it on similar lines to their friends and relations.

I: Really? I rather overdid it, all the same.

HE: Yes, of course you did; but when they visit a country for the first time as tourists, clutching their guidebooks, running from museum to cathedral, galloping from one town to the next, giving no more than ten minutes to the greatest masterpieces as otherwise they wouldn't have time to "do" everything, people barely see more than the clichés and commonplaces. Just think of it! The whole of Spain in three weeks!

I: Why "do" Spain in three weeks? Why not stay quietly in Madrid or Seville?

HE: You talk like someone with plenty of time and money. Put yourself in the places of Mlles. Mignot and Angioletti. They only have three weeks' vacation a year; they are not very well off. During these three weeks they want to store up as many sensations and memories as possible in order to feed parsimoniously on them during the remaining three hundred and forty-four days. They are filled with a morbid hunger. They stuff themselves with landscapes and masterpieces like squirrels laying up stores for the winter. I find it rather touching. Added to which, of course, they were taking part in an organized bus tour at "very modest" rates. In the company of three dozen old ladies, impecunious family men and bespectacled girl students. That ought to satisfy your constant demand for period pictures. Here's a good one: the vacation of a wage earner in quest of beauty in 1955, the vacation of the semi-intellectual who is poor but anxious to enrich his spirit and see in reality the works of art and landscapes of which he dreams and which he knows only through postcards or picturebooks. You can laugh as much as you like, and it may be absurd, but it is neither contemptible nor unworthy. Also it is only absurd in France where, as

Stendhal said, "poverty is absurd." Even from an organized bus tour made in the company of a few imbeciles one brings back something: either experience or ideas. Solange and Mlle. Angioletti preserved an enchanted memory of their excursion into Spain and this improved as the months went by. The Alhambra at Granada was engraved on their little hearts. Of all the beautiful things they saw as they raced by, a few remained with them and you can't deny that this forms a sort of enrichment of the spirit. They enjoyed it all so much that they promised themselves to do it again. They would save up enough money to go in the same way next year to Italy, then the following year to the Netherlands or Greece. I should add that in the bus Mlle. Angioletti made the acquaintance of a chemistry student whose mistress she became one beautiful scented night on a beach not far from Tarragona. Such adventures add greatly to the pleasures of travel. As the student dropped her when they got back to Paris, this little affair didn't have time to turn sour and merely enhanced her memories without adding any unpleasant undertones.

ı: And didn't Solange have a little flutter with a chemistry student too? I should rather like that snake of a Roberti to have been betrayed.

HE: I'm sorry, but he wasn't. During the whole trip she was as good as gold, and without the slightest difficulty. Her heart was full of her love; she thought of no one but Edouard. She longed to share her happiness with him. She felt a deep regret at being unable to wander at his side through the rooms of the Prado, at not having with her this highly intelligent man who would have revealed fascinating details about everything she wondered at, who would have introduced her to Spain. Her happiest moments were spent writing letters to him in the evenings at the hotel. She looked on the idyll of Mlle. Angioletti and the chemistry student with disdain. The student was rather scruffy and everything he said seemed to Solange intolerably crude and pretentious. By comparison she admired Roberti all the more. He was so handsome, so well groomed, so charming, so distinguished. God, how lucky she was to have been singled out by such a man! Not loved, of course, that would have been asking too much; but the mere fact that he liked her, that she occupied his mind just a little, that she received letters which he had taken the trouble to write, was already something incredible and unhoped for. Sometimes, in the bus, she would lose herself in daydreams which, aided by the bumping of the bus, would speedily conjure up thoughts which almost made her blush.

ı: There is one last thing I should like to know, after which we can leave Spain, as I'm beginning to be fed up with it. Did she and her friend talk about Roberti, discuss the situation at all?

HE: To begin with, Solange was very reserved and even prickly on this score. But the enforced intimacy of traveling together made her more confiding. The farther they moved into Spain, the more she felt a need to talk about her love. Mlle. Angioletti was well aware that Solange was having an affair with "a gentleman" and naturally she was on tenterhooks to hear about it, all the more since Solange was showing clear symptoms of being in love: she would be gay or sad without apparent reason; she would lapse into silence or chatter like a magpie. There was an enthralling romance behind all this and you can imagine how Mlle. Angioletti couldn't rest until she had heard every detail.

I: So Solange succumbed to the vulgar temptation of making confidences. A pity.

HE: It was inevitable. Even the most superior women succumb to this temptation. I would call it "zenana talk." This is doubtless because love is their speciality, their vocation, their art. They discuss love with each other the way painters discuss painting, poets poetry and doctors medicine. They will endlessly chew over some point of passion; they analyze the characters of the men in whom they are interested; they pick them to pieces before their friends, just like an engineer expounding his calculations to a colleague; they seek solutions together, consult each other, in short have a splendid time. They have all the fun of two technicians discussing method. Besides, as you must have observed, they are generally pretty discreet. There exists between them a kind of corporate solidarity and, in matters of love, it is as if they believed themselves to be more or less bound by a kind of professional secrecy.

I: These are delightful conclusions but, as I have already told you thirty times, I don't need them. I can draw them for myself. What I cannot invent is what the two girls actually said to each other.

HE: Well, piecemeal and bit by bit, Solange told her friend about Roberti. She described the married man, the busy man, somewhat aloof, rather indifferent. She explained how she loved him more than he loved her, but how even so it was all quite marvelous.

I: And what did Angioletti reply?

HE: Angioletti was enthralled. For her it was a true romance. She made the kind of comments one would expect: "Honey, it's utterly crazy. You're wasting the best years of your life. The man doesn't give a damn for you. You're making a fool of yourself. He'll never divorce in order to marry you. You ought to break it off. He's twice your age.

You've got to settle down sooner or later. If I were you, I'd have my eye on Legay, I would. He's a very nice boy too." And so on.

ɪ: In short she was way off the mark.

ʜᴇ: Clearly. But this never struck Solange who told herself: "She's right, I am crazy, but one cannot gainsay one's heart. I love Edouard and I'm happy." So she shook her head and said nothing. Since Roberti wasn't there to freeze her with some cynical remark, she let herself be pervaded by the sweetness of loving and being loved. Spain isn't far and three weeks' absence isn't long, but it is enough for the magic of separation to work, that is to say for pleasant memories to become magnified and bad ones to become blurred.

ɪ: The old story: absence makes the heart grow fonder.

ʜᴇ: Well, yes! The same phenomenon, moreover, occurred with Roberti, who was bored at Antibes and, what's more, had no one in whom he could confide. He made much of Agnes; he watched his sons flirting with girls on the beach with an indulgent eye; he was leading an idle and pleasant existence; the sun was tanning his skin which, he thought, made him look younger. But gradually the lack of occupation, the rest, the dry hot air of the South, the letters he went to fetch at the post office, all combined to turn his mind toward thoughts of love. As the weeks passed he recalled with ever-increasing insistence all the details of his affair with Solange. He counted over its joys, which from a distance now seemed fabulous. Each day he grew a little more forgetful of the constraints, the irritations, the empty conversation of his mistress, the countless material difficulties with which adultery was faced in Paris in 1955. He saw nothing but the beautiful, velvety and tender eyes of Solange, her smile when he looked down in victory at her face lying back beneath his; he breathed her perfume; he felt the softness of her skin.

ɪ: But Antibes in high summer is seething with girls in bikinis. Didn't that distract the old pig just a little?

ʜᴇ: Why no, it didn't. And he should have realized from this indifference that he was no longer the same man as the year before. One can only conclude that he had sworn not to examine himself too closely. The beauties on the beach always turned his thoughts toward Solange. He compared her body with theirs. He didn't find it more beautiful but far more desirable, which in turn led him to wax maudlin over this girl who was his secret, who understood him, whose flesh had such deep affinities with his own and in whom he inspired so powerful an attraction. In other words, and without his admitting it, his love made him as conceited as a young fool. He compared it with other possible loves and concluded it to be exceptional. Whenever a particularly beautiful and particularly naked woman passed close to him on the beach, his reaction was the following, or at least I can decode it for you as follows: "That beauty doesn't mean a thing to me: she probably has no temperament and she would never love me the way Solange does."

I: Not to mention that the beauties of Antibes, Juan-les-Pins and Cannes are expensive. We mustn't forget the stingy side of his character. Smart women are ruinous. With a little secretary one has the added pleasure of saving a lot of money.

HE: Of course, there was that consideration as well (although Roberti didn't express it to himself so clearly!) but love is made up of a mass of things, great and small, sublime and sordid. There was a great deal that was sordid in Roberti's love. That doesn't mean that it did not have moments, flashes of sublimity. And this occasional touch of sublimity was enough to make up for all the rest. After all, he suffered and suffered keenly, he was deeply unhappy in spite of his constant refusal to admit that he was in love and could suffer through love. But we haven't yet reached that point. We are still with the vacation of 1955. At that time he was utterly convinced that the only woman he loved was Agnes and he was still to be convinced of this for a long time to come. It is this confusion which makes his story so complex and pitiful. It seems to me glutinous with an indescribable treacle of false emotions.

I: One cannot say that an emotion is true or false. It is. It exists. So it has to be taken into account. A false emotion can modify the world and events just as well as a true one.

HE: Don't quibble over words. You know perfectly well what I mean. I call a true emotion an emotion which corresponds to the truth and a false one an emotion which corresponds to an illusion or a lie. And now with all this you've made me lose my thread.

I: You don't need me to lose your thread for you. You're an expert at losing it on your own. We were at Antibes. Roberti wasn't ogling the girls. He was thinking of Solange and telling himself how much he would like to sleep with her again.

HE: Yes, that's it. The nearer the end of the vacation drew, the more Edouard's daydreams took hold of him, impregnated him so to speak. The nearer the day of departure came, the more he gave his desire full rein. During the last few days he was seething with impatience. Of course he never showed it. He forced himself to behave in a way that grew colder and more detached the more impatient he felt. This impassivity formed part of his secret excitement.

I: Right. Now back to Paris. He meets his ladylove again. What happens?

HE: He was in such a hurry to see her that he rang her up within half an hour of his return. But he received a terrible blow. She wasn't there.

I: Where was she?

HE: Gone.

I: How do you mean, gone?

HE: Vanished, evaporated.

I: You'll have to explain this in detail. Gone where? Gone why? I'm all at sea. Here are two people who haven't seen each other for two months, whose one thought is to meet again, and one of them fails to turn up?

HE: It's a pleasure to tell you a story. I don't know anyone so responsive to dramatic situations. If only you could see your face at this moment! It's a perfect picture. Yes, old man, gone! Solange wasn't there. She had left Paris the night before.

I: But why? Had she run away? Didn't she want to see Roberti any more? I may say that's something I'd approve of.

HE: It was far simpler. Dietz had taken her off with him on a business trip. He needed an intelligent secretary to take notes of discussions, refresh his memory, find him the relevant documents and so on. It wasn't the first time he had taken Solange off like this. Actually it is one of the things that explains their friendship. I wouldn't say their intimacy because, with the way your mind works, God knows what you'd start imagining. But traveling together brings people closer. They end by talking of other things than work. They reach a stage, if not of confidences, then at least of discussing relatively personal topics. In trains and airplanes they tend to gossip. It isn't what they say that counts so much as a certain spontaneous trust. And gossiping with Dietz is never a matter of mere trivialities. You know him: he has a delicate way of guiding the conversation which enables him to ferret out people's worries or pleasures and discreetly console them or share in their happiness.

I: He's an excellent fellow, Dietz. It's a long time since I saw him. You should ask me to dine with him one of these days.

HE: With the greatest pleasure. Whenever you like. I'll telephone him tomorrow. At any rate it wouldn't be a bad thing for you to see him if you are going to write Roberti's story. Much as I was against your meeting Agnes, I think on the other hand you might find a talk with Dietz useful, even if you discussed other things than Roberti and Solange, even if you made only one or two glancing allusions to them. Agnes plays a part in the drama and it is always preferable for the artist not to see his models.

I: Thinking it over, I've come to the same conclusion. You see, I am being honest with you. Nature inhibits invention and it is through invention, not nature, that one renders truth.

HE: Whereas Dietz was just a witness of the drama. A distressed but objective witness.

I: Granted. Now tell me two things I absolutely have to know. The first is unimportant but necessary: where did Dietz take Solange and how long did the trip last?

HE: There you're asking too much of me! How can you expect me to remember details like that? I suppose it must have lasted about eight days. I seem to remember it took in visits to Belgium, Germany and Switzerland. Two days in Brussels, two in Frankfurt, two in Geneva, two in Zurich. Something like that.

I: Eight days! A whole week. Poor Roberti! You must give me a detailed account of it all, it will be fun. But now my second point: was Dietz aware of Solange's affair with Roberti?

HE: No. He was acute enough to guess that his secretary was in love with someone but he didn't know who and moreover he didn't care. The love affairs of his secretary *qua* secretary concerned him not at all, as you can imagine. To pry into (or even merely feel curious about) the sex life of his employees would have seemed to him contemptible. As for Solange, she had far too much respect for Dietz to confide in him. However, as I said, in conversation the form matters more than the content and the manner of saying things more than what is actually said. Without naming Roberti, without admitting anything precise, she tactfully and delicately painted so accurate a picture of her emotions that in return Dietz was able to proffer all kinds of sound and wise advice perfectly adapted to her heart and mind. Actually I've used the wrong word: it wasn't "advice." He simply talked to Solange (who was at such moments no longer a secretary but someone he was fond of and whose character he respected) about life, love, the passage of time, the waning of passion; he told her all about life, if you like, rather the way we are talking together here, and he made it very fascinating. They were excellent lessons he taught her, without any immediate aim but highly instructive. Solange listened to him carefully. She saw that here was an experienced and warmhearted man, a true friend, and she believed what he said even if she didn't fully understand all of it.

I: How very nice. There's something rather charming about this talk in the train between a pretty woman and a man who don't sleep together. But how did Solange take this unexpected trip on the eve of her lover's return? I presume she must have been appalled.

HE: No. Not appalled. At most put out, and then not for long. She was very apprehensive of seeing Roberti again. Up to a point, this postponement came as a deliverance. It gave her eight more days to prepare herself for the ineffable joy of touching him, hearing his voice, being locked in his arms. Besides, there could be no question of arguing against Dietz's wishes. Work was sacred. So she just took it as one of those gestures destiny sometimes makes when it wishes to test our constancy, one of those malicious tricks of fate it is wiser to bow to rather than resist. When she had set out on her vacation two months earlier, she had sadly but resignedly told herself: "I shall never see him again. He will forget all about me." She regarded these eight extra days of separation as a sort of ransom. Forfeiting them meant that she would surely see Roberti again. Our souls are full of such idiotic superstitions. She went even further. If he was to break with her, the break would at least have been put off for eight more days. She would have been granted a further week of illusion. In spite of the letters she received from her lover, in which he struggled to express a distorted and mannered kind of passion, she was as constantly apprehensive as if she had been without any news of him at all. Through his indifference and coldness he had so thoroughly convinced her that he didn't love her that she wondered at times if he wasn't just writing out of politeness or charity.

I: Are you quite certain about this last point? Aren't you letting yourself get carried away by your enthusiasm for psychology? For a woman, a love letter is gospel. She believes every word of it, even if it says the opposite of what its sender is in the habit of saying. I believe women instinctively feel what you explained just now about Solange's letters and epistolary style, namely that we are far more sincere, far more our true selves when we write than when we talk. Added to which the written word has an extra glamor. We believe far more readily what is written and signed than what is merely said. Moreover it corresponds to a reality. Lastly, it is rather more difficult to lie in writing. Men can do what they like with their tongues, which they have used from birth or almost. They find it harder to do violence to writing, which is not natural to them, even as antinatural as could be.

HE: I am not saying that Solange read Edouard's letters with skepticism. On the contrary she feasted on them; they brought her great joy. But sometimes, for no reason, she was seized with doubts. She thought it impossible for a man who showed so little eagerness to see her again, who was cold and remote when he didn't desire her, to be expressing his true feelings when he wrote things like: "I yearn to see you, my little periwinkle."

I: What a ludicrous style! I can see why she was worried.

HE: Come, come! You know very well it wasn't his style that worried her. On the contrary, she thought his style wonderful. Roberti's mannerisms seemed to her the height of elegance and poetic feeling. It was love and love alone which made her shiver in her shoes, love which fears everything and in which nothing is ever certain. Unlike ourselves, who are intelligent and completely detached, she didn't know that Roberti was revealing his true feelings far more in the letters he wrote than in the things he said. Come to that, he didn't know it either. He didn't realize that the same phenomenon which had surprised him in Solange was applying in his case as well, namely that through his letters she was discovering an unknown Roberti, a new being with a capacity for passion, a being who cared for her. He never suspected that into these letters which he laboriously composed for her, though they bored him and he even had to rack his brains to find nice things to say, he was putting more of his essential, true self than he had ever put into his talk. Here again we have a misunderstanding or a chain of misunderstandings well worth noting. You know that at Roberti's trial they read some of the letters he had written to Solange, particularly certain ones dating from this time, namely the vacation of 1955. The judges and jury were much impressed by their apparent sincerity. Roberti's lawyers naturally made the most of this to show how their client was completely "under Mlle. Mignot's thumb." Edouard himself was, I know, stunned by these arguments. As he told one of his lawyers, from whom I had it: "But all that was make-believe: I just wrote to please her."

I: Everyone knows this type of judicial error of interpretation. There are countless examples of it. The courts base their judgments on actions, that is appearances, and not on thoughts, that is what lies behind them. It can't be otherwise.

HE: Of course not. And the courts are right since actions, the concrete facts, express the truth of the man who has performed them even better than do his thoughts or intentions. They even express a more profound truth insofar as the man responsible is unaware of it. The action he has performed, even if he didn't particularly intend it, reflects him absolutely. To my mind the example of Roberti's letters read out at the trial is conclusive. When he wrote them he was convinced he was lying. Three years later, impartial third parties judged them to be sincere. And the third parties were right. It was he who was wrong. And when he said (he didn't actually, but he easily might have): "After all, when I write a letter no one knows better than I whether I am lying or telling the truth," he was wrong again. He was speaking as a man who didn't know himself, who had never known himself and for whom events which were nonetheless quite clear and explicit shed no light on himself. Read out three years later in the light of subsequent events, the letters of the 1955 vacation were in essence exactly what they purported to be: letters expressing the most passionate love. They were, in fact, pathetic letters. They heralded in their ardor all the madness and horror to come. I remember how one reporter wrote: "A man who sent such letters was capable of doing anything to defend his love." Roberti in his prison cell was staggered to read this assertion. Yet the journalist had hit on the truth. The journalist knew all the facts of the case; he was judging the problem with complete objectivity. His conclusion was impeccable. He saw the truth and Roberti didn't. I believe one must needs be very humble to bring oneself to concede that the world is right, contrary to one's own mind, feelings or perception; to tell oneself: "I am not as I believe myself in my heart of hearts to be, but as the world sees me and interprets me."

I: Oh oh! That's a dangerous argument.

HE: I don't see why.

I: It's a dangerous argument when applied to martyrs and artists. Imagine an artist of completely unrecognized genius who is discovered and admired only after his death. According to you he must die in despair, convinced that he has deluded himself all his life and in fact has never had the slightest talent. The same goes for the martyr, since he is held up to derision and condemned by the multitude. Imagine, finally, that there is only one just man in a totally corrupt world. Is the just man wrong?

HE: But I'm not talking of artists or martyrs or just men. Anyway none of these ever passes completely unrecognized. There is always a handful of appreciative connoisseurs who end by forming a group around them and, so to speak, serving them as a bulwark with their bodies (or their souls). I am talking about an average man, a man of average pride, inspired by no particular ideals, whose only mainstay is his egoism. I am talking of an ordinary man whose thoughts or intentions are white while his actions are black (or vice versa), and who is appalled when more account is taken of his actions than of his intentions. I simply want to show you how such a man commits an optical error, how he is in no position to form a judgment, how no one is in fact in a worse position, how he can only see half or a quarter of himself. This half or quarter obstructs the rest of the view. He is like a bad stage manager watching the play backstage, from the wings, and being astonished every time the audience boos or applauds.

ɪ: Tell me about Roberti, furious and champing at the bit, balked of his favorite distraction. It reminds me of that extraordinary passage in *Splendeurs et Misères* in which the Baron de Nucingen, stuffed with cantharides, waits in vain for Esther, who in the end never turns up. It's superbly comic! To begin with, how did he find out that Solange wasn't in Paris? A little picture of the man's discomfiture, please.

ʜᴇ: Well, the moment he arrived home he called Dietz's office. He was answered by Mlle. Angioletti (who incidentally was tremendously tickled at the idea of chatting to the man of whom her colleague had drawn such an impressive portrait). She told him Solange was "on a business trip" and that she didn't know exactly when she'd be back; probably in eight or ten days. Roberti thanked her in an indifferent tone of voice. Angioletti inquired who was calling. "Monsieur Edouard," replied Roberti, thinking to himself: "She'll take me for a café waiter."—"Can I take a message?" said Mlle. Angioletti sadistically. "No no, I'll ring back, thanks. If Mlle. Mignot returns earlier than you expect, just say I called." As he hung up he felt a great emptiness inside him. I apologize for this cliché but it expresses his feeling perfectly. It was as if the disappointment was extending from his mind to his body and spreading through his limbs. His arms were limp and his legs flabby. His chest felt tight. After which he had a violent attack of rage and resentment which lasted till the evening and which only the peaceful spectacle of his family could smooth away.

There is no disappointment one cannot overcome. Roberti got over his quite easily. On the whole he "made the best of a bad job." He told himself that, as it happened, these eight or ten days of solitude were an excellent opportunity to settle down to work again, bring himself up to date, renew contacts with his constituency, his colleagues in the Chamber, newspaper editors and so on. But there was in him a sort of anticipation or anxiety which occupied part of his mind and prevented him from giving his full attention to whatever he was doing. It was a feeling remotely akin to jealousy and it produced similar effects. From the mere fact that Solange hadn't been there to meet him, he suddenly felt ten times more eager to see her. He was, if you like, in the position of a man who would quite happily drop his girl friend, for whom he doesn't really care, but who, should she seem to be dropping him first, experiences a sudden revival of love and possessiveness which makes him move heaven and earth to keep her. We constantly see men drifting apart from their mistresses who begin to suffer because the latter have been smart enough to leave them just before they decided to take the initiative.

I: Yes. This kind of "spirit of contradiction of the heart" has always seemed to me very comic. Women know exactly how to play it. When it comes to love, men are primitive machines. You press a button and the old mechanism works just the same as it did on the first day of Creation. It's all very silly! So Solange hadn't written to Roberti to tell him of her absence?

HE: No, for two reasons: because Dietz had only decided to take her at the last moment and because she knew no address in Paris where she could leave messages for him. Roberti, with his usual excessive caution, had forbidden her to write to or telephone him either at home or at the Chamber of Deputies.

I: But what if she had something urgent to tell him? That she couldn't keep a date for instance?

HE: Well, he laid down the principle that nothing was urgent enough for her to telephone him. He preferred to chance her failing to keep a date rather than risk being compromised.

I: That's a particularly hideous detail you have kept hidden from me! You can't lift a single stone in this man's soul without finding an insect underneath it.

HE: His forbidding Solange to call him or write to him anywhere (except the post office at Antibes) had an added advantage in that it always left the initiative in his hands. Thus he would never be plagued by reckless phone calls or overfrequent meetings. He telephoned in his own good time: he fixed their meetings to suit himself.

I: What organization! I take off my hat to him! And Solange accepted it without protest? A model mistress!

HE: People will accept anything. To be obeyed, one only has to command. Nothing comes more naturally than obedience, if only because it offers people a simple world where everything is laid down in advance and no calls are made on their imaginations.

I: Oh look, all this is frightful! These little horrors of love make my blood run cold. If I hadn't a wife and children your story would make me want to retire to a monastery. Let's switch to something more pleasant. Tell me how Roberti whiled away the time until Solange's return.

HE: For eight days he was in a perfect state of melancholy, rage, humiliation and tenderness. I'm sure you can see the reasons for the melancholy, rage and tenderness. The humiliation stemmed from his reluctance to admit he was in love and felt a need to see the object of his love. Solange was never completely out of his thoughts. He was vexed, not at suffering (the word is too strong) but at being so preoccupied by someone for whom he believed he felt nothing but physical desire. With the pompous irony he often used when talking to himself, he wondered: "Can it be that I am the slave of my senses?" And he came to his usual conclusion: "No, I am not the *slave of my senses* but I have been thinking too much about Solange. I have been cherishing a desire I must at all costs root out. After which my mind will be free." He went even further. He would take her back once and once only to the Rue d'Argenson and there, in a final firework display, empty himself of all desire for her. "After that," he went on, "it will be easy to drop her. Farewell my lovely, I shall say. It has been marvelous but I've had enough. I no longer love you or I no longer desire you, whichever you prefer. It was great fun but all things have an end, especially the best things." Such notions gave him great pleasure. He would never be sufficiently revenged for the dirty trick she had played him by being away from Paris at the moment of his return.

I: The typical argument of a heel. The heel never forgives an unintentional offense. Or rather he takes an inevitable development as an offense. Roberti's little spirit was put out. It was rebelling against fate. A fine example to illustrate that stupid modern idea of rebellion at any price against anything. Go on.

HE: At the end of four or five days he telephoned Dietz's office again on the off chance. If Solange had returned earlier, it would be really too stupid not to find out. He had hallucinations in the street. Suddenly his heart would stop beating: he had seen her back. So she was in Paris then? He would hurry forward and overtake the back. It wasn't Solange, just a woman with a similar figure or who dressed in the same way. Ten times a day this would happen, he would pass ten replicas of Solange. He ended by seeing her everywhere. Once, at about six in the evening, he was seized with an irresistible and wholly illogical impulse to drop everything, rush to the Avenue Daumesnil and post himself outside her house. He was almost sure it would be a pure waste of time, that she was still in Zurich or Geneva and that he had only a chance in a million of seeing her unexpectedly step out of the doorway. But a chance in a million was worth the try. So he braved the Paris rush hour, drove as far as the Porte Dorée, parked his car and for three quarters of an hour prowled up and down below Solange's window. "She isn't there," he told himself. "I shan't meet her. These things only happen in novels. I must look pretty funny acting the bashful lover." Nonetheless he was happy. This prowl beneath the windows of his absent beloved helped greatly to calm him and brought him a melancholy contentment which he considerably enjoyed. The more the minutes ticked by, the more he persuaded himself he had come for nothing, for the sake of his *honor*. He had known even before setting out that he wouldn't see Solange and yet here he was. "This is what comes of having nothing else to do!" he thought. The spectacle of the Avenue Daumesnil enchanted him: it was familiar, reassuring and above all poetic. He enjoyed every moment of it. At bottom, what he had come in search of was not Solange but poetry. The poignant and exquisite poetry of anticipation, absence and a lover's solitude, for which his heart doubtless felt a need. Slowly he paced up and down the pavement. Three times running he passed a big red-faced young man with thinning hair and badly cut clothes who kept glaring at him.

ı: Valentin?

ʜᴇ: Yes, Valentin, who had recognized Roberti and was wild with rage at his impudence in coming to flout the Mignot family beneath their very windows.

ı: So what happened?

ʜᴇ: Nothing. Roberti merely wondered: "Why is this fellow staring at me like that? I don't know him."

ı: Didn't he guess it was Solange's brother?

ʜᴇ: Not for a moment. Although Solange had described him, he had completely forgotten about the young man. For him the Avenue Daumesnil was Kamchatka or Tierra del Fuego. It never entered his head that he might meet anyone he knew there. Valentin on the pavement of the Avenue Daumesnil was once again, for the hundredth time perhaps, destiny appearing to Roberti in a tangible guise and once again Roberti was looking the other way.

ı: You say he passed him three times.

ʜᴇ: Yes, because Valentin couldn't make up his mind. He had a wild longing to grab Roberti by the collar and bash his face in but didn't know how to set about it.

ı: Still, it's not so very difficult.

ʜᴇ: It's not so very easy either. One must have some apparent pretext. Valentin was held back by his fear of ridicule. That is why he contrived to turn back and pass Roberti three times. He was hoping the other would bump into him, tread on his heels or ask why he was staring at him with such a menacing air.

I: How idiotic!

HE: You told me yourself that Valentin was a man of the sixteenth century. He was behaving like a man of the sixteenth century seeking to fight a duel and endeavoring to provoke a quarrel. Remember how the gentlemen in Alexandre Dumas' novels are always whipping out their swords just because a passer-by has given them a dirty look.

I: True. My apologies. My apologies to Valentin.

HE: Unfortunately—or fortunately—Roberti was not a man of the sixteenth century and completely failed to understand why this fellow was carrying on like a fighting cock or a blustering bully. Besides, he was absorbed in his reflective and poetic mood. He barely noticed the other man. He was just sufficiently aware of him to wonder what he was up to. Finally Valentin grew tired of it. He went home full of rage and disgust and feeling sore about his abortive fight. He was sure Roberti knew perfectly well who he was and had pretended out of cunning or cowardice not to recognize him, but that one of these days a good opportunity would present itself to teach this bastard a lesson.

I: Did Valentin ever take a crack at Roberti in the end? I confess it would give me a lot of pleasure.

HE: I'm sorry but the right occasion never presented itself.

I: Too bad! He'd have deserved it. There's nothing like a good kick in the pants to put bastards in their right minds.

HE: Roberti also finally tired of hanging around. He went back to his car and slowly returned to the Rue Oudinot. The next morning he phoned Dietz's office again, and again the morning after. Each time he had the hope that it would be Solange—oh wonder!—who would answer, but this hope was unfulfilled. He was like the famous djin, the afreet in A Thousand and One Nights who was locked up in a bottle at the bottom of the sea and swore a succession of oaths to himself. For a hundred years he swore to cover with gold the man who would fish up the bottle, break the seal of Solomon which closed it and set him free. Gold? That wasn't enough: he would smother him with pearls, emeralds, topazes and diamonds. During the next hundred years he swore to bestow eternal beauty, youth and seductiveness on his rescuer. And so forth. Round about the fourth century of his captivity the afreet turned sour, became vicious and amused himself by swearing the most terrible things. Since heaven would not allow him to render good for good, he would render evil for good. "Whoever fishes up my bottle," he told himself, "I shall kill." And then one day little Mohammed or Mansur or Beshir (I can't remember the name) cast his net, dragged the bottle up onto the beach and opened it. Well, Roberti went through the same alternations as the afreet. Before picking up the telephone he would say to himself: "If it's she who replies, I will tell her I adore her, that I can't live without her, that she must come out to lunch with me; I shall present her with a Dior dress, and so on." Alas! It was never Solange. It was always the silly voice of Mlle. Angioletti.

I: Why a silly voice? That's a gratuitous statement. Gratuitously malicious. I shall leave this "silly voice" out of the novel. One should never write things gratuitously just for effect or to create atmosphere.

HE: But it isn't a gratuitous statement. I know Mlle. Angioletti had a silly voice because I heard it and, in the second place, when this girl answered the phone she felt she had to adopt a breathless, singsong tone which was quite ridiculous. In particular she spun out the word "yes" so that it became something like "yairs." At any rate, whatever the reason, her voice got on Roberti's nerves. He had taken a dislike to it for two reasons: because it meant Solange wasn't there and because it sounded to him not only silly but also supercilious. He imagined Mlle. Angioletti poking surreptitious fun at him. He was furious at appearing like a lovesick swain in the eyes of this little fool.

I: May I take over? One morning Roberti expected to hear the office idiot and he didn't. He heard Solange.

HE: Yes. One morning, about the ninth or tenth day, Solange answered the phone. She had got back the previous evening.

I: Wait! Don't tell me. I've already guessed. That very morning, the djin in the bottle took an oath to kill the man who set him free. So Roberti abused Solange.

HE: Well, more or less. But abuse is too strong. He didn't go as far as that. He contented himself with being cold. He was torn between great joy and violent anger. The moment he heard Solange's voice he was reassured. She was back, she was close by, he could see and touch her just as soon as he liked. And so, abruptly, all his longing to see and touch her fell away. Not a trace of it was left. He told himself how he had plenty of time, there was no hurry, and he must make this bitch pay dearly for the nine or ten days' anguish she had inflicted on him. Ironically he inquired if she had had a good trip, if she had enjoyed herself, whether her vacation had really been as successful as she had described it in her letters, and so on. In short he made small talk as if she were a stranger. He took care not to let her know in what turmoil he had waited for her, how passionately he had dreamed of her, how he had daily hungered to hold her in his arms. He was delighted to hear her disappointed and tremulous voice at the other end of the line. He saw her pretty face cloud over. "I can do whatever I like with her," he thought. "She loves me but I don't love her. If I loved her I would be upset, I would console her for the way I have hurt her. But I'm not moved in the least. I am a tiger whose appetite is aroused by the sight of blood. I find the keenest pleasure in tormenting this little slut, who fully deserves it anyway. Ah, just wait and see, my girl, how nasty I can be when I wish!" As a crowning touch of cruelty he didn't fix a date with her. Timidly Solange asked: "When can we meet? I've been thinking so much of this moment!"—"Soon," said Roberti in a bright, offhand way. "One of these days. I'll call you back. I should love to see you too." Politeness itself. The Comte de Valmont addressing the Présidente de Tourvel in *Les Liaisons Dangereuses*. But contrary to his expectations, once it was over this conversation didn't leave him very lighthearted. He even felt rather depressed.

Solange, for her part, was appalled. "He doesn't care for me any more," she thought. "I might have known. In two months he has completely forgotten me. And yet he wrote such sweet letters! He's so kind: he didn't want me to feel sad on my vacation. I can't ask for more. It's quite natural for such a man not to take to a little nitwit like me."

ı: Didn't Mlle. Angioletti tell her how he had telephoned every day? This news would surely have restored her morale.

HE: You know, when one is in love one is never an optimist. Yes, Mlle. Angioletti told Solange: "That man's got you under his skin, honey, he never stopped phoning while you were away. He couldn't wait for you to get back." But Solange didn't share her friend's conclusion. To her mind these daily phone calls proved nothing. She blamed herself for having gone away. Had she been there on the first day like a good submissive little woman, she told herself that such submission might have touched Roberti, he might have seen her right away, they might have gone at once to the Rue d'Argenson to set a fresh seal on their love. For this consideration also played its part. Solange's senses had something to say in the matter. During the past two months she had recalled, and more than once, the ecstasy she had known with Roberti. Besides, she was almost ready to believe that Mlle. Angioletti, despite her detailed information and assurances, was telling her white lies in order to soften the blow and leave her a ray of hope. She was convinced that her beautiful love affair was dead and buried, and what a lamentable, dismal way for it to end! Such things only ever happened to her. She was doomed to miserable failure. She never had any luck. She was just a poor wretch too stupid to hold on to happiness.

1: I don't much like the way you make Solange talk. You have caught Roberti's tone admirably, at least I think he talked and thought the way you say he did, but I don't have the same feeling with her. Every time you quote her words I am surprised at their insipidity. It's not that she always says just what one might expect but she says it in too conventional a way. It has frequently struck me and I've been on the point of mentioning it several times. Watch it. Perhaps it's because you don't "feel" Solange as well as you do Roberti. You know her less well so you invent her more and your invention is a bit pallid.

HE: Do you think so? Yet I knew her well. I often talked to her. I made a careful note of her turns of phrase. You know what an ear I have for little things like that.

1: When she asked Roberti: "When can we meet? I've been thinking so much about this moment!" it doesn't ring true.

HE: Why not?

1: Because it's too natural, too obvious. It's a cliché. It's what all women in love say, not only in life but also in bad novels.

HE: There you are! You've put your finger on it. Solange talked like a heroine of fiction. She repeated what she had read. She reproduced the outward forms of love according to third-rate hacks. Besides, most people talk like characters in bad novels or bad movies, particularly when they want to express intense emotions. These vulgar catch phrases are the first things that spring to their minds. Indeed, intense emotion is something rather rare, rather exceptional. The normal vocabulary is inadequate. So they turn elsewhere in search of the words they are incapable of finding for themselves. They turn in fact to the cheap literature which is the staple fare of the working classes. This doesn't mean they aren't sincere. Merely that they are humble and have more faith in these clichés than in their own abilities.

1: That's certainly an ingenious explanation. And you can add this: that when young ladies of modest circumstance and intelligence talk like the heroines in heart-throb magazines, they have a strong feeling that they are following in a great romantic tradition, a centuries-old tradition full of glamor. They are re-enacting "famous love stories." They are raising themselves to a level of high poetry or tragedy. They are Juliet, Mlle. de La Vallière, La Dame aux Camélias, Empress Soraya or Princess Margaret.

HE: Yes, that's probably so. But Solange didn't aim as high. These lofty analogies never entered her head. Besides, fairly soon, after six or eight months of association with Roberti, there occurred a sudden change in her speech. It was amusing to follow this transformation. Roberti's style made its mark on her. Gradually she dropped her magazine clichés in favor of her lover's verbal mannerisms. She began to speak and write like him. She began to call him: "My magician Merlin, my king of hearts, my lion, light of my life, my sacred flame, my beloved philosopher," and so on.

ı: Poor girl! If I'm right, she became even stupider than before.

HE: Not at all. But one might say that her vocabulary of love evolved on the same lines as awakening artistic awareness in an adolescent. The adolescent begins by having no taste at all. Then, little by little, taste forms. He ceases to admire the popular songs which once satisfied his thirst for beauty. He becomes harder to please. He progresses from the accordion to the cello. Naturally, in these early stages, he does not yet respond to works of real beauty but only to those in-between ones which still contain much that is flashy, loud and above all affected. Preciosity is not, as is commonly believed, the culmination or decadence of good taste, but the beginnings of it. Be that as it may, affectation marks an advance on vulgarity. It shows that the soul is maturing, that it has aspirations. Earlier we were talking about pedants. Well, I believe a pedant is a man who stops at this halfway stage between bad and good taste, who can go no further or no higher, who fails to see (or feel) that the final stage of the mind and spirit is utter simplicity, bareness, the sublime rendered with the least possible means, the sublime attained with such naturalness that one doesn't perceive the effort behind it.

ı: Right, that's enough. You always tend to be so long-winded. How long did Roberti hold out after his savage phone call? Two days, three days, a week?

HE: Much less than that. He spent a very bad day. He was highly dissatisfied with himself, and this was reflected in a vile temper. He was at once glad and furious at having hurt Solange. In the middle of the afternoon he calmed down and began to think how, after the way he had rebuffed her, she might easily take offense. What if she decided to break it off? That would be most annoying. Not that it would cause him any unhappiness, since he wasn't in love with her, but it would be hard to find another equally satisfactory mistress. It would take a long search. This led him to tot up the advantages offered by Solange: she had the most beautiful arms in the world, a ravishing face and a body which smelled delicious; she was a model of docility and gentleness; she practically never made any demands; she complied with all his sensual fantasies and even anticipated them; added to which she loved him and this deserved a little consideration. Roberti was touched by this love he inspired. He felt grateful for it. When one is middle-aged it is delightful and flattering to be loved, and loved to distraction. One's personality acquires increased stature so to speak from the passion one has aroused. One cannot lightheartedly destroy it. After fifty, one has passed the spendthrift stage. At all events there could be no question of a break before he had taken Solange back once again to the Rue d'Argenson. All these fine arguments which seemed to him the height of cynical lucidity were, of course, so many lies. They were the deceptive paint with which he daubed the terrifying face of love. By six that evening he was feeling so ill at ease that he reached a decision which didn't really surprise him; he would go and wait for Solange outside her office. By six-twenty he was in the Avenue de l'Opéra anxiously watching the door through which the object of his thoughts would shortly emerge. He experienced again that emptiness in his mind and limbs which had so greatly humiliated him a few days before. His heart was pounding. He could barely breathe.

ı: In other words, he was wild with excitement.

HE: Yes, but it was a painful excitement, very hard to bear.

ı: Excitement is never pleasant, as we all know.

HE: He had such a longing (or need) to see Solange that to ward off bad luck he told himself: "Today she has left earlier than usual. I know it. I should have thought of it before. I'll wait till seven. At seven on the dot I'll go home." He looked at his watch every thirty seconds.

ı: And Solange suddenly appeared.

HE: She appeared. She looked what is known as completely woebegone. She walked with her head bowed. She never saw Roberti until she was just a few feet from him. He wasn't exactly beaming either. His features were drawn, he was pale and his hands were trembling.

ı: Oh, but that's love with a vengeance—two people who adore each other and meet looking as if they were at a funeral.

HE: Yes, it's love. Roberti said with a tight smile: "Good evening. It's really rather too long since we met, don't you agree?" Solange was petrified. She had spent the whole day telling herself over and over how she would never see him again, and now here he was! But she was still so full of fear that she dared not show her joy. Why was he here? To finish off his morning's work no doubt, come to confirm in person a rupture which she believed inevitable. He was here because he was a loyal and upright man who preferred to have things out in the open, who wanted to leave no trace of hope in a heart in which he had decided to take no further interest. But Roberti, calmed by Solange's presence and the sudden switch from waiting to action, took her arm and squeezed it. Impossible to misinterpret such a gesture. It was a gesture of love. He loved her. It was because he loved her that he had been so unpleasant that morning on the telephone. They hurried off along the pavement of the Avenue de l'Opéra. She let herself go against him, all soft and weak at the knees. Her throat was tight. All she could say was: "Oh my darling, my darling!" Roberti was enchanted and at the same time furious.

I: Why furious? Explain.

HE: You know quite well why. Because he was there in the Avenue de l'Opéra at seven P.M., and this meant that he had capitulated.

I: But it's wonderful to capitulate to love. Anyway, can one claim to have capitulated when one has merely become a little less unkind and this has brought such joy to someone one loves?

HE: That is the reasoning of a man who is not in love. Love is war, with all the follies and horrors that war involves. Roberti, who was in his way a petty despot, a petty conqueror, wanted a complete triumph, the unconditional surrender of the enemy. And here, in this battle, he had been weak. He had retreated.

I: Forgive me, but since we're going in for military metaphors, I'd say rather that he had adapted to love as to the lie of the land. He didn't capitulate to the enemy; he capitulated to himself. That's very different.

HE: It wasn't any different for him. He felt it as a defeat. Whence a touch of bad temper. But only a touch. A faint exasperation underlying his delight. But his delight was far greater than his exasperation.

I: It seems to me that the attitude of Solange, clearly overwhelmed at seeing him again, scarcely believing her eyes, reeling with joy, should have reassured him as to his victory, since he was so set on being the victor.

HE: Precisely. In a way this increased his exasperation. It showed him he had misjudged the love he inspired, that this love was far deeper and stronger than he had thought, that he had overestimated the enemy. Had she greeted him coldly he would have been less annoyed since then his impulsive action would have taken on the air of a rewarding maneuver.

I: God, what subtleties! How exhausting this man is!

HE: But suddenly, after perhaps a quarter of an hour, he was touched. The remaining ice in him melted away. He was uplifted on a great surge of pity and tenderness. Solange was leaning on him with her full weight, as if her legs didn't belong to her; so far as their walking side by side and the Avenue de l'Opéra permitted, she molded her body to his, pressed up to him, clung to him. She was, after all, a heady experience—this ravishing young woman who lived only through him, this heart in which he caused the rain to rain and the sun to shine. Her self-abandonment against him was like the deliverance of one who has suffered deeply and whose pain suddenly ceases. There was a sort of animal quality about it which was most moving. Her despair was released on the wings of a deep sigh which spoke far more eloquently than any poem and gave Roberti a thrill of joy. So much so that he was seized with an idea or, more precisely, an impulse. This came to him very strangely, as if his heart were overflowing with gaiety and he felt an unexpected need to make some kind of sacrifice to the god of Love. The happiness he was giving Solange was to him so moving that he felt an urge to make it even greater, to overwhelm her, treat her to an unwonted display of ostentation. He said astonishing, unlooked-for things which staggered him as he spoke them even more than they did Solange as she heard them: "We won't go any more to the Rue d'Argenson. It's too wretched, hiding ourselves away in that hotel for two hours at a time. I'll rent a studio, just a small room somewhere which nobody else will know about, which will be our refuge, our little domain, our secret garden."

ı: What? He suggested renting a love nest?

ʜᴇ: Yes. And it was a suggestion which truly came from the depths of his heart, from its deepest and most secret recesses. Never once before had he even thought of such a thing.

ı: One moment, one moment please. I can't be satisfied with such a bald statement. The fact that a man is amazed to hear himself saying monstrous things is just not enough. I need explanations. What sort of behavior is this, carrying on like the worst possible kind of bad novelist? Do you realize Roberti has all at once decided to rent a studio? But it's revolutionary, an earthquake! And you just drop it like a frog into my pocket.

ʜᴇ: I'm simply describing things as they occurred. It often happens that people say things which surprise them, suddenly adopt attitudes which a moment before would have struck them as hopelessly absurd. I can't see what you find so surprising in this business of renting a studio. The things we say, the promises we make, don't automatically pass through the sieve of reason. The unconscious doesn't escape from its cage only when we are asleep and dreaming. I think that, with the studio, it was a case of Roberti's real love momentarily escaping—this love which he fended off with all his might and with all the sophistry of reason, this love which he kept under lock and key in a dark cellar deep within himself, this love which he denied. The voice of this love drowned Roberti's voice and said something different from what he meant to say. Besides, after having made the incredible suggestion of a studio, and you can imagine the joy with which this was welcomed by the interested party, he took himself to task: "What have I said! Why don't I think before I speak! A studio! I'm utterly mad. Now I've got to find this studio. What a nightmare!" But even the thought of this was not enough to dampen his enthusiasm. His heart was warmed by Solange's delight, which was almost as great, I may say, as if he had asked her to marry him. He even sought arguments to prove to himself that in actual fact he hadn't been so mad after all. A hotel was degrading, ugly. She deserved something better than these rapid and cynically down-to-earth sessions. The Rue d'Argenson, for all its comfort and discretion, reeked of furtive middle-class adultery in a way that could easily hurt a sensitive soul. Solange was too young, too pure, too loving to be indefinitely treated like an oversexed housewife or a tart. These were the noble, that is to say the true reasons he found. But after leaving her he sought for the repose of his soul to find base and false reasons which would bolster up his self-deception. Hotels were dangerous, especially the one in the Rue d'Argenson, in the heart of Paris. Anyone might see him going in or out. Look at Gallardin. That might have turned out to be a very nasty business: it was a warning. A hotel is expensive, whereas a studio which he could visit whenever he liked, which he could "amortize," would cost him considerably less.

i: But heavens, renting an apartment for the secret entertainment of the woman one loves is an enormous step to take. A revealing step. It seems to me, a man who goes that far shouldn't have any more illusions as to his pretended indifference.

he: Oh come! As if you didn't know that men will believe anything they want to believe, especially arguments they have concocted for themselves, for their own self-deception. We've seen it happen time and again. And here I am only speaking of the man who lies to himself and pounces voraciously on his lies; but there are also those who lie to others and who one might think know perfectly well in their hearts what they are doing. Yet no; they are the first to be deceived by their own propaganda. So you can imagine how it was with Roberti! He told himself quite gaily and with some inner merriment: "I'm going to have my own *garçonnière*. At last! How have I managed to live without one up to now? It will come in handy for my future mistresses. My whole sex life will be much simpler from now on. There will be sherry and biscuits in a cupboard in the best tradition." These were the arguments of the married man who has nowhere to take his conquests. Finally, the *garçonnière* is a stage in the rake's progress. It is the modern equivalent of the *pavillons* of the nobility under Louis XV. You can imagine how such a comparison appealed to Edouard's taste. He never paused to think that he had managed without this commodity until he was fifty and that, had Solange never existed, would probably have managed without it all his life.

1: Right. He found a studio. How? Where? Finding a studio in 1955 was the very devil on account of the housing crisis. How the studio was found and a description of it, please. This is important and indispensable.

HE: What it was difficult to find in Paris in 1955 (and still is) was an unfurnished apartment. But even at the height of the postwar housing crisis there was never the slightest difficulty in finding furnished ones, for the simple reason that these rents were not controlled and were subject merely to the laws of supply and demand. The landlords made their tenants pay whatever they chose. You remember how it used to be. A fellow had two unoccupied rooms somewhere; he installed a kitchen table, three rickety chairs, an iron bedstead and a horsehair mattress and called the thing a "furnished apartment." In return for which he demanded thirty thousand francs a month.

Roberti didn't have to make much effort. All he did was open a newspaper and pick out a few advertisements. He visited three or four places. Finally he settled on a "living room, bathroom, kitchenette" for the very reasonable sum of sixteen thousand francs a month.

1: Dirt cheap! At that price it can't have been Versailles. Always frugal, this Roberti. A regular family man!

HE: No, it wasn't Versailles. It was on the fourth floor of a cheap brick building in the Square Saint-Lambert, in the Fifteenth Arrondissement. Roberti had rather fancied it, certainly not because it was pretty or even gay, but it was secluded. Whoever among our acquaintances would go for a stroll in the Square Saint-Lambert? For Parisians, at least for the smart set, the Square Saint-Lambert is an outer suburb. So there was little likelihood of being recognized.

1: And what was the "living room" like?

HE: Dingy, obviously. A small room with one small window and a common, flowered wallpaper streaked with damp marks. There was a sort of divan, a broken armchair, a faded carpet and a rustic lamp, the stand of which was carved in imitation of the screw of a wine press. On one of the walls the landlord had hung a hideous picture representing the Sacré Coeur on Montmartre, a subject of which the least one could say is that it has been depicted a great deal by both the greatest painters and the most insignificant.

I: It sounds like an ideal setting for suicide. But how do you know all this? Were you ever there?

HE: There was much talk about this studio during the trial. It was described over and over. I'm just reconstructing it for you.

I: How sinister! And you say Roberti liked it? It's not possible.

HE: He didn't dislike it. He found this desolate spot had a certain charm. Many men, you know, have a secret liking for sordid places. Roberti was one of them. He had a taste for the sordid which can go very well with delicacy and a love of beautiful things. It is a more common trait than we think. In my view a taste for the sordid stems from a youth of poverty, reflecting a nostalgia for it, expressing a wish to revive it. We have an example of this in the person of Guyot.

I: Guyot? What Guyot? Victor Guyot of Lyon?

HE: Yes, Victor Guyot. He's a millionaire several times over, as you know. Well, every time he visits Paris, instead of going to the Claridge, the Meurice or the Crillon, he goes to a shabby little hotel in the Batignolles district where he takes a ramshackle room. For a long time I wondered why. He does it to recapture the setting and smell of his youth, his beautiful youth. I know another man as rich as Croesus who takes all his mistresses to a crapulous roominghouse in the Rue de Dunkerque where he used to drag his conquests twenty years ago. He clings to this squalid furnished room which witnessed his penurious but triumphant youth. I once asked him about it; he confided that he gave a more brilliant performance there than anywhere else. The dirt, the poverty, the atmosphere of debauchery and prostitution redoubled his ardor. Note that there is surely something poignant and poetic in having a beautiful young woman in a squalid room. For a certain type of man everything which saddens love intensifies it; everything which tints it with tragedy and tends indirectly to humiliate the object of his desire increases the rapture.

I: According to you, would a taste for the sordid be a form of sadism?

HE: A minor, very muted but undeniable form.

I: From which I deduce that Roberti could be a bit sadistic on occasions.

HE: I think, in fact, that there was a hint of sadism about him, but it was a tiny, imperceptible one which manifested itself in an on the whole fairly innocuous form, such as this odd pleasure he took in the lamentable appearance of the studio in the Square Saint-Lambert. It was an almost symbolic sadism of which, no doubt, he was not even aware. So far as I am concerned, I discovered it more by deduction than observation. Probably this reasoning of mine as I have just traced it was never followed by Roberti himself.

I: But tell me, this is most interesting. It sheds quite a bit of light. If Roberti had tendencies toward sadism, Solange must conversely have had a certain vocation for masochism. This would explain their physical compatibility. They were complementary as lovers. The one liked causing pain and the other was not averse to suffering.

HE: It wasn't perhaps quite as simple as that.

I: No, it certainly wasn't as simple, as clear-cut, but I'm sure I'm not wrong. For instance, when Roberti did the honors of the love nest in the Fifteenth Arrondissement, I bet that deep down she felt humiliated and rather pleasantly titillated by this humiliation. Don't you agree?

HE: No. I don't think so. I don't believe questions of feeling have so logical, so arithmetical a way with them. Obviously Solange didn't find the studio very gay or pretty but she didn't dwell on this painful impression. For her the significance of the place meant far more than its appearance. This room, miserable as it was, meant that for Roberti she represented something more than an ordinary mistress to be taken up and dropped at his convenience. It offered proof that he *cared* for her. Besides, don't forget that, like most people, Solange had neither imagination nor a critical spirit. The studio appeared to her exactly what it was, that is depressing and ugly, but this was just a vague and general impression which, if it shocked her, she immediately brushed aside as sacrilegious. She was even a little hurt by the jokes Roberti saw fit to make about the furniture, the wallpaper and the hideous picture of the Sacré Coeur.

I: Ah! So he made jokes?

HE: Yes. That was his way. The way of a superior man who eyes the world with amusement, for whom nothing is to be taken seriously, who never lets himself be impressed, who demystifies everything with wisecracks.

I: "Demystifies"? Now you're beginning to quote fashionable jargon. Why not "desacrilizes" while you're about it?

HE: I apologize. I had no other word to hand. I won't do it again.

I: "Edouard desacrilized the studio in the Square Saint-Lambert with his sallies at the furniture and wallpaper." There's a splendid sentence for a novel! That's how people write nowadays. It's too awful! Even good minds like yours end by becoming contaminated by this rubbish and use it "because they have no other words at hand." "Are you cognizant" (to use your parlance) of what this means? The French language is invaded. I proclaim a state of emergency.

HE: Very well, but we'll defend it another day. We can't do everything at once. Let's first finish with Roberti. I was saying how Solange was chagrined by his jokes. She didn't respond at all to this kind of wit, she couldn't understand it. Roberti was struck by the ugliness of the studio: by joking he thought to mitigate this ugliness in some way, make it laughable and hence touching. Now this was clumsy. His jokes achieved the opposite effect. Instead of abolishing the studio's ugliness, they opened Solange's eyes to it. "If he finds this place awful," she thought, "then it is. He's never wrong." And that is the way one makes mistakes through an excess of intelligence. An excess of vanity too, for jokes almost always spring from a sense of vanity: an urge to shine at the expense of someone or something and show how superior one is by setting oneself up in judgment.

I: Finally, was she pleased or wasn't she? I've got quite lost in your subtle analysis.

HE: Oh, she was very pleased. Thrilled. In spite of Roberti's stupid attempts at wit, she was in seventh heaven. Bubbling over with gratitude. She prattled away in her happy excitement: "Here it's our home. We are at home. On Tuesday or Wednesday evenings we shall come home here. Now you won't have to ask where shall we meet any more. You'll just say: 'See you at home.' How wonderful to think I have a *home* with the man I love." This childish effusion charmed Roberti, who saw in this studio one further secret, a perilous secret certainly but a particularly delicious one.

I: If you don't mind I should like, before we go any further, to turn back just a little. I have two questions to ask. First, I am very surprised that Roberti should have let Solange take his arm in the Avenue de l'Opéra. I didn't raise this point at the time because you were in full spate, but I'd be very glad if you would elucidate it now.

HE: Really, you don't miss a thing! You mustn't be surprised after this if you don't get to bed at all tonight. He gave Solange his arm in the Avenue de l'Opéra because he was in such a state of nerves that he no longer quite knew what he was doing.

I: No. Find something else.

HE: You're right. That isn't absolutely correct. Even when in the worst state of nerves he always knew what he was doing. What happened, I think, is that he gave way to an impulse of love, said to himself something like: "The hell with it, I don't care! After all, what does it matter if anyone sees me?" It was seven P.M.; the pavements were crowded. Perhaps he thought he was invisible in the rush of clerks and typists leaving their offices. Anyway, love has to put in an occasional appearance when one is in love! One must now and then do something rash. He had a longing to touch Solange; he had a longing to impart to her the warmth of feeling he had for her at that moment; and finally he wanted to *please himself*. And for him the greatest pleasure was to touch this woman whom he hadn't seen for two whole months, to feel her clinging to him in adoration.

I: That's better. Second question: wasn't he vexed, let's say even jealous, at knowing that his girl had been on an eight- or ten-day trip with Dietz? Did Solange tell him about this trip?

HE: No, he wasn't jealous at all. As I've already told you, he hadn't a jealous nature. In fact, this lack of jealousy over Dietz and Solange's trip together provided him with an added reason for thinking he wasn't in love. Besides, she told him all about it. She spoke so judiciously about Dietz that, right from the start, Roberti was convinced there was nothing between her and his friend. There are some people in whose fidelity we have complete confidence. Roberti had such confidence in Solange. She gave him no grounds for jealousy, both through her candor, which was undeniable, and through the naïveté with which she showed how much she depended on him. Sometimes in his reveries he imagined she was deceiving him; he tried to picture her in the arms of someone else but, whatever the realism he put into it, such images remained unreal. They didn't fit in at all with his inner conviction and with the reality.

I: I note in passing that it did occur to him all the same that she might have been unfaithful.

HE: Note it if you like. So what? It was the kind of cynical reflection he was fond of; he went out of his way to make them as a form of intellectual hygiene and they gave him a high opinion of his lucidity. Intelligent men are as a rule rather pleased when low suspicions come their way. They tell themselves that for all their high-mindedness they are not blind; that even if they have their heads in the clouds they can still spot the little smuts of life. This was the case with Roberti. I think I have demonstrated it pretty thoroughly. He constantly forced himself to see the base or petty side of things. He thought this an excellent sort of cold douche which should always be taken to restore the balance between the abject reality and his aspirations toward the ideal. This had even become pathological to the extent that every time he hit on some consideration or fact capable of damaging one of his fine ideas, he felt a bitter jubilation. It seems to me that this is a typical characteristic of twentieth-century man. We are witnessing, among so many other things, the decadence of skepticism. What in fact is skepticism, fundamentally? An instrument devised to lead us to the truth by putting errors in doubt. What, through overuse, has it become? The opposite. It leads to error by making us systematically doubt the truth. Skepticism has attained the same degree of superstition that credulity once did. I can see no difference between the twentieth-century skeptic and the credulous man of the Middle Ages.

Instead of noting how Roberti thought Solange might be unfaithful to him, which means nothing, you would do better to note that he had on the contrary a deep and unshakable conviction that she was faithful to him, which is interesting and true. Also because this conviction wasn't to last forever. You will see it gradually waver and dissolve. The day was to come when he would be well and truly jealous, and when he would have profound reasons, unknown to Solange, for being so. His soul would be sickened by jealousy, a dirty sentiment with which one dishonors oneself in one's own eyes, because it feeds on low suspicions and doesn't even spare the innocent. True love engenders jealousy the way a hidden wound engenders the pus which makes it dangerous and prevents its cure. Roberti was to treat his jealousy like a sick man who won't admit to his sickness. Just as the hypochondriac is a comic figure, so is the hypoeupeptic a tragic one. He has gangrene and says: "I have no gangrene." From time to time nature gets the upper hand and then he can't help taking a little trouble about himself, which postpones death. But he treats himself carelessly. He treats himself like an ignoramus and finally he dies, carried off by the ailment he persistently denied. The hypochondriac is a coward, which makes us laugh, but fear preserves. The hypoeupeptic is a vain man and vanity kills, which makes us shiver.

I: I demand a one-minute silence.

HE: Why?

I: Because you've just made a discovery.

HE: I? What have I discovered?

I: Something very fine, something which is at once very old and very new, but to which nobody has ever troubled to give a name.

HE: I didn't do it on purpose. I don't even see what you're driving at.

I: At the hypoeupeptic, the man who brags of his good health.

HE: But I've never stopped talking about him for the past two hours.

I: Yes, but you never found the word. Roberti was a hypoeupeptic. You have named it. Thanks to you, it now exists. Thanks to you what was just a feeling, just haphazardly remarked, a casual rediscovery for the men of each succeeding century, has now become an idea. You have labeled it. You have put it in the cupboard in which humanity piles its wares, opening it every now and then to check them over. You have trapped an idea which has been running free since the world began in the great virgin forest of ideas, which has been fleetingly glimpsed but with which no one has so far really come to grips. You have slipped a cord round its neck and put it in the big zoo of captive ideas. Bravo, you have done well.

HE: You're pulling my leg.

I: I swear I'm not. I swear I'm sincere. The proof is that I am beginning to talk in metaphors like you. Metaphors are always a proof of sincerity. You ought to know that, you who make a vice of sincerity with metaphors to match.

HE: It's really rather funny! One does one's level best to be clear, copious, comprehensive, one goes to the heart of things, descends into men's souls, digs down into the center of the earth at the risk of dying of exhaustion or asphyxia, and no one has a word of thanks. Everyone finds it quite natural; it's the least one could do. Only chance, on the other hand, to invent a well-turned, striking, apt expression which comes to you out of the blue, without your having paused for a second's thought, and everyone goes mad. You must admit it's discouraging.

I: Why no. It's life. Great arguments, great outpourings serve only to prepare for one exquisite little moment. You forget that this little moment wouldn't be exquisite were it not preceded by the great outpourings, by digging down to the heart of the earth and the asphyxiation of the digger. You toil like a slave for twenty years and suddenly you are rewarded with poetry. The world doesn't give a damn for your toil and is right not to. All it takes into consideration is the poetry. It isn't fair but it is correct. The public acclaims the gift, the unique marvel. It isn't interested in mere competence. I find that rather comforting, don't you?

HE: No. Because the public as a rule is way off the mark. And with a bit of luck anybody can procure for it that exquisite moment of yours. Whereas the toil, the serious side, is another matter.

I: Whatever you say, one also has to be forgiven for one's hard work. Hard work engenders pride in those who accomplish it. If you so much as betray a hint of this pride you are done for. The world only likes and welcomes the lazy, who now and then get a good idea out of the blue and immediately dish it up uncooked. Why? Because the lazy are reassuring, because their softness and flabbiness gives their public a pleasant feeling of superiority and they confirm the idiotic tradition, the cliché of carefree bohemian genius making light of its gifts, squandering them, and so embedded in its vices as to lack any self-pride. Not to mention that the minor impulses of the lazy are much easier to understand than the great and elaborate products of hard labor.

HE: Oh, be quiet. You depress me. You are showing me once again something I know but, thank God, periodically forget: namely the immeasurable futility of men, who care only for tinsel and trash. One only ever wins fame for trifles and as a result of misunderstandings.

I: What does that matter? The essential is to be at peace with one's conscience. For someone who isn't a public figure I find you very gloomy and pessimistic. What would you have me say, I who whenever I publish a book am nearly always praised for what is bad or second-rate in it and dragged through the mud for what is good in it? Be like me. Consign them all to hell. And go on singing. Those who say you sing flat when you sing true are just tone-deaf. You with your good ear know perfectly well when you are singing flat and when you are singing true.

To return to your hypoeupeptic, your imaginary healthy man, this is a remarkable discovery which doesn't confine itself to the emotion called love. From what I now know of Roberti, I have an impression that this definition is applicable to every aspect of the man. To believe oneself to be well when one is sick is not only the way of a lover; it is also and above all the way of a politician who is constantly posturing, promoting himself, lying, making propaganda to earn from his voters a good opinion of himself and his politics. In his outward behavior the politician is obliged to be optimistic. He is a professional optimist. But by dint of simulating optimism he ends up by really feeling it. His optimism passes from his speeches into his heart. He becomes the dupe of his own poses. I imagine this was the case with Roberti. He was a man who must surely have long been in the habit of lying to himself. Just think! Twenty-five years of political life behind him! Twenty-five years of exaggerating, of bad faith, of spouting rubbish for the edification of the public, of more or less justified attacks against rival parties. All this leaves its mark. It warps the soul. The distortions of one's speeches become a distortion of the mind. Alas, we don't even need to go back into the past to find Roberti. We have the spectacle of him before us every day. The whole world today is furiously optimistic and false, to such an extent that one is surfeited, nauseated to the point of vomiting. Everything is fine, everything is splendid, men are multiplying like rabbits, they are buying more and more television sets thanks to which they can be told that they have never been so intelligent, never so happy, never so civilized, that they are producing more corn and motorcars than their neighbors, that the government is wonderful, that war is abominable but will of course be avoided and so on. I don't know what the Ancien Régime was like but at least in those days they only bothered to stuff the head of one person, the king, on whom the politicians depended and who had to be convinced that everything was rosy, who had to be steered through a cozy little life untouched by any emotion, perfectly smooth and flat, perfectly blind, so that they might preserve their power and calmly continue in their malpractices. Under the Ancien Régime the plebes may perhaps have been unhappy but they lived with the truth. Now that the plebes are king, or supposed to be so thanks to the universal vote; it is the plebes who are stuffed with stories, flattered, lulled to sleep and made blind. Just as there can be no monarchy without obsequious flattery, so there can be no democracy without lies. As a result the modern world, which is more or less entirely democratic, has become one gigantic lie factory. The lying of the men in power and their underlings verges on metaphysics. It tends to convince people that we shall end by banishing all emotion from the surface of the earth and in fact are already well on the way toward this prodigious triumph. Just a little patience. Just a little confidence. Just a few more electric gadgets. The presidents and assemblies of the five continents are approaching the goal. All peoples are going to live like kings. In other words in a state of stolid indifference. Not the indifference of the Stoics, of course, but that of cataleptics. All this is absurd and will no doubt become frightful. The modern world is hypoeupeptic. It is the most hideous flaunter of good health humanity has ever seen. Can you imagine what a world without emotions means? It is a diabolical concept expressing hatred of the divine creation. It is a concept insinuated by the Devil. The modern world is a gigantic Faust busy selling its soul for a washing machine. The washing machine stands between man and the terrifying face of death. It denies death and hence eternal life. It confers youth, beauty and power on nature. It is the shape Mephisto has adopted in the twentieth century. The pact is not yet concluded but it is on the point of being so. The poor fool who signs the installment plan for his beautiful washing machine all in chromium and enamel reminds me irresistibly of the other poor fool signing the parchment with his blood.

HE: Glory, what a tirade!

I: Wait. It isn't over. I was working my way round to Roberti but let myself get carried away. . . .

HE: Yes, I rather think you did. I was glad to see it. Don't you think you tended to slander the poor washing machine? It's apparently very useful. Housewives are thrilled with it.

1: For heaven's sake don't be disingenuous! You understood perfectly what I meant. And anyway it brings grist to your mill since I was about to reach the following conclusion—that so far as love is concerned Roberti was an admirable representative of the contemporary world, which he illustrated and copied. As you have said a number of times already, he was a man of the second half of the twentieth century, who even in his most intimate behavior reflected the age he lived in. I see now how much he resembled Faust. I see that he is the Faust of our time, not only in the coincidences of his life but also in the depths of his soul.

It was a quarter to eleven. Our dinner for two had lasted as long as a banquet. Some people maintain that one shouldn't talk when one is eating well, that one should devote oneself wholly and singlemindedly to the oysters or the black pudding. They are guzzlers and fools. To my mind, good conversation adds savor to the feast, gives it extra spice, makes what was merely good delicious. It is a conclusion I always reach at dinners where I am bored. However succulent the dishes being served, I subside into gloom. No lobster is worth an hour's boredom: it is too high a price to pay. In the old days, when I was young and poor and in need of at least one square meal a week, I would sometimes accept invitations to dinners which I knew beforehand would be deadly. I would sit and eat like an ogre, I would gorge myself for three or four hours, but I could never help feeling ashamed; by thus bartering my time and conversation for roast chicken, by thus lending my presence against payment in kind, I was acutely conscious of indulging in a form of prostitution.

The waiters had cleared our table. My companion beckoned to the cigar girl, who came up with a pile of beautiful white and gold boxes which she opened. We selected fat Havanas, firm and heavy, exuding an exotic aroma. The first puff at a good cigar after a luxurious meal has always struck me as one of the supreme moments of civilization. I am surprised that Baudelaire didn't devote a paragraph to it in his *Paradis Artificiels*. The evening was so warm that we had the impression of being indoors rather than smoking in a garden. There was not a breath of wind to consume our cigars for us. The smoke hung around us like incense. "The incense of Havana!" I thought. One curious (and rather memorable) thing: a dragonfly settled quite undismayed on the tablecloth. I eyed it with great benevolence but it stayed for only a second. Its wings vibrated as rapidly as a hummingbird's and its body was exactly the color known as Prussian blue, glinting darkly. What a charming insect! It would seem as monstrous to squash it as to loose off a cartridgeful of buckshot at a doe.

The other tables had emptied. Diners who had arrived after us were leaving. This gave us a fleeting pleasure. By devoting so brief a time to their dinner these people didn't know, as we did, how to make the most of things, extract the greatest possible delight from them. They were in a hurry, the way people are nowadays; not wise men like us who found the means, in the heart of Paris, to talk ourselves hoarse like provincial gentlemen of the eighteenth century. Gentlemen of elaborate wit, of course, well suited to collaborate on Diderot's *Encyclopedia* were they but asked! Glued to our seats with our eyes half closed and our right hands limply clasping the warm bodies of our cigars, we sat for a few moments without speaking, which certainly did us both good. I remember how the musicians weren't playing just then; they were enjoying a break before gathering up strength for some tempestuous *Sabre Dance* or *Wine, Women and Song*. The other sounds of the restaurant were also muted; there was even a sudden silence.

ı: Now that Solange and Roberti had a hideout, I presume everything went like clockwork. Influence of the studio on adultery. No more call for self-restraint. Directly one has a moment to spare, one rushes to the Square Saint-Lambert and plunges into ecstasy. No?

HE: Is that how you see things?

ı: No, no, I don't see anything. I am simply propounding a theory. I am suggesting in principle that when a man rents a studio in order to take one particular woman there to the exclusion of all others, when he acquires a sanctuary for adultery so to speak, he makes the most of it. When this happens, one of two things is possible.

HE: The first being . . . ?

ı: First thing, adultery gets organized. It moves into top gear and becomes routine. You visit the studio every Wednesday from five to seven. It is an added convenience. You save time. Each of you goes there separately, consequently you don't risk being seen together in the street and so on. When the pair consist of a practical man and a meek woman the arrangement is perfect, insipid and repellent. It can last for ten years, twenty years, a lifetime. I want to stress this aspect of the problem. Most men who lead a "double life" do it this way.

HE: I like you when you get dogmatic. The second thing?

ı: Second thing, the studio is a daily temptation. So one gets completely disorganized. The normal man who rents a studio no longer goes home, he becomes peevish toward everyone around him, he sleeps out, he wallows in Oriental (and emotional) lust. He *makes the most* of his hideout. He spends all the time he can there. That is the true double life. But it doesn't remain double for long. This kind of double life is like two communicating vessels. When one fills, the other empties. The family man led into debauchery spends more and more time at the studio with his mistress and less and less time at home with his wife and children. It often ends in divorce, after all kinds of extremely dreary and conventional bourgeois dramas.

HE: In which of the two categories you have defined do you place Roberti?

I: With that bird it's hard to guess. Instinctively I'd say the first. On the other hand there is the fact that he rented the studio at all, which is tremendous. And then, according to you, he was very much in love with the Mignot girl. Frankly I don't know. There are also secondary considerations. While the studio is a convenience, it can easily become an inconvenience after a few months, as often happens with love which needs setbacks, frustration, pinpricks, delays and failures to make it last for a while. It seems to me that a normal man who in his fifties rents a studio must be dazzled by it and overindulge in it. There! Roberti surely overindulged in his studio. At least in the early days.

HE: Your deduction is wrong.

I: Why?

HE: Because you introduced a false premise: Roberti was not a normal man. He was a tragic man.

I: A tragic man! I've a horror of these big words. You would be hard put to it if I challenged you to explain what a tragic man is. Or else you would treat me to a high-flown pronouncement in the jargon of a contemporary thinker. "Tragic man"! It's a perfect expression for film critics or those who analyze the novelists of the thirties.

HE: Not at all. I can easily give you a definition of the tragic man. To my mind he's a fellow who only does what he dislikes doing by virtue of a high principle, a high ideal or a noble sentiment. Whereas the normal (or, if you like, comic) man is on the contrary a fellow who only does what he likes doing by virtue of a mass of little ideals, small principles or small sentiments.

I: Ah, not bad! But in what was Roberti a tragic man? Where was his high principle? Where was his high ideal? I must admit I see him rather as a comic man, and so a normal one according to your description. I see in him a mass of small sentiments, a mass of silly little principles which turn his behavior into something absurd and lamentable.

HE: Yes, at first sight. But if you dig deeper, what do you find? You find a man overwhelmed by love and struggling against this love with all his might.

I: Really?

HE: Struggling in his own way, according to his temperament. To us his battle seems absurd and hard to understand, but he fought it nonetheless. He was not a hero engaged in a straightforward and honorable duel; he was a civilian abruptly flung without training or discipline into a confused and equivocal war. What would the hero do? Slay his love with one blow of his sword, in other words cease then and there to have anything to do with his beloved, for he knows he must conquer or die. What does the civilian do? He maneuvers, he compromises, he wants to keep everything, both love and life. I don't think I need develop this any further.

ı: Actually, I would like you to develop a bit more. It's well worth it and you are being very terse. I like this idea of Roberti as a civilian of love. I would even say a reserve officer, an infantry lieutenant, suddenly drafted at fifty and sent to the front line where the fire is the most deadly. At fifty one should no longer be draftable, or else in the territorial army guarding the railways.

HE: Ha! Are you developing a taste for metaphors too? That would be fun. *Graecia capta coepit ferum victorem.* Take a note of this: that the civilian is ignorant of the fundamental law of warfare, namely that cowardice doesn't pay. The civilian believes in strategy. He imagines one can conquer the enemy by leading him into ambushes where he destroys himself singlehanded, with no need to risk one's life or even dirty one's hands. Naturally the civilian knows war is dangerous but he doesn't know that it is even more dangerous than he thinks. He doesn't know that in the end it always comes to hand-to-hand fighting, in which guile is no longer possible. One has used up all one's cartridges and finds oneself facing the enemy alone with one's bayonet, that is to say *cold steel*, just as in the days of Leonidas, Gideon, Mucius Scaevola or Roland at Roncevaux. The professional fighter knows this. So he proceeds to close combat as quickly as possible, in order to shorten the interminable vigils in the mud of the trenches and all the preliminary dangers. The fundamental trouble with Roberti was that he never knew (knew with his reason) precisely what he wanted, or if you prefer it he wanted everything, which comes to the same thing. He had forgotten (if ever he had known) that one is obliged at every moment of one's life to make a choice, that is to say to reject something which appeals to one a little less than what one retains. He took himself for a sort of Leonardo da Vinci of the heart, capable of reconciling every form of happiness; Leonardo triumphed successively in painting, sculpture, architecture and ballistics; whatever he touched, his genius burst out and carried him to the front rank. It seems to me that Edouard must have had a similar idea about his emotional powers.

Had I to place him in one of your two categories, I would plump rather for the first one. The existence of the studio didn't alter his way of life. Solange's disappointment was all the greater for it. She had believed that her life was going to change. She didn't know exactly how, but she told herself she would no longer have to put up with those furtive visits to the hotel in the Rue d'Argenson, that her liaison was somehow being promoted; she would arrange the furniture, she would make the studio look fresh and welcoming, she would fill it with femininity and youth; Roberti would come to find the place attractive and enjoy being there. As a beginning she bought a vase and some flowers, and what flowers! Roses, if you please, at three francs apiece, beautiful crimson velvety roses which looked as out of place in the Square Saint-Lambert as a Boulle cupboard of bronze-encrusted tortoise shell or a Savonnerie carpet. After which, she had a touching idea. She pinched three embroidered doilies from her home, those crocheted things, you know, that one sees (or used to see thirty years ago) in middle-class sitting rooms, set out on mantelpieces or on tables, and she brought them along with her.

I: Are you positive about this? It gives an insight into habits and character of vital importance. Do you realize? We are in 1955, Solange is twenty-five years old, she's a modern girl who has had lovers, who dresses like a fashion plate, who goes from Paris to Zurich and back in eight days via Brussels and Frankfurt; and her ideal form of decoration is an embroidered doily in the style of 1890. How fascinating! Thank you. I have seldom been shown into a more secret recess of the human heart.

HE: If you went to Moscow, old man, you would see such recesses everywhere. Moscow is full of lace window curtains and flowerpots.

I: Forgive me, but the Muscovites have a nostalgia for the good old days when the nobles had them flogged and the Tsar lived with his dear Rasputin, hence the window curtains and flowerpots. Besides, Moscow is the least modern city in the world. They live there the way they did in 1920. Whereas Solange is quite another matter. For her the crocheted doily was atavism, tradition. It was one of the indestructible relics of the old French popular civilization living on in her soul. She found it beautiful, the most beautiful thing of all, because it descended from her ancestors. When she was a child she was shown the doilies as being infinitely precious objects of art which she was forbidden to touch. The doily ennobled the common mantelpiece on which it was placed, or the dining-room table, or the whatnot on which half a dozen hideous ornaments sat dying of boredom. At twenty-five she committed the major sacrilege of stealing three doilies to lay them at her lover's feet as a sign of her complete submission and boundless love. To him she sacrificed her past and the past of her tribe, she offered him the idols of her childhood; to him she immolated what was the most serious thing in her life. Because the fashion-magazine editors, trips to Zurich or Spain were not serious, were just meaningless trifles, picturesque and ephemeral trimmings of life in 1955. The foundation of Mlle. Solange Mignot's soul was a doily embroidered by her grandmother or great-grandmother and piously preserved from generation to generation. It is absurd but not without grandeur. It is a symbol of France eternal. This embroidered doily was for Solange something of true worth, whereas airplane trips and sack dresses were false values. I should like you to tell me how Roberti reacted to these doilies. Did the idiot at least understand what they stood for?

HE: Your disquisition on the doily is brilliant but aren't you making it up?

I: Yes, I am, insofar as I have analyzed at length something the heroine only felt in a very confused and fleeting way. But that's what I'm here for, aren't I? Fiction is my profession. This doesn't, as you imply, mean contriving false interpretations of men's acts; it means trying to see the undersides of their souls, trying to pin down the truth and essence behind trite or odd behavior. If you're not satisfied, just look at Balzac and Proust, who *make up* for page after page. I loathe that superior air which people adopt when they tell someone trying to see things clearly that he's making it up. It's what people without imagination or insight always smugly retort when one tells them something out of the ordinary.

HE: I have a feeling you have accused me several times since this morning of "making things up" too.

I: That may be, but I have the right to do so, because I know what I'm talking about. I know what it is to write good fiction or bad.

HE: Oh, but that's simply splendid! Such bad faith takes the cake!

I: You haven't answered me: what was Roberti's reaction to the doilies? Did he burst out laughing or what?

HE: His reaction was not very favorable. Behind the doilies he suddenly saw the whole Mignot family, a whole class of society; he realized Solange's origins. And then—listen carefully, as it's very revealing of the man—*he was shocked.*

I: Shocked by what, exactly? The fact that she had stolen the doilies?

HE: Of course not. On the contrary. That she had stolen something for him, and from her parents to boot, could only tickle his vanity. It was a sort of renunciation of the Mignot family for himself. With her three doilies, Solange came over to him bag and baggage. Whatever we learn from those moral fables in which we see high-minded monarchs withering traitors with scorn, betrayal is always gratifying because it confirms its beneficiary in the idea of his righteousness or power. I would go so far as to say that the more unjust a man's cause, the more warmly he welcomes traitors; he recruits them, he creates them: every traitor who comes over to him is an added guarantee; his cause can't be so unjust after all, since it brings him adherents who sell their souls to espouse it. The upholder of bad causes needs frequent reassurance and traitors give him this. Will you allow me to digress just a little more? A bond of mutual esteem is tacitly set up between the traitor and the man to whom he sells himself. On the face of it, each grants the other the respect neither deserves.

No, Roberti was not shocked because Solange had stolen the doilies. He was shocked at seeing her and the doilies together, seeing her bringing in these little horrors and thinking them marvelous. He was shocked because the doilies suddenly told him quite clearly that his beloved, this woman to whom he was so drawn, came as it were from a concierge's lodge and had preserved, if not its ways, at least its sentiments. The doilies stood for everything he loathed and despised. They were the props of a revue sketch intruding into a novel by Stendhal. They were like a housewife bumping into the Princess of Cleves. The three doilies were plainly turning his adventure into a farce. He felt ashamed of himself, ashamed of never rising higher in his liaisons than shopgirls, secretaries, suburbans; he thought with envy of those leaders of the old regime, that is to say the distant Third Republic, who took as their mistresses countesses or actresses from the Comédie Française, in other words beautiful sumptuous animals who could be proudly flaunted in the face of all Paris and whose possession enhanced a man's prestige.

I: Having such ideas at fifty! How ghastly!

HE: Yes, isn't it? The ideas of a young snob. Whenever he had them, his soul closed like an oyster, his mind seized up. He became incapable of saying anything, he could only give a tight smile; he was like a jar filled with gall. However, these gusts of bitterness were only intermittent; they didn't last.

I: He always reveals cheap reactions. Never a generous impulse. And worse, not even a faint impulse of charity, understanding or indulgence. His instinct was corrupt. And yet a constantly false instinct is something rare. You who love talking about the Devil, don't you believe that here already is a mild case of diabolical possession in this instinct which always and unerringly took the wrong direction. I seem to remember that in *Faust* Goethe shows us a mass of lesser little devils of the fourth or fifth rank, each of which has a precise and clearly defined task. Mephisto himself is far from being the supreme boss. Satan sends him to Faust the way the chief of police would send a detective to arrest a delinquent. On his reaching fourteen, the beginning of puberty, the time when one begins to ponder, to think about God, about men and women, I can easily imagine the Devil on the off chance, in order to get his foot in the door (one never knows!), insinuating into Roberti's soul a little suburban Beelzebub, a poor demon who had risen no higher than the rank of corporal, with the mission of seizing every chance to direct his instinct into petty channels. An easy and routine enough mission, demanding no special aptitude, no spirit of initiative. What do you think of this idea? Mind you, it is not very hard to drive out suburban Beelzebubs. It just calls for a slight *effort*. An effort to be generous, patient, warmhearted, delicate. The effort deliberately to renounce one's personal pleasures, systematically to sacrifice one's comfort, never to make demands, to convince oneself that neither society nor the individual owes one anything. After two years of such exercise one becomes a fine character or, if not too fine at heart, then at least very pleasant and courteous. Roberti, if I understand correctly, never made that effort. He always accepted himself just as he was. That is the *modern* attitude. And people today haven't even the excuse of blindness. They go open-eyed to damnation. Right. That's enough about the three doilies. What did Roberti finally do?

HE: The worst thing possible. He joked. Starting with the three doilies he mockingly described the lodge of Solange's grandmother, he re-created it. He explained in his best ironic and elusive vein what the three doilies represented, namely a narrow, absurd and pitiful way of life. He referred to the innocuous and unexpected little luxuries of the poorer classes. Finally he turned savage. He could see he was hurting Solange terribly, but he told himself it was necessary to form her taste. He had to be a bit harsh if he was to turn this commoner into a duchess. This was clearly false reasoning. In fact, he had taken the gift of the doilies as an insult and was avenging himself. Solange had *let him down*—unwittingly, of course, but we punish involuntary failings based on ignorance just as severely as deliberate insults. It's in the nature of things. This is how those poor wretches who haven't the good fortune to be well educated learn about life, through being rebuffed. I would add in passing (but perhaps you have already noticed) that Roberti enjoyed being unkind to Solange. He was amused by the power he had over her, the way one is by some new faculty one has acquired or has always possessed unawares until some chance circumstance suddenly reveals it. He measured his power to make her suffer by the way her expression would change according to the harshness of his words. It was delightful and even, I would say, rather impressive to watch, something like the wind passing over a field of corn. By ruling emotionally over a human being in this way, he was taking his revenge, I imagine, for past disappointments and failures. But he wasn't fundamentally spiteful. Usually, after a few vicious remarks, he would soften toward this girl made utterly defenseless by love. His way of making love with her was a reflection of his feelings. He would display a certain brutality; he would "humiliate her physically," if I may so put it, he would take her submissive body like a conqueror and this, from what I can gather, she enjoyed as well. After which came torpor, caresses and consolations which both of them valued highly. To finish with the doily episode, Roberti was so vile that Solange burst into tears, snatched up the three little horrors and flung them out of the window.

ı: Out of the window? Into the Square Saint-Lambert? What a splendid gesture! Down the doilies fluttered onto the heads of the passersby! Bravo, Solange.

ʜᴇ: Yes, indeed! Roberti was abashed. Completely put to shame. He felt he had gone too far. So he did what all lovers do when they want to be forgiven. But he did it with a touch of servility, the servility of one who has overstepped the mark and suddenly feels scared of losing everything. He became too affable, too fulsome, too consoling; he more or less apologized, said he had been a beast, that for the sake of a joke he had run her mother down, that the doilies were actually a very nice idea which he had failed to appreciate because men never understood anything, and so on. And then, willy-nilly, since they were both alone within four walls sitting on a divan, things took another turn. But when they parted, Solange's heart was bleeding badly and she felt suicidally wretched. She had forgiven Roberti, of course, for various reasons including the fact that women always forgive a man the injury he does them when they sense love at the back of it, when they feel that it's love which has made him unkind (and they are never mistaken about this); but she couldn't bring herself to feel happy either. She went home full of sinister forebodings as to the future and once again, after dinner, sobbed herself to sleep.

I: And what about the roses? Roses at three francs each, after all! Wasn't the tiger Roberti touched by the roses?

HE: He was barely aware of them. Men never notice flowers, especially men like Roberti who care only for antique furniture. Women want flowers because they need to steep themselves in nature much more often than men. Perhaps they have lagged imperceptibly behind and are just a little closer to animals than we are. They have to have trees, foliage, grass, orchards. What do flowers represent? Nature in Paris. And not only that: they are also the most beautiful form nature can assume. Anyway, whatever the reason, Roberti didn't go to the Square Saint-Lambert to look at roses.

I: No. That was the whole problem.

HE: Of course. Solange, for her part, would gladly have gone to the Square Saint-Lambert for the mere pleasure of it, that is to say precisely for something other than "pleasure": for tenderness, unburdening of the heart, feasting her eyes on the spectacle of her happiness, talk. She would have liked to pass imperceptibly from tenderness to sensuality. When she joined her lover she always hoped he wouldn't be in too much of a hurry to take her, that they would first devote an hour or two to sweet nothings, to love talk, in short to "living together," but this hope was always dashed. Roberti's desire was violent and pressing. He knew so well the rapture he would find in Solange's arms that, as soon as she was near him, he was incapable of delaying it for a moment. Since she too was in a high state of excitement she didn't demur and almost all their time was spent in carnal frenzy. Solange would put as much fire into this as Roberti, she would touch the heights of ecstasy; but later on, when they had separated, she would sink into deep depression. Indeed, the only common memories she shared with him were those of sensual extravagance. There was scarcely anything else onto which her dreams of love could fasten; no conversation, no walks together, no helpless laughter, no quarrels, no reconciliations, no bad movies they had seen together and had so enjoyed making fun of. When she weighed up her love she saw nothing in it but embraces—miraculously successful, certainly, but this seemed to her rather monstrous and in a sense degrading. She felt thereby reduced to the almost shameful status of a female animal or a prostitute. Here we are deep into the invisible and, to my mind, most secret corners of the soul. Solange, who was proud of her love, wanted to make this love a beautiful and immaculate work of art and with her feminine instinct knew how to set about it; she tried desperately to forge memories for herself but to no avail. Love, to her, was a huge sort of photograph album where she figured on every page in her lover's company; in the Alps, before the Arch of Constantine in Rome, in a Brittany fishing port and so on. Other photos would show her naked in her bath with her lover elegantly shaving beside her. In others again she could be seen busy in the kitchen with a scarf round her hair. In other words the whole of life with its joys, obligations, constraints, day-to-day realities. Everything which leads one in old age to say: "I've had a good life, I have no regrets." But poor Solange didn't paste many clichés into her album of ideal photographs because Roberti (just as secretly) opposed his will to hers. He wanted no memories forged at any price. The only ones which counted for him were precisely those which made her so sad. In this way he had the illusion of being barely unfaithful to Agnes, his home and his life as he had conceived and organized it. He locked Solange away in a tiny portion of his time and heart, he pared down her place there as far as he possibly could. Not to mention another more conscious and practical consideration: he told himself how one may talk, lunch in restaurants, climb the Alps or walk beneath Constantine's Arch with anyone, but that to make love the way he did with Solange was something unique. Since he saw little of her, he took care not to impair these moments with trivialities. All the more since her conversation was not exactly diverting and he himself didn't have much to say to her: he hardly knew her (although thanks to the enjoyment of her body and the few letters he had received from her, he had a general, synthetic but fairly accurate idea of her heart). In short we have here, if you like, two rather pathetic people: a child whose life was pretty empty and an adult whose life was pretty full. The adult treated the child with neglect; he only spared her odd scraps of his time and found that quite sufficient. When Roberti offered Solange the studio, she was filled with the same joy as children who have built themselves a hut at the bottom of the garden where they can go and hide, spending hours there in happy aimlessness, just enjoying feeling at home in a place that is truly their own. But Roberti had left childhood far behind him: he had forgotten those huts made of branches which for children add so much delight to their vacations.

I: What annoys me about Solange is her egoism. You may say it's the egoism of a child. Even so, one's no longer a child at twenty-five.

HE: I don't get your point. Love begets egoism. It's the normal thing. One suffers selfishly, for oneself, because one is as it were being flayed alive. When you torture somebody, you can't blame him for "suffering selfishly." It's his own flesh being burned, his own bones being crushed. He cries out with the pain. But this pain is real, immediate, it drives him back on himself, it cuts him off from the world, it is so violent that it prevents him from thinking of anything else, particularly the sufferings of other men. Anyone who suffers from love the way Solange did for three years hasn't a sufficient amount of spirit left to suffer for anything else. It is beyond the bounds of human nature.

ı: Your mania for explaining and excusing everyone and everything sometimes goes a bit too far. You mustn't take me for a complete idiot. Your Solange wasn't as unhappy as all that. The way you talk, anyone would think she was one huge gaping wound. But that wasn't true. She had quite a number of little joys, even if these only meant going for a fling once or twice a week at the Square Saint-Lambert. And reverting to the affair of the doilies for the very last time, I am certain of one thing—that she was never for a second brushed by remorse for having committed a form of sacrilege by stealing from her parents a precious memento which they held dear. She was merely upset by Roberti's mockery. When she sobbed herself to sleep after a session at the Square Saint-Lambert, she was just feeling sorry for herself, and for herself alone. It's the sign of a soft and complacent soul which rather enjoys being beaten, which cherishes its wounds and above all *exaggerates its woes*. I can't tell you how much I hate all that. Do you know what it finally boils down to? To bedaubing oneself with romanticism in order to conceal one's cowardice.

HE: Yes, it's quite possible. But we are always meeting people who exaggerate their woes. As a result of which they are exaggeratedly unhappy. A misfortune needn't in itself be very great. It all depends on one's attitude toward it. This is where love comes in. Solange when not in love with Roberti was a person full of moderation and good sense. But as soon as she fell in love she became excessive and lost her head, she exaggerated her woes. These may not have appeared to her as the most frightful a human being could endure, but they took complete possession of her soul. For her, they were the height of misfortune. And you can moralize to your heart's content, philosophize and summon Epictetus and the Stoics to the rescue, but the fact remains that poor Solange Mignot, exaggeration or not, was very unhappy. Finally I would point out that the cowardice of women is very different from that of men. Men get sucked down by cowardice and generally wind up by being completely drowned in it, because with a cowardly man his cowardice is innate, congenital. With women, cowardice is nearly always a temporary state due to love; it vanishes at the same time, in the same moment, as love does. They then revert to being as hard as steel, implacable, savage, pitiless, like the proper little Attilas they all are. I've an idea. You surely remember, in Corneille, the famous question Don Diego asks of his son the Cid: *"Rodrigue, as-tu du coeur?"* "Have you heart?" "Heart" here stands for courage but this substitution of words is revealing. Don Diego is addressing a man and a man is courageous when he has heart. Whereas women are courageous when they have no heart. Imagine, for instance, the Infanta saying to Chimène: "Chimène, have you heart?" That would mean the exact opposite. It would mean "Chimène, are you still cowardly? Are you cowardly to the extent of loving the man who has killed your father as much as you did before?" Solange's cowardice lasted for three years, that is the length of time her passion lasted, and then one day the feminine genius resumed possession of her soul or, rather, underwent its transformation. This transformation took place at top speed, from one day, almost from one moment, to the next. All at once Solange no longer had any heart.

i: Look, I feel there's something wrong about this. Aren't you confusing different periods? Solange couldn't be "very unhappy" three or four months after her affair began. It isn't plausible. She was still enjoying the thrill of discovery. She was certainly still feeding on illusions. She was telling herself how Roberti was going to grow more and more attached to her, how he was going to free himself increasingly from his other occupations in order to devote himself to her. She was still full of optimism. She believed that they were groping, feeling their way toward each other but that one of these days they would find each other. In six months' time, for example. And she had the studio. That was something solid. However silly, she wasn't altogether incapable of using her head. When a man rents an apartment to entertain a woman, the latter must feel her position considerably strengthened, surely?

he: No. Not Solange. By the end of six months she had no further doubts as to the studio's significance. Roberti had never made the slightest effort to turn it in any way, however small, into a kind of home or even haven. At heart he was even well content that it should be such a dreary and shabby place. That way he was hardly tempted to go there for any reason other than the one we know.

i: Wait, wait. I'm beginning to see what bothers me. There's a contradiction between your story and what really happened.

he: What contradiction? It's not possible. There can't be a contradiction when one confines oneself, as I am doing, to describing events and feelings. Or else it's one of those organic contradictions of life and there's nothing I can do about it. You'll just have to put up with it. I have always been repelled by Aristotle's famous dictum that something cannot be true at the same time as its opposite. There are heaps of things that are true at the same time as their opposites. If you are shocked by the word "true," let's say "coexistent"—which amounts to more or less the same thing. Life is made up of the juxtaposition of a number of irreconcilable truths.

I: Aren't you ashamed to employ such miserable arguments? Aren't you ashamed to use Aristotle, poor old man, as a punching bag? Go stand in a corner, your bad faith is simply disgusting.

HE: But for God's sake what contradiction are you talking about?

I: Listen. You tell me that on the one hand Solange was very unhappy because she didn't see Roberti as much as she would have liked, because he appeared to desire nothing from her but her body, because once he had had his fun he was in a hurry to be off. Right. But on the other hand we know (and you yourself have alluded to it several times) that his mind had begun to color hers, that she was becoming a bluestocking, had started to read good (and less good) books, had begun to listen to Vivaldi concertos, to be a fan of the *divine Mozart*, visit art exhibitions, in short "improve her mind," "develop her taste." Don't tell me this thirst for art and culture suddenly descended on her at twenty-five, that she all at once discovered a splendid appetite for beauty with a capital B. For myself I conclude that Roberti not only felt a desire to educate her but that he even took time to do so or at least mapped out this education for her. And this necessarily implies talk, visits to museums and concerts, in short times devoted to other things than fornication. To adopt your own analogies, this must have ended by constituting for better or worse, willy-nilly, according to the circumstances and opportunity, a photograph album, a casket of souvenirs. I think you ought to clarify this point for me.

HE: Perhaps I have left something out, but I wanted you above all to grasp the sense of extreme emotional abandonment felt by Solange. And I see I have succeeded quite well since you are getting so worked up in protest. I will clarify the problem for you. Among the many varieties of lover, have you ever chanced to observe what I call the Pygmalion lover?

I: I suppose you mean the type who cannot be in love with a woman without immediately turning into a pedagogue or a teacher of deportment? Yes, I've known several men like that. It's absurd but rather touching.

HE: It's certainly absurd but it isn't touching. For a long time I used to wonder whether it was a form of altruism or on the contrary of egoism. Finally I came to regard it as a subtle form of egoism. Pygmalion lovers are not the disinterested missionaries of culture they doubtless believe they are, but people who want to fashion themselves an audience and wallow in the joys of pedagogy. To instruct a pretty girl whom one has taken to bed, unveil the world of ideas to her wondering eyes, "raise her to one's own level," is a wonderful way of satisfying one's vanity. One then tells oneself how one is truly master of the girl in question, ruling without rival over her body, mind and probably heart. One knows oneself to be not only loved but also admired. In a way, the Pygmalion lover leads the girl onto the ground he has selected for her conquest, her total defeat, her reduction to the state of a dog quivering with awe. I am only sketching this briefly, I don't give you the inner workings of Pygmalion love, but you are perceptive enough to spare me the finer details. The Pygmalion lover is unaware of his egoism and vanity. He acts by instinct, he heads instinctively for what makes him happy. The type of woman on whom he battens is not very distinguished. She is never a society woman, for example, who would laugh at him; nor is she intelligent or educated. Neither is she a working-class girl whose supreme joy is to go out dancing on Saturday nights, nor a shopgirl from one of the big stores who thinks of nothing but aping the chic of *Vogue* fashion models. His women are confined precisely to the girls of that in-between class who have a whiff of education, certain aspirations and who suffer from their humble condition. They are the countless Madame Bovarys who people ministries and offices, who are private secretaries, stenographers or clerks, who rub elbows daily with people from more well-to-do circles than their own and with whom they are by force of circumstance on familiar terms, which only makes them more discontented still, because this familiarity is purely external and based on nothing real. That is why secretaries are the ideal prey for the Pygmalion lover. Do you follow me?

I: I am one step ahead. It was already plain to me, even before you warmed to the theme, that Roberti was a Pygmalion lover of the first water. Besides, he had started with Agnes. You gave me a full account of how he educated Agnes during the early years of their marriage.

HE: He had assuredly started before Agnes. I am sure that even at twenty he was practicing Pygmalionism with his young conquests, telling them about Nietzsche's philosophy (very fashionable among the youth of 1930), Schubert's music, his dear Gide and so on. He doubtless played records to them on those old gramophones which had to be wound up every three minutes, you remember. I'm convinced that he tried to improve the minds of the women in whom he took an interest (I mean who were more to him than just passing fancies), that he took them by the hand and led them down the wonderful path of Knowledge. Agnes was his masterpiece. With her he had all the time he needed to make her perfect, that is to say impart to her mind the knowledge in his own, instruct her in painting, music, poetry, philosophy and even politics. Hence his deep affection for her. But by 1955 she had long ceased to be a pupil. Insofar as she was Pygmalion's statue, if you will allow this image, she had been relegated to the attic. From being his pupil she had in the fullest sense become his companion or, if you prefer, his foil; her mind was as familiar to him as his own.

I: It's really rather comic, this mania for pedagogy!

HE: When you come to think of it, it's not so surprising. A desire to govern the thoughts of the object of one's passion is an old tendency of human nature. It is one of the chief characteristics of love in Plato. In Greece in the fifth century B.C., the master instructed his disciple conjointly in love and philosophy. The two went hand in hand.

I: Oh come now! That was a very special kind of love! Sodomy hasn't figured in the college curriculum (at least not officially) for twenty-five centuries. It's really too ludicrous to compare Roberti with Socrates!

HE: Admittedly Socrates is stretching the point a bit far. But, sodomy or no, there is truth in what I say. Masculine love, when it is aimed at someone younger, more frail and with a lot to learn nearly always resembles paternal love. Very well, let's leave Socrates out of it. Let's say that Roberti had the soul of a teacher in a girls' school. Heaven knows he had been through enough pupils! He had been a young teacher; he had become an old one. Being an old teacher doesn't mean one doesn't have young pupils, and even less that one doesn't like having them. The candidates' age for passing out of the college of love remains the same. Eighteen to twenty-eight.

I: Would-be "licentiates" . . .

HE: I say, that's not bad!

I: What I should like to know is how Pygmalionism reveals itself in a man as busy as Roberti who, from the moment he becomes Solange Mignot's lover, is further possessed by such a terror of being found out.

HE: Don't rush me. I'm coming to it. Yes, the Pygmalion side of him was rather difficult to reconcile with his general attitude toward

Solange, but he managed it more or less. From time to time they had "good talks," they "turned over ideas"; but on these occasions Solange didn't do much talking. She was deeply conscious of her ignorance. Everything her lover told her seemed to her marvelous and fascinating. She thought he knew everything, that she would never manage to sustain a serious argument with him, that her only role was to be all ears. And so it happened that instead of talking about love, as would have been normal and delightful (making a duet in which each could have poured out his heart) Roberti held forth in a monologue. He poured out his mind and his conceit. His mind postured. Solange, as she listened, was discouraged from speaking: what she had to say, compared with what she was hearing, was far too childish and insignificant. What were her sufferings, her outbursts of tenderness, her girlish ideas, compared with Scarlatti's sonatas or the *Après-Midi d'un Faune?* And what then? Perhaps, with time, Roberti adopted a professorial, pedantic tone. At all events Solange never had the feeling of *sharing* her life with him. She had the impression he was giving her much by introducing her to Bellini's painting or Baudelaire's poetry, while she had nothing to offer in exchange. Perhaps he contrived to make it clear that he was quite indifferent to her tenderness, that this was a worthless commodity for a superior man such as he, full of knowledge and profound thoughts.

You know how women are. They can't bear not giving anything to those they love. Nothing touches them so deeply as when a man says: "I need you." They will do absolutely anything, gladly commit the wildest sacrifice. Now Roberti doubtless needed Solange (and for other things than you know what) but he never told her so and always took steps to see that she should never be aware of it. In her excessive humility, poor girl, she was always convinced that for him she meant nothing more than a pleasant habit, a pastime scarcely superior to bridge or golf. When he told her he loved her, something really strange occurred: neither he nor she believed it; each took the words as being just a polite gesture, one of these remarks one is simply obliged to make in certain circumstances or else appear a boor. And both were deceived; it was the truth. A truth which, had they glimpsed it, would have driven them both wild with a happiness they never knew.

I: That's all very fine but it still doesn't explain how Roberti found time to educate her. The occasional little discussion on Gauguin or Debussy was not enough.

HE: He sometimes took her to exhibitions of painting at the Louvre, the Orangerie or the Galerie Charpentier. At other times he took her to concerts at the Châtelet or the Salle Pleyel. He would sidle furtively through these outings. Having arranged to meet her outside the art gallery or concert hall, he would arrive at the last minute clutching the tickets, grab her by the arm and dive in. He went to concerts the same way as he went to the hotel and to museums the same way as to the Bois de Boulogne. He slunk with his mistress through the Louvre as if it were a public garden. He never gave her his arm. He would be all the time glancing to right or left to see if anyone he knew might be there. In which case he could instantly pretend to ignore the presence of Solange, who, after all, was just another visitor.

ı: And did she really accept this? Did she consent to go out with this man who never stopped trembling, feeling ashamed of her, displaying an ignoble cowardice? Poor girl!

HE: Yes, she accepted it, she even did so with a good grace. Every time Roberti suggested going to look at pictures or listen to some music (and this was hardly ever more than once a month) she was thrilled. Don't forget, we are looking at all these events and emotions objectively and in retrospect. In life nothing is quite so explicit. We are constantly deceived as to the meaning of things, because this meaning is concealed under all kinds of appearances and also because everything about us is in motion. Motion is the great enemy of reflection. The past is simple and intelligible, transparent, because it is immobile (or immobilized). Solange was happy to be with Roberti; for her his presence was so overpowering, so sweet, that nothing else mattered. Besides, Edouard was careful not to hurt her by making his precautions conspicuous. He never actually looked like a hunted beast. The glances he gave to right and left were furtive. He hoped that most of his little wiles passed unnoticed. And indeed, during the early months of their affair, Solange was completely taken in. Then little by little she became —how shall I put it?—"sensitized". She began to realize the permanent torture to which Roberti was subjected whenever he found himself in her company in a public place; she learned to sense even his faintest movements of fear, to intercept his sidelong glances, and she began to anticipate them, dread them, suffer from them. She would guess from some sudden awkwardness of his that he was once more on the alert after having relaxed in the most charming confidence for the past quarter of an hour. She was not hurt by it. Merely saddened. In a moment I will tell you of an incredible trick he played on her during the Easter vacation of 1957 and how she put up with it, still so great was her love for him at that time.

Oddly enough, and typical of Roberti's character, he enjoyed going out with Solange in spite of the all the more or less imaginary dangers he scented around him. He would go to meet her in a blend of happiness and boredom which increased and became almost exquisite when from afar he saw his mistress waiting at the appointed spot. It was abundantly clear that she would never stand him up, from which he would have been able to draw some moral advantage. She was always there, whatever difficulty she had encountered on the way. She would have come even were she dying. The "alternation of the heart" is a well-known factor listed for at least forty years in the old catalogue of psychology. But what would you say to a *simultaneous alternation* were I to venture to link these two terms? This was the case with Roberti when he arrived at a meeting place. "What drudgery this is going to be," he told himself. "The next two hours are going to be deadly. Fifty people are going to see me with this little blonde! I'm quite mad." He no longer had any wish to see Solange, he bitterly regretted having given way to the proprieties which require that one takes one's mistress out from time to time. Then she would approach him with a luminous smile (forgive the cliché, but I can find nothing better: her smile lit up her face and flooded Roberti's soul with light). After ten minutes the close proximity of these two had done its work and Edouard was feeling completely happy. Later he remembered these outings with nostalgia and, in prison, regretted that there hadn't been more of them. He in turn lamented having failed to accumulate more memories of this kind. He had only a very few of them to cling to as he gloomily brooded in the condemned cell. He told me one day that the image he took most pleasure in evoking was that of Solange one summer afternoon two years before. They were due to meet one Saturday in the courtyard of the Louvre. She was waiting for him (as she always arrived five or ten minutes early, knowing him to be so busy and not wanting to waste one moment of his presence by being foolishly late). He had seen her from a distance and his heart had begun to beat. Her white-clad figure, her fair hair, her hat with the wide, turned-down brim in fashion that year, her slender figure, her full skirt were engraved indelibly on his memory. There was an infinite poetry about it all, a poignancy which had even struck him at the time. For the space of a moment he had suspected that being so overwhelmed must surely mean he was in love, but he had immediately rationalized this thought out of existence. A man of fifty doesn't suddenly begin to believe himself in love because he feels excited at the sight of his pretty mistress caught in a ray of sunlight in the middle of the courtyard of the Louvre! It was just a second's illusion. Yielding to such illusions amounts, in its way, to being superstitious. Now a Radical deputy abominates superstition. And yet, in that brief moment, love had revealed itself to Roberti. He had declined to see it. He had turned away his head. Looking back years later, he understood this very clearly in his prison. He saw Solange again standing in her wide skirt and hat; saw again her rather slender but prettily shaped legs in a sunshine two years older, and a wave of tenderness and despair swept over him. These are the real memories of love, I am sure of it. It is images like these which cling like perfume, which never leave you, which you carry with you to the grave. Poor Roberti. To my mind he paid a heavy price. He had a share of his hell on earth, which makes me hope for his sake that perhaps he was not completely damned, that God left him a ray of hope in the depths of his abasement.

I: Do you really think that hell on earth is made up of memories of love?

HE: No, of course not. But just picture poor Roberti in his cell, before or after his trial, in search of things past and finally realizing, when it was too late, that, far from having no feelings as he had believed for the woman who had been utterly his, body and soul, for three years, he had on the contrary loved her passionately, that he loved her still behind the heavy, iron-studded oak door of his cell, that the opportunity of possessing this woman to his dying day had depended on him alone, that he had been the blindest of men. It must be terrible to realize that for three years one has been holding happiness close without knowing it to be in fact happiness and that one has thrown away this fabulous jewel as if it were just one of the common gewgaws of life. Picture him alone with his thoughts, all the more consumed by love now that nothing more could be done: not only was he irrevocably separated from his beloved by a power stronger than he, made up of society, justice, the law courts, morality and the police, against which one is utterly impotent, but also his beloved loved him no more, despised him, belonged to another. And I am forgetting something else which further increased his despair: apart from a few bewitching images like that of Solange in the courtyard of the Louvre (bewitching and even perfect, but very rare), almost all his memories were poisoned, and poisoned by himself. Each time he searched his memory for a picture of happiness shared with Solange, in order to feast on it in his solitude, to bring some light into his cell, all he found was a shapeless blur for which he alone was responsible. For once you must forgive me this comparison: it isn't mine but Roberti's, from whom I had it. Because I often went to see him in prison; I was even the only person besides Agnes to visit him; on those occasions he would let himself go; we had endless talks together; he treated me almost like his confessor. I developed an increasing affection for him the longer his captivity lasted. It was then that I truly got to know him and my feeling of friendship for him became something for which I was glad, in which I took pleasure, which was something more than habit. His mind had become considerably sharpened during these long days of bitter brooding. Sharpened and I would even say purged. Six months of prison had enabled him to see the past fifteen years of his life in perspective. But it was only an intellectual reassessment, not a sentimental one. He could at last see events in their true light, but they still caused him suffering, suffering even greater. Reverting to this comparison of a shapeless blur, according to him whenever he saw Solange she would try to make their meeting a work of art, a conventional picture perhaps, too sickly sentimental, but very well drawn, very well composed, and he would always ruin this picture by some incongruous touch of meanness, both because he had good taste and found these oleographs absurd, and because he didn't want to build up such memories at any price. Oh, not one incongruous touch; twenty, a hundred, a whole crisscross of lines and smears, waspish brush strokes which destroyed the picture as Solange drew it, turning it into a meaningless mess of lines and colors, making it something ludicrous and laughable. In short he indulged in vandalism. To be in prison, to be completely devoured by love yet as it were to have no memory of love is a strange situation, you must admit. And I am omitting all the other reasons that could augment Roberti's grief: the scandal, the worry of knowing his wife and children to be in a precarious state, the desertion of all his friends (except me), the contempt of the world at large. Don't you think these were grounds enough for despair?

    I: No. Frankly I don't.

    HE: It's all very well for you to talk, lolling there with your cigar.

    I: That's the only way one *can* talk. Otherwise one makes mistakes. You show me Roberti in his cell, you conjure up doors of oak studded with iron. That's not entirely correct from what I know (for I do know a few things, after all). Roberti spent nearly all his period of detention in the infirmary, which is far less painful physically (and even morally) than a cell. And anyway what are these iron-studded oak doors doing? We no longer live in the Middle Ages. Prisons today are like factories. They are all grills and steel. You may say that's no more cheerful than the Castel Sant' Angelo or the Bastille, but at least it's less frightening, less romantic and less unhealthy.

    Second, I think that when one finds oneself flung into prison overnight, one's world alters completely. Meaning what? That one is uprooted, that one's life adopts an entirely new, a much slower, more contemplative course. As a result, after a few days one's soul changes. Provided he is not just a common ruffian, provided he has intellectual resources, a man justly condemned to prison cannot be so very different from a Trappist monk, minus his faith. Does this comparison shock you? Wait till I've finished. A Trappist withdraws from the world in answer to a decree of his will. Once this act is accomplished he sees himself set face to face with the Absolute. The Absolute brings his soul a peace which the outside world cannot even suspect. The Absolute ceaselessly fortifies him in his resolve. I am sure that prison fortifies in the same way as the cloister. There is a life of the prison just as there is a life of the cloister, made up of a number of humble or menial tasks which amply fill the days and effectively divert the passions. You will never make me believe that a man like Roberti didn't adapt himself to prison after a certain while (to prison and the prison infirmary). As a man he was far too practical, too deliberate, to knock his head against the wall. If you want the core of my thought, I think that he *settled down* in his cell and then, in the infirmary, that he tried to give his corner a certain distinction, a certain style, by hanging up a reproduction of some old master or tastefully setting out a few books or some ornament they allowed him to have as a special favor. Am I wrong?

HE: No, you're not wrong. . . .

I: Don't waste your time giving me details. I can see him in his bed in the infirmary as clearly as if I were sitting beside it. There's a pile of books on his bedside table. He's wearing his smart tortoise-shell spectacles, he might be a minister convalescing in an expensive clinic.

HE: Hmm! There you're going too far. You can only see him in your mind's eye. I actually did see him. For a time he was just as you have described him, I don't deny it. He took care of his appearance, not in order to show off as you insinuate, but for his own satisfaction. This personal tidiness, this well-groomed air which he maintained almost to the end, was a great help to him. Eau de cologne was his opium, his cocaine. He held out thanks to eau de cologne. But don't forget that I saw him in death as well and then, what a transformation in my poor friend! With hair uncombed, three or four days' growth of gray stubble and a waxen pallor, he looked an old man. I have often noticed that when a man dies he ages twenty or thirty years in a flash. Death strips him of all artifice. All at once one sees that he has hardly any teeth left, that his flesh is flabby and (most horrible of all) that his mouth has caved in, appearing seamed with deep vertical wrinkles. Death sets the body on a level with the soul, and this is always impressive to behold. That is doubtless why bodies are prepared for interment. It is unseemly for them to be laid in the earth with their true features. When Roberti died he was fifty-three, which is not old, but his soul was at least ninety. In death his face was that of a man of ninety. I shan't forget it in a hurry. He was at once thin and bloated. Incidentally, they buried him pretty quickly. He was already decomposing fast. That is what befell the mad lover of Solange Mignot, whose body only a year before had been loved and desired like that of a young man. As for Solange, she was as beautiful and dazzling as ever, if not more so. She was twenty-eight. She had just given birth to the child for which she had so greatly longed and which he had always refused to give her.

I: Brr! Suddenly you've given me goose pimples! What drives you to ruin all your effects like this? What impelled you to describe Roberti's death at this juncture? You obviously have no sense of composition.

HE: I love ruining my effects. To me it's the quintessence, the height of elegance where art is concerned. Don't you agree? Novelists who carefully deliver their *coups de théâtre*, artfully hold back their dividends (how much? fifteen per cent?), who wait till the end of their book to unveil the enigma, have always seemed to me like shopkeepers anxious not to lose a penny on their wares. My idea of the artist is quite different. For me he is a duke, a prince who gives on the spur of the moment, out of an excess of generosity, for generosity cannot but be excessive. Besides, you annoyed me with your description of Roberti contented in prison.

I: I never said he was content. I said he had conformed to it, that's all. And conformed without too much difficulty. Sitting here smoking my cigar under the trees of the Pavillon Royal and digesting my *foie gras*, completely relaxed, I can see something you didn't spot during your visits to him in prison. I see the Inevitable, with which he was imbued after two or three weeks. I see him coming to terms with the Inevitable, preparing for his fate. I see him withdrawn (or cut off) from the world, knowing there was nothing more to be done, passing from action (disorganized, ridiculous and crazy) to contemplation. I see him to some extent at peace. Note in passing that I am sparing you the usual remarks about the reconciliation punishment brings to guilty souls. In short, to my way of thinking, Roberti in prison didn't feel utter despair.

HE: Well, you're wrong. You are being misled by appearances. Your idea of despair is oversimplified. Despair is not a great wave breaking over a man's head, a sudden invasion, a crippling disease which strips away all one's resilience at one blow. I myself picture despair rather like a microbe wreaking its havoc in a corner of one's organism. I might add that the same thing happens with despair as with almost all the feelings and passions: its victim remains unaware of it for a long time. He has no idea the microbe is at work. Then one day he perceives that nothing, not a trace of hope is left in him. It has all been eaten away. He is like a house attacked and devoured by termites. The house crumbles into dust. The man crumbles into dust. With Roberti, despair followed this secret process. At least, that is how I explain his death. Otherwise it remains incomprehensible. Nothing compelled him to die at the age of fifty-three. Of course, the doctors talked about a duodenal ulcer, old internal injuries and other things of that kind, most of which I've forgotten, but anyway it didn't mean a thing. He was sick, certainly, but he had nothing wrong with him that couldn't be cured, given any desire to live. He died of his soul. In this connection one always comes back to the example of Napoleon on Saint Helena. Napoleon died at fifty-two because he was on Saint Helena. Had he remained Emperor, had he continued to consume his "yearly income of a hundred thousand men" as he used to put it, he would have lived much longer, until 1850 or possibly 1860. You laughed at me just now for mentioning Socrates. I suppose Napoleon will also provoke your mirth. Yet Roberti, however wretched he was, however forgotten, however ignored he will always be, died like Napoleon. He had his Saint Helena. If you want my opinion, I even think he died a little better than Napoleon, for despair diminished the great man whereas it made the little man slightly greater.

I allowed a brief silence to fall after these last words, not that I was weary of arguing or interrupting (on the contrary, as midnight approaches one acquires a new lease of energy) but I had found him too lyrical for my taste. I don't like pointless references to Napoleon. In order to bring him back to a sense of modesty I murmured: "What a beautiful night!" stressing the first syllable of "*beautiful*" strongly enough for him to understand. In truth it was. It had grown much cooler, which made it all the more pleasant. A film of mist lay over the hedge and, visible through its foliage where they caught the lamplight, the roofs of the cars parked along the pavement. It was the dew which had fallen as we talked and which we ourselves hadn't felt, as if it had spared the terrace of the Pavillon Royal, as if this establishment, for the comfort of its patrons, had signed an agreement with nature and was preserved from the discomforts of the night.

My cigar was but half consumed, for I had only been taking brief puffs at it. It still had plenty of aroma. I have habits of economy too deep-rooted to throw away a cigar before it is reduced to a sticky, extinct stump. Moreover true connoisseurs know there is a certain charm in smoking a Havana to the end, savoring it to the dregs, the bitter black nicotine of it, after having relished its prime.

Normally I don't much care for sitting on after a meal, but that night I took a keen pleasure in it for various reasons which I have given here and there and which have possibly not been forgotten. I was, God forgive me, even filled by that sort of unease, that twinge of anxiety one feels at the idea that a happy time is drawing to an end and that one will shortly have to part company with a friend with whom one has joyously traveled a long and difficult road. Such are the little daily despairs of friendship and with me, when it is very deep, friendship always assumes the guise of a disputatious complicity. Together he and I had covered at least four fifths of a complicated journey and never before, in spite of all our arguments, had we viewed the country through which we had passed in such harmony. We had only an hour or two left to spend together and all at once this seemed to me a tragedy. What curious forms our sensibilities can assume! My life is full of them. I hardly ever refer to them, for they aren't the kind of things one talks about. Nobody understands them; they are too tenuous. Perhaps they are nothing at all.

HE: Didn't we mention Madame de Staël earlier?

I: Possibly. I don't remember.

HE: Yes we did, in connection with the beginnings of love.

I: You're right.

HE: And do you know why the beginnings of love are the best moment of all? Not because one is discovering a person different from or similar to oneself, not because one is captivated by these differences or similarities, and not because "beauty is a promise of happiness" either, but because of the result of all that. Love in its beginnings gives the man it attacks such energy and activity that he will pay any price to draw as close as he can to the object of his passion and finds no difficulty too great to overcome. Madame de Staël's remark was that of a woman who had seen her lovers in the throes. During the first weeks of an affair the lover moves heaven and earth to be with his beloved and achieves this by virtue of the axiom that we always get what we really want. Later this determination flags. Being more accessible, love gradually ceases to be his foremost preoccupation. The daily round of life floats back to the surface. It takes hold of the man and then the woman's troubles begin. This refers above all, as you must realize, to unmarried love (but a similar process can be observed in married couples).

After a few months or sometimes a year, one can no longer truly say that love is still in its beginnings; it has turned into a habit and, what is worse, a frustrated one. It still represents great happiness, no doubt, but one to which all sorts of painful ideas attach themselves. With a little Prometheus well and truly bound like Roberti, that is to say bound by his occupations, his need to maintain his social position, his affections, his wife, his fear of gossip and the gutter press, his spasmodic ambitions, his thousand overlapping projects, love provokes a permanent conflict which makes it a torment, and a torment that is seldom exquisite. Now love is something important: we are always afraid of not taking it sufficiently into consideration, of sacrificing it to some less precious occupation. Whence a continual malaise in the mind and heart of the busy man who spends his whole time in subtle calculations, trying to maintain an exact balance between his sentiments and his reason, in other words between his personal happiness and his position in the world. Throughout each day Roberti was intermittently seized with fleeting but piercing longings to see Solange, touch her, inhale her, but whenever he was in her company thirty regrets and preoccupations would intervene to mar his pleasure. It was as if, in these rare moments when he had her to himself, his whole public life rose up before him and stared at him reprovingly, so that he never knew perfect felicity and little by little love took on the aspect of a wholesale complication. It pressed down with considerable weight on the whole of life. In the beginning, life obstructs love; there is no problem then, one just sets life aside, performs miracles, has what seems the gift of ubiquity, invents superb lies. Later on it is love which obstructs life and one has to retrace one's steps in the opposite direction, but it is a hard road, a devilish steep slope to climb. One starts to lie to the woman on whose account one once lied to others. To sacrifice her one spends those treasures of the imagination which formerly one had employed in sacrificing everything else to her. And there you are. Certain obstacles foster love while others strangle it. In three years a thousand little vexations obliterate a great love which would once have victoriously braved adversity, imprisonment and death. Gnats always triumph over lions.

For two people in the position of Roberti and Solange, the greatest obstacle to love was invisible: their respective ages. They were convinced (and would have been shocked to hear the contrary) that this difference in age was a negligible factor, unimportant, an absurd prejudice; they believed that love sets the most disparate people on an equal footing (which is untrue in any sense, but love among its other illusions numbers that of equality). Moreover each thought the other's age was the most charming and desirable age to be. Edouard loved Solange's firm fresh skin, the scent of her breath, her lack of experience, her youthful mind; and Solange was deeply convinced that at fifty a man is in his prime, the time when he is most splendid, most seductive, most intelligent, most understanding, most vigorous in love. But she did not know and he had probably forgotten that time doesn't pass in the same way when one is twenty-five as when one is fifty. At fifty the weeks last a day. At twenty-five the days last a week, they are encumbered with long, seemingly interminable stretches of boredom. Life is impossible to fill. One hasn't sufficient thoughts, sufficient things to do to occupy a whole day. Each minute is a lifetime in itself, unconnected with the preceding one and the one to come by those countless little bridges set up by the full activity of maturity.

I: Yes. We get used to time. We tame it with the years. It loses its value through the excessive use we make of it. By dint of passing the hours, we pass them more and more quickly.

HE: On the other hand, in the minds of the mature this telescoping of time produces strange mirages. Certain moments, certain hours stand out from the morass. What time loses in quantity it makes up for in quality. It is as if, in the dizzy course one runs, one suddenly comes to a halt. Time "suspends its flight." Out of each week swallowed up in the past, there survive two or three exquisite or horrible hours during which one had the feeling of *living*, while the rest of the time one merely existed. The hours Roberti spent at the studio with Solange brought him an excitement so violent, such a physical and emotional shock, that he had the illusion in memory of having done nothing else the whole week but devote himself to love. I have always thought that it isn't so much because they have more energy that the young make love more often than the middle-aged, as because they don't know how to cling to moments of happiness or draw prolonged sustenance from them. They never glimpse the moment of eternity they hold in their arms. They see nothing in such moments but a brief windfall, largely atoned for by acres of boredom before and after.

In short at fifty the hours are brief and at twenty-five they are interminable. This produces two kinds of people very alien to each other, who may by all means be in tacit agreement on every possible subject, perfectly akin as regards their philosophy, sensibilities, religion, outlook on life and ambitions, but who differ *by their very nature*. They dwell on two separate planets. On one of these time passes quickly; on the other, slowly. To my mind this difference is where what is known as the "gulf between the generations" lies. This gulf, moreover, is bridged automatically when the younger generation reaches thirty, which is the age when time suddenly begins to accelerate because life has insidiously become filled up. I believe a man of thirty is much closer to an old man of seventy than he is to a lad who has just attained his majority. At thirty he begins to speak the language of those for whom time has become devalued and who, alas, no longer know what boredom means. Roberti and Solange were like an affair between an earth-dweller and a Martian. Two separate worlds, you see. Two worlds not governed by the same laws of nature, where the same things have different values, where life has neither the same flavor nor the same *shape*. At fifty, one is seized with panic on seeing how the days are swallowed up and the weeks flash by like rockets. The twelve months of the year crash down one after the other like oaks in a forest set upon by woodcutters. It is as if the time between one Christmas and the next had elapsed in the space of a few nights. At fifty, one knows one has lived more years than are left to one. One has been caught up for the past twenty years (twenty years which flew like the wind) in a relentless whirlpool sucking one down toward death. However one tries to forget about death, however one tries to carry on as usual, one cannot help being brought face to face with it now and then; each time this happens it has grown a bit larger, it has drawn nearer by the distance one has covered and is covering with increasing speed.

Once past a certain fateful age, this speed with which life passes is terrifying. Some people are obsessed by it. Roberti was such a one, who at times could almost see himself visibly growing older. It was something he often used to talk about to me in a detached, faintly ironic way, like a true philosopher concealing under banter a despair against which he is helpless. He had hit on a striking image: he compared himself with a passenger looking in the rear mirror of a car racing at ninety miles an hour and watching the road receding at breakneck speed. Such was his "tragic conception of life" and I could understand how, with his acute awareness of the wretchedness of the human condition, many things seemed to him unimportant, beginning with the heartaches he inflicted on Solange. He himself was beset by a sorrow far more irreparable. That is why men of a certain age never make very pleasant lovers for young women. Their metaphysical torments impoverish the love they are still capable of feeling. To anesthetize himself, Roberti filled his days with a thousand different occupations and obligations and this was a mistake, since by being so congested they appeared briefer still. He would go to bed at midnight or one o'clock oppressed with the feeling that he hadn't performed half his various tasks, that the morrow would thus be doubly overburdened and life was being frittered away without bringing any real happiness.

There is only one way to hold time at bay: by creating a vacuum within and around oneself, putting an end to one's occupations and diversions; in short, cultivating boredom. But we fear boredom because, when not applied to anything in particular, our minds instinctively turn to the contemplation of death. To my mind this fear is groundless. Viewed from the angle of boredom, death does not appear almost more hideous but on the contrary is imbued with nobility and resignation.

It is no longer the abyss toward which Roberti's allegorical car is hurtling at ninety miles an hour, it is no longer a murderer lying in wait for you at a street corner; it is the end—rather sad, to be sure, but noble and uplifting—of a novel one has written as best one could, it is the closing lines of a poem, the total return to the self which heralds our mysterious return to the bosom of the Creator.

Death terrifies people because they look forward to the time when they will no longer have the strength to clasp the world to themselves, when the world will wrench itself from their grasp, when their work, friends, possessions, pleasures and obligations will slip from their hands. They picture as intolerable the few hours, the few days of solitude (preluding the solitude of the tomb) through which they will pass before their eyes close forever. They cannot bear the idea of being left face to face with themselves without a go-between, for it is too long since they lost themselves from sight. They have forgotten what they are. They are afraid of this being which is themselves and which they no longer know. It is for all these reasons that I advocate boredom. Besides the fact that it prolongs the hours for the middle-aged (already a considerable factor), it gives them an opportunity to re-examine their own souls into which they hardly ever venture, to become familiar with them, *learn to love them* in anticipation of the time when, stripped bare, these will be all they possess.

Anyway Roberti, as I have said, was never bored. He was stuffed as full as could be with the common prejudice against boredom. For all his subtle mind, his love of paradox, he believed like any fool that it is degrading to be bored. He took pride in the fact that his days were corpses on which his activities swarmed like maggots. God, how sorry I feel for people who are never bored! I felt sorry for Roberti and tried to enlighten him. There were even times when he saw my point, but by then it was doubtless too late. He no longer had the courage or, rather, the audacity to unburden his life. This life did gradually unburden itself during the three years his affair with Solange lasted, but neither Edouard's will nor his reason played any part in this, so that it unburdened itself badly, not of the futilities—the dinner parties, entertainments, first nights, arid discussions in the lobbies of the Chamber—but conversely of those stern undertakings which demand application and leave a sense of gratification once they have been fulfilled. Moreover (and this is revealing), up to the last minute of his life as a free man Edouard never knew what boredom was. Love slowly and secretly destroyed his taste for work (because love needs considerable room in a soul and must destroy something else before it can move in); it left the trivial side of him intact. Diversion, according to Pascal, is everything which *deflects*, our business as well as our recreation, but recreation is no less of a diversion than business. To the many causes which made Roberti's love a fatal one and sped him on his way to hell, we must certainly add this perpetual diversion in which he was steeped and which he either would not or could not do without.

This increased Solange's troubles. She suffered directly from it. In fact, after the first few months, he had fitted her into his timetable as if she were a new job he had taken on in addition to all the others he already held. He saw her twice a week; he rang her up nearly every day and considered that this made everything all right. He believed in all good faith that he was granting her a good deal of his time. But for her it was nothing: her days, interminable and barren, her lonely and unhappy nights, her dreary evenings spent at home, were a bitter price to pay for these meetings and phone calls. Like all women she needed the presence of her lover, an active, constant presence. She needed to see him, touch him, hear his voice; she needed cajoling. She had to have the corporeal side of love the whole time, that is to say the face, the smile, the voice, the big and gentle hands of the man she loved, failing which the world was mere ice and darkness. She suffered from not being able at any moment to press up close to Edouard in the same way, I suppose, as people suffer who have had a limb amputated and continue to feel pain in the limb they have lost.

Where love was concerned Solange was "like the birds of the air" (so said Mlle. Angioletti). She lacked what women most ardently desire: *status*. When she was with Roberti she was never sure of anything and when she left him she always wondered whether she would ever see him again, so unpredictable and so fearful was he of committing himself in the slightest way. Had he so much as fixed certain days for their meetings—Tuesdays and Fridays, for instance—she would have at least known where she stood and ceased to hope without rhyme or reason; but he would always let her know at the last minute when he had a moment to spare. Sometimes only a day would elapse between two meetings, sometimes three or four. So that she never dared accept another invitation for fear of having to break it at the last moment. By a rule of compensation which is often to be observed in love, the more her heart was full, the more her life was empty.

I have told you how she greatly longed to have a child. She tried, the way everyone does, to attribute rational or sentimental causes to this desire which was above all physiological. I defy you to guess the conclusion she drew. It never occurred to her (for she was a generous soul) that if Roberti made her a mother she would have certain rights over him, grounds for pressure or blackmail. Not a bit of it. She ingenuously told herself that a child would occupy her time and keep her company. I suppose such notions are hard to understand when one is a man and may even appear improbable; yet they are true. Men normally regard children as a source of trouble and complications. Women look on them as the meaning of their lives. Children fill their days and hearts with a mass of delectable cares. Children absorb the tenderness of their hearts and the substance of their bodies. Solange would dream sadly of the child Roberti did not give her and which he might perhaps resolve to give her one day. How divine that day would be. She thought not uncomplacently of the scandal to which it would give rise at home. This time she really would be forced to leave the paternal roof. Edouard would have no choice but to install her in the studio in the Square Saint-Lambert, which she would transform into a charming spot. It would no longer be that rather squalid hotel room to which he reduced it but a home, a place that was alive and where at last one could have normal feelings. Love would assume its proper place there among the other activities of life. It would cease to be this frantic fornication, monstrous in that the relations between the two lovers hardly extended beyond it.

It is always depressing to detect the seeds of death in things which are just beginning, especially when these are beautiful, like a love affair into which one flings oneself with delirious enthusiasm. It reminds us too acutely of the misery of the human condition; it reminds us too clearly that men are condemned to know no happiness that is not fleeting, that they can count on nothing, that life and death—alas!—always go hand in hand and everything is doomed to annihilation from birth. Roberti's and Solange's love was secretly poisoned (and from the very first day) by the *conception of duration*, which was different for each of two lovers so wide apart in age and position. Solange's love finally wilted away because Roberti failed to nourish it with his presence. As this love was very deep it resisted for three years. Possibly, in spite of the horrors of its end, it never completely died. It became anemic; life ebbed out of it, eaten away by that disease which terrifies women and is called loneliness.

Roberti's love, while it increased, turned sour for the opposite reason. Men are no doubt less materialistic than women; they are more readily content with the symbols of things than with the things themselves, that is to say when they are in love they don't feel as great a need as women do for the presence of the loved one. He thought about Solange on the whole deeply and continuously, and resented her for preoccupying his mind in this way. It was almost as absorbing as actually seeing her. He believed he didn't love her but he reckoned that, having seduced her, he had certain obligations toward her and found this idea intolerable. Nothing is so hateful as having obligations, especially when one is a man like Edouard. So there were days when he had no wish to think of her but thought of her in spite of himself. He knew she was longing for him to telephone her as fervently as a traveler dying of thirst longs for a drop of water. So he would put off this phone call from one hour to the next. The feeling that he owed it to her exasperated him; he would invent excellent reasons for not making it, he would arm himself with indifference. But this made days filled with thoughts of Solange, and these thoughts were not pleasant.

A revealing example of the difference in language that tempered their relations has just occurred to me. To my mind it admirably brings out how impossible it is for a man of fifty and a woman of twenty-five to understand each other clearly. Whenever they visited the Square Saint-Lambert, Roberti never failed to telephone the next morning to ask his love if she had slept well. This inquiry astonished her, for one always sleeps well at twenty-five and she couldn't imagine how sleep could pose the slightest problem. "Better than usual?" he would insist. "I slept like a log!" she would reply. This delighted him. It filled him with pride. He saw himself as a magician: he had sent a woman to sleep! An interesting feature, don't you think? Typical of a man of fifty: the young never ask if one has slept well; feats of love come so naturally to them that they scorn to find out whether they have exhausted their partners.

I: Well, you can't complain. I haven't interrupted you for a long time.

HE: From which I conclude you were interested?

I: Yes, I was. Even so, I couldn't help regretting something all the time you were talking.

HE: Oh yes? What was that?

I: Not seeing Roberti. Not seeing him physically.

HE: But you knew him. I am not going to start describing a man you met several times.

I: I probably saw him only three or four times in my life, and that was years ago. I have a vague recollection of his general appearance. He was rather tall, rather big, rather soft-looking, if I remember. Didn't he have a slight stoop?

HE: Yes, a slight one, that's correct. It was his round shoulders which made him somehow, as you've said, soft-looking. This wasn't due to any malformation at birth but to his short sight, which had given him the habit of bending excessively low over his papers when working at his desk.

ɪ: And his face? As a rule I can hardly ever remember faces; when I try to recall Roberti's, it's a complete blur. I can only remember his gray—well, pepper-and-salt—hair, which was rather striking. It's odd; you told me his hair was fine and thin, but that's not how I recollect it. I see it as rather thick on the contrary, a rather strong, even dense head of hair.

ʜᴇ: Well you're wrong, and it just shows what a skillful way he had with a comb.

ɪ: I also remember his eyes. They were big, weren't they? But what color? The color of eyes is something I never remember. I can only recall their expression.

ʜᴇ: They were chestnut, burnt sienna. You don't remember their color because most of the time he wore glasses.

ɪ: And didn't he have a rather large head? His face is completely devoured by shadows. Describe it. I need it. These ideas about death and the swift passage of time which you have put so clearly—I need to fill them in with the exact features of a man of fifty.

ʜᴇ: For me he had a rather fine head, certainly appealing to women: a very white skin which easily turned waxy when he was ill or depressed; a big nose, strong and straight; a forehead which looked high because his hair formed a widow's peak. His chin was deceptive for it was firmer than his character, more pronounced, well rounded under the handsomely curved mouth. He had pale lips and superb teeth. I think that what made his appearance particularly arresting were his languorous eyes and ironic mouth. These formed a charming contrast which appealed greatly to women and his constituents. On account of his round shoulders he held his head slightly forward and to one side which gave him an energetic air, the look of a fighter who grapples with life and forges straight ahead. He walked—how shall I put it?— with a sort of light heaviness. One felt that he filled his suits well (and these were always perfectly cut) but one couldn't tell whether it was with muscle or fat. Well, fat is going too far. Let us say flesh, rather. Roberti was a very "fleshy" man, almost pulpy in spite of his fifty years. His waist was thick or, if you like, had thickened with the years, but no more than that: it wasn't enough to make him fat. He looked forty, forty-five at a pinch. Always well shaved, dapper and smelling fresh. A soft skin, smooth limbs with thick thighs which visibly swelled his trousers, and big hands. There. Does that suit you?

i: Yes. Thanks. You hadn't yet given me a full-length portrait of him. I realize that's what has been bothering me all along. Now I can mentally place the fair Solange Mignot alongside the man you've described, and they seem to me to make a very well-matched pair. Not at all like Beauty and the Beast, as I had been more or less inclined to imagine.

he: Good. Now I'll take up the threads of my story again. And I am going to do something that will please you: I am going to skip three or four months. We had in fact got to September or October 1955; at least that was more or less the date of the affair of the lace doilies. Nothing particularly interesting happened after that until January 1956.

i: Ah, that's the way I like to hear you talk! Let's skip three, four months, two years! Let's stick to essentials, be brief, violent, dramatic! What happened in January 1956?

he: Don't you remember?

i: I do not. I published a book on political morale that year, *The Taxis of the Marne.*

he: Roberti read it. He spoke to me about it several times. It was a book which greatly impressed him.

i: Is that so? He liked it?

he: Well, well! The wolf of letters turns into a spaniel and begs for sugar. If, when I began to tell you this story at two o'clock this afternoon, I had mentioned that Roberti was one of your readers, that he liked and agreed with some of your ideas, that thanks to you he had become aware of several little things, admit that you would have viewed him with a different eye. Admit you would have been more indulgent and sympathetic toward him.

i: I really don't know what to reply. I could act stupid and lose my temper. But I am more honest. Yes, I think that to begin with I would have viewed Roberti with a different eye. An artist must necessarily have affinities with those who admire his art; he feels a certain intimacy with them; I would even say he feels himself responsible up to a point for their actions and thoughts. But it wouldn't have lasted very long. The portrait of his character such as you have drawn it would soon have turned me against him. In 1956 he was in his fifty-first year. I was thirty-six. Such of my books as he had read may possibly have influenced his mind; at any rate they didn't form it. They didn't make a different man of him. I should add that the success of *The Taxis of the Marne,* like most successes, was based on misunderstandings.

It's possible Roberti liked the book for quite the wrong reasons. I have often found myself praised by people whose approval caused me considerable pain!

HE: You may reassure yourself that this wasn't the case here. Roberti liked *The Taxis* instinctively. He read it in the right spirit. He was so pleased by its general attitude that he even accepted the wild exaggerations and crying injustices you sometimes put into it. And he did a lot of propaganda for you. He made masses of people buy your book, particularly his fellow deputies. He gave it away to his friends. You were widely read in the Chamber.

I: You're a dirty dog. A really dirty dog. You shouldn't have told me that. Now I'm going to feel embarrassed. As a moralist, my objective calm has been undermined. You have raised a point of conscience I could have done without. You are a sadist. Here I am all at once linked with Roberti when it was the very last thing I was expecting.

HE: I'm terribly sorry, but nothing should be withheld. There were a few thoughts in Roberti's mind which he derived from you. You just have to lump it. He may well have taken with him into the grave a few snatches of sentences you yourself had written, which had lingered in his memory. He had been touched by your music.

I: Well, I shall try to forget it. What happened in January 1956? *The Taxis* only came out in September.

HE: Don't you really remember?

I: I wouldn't say I didn't if I didn't.

HE: There was a general election. The nation went to the polls.

I: So what? How am I supposed to take that? Roberti was re-elected. It has nothing to do with his affair with Mlle. Mignot.

HE: Yes, he was re-elected, but it does have something to do with his love life and I should like to tell you how his re-election came about.

I: Why?

HE: Because it was his last victory. After that, everything began to decline and become corrupted. But at the elections of January 1956 he was really on top of his form. The mastery he displayed was really astounding. At that time he was still upborne by love and this made him light; afterward love began to be upborne by him and it grew heavier and heavier until it crushed him. We are quite wrong to say "Lucky at cards, unlucky in love." It isn't true; love brings luck, perhaps because one has a great longing to be admired by the person one loves. Do you remember the 1956 elections?

I: I? What do you take me for? The 1956 elections? I have better fish to fry.

HE: Well I'm sorry, but I who haven't so many fish to fry remember the 1956 elections very clearly. They were the last before the fall of the Fourth Republic. Try to think back a bit. They were dominated by one main electoral group, the Republican Front, which included the Socialist Party, a section of the Radical Party and several minor left-wing, non-Communist parties. This Republican Front didn't survive the election, however. Everyone expected a Mendès-France government to emerge from it but the Socialists won the largest number of seats. As a result, it was Mollet who was entrusted by President Coty to form the government. Mendès had been counting on getting the Ministry of Foreign Affairs or of Finance, but he didn't; he was offered the Ministry of National Economy, which he turned down. In the end he agreed to become minister without portfolio, which was pretty meager and rather humiliating for such a man. He resigned a few months later.

At the time of the elections Roberti's position was very tricky. He was a Radical, as you know, and the Radical Party had just split in two. Mendès was no longer head of the Executive Committee. He had carried with him almost half the party, that is to say the left-wing, progressive half. The other half, being more cautious and reactionary, had remained under the banner of Bourgès-Maunoury.

I: Push on a bit faster, will you? I'm not going to put all these names in my novel. If anyone still reads it in fifty years' time, they won't have the faintest idea who they are.

HE: I am pushing on but even so I had to outline the general picture. As for names, don't worry: they'll create a very good effect in fifty or a hundred years' time. People will think you invented them, the way Balzac invented Rastignac, De Marsay, Senator Malin de Gondreville, Baudoyer, Des Lupeaulx, etc.

I: What I simply want to know is, did Roberti come out for Bourgès or Mendès?

HE: It's not nearly as simple as that. In any party a man like Roberti is on good terms with everyone. That is his strength and his weakness. Or more exactly, to be on good terms with everyone is the strength of the weak, their way of avoiding being crushed between strong rival forces in their struggles for power.

I: In other words he sat on the fence. But there comes a moment when even the most prudent have to make a choice. There's something comic, when you think of it, about this split in the Radical Party, the party of prudent men, the staunch enemies of clear-cut positions. Poor Radicals! How upset they must have been.

HE: One shouldn't slander anyone, not even politicians. What upset them was not so much having to choose between one trend and another as seeing the party falling to pieces, the Young Turks on one side under the banner of Mendès, and the Old Crabs under that of Bourgès. The Radical middlemen, anxious not to lose too many feathers, tried to pick up the pieces.

I: My word, you talk like a parliamentary journalist! What on earth are these middlemen doing losing feathers as they pick up the pieces? I don't understand such rubbish!

HE: You understand it perfectly. Don't interrupt the whole time. The political vocabulary, like the sporting vocabulary, is perfectly adapted to its object. I can't see why I shouldn't make use of it. Roberti, of course, was in the middle of the middlemen. He had ties of friendship with Mendès, who had incidentally supported him on occasion in the days of Herriot. But when Mendès left he didn't follow him, albeit without making any overt act of allegiance to the Bourgès clan. Besides, at that time the party was not yet divided in two. Theoretically it was intact. The actual split only took place after the election.

I: Dear me!

HE: That's the way politics are. A delicate tapestry in petit point.

I: Politics, no. A certain kind of politics. It has a name in the colloquial journalistic vocabulary: it's known as gerrymandering.

HE: All right. But gerrymandering is only gerrymandering at a lower level. On the higher one of major national interests, it becomes *statesmanship* or *subtlety*. The name changes, the function remains the same. Would you say that Cardinals de Retz or Mazarin gerrymandered? Did Louis XI gerrymander with the Duke of Burgundy? If one wishes to gerrymander in the noble sense, for history, one has to begin by doing so in the pejorative sense, for oneself, in order to attain those high-ranking positions where history is within one's grasp. Especially when one is living in a democracy.

The election campaign of January 1956 was known as the campaign of the Phrygian bonnet. In fact, the candidates nominated by the Republican Front wore a little Phrygian bonnet in their buttonholes. The Phrygian bonnet was printed on their posters. In the daily and weekly papers which supported them, their names were accompanied by a little emblem representing a Phrygian bonnet. Roberti had a keen enough political flair to sense that the Republican Front had a good start. He was standing as a Radical for I forget which Paris constituency. Against him was a list of Republican Front nominees, in the drawing up of which he had played a part. I'll explain how. He had retained enough friends in the Mendès faction to whom he had made various promises of rallying to their side in the end, after the elections, for them to have nominated only obscure or inexperienced Radicals who would offer him and his supporters comparatively little competition.

His campaign was a miracle of adroitness and political tact. During the two weeks it lasted, he displayed phenomenal energy. He spoke every evening in various school halls before fairly large gatherings. Throughout the day he built up his "contacts." He saw all kinds of useful people: trade-union secretaries or chairmen of Radical committees, war veterans, representatives of trade associations, lawyers, doctors, even clerics, which wasn't bad going for a Radical. He had taken the precaution of breaking off every kind of connection with the Radical Party (or at least its prominent adherents or dissidents) a week before the campaign opened. His plan was to stand under the traditional Radical banner, while letting it be understood that he was very close to the radicalism of the Mendès faction. He didn't wear the Phrygian bonnet in his buttonhole but behind his lapel. At certain meetings he never hesitated to turn back this lapel, which always created a sensation. His colleagues on the list were both terrified and thrilled by such audacity. I have said that he saw no one, but this didn't prevent him from telling his constituents, according to the circumstances: "I have just been having a word with President Mendès . . ." or "As President Bourgès-Maunoury said to me only an hour ago . . ." These references, these famous names carelessly dropped into the debate at a given moment, won Edouard and his list thousands of votes.

ɪ: Did he also refer to Edgar Faure? From all you have told me, I'm beginning to think it wasn't so easy to be a Radical in 1956.

ʜᴇ: No, it wasn't at all easy. It really called for considerable agility. As to Edgar Faure, Roberti would become at once vague and poetic if anyone raised his name. Edgar Faure was a highly dangerous weapon to wield: he was too clever, had too many enemies, and his expulsion from the Radical Party was still quite recent. Edgar Faure was Roberti's last ditch, when he was faced with argumentative or captious intellectuals. He normally extricated himself by shedding a crocodile tear over "dear Edgar" who was so widely missed, with whom he "couldn't agree" but had nevertheless maintained close ties of friendship. Most often it was Daladier whom he invoked, the old white-haired sage sanctified as it were by the defeat of 1940, a sort of tutelary deity of the Radical Party, to be on close terms with whom did him much honor. If things got really difficult he took cover behind René Mayer, a remote, powerful, mysterious and sphinxlike figure pronouncing oracles from his lofty throne of the Wagons-Lits.

For the Roberti family, Papa's election campaigns were a source of great delight and excitement. Agnes and the boys never missed a single one of the school-hall meetings. They sat in the back row and clapped till their hands were sore. These were almost the only occasions when they could admire the head of the family in all his glory and they made sure they never missed one of them. During the preceding months Agnes wrote thousands of addresses on thousands of envelopes. The boys took electioneering leaflets from door to door. They were all borne along on a tide of enthusiasm. I should add that Roberti steered things with a master hand. He often told me that the election campaigns were the most amusing part, the cream of political life. It is then that a politician really feels alive, it seems, for not only within the space of three or four weeks does he pass through all the social strata of his constituency and penetrate, so to speak, to the very bedrock of Paris, but also he weaves a web of countless intrigues, the success or failure of which is not sufficiently delayed for him to have time to get bored. He is at work on live, immediately tangible material. All kinds of people pass through his hands in the course of the day, from public figures to the little electoral agent coming to offer a dozen votes in return for some promise or even just a glass of wine.

Granted, there is nothing more enthralling, nothing more consistently meaty than an electoral campaign. There is never a dull moment. There is something to fill every second of the day. It is perpetual activity with all the uncertainty of activity, that is to say eight abortive ventures for every two that succeed; but one has no time to think of oneself. Roberti was never in such good form as during his elections, as if activity were a tonic, as if countless little activities reacted on his organism like countless little injections of vitamins or camphor. He was on his feet eighteen hours a day, managing to attend to everything, leaving nothing to chance and even, if need be, wasting his time in idle discussions with one or another group of tradesmen or trade unionists, if ever a discussion can be idle when its object is to win supporters. At any rate, there was one part of it he always welcomed with joy: that of receiving at his committee rooms an interminable flow of what one might call the "little folk," hundreds of people whom he didn't know but who knew and trusted him. This, I believe, is the fine, I would even say noble, side of being a deputy and few people suspect it. Roberti had long-standing and faithful constituents; he also had new ones; all had in common the fact that when they stood before him they appeared as weak and defenseless as children. They were in part entrusting him with their fate, they were giving him their mandate because they knew him to be more intelligent, cleverer and stronger than they. They looked on him as their defender and natural protector; they counted on him to speak for them, to speak better than they could, to *do his best* to preserve their liberties and happiness. He found this infinitely touching and was keenly aware of his obligations to these people so confident in his own good will; he felt responsible for them the way a father does for his children. A fraction of the French people were handing him a fraction of the State as a sacred trust because they considered him the most worthy of it. Even under weak, outworn, decadent regimes like the Fourth Republic politics can, you see, preserve certain honorable and— why not say it?—noble qualities.

Edouard liked best by far the public meetings in the evenings at the school halls, in which he was a truly political animal. Amateur candidates, in fact, do their best to avoid this kind of contact with the electoral body. It scares them and they don't know how to address it; they are afraid of being left tongue-tied by hecklers. Roberti, however, arranged a daily meeting which lasted from nine P.M. to midnight and sometimes even carried on till one o'clock, for when all the speeches had been made, all objections crushed and most of the audience had left, he would linger on palavering with some old man thirsting for further details or some opponent he was trying to win over.

The speeches he made at these meetings were remarkable: well composed, colorful, interesting, lively, skillfully interlarded with anecdotes and jokes which provoked laughter. This got around. The halls would gradually fill up until they were overflowing by the time it was his turn to take the stand. His evening speeches, which began about ten-thirty, lasted roughly an hour. They were his reward for a day of herculean labor. From his very first words he would "feel" his audience, as speakers call it. He could tell at once whether the crowd he was facing was already won over or reserved or even resentful. It was a rare occasion when his charm hadn't begun to work after ten minutes. At every moment he followed the effect of his words on his listeners' minds. He watched conviction slowly spreading through the hearts of the little crowd he held under his magnetic sway. He knew all the rhetorical tricks to trigger off rounds of applause; and once these get going they develop into a ceaseless spate of interruptions. Sometimes, at the height of an ovation, he would indulge in the luxury of raising his hand to cut it short. He would let his voice swell, simulate anger, become scarlet in the face and bang his fist on the table. I won't describe his methods in detail. They were those of any gifted and intelligent orator, and he had them to perfection. Where he was superb was when someone contradicted him. He would give his opponent full rein without interrupting even once. He heard him through attentively, resting his forehead in his hand, taking notes; he allowed the fellow's confidence to grow, so that the latter would speak progressively louder and wind up with some fine phrases which earned a round of applause. Roberti would wait till silence was restored and then, in a very gentle, barely audible voice (warm with good will), he would refute one objection after the other. He had a close-knit dialectic and an undeniable gift for bringing out the absurdity of certain attacks. Gradually his voice would swell, the veins in his forehead would stand out, his cheeks would flush and he would end by pulverizing his adversary with scorn and sarcasm which not only rallied his audience but convulsed it with laughter. It was a splendid sight, I promise you. On such occasions he was Raimu, he was Brasseur, in other words a great actor endowed with a prodigious dramatic temperament. It is odd that he never exploited this talent on the floor of the Chamber but, so far as I know, only ever made use of it before the commonplace public that attends election meetings. Perhaps he was a bit scared of his colleagues, whereas he was completely at ease with his constituents. It is one thing to talk to people who know nothing of eloquence, and quite another to play a part in front of five hundred actors who know all the tricks of the trade and are not easily taken in.

I often went to Edouard's election meetings so I know what I'm talking about. I never found them dull. I used to go with Agnes and the boys. Thus I was in a position to feel the sort of enchantment of these halls at nighttime and the reasons why Edouard loved it all. I too fell for the yellowish glow from the weak lights, the dirty gray walls on which the teachers pin up their pupils' clumsy watercolors which all look the same and people nowadays consider as artistic expression in its purest state. I knew those strenuous evenings when three or four hundred people crammed into the hall, three quarters of them standing packed like sardines, pickled in the thick smoke from cigarettes and pipes, the whole exuding a heat fierce enough to bowl you over in the middle of January with snow falling outside. Yes, I knew all that and from where I sat I too could taste its delights. From the pleasure it gave me I could imagine what it must mean for the candidate in whose honor this festivity was arranged, who was its star turn, organizer, conqueror and beneficiary. I can still see the halls festooned with streamers, banners and electioneering posters. I can see the four or five official bouncers with their bulging muscles bursting through their threadbare jackets, parading their ugly mugs at five francs an hour. They were old friends of Roberti's, who signed them on regularly and was faithful to them. They were fond of him though they scarcely ever had any occasion to display their devotion, for it was indeed rare for anyone to try to break up the placid meetings of the Radicals and Radical Socialists. In January '56 it was more the Republican Front candidates who were given rough treatment and sometimes even beaten up. That, then, is what an election campaign is like and one can understand how politicians adore it. One can understand how they adore politics for providing them with such vivid entertainment. One can even understand the man who is perpetually blackballed but still tirelessly goes on offering himself for nomination.

I: Well, you certainly seem to know the whole thing inside out. Didn't you ever stage a little campaign on your own account, way back, in secret, in some remote district (Guadeloupe, perhaps!) and unbeknownst to your friends? I'm beginning to wonder.

HE: No, no, you needn't worry. I never do anything. I am an onlooker, I record and sometimes recount. That is my sole function in this world.

I: And what did Roberti think when he saw you attending his meetings so assiduously? Wasn't he disturbed by your presence, I mean the presence of a friend who knew him inside out and was possibly judging him?

HE: Not a bit. Far from it. To the best of my knowledge candidates love to see their friends in the hall. They are like actors; their sensibilities are heightened and they tell themselves their friends aren't judging them from the moral standpoint but more, in a sense, from that of dramatic art; that it isn't what they say that matters but their performance, their presentation, their skill in gesture and vocal inflections. Sometimes, after meetings, Roberti would say to me: "I wasn't bad tonight, eh?" exactly like an actor when one goes to congratulate him in his dressing room after a first night and finds him exhausted by having "given" everything he has. There is also the fact that, during elections, every sign of solidarity seems tremendously precious. One never stops counting up one's troops. It is a triumph every time one wins a new supporter; it is always a disaster to lose one. Lastly, remember that people are superstitious: Edouard reckoned that I brought him luck; he told me he was more sparkling when I was present.

Observing him, I discovered a secret of politics: one must never be in advance of public opinion. The public dislikes prophets; it regards them as humbugs and, when the event they have predicted comes true, it no longer remembers their predictions. At his meetings Roberti spoke like yesterday's newspaper. In this way he delighted ninety-nine per cent of his audience. Great art, to my mind—the simple great art of a virtuoso who doesn't scorn to play popular tunes on his Stradivarius for the Sunday public.

I: All this is amusing, odd and probably true, but isn't it rather beside the point?

HE: Not at all. I can't understand such a stupid objection coming from you. For Roberti love was a mortal disease. If we are to measure the extent and ravages of this disease we have first of all to take a look at the man when he was healthy. The election campaign of January '56 shows us Roberti in good health, as he was *before love*. On the other hand it isn't enough for me simply to say "Roberti was a deputy": I have to show you *how* he was a deputy, what it meant for him, what place this calling (or function) occupied in his life, in what way his mind and heart had been shaped by it. You're being unfair: you refuse to see this honorable, positive side of his character; you just look the other way. All you want to see is the stages of his destruction. I am afraid that, basically, you only feel contempt for the man. You condemn him on the strength of his transgressions; you don't take the time to develop charitable leanings toward him. In every human being one studies carefully one can detect the mighty seeds of salvation. The miserable wretch Roberti became was not just nothingness; he existed; at times he was enchanting. We are not studying insect life. Besides, I only ask for a moment's patience, for a last memento. At the '56 elections I acted two or three times as his "baron," and it was most amusing. Do you know what a baron is?

I: I haven't the faintest idea.

HE: In political slang, the baron is the candidate's stool pigeon.

I: I see. The hired idiot who asks easy questions so that the speaker can shine at his expense.

HE: Forgive me, no: the baron is far more than that. There's an art in being a baron which isn't given to everyone. The last thing he must do is appear to be a stool pigeon; his job is to contradict the candidate, so the objections he raises must never be too easy to refute. His attitude is most important, too. The virtuoso, the consummate baron (which, without flattering myself, I was!) begins by being arrogant and cantankerous. He attacks the candidate with biting sarcasm; he hurls implied insults; he poses as a superior man. In the eyes of the gathering he is disagreeable and in bad faith, like all the candidate's opponents in principle, the candidate of course being a lamb clad in guileless honesty and white raiment. As the candidate replies and explains, the baron changes his features, falters, weakens and begins to stammer. When the candidate has finished he cries: "Sir, I came here admittedly with the intention of doing you harm, but I didn't know you. I didn't know you had such sound and just ideas. You have won me over. You are really an excellent fellow. The country needs men like you. You will get my vote!" The audience is deeply impressed. It applauds fit to burst. As a rule a good baron carries fifty votes for the candidate at every meeting.

I: What tomfoolery!

HE: There are a thousand such tomfooleries in every democracy. This one has been practiced since the days of antiquity. I feel sure the election campaigns in Athens were no different from what they are in Paris today. The public is a great child, won over by any Punch and Judy show. People seeking to please children don't despise them when they spin them fairy tales; on the contrary they love them; they are out to win their confidence and friendship. I prefer the tomfoolery of democrats to the bloody tragedies of tyrants. Not to mention that tyrants, too, go in for tomfoolery. The difference is that they forbid anyone to refer to it on pain of death.

So I often went with Agnes and the boys to Edouard's public meetings, as I have said. The four of them made a charming picture. The three boys were naturally thrilled, brimming over with admiration for their father. They applauded the whole time, until their hands were quite scarlet: "Bravo! Vote for Roberti! We want Roberti! Down with the Independents! Down with the Communists!" they shouted. They booed any heckler who rose to speak. Agnes was less demonstrative but her attitude was equally touching: she devoured Edouard with her eyes; gazing proudly up at him she drank in his words even though, from having heard him a thousand times before, she knew exactly what he was going to say. She laughed at his sallies as gaily as a young girl. In short she was like a mother who never wearies of marveling at her son's exploits, who can never get over having brought such a hero into the world. After more than twenty years of marriage, Roberti impressed her as much as ever. Not for an empire would she have missed an election meeting. When he got home at two in the morning he would find a cold meal waiting for him, prepared with love. In these circumstances Agnes was the ideal wife, immaculate, discreet, admiring, full of optimism and encouragement; she surrounded her husband as far as was possible with devoted care. She backed him up in his great effort with admirable efficiency. It was at such times that Edouard saw how much she meant to him; she was his companion in the fullest sense of the word; she was the one being who shared his thoughts and his every ambition; she was his very flesh; she was himself. Compared with her his lapses, his adulteries, Solange herself meant little, so little that he didn't even feel ashamed of them: he never thought of them, they didn't exist. On the whole surface of the earth there was no other being as devoted to him as Agnes.

I: I might point out, incidentally, that you don't often mention Agnes. I am glad to see this dear creature emerging at last!

HE: I don't often mention her because there isn't much to say about her. Roberti and Agnes were a very united couple, like countless others. They hardly ever quarreled. Agnes had long since acquired the habit of looking up to Edouard. She had in him the complete faith of a devoted and happy wife. No echo of his casual affairs had ever penetrated his home. As for her character, I have already outlined it. That must do for the time being. You will see her later on, at the time of the drama, in all her grandeur, I would almost say all her glory. You, with your passion for sticking to the *subject*, should understand that she doesn't as yet play any part in it. She will appear presently; she only comes on stage in the fifth act of the tragedy.

I: What with all this, we have lost sight of the fair Solange. What has become of her? I can't help feeling Roberti didn't take her very often to the Square Saint-Lambert during January 1956.

HE: No indeed, poor thing! The '56 elections were a pretty severe strain on her. She followed them from a distance, through binoculars so to speak. For the first time she felt really excluded from Roberti's life; she saw what a minute place she occupied in this life, which was centered round Agnes, the children and his political career. She was way out on the periphery. During the two weeks of the election campaign proper, Edouard contrived to call her about every other day. At the outset she fervently longed for him to be re-elected. She felt highly honored at having a man whose photograph sometimes appeared in the newspapers for a lover. Then her interest gradually waned. She would have given anything to be for him what Agnes in fact was: the companion who saw to everything, who loved, encouraged, consoled, protected and *brought good luck*. Particularly this last. She would have loved to be Roberti's mascot, to exercise a beneficent influence on his destiny. But once the campaign started in earnest, he had withdrawn from her. He had thrown himself alone into the battle, like a man strong and self-reliant enough to dispense with any outside help. Not only did he have no need of Solange but also her presence would have embarrassed him. She had imagined he would see her fairly often, how they would meet at midnight, were it only to chat over a coffee, how he would describe to her the events of these days as to a loving confidante, how he would let her share in his hopes. Not that she cherished any ambition of giving him counsel or advice, but she would have listened to him in silence with love and admiration. She would have been the vessel into which he could pour his innermost feelings. Thus she would have *shared* in an important phase in the life of the being she treasured above all else in the world.

I: I find that rather touching.

HE: Yes, it was touching, but totally devoid of common sense. Not only were Roberti's days filled to overflowing, but also he had no wish to see Solange. He was entirely taken up with the business in hand; nothing could distract him from it. At midnight it was his friends in the party, come to speak at his meetings, whom he met in the café, together with a few faithful hangers-on among his constituents. There they would mull over the day's labors, reach conclusions, sketch out plans for the next day, discuss their opponents' chances or the setbacks they had suffered. After which Edouard went home, snuggled down in his bed and slept, if I may so put it, with "concentration." I have told you how on such occasions he was on top of his form. This meant among other things that he slept little but deeply. Five hours' sleep was worth a normal eight. At seven-thirty Germaine came into the conjugal bedroom with the toast and coffee and said "Wake up, M'sieur, the country needs you. Here are the papers." By eight-twenty Edouard was washed, shaved and fully equipped from top to toe. He had thirty appointments ahead of him, a hundred phone calls to make, two conferences at his headquarters. The days were so crammed with events that they seemed to last a century, although they were gone in a flash. It was midnight again before he had even had time to turn round, and yet he had the impression he hadn't been to bed for a month. At midnight he was as wide awake as a hare but wanted only one thing (to which incidentally he treated himself): a long confabulation with his friends, at which they cheered each other on and treated each other to hope and heroics as liberally as to beer and brandy. Sometimes they even wolfed a monster plate of sauerkraut. Sauerkraut is the sustenance of men of action.

There were days when Roberti didn't think once of Solange. She was as remote from him as some mistress he had had ten years earlier and whose name, even whose odor, he had forgotten. I think she sensed this after her fashion, that is to say in a confused and equivocal way, more physical than rational. She subsided into a mood of despondency, she felt hopelessly out of things. If only she had had no news of him at all, if only she had been able to imagine he was away and wasn't writing! But he was in the news. She knew he was living life to the full, close at hand, in a whirl of activity, and that she was completely excluded from this activity which seemed to her the most desirable and essential thing on earth. Such bouts of dejection have just as strong an effect on the mind as an actual illness. They are far more debilitating than rational depression, since they cannot be countered with logic. "He doesn't love me," she told herself. "He has never loved me. If he did, he wouldn't keep me at a distance like this. What rotten luck I have. I'm sure I could have had many boys whom I could have made happy with my love. And I had to go and fall for this one, who doesn't care."

I: A "boy" of fifty!

HE: Solange's vocabulary. Young people's vocabulary.

I: "Boy" has been synonymous with "lover" since about 1950. Etymologically, it must be a survival of the homosexual idiom fashionable in the thirties.

HE: Why no. It's been going on since the Middle Ages. All girls call their lovers "boys." It's only mature women who say "the man I love." Solange, in spite of her blossoming, her sufferings and all the rest, had still preserved many of the qualities of a young girl. At least she had retained a young girl's modes of expression.

On about the twelfth day of the campaign her heart was transfixed. As she opened a magazine which ran a feature on the election and the various candidates, a profile on Roberti suddenly leaped out of the page at her. It held Edouard up as a model family man; it described him as the best of fathers and husbands; it traced the various stages in his married life and political career. There was a photograph of him and his wife, he with his arm affectionately round her waist, she tenderly looking up at him, and also photos of the children. The article was clearly slanted but Solange, who knew no more of the world than a denizen of the Avenue Daumesnil who had never left her burrow and who, like most simple and unimaginative people, readily believed the printed word, took it all quite seriously and even as a bitter blow. She was thunderstruck. Hitherto her lover's wife and the children she had given him had been abstract notions for her. All the more in that Roberti had never discussed Agnes with her and she, from delicacy and shyness, had never dared broach this topic. The article came as a great shock. It filled her with discouragement. Her lover's life seemed to her an impregnable fortress. This life so full, so apparently happy, left not the smallest place for her. She then had a reaction which was very out of character: she began to envy and hate Agnes, which made her unhappier still. So this was the woman for whom Roberti felt more love than for herself! She, Solange, would always be vanquished by the lawful wife, whose aegis was the sacrament of marriage and who shared Edouard's life in the fullest, deepest sense. She apprehended something else from these abhorred photographs which filled her with pain whenever she looked at them: that Roberti was afraid of Agnes. And what kind of fear? The most abject: that of a man anxious not to lose the advantages he has gained. The fear of the secure and contented bourgeois. She understood all this in a flash and forgot it immediately after, as often happens with people who are not in the habit of using their brains. The truth dazzles them for a second and then withdraws, leaving no trace. They even lose all memory of its passing. What it left in Solange's heart was a dull ache without any precise shape, without features, just the feeling that there existed deep within her, at a depth to which she had never descended and never would, an explanation for this grief.

Absence of the loved one causes an intolerable anxiety in a heart that loves. With Solange, such anxiety was brought to a peak by reading this article. She had an intuition that she would never see her lover again and, as you can imagine, the age-old reaction came into play. Nothing in the world seemed more precious than to see him once more, even from afar; nothing seemed more precious than to feast her eyes one last time on those adored features, so that she could etch them into her memory forever and bear them off with her into the solitude which was henceforward to be her lot. This intuition was completely false, but love often induces such hallucinations.

ɪ: Don't tell me she went to one of Roberti's meetings?

ʜᴇ: Yes, she did. What else would you have her do? She went to the last one of the campaign. She thought there would be so many people that she would be lost in the crowd. She would conceal herself in the back row; no one would notice her but she would at least be able to see and hear for one last time the man on whose account she was suffering. She would also doubtless see Agnes, her "rival," and the three boys, for whom she felt a deep curiosity and a sort of tenderness. She was quite aware that Roberti, had he got wind of it, would have hated this step she was taking but she didn't care; she was convinced she had nothing more to lose. What did it matter whether he was angry with her or not since, whatever happened, she would never see him again? In short she acted in desperation. . . .

ɪ: I don't understand.

ʜᴇ: What don't you understand? It's perfectly clear.

ɪ: I don't understand this panic. Roberti called her every other day. She must have realized he had no time for her. Am I to conclude that she hadn't much faith in him?

ʜᴇ: Exactly. She had no faith. She had long since guessed with her instinct that he was a prize liar and she also believed he loved her as little as could be. He called her, yes, but she told herself how one day he would stop calling and it would all be over. She was sure this was how he would break with her, that is to say by quite simply running away like a coward or, rather, like a man who has a horror of "dramas." Plop! He would simply dive out of sight. The last embrace he gave her would be as burning as all the others. She would have no means of knowing it was to be the last.

Moreover Roberti's phone calls were very brief. I don't say they were terse, but remote and indifferent. Wasn't he merely telephoning out of politeness, because one owes a measure of consideration to a woman one has slept with? At the other end of the wire he would call her "darling," hypocritically complain of "having his hands full with these elections," of "working like a dog," of no longer having "any time to live"; he would apologize for being so brief and hint lewdly at the time when they could at last return to the Square Saint-Lambert; he would say with his personal affectation of speech: "I languish for you"; but Solange heard above all the undertone of gaiety in his voice which gave the lie to all these pretty phrases. She was certain he was extremely happy, with a happiness in which she had no share, and this made her literally desperate. Spending the whole day and part of the night contemplating one's love, scrutinizing it, finding in it no grounds for rejoicing but on the contrary every reason for suffering, ends by driving one mad; one loses all sense of proportion. There comes a moment finally when one can no longer sit in idleness but feels impelled to do something, no matter what, take even the most stupid and preposterous action: in a lover's eyes anything is better than inertia, passivity and solitude. The way I see it, such moral ordeals are too violent. Excessive anxieties are not good for love: instead of consolidating it they hasten its destruction. Love is not a superhuman, that is to say infinite, sentiment; like all sentiments it could if necessary be measured in terms of mathematics or physics. There is a limit to its powers of resistance. The

1956 elections dealt the first serious blow to Solange's love. Had she been less young, had she had less good will and possibly more character, had she been better versed in the world and in life, she would have broken it off. But at twenty-five one puts up with everything. The heart is as resilient as the body. One is also very tolerant. One believes one must have patience, that one shouldn't rely on appearances, that one should persevere in one's undertakings, that endurance is always rewarded.

One finds it difficult, finally, to acknowledge that one has been cherishing illusions, that one has been wrong. One strives to make true what everything around one proclaims to be false. The important thing at twenty-five is to build the future. One is unconcerned as to whether the foundations of this future are firm. I always maintain that the young are far more patient than the old or mature and I'm not wrong, in spite of the general view. Youth has endless patience which is all the more to its credit in that time, for youth, drags by with desperate slowness.

I: Hmm! You are verging on paradox. I think rather that the young are patient in theory but impatient in practice. They have a sort of second-degree patience which one might equally call hope. All right. May I have a picture of Solange at the election meeting?

HE: Well, as I've told you, she picked the final one. I was there too. Of the fifteen meetings Roberti held this was probably the most successful. There were over six hundred people packed like sardines, rippling with eddies, explosions of excitement and indignation, cheering and laughter. Roberti was particularly brilliant. He spoke like an angel. His speech was magnificently lucid, intelligent and convincing. Every two minutes he was interrupted by a huge ovation. A triumph! At one moment, I don't know why, I looked round and from where I was sitting saw an elegant figure not unfamiliar to me. It was Solange, who had managed to worm her way into the hall though the audience was blocking the doorway and even overflowing into the street!

I: What effect did it have on you, seeing her there, fifteen feet away from Agnes?

HE: Oh, you know, nothing has any effect on me. The most unexpected occurrences, the most romantic situations never surprise me. It's my nature. And as I am never surprised I keep my power of observation intact in every circumstance. That is how God made me. I am as impassive as a camera. So I saw Solange and felt no surprise at seeing her. Indeed, I was scarcely even conscious of the piquancy of the situation. Her expression was grave and inscrutable. I waited, expecting the electric atmosphere in the hall to produce some reaction; but her troubles were too heavy for her to succumb to the general enthusiasm. The more those around her shouted and waved, the more numbed by her gloomy forebodings she became.

Inwardly she compared the drama she thought she was living through with the joyous masquerade in which she suddenly found herself caught up. These two situations had nothing in common and, as I see it, she must have felt the contempt of those who are deeply unhappy for those who have no inkling of their unhappiness, the contempt of tragic figures for those tranquil beings who have never experienced tragedy. Doubtless she also felt contempt for Edouard, who looked as if he were hugely enjoying his intense activity up there on the platform, whereas her own heart was bleeding.

How different it would all have been if, instead of coming to this meeting on the sly, like a gate-crasher, she had come on Roberti's invitation! How deliriously she would have shared in his success! Mark you, she was also intimidated by all these people, by this full deployment of republican and electioneering pomp. I'm sure she never heard one word of all that was said during the meeting. What fell upon her ears was just a string of meaningless sounds. When all the speeches had been given, all objections refuted, when the final cheers had died away and the audience had begun to leave, she was seized with an irresistible impulse. Instead of getting up to go as well, she followed a group of people making for the table (consisting of a long plank on trestles) behind which Roberti presided with his fellow candidates. Agnes, the boys and I had remained seated on our bench at the back. You can imagine how carefully I was watching Edouard. I wanted to see his expression when he spotted Solange, who was the last in the line waiting to see him that evening.

I: One moment. I want you to be more precise here. "Irresistible impulse" is too vague. It doesn't mean a thing. To my mind, Solange was not in the least impelled by an irresistible impulse but felt an urge to show herself to Roberti, to prove to him by her presence that she still existed, that she was a human being and not something to be lightly cast aside. I even believe she was not wholly displeased at the thought that he would find the sight of her highly embarrassing. Or else (another possibility) she told herself he would be glad to see her, glad to know she had admired him in all his glory. In short I believe a little analysis is called for here that you have glossed over with your "irresistible impulse," which the more I think of the less I like.

HE: But you're perfectly right. Absolutely right. On reflection, one thing struck me to which I didn't attach any particular importance at the time: Solange walked up to Roberti with a very firm step, like someone who knows full well what she is doing, with no hint of the sleepwalker about her. And when she reached him she gave him a ravishing smile: she told him, so far as I could hear, something on the following lines which she had surely thought up in advance: "I simply had to congratulate you, Monsieur. You were splendid. I want you to know I shall vote for you tomorrow!" For a fraction of a second Roberti was completely thrown off balance. Seeing his mistress before him in these surroundings set his heart pounding madly. But he immediately recovered his poise. He bowed and said: "Thank you, Mademoiselle. But how can a charming young lady like yourself waste her time coming to listen to dreary political discussions? Women are really past understanding. I feel very proud to have captured your interest." As he spoke I clearly saw the glance he threw toward Agnes. I equally sensed (but this was perhaps because I knew what was going on) an instant complicity between the lover and his mistress. I saw their secret dancing before my eyes.

The faculty of divination is for me a subject of endless wonder. I may say that Agnes, alerted by some obscure intuition, looked up at Solange at the very moment when she approached Roberti and said to me half-jokingly, half-anxiously: "Did you see that? Edouard's made a conquest. And she's not at all bad, that girl, in a doll-like way. Her legs are a bit bony." Just then we were alone, she and I, side by side. The boys had left us to go and chat with the bouncers, who were sitting like four large dogs against the radiator. As you know, some remarks are merely the surface outcrop of some deeply buried thought or feeling; they are its sign, its symbol, its summary, its algebraic formula. The skilled mathematician or chemist can instantly review in his mind all the calculations comprised in a formula. Similarly, underlying the words Agnes actually spoke, I could read all the things that she left unsaid, namely: "I can understand a young and pretty girl being seduced by Edouard. With his charm, his position, his politics, the people he sees, he'd have every opportunity to be unfaithful. That would be frightful. I have reached the age of women whose husbands are unfaithful. This girl has everything to make a middle-aged man like Edouard fall in love with her. Men always tumble into the arms of girls who act as if they admired them."

I was all the more astonished in that as a rule Agnes didn't pass remarks. She was a very gentle, calm woman; far from being inclined to make sarcastic comments, she was the least suspicious, the most easygoing person you could imagine. She then lapsed into a brown study which lasted two or three minutes, during which her face clouded over.

For her these election meetings were routine, as were also the lines of voters filing up to the table after the meetings were over in order to congratulate Edouard or have a few words with him. There had been young women before, even pretty ones, in these lines. Agnes had never so much as glanced at them. But she didn't overlook Solange. Don't you dare claim, after this, that people are walled up inside themselves! The world echoes in our hearts and we only have to heed these murmured counsels, these feathers which brush our consciousness, to be well versed in all those things that can make us happy or unhappy.

Stranger still is the fact that Solange's image haunted Agnes for several days. In truth, it never actually deserted her. She confided as much to me later on. Solange had become engraved in a corner of her memory, one of those shadowy corners which are closer to the heart than the mind. I also remember something else: an hour later I can see the three of us, Edouard, Agnes and me, supping together at a table in the Café de la Régence in the Place du Théâtre-Français, to celebrate the end of the campaign. Over the dessert the conversation, which had been rather gay and lively, suddenly flagged. In an indifferent (but artificial) voice Agnes asked Edouard: "By the way, who was that luscious blonde who went up to congratulate you? She seemed to appeal to you." I distinctly saw Edouard blush. "How d'you expect me to know?" he replied. "Some voter, obviously. I can't be turning down women's votes just because they are blondes. Yes, she wasn't bad. A bit common, I thought." What do you think of this technique in lying? Is it light enough, delicate enough in touch? Just what was needed to allay a wife's suspicions. An offhand reply, with a wonderful blend of indifference and disdain. Like me, Edouard had sensed Agnes' immediate antipathy for Solange, an antipathy without reason, without bounds, since she couldn't suspect that Solange was anything but just another voter. When the scandal broke, and up to the moment when the investigation and trial undeceived her, Agnes believed that her husband's relations with Solange had begun on the night of the last election meeting of January '56, that he had seen her that night for the first time and fallen for her on the spot. She recalled the scene, that is to say the empty school hall, the yellow light, Solange's pretty smile and so on, all of which had been indelibly engraved in her mind; and she thought how she had had a genuine presentiment. When she discovered that Edouard had by then been Solange's lover for eight months it brought her an added cause for anguish, as if her misfortune were made all the greater by the fact that it had lasted eight months longer than she had thought, eight months during which she had suspected nothing whatsoever, during which her heart had given her no warning.

I: What I should like to know now is how Roberti reacted to Solange.

HE: Actually, far better than one would have expected. Once his alarm had subsided he responded to the romantic side of the situation. He was rather pleased to think she had had a chance to see him in his glory. And then he found the fact of her coming like that, unannounced, agreeably titillating. He understood all the curiosity and interest implicit in such a step. In short he felt resentful for twenty-four hours and then, since Agnes had apparently forgotten the "luscious blonde," he wasted no time in forgetting her tart questions. He told himself in the carefree way of rational men who deny all signs and portents, telepathy and second sight, that there was clearly no cause for worry. Once again he had slipped through the net. Finally Solange, without doing so on purpose, had chosen the best possible day to make her appearance, namely the penultimate day of the campaign. It was a Saturday evening. The next day, Sunday, was polling day. As you can imagine, that day was long and full. Edouard and I had gone round all the polling booths. Hour after hour he saw the pile of voting papers bearing his name diminish. An intoxicating sight! Toward five P.M. the officials greeted him with a respect which augured well. At six P.M. the polling closed and by seven the first results were out. We then raced round the various counting centers, skimming from one Town Hall to the next. A majority for Roberti's Radical list became immediately apparent. By nine o'clock, although many votes still remained to be counted, his election was assured. Notwithstanding this we were still gossiping at midnight with the mayor of the Fifteenth Arrondissement, who couldn't say enough by way of congratulation. For a successful candidate election night is an exquisite moment. He wishes it would never end. We didn't get to bed until four-thirty the next morning, after having relished every drop in the cup of happiness fate had meted out that night to Roberti.

I said Solange had chosen her day well. Indeed, from Monday on, everything had calmed down again. The time of action was over. Love then made a violent return into Roberti's heart and body. The image of his mistress, the dazzling and tender smile she had given him two days before, her perfume which had wafted over him for thirty seconds, her cover-girl elegance, the little hand he had squeezed and which she had allowed to linger briefly in his, thereby showing she had preserved her faith in him—all this finally compelled his recognition. The last traces of anger or resentment abruptly fell away to give place to one of

those outbursts of tenderness and desire which would seize him whenever he happened not to have seen her for some time. This tenderness
and desire were so intermingled that he would have been incapable of
defining what part each of them played. He realized that it was three
weeks since he had touched Solange's body, breathed in her scent or
heard her glad voice call him "my love." These three weeks, filled with
so much activity and so many words, suddenly seemed like three centuries. He wondered how he could have lived so long without his bi-
weekly stimulant, his drug, his hashish of love—for this is more or less
what Solange had become for him, both through her youth and her
ardor, which proves that at bottom and without his knowing it he had
become attached to her as one does to a prostitute. He couldn't wait a
day longer before rushing to the Square Saint-Lambert. He forced her
to leave her work at five P.M. She simulated a headache with the possibility of flu which didn't deceive Mlle. Angioletti, who even said with
a broad wink, like the understanding girl she was: "Don't worry, honey!
If the boss asks for you I'll tell him you could hardly stand. Everyone's
got colds just now." Solange was so relieved that she couldn't keep up
the pretense of her headache any longer. She burst out laughing. Angioletti then said in the pensive tones of a young woman anxious to
convey an impression of wide experience: "Really, honey, how much
softer can you get? You'd go round the world for that man. He just
has to call and you come running. You ought to keep him dangling a
bit, he'd be much nicer to you then. All men are selfish, let me tell you.
You've got to string them along a little or they don't respect you.
At any rate, don't do anything foolish."

The good little Angioletti hadn't finished with the Mignot family
that evening, for one hour after Solange's departure for Cythera she
received a phone call from Citizen Valentin suggesting that she "have
a nip" with him after the office. Not that he suddenly felt a desire to
woo her (he had taken a dislike to her since her gaffe long ago at the
Café Napolitain), but he planned to interrogate her. He too had seen
the magazine containing the article on Roberti. He had been struck by
the resemblance between this man and his sister's lover. In his heart he
already knew they were one and the same; he had sensed it intuitively
on reading the magazine, but even so he clung to a dim hope. Oddly
enough, it was the idea that Solange's lover might be a deputy which
upset him most. Not only did this man, according to the magazine,
enjoy all the possible fruits of happiness—a devoted wife, fine children
and money—but also he was *well known*. In Valentin's eyes, his fame
constituted an added offense.

I: For what reason, do you suppose?

HE: I don't know. Perhaps because he felt small and weak in the face of a man as powerful as a member of the Chamber of Deputies of the Fourth Republic could be. Perhaps also because he told himself it was really rotten luck that Roberti should have taken his sister for a mistress when he was surrounded by countesses, society women and actresses who would have suited him far better and whose true role in life was to wallow in adultery with public figures. The perversity of digging out Solange, that poor defenseless daughter of a post-office clerk! Valentin felt the hatred of the yokels of yore against the overlord who cynically made use of his *droit du seigneur*. Given that Roberti was a deputy, there could be no hope of his one day "making an honest woman of her," that is to say divorcing his wife in order to marry Solange, which would have been a possibility had he but been an industrialist or a merchant, in other words anonymous. Finally the very name "Roberti" irked Valentin on account of its Italian ring. He almost thought of him as a foreigner.

He had little difficulty in persuading Angioletti to talk; she was well-meaning and simple-minded and after two Cinzanos told him all she knew, including the mock headache. The poor little fool was utterly confiding. She was a hundred miles from imagining Valentin's Corsican character and sixteenth-century ideas. She took him for one of those brothers of our own time who are tolerant, accommodating and quite indifferent as to their sisters' virtue. She even thought it a good thing for Valentin to know everything she knew; it couldn't do anyone any harm and particularly not Solange, since in this way he would be in a better position to help her and give her useful advice. She was very surprised when, after interviewing her for three quarters of an hour, Valentin got up and walked out on her. He was scarlet in the face and frowning darkly; he wore such an expression of suffering that, for all her obtuseness, Mlle. Angioletti herself noticed it. But even this wasn't enough to make her realize the havoc her revelations had caused. She simply told herself that Solange's brother was decidedly "weird" and "a real nut," which no doubt didn't prevent him from being a nice boy. After which, slightly tipsy, she went home to set her hair—an activity which frequently occupied her, it would seem.

As for Valentin, he strode off into the icy January wind along the Boulevard des Capucines. He had such a baleful, almost wild air that passers-by turned to stare at him. He kept repeating between clenched teeth: "A fine lot, the representatives of the people! What a rotten government!" He dreamed of a successful sixth of February, with the people taking the Palais-Bourbon by storm and lining up the worthless gravediggers of France against the wall.

I: Even so, Mlle. Angioletti wasn't wholly in the wrong: your Valentin *was* a bit of a nut. Setting fire to Parliament because his sister sleeps with a deputy is going just a bit far!

HE: You obviously don't know hot-tempered people. That's the way they are. They don't set fire to anything: it's they who are on fire. So they think mad thoughts, they say whatever enters their heads. Following which their rage subsides and they are left with a great feeling of sadness. That is what happened in Valentin's heart. For fifteen minutes he was blinded by rage, it transformed his imagination into a picture by Breughel or Hieronymus Bosch; then he recovered his sight and felt deeply unhappy. So unhappy that he almost decided to stop thinking about Solange, her love life, her wretched "fellow," and wash his hands of the whole loathsome business.

I: What seems fine to me about Valentin, at least as you've described him, is this capacity for suffering. It is rare and impressive. It is no longer the way of our century. He "took part" in his sister's life the way nowadays only those who truly love take part in the life of the loved one. He was as concerned with what his sister did as if she were his wife. You can heap as much ridicule on him as you like, show him to be fat, red-faced, irascible, flitting through the dark like an owl, narrow-minded and so on, but you'll never manage to cover up this admirable trait, this trait of antiquity. Of all the characters in Roberti's story Valentin is to my mind the one with the most soul or, if you like, the one with the most generous soul, I mean a soul which never suffered for selfish motives. I suppose that at bottom his thoughts ran like this: "Solange is disgracing and degrading herself and no one can be happy in disgrace and degradation. Consequently she must be extricated from her mess, whatever ordeals have to be gone through to achieve this, including the incomprehension and hatred of the person one is seeking to save." He intrepidly interfered with what didn't concern him in the manner of a holy man for whom nothing exists— neither tact nor tolerance, neither fear of opinion nor pity—outside the salvation of his neighbor whose heart he holds as dear as his own. Clearly this doesn't make for an easy character but easy characters throng the streets nowadays. Indifference has descended on the world, which is possibly one of the sorriest aspects of our time. Twentieth-century men have become anglers who sit staring at their floats while someone drowns a few feet away. Valentin, now, was not an angler.

He was a master of wolfhounds. What did he do after Mlle. Angioletti's revelations, for such a man must have done something?

HE: He did what people do when they are impelled by violent feelings about someone: he wanted to fix this someone in space, so as to know where to reach him in case of need. He opened the telephone directory at the letter R and felt a bitter joy on reading: "Roberti, Edouard, Deputy, Rue Oudinot, Invalides 47–46."

I: And then?

HE: And then nothing. The line of print in the directory set his heart thudding, like some hideous spectacle impossible to bear a minute longer and yet which has to be borne, like certain horrors one forces oneself to watch out of a sense of duty; out of a sort of piety, too, toward one's memories or toward the dead, lest one should ever forget. Moreover in such cases our memory is implacable; one glance and we are haunted forever by what we have seen. Valentin didn't note down Roberti's address, nor his telephone number. It wasn't necessary: they would remain with him forever. He closed the directory knowing that one day he would make use of both.

I: Well, that's all very fine but the picture isn't complete. For it to be so, you must as a parallel show me Solange, the object of this cult, this passion, in her lover's arms.

HE: I was about to do so. On leaving the office at five that afternoon she literally flew. She took a taxi. Roberti and she met in a wild frenzy, thinking they could never have enough of each other, which however they finally did and even rather sooner than they had expected. This left them a little time to talk. Roberti described one or two episodes in his campaign but his companion disappointed him. She was still too elated to take an interest in things which were so remote from her love and had even come close to destroying it. Her mind was elsewhere. Roberti finally perceived this, despite the pleasure he took in describing his exploits. Solange gazed at him with burning attention like an animal one talks to which, despite its willingness, understands not a word of what one is saying. Thoughtlessly he then taxed her with the stupidest, most reckless item in the questionnaire of love: "What are you thinking about?" Solange raised herself on one elbow, looked at him pensively and replied: "You've got fine children, you know. Especially the tall one. It's amazing how closely he resembles you."

You know Stendhal's phrase: "A pistol shot in the middle of a concert." That is exactly the effect these words produced: a pistol shot in the middle of a concert of love. They shocked Roberti beyond words. In the same tone fraught at once with curiosity, passion and reverie,

Solange added: "Why do you never talk to me about your children? I'm sure I should be very fond of them if I knew them. And your wife? You've never told me anything about her. I don't even know if you love her."

There was cynicism on her part in contemplating that he might go to bed with her while continuing to love another woman. Had she realized he was using her as he would a tart, and didn't she care? This Solange, who seemed to him to burn with so bright a flame, was she then just an ordinary slut? Will you believe me when I tell you this pained him? Yes, he was pained to learn that possibly she was no purer than he, in other words that she came to terms with life. These are strange exigencies coming from a hypocritical roué and they may well provoke laughter, yet our hearts can be like that: in the midst of evil they can have these incongruous patches of delicacy! Solange, for Roberti, was at once transparent and opaque. He played on her as on an instrument of which he was the complete master; but from time to time he was amazed to hear an unfamiliar sound.

Her questioning about Agnes and the boys was something new and not a little disturbing. It was a bridge (or at least let's call it a gangplank) which this intrepid creature was throwing between his secret life and his family life. He was highly embarrassed. On the one hand he didn't wish to snub her, as he felt a great weakness for her that day; on the other hand he didn't want conversations of this nature to become an established thing at any price. He foresaw that he couldn't avoid disowning Agnes sooner or later and that would be a kind of sin. So he did what he did most of the time: he evaded the issue. He said something like: "When I am with you I can think of nothing, of no one else. You and I are something apart. Outside time, outside life," etc. You can see how it went on.

I: And was she content with that?

HE: She was always taken in by these fine specious phrases with which Roberti disguised his uncertainties. Naturally it didn't suit her purpose. She took no particular pleasure in the fact that her adventure was "outside time and life." She would have much preferred the contrary. But false poetry, pretentious and empty phrases have considerable power, especially when spoken by a man one admires. "He must be right," she thought. "I am just not *developed* enough to understand." She thought she was stupid, that she had a vulgar heart, that there was "something lacking in her," that is to say the exquisite awareness of true lovers whereby they see love in its disconcerting and fleeting truth. She was close to imagining that, in loving her outside time and life, Edouard

loved her more than she loved him—she who wanted so desperately
to penetrate all his time and all his life with her love. She believed
that at fifty one knows the secret of love while at twenty-five one is
still ignorant of it.

But lies, where the emotions are concerned, share the same fate as
bad literature: they impose themselves momentarily, so long as the fashion lasts, and then good (or common) sense resumes control and one
is astonished at the aberrations they led one into. In January 1956
Roberti was very much the fashion in Solange's heart and mind; he
was her oracle, in the same way as a student will adhere fanatically to
the flimsiest and most inept pronouncements of some second-rate writer
whom he believes to be the great thinker of his day.

To Solange's questions about Agnes and his home life Roberti always opposed a hostility and stubborn silence which wore her curiosity
out after six months. Let us be clear: the curiosity remained in her
heart but, in face of the scant success her attempts achieved, she finally
ceased to give it expression. She could see she was only tormenting him.

I: And didn't she bear him any grudge?

HE: No. She bore him no grudge so long as she loved him. Edouard's
attitude irritated her, she suffered from the way he stubbornly persisted
in concealing an aspect of his life in which she was so passionately interested and in which, had she been able to see into it, she would have
read her fate; but she didn't resent him for it. It was just one of the
obstacles of nature. She struggled against this insuperable obstacle but
bore no ill-will against nature. Her curiosity broke itself on the mystery
of her lover's private life. It was something she would never fathom.
And wasn't life compounded of things one would never know, of forbidden things, especially when one was a poor kid from the Avenue
Daumesnil, quite green, naïve and ignorant? Child as she was, Solange
had at least learned one thing: that one never gets what one desires at
the moment when one desires it. It may sometimes come later, but
then it is too late and one no longer wants it. After January '56 she
knew instinctively that Roberti would never say a word, a single word,
about his wife and children; that on this point she had ventured into
the realms of the impossible. It didn't prevent her from questioning
him several times during the ensuing months with childish persistence,
always in the provocative tone of voice of someone who knows he is
asking futile questions and feels frustrated in advance. Later, when her
love had declined, she recalled Roberti's determination never to confide anything about his family life and made what she called this lack
of trust an additional argument for breaking with him. But when one

reaches such a stage, everything serves to strengthen the decision one has taken.

I don't want to close this episode without giving you the note of irony whereby it qualifies for the human race's Great Book of Misunderstanding. When all was over, when the scandal and horror had exploded and Agnes had learned all, one of the things she said to Edouard in her anguish and indignation was this: "Ah! You must have had good laughs together over me, you and that bitch! To think of the two of you discussing me! The humiliation of it!" Roberti stood before her mute, pale, his face all crumpled by the tragedy, his thoughts miles away, his heart unresponding. This reproach made him shudder; he saw it as the height of injustice. He couldn't prevent himself from replying in a strangled voice, knowing full well that such a controversy was ludicrous compared with the immensity of the disaster: "Never! She and I never ever spoke of you!"

Up on their platform the musicians were beginning to get bored. They paused frequently between numbers. The first violin put on his scarf, although the temperature at this late hour was still as mild as when we had arrived. There was nobody left save a few belated diners at two or three tables and, from what I could see, their conversation was beginning to sag. The double-bass player went to fetch the big black case in which he interred his instrument with all the care of an undertaker. The maîtres d'hôtel were wandering slowly between the empty tables, but being extremely well trained they pretended not to see us. My companion asked for his bill, which was promptly brought to him. It had seemingly been prepared a long time back. The silence of night had descended on the Bois. I was suddenly made conscious of this from the sound of a car passing. There was no more birdsong. The last diners were chatting in undertones. As for the orchestra, it was playing its good-night symphony. Only the pianist had remained at his post. One by one his colleagues had discreetly left the platform. This piano suited such a moment to perfection. The player's fingers seemed as nimble as ever. As gently as a young girl or an old American pianist he was playing a tune of the mid-thirties whose title, twenty-six years distant, came back to me with a rush: *You Are My Lucky Star.* . . but he was playing it in his own way, with all kinds of embellishments and flourishes; he added sighs and codas; he played it through ten times over in different keys or rhythms; around this thin little melody he built up an entirely baroque and charming structure. To whom could this obscure pianist be seeking to demonstrate that he had talent and imagination? Himself, no doubt, at the close of this long evening during which he had simply sat earning his fee. He was like an army bugler at the end of a dreary day taken up with barracks duties, blowing an elaborately fantastic version of *Lights Out* so that his day should not be wholly and irremediably wasted, so that it should include its moment of pleasure

HE: Would you like us to take another jump forward in Roberti's story?

I: I wonder. I rather enjoyed the details about his political life. I was hoping you would describe the setting up of the Republican Front Chamber. The more so as 1956 was also the year, if I remember correctly, when something over fifty Poujadist deputies were elected. Fifty loudmouthed cabbage growers, dairymen, butchers and grocers in the Assembly proclaiming how they were going to knock the government sideways, saying "Pleased to meet you" and "My regards to the missus," shouting "Shut your mouth!" at members speaking on the floor, virulent against the enemies of the small tradesman (who isn't as small as all that), vulgarly quarreling as if they were at market—don't you think that deserves sketching in? The introduction of these ruffians into the Chamber, which after all is like a rather select club, must really have been something!

HE: I should like nothing better. But I must point out two things. First, that it has already been described. Look at the newspapers of the time. The gossip writers and parliamentary correspondents gave it everything they had. Second, if you start me off on that, God knows when I'd ever stop. It's exactly the sort of thing which inspires me and we should land ourselves in a fine mess as it's completely beside the point. Roberti never had the slightest contact with the Poujadist deputies. They were really too bad company. No one had any contact with them, come to that. They formed an isolated group, noisy but ineffectual. When they first descended on the Palais-Bourbon everyone was scared stiff; a fortnight later they were just a joke. These grocers were no members of the national convention. They were just buffoons.

There is also this. When the new members had been enthroned, when they had taken their seats and their lockers in the cloakroom, when the old hands had spotted and congratulated each other and the new hands had concealed their wonder under expressions of boredom, Roberti was surprised not to feel a deeper satisfaction. The compliments of his colleagues, the respectful familiarity of the ushers, all the parliamentary pomp left him for the first time in his life so cold that he asked himself: "My God, am I no longer going to find this any fun?" But a rational man doesn't dwell on such states of mind, the fruit of a fleeting melancholy and most of the time without significance. So he banished this thought from his head. But he didn't succeed in banishing it from his heart. The excitement of the election campaign had died away; its triumph brought him no pleasure. A new term of office was beginning, which was exactly like the previous ones. There would be ministerial crises and Roberti would not become a minister. Besides, he had no desire to become one. Being a minister would have been a damned nuisance: he would hardly be able to see Solange at all.

Like all weak men he had occasional fits of metaphysical discouragement. Like all weak men, I say, but also like all men not driven by a desire to achieve some vital task which they pursue without illusions, since it is but earthly and contingent, yet nevertheless with passion, energy and hope. His task, if he set himself a task at all, was a small one, three quarters of it based on egoism, its principal aim being the personal aggrandizement of Roberti. So at times he was oppressed by ideas reflecting those of Ecclesiastes: "Vanity of vanities, all is vanity." What was the point of exerting oneself? What would remain of it? His soul was not so base that he regarded making money and cutting a dash as an end in itself. That was insufficient, yet it was the only result he had procured in fifty years of living. Such, more or less, were his thoughts on the day the new Chamber first assembled. While its oldest member was making the opening speech of the session he sat dreaming with his elbows propped on his bench. He had heard these patriotic clichés a thousand times before. He counted up all the silly things which had been said on the floor since he had been a member. With how many shouts of indignation had the great chamber rung? It would have been impossible to enumerate all the passions that had electrified this place, and what now remained of these dead, forgotten, absurd passions? Nothing, nothing, nothing. Time had passed over them like a steam roller. . . .

ɪ: I have long observed that metaphysical anxiety is a great stand-by for failures.

ʜᴇ: Yes, it's their habitual justification. When one has done nothing good with one's life one takes revenge by scorning the futile agitation even though it land him a spell in the clink. As for me, I listened with deep contentment, tilting back my chair and refraining from talking. I let this old tune, deployed with such unexpected lavishness, wash over me; I gazed up at the blue foliage of the trees above my head. It was barely stirring. As if he had divined my secret tastes the pianist, after a few nostalgic capers on the keys, broke into *The Maxixe* which struck my ears at the least expected moment and woke me out of the happy and brief torpor in which I had been immersed. He had recaptured all his gusto. *The Maxixe* rang out like a march or a dazzling finale; I closed my eyes so as not to miss a note. The pianist took up the theme five times, ten times, with ever more complicated harmonies, ending with a series of chords which left as little doubt as to his intentions as those insistent, artificial and repeated chords with which Beethoven ended some of his symphonies to show that all was well and truly over, that there was nothing more to come. After which came the dry slam of the lid of the piano as he shut it down. I opened my eyes to see M. Sébastien advancing with a smile toward our table.

This smile impressed me with its cordiality. It was a smile so gentle, so luminous (not merely confined to the lips but lighting up his whole face) that for a moment I thought I could see the wise, tranquil and kindly soul of our friend in its entirety. I read his past and his future and thought—I remember this clearly—that such a man had nothing left to fear of fate, that Providence enfolded and protected him because he was devoid of even the faintest trace of malice. Of course I know one shouldn't jump to conclusions in this way—as a rule I hardly ever do—but there are certain privileged beings, places and moments which from time to time in one's life tell an amazing and true story in which one cannot but immediately believe. This is what happened to me that night with M. Sébastien. I felt a certainty that at heart he was just as his smile depicted him: an unknown great man, a philosopher out of the common run, one of those beings through whom humanity daily redeems itself unawares. He had come to say good-by. But for the lateness of the hour we would gladly have resumed our talk with him. He asked if we would like him to send a boy to hail us a taxi but we declined this invitation, feeling a desire to stretch our legs. Take a stroll round the lake, for example. The sky was as clear as it had been twelve hours earlier above the Jardin des Plantes. It wasn't black but blue; the Bois was not dark. The moonlight made the leaves shimmer. We shook M. Sébastien warmly by the hand, distributed tips to the various waiters and set out.

A walk round the lake was not a bad idea. Myself, I felt a need for movement. It was long past midnight. There were several strollers none-theless and of the most unexpected kind. As we reached the edge of the lake, near the place where the boats are stacked, we made out a fat woman sitting on an iron chair, motionless, pensive, staring at the calm water on which the ducks lay sleeping. Farther on were a couple of young people talking in the shadows; then a man with an old dog. In front of us walked three boys absorbed in a fierce but harmless dispute. Such is Paris on spring or summer nights: there is no corner completely deserted, no street down which a car does not occasionally pass. What-ever the hour, someone is still awake, someone is inhaling the night air, airing his troubles, his desires or his curiosity, seeking an encounter or solitude, indulging a need to feel the city throbbing all around him. These Parisians who had come to refresh themselves and dream, whose breathing and footsteps I could hear, imbued me, I don't know why, with a poetry which my companion shared, it seemed, since for a while we didn't speak, listening to the lapping of the lake against its banks and the swish of the sand under our feet, contemplating the black water which in the reflected moonlight looked as thick as oil, breathing in the soft scent of the trees and the smells of the lake heightened by the night. It was no longer *today*; the past rose up within us. We might just as well have been walking in the France of 1780; the passers-by were shadows; their whisperings came from the back of beyond. One gets a similar feeling wandering on a cold and gray autumn afternoon through the park of Versailles, where the landscape is exactly as it was two hundred years ago and where so many memories have imprinted themselves that one could almost believe one had lived there oneself in the old days and left there the better part of one's soul.

of the human antheap. But in the present case it's not exactly the same thing. It was nobler or, if you like, more disinterested, for Roberti had no particular setback to swallow. On the contrary he was still full of his success at the election and this should have disposed him to take a keen delight in each pleasure of the inaugural session, which merely strikes outsiders as tedious but is full of titillating details for initiates. After the inaugural speech the members gather in the lobbies to elect the president and tellers. A rather bitter (albeit hypocritical) battle always now takes place. Many people would like to be tellers, for this office entitles them to superb free apartments. Well, even the election of these officials and the maneuvering of the candidates failed to lift Edouard out of his romantic brooding. It all appeared to him trivial, unimportant, utterly absurd.

I am going into all this at some length to fix the date, to show you how Roberti first began to veer toward darkness. Now I am going to tell you a story drawn from my own memories. I was seventeen and in my last year at the *lycée*, doing philosophy. I had passed my first graduation exams quite comfortably; I had always worked in a very satisfactory way but suddenly, in spite of the subject's interest, I left off doing anything. This was because I had been seized with one of those ravenous appetites for reading which now and then come over me. I passionately devoured all the good writers: Balzac, Stendhal, Proust, Diderot, Tolstoy, Thackeray, etc., even philosophers didn't come amiss (alas, they were not those of the curriculum but Schopenhauer, Nietzsche, Plato and Spinoza!). By comparison the elementary philosophy course struck me as most insipid. And that's not all. Concurrently I had embarked on an idyll with a young lady who would certainly not appeal to me today but in whom I then saw celestial beauty, a lively wit and the tenderest of hearts. She had what I at the time thought the most beautiful name in the world: Suzanne. Whenever I had a spare moment I rushed off to meet her. We would go on interminable walks through the streets. I was shy but ardent; she loved me, she allowed me liberties; sometimes she would take me to her home when her parents had gone out. In short we had become lovers; this lasted throughout the school year. The vacation separated us forever.

ɪ: Your autobiography is very interesting, but where is it leading us?

ʜᴇ: To this. My affair with Suzanne, added to the great thoughts I was gleaning from my novelists and philosophers, had completely turned my head. I entirely lost sight of reality, which consisted of applying myself to my philosophy course, listening to the professors' lectures, writing essays and passing my second exam with honors. I had become far more of a philosopher than the *lycée* required. My thesis by and large was the following. Going to class is stupid. It serves no purpose. It is against nature. What is true and right is reading Balzac and making love with my pretty Suzanne. With her I learn far more about the human heart than I do from listening to M. Perrucheau. If you set M. Perrucheau against Suzanne, Balzac and Nietzsche, M. Perrucheau doesn't weigh very much, poor man; and that June I lamentably flunked the graduation exam.

A similar phenomenon occurred with Roberti, but for him the stakes were very different. When the Chamber reassembled in 1956 his instinct, his heart, without his being aware of it, set up Solange Mignot against M. Le Trocquer, President of the National Assembly. Oddly enough, M. Le Trocquer further resembled my professor M. Perrucheau, who was bald like him, with a square head and a hard expression. Whenever I contemplate Edouard on his bench and M. Le Trocquer on his dais, I cannot help thinking of my old philosophy class and likening the deputies of this new term to unruly students. At fifty Roberti experienced roughly the same feelings as I did at seventeen. The Assembly seemed as ridiculous to him as school did to me. He had reached one of those critical stages in life when an inner transformation takes place. Indeed, I underwent a transformation at seventeen; I precociously became a man. This revealed itself in an inability to put up any longer with school, student life, the dusty rubbish with which they stuff children's brains. In the same way Roberti at fifty reached a plateau of life; he underwent one of those cyclic revolutions which are like milestones in human existence. Was it belated? Possibly, although fifty is a very tricky age. Certain ages are more vulnerable than others: eighteen, thirty, fifty, seventy. In between, one is moderately tranquil.

To continue. I had asked your leave to take a jump forward in our story. Here it is. It is a jump of four months. In the Easter vacation of 1956 something unique cropped up in the story of Roberti and Solange, something which never occurred again. They spent ten whole days together. They lived like a genuine lover and his mistress, almost like a married couple.

ɪ: You don't say!

ʜᴇ: It happened like this. One day Roberti told her: "I'm going to take ten days' vacation." It was a parliamentary recess. She greeted this statement as if it were the announcement of a catastrophe. She hardly ever saw him, but the idea that he would be away, that for ten days there would be nothing for her, neither phone call nor excursion to the

Square Saint-Lambert, was intolerable. Roberti in Paris, however intangible, was at any rate better than Roberti vanished into the outside world. She never saw him more than twice a week but at least *she knew where he was*, which is always a kind of consolation for women. In Paris he was immersed in occupations of which she was jealous in the same way as she was jealous of Agnes, but it was a jealousy to which she had grown accustomed and the objects of it formed part of the *given world* by the same token as Roberti's eyes or the shape of his smile. Whereas the vacations, the travels and diversions of the man one loves are a mystery full of horror. What adventures would Edouard encounter wherever he was going? What women who would wean him away from her? After ten months he had retained for Solange the fascination of things one cannot understand. If you prefer, she had an "intuition" of what he was, namely a quicksand, never sure, in which love ran the constant risk of foundering if it wasn't careful; but she understood nothing of his subtleties, his lies, his procedures, his fears, his evasions, that philosophy he had of remorselessly clutching at every happiness to pass within his reach. For her, so upright and candid, life was simplicity itself. If I had to sum up her moral outlook, I would express it in the formula: "A great happiness dispenses with small pleasures." In its intransigence and exclusivity this is a feminine principle, as you can see. No man exists, I believe, for whom a great happiness dispenses entirely with small pleasures. And least of all Roberti, who was a thousand miles from realizing that he was in possession of a great happiness.

She made a great effort to appear indifferent. "I'm going to take a vacation too," she replied. "I still have a week due to me from last year." She even tried, poor child, to give these words an undertone of defiance, of bravado, to show she was a free woman. "Well, well," said Roberti very softly, with a mocking smile, putting his head on one side. "And where do you plan to go?" Solange had no idea. The mountains, perhaps, where you get the best snow in April. Suddenly she looked up and saw Edouard's smile, which was ironic, certainly, but also very benign, very gentle. Her heart began to beat wildly. Was he really going to propose taking her, Solange, on a vacation with him? She couldn't believe it and yet at the same time she was sure of it. Unexpected strokes of luck are always greeted by this mixture of certainty and incredulity which is like an explosion, a conflagration in the heart.

1: Good. Very well, then. That's enough. She is wild with joy. But that isn't what's important. What's important is to know how Roberti snatched a ten days' vacation from destiny. How did this model husband, this exemplary father get his dear wife and children to swallow such a separation? How and why? For after all, if he believed himself indifferent to Solange he wasn't lightly going to commit three or four indiscretions in a row: disrupt the traditional Easter vacation with the family, slink off with a light-o'-love, create a dangerous precedent and so on.

HE: Ah, here we enter into the realms of nuance, subtlety, shadows and the impalpable! Yes, you're right. Edouard rarely separated from Agnes and his sons. And yet this did sometimes happen. As a rule it was Agnes who nudged him into taking a few days' vacation alone. For her this was a sacrifice since she was really *attached* to him. Attached in the strongest sense; thousands of ties bound her to him. She drew daily sustenance from his presence, from his words, however insignificant, from his gestures, his way of putting on his jacket, the position of his glasses halfway down his nose, his opinions on people and events to which she listened religiously. But she believed it her duty to urge him from time to time to "get a bit of air," believed it was wise to offer him these little gifts of solitude because men, unlike women and be it only once a year, need to find themselves alone and face to face with themselves, just as some martyrs to liver complaints need to take a cure at Vichy every summer. She had also noticed that Edouard was tired and their home was not very restful. Three adolescents of the male sex, full of vigor, full of fire, endlessly squabbling, eternally asking unanswerable questions, are annihilating for a man who works hard or is at least supposed to. In short, she insisted that Edouard should go away somewhere, no matter where, by himself. Easter was the ideal time. For her part she would go to Arcachon with the children. "You'll find it fearfully dull coming with us," she told him. "You need a rest and a change. The winter has been very exhausting for you what with the election campaign. Have a change of surroundings. Go and spend ten days somewhere where you'll enjoy yourself." With the broad smile of a wife who holds undisputed sway she added: "I'll vouchsafe it to you, darling. You can go back to nature. If you're unfaithful to me, I don't want to know about it." "Vouchsafe" was one of her pet expressions! She always had a rather old-fashioned vocabulary (explainable by her provincial origins, for in the provinces words go far less rapidly out of fashion than in Paris) to whose charm I have always keenly responded.

The instant he heard this proposal Edouard thought: "Ten days with Solange!" "Thought" isn't even the word. His instinct, his body, his flesh so to speak projected this idea into his head with such force that he felt giddy, though naturally he never betrayed it. On the contrary he compelled a sour expression onto his face. "Go away all by myself? What an idea! But I haven't the faintest wish to. And where?" and so on and so forth. He was unbeatable when it came to this type of mitigated refusal, that is to say firm enough for him not to appear pleased and mild enough to induce Agnes to insist. Perfect naturalness. The striking portrait of an undecided man who is slightly tempted but not unduly, who allows himself to be overruled, who yields in order to please. Agnes knew him pretty well, as you can imagine, after spending so many years with him. She clearly saw that the prospect of a bachelor vacation was a welcome one. "How good he is," she told herself with a rush of emotion; "he's trying to make me believe he doesn't want to be alone because he knows I don't like being apart from him." And that is how people bring about their own misfortune. Edouard stood firm for forty-eight hours, during which he knew all the voluptuousness of lying, dissimulation, hypocrisy, remorse over his wife's simplicity and devotion combined with lascivious anticipation. He resisted inch by inch, vigorously putting up the feeblest of arguments and then, weary of the struggle, giving in. And Agnes, who was really a pearl among wives, rejoiced with all the purity of her heart. As a distraction, for the fun of it, she even invited Edouard to join her in hunting for somewhere for him to go; she didn't want him to hide himself away just anywhere but to select the place most likely to beguile and divert him. Cannes, Monaco, Biarritz, Madrid, Florence? She was exalted by her sacrifice. She wanted to make it even greater by some mad act of generosity. "Go to Florence, darling," she cried, "go to Italy. It's ages since you were there and you've always longed to go back. Now is your chance. It would make me so happy!"

I: Stop, stop! I'm choking. Weak spirits like mine can't stand the angel and the devil face to face for more than five minutes. Your account of this makes my hair stand on end, gives me goose flesh. I find it as disgusting as watching an operation.

HE: And yet, to be frank, there's nothing in it to make such a fuss about. Most people have horrible secret stirrings of this nature twenty times a day, but they don't admit it and the novelists, whose business it is to do so, don't either. It remains buried forever, nobody knows of it, and that is how humanity as a whole preserves some self-esteem. Every individual, knowing himself for what he is, thinks that in his way he is unique, a monster of evil inclinations. How far is one responsible for all the ugly thoughts that flit through one's mind? The soul often functions like an adding machine or a cash register. It automatically carries out emotional operations the results of which, on close examination, make the hair stand on one's head; as a rule they are of no importance, thank God. If you consider the various cogs meshing together in Roberti's soul, namely love, lust, marital devotion, the genuine desire to cause as little hurt as possible and so on, you cease to be astonished and hardly even feel shocked.

I: But what about these forty-eight hours of putting on a shameless act?

HE: That's art, finessing. Almost a game.

I: Sometimes, you know, you are amazingly indulgent. Admittedly one isn't responsible for one's fleeting ugly thoughts, as you put it, but one is for the cogs which mesh to produce them. Some people, you may have observed, control their cogs, jam them or are brave enough to change their direction. I don't even have to look very far to find one. Take me, for instance: I am visited by ugly thoughts like everyone else but not at the rate of twenty a day, I promise you. And I watch out for them as best I can. When I see one beginning to sprout I waste no time rooting it out. Sincerely and impartially, I don't believe my little soul produces more than one fleeting ugliness a week, which makes fifty-two a year. Not that this is saintliness but at least it's not unseemly for a man. And I can't be alone in this. Roberti was a rather special case of softness and complacency.

HE: Let me give you another trait, incomprehensible but true. The fact that it was Agnes who had the idea of his going away filled him with affection and gratitude toward her, and this mitigated his remorse. It is all highly complicated and I should need at least half an hour to take the machinery properly to pieces. Oh well . . . However fascinating, one can't go on about it forever.

I: Where did he go off to with Solange in the end?

HE: Italy.

I: Damn it, a regular honeymoon! And in the best tradition.

HE: You are more right than you know. They went by car. One morning at six A.M. Roberti picked up Solange, who was waiting for him on the pavement of the Avenue Daumesnil with her suitcase. It was a superb spring morning, not a cloud in the sky, the air was soft, little activity as yet in the streets, in short their departure was the greatest possible success.

I: I suppose Citizen Valentin was watching this touching scene behind the muslin curtains of his window and gnashing his teeth.

HE: I don't know about that. But what I do know is that he forbade his mother to write a single word to Solange during the whole time she was away. This incidentally was no great deprivation for Mother Mignot, who was indolent and found it an endless torture to write a letter of five lines. Solange was hurt by this since, in the midst of all her family difficulties, she had preserved an on the whole affectionate relationship with her mother.

The couple's escapade to Italy was discussed at length at Roberti's trial. Every detail of it was revealed. How they stopped at Mâcon for lunch, how they spent the night at Nice and even how they crossed the border at Ventimiglia, for that was the route he had chosen in preference to Switzerland and the St. Bernhard Pass, which would have been quicker.

I: I presume that Solange at last felt really happy? For a woman "being happy" means so much!

HE: Yes, of course. The prospect of ten days' vacation alone with Edouard seemed to her the most supreme of human joys. She was so happy that, contrary to her wont, she kept up a continuous chatter. She said whatever came into her head just for the pleasure of hearing her own voice and that of her lover replying. She had taken possession of the car as if it were a house. She had the map and the Michelin guide on her knees. To complete her happiness there was the constant reflection that she had no need to count the seconds, no call to hasten to the essential part of love; she had endless time in front of her. It was a feeling of such sweetness that the tears frequently rose to her eyes. For the first time she wasn't forced to economize with life. On the contrary life was inexhaustible; there was such a wealth of it that hundreds of moments could be squandered. That is true happiness: squandering! Now at last she held this happiness which had been so stubbornly denied her ever since she fell in love with Edouard. She contemplated the ten days ahead through her young eyes, that is to say as a long, long time during which she would have ample opportunity to gratify her frantic yearning for quietude and intimacy. One has to admire the way women are; what pleased her most was the thought that these ten days would contain utterly empty moments, that she and Roberti would often have occasion to feel as bored as an elderly couple with nothing left to say to each other, sharing nothing save their time. To be bored in the company of the man one loves—what a dream! She pictured herself sitting on the terrace of some *trattoria* in one of those beautiful Italian towns which she knew from American Technicolor movies! They sat in silence side by side, silent as carp, overcome by the torpor of living together, their minds completely empty, watching life flow drearily past. Such an evocation made her almost swoon with tenderness. She enacted the pantomime of marriage in anticipation. At moments Edouard's big hand would be placed gently over her own; she would look up at him; she would see his affectionate smile; it was the smile of a husband who forms one single being with his wife and feels no more need to make conversation to her than he does to make it to himself. Ah, what wonderful repose for the heart!

I: And what was Roberti thinking as he sat at the wheel of his car, doing a steady seventy down the road through Burgundy?

HE: Oh, with him it wasn't so simple. He was reproaching himself, of course. He must have been crazy to saddle himself with Solange! How was he going to put up with this parakeet twenty-four hours a day for the next ten days! Traveling with one's mistress is a monumental act of stupidity. One should always go alone if one can, so as to be available for whatever adventures offer themselves. He had departed from this sacred principle. By inviting Solange to go with him to Italy he had deliberately turned down in advance the favors of the pretty American he would undoubtedly have met in Siena or Florence, guidebook in hand and ripe for a bit of sex, as all American women traveling in Europe are well known to be.

Then his self-reproach abated. After all, this trip was rather fun, there was a certain spice to it. Solange's obvious joy irritated him, he felt an urge to cut it short with a few sarcasms, but on the whole he was well enough content with this joy, there was something strangely consoling about it. From time to time he would turn and look at her. She was very pretty, very young. She looked about sixteen. He felt much younger himself. To hell with parsimony: he would change his skin for ten days! He had never paid much heed to what Solange said: getting to know her young mind would have its charms. Certainly she was no intellectual, poor sweet, she had no profound views on mankind and the world but notwithstanding she was vivacious, full of good will and common sense. At fifty (and even thirty) one is curious to know what goes on in the heads of one's juniors. Indulgently one contemplates the forming of experience, the blossoming of ideas, the different outlook, the fresh thoughts, the emotional clumsiness. "All in all," his thoughts ran, "this child will take me out of myself far better than Italy could. I really know nothing about her. I shall discover her soul. At least that will provide some distraction. And if it isn't a distraction, if she bores me, I can drop her when we get back to Paris. That way the trip will be entirely beneficial." In spite of his resenting it, Solange's glad chatter slowly took hold of him, relaxed him, penetrated his stony heart. By the time they had covered a hundred and fifty miles he felt perfectly content; her presence had done its work; he had grown used to the idea of having her beside him. When they left Paris she was still a stranger; by Avallon she was a creature still mysterious but quite familiar, very close to him, with whom he had secret understandings which he shared with no other woman. By Saulieu he had reached the point of congratulating himself on having his exquisite mistress all to himself for ten whole days; she was so sweet, so compliant, and even her chatter was by no means empty-headed. With her at least he was sure of himself, he knew his sensibilities wouldn't play any dirty tricks on him.

Near Mâcon they had lunch in a sort of country house converted into an hotel where the Lyons bourgeoisie came for illicit weekends. They breathed in the first scents of spring and the river Saône. Solange was ingenuously thrilled by the place, which seemed to her the height of discreet chic, and Roberti was enchanted at her being so thrilled. It was most gratifying to have laid hands on someone so easily dazzled, someone who so enjoyed being dazzled, who had from the outset bestowed on him her unconditional admiration. He played the prince bearing off the shepherdess into fairyland, his charm further enhanced by the glamor of wealth. It's an infinitely delightful part to play, even for a man in his fifties. Above all for a man in his fifties, perhaps, for at that age one begins more or less consciously to count on one's checkbook to affirm one's power over women.

They reached Nice at nightfall. After depositing their luggage at the hotel (the Ruhl, naturally, for one night!) they dined in a restaurant on the harbor and then took a long walk down the Promenade des Anglais in a state of profound euphoria, tired by their journey, relaxed by their meal, listening to the muted lapping of the waves—*vlooff, vlooff, vlooff*—letting desire mount slowly, with their arms round each other's waist, holding each other so tight that it made walking awkward.

ı: Fascinating! But that's enough. There is something of greater interest. That night at the Ruhl. It was the first time Solange and Roberti spent a whole night together in the same bed. Quite an event. Describe it.

HE: It was also the first time Solange had spent a whole night in the same bed with any man and the first time in years that Roberti had spent a night with any woman other than Agnes beside him. The prospect did not please him. First because at his age he had certain deep-rooted nocturnal habits such as putting cotton wool in his ears; second, he was afraid of snoring; third, he told himself he would sleep very badly with Solange snuggled up in his arms. He thought apprehensively of how he would appear in the morning, yellow-skinned, unshaven, his hair tousled and a pepper-and-salt stubble on his chin. He would have to get up first, while his partner was still asleep, and meticulously wash and shave. How tiresome and complicated for a gentleman fond of his creature comforts! Again, he knew from experience that after making love he would only have one idea in his head—to flee, be alone with his body and mind released from all desire—but now he would be cornered, trapped.

For Solange it was very different. She was preparing herself for a ceremony. She was filled with a new anxiety, deeper than the anxiety of love and even different in nature. Almost a religious anxiety such as one may feel on approaching a sacred rite. She was sure she wouldn't sleep a wink that night. Nor did she wish to. She didn't want sleep, foolish sleep of which we have enough and to spare, to snatch her away from contemplation of her happiness, that is to say of Roberti lying asleep beside her in total abandon, wholly offered up to her gaze, in the full truth of his defenseless face. *She was going to see Roberti sleeping.* This was one of her heart's most steadfast desires, which she had cherished for nearly a year. She thought how she would never know him so long as she hadn't seen him asleep, how the fact of seeing her lover asleep would bring her a revelation. At the same time she would protect this sleep. Roberti in sleep would at last be a weak and defenseless being and thus moving beyond words. For the first time she wouldn't have to watch herself in his company, she could give free rein to the impulses of her love without fear of appearing ridiculous. For the first time she would truly be in possession of her lover, he would be entirely hers; she would as it were hold his soul in the hollow of her palm.

I: Well, I must say there's nothing you don't know! So that's why women always say to their lovers: "I should so much like to see you asleep"!

HE: Probably. Have you noticed how in every love story there are about twenty constantly recurring phrases? Were someone to list and seriously analyze them we would have a complete picture of love. Twenty phrases, twenty commonplaces, twenty foolish remarks everyone knows and has made sum up the human heart. Poor us!

I: And so she finally saw her darling asleep?

HE: Yes, of course, she saw him asleep and then fell asleep in turn, a sleep of the dead. If Roberti snored, which is very likely, she never heard it. The next morning there were all the delights of waking and breakfast: Roberti freshly shaved and abundantly powdered, wrapped in a sumptuous floral dressing gown (a birthday present from Agnes two years before), his feet in shining slippers; Solange half opening one eye, still warm from the night, her beautiful blonde hair streaming over her soft round cheek; the sunlight flooding into the beautiful bedroom of the Hotel Ruhl, the cars passing along the Promenade des Anglais fifty feet below, the sea wrinkled like an elephant's skin, the soft pure air drifting in through the window and faintly stirring the curtains. I shall spare you further details of this classic genre picture; you can reconstruct it at leisure in your study. I shall also spare you the departure from Nice, with Roberti distributing meager tips with all the elegance of a marquis. I shall come straightaway to the border, namely Ventimiglia, because here the plot thickens. Solange was gay as a lark but this didn't last long. You'll never guess the trick he played on her.

ɪ: I always find it difficult to imagine horrors.

ʜᴇ: When they reached the border post Solange, from an imperceptible movement, sensed that Edouard was ill at ease. And indeed he was, for he had just spotted a car with a Paris number plate, inside which he thought he recognized a distant acquaintance. She was sensitized to the nth degree where this sort of thing was concerned. On the instant she began to suffer. She had no need to watch in order to follow second by second the increasing anxiety in her lover's soul whenever, in her company, he rightly or wrongly thought he was being stared at by some bystander. Each time she felt an anguish verging on despair, for to her it was as if their love were collapsing. It wasn't so much that Roberti was ashamed of her but this abject fear which seized him and against which she was helpless cut her to the quick. Had she not so loved and admired him in other respects she would have despised him for this. She would have given anything for him occasionally to do something rash. For no reason, for the pleasure of it, as a sort of gift! Instead of which he turned into a statue. This perfect man of the world, this exquisite lover so full of delicate thoughts only a moment before, became a stranger. He became petrified, convulsed, his mouth grew pinched, he fell completely silent or else issued orders in a low and breathless voice like a warrant officer surrounded by the enemy bidding his men beat a silent retreat: "Let go of my arm. Turn your head to the left. Put a few feet between us. Try to look as if we weren't together" and so on. Anyone less simple-minded than Solange wouldn't have put up with such behavior twice running. But she went no further than dreading them as disasters and suffering from them. Sometimes she thought there was no other woman in the world with whom Roberti would have dared carry on in this way, and this gave rise to two contradictory emotions within her: it consoled her and appalled her at the same time.

ɪ: I simply can't understand this trait in his character. Such panic seems almost pathological. Here was a fairly rational man on the whole who in one particular respect behaved like a complete lunatic or at least like the victim of an obsession.

ʜᴇ: There's nothing to understand about it. That's just the way it was. If I say he had big hands you don't ask me why. Well, this terror which seized him when he saw a familiar figure looming on the horizon is the same thing. Just part of him. A psychoanalyst would perhaps explain it by a childhood trauma or something of that nature but would that get us any further? We constantly see rational men who in one particular respect act as if they were raving. Seeking the origin of the neurosis is of no interest; that's the doctors' business: they dig it out and everything is explained but nothing is solved. What is interesting is to show its effects, how it turns the life of the man so afflicted into something strange, picturesque, unique, and how his reason covers it up with explanations and justifications and to some extent assimilates it.

ɪ: All right, all right! I have the impression that right now you're pulling the wool over my eyes. You don't convince me but I must be tired, I can find no objection to raise. There must surely be one. It will occur to me later. Let's get back to Ventimiglia. Roberti must have been sorely perplexed. With Solange sitting beside him in the car there was no possible way of acting as if he didn't know her.

ʜᴇ: Yes, there was one.

ɪ: What?

ʜᴇ: Making her surreptitiously get out and cross the border on foot.

ɪ: No! It's not possible! Don't tell me he did that!

ʜᴇ: At any rate he tried. Directly he saw the car from Paris (he had an eagle eye for that) the idea took root in his mind. In an altered voice he asked Solange: "Darling, will you be very sweet? Will you do me a great favor?" She immediately understood what he was on about. Roberti was crucified; but what tortured him most was not the monstrous thing he was preparing to ask his girl friend to do, it was the thought that the passengers in the other car were possibly eying him at this very moment and putting two and two together, and how they would spread it all over the place that they had caught him red-handed on the loose with a ladylove. "Over there, three cars away from us," he continued, "are some people I know. It would be catastrophic if they saw you with me. Here is what you must do, my darling. Get out of the car quite naturally. Look, a lot of people are getting out to go and change their money or visit the customs. I'll pick you up the other side of the border. It's no distance to walk. Barely a hundred yards."

I: No, no, no! It's not possible! And the poor little fool did it? She crossed the border on foot?

HE: Well, no. For once she rebelled. She looked Roberti full in the eyes. She was deathly pale and so tense that she almost scared him, giving him a suspicion that he had gone too far. She only said one word, in an icy voice which he had never heard before: "No!" Even so he tried to quibble, to convince her, to show her how trivial it was; he accused her of "being difficult" . . .

I: That's the last straw.

HE: The imminence and magnitude of the danger stripped him of any kind of decency. It was a terrifying spectacle. He began to produce the selfish arguments of a petrified shopkeeper, to implore her, to talk of his own interests: what could it mean to her to walk a hundred yards? Less than nothing. Whereas for him the consequences of this business might easily be lamentable. After all, he was a deputy, he had his reputation to think of. But Solange was filled with an invincible determination. Before this insensate spectacle, this panic out of all proportion with its object, she only added one more thing: "I won't budge!" What is strange and shows the truly incomprehensible way in which, for us men, the feminine mind works is that at this very moment when she was putting up such a stubborn resistance her heart almost relented. "He must love me," she thought, "if he asks me to do such things!" In the end Roberti obtained one result. Realizing she would never leave the car he begged her at least to hide. So she crouched down on the floor: that way, from outside, he looked as if he were the vehicle's only occupant. His face was livid. The best part of it, as it turned out, was that he didn't know the people who had given him such a fright at all. Indeed, he saw them close up at the customs post. It was a petty bourgeois accompanied by his family, grandmamma and grandpapa included. Roberti was so relieved that he didn't even feel the desire to laugh. Fleetingly he regretted his attitude toward Solange. She was surely going to sulk for the next sixty miles or, worse, cry. What hell! Anyhow, that would be better than an unfortunate encounter.

I: Glory! One would hardly say this trip was beginning very well!

HE: Oh, in love all is forgiven. The more so since Roberti, when he took the trouble, was adept at getting himself forgiven for his little horrors. Once the danger was past he readily made fun of himself. He took the line of self-mockery. He set out to be affectionate, amusing, considerate, loving. He made jokes, he commented on the landscape of the Italian Riviera, which is far less attractive than the French one. In other words he carried on as before. But Solange had been too upset to give in so easily. She remained mute and hunched up, lost in her gloomy thoughts. She couldn't help thinking how such scenes as the one at the customs, if repeated, would end by killing the love within her. She experienced the death of this love in anticipation and it caused her the deepest pain, like the death of someone very dear.

i: Oh oh, such thoughts are dangerous! When one has them it means love is on the wane.

he: Yes, but she had no idea of this. In any case, her depression gradually fell away. What chiefly lifted her out of it, and note this as you can make an amusing comment on it, was her own good nature. After sixty miles she told herself it was really too silly to spoil this marvelous trip by gloom and bad temper; she must make an effort, "pull her weight," all sins should be forgiven, Edouard was "like that," which didn't prevent him from having all sorts of fine qualities and anyway she loved him in spite of everything. Roberti had a happy inspiration. At Genoa he stopped outside a florist's shop, got out without saying a word and came back with a huge bunch of Parma violets superbly packed in a celluloid box. This sealed their reconciliation. The prattling recommenced as if nothing had happened.

On the whole this trip to Italy, despite the dark portents of the border, was a great success. There was only one incident at Florence which I shall mention. Edouard and Solange were extremely happy nearly all the time.

i: Look, you don't have to describe this trip to me in detail, it isn't necessary. Just give me a general picture. I don't need you to paint the Italian landscape for me; I know it. Nor do I need you to show me round the museums. I've been to them, I know what's in them. What chiefly interests me is the places they visited. Their itinerary, followed by their thoughts or doings.

he: Their itinerary was very simple. They drove down to Pisa, where they spent the first night. The next morning they contemplated the Leaning Tower, the Cathedral and the Baptistery, which are particularly beautiful on spring mornings under a pale blue sky. I still retain an extraordinary memory of these three monuments myself, although it's over ten years since I saw them. They look dead. They are three white corpses standing in an empty square. And do you remember the slender columns of the Campo Santo? Like bones, they're so thin and fragile. Bleached tibias from the little legs of thousands of children massacred in the Middle Ages. From Pisa they went to Florence, where they spent three days, then on to Venice and from there back to Paris.

It's wrong of you not to let me describe these travels in Italy in detail. You'd enjoy it since, viewed from a distance and impartially by people not intoxicated with love, they are rather comic and pitiful. Roberti indulged in an orgy of pedantry. He belonged to that category of the semicultured who genuinely admire beautiful things but discuss them with absurd enthusiasm and often passing the most outrageous comments. For him Solange was the ideal prey. He applied himself to making her share his "fervor," which was all the easier in that she too was drawn by beauty. So you can imagine the number of idiotic remarks they were able to make in the museums. You can picture them gazing at the Botticellis in the Uffizi; silent, ecstatic, moist-eyed. Solange was captivated by Botticelli on sight. She declared him to be "her" painter. After which she went crazy about Mantegna. But Edouard was keeping watch. She must not stop short there; he next initiated her into the mysteries of Bellini. In the evenings they would dine on the terrace of some *trattoria*, worn out by the day's frenzied sightseeing. They ate *tagliatelli* and drank Chianti out of bottles enveloped in straw. Sometimes a guitar player would come to their table and croon a Neapolitan song.

To say that Solange was thrilled would be an understatement. For her this descent into Italy was a stupendous new world unveiled to her soul. The world of happiness, of Beauty, of *joie de vivre*, of love. Roberti was tireless and she had no less thirst than he for the sublime. Each new work of art she discovered delighted her like some wonderful gift which had been awaiting her since the *quattrocento*, which had been expressly put together for her by Michelangelo, Leonardo, Benozzo Gozzoli or someone of that stamp, toward whom she cherished a feeling of real kinship. And then there was the enchantment of never straying an inch from Edouard who was so marvelous at explaining everything, who said all there was to say, who made her see these marvels the way they should be seen. Thanks to him nothing escaped her. He increased even more in stature in her eyes. He knew countless out-of-the-way facts. His talk was an incredible blend of bathetic art criticism and humor. Solange listened with passionate attention. After forty-eight hours she was talking the same language, minus the humor.

I: It would be nice if you could give me a few examples of this jargon. Are you up to it? Could you reconstruct it in cold blood?

HE: One can always try. Thus Edouard claimed that a picture is heard more than it is seen, which didn't however prevent him from perorating, explaining how some patch of blue represented C sharp or some wash of red a diminished seventh.

I: Bless my soul! After all, it may be true.

HE: Yes, but there's nothing new about it. And by dint of listening to pictures he all but reached the point of closing his eyes in front of them. In any event, he listened to them less than to his own voice. He spoke of Carpaccio's insolence, Tiepolo's pantheism, Titian's renunciation, Giotto's asceticism. He found Veronese lightweight, not profound enough, too sumptuous to be honest; he drew a parallel—God knows why—between him and Cézanne, and poor Veronese didn't emerge any greater from the comparison. He saw in Michelangelo a "metaphysics of muscles." Naturally, like all arty people of this type, he would give the whole of Italian painting for one tiny landscape by Guardi run up in ten strokes of the brush. He said how in Tuscany "beauty comes to eat from your hand." The architectural background in some painting by Raphael was for him the exact translation of Chapter Four of Kant's *Critique of Pure Reason.*

I: Ow, ow, ow!

HE: In front of Uccello's battle scenes he claimed, with a subtle smile, that he could hear the band of the 27th Rifles blaring with all its brass and big bass drum. He flatly despised Caravaggio, far too theatrical for his taste and just about fit to paint the scenery in the Châtelet theater. To show his freedom of mind he didn't hesitate to declare Fra Angelico overrated: an old radical like him found it hard to tolerate such suavity. But Tintoretto, Cimabue, Pisanello, Lucca della Robbia, Masaccio, Filippo Lippi, Piero della Francesca! What artists! The slightest line drawn by them communicated that anguished joy, that divine swooning, that choking sensation, that embrace of things eternal! One particular exclamation frequently cropped up in Edouard's expositions: "It's suffocatingly beautiful!" I'm sorry, "exclamation" isn't quite the right word; I should have said "observation" or "objective comment." In fact he spoke these words in an at once convinced and detached tone which denoted something indisputable, accepted, obvious, like the military genius of Napoleon or the depth of the Atlantic Ocean. The whole of Italy was "suffocatingly beautiful," so that he and Solange lived in a continuous state of exaltation. They swooned in ecstasy a hundred times a day, to such a point that there were occasions when even Edouard felt jaded and, hearing Solange shamelessly capping his own hyperboles, suspected it was all faintly absurd.

I: Aha! So Solange went in for it too! It would be fun to hear some more of this.

HE: Short of being a complete Philistine, what else could she have done? Imagine a Frenchman going to London without knowing one word of English. He must at all costs learn the everyday words and expressions, and fast. So he buys a manual of useful phrases, he tries to decipher the newspaper, he bravely speaks to the bus conductors. Someone quite uncultured, flung abruptly into the world of art or science, offers a similar spectacle. The first thing for her to do, before even attempting to understand what it was all about, was to pick up the words and idioms, the jargon of the connoisseurs; she thought this language would give her the key to art, just as English gives the key to life in England.

ɪ: It's less difficult than English!

ʜᴇ: Far less! But one reaches the horrifying result that jargon, in the mouths of the ignorant, becomes superjargon. It is the caricature of a caricature. I don't believe art lovers understand much of what they say but at least they do a little; it's not totally devoid of meaning for them. Whereas their imitators who hasten to adopt all their mannerisms in order to gain entry into the community of the elect understand nothing at all. They gargle with impressive words, metaphors, enthusiasms, they get drunk on the poetico-philosophico-sentimental dialect whereby people of average intelligence express their esthetic emotions.

Solange, as I said, had admirably picked up her friend's phraseology, which seemed to her marvelous. The first day she didn't dare say very much; the second day she made timid use of a few official words of admiration; then she grew bolder with surprising rapidity. By the third day she was chatting with almost the same ease as Edouard in front of masterpieces. In this way, she thought, she was putting herself on his level. Beauty made her suffocate, too, at every turn. And this was the origin of what you referred to earlier, that is to say the manner she acquired of a bluestocking, a pedant, a miniature Madame Verdurin. By taking her with him for ten days to Italy Roberti ruined her beyond redemption. Uninformed as any daughter of the people, with her instinct intact, with her limited but honest mind, her sincere and unaffected heart, Solange was charming. Holding forth on Ghirlandaio, on Debussy's music (which bored her to death) or Éluard's poetry (of which she didn't understand a word), she certainly preserved a great deal of her charm but she also became ridiculous and, frankly, a hideous bore. Such is the gift Edouard made her. An invaluable gift in her eyes, moreover, thanks to which I suppose she will cherish a tender thought for him all her life. He will have been the man who opened her mind, who introduced her to beauty, who broke down her narrow horizon.

ɪ: In other words, out of an ignoramus he made a fool. What an illustration of modern life and "culture for the masses"! Faust educates

Marguerite. He gives her the education of the Devil insofar as he stuffs her mind with nonsense.

HE: Education of the Devil or not, they were very happy during this trip to Italy save for once, the last day they spent in Florence. They had explored the Pitti Palace and the Medici Chapel from top to bottom. It must have been five-thirty or six in the evening. The day was still very bright and beautiful. As they both felt ready to drop, they went to sit on a nearby terrace and ordered *due caffè freddi*. The delicious thing about Italy is that when you come out of a museum what you see in the street is just as beautiful as what you saw during the previous two hours. Besides, there is the sun, hot, lavish, seemingly more vital than anywhere else. So Roberti and Solange on their café terrace were in a state of perfect contentment. They had "communed with beauty," their bodies felt pleasantly weary, Edouard was expatiating about Lorenzo di Medici, unless it was Signor Niccolo Machiavelli or that dreadful Savonarola who made a bonfire of the masters' canvases as if they were so many faggots, when suddenly . . .

I: Let me go on for you because it isn't hard to guess: when suddenly who should he see before his table, looming dark against the sunlight, tall as the Eiffel Tower, smiling with outstretched hand, delighted at this chance encounter, but . . . ?

HE: Maître Noël Amouroux, a leading lawyer from Paris who also loved Italy at Eastertime.

I: Wow! Who was this Amouroux?

HE: An acquaintance. A man of his own age, who had been his comrade in the old days in law school, whom he saw every now and then; one of those people one doesn't really know at all but who are familiar, whom one keeps meeting throughout one's life as if they were distantly accompanying one to the grave.

I: In short, a pest.

HE: In the circumstances poor Edouard was completely taken aback. He turned white as a sheet. "My dear Roberti, what a pleasant surprise!" Amouroux was saying. "How delightful to meet Madame Roberti at last! The other day I was dining at Georgette Elgey's and she talked a lot about you. I had no idea you were so beautiful, Madame." Solange felt a strong desire to laugh and admittedly it was funny. But Edouard felt sick.

I: Even so, for a politician he lacked aplomb. He only had to fall in line with the worthy Amouroux. What would have been the harm in that, might I ask?

HE: There are some things people are capable of and others of which they aren't. For Roberti, being seen with Solange by somebody liable to repeat it was the worst possible horror. He was seized with panic. He was filled with the terror of a rat in a trap. I can't help it if that's the way he was. When Don Quixote launched into his tales of chivalry no one could stop him. The same went for Roberti as far as his secret life was concerned. In even the most rational, most composed of men there remains one dark corner where rationality never penetrates. The rat in the trap has only one object: to get out, escape no matter how, put as much space as possible between himself and this nightmare. Amouroux's appearance put all Edouard's thoughts to instant rout. He was seized with a mad impulse. He got up without saying a word.

I: Incredible!

HE: He fled. He ran away like a frightened soldier who deserts. That's fear for you.

I: And how did Amouroux react to his departure?

HE: Well, he was stupefied, naturally. He stared at Solange with popping eyes. She was in an impossible position, poor thing. Roberti's flight had so flabbergasted her that she too lacked the presence of mind to say something like: "My husband is rather on edge, he's been overworking lately, you mustn't mind him." Her eyes filled with tears while at the same time she was seized with a sort of rancor against the man whose cowardice let her in for such humiliations. With the most praiseworthy calm she said to Amouroux: "Excuse me, but I am not Mme. Roberti. I'm not surprised you expected me to look different." I believe the most embarrassed of the two was actually Amouroux, who didn't know which way to turn. Solange was so deeply hurt that she didn't return to the hotel for three or four hours. She walked round the streets of Florence, filled with a sadness which further enhanced the beauty of the city. She felt so unhappy that she went for a moment into the cathedral (dome by Brunelleschi, Pietà by Michelangelo) thinking she might draw some solace from it. But there were no chairs, nowhere to kneel. Nothing but American tourists chattering in undertones. And the cathedral itself was too beautiful for one to collect one's thoughts in it, especially if, like Solange, one hadn't been to church for ten years.

Back at the hotel she gloomily mounted to their room. Edouard lay stretched out on the bed fully dressed, his collar unbuttoned, his shoes unlaced, his eyes opaque, his complexion waxy. The room was dark save for a funereal light cast by the bedside lamp.

I: A nice bit of staging!

HE: It wasn't entirely staged. The incident had made him ill. He had been sick. His nervous system, which was delicate, played such tricks on him at times. His breathing was harsh and painful, so contracted was his sympathetic nerve. "Don't put the light on," he said to Solange. She was immediately touched. She ran to the bed and took him in her arms. "I wish I could die," moaned Edouard. "Be quiet," she said. "You mustn't say such things, darling."—"What happened just now was too ghastly," he went on. What was ghastly? Having been recognized by Amouroux or having run like a rabbit? Both, no doubt. But Solange took this remark as an expression of repentance. Tenderly, maternally, with unimaginable gentleness, she set about consoling him. "You mustn't let yourself get into such a state," she said. "After all, I could be anybody. I don't carry a label on my back explaining who I am." In short the matter ended as might be foreseen: these floods of tenderness cheered the piteous Edouard wonderfully. The next morning they set out for Venice singing. Never had the Tuscan landscape been so sublime: with its gentle valleys, its little round trees standing out on the hilltops against the sky and its pale colors, it seemed to have been painted by the greatest of the masters.

ɪ: Right. Spare me their stay in Venice. Spare me the gondolas, the night balmy with the smells from the drains in the Grand Canal, Guardi and Canaletto whom the excellent Edouard must have cited every three minutes, the pigeons in the Piazza San Marco, the Venice of honeymoons. Anyway I dislike Venice. Did you know Jean-Paul de Dadelsen?

ʜᴇ: The Dadelsen who died about two years ago? No, alas, I never knew him. But I often heard about him. I met him once or twice. I believe he was a splendid person.

ɪ: He was a good friend. I was very fond of him. He used to say that Venice is a Camembert cheese.

ʜᴇ: A Camembert? What an odd idea!

ɪ: Yes, an enormous Camembert, too ripe, too old, with the tourists swarming in it like maggots. A runny Camembert oozing out on every side. That's more or less how I feel about it too. So if you please, no Venice. I just couldn't take the ecstasies of Mlle. Mignot and her lover in the city of the doges. It isn't Guardi, it's Ziem. My contempt for that type of painting verges on hatred. Do you know what I'd like? One detail you have omitted and which is of prime importance. Did Roberti write to his wife? And what sort of letters?

ʜᴇ: But of course he wrote to her. Every other day. And they were charming letters full of affection, in which he resented being so far away from her and explained how Italy when one is all alone without one's Agnes "is not the same," how he only stayed away because it was sensible, because he needed a change of scene, but how he couldn't

wait to get home. He asked for detailed news of the whole household. He was worried at receiving so few letters. In fact he had found no letter from Agnes at the post office in Florence and this had rather spoiled his stay there. He vaguely wondered whether his wife, by some hideous miracle, hadn't got wind of the truth. Happily three letters were awaiting him at the post office in Venice, which testified to her faith in him and unswerving love. The dear thing had no suspicions at all. She was as tranquil as could be. These three letters contributed greatly to the gaiety Roberti displayed during the days they spent in Venice. Don't rush to condemn him: it wasn't so much the gaiety inspired by a successful imposture as that of knowing the peace of mind and heart of someone one sincerely loves, who would suffer great pain did she but know how one was capable of treating her. That is how men are; good and evil do not dwell in their souls side by side; they are closely interwoven, welded together, grafted one on the other in such a way that most often it is impossible to separate them. Thanks to Agnes' letters these days in Venice were full of enchantment for Solange: Edouard had no more weight on his heart; he was gay, blithe, amusing, considerate, as young as she and so kind that she was overcome with love for him. He gave her presents: silver bracelets, elaborate earrings, gilt leather sandals. She thought that, thanks to this trip, his love had grown, that at last she was making him happy.

I: And then one day the trip was over. They had to pack their bags, fill up the car, bid farewell to the land of Dante and return to Paris. How sad!

HE: Nonsense! You mustn't exaggerate its sadness. In the first place, I don't know if you've ever noticed but it is never sad to come back to Paris whereas it is always frightful to tear oneself away from it. While well content with his escapade, Roberti wasn't sorry its end had come. Ten days closeted with Solange were all very well but more of her would have been tedious. Her range of topics was too limited, poor child, and her chatter, which was as pretty as a twittering of birds, was often insipid. Moreover he had had her at leisure to himself. In that respect he was fully sated. A little rest wouldn't come amiss. In Paris he could relax without his prestige thereby suffering. On top of which a middle-aged man, settled in life and dependent on a whole mass of things, doubtless has many little habits and fads that he soon begins to miss when he goes on vacation and into which he is only too glad to slip once more. I shan't, of course, enlarge on the pleasure of seeing Agnes and the children again, which was great, even considerable. In the final count it was with them alone that he felt on terra firma. Any-

where else, even in Italy with his mistress, the ground was unsafe.

I: When I said "How sad!" I wasn't thinking of Roberti. I was thinking of Solange. She must have been very unhappy when they had to pack their bags. It was the end of her fairy tale.

HE: Well, yes and no. She told herself that the trip to Italy marked the beginning of a new era in her relations with Edouard, that after these ten whole days of living together things would never be as they were before. In its way, their return too was a success. Between Venice and Paris there is plenty of time for talk and Roberti didn't stint himself. All things considered, he was well enough pleased with Solange; he was pleased that she had liked his painters; he was pleased with the equanimity, the docility she had shown, the thirst to learn and "thrill to beautiful things." In truth, he felt much closer to her than ten days before. He told himself (perilous thought) that if she had the good fortune to live with him as his wife or companion he would make an accomplished young woman of her within less than a year. Her mind was qualified to understand everything. All she had lacked was a suitable mentor. She was ignorant but in no way stupid or narrow-minded. Her natural intelligence, her good will, her love would enable her to make giant strides, were anyone to trouble to open up for her a few avenues in the vast forest of culture. Sweet regrets . . . ! As he drove he recited snatches of poems by Nerval, Apollinaire, Rimbaud or Valéry. There was a radio in the car thanks to which they could occasionally relish a Mozart symphony or a melody by Fauré. Solange listened to it all with a grave and earnest air which would have made you, with your heart of stone, burst out laughing, but it gave Edouard the pure exaltation of a busy pedagogue. He told her how he would give her books and records in order to consolidate these first steps. Books and records are priceless gifts for someone like Solange, a native of the Avenue Daumesnil, daughter of a retired post-office clerk into whose home culture has never set its foot. She was just as excited as if she had been promised a diamond. Thanks to these books and records she was going to enter a new world, change her setting in a way, enjoy social promotion. Above all she would be able to exchange ideas with this cultivated and profound man. If she applied herself she would soon cease to be the dull little girl who only knew how to listen; she would be able to converse with him, she would be worthy of him; at least she would try.

I: How did the return to Agnes and the family go?

HE: As anticipated. Hugs and kisses, an account of his travels, descriptions of Florence and Venice in the spring, impressions of Italy and so on. And yet Roberti was surprised not to take more pleasure in

it. He had dropped Solange off in the Avenue Daumesnil with a tinge of regret. He had sat watching her for a long time before he drove away and had found her prettier than ever, all tousled from the journey. The Italian sun had lightly tanned her skin. Her fair hair hung quite straight; just at the roots it had resumed its natural chestnut color and she had woven it into two little plaits which were enchanting. As he left her the idea flitted through his mind that the most beautiful memory of his life was coming to an end. He had held her close with a sort of despair which he couldn't get over (in both senses of the phrase: he was amazed by it and he couldn't manage to shake it off).

He did his best to reply in detail to the happy and eager questions of Agnes and the boys but his tone was forced, he answered mechanically like someone quite indifferent, fulfilling the demands of conversation out of politeness. He was impregnated with Solange. I mean not only did his body carry traces of his mistress's scent but his soul had been infected as well. We always speak of *"esprit de l'escalier"*; we never speak of *"sentiment de l'escalier."* And yet this is one of the commonest phenomena. I would even say it is practically universal. It is almost never at the time that the heart decides or measures the extent to which it is invaded but only later on, subsequently, when the delicious or horrible moment has become that useless thing, a memory. In the case in hand, Roberti provides us with a good example. Destiny had granted him ten days of happiness and consequently all the leisure to recognize this happiness, identify it, compare it with the other happinesses his life had brought him—and not once during these ten days had it ever crossed his mind that he was happy. He was gay, enjoying himself, taking a sentimental vacation, indulging in a secret feast, an orgy of works of art and sensual pleasure, but was any of it what is customarily called happiness? No, no, certainly not! It was just the lush fruit of a skillful piece of organization on his part and foolproof precautions. The trip had been marred by two unpleasant incidents; the rest of the time he had trotted round the museums and gazed at ancient stones in the company of a young woman to whom he didn't believe himself very attached and now suddenly, after it was all over, this succession of banal activities and second-rate feelings, in comparison with the whole of his life, was transformed into a privileged interlude, a treasure of the heart. This left a taste he had never before known: the taste of ambrosia, perhaps, in the mouths of the Greek gods.

Later on, in solitude, he tried to analyze this curious state. He was forced to conclude that his will played no part in it, that this acute feeling of a happiness now past came from being deprived of this happiness, but he immediately summoned his faithful Reason, his trusty common sense to the rescue and to the best of his ability reconstructed his familiar lie: that one mustn't dwell on fleeting sensations; that his sadness at parting with Solange meant nothing, no more than his happiness at having had her all to himself for ten days on end. This sadness and happiness were physiological, skin-deep, no more far-reaching than the fits of depression one gets when tired or the gaiety induced by a good night's sleep. By the next day it would be forgotten. But the next day it was not forgotten, nor yet the day after, nor yet the following week. Roberti couldn't expel from his heart the nostalgia implanted in it by his trip to Italy.

Do you mind if we pause here for a moment? In people's lives there are hinges, moments when the door swings open and they unwittingly find themselves without a second's warning (or else warned in so obscure a way that they fail to recognize it) in another room of the sort of vast shapeless mansion of which each man's life consists. Thus they pass through thirty, fifty, two hundred rooms between birth and death. Some terminate their visit on a flat roof under the open sky, others in an underground cell into which light only filters on sufferance through a shaft enclosed by iron bars, others in a state apartment, others in a desolate shed open to all the winds. . . .

I: And so on and so forth; you needn't list any more. I'm with you.

HE: Good. Anyway it's not so much the last room in the house that interests me for the moment but the tenant's progress, the "direction of his visit," as they say in museums, the rooms through which he passes, those in which he stays for ten minutes and those in which he settles down for ten years, the great halls and the lumber rooms, the dark corridors, the unexpected alcoves. I imagine all these places as filled with pictures, frescoes, miniatures, photographs portraying the man's life, but the man doesn't see them, or doesn't look at them properly; at any rate he doesn't understand their significance while he is in the room. He only understands once he has passed into the next room, which prevents him from paying the necessary attention to the paintings there. And so it goes on to the end. Our man is always one room behind.

Since I first began talking about Roberti it seems to me he has progressed quite a long way through the mansion of his life, he has passed through a fair number of places. On his return from Italy a new door opened; he entered a new room of his inner castle. Effigies of Agnes and the children were painted on the walls, but badly, in pale colors; badly drawn as well; the features of his dear ones were no longer quite the same. They were not caricatures, but faded and insipid portraits, tarnished by time and damp, distorted, almost unrecognizable. He took no pleasure in contemplating them; on the contrary their dilapidation distressed him, pierced him to the heart. He preferred to turn his gaze to a beautiful painting, bold in coloring, rich in texture, powerfully drawn, a picture worthy of Titian or Tintoretto depicting a blonde young woman with large chestnut eyes and a modest smile, whose slightly thick neck, fair complexion, splendid bosom, rounded shoulders and pose were nevertheless so many promises or tokens of sensuality.

ɪ: Tell me, is this picture a nude?

ʜᴇ: It looks like one to me.

ɪ: Obviously it's a nude. No other possibility. But not a nude by Titian, if you don't mind. Don't bring Titian into this business. It's a nude by Bouguereau or Gérôme, a lewd and lascivious nude done by a bad painter who mixes art with pornography, a nude from the official Salon of French Artists of 1890, in other words something as obscene as the complete works of the Marquis de Sade.

ʜᴇ: Very well, if you like. It's not something I'm disposed to argue about, even though poor Edouard had fairly good taste in painting.

ɪ: Wait, though. It's not a question of painting. It's a question of his mental fantasies or, more precisely, your pretentiously poetic metaphors. Do you know what I think? Your portrait of Solange in the costume of Eve is not even Bouguereau; it's one of those pictures the old-time Americans used to hang in the saloons of the Far West depicting a sleeping woman in relief, with a rubber stomach and breasts in imitation of flesh and a mechanism inside to create the illusion that she is breathing. That is what Roberti devoured with his eyes in the eighteenth or sixty-fourth room of his life. That is what plunged him into ecstasy. He thought it was real. How pitiful and ghastly! To me it's as sinister as a midnight visit to a waxworks museum by candlelight.

ʜᴇ: Oh come, come, don't get so worked up. You've been listening to me very nicely for three or four hours. I hope you're not suddenly going to start being difficult again. Let me go along with my touch of poetry when the spirit happens to move me! Don't destroy my effects. Especially since I am certain there is basically a measure of truth in my allegory of rooms with paintings on the walls. Possibly it's a rather bold image but that is the way I see life. And during the last three years of his life Roberti often gave me the impression of a man lost in a labyrinth of corridors, plunging ever deeper into one of those strange and seedy, vast and ill-furnished palaces, the exploration of which only ends with death. I saw him wandering from room to room,

the doors creaking as he passed, himself impelled by some huge invisible
hand forcing him onward in pursuit of love—love like a bird with clipped
wings clumsily fluttering, only asking to be caught, yet one dares not
grasp it because one senses that, once caught, one won't know what to
do with it, that one will only have a single choice: either to live with
this inconvenient little creature forever or else to wring its neck. Do
you know of anything more poignant than indecision? It's the supreme
ill, whether it applies to love of God or love of a human being. The
undecided cause the worst damage because they shift from day to day.
Human monsters are most of the time merely uncertain people forced
back on atrocious behavior to alleviate situations which their weak characters have allowed to become untenable.

i: I'm sorry, but for me allegories might as well be Chinese. With
your permission I will translate your trudging through dilapidated palaces. This is how I see it (correct me if I'm wrong): after the trip to
Italy Roberti began to feel undermined by love. He continued to deny
it to himself but with less and less conviction. The fair Solange loomed
ever larger in his sight, in his soul. Gradually she began to replace the
outside world for him. That's it, isn't it?

HE: Yes, that's it, but you're going too fast. Roberti was by nature
slow to change, and the lie he carefully fostered increased his slowness
all the more. He admitted to nothing. All he recognized was the fact
that he wasn't overjoyed to return to his family after ten days' absence.
This was something new. It was the first time his family's exuberance
left him cold and even bored. During all the hugging and kissing and
questioning about his travels his mind was elsewhere. He almost dared
to think (mind you, I say "almost" and that is already a lot) that he was
happier the day before in his car, chattering about poetry and music
with his little parakeet. He felt a nostalgia for his little parakeet. A
bold-minded man would, I suppose, have drawn the natural conclusion
from such a thought, namely that he must leave his family and set up
with his little parakeet; but Edouard's mind was not bold in any sphere,
particularly not in that of the emotions. Moreover he had a sense of
duty, and a pretty punctilious one. He regarded it as a point of honor
that nothing should change in his attitude toward Agnes and the boys,
whatever the state of his heart.

i: Well, I never! By the way, you reproached me for going too fast
but what about the way you're rushing ahead! You've taken the bit
between your teeth! Have we already got as far as such thoughts with
Roberti?

HE: Ah, it's the same old problem: the difficulty of putting into words the undulating, reptilian, amoeboid movements of the soul, which swims around like a marine monster in the deepest parts of the ocean. Whatever one does, however accurate and complete one tries to be, one is constantly forced to summarize, compress and race ahead, failing which nobody understands. In a sense I am tracing you a simple graph representing dark and shapeless masses. Yes, he had already reached this stage from one point of view, but from another he hadn't yet done so. He had reached it so far as his heart was concerned but his reason wouldn't allow it. Here we are, back with our old controversy over what is in fact true. You maintain that what is true is what we are aware of and that a feeling doesn't exist if we aren't conscious of it. I don't share this view. And the whole story of Roberti corroborates my theory. He thought in a certain way and strove to make his actions conform to his thoughts; then one day he perceived that an immense change had taken place within him, at which he had never so much as deigned to glance during all the time it was going on. This intelligent man, adept since youth in introspection and psychology, continually averted his eyes from that part of his soul in which something really vital was happening.

Allow me for once to employ a pedantic vocabulary. There is an objective truth of souls and a subjective one. For Edouard the objective truth was this: ten days of complete intimacy, twenty-four hours round the clock, with Solange had woven a mass of little bonds between himself and this woman. How can I express it? He had come to suspect that a close relationship was possible between himself and another woman besides Agnes. I believe I told you how nothing reassured him so much, how he loved nothing so much as familiarity. For him this sentiment was the most powerful lever where love was concerned. Up to the trip to Italy he had come to know Solange very well (she had long since ceased to scare him, she now formed part of his daily occupations and consequently he no longer had the impression when he took her to the Square Saint-Lambert that he was committing a sin); but after the trip he began not infrequently to think he might be moderately happy with her should fate for some reason lead him to live with her permanently.

I: What reason?

HE: Oh, the sort of reasons one invents when daydreaming. For example, poor Agnes taking a train somewhere, the train being derailed and Agnes being killed. He'd be absolutely grief-stricken but one is helpless against such acts of God! Or else watching Agnes' love for him gradually decline until she asked for a divorce. And so on.

ı: Well, I must say!

HE: Don't attach any importance to these fantasies whatever you do. They didn't mean a thing. His mind was just rambling, playing a game, fooling. What surprised Roberti most during the months following his return from Italy was the increasingly marked tepidness he felt toward Agnes. Oddly enough this in no way diminished his affection for her. It was the physical side that was dying and nothing else. Not tenderness. On the contrary, sometimes when he had succumbed to the innocuous daydreams I have described he would be overcome by a terrible remorse on finding his mind turning so complacently to such fancies. He imagined Agnes suddenly perceiving that he was no longer the man she loved and who loved her, that he had become an enemy, that he perhaps wanted to be rid of her. The horror of it! He looked at her asleep in their conjugal bed and the tears all but rose to his eyes at the sight of such trust and surrender. Observing her in the different attitudes of life he was moved by her homely face, her ringlets, her vivacity and, when she was in a good mood, her cheerfulness. He trembled to think there were people who could murder their spouses. He himself would never be capable of causing this good creature any harm.

Here again, don't misconstrue these notions. There is nobody who doesn't experience similar nightmares of the mind or heart. Indeed, nightmares are exactly what they are; we are no more responsible for them, although they occur in a waking state, than we are for those which visit us when asleep. We feel remorse for the latter as well, which is hardly reasonable. Like a character in a tragedy Roberti told himself in so many words: "I love Agnes, it is my wish, it is my duty." But such exhortations are not enough to lead one back to the path of rectitude. Whatever the makers of paradoxes, popular authors and well-meaning moralists maintain, it is impossible to love two women at the same time. And this is always the way it goes, at least in our Christian and monogamous world: the new love always sucks the blood of the old, it is its vampire.

Roberti professed one unshakable principle which I would formulate thus: "The vital thing, whatever happens, is to preserve the love I have for Agnes and she has for me." Thanks to this he had managed never to love the various mistresses he had had since his marriage. A principle over twenty years old is deep-rooted. It doesn't easily let itself die. It resists the truth, the conspiracy of events, the evidence. Besides, what is the evidence? A breath of air, a revelation as fleeting and incredible as the apparition of an angel to one of the blessed. The evidence is only evident for those eyes that expect it and are ready to see it. What was the evidence after the Easter vacation of 1956? For me it was the fact that his desire for Solange, the habit of her body he had acquired over the past year strengthened by ten days of complete intimacy, had diluted, etiolated his love for Agnes, already virtually emptied of its essential substance. What preoccupied his heart? Thoughts of Solange and not of Agnes. What memories lingered in his hands, in his flesh? Memories of Solange's body. Such is the vampirism of love.

Of course he didn't think of Solange the whole time, yet she was never completely out of his thoughts; she had become part of his nature rather like a newly acquired trait of character, if you see what I mean, or some physical constraint—rheumatism or a heaviness in the limbs—which sets in one day and never leaves you thereafter. You aren't continuously aware of such things, you forget them for hours on end during the day, but they are still there; they are discreetly and permanently with you. As soon as you aren't absorbed by some task or distracted by some entertainment they reappear, make themselves felt, spread through your body. Yet Edouard never saw what was staring him in the face: that the image of Solange was superimposing itself on that of Agnes and obliterating it.

I: But *you* realized it, *you* saw everything with your eagle eye. What did you do to protect the happiness of your friend Agnes and save your friend Edouard from self-destruction? I apologize for this brutal and probably insolent question but you have to answer it since you too form a part of Roberti's story. You are one of its characters. You are a man, after all; not the eye of God dispassionately watching events on earth. Tell me, what did you do as a man of duty? You can't have remained a simple spectator, for the objective spectator of a tragedy is nothing short of the worst kind of Pharisee. I know you. You are no Pharisee. Tell me.

HE: You are right. You have touched me on a raw spot. It seems to me that I did what I could but not everything I should have done. Time and again I put Edouard on his guard, not against adultery, for his adulteries were nothing very serious, but against *love in adultery*. Time and again I tried to make him see for himself the truth that I could see. Will you believe me when I tell you I failed? There was nothing to be done. Nothing! In this respect he was the stubbornest and blindest man I've ever had to deal with. His constant reply was: "Solange is nothing. Just a diversion. I'm fond of her. She's a good girl but stupid. How do you suppose I could ever be in love with a stupid woman?" Time and again, I tell you, I returned to the charge. I was emphatic but I never dared be emotional. I didn't have it in me to adjure a man of fifty-one to renounce his girl friend, think of his family and so on, with a trembling voice and flights of rhetoric. Impossible! My fault, I see it now of course, was to have confined myself to him. I should have talked to Agnes as well. But how? I tried, I swear, to give her guarded advice; I urged her to suggest that Edouard travel more, to go away with him for three months, for instance, visit America; I explained to her that after twenty years of marriage one has to be doubly vigilant. Each time she laughed in my face. She was as sure of Edouard as of herself. She even went so far as to tell me he was a model husband, that there was none like him, that he had never deceived her and wasn't going to start doing so now, what with his growing boys, his position and the rest of it. I should have talked to Solange but I knew her so little; she would have politely told me to mind my own business; and damn it, it wasn't for me to act Armand's father in *La Dame aux Camélias* on Roberti's account! I should have talked to Valentin but I didn't know him; I should have talked to Dietz but was restrained by prudence. Finally, I confess I never foresaw that Roberti would blow the whole thing sky-high. I could only foresee two possible endings: either a divorce or a rupture with Solange, followed by a well-seasoned spell of unhappiness. But after all, who doesn't have unhappy love affairs? Sooner or later Roberti would have got over it, after three months or two years. There's my confession of guilt. Condemn me or absolve me. As far as I am concerned, I don't entirely condemn myself but I don't wholly absolve myself either. It's very difficult, you know, to cut across someone's destiny when that destiny is already three quarters accomplished. I may have the eye of an eagle, but not the eye of a prophet; it's true that when things happen I see them long before anyone else does, but even so I can't foresee them.

ı: My apologies. Forgive me for having tormented you. To begin with, it's not for me to judge you. But I do feel you did your best in this affair. Forgive me for having doubted you. Truthfully, I don't see what more you could have done, short of turning into a troublemaker, one of those odious busybodies who unfailingly provoke catastrophes which might otherwise have been avoided.

HE: There's something else I can see now, after the event, regarding the relative ease, the relative rapidity with which Solange wiped Agnes out of Roberti's heart, and this is that the process had started much earlier, long before April 1955 when he met Solange; in 1936 or 1937 in fact, at the time of his first infidelities. The way for this operation had been prepared by all the other women whose bodies or hearts he had enjoyed and who had gently, insidiously blunted his love for his wife. Such are the effects of adultery, or rather of the habit of adultery, slow but persistent like water wearing away a stone. In caressing many other women Edouard had unwittingly forgotten his wife. Even innocuous and secret adulteries such as he had always practiced are not without importance. They work in silence, they effectively pave the way for tragedy in that they lull the vigilance of the man who commits them, giving him an illusory confidence in his heart at the same time as they accustom him to the taste of other flesh.

ɪ: Did he see more of Solange after the Italian vacation?

ʜᴇ: How can you ask such a question? Haven't you understood the man at all? Right to the end he never saw her more than twice a week at the outside. Even if in his heart everything had changed, was knocked sideways and transformed, nothing had changed in his rational mind nor consequently in his habits, for with him reason always had the last word; it was reason that decided, dictating all his attitudes and actions. He had long since learned to mistrust his heart, in which he had no confidence. Can one listen to one's heart when one goes in for politics?

ɪ: Lord, yes. Why not? Lamartine did, Clemenceau too, and even Robespierre. . . .

ʜᴇ: Well, look where that got them! Clemenceau never became President of the Republic as he deserved a hundred times over, Lamartine died in penury and as for Robespierre, the guillotine! And who are you quoting, anyway? Geniuses, great citizens, poets. Roberti was not a great citizen, poor fellow. He knew his limitations more or less. And his heart, too, he knew. He had known for thirty years that he should never trust that capricious organ. Thirty years in politics had taught him always to mistrust his first impulse, and even his second or third. A man like him, who has constantly held himself in check for thirty years, molded his character in a certain way and persistently forced himself never to follow his instincts when called upon to take a decision in any sphere of life, may well be said to have changed his personality. And I might add that a personality forged with determination for thirty years is the man himself. His determination is as strong as his nature and even stronger since it changes his nature, replacing one kind of nature with another. Granted, the heart has its reasons which reason knows not. But Roberti's success (well, success in a manner of speaking) was that in the long run his heart had ended by having no reasons left: he had killed them all off through the political training he had given himself. I'm not saying he was a heartless man. He wasn't. But

454

he was a man convinced that every time it spoke his heart automatically said something foolish.

Sometimes in a closely united and albeit intelligent family there is one member who, without being a scapegoat or even a butt, is by common consent treated less well than the others. He is regarded as the fool of the family and rather looked down on; whenever he opens his mouth to give an opinion or express his feelings, to say whether he is happy or unhappy, speak of his pleasures or regrets, he is instantly cut short. "Shut up," they say. "You're just a bore."—"Here's Gustave about to say something silly," cries someone else to the world at large. Normally poor Gustave, who is a good-natured lad, takes no offense; he joins in with those making fun of him and his laughter is no less loud than theirs. But in the long run these on the whole cruel jibes (unconsciously cruel since their authors merely think they are joking or maintaining an amusing tradition)—these jibes, I say, end by making him timid and silent. The day comes when he's convinced that he really is an idiot, that every word he utters is nonsense, that for him the best course on every occasion is to keep his mouth shut. This has an effect on his character, which becomes pusillanimous. I have known one or two such families in which there was a Gustave, basically no stupider or weaker than the rest but whom the latter had made genuinely foolish and timid through their chaffing.

Roberti's heart was the same; it was tiny, atrophied and shrinking in the face of his haughty and mocking reason. His heart was Gustave the idiot with his meaningless prattle, Gustave the goon, who has been taught to be abject and has become an animal, a brute beast, as they used to say in the seventeenth century. "Gustave, go and lie down!" Roberti's heart had lain down. It played possum beneath a pile of cushions, dust sheets, blankets, eiderdowns, feather mattresses. It was like those craven souls who pull the sheet over their heads at night because they have heard footsteps in the room. They don't want to see the ghost, which is just a common burglar who'd take to his heels if he knew the bed was occupied.

No, keep quiet. Don't interrupt. I know what you're going to say: not only am I producing a shower of metaphors but I'm also repeating myself for the hundredth time. It's true. But remember that life, too, inexhaustibly repeats itself without the slightest regard for style or composition. Life harps on the same theme and we are sickened by its harping. Men are like the crows, mice, dogs, chimpanzees on which the philosophers or biologists of forty years ago used to conduct elementary experiments of practical psychology whereby they attempted to establish a theory of habit. In my young days we used to study that at the Sorbonne; it was a deadly bore. I particularly remember one wretched crow which had been taught to go and take its food from a screw of paper stuck in the ground, always in the same spot in the middle of five or six other empty screws of paper. After a few days poking about the crow would hop unerringly straight to the paper containing the food. The crow when it's at liberty, the crow prior to the psychologists of the Berlin school, is to the best of my knowledge a rather wide-awake bird. It knows among other things the meaning of a gun in a man's hand, and even the meaning of the pale glint of the winter sun on a gun barrel a mile away. Following the psychologists, the crow is an imbecile, a capon, a machine, an automaton, in which habit has replaced intelligence or, if you prefer, instinct. This crow is man, my friend, and what I've just told you—it has only now struck me—is as fine as a fable by La Fontaine. Throughout his life man prods his beak into the same screw of paper. Because he has found food in this paper once, ten or a hundred times, he believes he will find it there always. And then one day it is poison. Do you now understand what I mean when I say that life harps on the same theme? We are offered the daily spectacle of two thousand million souls in two thousand million screws of paper. During the three years his affair with Solange lasted, Roberti almost continually did the same thing. It was this selfsame thing which gave his love an original, unique form. Because of this same thing constantly repeated, this insane but logical attitude on which I too have to harp if I am to give you a truthful picture, there occurred a tragedy, an absurd tragedy, a tragedy of the commonest kind and yet least celebrated by the poets: that of failure in self-understanding, the tragedy of the man who looks aside.

"Ah! Smite your heart, it's there that genius lies!" This line of Vigny's is admirable and I for one constantly find how true it rings. Roberti is a deplorable illustration of it. He never smote his heart. Nothing but his brow, like Archimedes, every now and then crying: "Eureka!" Adventures like his are instructive; were I a priest I would describe it from the pulpit to my parishioners, to show how reason is the instrument of the Devil or, rather, the favorite door whereby he enters into men's consciences, and how the heart is the bolt with which God had provided us to close this door when need be. The genius in the heart is not only the genius of an artist creating songs of despair from his sufferings; it is for each and all of us the simple genius of life, the intuition of what is right or beneficial for ourselves and others.

While I'm about it I'm also going to explain my propensity for metaphors which you find so irritating. To begin with, it is part of my nature. We are as we are, we talk as best we can. For me it is necessary to grasp parallels in this world. One thing illuminates another. What is obscure in any particular domain becomes crystal-clear when related to another fact, another event in a different domain which appears to hold no mystery. Second, I believe that the universe contains very few combinations, very few principles, but an infinite number of different examples to illustrate these. In short, my predilection for metaphor derives, I dare say, from a sort of mathematical or Cartesian mind. With metaphors I can reduce the unknown to the known. By which token poetry is as good a method as any other (and even, to my mind, better) for solving riddles. The metaphor is my personal geometry, my private algebra. Deprive me of it and by the same token you deprive me of my means of reasoning.

Had Roberti been a great man, had they cut out his heart after his death and sealed it in an urn as they do for famous men, this urn would have been a most fraudulent receptacle. Not that it would have only contained air, but it would assuredly not have contained the real driving force of this man's life. Merely an organ like any other, no more significant than his pancreas or his spleen. Have you ever fallen in love with a woman on sight?

I: If I have, I don't remember it. Perhaps when I was very young, sixteen or seventeen. But does one really know what one feels at that age? What they call love at first sight is just an unexpected rush of desire which one mistakes for love. What about you?

HE: I, never. I don't know what it means. The story of Romeo and Juliet has always seemed to me a children's drama, comparable to those one reads about in the newspapers: a little boy who kills his friend while playing with a loaded gun; or a little girl who falls over a cliff playing hide-and-seek. Romeo and Juliet had the luck to meet the aging Shakespeare, who went wild about them and packed them full of poetry. But the essence of the affair doesn't ring true. Or rather, once past twenty, there is and can be no Romeo and Juliet.

I: Kindly explain what Romeo and Juliet have to do with it?

HE: I mentioned them because I believe the deepest and most lasting loves are those in which the lovers feel a perfect familiarity with each other. When such loves go to pieces they lead to the most genuine tragedies. Two people were welded together in the flesh, two minds were intertwined. The rupture is then like the blow of an ax ripping everything apart. I simply fail to imagine how a man can be reduced to despair on breaking with a woman he hasn't known, as it is said in the Bible that a man knows a woman, since most often the woman's heart opens up at the same time as her body. And this brings me back to Roberti. On his return from Italy he *knew* Solange at last. He had come to terms with her. She had at last won her place in his dwelling like the concubine of the Hebrew patriarch, the serving girl who supplants the highborn wife because she is young, fresh, respectful and also because she is by condition servile. During the ten days of the trip to Italy and with nothing outwardly to reveal it, the mysterious osmosis known as love had occurred. The way for this had certainly been prepared by the previous eleven or twelve months which the affair had lasted, but it hadn't actually taken place; it still might not have done so. But by the return from Italy it was complete. Roberti (don't forget it's he I am referring to, not Solange) had the vague feeling, although his thoughts continually shied away from it, that he now had more things in common with his mistress than with his wife.

ɪ: What things?

ʜᴇ: Ah, what things! They're hard to define. Imperceptible and all-powerful things, many of them having moreover to do with the senses. After all, it is taste, habit and sensual complicity, the secret rites, the allusions to some exceptional triumph, the foolish or salacious vocabulary of lovers when they are alone, the pet words and gestures, which make love something other than friendship. In a year and ten days Roberti and Solange had by dint of such things, by the attraction of their two bodies, built up between them a secret life, something which could have been studied by sociologists. Their love had a history which was their private asset; they both knew it inside out and would tell it to each other in the form of winks, for instance, or remarks unintelligible to anyone else. One night in Venice, for example, Roberti had asked Solange in their hotel bedroom to adopt the pose of Susannah in Tintoretto's famous picture, whence the expression "doing a Susannah" which Edouard would sometimes cap with "and the Elder!" while proving the reverse.

ɪ: Right. I get it. But all this is not enough to produce love. It's no more than ordinary love play.

ʜᴇ: Well, I can't give you any more positive explanation. I don't have one. But what I can assert is that the physical intimacy Roberti enjoyed with Solange had triumphed over the sentimental and intellectual intimacy he shared with Agnes; that the twenty years he had lived with Agnes barely existed any longer beside the ten days he had just spent with Solange. In true love stories one is almost always forced back on the device of Montaigne and La Boétie: "Because it was he, because it was I." Place Jacqueline Thingummy and Albert Whatsisname in the same, precisely the same conditions as Roberti and Solange. Throw in the same ingredients, the twelve months of meetings, the Square Saint-Lambert, the trip to Italy and the rest, and love doesn't blossom. Why not? Because it wasn't he and because it wasn't she. One last point. There is a mystery in the beginning of love. I mean the true beginning, the one which may for instance occur after a normal affair of a year. It's the same mystery as the birth of a flame. Why does a stick of dry wood suddenly burst into flame? I can describe the match and the phosphorus against which you rub it, I can measure the degree of dryness of the wood and so on, but the mystery of the flame remains intact. It's silly, I know, to talk of "the mystery of love," but find a better expression if you can. If I say "crystallization" like Stendhal, will you be any better off? When I ask you to reveal the secret of artistic creation, you reply: "It begins by a line of melody in my head and then I feel a desire to use half a dozen words such as 'spoon,' 'bowl,' 'hair,' 'Pegasus,' 'guerrilla,' 'pitcher plant.'" When I ask you what this line of melody means, you reply that it means nothing, that it is no more than a faint theme impossible to transcribe, which has sound and meaning only for yourself and then only inside yourself. When I ask you why this word rather than that, you reply that you have no idea, that that's the way it is. Whereupon you take paper and write a book of two, three, four hundred pages which, when finished, rings from beginning to end with the melody you had in your head at the start, into which you have inserted the pitcher plant, the guerrilla and the bowl unless you cut them out when revising the text. When you begin a book, you say—and this always astonishes me—that you have no character or plot in mind, that those are secondary and interchangeable, that what is primordial is the desire to write it and that this desire one either has or hasn't.

Well, since you are questioning me so closely about love which is also a creation, since you are forcing me back on my last defenses, I can only give you a similar reply. Artists have their secrets which they don't know themselves, of which they only have an inkling. Lovers have a similar secret they know no better; it reveals itself only through the effects it has on their hearts and actions, that is to say external effects. For the heart, in love, is still external. It envelops the secret lying deep within it like a diamond at the bottom of a leather bag or a lump of radium inside a lead box. One cannot see the diamond through the leather; no ray of radium passes through the lead. No more does the secret pierce through the heart, and you can only study love in the manner of a critic studying a text. Take the greatest critic of all, Sainte-

Beuve; what more does he do than nibble at the edges of the text he is concerned with? He traces the author's origins, sketches his biography, lists his mistresses, counts up the various stages in his career. And what then? None of these is of the slightest importance or interest. They explain nothing. Even with my own love which inhabits and enfolds me, by which I live or die with every pulse of my blood, I only see its effects as it were. It is through the effects that I am informed as to the cause, which is my secret, lying buried so deep that my intellect—that snake, that eel which slithers down the narrowest holes—still fails to reach it. A man in love no more knows the secret of his love than a poet knows the secret of his poem. Besides, once the poem is finished, once the love is ended, the same phenomenon occurs: neither the lover nor the poet can conceive, the one how he could have loved, the other how he could have written. The normal man resumes his place, the man who lives as opposed to the other, temporary monster who has created. Those are the real secrets. They belong to no one, not even to those who are their repositories. Who planted the secret of art in your soul? Who planted that of love in Roberti's heart? The expression "God alone knows . . ." here assumes its full meaning. *God alone knows* what it is all about, and He has never condescended to tell us.

I may add that, for me, nothing is so false and silly as those popular songs about the lady who spends one night of madness with a dark handsome stranger, said handsome stranger disappearing at dawn while the lady is left with an incurable ache in her heart. They are just as puerile as the story of Romeo and Juliet. For the lady to retain a bitter-sweet pang in her heart, well and good; but blank despair, no, it's rubbish, a romantic fiction for radio audiences. I only believe in love's despair when the way for it has long been paved, when the sufferer has known complete intimacy with another being, has penetrated the latter's mind through the medium of the body. And that doesn't come about in a week. Roberti's despair was prepared over three years; during this time, once love had declared itself, his mind worked in the same way as that of an artist, namely in the dark, in the subconscious, without the guidance of the will. How often have you, an artist, not told me how you think while you sleep, how some passage in a book you have wrestled over for three fruitless, floundering hours, writing the purest nonsense or things beside the point, suddenly seems as clear as daylight the next morning? Everything is then simple, everything flows spontaneously. I quote your own expression: "You coast down the slope." This unexpected facility is the reward of the night, during which your brain continued to work while you were fast asleep. Another metaphor, if I may. Roberti slept for three years and during this time his heart worked like an electric turbine.

I: Listen, you know me. I am fairly honest on the whole. Your disquisition seems to me accurate and reasonably convincing. But something doesn't fit: Romeo and Juliet. After all, they died, poor children. And before dying they had slept together. So they knew what they were about.

HE: Slept together, I grant you. But Juliet was fifteen and Romeo seventeen or thereabouts. Does one make love at that age?

I: So I've heard.

HE: Oh come! At most, you sleep together. You thrill to the feel of your partner's skin. But that's mere fumbling—primitive, clumsy, brutish and infantile.

I: Even in Verona in the fifteenth century?

HE: Exactly. Suppose we rewrite Shakespeare? The Capulets say to the Montagus: "Let's kiss and make up, and our two lovebirds shall marry." What happens? Five years later Romeo is cuckolded because Juliet meets a gentleman in his mid-thirties who teaches her real ecstasy. As for Romeo, wretched youth, trapped into marriage at seventeen, I hope you don't expect him to stick to it all his life? In the first place, all Juliet's friends are crazy about him as you can imagine, such a romantic hero! At twenty he's the father of two or three chubby *bambini* and the most notorious skirt-chaser in the Via Veneto. At thirty he keeps a superluxury courtesan who is ruining him as fast as she can and returns home drunk every evening to his *palazzo* (when he returns home at all).

I: Shut up. You revolt me. The idea of slandering Romeo and Juliet like this! You can't deny that in the end they committed suicide.

HE: Only by mistake, like two ninnies. It's a children's drama, I tell you. Or a drama of impatience. Or else a drama of stupidity. It has nothing to do with love. But then Shakespeare stepped in and men of genius set everything upside down. They can make you believe the moon is made of cheese.

I: You're quite disgusting. Nothing is sacred in your eyes.

HE: That's a good one! What about you? My ears are still ringing with your vilification of the Princess of Cleves. I can see your game. You don't know what to reply so you attack me. I needed Romeo and Juliet to illustrate the difference between true and false love. Beside that of Roberti and Solange, the love of Romeo and Juliet is like a *trompe l'oeil* painting compared with a vista of genuine stone or marble columns. Or rather, it is a poetic divertissement, a concerto, an exquisite sonata for violin and piano opening with an *Allegro gracioso* and closing with a heartrending *Andante*. We listen to it as if it were Beethoven but, once it is over and the tears are wiped away, if we reflect for two minutes we see it was just another piece of music. In spite of their suicide, Romeo and Juliet ascended to the celestial incubator for babies who die before baptism. On their arrival the angels and archangels, the Thrones and Dominions, flung wide the portals of Limbo carved out of sapphire, diamond, platinum, onyx and pearl by Rodin, Michelangelo, Phidias, Donatello, Cellini and other less exalted colleagues.

1: Even so, I should like to have written *Romeo and Juliet*. Just think! In two or three hundred years' time people would refer to the "divine Dutourd" or the "great Jean," whereas in fact where shall I be then? In Limbo, playing canasta with three other babies like myself. Because whatever you say, truth is less rewarding than poetry and vistas of genuine columns are less rewarding than a *trompe l'oeil* fresco by Raphael.

HE: Well, if these aren't grandiose ideas!

1: Why not? I've the right to dream too, haven't I? For twenty years I've worked like a beaver, writing from four to five hours a day. You make every allowance for drug addicts or sex maniacs but none at all for poor megalomaniacs like me, who console themselves with their dreams of posterity for wasting half their lives earning a meager pittance. If one metes out all one's forgiveness to one's enemies, one has none left for one's friends. Alas, will they ever talk of "Roberti and Solange" the way they talk of "Romeo and Juliet" or even "Faust and Marguerite"? This unhappy pair will never pass into the folklore of humanity. Perhaps precisely because they are too true, not sufficiently painted in *trompe l'oeil*, not distorted enough with that lovely distortion which makes works of art perfect and by means of which one attains the purest music.

HE: Oh hell and damnation! I too have credentials: weeping and wailing or gnashing one's teeth are equally cowardly. Tackle your long and arduous task with energy! Roberti and Solange are the truth about love; they are as complex as nature itself. Following which, take posterity and wring its neck. What is posterity for a man of letters? Having his name in a dictionary and being read by two thousand people a year for twenty centuries. Absurd!

1: There must be something else as well to make one long so much for this damned posterity! Right. We've wandered enough. Back to the subject. Outline, define this subject and let's stick to it to the end.

HE: I have an excellent point of reference for the end. The Fourth Republic collapsed on the thirteenth of May, 1958. This date coincided, within two to three months, with the collapse of Roberti. Poor man, his private shipwreck was swallowed up in the general one as if, infinitesimal as he was, he embodied one kind of France which was on the way out, giving place to a new France, a different nation in which there were more young men than old men or middle-aged ones. Thus the subject is two years of love.

I: One thing I'd find useful, to begin with, is a report on Solange's heart after her return from Italy.

HE: Don't be impatient! You're always asking for what I'm on the point of giving you; there's no pleasure in making you a present. I was just about to let you have this report. And it's all the more interesting, all the more pathetic, in that after Easter 1956 the identical phenomenon occurred in both mistress and lover. The phenomenon of total misunderstanding, so complete in its way that, however I try, I can recall no other example of it in any of the love stories I know. While Roberti was striving to convince himself that he wasn't in love when objectively he was showing every symptom of it, Solange on her side was striving no less assiduously to convince herself that she was in love when the process of decrystallization had already begun in her heart.

I: Already, after a year? That's pretty quick!

HE: Love almost always makes me think of those escalators in big stores: one goes up while, parallel with it, the other goes down.

I: Escalators cross halfway.

HE: Yes, but only for a second. And I wasn't there to pin down the exact moment when Roberti and Solange crossed, when their mutual love was equal. I can only show you the escalators relentlessly grinding on. Once back from Italy Solange began to think of Edouard in a different way. Naturally her memory was full of delicious times spent in Florence and Venice—pictures, *trattorias*, palaces—but she also recalled with strange insistence the two incidents at the border and in Florence. You know how events develop in the memory or, rather, how memory takes hold of events and subjects them to a sort of chemical change. Sometimes, in being worked on by the mind, they become altered, distorted; sometimes through our dwelling on them their meaning becomes dazzlingly clear and they turn into symbols. These two incidents progressed for months in Solange's soul, slowly, slowly, like two tortoises. Why these two particular ones rather than any previous incidents of the same nature? Probably because they were linked with a period of happiness such as she had never before known with Edouard. Due to them this period was not wholly perfect. Note this carefully—it is very strange. Normally one might think that on her return from Italy and during the ensuing months she would have preserved a general impression of happiness and, as a result, a wholehearted gratitude. But no, her gratitude was not wholehearted; resentment persisted alongside of it. She even came to weigh her love for Roberti. This love was changing. It was gradually assuming the features of banality. It was turning into the sober passion a young woman may feel for an aging man, a passion all too familiar and docketed, a thousand times described, a hundred thousand times experienced.

Pay careful heed, I repeat, to the way in which I am describing things. For all its slowness, it is still a swift and lucid interpretation of feelings far slower and rarely acknowledged by those concerned. I am afraid that even the most dense and teeming novel can never be more than a crude sketch compared with the life it seeks to reproduce. What wouldn't I give to be able to let you have a minute by minute description of the decline of love in Solange, the way a scientist watches a living tissue disintegrate! But men's souls are as little explored as the earth was three thousand years ago. The maps which their accredited geographers attempt to make of them are far less accurate than the ancient projections of Mercator.

There, then, was Solange, and there Roberti. One was already descending the slope of love; the other was climbing it at full speed, and neither was aware of having embarked on this irrevocable process. For the next two years each of them was to make ever-increasing efforts to maintain the initial fiction in his own eyes. This dual, identical attitude is perhaps a reflection of the fact that human beings have a horror of change, seeking to remain as far as possible the same as they have always been, never admitting that their hearts ceaselessly give the lie to their reason. They find this humiliating. Moreover in such circumstances the feminine mind is bolder (or less set) than the masculine one, and we nearly always see the woman's disillusionment precede the man's. Women persist less long in the falsehood of love and, since most of them are able to take lightning decisions, they are never chary about breaking off an affair as brutally as need be. Have you ever noticed, when reading the papers, how eight out of ten crimes of passion are committed by men? If one troubled to study these crimes through a magnifying glass one would see that in at least three cases in four the man who perpetrates them no longer loves the woman he kills or on whose account he kills. But he doesn't know this, or doesn't know it yet. The woman was three months or a fortnight or even only twenty-

four hours ahead of him. He, poor foolish murderer, was still loitering
down the flower-decked paths of habitual passion, dawdling beneath the
illusory rose arbors of sentiment, without seeing that the blooms had
withered and the roses had become hips.

One thing more, which I have already told you but must repeat in
order to pinpoint the reactions of two people as dissimilar as Roberti
and Solange, is that twelve months were a very long time for a young
woman of twenty-five . . .

I: She could well be twenty-six by now, couldn't she?

HE: Twenty-six, then, if you like. Twelve months, for Solange, were
almost a lifetime or, if not a lifetime, a considerable portion of her life.
Twelve months of love for a young woman is a love of long duration,
a love with an almost historic complexion. It is already an institution.
It is becoming a legend. It appears like a picture, a vast fresco. For a
man of fifty-one, on the other hand, twelve months are nothing. A
mere prelude, a brief encounter, barely long enough for him to feel the
first stirrings of emotion, to recognize it as such amid the clutter in his
soul where so many other emotions have already accumulated,
flourished, grown old and died, leaving skeletons or bad smells behind.
Twelve months are a day, a minute; one holds them, these twelve
months, in the hollow of one's hand; one regards them as one would
a miniature, a crude pencil sketch which may possibly develop into a
picture, but a picture it will take years to complete.

To go back to the incidents at the border and in Florence, these
would fill a large space in the fresco I have taken to symbolize Solange's
love; they would form two major details of it, given marked prominence
by the artist; two grotesque and grimacing figures near the foreground.
But they wouldn't appear at all in the sketch I have taken to symbolize
Roberti's love, which would merely consist of a few thick, wavy lines in
charcoal or crayon, barely stressed and only hinting at volume rather
than reproducing it—a few tentative lines which one would debate
whether to erase or accentuate or redraw later on, when the time came
to trace the exact outlines of the truth and *render a likeness*.

Roberti had purely and simply forgotten these two incidents, which
was after all quite natural. There's no pleasure in recalling dirty tricks
you have played under the stress of danger. You expunge them from
your memory. When you behave badly toward someone, you do one of
two things: either you forget or you bear a grudge against your victim.
Up to a point I find it to Roberti's credit that he bore no resentment
toward Solange. He had every reason for doing so. Whenever the border
at Ventimiglia or the tall figure of Amouroux chanced to cross his

mind, subjecting him to gusts of retrospective remorse, he was quick to dispel such unwelcome images. He told himself they meant nothing, that Solange had thought no more of them, that she surely had no idea of their moral portent. The fact that she was as tender and loving as ever proved it. In short he underestimated his adversary. To employ a popular expression, he "took her for stupider than she was." In other words he relied on love, which is all-forgiving and banishes whatever jars its illusions. But Solange had already ceased to love him with that kind of love.

The causes of decrystallization are very strange, I would even say disconcerting, to observe. What would appear to fortify love is what in fact begins to weaken it. Thus Roberti's Pygmalionism in Italy, his burst of fearsome pedagogic activity, had filled Solange with admiration and respect; she herself believed her love had drawn fresh vigor from the spectacle of her lover's dedicated determination to open her eyes and mind. But Roberti was no longer young enough to play this role with impunity. When one is twenty or thirty there's no danger in appearing a fount of knowledge to the girl one loves. The girl admires this in the same way as she would admire a handsome body and well-developed muscles: one is an oak to which the bindweed of love clings. But several times in Florence and Venice, or during their travels, Solange had caught herself listening to Edouard as one listens to a professor. And not just a professor. A father.

ı: So what? I don't see any cause for decrystallization in that. Three out of every four young girls have the desire to go to bed with their papas. Dr. Freud has explained it at some length. Not to mention that love and pedagogy go very well hand in hand. We already touched on this subject before with regard to Socrates, spiritual father of a number of young citizens and sleeping with them between philosophy lectures.

HE: If I remember, we also said that there was a difference in sensibility between the fifth century B.C. and the twentieth century A.D. Similarly there is a difference between Socratic love and the other kind. At any rate Solange had nothing, absolutely nothing, in common with the young prodigies of the groves of Academe. While he inspired her admiration and gratitude for undertaking her education in art and poetry, Roberti assumed in her eyes the guise, not of an old man but let's say of one considerably her senior. Besides, all that art, all that poetry and music descending like an avalanche had possibly rather fatigued little Solange's brain. It was all so sudden and such very hard going. Of course there had been sexy enough interludes in the hotel bedrooms, but these interludes themselves had a grave, almost religious connotation, since sexual license, when it leads to the wildest transports, is not exactly gay: its pleasures are all the more acute for being presided over by a touch of solemnity and sadness. In short, if Solange was happy she could hardly be said to be enjoying herself. Imagine, they didn't once go to a movie during all those ten days! She, for her part, would have very much liked to. She would have loved to treat herself to one of those ludicrously bad Italian costume movies featuring some splendid love story of antiquity. But Roberti considered they weren't there to go to the movies; they must gorge themselves as fully as possible on beauty or at least on local color.

Back in Paris, Solange felt she had grown older. She didn't precisely have an *urge for fun,* nevertheless she felt a desire in some way or other to recapture her youth. What form did this youth of hers take? How did it express itself? In helpless giggles with Mlle. Angioletti, for instance; in the songs of Yves Montand or Patachou, which she scarcely dared to hum in front of Edouard for fear of his mocking her "low-class" tastes; in outings with old girl friends from secretarial college and their young men; in visits to the movies, for she was highly addicted to the movies, especially detective stories. Finally, she had a secret: once a week she went to a dancing class in the Avenue Daumesnil, where she felt perfectly at home since it was only attended by people of her own age, from her own neighborhood and milieu. I won't discuss her family. As you can guess, a sort of *modus vivendi* had been established between her and her parents thanks to which life had become tolerable and even, at moments, pleasant. Indeed, no one can sulk forever. As a woman Mother Mignot couldn't help being inquisitive about her daughter's amours. Although the latter betrayed little of her feelings, they did have one or two heart-to-heart talks. Mother Mignot showed herself "sad but resigned." She was fairly indifferent by nature but this didn't preclude maternal love, which manifested itself in confabulations and computations and even a certain feminine complicity. Mother Mignot deplored her daughter's liaison but acknowledged it. She gave Solange idiotic advice which left them both tearful. Father Mignot, on the other hand, was an ostrich who took refuge behind his newspaper. He was well enough content now that nothing more was being openly said about it. Lastly Valentin, who was the only member of this family with a soul worthy of the name and who suffered in consequence, had taken the line of concealing his unhappiness. In short, on her return from Italy Solange in some measure slipped back into her youthful skin, for which she was thankful. She kissed everybody, including Valentin, with whom she hardly spoke any more but whom she loved as much as ever. This kiss was prettily given and prettily received. Thanks to it, brother and sister were to some extent brought together again. Both were touched. It set the seal on a reconciliation between them.

The day after her return, she felt such a longing for youth and the simple life that she did something totally unexpected. She telephoned Legay. All at once, just like that, she wanted to see this nice, amiable, uncomplicated, ignorant young man again, wanted to gossip with him, have a drink with him somewhere—perhaps at the dear old Café Napolitain on the boulevards. Six months earlier the idea of doing such a thing would have dumbfounded her, for she then found him intolerably dim and silly. But now she was discovering that, like herself, he was young. She wanted to talk to someone who loved her, for she was sure (and you know how sharp women are on this score) that he still loved her and would do so for a long time to come, sure that she had left a mark on his heart that wouldn't easily be effaced. She felt sorry for him; she thought that by offering to meet him like this she was doing him a good turn. Added to which she looked forward, not without a certain smugness, to dazzling him with her artistic culture and knowledge of French literature.

Legay naturally didn't need to be asked twice. At the appointed hour he was at the Napolitain with a beating heart but not altogether surprised, for some intuition told him that, in spite of everything, Solange was not lost to him. Their reunion was slightly strained to begin with, but the old familiarity soon returned. She gazed at his honest face almost tenderly. She was charmed by his youth, his naïveté, his lack of moodiness and even his bouts of silence. He told her all about his research into extra-thin television sets, which wasn't going so well: at this time he was still stymied by the intersecting copper wires. He let himself go at some length about it, he was fearfully boring, but for him this was a privileged day: whatever he said, no matter how deadly, Solange was determined to find it all fascinating. He discreetly inquired after her news, to which she replied no less discreetly. Touched, I say, that's what she was. Isn't it quaint? With Legay she felt on an equal footing; she even enjoyed a measure of superiority since he loved her. She treated him affectionately. She called him "my dear boy," like an elder sister or a duchess. "I'm very fond of you, Jacques," she told him. "You are my friend, aren't you? I have no men friends, yet friendship between men and women should be possible. Say you'll be my friend. We ought to meet more often."

Even the most candid of women are still monsters of falsehood: do you know what the sweet and sincere Solange dared to say to poor

Legay? "You mustn't drop me like this again." Yes, old man, that's what she said with complete naturalness, with absolute conviction. And he, poor cretin, swallowed this whopper like a fish taking a fly. The memories of those in love really do suffer the oddest eclipses: he thought that possibly it was indeed he after all who had "dropped" her. For eight months he had hardly stuck his nose outside his studio. On getting home from work he would shut himself in and wrestle with his invention, devoting every evening to it and weekends as well. He hadn't even seen his dear friend Valentin for over six weeks. He got hopelessly involved in a sort of embarrassed self-justification which Solange pretended indulgently to accept.

i: He must have left this meeting crazy with love, didn't he?

HE: No, not crazy with love but filled with hope, filled with joy. Besides, men (particularly young ones) take everything at face value. Solange had used the word "friend"; in his heart of hearts Legay dared go no further than that. To be Solange's friend was rather chilling, no doubt, but it was better than nothing. From friendship they would in time pass to love, and there he would be on his own ground. He could see in his heart treasures which had never yet been laid out but which would be one day, for Solange. Through the channel of friendship he would filter a little of the love that was choking him. It would take time but he was in no hurry. His invention kept him company like a mother. This invention over which he had struggled for so many months, and was still to struggle for a long time to come, had further taught him that miracles don't exist, that we only get what we want through ceaseless toil and a determination constantly focused on the one object. When Solange arranged this unexpected date at the Café Napolitain he had taken care to stifle the absurd hope that she would fall straightaway into his arms. He knew it was just a matter of renewing old ties. But it was the first in a long series of steps which would lead him, he was quite certain, to a grand sentimental finale.

In one way this meeting brought him luck. A long talk with the object of one's passion produces an effect comparable to that of benzedrine or a pep pill. On leaving Mlle. Mignot, Legay's mind felt wonderfully light; thanks to this sudden eruption of love after eight months of arid labor, his brain was in such a turmoil that a vital point concerning extra-thin television sets came clear to him without more ado: copper was too coarse a material for constructing the network of the screen. It was platinum he needed. Why hadn't he thought of it before? That's what comes of having one's nose pressed too close to one's work: one fails to see the obvious. Platinum! He would buy platinum. But how?

Where was the money to come from? Hell, that was a minor problem. He would draw up the strictest budget, he wouldn't spend a penny more than he need. He would live on pickled herrings and spaghetti, he would wear his suits till they fell in rags, he would go without everything. He hadn't felt so joyful for a long time.

1: Poor Legay! He's not a man of our time any more than Valentin. In his place, any other young man would have begun by taking out a patent: then he'd have called on all the leading television manufacturers to obtain financial backing and, as the economists say, "outlets." Instead of which he stayed in his burrow, slaving like an artist who knows nothing beyond his own inner world.

HE: Yes, there you put your finger on one of my oldest theories. I believe that the majority of men are convinced they are alone in the world. They are unaware of the existence of a *community* of great usefulness, which functions like a machine provided one understands the controls. No one has ever told them. No one (especially not their parents) has ever taken the trouble to give them a general picture of the resources offered by the world. I once knew an old fellow who never went to court in his life and often let himself be fleeced because he didn't know the existence of a legal system whose purpose is, in principle, to protect honest men against rogues. He was equally ignorant of the existence of solicitors, lawyers and notaries. Well, when I say ignorant, don't take me too literally. He wasn't entirely unaware of them but he didn't know how to get in touch with a solicitor nor exactly what solicitors are for. He thought his own good sense and the justice of his cause would always provide him with adequate protection from disaster. It seems incredible but I swear there are millions of people in the same position. Some of them don't even send for the doctor and let themselves die because they don't realize that medicine has progressed since the days of the clyster and the cupping glass.

Legay belonged to the category of social marmot typified less by ignorance than by lack of imagination. He certainly had a touch of genius in his own sphere but no kind of talent in any other; considerable ability and no experience of life. Whence the deep obscurity from which he has never emerged despite his truly remarkable discovery. In one sense there is something touching about this childishness vis-à-vis the world. Just as there are ill-starred poets, so there are ill-starred engineers. One could list Legay under this heading, with the proviso that one can be ill-starred without necessarily being unhappy. Legay found happiness down a different road from the one on which he first set out. Fundamentally, I think, he wasn't genuinely creative but just accidentally so. You know Vigny's definition: Genius consists of fulfilling in one's maturity a great idea of one's youth. Legay fulfilled the great idea of his youth when he was young and then it was over. His invention perfected, sold and lost to him, he turned to love and with requited, happy, uneventful love he remained; he became a kind husband and a good father. He had "responsibilities." By an odd coincidence, so long as he was a friend of Valentin's he was a man of another age, as if his comrade's turbulent and ancient soul exerted some mysterious influence over him. But when Valentin was no longer there to infect him so strangely with his dark passions, he reverted to being a little man of our time, harried by the countless absurd preoccupations which form the inescapable counterpoint to happiness in the twentieth century: income-tax returns, a fixed monthly salary, children to be clothed and educated, the steady rise in the price of vegetables, national-insurance contributions and so on. How old is he today? Thirty plus. Obviously one can't predetermine the fate of one still so young, but I would bet my last penny that his fine invention of extra-thin television sets will remain something unique in his existence, that for the rest of his life he will be a sort of *veteran of Genius*, to coin a phrase, and that when he is seventy and retired he will nostalgically look back on the great achievement of his youth, never subsequently repeated. You see, the truly ill-starred artist is not the one who dies in penury and despair after producing a mass of unappreciated works during a lifetime of misery; he is the man like Legay who, just when his talent blossoms, finds happiness and succumbs to temptation. How strange Solange's fate has been: this gentle, basically good girl will have been the evil genius of two men. In contrasting ways she will have caused the downfall of them both. I am going to say something which you may not understand right away but which will become clear later on: she behaved with Legay as she should have behaved with Roberti and vice versa. Had she made Legay suffer as she did Roberti, Legay would have emerged from it fortified and saved. Similarly Roberti would have been saved had she given him what she gave Legay. Nothing, alas, ever goes the way it should and lack of understanding reigns supreme over all human relations. The irony of it all was that Solange, full of her experience of slavery with Roberti, came to Legay with an exactingness and I would even say a moral fiber she had completely lacked before. The root of the matter, of course, was that she loved Roberti madly (in the fullest sense) and Legay soberly.

I apologize for these considerations, which are rather looking ahead to say the least. We were at the reunion with Legay. This marked a new stage in his relations with Solange. During the next two years they saw a good deal of each other, not only just over drinks but also going to the movies and even the theater. To add spice to the situation, Solange took it into her head to educate Legay in literature and art. She repeated to him what she had picked up from Roberti as if she had always known it. She talked about Baudelaire and Jules Laforgue, Manet and Renoir, and of course *the divine Mozart*. She lent him books Roberti had given her. Legay admired her hugely for possessing all this knowledge and taste. For himself, he was as blind to painting and as deaf to music as could be. Literature bored him. He strove to "cultivate himself" in order to be worthy of Mlle. Mignot one day. This cost him an immense effort. At night, after a grueling day's work, he would read two and a half pages of *Crime and Punishment* or *War and Peace* with drooping eyelids and drop off like a log. He was neither stupid nor obtuse but his form of intellect was not apt for literature or the arts— something always surprising to the French, who never think of anyone as intelligent unless he is a man of letters or an art critic.

Solange had a protective feeling toward him. She was sure she was far more intelligent than he and this attached her to him. Silly little bluestocking as she had become, she nonetheless recognized Legay's qualities, his common sense, his instinct for what was true and good, his unfettered mind when it came to anything other than art or poetry. For instance he was quite a subtle judge of movies. His political views were far from shortsighted; to say nothing of his scientific mind, which was genuine and even quite profound, albeit empirical. Had he been born in other circumstances or allowed to go to university, he might have risen to a teaching post in an engineering college, for example.

"Friendship should be possible between men and women," she had said. For two years this commonplace, this nonsense held true between them. Since she was certain of only having one single and unique love in her heart, she believed that she felt nothing but friendship for Legay and, things being thus perfectly clear and simple between them, she saw him with increasing pleasure and frequency as the months went by. For her he fairly rapidly became an agreeable habit. He was the well of pure water at which she came to drink when her amours with Roberti had burned her throat too badly. He was also her confidant, but one of a rather special kind, that is to say she never told him anything about Edouard or her love. She simply talked about herself, about her soul as she saw it, sad and unsatisfied most of the time. She posed as a romantic heroine but kept her secret, as women are so adept at doing. Behind her ambiguous remarks Legay devined a checkered and vivid drama, and naturally such mysteries greatly stimulated his love, nourishing it and increasing its capacity. The more so in that he was careful to show nothing of this, adhering as conscientiously as he could to the role of friendship that had been assigned to him.

Another quality: he had a soothing presence. Some people possess this virtue, which is hard to analyze. They merely have to be present and after fifteen minutes one feels happy, one's heart is unburdened or appeased. They have done nothing; sometimes not even spoken. It is as if they gave off healing rays. Little by little, whenever Solange felt particularly torn in two by her love, she adopted the habit of telephoning Legay. He was always there, faithful at his post. He sensed that his stock was rising. He knew she "loved another" (he didn't know who) but was perspicacious enough to see that this love was changing, weakening and would eventually die. Sometimes he felt he was crouching in the shadows like a big patient cat waiting for its prey, which sooner or later would inevitably fall into its clutches. A high-flown analogy, since Solange in no way resembled a mouse! The mouse was the love she might perhaps come to feel for him in the future.

I: Poor Roberti! Now I'm beginning to feel sorry for him. You're preparing his downfall a long way ahead, you brute!

HE: Well, what do you expect? One has to show the beginnings of things if one wants to understand their development. A novelist should work like a historian and unearth the remotest causes. Now that I can see things historically, from a distance, I can date the beginning of Solange's love for Legay from her return after the Easter vacation of 1956. The love she felt for him was utterly different in nature from the love she bore Roberti; I must nevertheless point out an unexpected parallel. Do you remember how I said that she loved Roberti for two years before their affair began? Similarly she treated Legay as a "friend" for an equal length of time, from '56 to '58, during which time this new love took shape within her.

I: Did she tell Roberti about these periodical meetings with Legay, these outings, this budding intimacy?

HE: Naturally. She saw no harm in it. She would have considered it infamous to lie to Edouard. She told him all about her talks with Legay, of whom she drew a slightly malicious portrait, representing him as an old friend she had known for years, a little bit in love with her, of course, but so respectful, so utterly devoid of hope . . . !

I: And naturally Roberti wasn't in the least perturbed?

HE: Not in the least. He compared his place in Solange's heart with Legay's and his vanity was pleasantly tickled. He was glad this wretched

473

young man should be inflamed with love for his mistress while inspiring nothing in her but pity. He formed an excellent foil. That, at least, is the conclusion he drew from Solange's confidences. He was so sure of the hold he had over her that he feared no one, least of all Legay. It was often he who condescendingly asked her for news of him. He even went so far as to advise her to see him more often, as if Legay were a chaperon. He thought the latter must greatly admire and envy him for having kindled so violent a flame in such a pretty girl. It made him almost feel friendly toward Legay! And after all, can anything be less dangerous, can anything be less romantic than a childhood friend?

I: But Legay wasn't a childhood friend of Solange's, he was a pal of her brother's. There's a slight difference.

HE: It didn't seem so to Edouard, who had more or less got it into his head that he was a childhood friend.

I: This poor man brought about his own downfall with a vengeance.

HE: Yes, one could say that. But who doesn't bring about his own downfall in this way? We are responsible for everything that happens to us. One last detail: Roberti was grateful to Legay for keeping Solange company. In a sense he unloaded his obligations as a lover onto this harmless nitwit. Legay gave him an easy conscience. Solange wasn't alone in the world. Apart from himself there existed someone else to take her out for walks and talks. In short, as you can see, he behaved like a husband naïvely delighted to have a friend to represent him at his wife's side at social functions which he finds tedious. All in all, Legay was a godsend: Roberti shared Solange with him, enjoying all the advantages of this tacit association, while Legay had all the disadvantages. For Roberti the little bacchante of the Square Saint-Lambert; for Legay the silent and insipid young woman. In which, besides, he was mistaken, for whereas Solange was inclined to be dumb with Roberti, who talked a great deal and intimidated her, she was highly voluble and completely at her ease with Legay; with him it was her turn to intimidate. She "did a Roberti."

I: Don't you find two years of friendship with Legay rather excessive? I'm surprised that Solange should have deluded herself all that time as to her feelings, that she should have gone on loving Roberti and not realized sooner that it was Legay who attracted her from now on.

HE: In the first place, that's the way it was. Second, you forget one essential factor: the sensual appeal Roberti had for her and which had in no way diminished—in fact it never did, it remained unimpaired to the very end. Edouard only had to be beside her and she would instantly feel weak, all atremble and hot with desire. No other man had made or ever would make such an impression on her body. Solange's body *loved* Roberti's body passionately and the thrill she felt in his arms was so piercing that it even reached her heart. It was the same, or almost so, with Roberti, who had a feminine sensibility in this respect. The mere sight of Solange filled him with a desire so violent and persistent as to be quite abnormal for a man of fifty.

All kinds of things have been said about physical and spiritual love. Some maintain they are one and the same, others that they are totally separate. Me, I would certainly never dare commit myself on so grave a problem. Nevertheless the example of Solange and Roberti would tend to show that perfect physical conformity isn't enough to sustain love for very long. After two or three years one of the partners, for all his physical satisfaction, feels only the more keenly the void in his soul. And then as always, however agonizing the choice, the soul gets the better of the body, it is the soul which triumphs.

Two or three years, I say. That, to my mind, is roughly the duration of the illusion which consists in believing that loving someone's body means also loving his soul. In 1955, 1956 and even to the end of 1957, the mere idea of allowing any man other than Roberti to touch her filled Solange with horror. She ran no risk when he wasn't there. No man, however seductive, had the slightest power over her senses.

I: Not even Legay?

HE: Not even Legay. Especially not Legay. She trusted him but felt no attraction. She loved his soul, or at least was learning to love this young and charming soul, simple, honest and uncorrupted as it was. She was growing attached to it. This was the path whereby love made its way into her. That sort of love bears no relation to the abrupt sensual explosions induced by brief, violent and ill-assorted passions. She could see that Legay loved her. From time to time he grew bold enough to take her hand and squeeze it. She permitted this with an indulgent smile. Squeezing her hand wasn't overdoing it and, in her eyes, didn't mean very much. In Legay's eyes it meant a great deal; for him it was a pledge; more, each squeeze of her hand represented a successive stage in his love, each time it brought him intense happiness.

I: Obviously. The greatest thrills of love are provided by mere nothings; it's an old story. The wildest conceivable orgy doesn't induce half the pleasure one gets from furtively breathing the perfume on the neck of one's beloved.

HE: Well, toward the middle of 1957, Legay had reached this pitch of love. Contact with Solange's little hand represented for him a priceless gift of the heart and senses. Once he even planted a swift kiss on it.

Such wild temerity gave him palpitations for the next fifteen minutes. Solange withdrew her hand at once and frowned. This time he had overstepped the mark, for a friend. She read him a little lecture, the main burden of which was that he "mustn't do anything to spoil things between them," that "it was all so clear and pure" and so on. Poor Legay was put to shame. He would have loved to "spoil things between them." But he was scared; he apologized with such apparent sincerity that she was touched. "Don't hold it against me, Solange," he begged. "I feel we are such good friends!" He didn't dare to mention love but put such warmth into the word "friends" that it would have been hard to mistake his meaning. In such circumstances women are wonderfully hypocritical: Solange had understood him perfectly but absolved her swain because he had said "friends." Moreover this love disguised as friendship like a wolf in sheep's clothing caused her less and less displeasure. On another occasion Legay brushed her cheek with his lips under cover of wishing her a more affectionate good night than usual and she pretended not to notice.

I: One person who must have been glad about this was Valentin.

HE: Ah, there you've touched on an interesting point. Actually Valentin knew nothing, literally nothing, about the little intrigue between his sister and his pal.

I: What! Did neither of them eventually tell him, when it would have made him so happy? How cruel!

HE: Neither of them. After Easter 1956, when she took up again with Legay, Solange did so surreptitiously. I would even say she did so *against* Valentin. She wanted to see Legay again, but she didn't want to please Valentin. She still felt too resentful toward him. She pictured her brother's delight at such news and the thought of it exasperated her. Valentin would immediately have started forcing the pace, planning a wedding, arranging more frequent meetings between her and his friend, all of which would have driven her wild. She asked Legay to give her his promise, which he kept, not to breathe a word about their meetings. In this affair her instinct was as farseeing as that of a beetle or a bee. At a time when she herself was as yet unaware that she would one day love Legay, she still preserved this love which would have been nipped in the bud had Valentin got the slightest wind of these meetings.

Another no less striking proof of instinct: when she described her talks with Legay to Roberti, the latter always asked whether they had discussed him. "He knows I care for someone," she would reply, or else: "He knows I'm not free" or again: "He's fully aware I have a lover whom I adore." But this wasn't sufficient for Edouard's vanity. He would have liked her to say more, to let her "old friend" know what exceptional thrills he gave her and the kind of loving with which she repaid him. Yes, he would have liked to have had one witness in the world of his happiness and prowess. He even went so far as to say during one of her accounts: "Don't mention me by name but you can tell him everything else."

I: Oh, oh! This is no longer vanity, it's sadism.

HE: Whatever it was, here again Solange's instinct came into play. Not only did she not mention Roberti's name, but she also took care not to impart even the smallest detail about her amours to Legay. It would anyway have been contrary to her general attitude, which was that of a mysterious figure, the ethereal heroine of an unknown novel. Although she could be quite shameless in her behavior and sometimes even her speech at the Square Saint-Lambert, she was really very prim, with all the natural modesty of the lower orders, I would say. For her there were some things one "just doesn't talk about," especially to a man one merely looks on as a friend. If Legay subsequently learned a number of facts about the relations between Roberti and Solange, it wasn't from her. But by the time he learned them he was too deeply in love for such revelations to be able to destroy his feelings or even impair them. On the contrary they only fortified them by adding a touch of pain and pity.

I: Do you know, there's one thing your story cruelly lacks every now and then? Portraits.

HE: Does that really trouble you? To my mind it's of no importance. As a rule the body so closely resembles the soul it contains that if you describe the soul you see the face with all the requisite clarity. That's why I never think of painting full-length portraits. Besides, I saw all the characters in Roberti's story and it never occurs to me to describe people I know.

I: Yes, but I didn't know them. Not all of them anyway. Legay, for instance. I've absolutely no idea of how he looked. Or rather, I do have a notion but it's a false one. I once knew someone called Legay: he was short, skinny and pushing, looking at once sly and stupid, with a wide hypocritical smile. When you say "Legay" this image rises up in my mind. You've no idea how confusing it is. What did Solange's Legay look like? Was he "a nice lad from back home," likable and insipid? Was he good-looking, was he ugly, was he tall, was he fair?

HE: But he was a splendid young man, I'm sure I told you. Nearly six feet tall; a handsome, broad, welcoming face with an earnest, gentle, humorous expression; fine blue eyes but of a delicate light blue which gave him a look of great charm; one of those faces in which one doesn't at first spot the intelligence because it is concealed by goodness. But make no mistake, the intelligence is there and if one looks carefully one sees it in a sudden sharp glance or a smile which lights up the whole face. His hair was a fairish chestnut. The dominant impression was placidity. Such placidity that one thought: "It can't be true; this young man has great strength hidden somewhere within him."

I: And the nose?

HE: Ah, the nose was less successful. It was small and straight. Due to this nose, which in itself was certainly very well shaped, Legay's face was handsome but lacking in character. His well-shaped nose was bestowed on him by a wicked fairy.

I: Then he and Solange made a very handsome pair, I presume.

HE: Very. One day Roberti chanced to see them together and it gave him a nasty shock. I'll tell you about it later, when we come to it.

I: I find it hard to understand how such a good-looking boy should waste his time playing at "friends" with Solange. As you've described him, he must have had as much success with women as he wanted.

HE: No, why? One doesn't appeal to women just because one is good-looking. Added to which I don't think he was very given to fun and games. He was affectionate and sentimental. He can't have had many mistresses before he married. He was preserved by his creative mind, by the time he spent in earning his living and perfecting his invention. You know as well as I do that creative men aren't apt to be womanizers. They don't have the time, and little inclination either. Finally, he loved Solange. Loved her truly. The creative urge on the one hand and love on the other are quite enough to fill a heart like Legay's. As for fun and games, it won't be any news to you to be told that one can easily go without it for months. Chastity is far less hard to bear than many maintain, especially men, who in this respect are consummate liars. Most of the time an active love life is primarily the result of laziness. Someone creative, whether engineer or artist, who has his whole time and mind filled by his creation, can if need be go thirty or forty weeks without seeing or touching a woman and barely notice it.

I: Thirty or forty weeks! As much as that, you think? It seems rather a long time to me even so, especially for a stalwart young six-footer. I suppose it's possible, though. Of course, generally speaking I agree with you about chastity being less hard to bear than people make out and far more common than people think, above all among artists. As to engineers, I can't say.

HE: It's the same. At any rate it was so with Legay. The few mistresses he had had before he fell in love with Solange were either older women or else plain ones. From which I deduce that with him the sex urge was not one of those animal explosions so frequent among young people but rather an extension of friendship or affection. Besides, you have probably observed how good-looking men like Legay nearly always marry ugly ducklings. Because beauty and desire are two different and almost totally unconnected things. As a rule a good-looking man inspires little desire in women. When you see a handsome man married to an ugly woman, you can be sure that they are two people who found themselves left on the shelf and so got together. Legay had no amorous appeal, if I may so put it. Perhaps this was due in part to his too-well-shaped nose. To be truly loved he needed someone who had first made a prolonged acquaintance with his soul, which fully deserved loving. Solange spent two years getting to know this soul. One further thing which has perhaps to be taken into account is that Solange, after three years of an adulterous association, needed repose. Repose of the heart, peace of mind, a desire to become pure again. Not to mention that maternal instinct which yearned for fulfillment. Purity is as contagious as impurity. With Roberti she had lived in impurity of mind and body. One day she realized that Legay's purity had had its effect on her and this seemed to her something wonderfully new, a highly desirable state.

I: So for two years Valentin never knew his sister was secretly seeing Legay? That Solange never told him I'll allow, but what about Legay? Did he conceal this amazing news from his bosom pal? It's barely conceivable.

HE: It's barely conceivable but he did. When a man has to choose between his bosom pal and the woman he loves, the pal counts for little. Solange had expressly insisted that Valentin should never know. So Valentin never did. Besides, here again lack of understanding reigned supreme, which simplified matters. In fact, Valentin no longer felt quite at ease with Legay since Solange became Roberti's mistress. He had promised him too categorically that he would become his brother-in-law and felt as if he had perjured himself, as if he were responsible for the vagaries of his little sister's heart! But this brother of yore, this Corsican brother, had a sense of responsibility extending far beyond what is nowadays expected. So when he went out with Legay or visited him in his studio he avoided talking about Solange. Legay was careful not to ask for news of her and Valentin was careful not to give any. They carried on as if she didn't exist. There was no shortage of other topics. Once or twice Valentin suggested they meet on a day when

Legay had arranged to see Solange. "I'm sorry but I've already got a date," he would say with a wink, which plunged the unhappy Valentin into gloom, convinced as he was that his friend had found another fiancée.

Viewed from a distance, all this is really poignant, as one can now see one of the mainsprings of the tragedy in which the story of Roberti and Solange's love ended. But for the stubborn persistence with which Solange hid her relations with Legay from Valentin, quite possibly nothing might have happened. The affair with Roberti would have broken up as so many other, equally flaming and sordid but not everlasting affairs have done. It would have broken up in tears and despair, maybe, but not in blood, scandal, disgrace and everything which entitles one to say a man's life was accursed. Had Valentin known for those two years that his sister was seeing Legay fairly regularly, that she enjoyed confiding in him and being with him, perhaps he might have summoned up patience and lived less in a state of rage throughout those two years. Perhaps he might have *come to terms* with fate and men's souls. But there it is. Destiny didn't permit it and, in the circumstances, one might say that Solange aided destiny considerably. Out of rancor she brought disaster on her brother, whom she loved deeply in spite of everything. Her rancor counted for little beside her love for him and yet this little lever set the vast mass of her love for him tottering.

ɪ: Did her dear Valentin, whom I like so much, have any sex life? It's a question which tantalizes me, I don't know why. You who know everything must know about this too.

ʜᴇ: Actually I don't. I'm sorry. It would be interesting to shed some light on this point, I agree. But one can try to make some deductions. If he did have a love life, it can't have been very intense. A young man who puts so much passion into interfering in other people's affairs is unlikely to expend much on his own account. Second, he was fat and prematurely bald. At first glance that doesn't make for an enthusiastic lover.

ɪ: Yes, but you've told me how he had a red and hence full-blooded, possibly plethoric face; how he had a huge appetite, etc.

ʜᴇ: Listen, I'm truly sorry but I can't tell you any more than that. I didn't hire a private detective to follow him and keep me informed as to his adventures. Don't forget his longing to get married either. A man as honorably intent on this as he was doesn't flit from woman to woman. I don't believe he had any girl friend; in my opinion, when the urge became too obsessive, he shuffled off to the Rue Delambre or the Rue Lepic. . . .

1: Yes, probably. You're right. Brr! It doesn't add up to a very gay life. Poor Valentin! Between the bank, his sister's eccentricities and the whores of the Rue Delambre, his passage on earth wasn't very uplifting. A man of the Renaissance reduced to such miseries!

HE: The place of a man of the Renaissance is not in the twentieth century. When you land in the wrong age like Valentin you must expect the worst. Especially if you are stupid or narrow-minded. In great periods of history even stupidity had a certain grandeur because the fools were led by superior men and bound by exacting traditions. In base periods there are no superior men (or at least they are not the lawmakers) and no traditions. So then fools are left to their own initiative. It follows that their lives are far more dangerous, and they themselves are far more dangerous too.

I don't conceal from myself the fact that there was something monstrous in talking the way we did, all that day and all that night. Never in my life had I talked so long with anyone and I shall never do so again. Such conversations belong to another age, when men were better suited for them. As we strolled round the lake I remember how a comparison came to my mind: I thought of the famous duel between Roland and Oliver which lasted five days and four nights, according to Victor Hugo, and I all but burst out laughing at the thought of it.

> *Their swords wrenched from their hands,*
> *their helmets gone,*
> *Silent, gasping with horror, they fight on,*
> *Smiting with mighty tree trunks like two giants.*

That, to me, is how we appeared after I forget how many hours of uninterrupted talk! I looked at my watch: it had stopped. One extraordinary thing, I didn't feel tired and neither did he. Here or there, wherever it might be, in the Bois or elsewhere, Roberti's story had to be pursued unfalteringly to the end. All the same I suggested that we sit down on two iron seats set before the dark waters of the lake. The Bois was deserted and silent. It must have been two in the morning: too late even for dirty old men! We were entirely alone in this false nature so skillfully imitated by man, this romantic parody of forest and still water. Night is a blessing for cities—as if it cleansed them every twenty-four hours. Nothing smelled so good as the Bois de Boulogne; a few hours of darkness had sufficed to rid it of the odor of men. We felt perfectly at home on our iron seats.

ɪ: Your remark about men of the Renaissance who have strayed into the twentieth century reminds me of your friend Roberti's great opus which you told me about this afternoon, though I've forgotten its title. A sort of Bossuet-ish title.

ʜᴇ: His *History of Variations in Moral Outlook.* Lord, yes, so it does. It was a rather Robertian remark. He might well have made out a card comparing stupidity under Lorenzo di Medici with stupidity under Président Coty.

ɪ: What became of this *History of Variations* in the great shipwreck of love?

ʜᴇ: Nothing. What would you expect to happen? Roberti was no writer. He had an undeniable gift of gab; the minute he opened his mouth ideas came easily, he was never at a loss for them, but when it came to writing it was quite another matter. Formulation in particular caused him agonies. Setting out thoughts in logical sequence, pursuing an argument through to the end, was for him a superhuman effort as soon as he held a pen. In the time it took him to write down one sentence he would lose the next one. Alas, I know this type of impotence well since I suffer from it as much as he did, poor man. My mind runs ahead of my hand; it won't wait for it. If I want to get something down in writing I have to make an abbreviated version in cable-ese, otherwise it all evaporates. "Take your notes," you will say, "and expand them afterward at your leisure." But that is precisely where one recognizes the gifted writer. I can never get beyond the note in cable-ese. When I want to transform a note into a sentence or paragraph, it's a herculean labor. For me, setting out a sentence is as difficult as chiseling a stone. I scrape at it, polish it assiduously, kill myself trying to give it shape or proportion and when by luck I achieve this, what do I find? That the shape is banal, common, vulgar, stereotyped. It's tragic!

I am telling you all this because I think Roberti encountered the same difficulties as I do when it came to passing from the note in cable-ese to literary "treatment." You yourself have told me a hundred times how it isn't hard to be intelligent; everyone has ideas. But to bring one's ideas to life, give them birth, make vital and active beings of them . . . ! That's why I admire you with your gift, even though you are certainly less intelligent than I am and have far fewer ideas.

I: Hum! I don't know how I ought to take that.

HE: Take it well, take it well! For I say it with the most sincere and unquestionable feeling, to wit envy. I would gladly exchange all my ideas for your little music and my philosophic turn of mind for your bird brain. When one has the little music one needs nothing else. One can even treat oneself to the luxury of being an egregious ass and it doesn't matter.

I: Listen, I'm devoted to compliments, I never weary of them, but I think you ought to stop there. "Egregious ass" is about the limit of what I can take. Let's get back to the *History of Variations*.

HE: Why the hell are you so interested in that wretched literary project which never got beyond daydreams and rough drafts? I don't say it isn't amusing to bring it up occasionally, but it's not worth making a great song about. The *History of Variations* was nothing. I told you all there was to tell about it this afternoon. It was the symbol of Edouard's missed vocation. It was the confused attempt of the amateur who believes, in his simple pride, that if he cared to take the trouble he could be as great as Rembrandt. But there you are, he didn't take the trouble. He wasn't consumed by a sacred flame. Above all he hadn't, in the first place, the talent (or awareness of talent) which gives one the courage to grasp the work with both hands, fling oneself into a titanic struggle at the end of which one obscurely knows one will emerge the victor. So he fiddled about. He scribbled out cards in his spare moments. A book doesn't get written in spare moments but on the contrary in moments wrested at great cost, the way the land is wrested from the sea in Holland. Roberti preserved the illusion that his book would materialize in time, painlessly; that one day all the work would be done and *there would be nothing left to do but write it*. You who know what the work of artistic creation involves, the perseverance and strength of spirit one has to apply to it, should readily understand the utter futility of such an attitude. It merely leads to disgust with oneself, disgust with the work in question and despair. Petty disgusts and petty despair, of course. No grounds for suicide. When he thought of the *History of Variations*, Roberti felt an unmitigated boredom. He contemplated the short way he had come and the endless distance it remained for him to cover. The cards he made became fewer and fewer. Finally, his pre-occupation with Solange brought the thing to a complete standstill. To revert to your earlier idea, one needs to be an artist through and through to prefer one's work to life. Life is such fun, so fascinating! It projects sentiments through one like a magic lantern. It is there, ready-made, ready-armed, picturesque, offering a thousand different points of departure. It is one vast gear and you only have to slip into it. It up-lifts you, transports you, leads you, does nine tenths of the work. Most men take life the way one takes a bus. Between the *History of Variations* and Solange there was no common yardstick. The fact that Solange existed illuminated Roberti's mornings and promised excitements to come. Thanks to her, each day enclosed a treasure awaiting discovery. Each day brought a gift, and a beguiling one. How can you expect a normally constituted man (that is to say not a monster such as artists are) to resist that? It's not possible. Art alone is stronger than life and gives one the courage to scorn it. So that was the end of the *History of Variations*. Unwittingly, Solange had killed this embryo. She destroyed what frail chance it had of reaching fulfillment.

Anyway, what doesn't love destroy? It battens on people's souls like a cloud of locusts. It transforms a verdant countryside into a Sahara where nothing grows. A man possessed by love becomes a wasteland ravaged by sun and simoom. I observed this in Roberti. Love not only distorted him, since it made a different man of him, but it also numbed him, imbued him with inertia. You ask for news of the *History of Variations*; you might also ask for news of all his undertakings. It was the same story. Without realizing that he was becoming increasingly taken up with Solange, he gradually lost interest in all his occupations; he let things slide; he allowed his position and affairs to decline. He was, as you know, legal adviser to several companies. Prior to Solange he was very assiduous, very punctilious in his duties (which it must be said were hardly time-consuming although they demanded a certain conti-nuity of attention); then Solange moved into his life and he found they had lost their savor. The new cases which arose bored him; he went through his files less and less often; he canceled appointments; he let business on hand drag; he had to be prompted ten times before he could be stirred into action. Things muddled along like this for one, two, two years and a half. People didn't dare make too pointed re-marks: he was a deputy, they were used to him and liked him; but the companies employing him were put to great inconvenience. They began to cast around for ways to dispense with so lethargic an adviser; little by little they acquired the habit of entrusting their problems to someone else, and so almost imperceptibly Roberti was replaced. You know how these things are done in such organizations or commercial enterprises. When they want to get rid of someone painlessly, they give him less and less work until the moment comes when the condemned man is reduced to throwing in the sponge. It's a kind of progressive strangulation. At the right moment the company's president has an interview with the victim. With perfect politeness, in a voice choking with regret, he tells him: "You see, my friend, your job with this firm is redundant. You yourself admit it and we're desperately sorry. We're terribly sad at having to part with you but there's really no other solution. It's nobody's fault. Our business has developed in such a way that your position, which at one time was most important, has now become pointless," etc. There's nothing one can reply. This is what happened to Roberti, with minor variations, at the beginning of 1958 in all the companies where he held a sinecure. Even sinecures were too much for him. He had reached the stage of aspiring to nothing but total inertia. One thing which had never happened to him before was that he no longer even replied to letters bringing requests from his constituents. They accumulated on his desk. In his own words, he "let them grow old." In this way they grew one or two months old, after which he tore them up and threw them into the wastepaper basket. One feels no remorse at throwing away a letter two months old: it is too late to answer it. In 1957 he began to go less often to the Assembly, then to skip the meetings of the Arts and Letters Committee although he had been re-elected its vice-chairman. One day one of his party colleagues astounded him by saying: "What's up, my dear Roberti? We no longer see you, no longer hear you. . . ." He was thunderstruck, but for all that this inquiry didn't wake him from his torpor. He knew he had considerably slackened off but didn't think it had been noticed or that it was already a matter for gossip in political circles. This notion infuriated him, a strange reaction in a man so prudent, always so careful of others' opinions, always so prompt to correct an unfavorable attitude; it awakened the spirit of contradiction in him. The fact is that, for the first time in his life, criticism was being aimed at the private man through the public man and he resented this as an intolerable intrusion into his personal life. He immediately absolved himself by means of such arguments as: "I am the sole judge of my behavior, I don't have to account to anyone, I am an old virtuoso of politics: a little respite can't do me any harm. One of these days I'll take myself in hand: I'll make a strong speech on the Budget or the war in Algeria and everyone will see I've lost none of my old astuteness. After all, damn it! I've been working like a galley slave for thirty years, I've a right to a bit of rest. I had no youth so I'm having it now. It has long been due to me. None of this is serious. I still have plenty of resources. I know damn well I'm letting myself drift. The main thing is to know it, but I also know myself; next month or next year I'll tell myself: 'Enough of this, you've had your fun, now back to serious business!' I am a man of unexpected resilience. When all would be lost for another, I only have to make an effort of will because basically nothing touches me: I play with life. It's quite simple. If I'm doing nothing just now, it's because I don't want to do anything. I'm enjoying one of life's vacations. Two years' vacation after half a century's hard labor isn't overdoing it. And certainly my constitution needs it."

I: I notice you're fond of using that figure of speech known as "prosopopoeia," which by definition consists of putting words in the mouths of dead or absent people.

HE: Yes it's true, I'm very fond of prosopopoeia, I find it suits me. It's the repressed novelist in me.

I: I've found a good name for the one you've just produced.

HE: What's that?

I: "Pharisopopoeia."

HE: Well . . . yes and no. In this particular case I showed you a Roberti who was lying to himself, certainly, but not altogether. At least he had an excuse for lying: that of his past character. At fifty a man finds it hard to believe his soul can still change. He has fifty years of self-experience behind him, he believes he knows himself, he believes he can judge what is to come by what has already been. He has forgotten all his previous transformations, or rather thinks he has done with transformations and reached his *final state*, as engravers say. He's wrong, of course. Between fifty and eighty there are still thirty years to be lived, during which one has plenty of opportunity to change three or four more times, and in as far-reaching a way as one did between twenty and forty.

You have often heard talk of the *logic of the emotions*. This logic pinpoints the way self-deception works and shows us how the minds of intelligent people who can't think straight function: their reasoning is impeccable; they are in full control of it at every stage, but what is at fault is their initial premise. They start off with this instinctively, with their eyes shut, in the direction they wish to go, which is obviously not that of the truth. Roberti, at the very outset, didn't admit that for the first time in his life he had been assailed by love, convinced as he was by fifty years of emotional frigidity, which is impervious to love; hence he denied the great transformation love had made him undergo; he took no account of it; for him it didn't exist. He considered himself the same as he had always been. He unreservedly likened the Roberti of 1957 to the Roberti of 1954 or 1935, to the familiar character whose strengths and weaknesses he knew and to whose movements he was *accustomed*. For fifty years he had known a Roberti whose chief characteristic was the absence of all passion, that is to say a man capable of doing what he wanted when he wanted. He had learned to rely on this. He introduced this element, which seemed to him primordial, into all his assessments. When he tries to foresee some future event, a rational man weighs up the probabilities as accurately as he can. In similar circumstances another man less rational than Roberti, someone more thoughtless or irresponsible, would have ignored the probabilities and seen himself as he truly was at that time.

The older I grow, the more convinced I become that the passions enter men's souls stealthily, through secret doorways, and that we only recognize their presence very late in the day (when we recognize it at all). There are some men, even, in whom the passions preserve their incognito to the very end, who only snatch off their masks at the very last moment, astonished to discover as they lie dying that they have been ambitious or lecherous, cruel or avaricious, and that this has led them to do things the enormity of which they hadn't appreciated at the time. The case of Roberti seems odd to us because *as a rule* love is the least masked of all the passions. But with him love was masked, like ambition or avarice in other men.

My prosopopoeia dates from about the end of 1957. It means that at that time Roberti didn't believe himself to be any more in love than in 1955. Yet he had had two whole years in which to identify his love. Note in this connection that there is a contradiction in his attitude toward himself. At the same time as he was telling himself: "I can take myself in hand when I wish to," etc., he felt that he was no longer the same man as three years before. He suspected that his soul had become enriched. Deep down he was well content with this new being he was denying. Other people didn't understand what was going on inside him but he himself had a confused intuition that it was something good, that the way he was now, namely dull and supine, was somehow better than his old self. He had a suspicion that he had "killed the old Roberti." All this is obscure and I'm explaining myself badly, I fear. But the contradictions of the soul are always very hard to elucidate. The more so when, as here, the contradiction is total: he had killed the old Roberti while nevertheless continuing to regard himself in the light of the old Roberti. I hope you have understood, as I'm incapable of making myself any clearer.

I: I've understood perfectly, thanks. One can like clarity and be still capable of understanding obscurities. Besides, what does it mean—"obscure"? Most of the time I translate "obscure" as "muddled." When a man is obscure, it is almost never through profundity so much as incapacity, because he expresses himself badly or in an involved way. It happens to you sometimes.

You say "old Roberti." You say "new Roberti." You say he secretly preferred the new Roberti to the old, whom he had killed. Right. But I, the impartial onlooker, I who have spent so long listening to you and by now have made a fair inroad into Roberti's soul, do not share this view. I'll give you the opinion of the outside world after weighing up all the pros and cons: the old Roberti was better than the new. I will now do penance. I have misjudged the man. When you showed him to me this afternoon in his enduring truth and I abused him, I was wrong. This run-of-the-mill deputy, this paterfamilias, this renegade husband, was somebody after all. He had free will. He used it to do one cheap thing after another, to excel himself in caution, to tremble in his shoes, but it all formed a coherent whole. Fifty isn't old for a politician. I wouldn't call it young, but almost so: every ambition is still open to him. A second-rate but intelligent man like Roberti, familiar with the political underworld and knowing how to exploit it as he did during the 1956 elections, can aspire to a very high position and, what's more, attain it. This is another way of killing one's old self. That is to say one doesn't kill it but improves it. True, all power corrupts, but it also increases the stature of the man who wields it. Roberti's goal, like that of every politician, was power. I am beginning to think that had he won it, had the party game permitted him to land some small ministerial post, and then another more important one and so on to the top, he would have been saved.

HE: How funny to hear you talk like that! It's like hearing myself twelve hours later. You take a long time to get the hang of things. You're as slow as public opinion. But this is now over. I too, by telling you Roberti's story, have made inroads into his soul. I have rediscovered him. Incidentally you have helped me to rediscover him thanks to the abuse for which you are now reproaching yourself.

I: Yes, I am reproaching myself (but only a little). For what is going to become of him now? He's a man who has already lost his free will. Like so many others he is a victim of love, no doubt with his own special characteristics, but all it ever boils down to is just another victim added to the long list of names inscribed on the cenotaph of unhappy lovers. This picture you have drawn of him imbued with lethargy gives me cold shivers. I can see exactly what is to follow. I suppose the little horrors we have hitherto encountered on our way are nothing to those looming ahead. You're as artful as a professional novelist. You made me hate Roberti happy; he's not yet unhappy and already I'm feeling sorry for him.

HE: Nonsense! You're going too fast. Or rather it's I who have gone too fast. Lethargy didn't pounce on him like a wolf. It crept up on him gradually. Were I as artful as you maintain, I would have shown you the progress of lethargy, its manifold workings, its long process of disintegrating life, whereas I gave you only a rough sketch, a synthetic picture. I suddenly set Roberti's inertia before you. Why? I don't exactly know. Perhaps because I felt a sudden need to give you a striking example of one of the basic effects of love, which is indeed to precipitate inertia in the person affected. It's not so much that one exhausts one's body and soul in copulation as that one is wholly occupied by love. One needs leisure in which to *ponder one's love.* So one creates it for oneself. If Roberti neglected his work, it wasn't in order to relax but because he needed time for his daydreams.

I: Do you believe daydreams can succeed in devouring life, in taking its place? That is something which strikes me, the opposite of a dreamer, as quite impossible.

HE: No one, not even you, is the opposite of a dreamer. You must certainly know what it is to be so immersed in some novel that while reading it you forget the real world. Try to recollect your efforts to extricate yourself from the book, to look round once again at life, at your own life.

I: True. Provided the novel is very long and very absorbing.

HE: No novel is as long or absorbing as a love affair in which, furthermore, one is one of the protagonists.

I: Wait, wait! The novel shows me the same world out of which it has snatched me; in it I find this same world, more complete, simpler, more comprehensible, more true.

HE: It's the same with daydreaming, which makes straight for the essential, endlessly caressing this essential and never having enough of it.

I: Even so, Roberti didn't spend all his sixteen or eighteen waking hours daydreaming.

HE: No, of course not, but the dream was inside him like a permanent

temptation. Thinking about Solange, about the Square Saint-Lambert
and what they did there, was a source of great delight, abounding in
charm, as restful as an hour's reading after work. So he would close his
eyes for a moment and be lost. Lost for at least an hour, for when one
daydreams time passes in a flash, almost as quickly as when one is
asleep. From a detailed evocation of his mistress and the joys she gave
him he would switch to less clear-cut images and his mind would be
sucked down. At this stage of reverie, conscious thought becomes fine-
drawn, beaten thin, stretched taut. It doesn't fall asleep; it drowses in
that half slumber in which everything in one's being is languid but the
perceptions remain unimpaired. One hears sounds, one constantly half
opens one's eyes but is nevertheless in a doze. Do you now see more
clearly the corrupting effect of love on Roberti? Reveries provoke a sort
of moral catalepsy.

i: I see. At least, I have an inkling. I presume his daydreams were
always more or less erotic to begin with?

he: Yes, most of the time. Erotic daydreams were in any case best
qualified to induce mental torpor. Similarly they bolstered up Edouard's
self-deception, for when he occasionally stood back and identified them,
he told himself that all he cared for in Solange was the use he made of
her pretty body and that this was a far cry from love. In fact, his reveries
were entirely self-centered. When one dreams lovingly of a woman all
kinds of things enter into it and first and foremost consideration for the
woman in question. Edouard in his reveries evoked Solange, naturally,
but only as an object of pleasure. She was an object perfectly adapted to
his body, I would even say a unique object, but still only an object. He
regarded her as a means and not as an end: the means of enjoying an
exceptional sexual thrill. He seldom thought of her soul and then only
in a random, fleeting way, just as one sometimes lets one's mind idly
wander in speculation as to what ideas may revolve in the head of a
cat or a dog.

His daydreams were set in motion in the following way: whenever
he was bored or saw that he was about to be bored, either by having
to examine some dry legal brief or reply to a letter from some impor-
tunate constituent, Edouard would sit back in his chair or rest his elbows on his desk with his chin in his hand and his glasses pushed up
on his forehead and conjure up scenes in the Square Saint-Lambert. He
didn't even need to close his eyes to see the studio in half darkness
and the dim shape of his mistress. Away from her, he still toyed with
her in his thoughts; he luxuriated in her odor, more familiar than that
of his own wife. He reconstructed her gestures, her caresses, her sighs;

he reveled in the habit she had developed of his body and the skill she had acquired in flooding this body with pleasure. And that's not all. He would think up new refinements for the next occasion, new perfections, the sort of complicated things described in pornographic books. He knew that in this respect Solange would go with him as far as he wished.

It would be interesting to make a study of these erotic reveries, since they proceeded in roughly the same way as an artist's reveries while thinking about his work. I venture the term "masterpiece of the flesh." What do you think of it? It corresponds fairly well to Roberti's approach, since his mind was preoccupied by love much as the composition of a picture or a sonata preoccupies the mind of a painter or a composer. The work of flesh with Solange had become quite simply a work of creation; a long and exacting work, if I may so put it, growing ever more absorbing as the weeks went by. The work of his life, the masterwork of carnal love. Love drives people mad to the extent to which it becomes a fixed, that is to say recurrent, idea, a peg on which the increasingly unoccupied mind can be hung. Strongly sexual love in particular never misses its man. At fifty-two Roberti was pretty severely infected with sexual mania, which had taken two years to develop in him. Some artists become mad in the same way. Overintense brooding on a creative work of the mind finally induces the same lack of balance. There's no shortage of artists so absorbed in their work that they wreck their homes, lurch from catastrophe to catastrophe and die in penury. But that type of madness is respectable since its object is selfless and spiritual, whereas the object of sexual madness is selfish and faintly absurd. "Sexual perfectionism" is a monomania of the same nature as that which consists of eternally furnishing an apartment: one simply *must* have another ornament here, another table there and so on.

ı: I'm not convinced.

HE: Well then, what have I forgotten?

ı: I see a contradiction in your analysis. A man infected with sexual mania is not content with two meetings a week. For you told me, I think, that right to the end Roberti never went to the Square Saint-Lambert more than twice a week.

HE: Yes, so I said and I say it again. Some weeks, even, he only went there once. So?

ı: So this temperance, this diet, doesn't accord with sexual mania.

HE: On the contrary it accords very well. It is even in this that the whole interest of the matter lies. Let's argue it out.

ı: By all means.

HE: Supposing Roberti visited the Square Saint-Lambert every day (granted that his strength permitted such feats at his age). What then?

I: I see. He would no longer have the time or inclination to dream. All his thoughts would be absorbed by action.

HE: That's it, more or less. But we must go into details. To begin with, Roberti was a dreamer, in other words he was prone to daydreaming, he enjoyed it. Second, sexual mania in a man of fifty doesn't assume the same forms as in a younger man. The latter is not subtle; he simply needs a brutish and frequent appeasement of his senses. The older man prefers quality to quantity. Whence these long reveries during which he prepares for the combat of love, picturing it as it unfolds in its various stages, ordaining and savoring its gradations. However inclined a man in his fifties may be, he could never claim to the ardor of a young buck; his victories are all the more dazzling for being carried off with less means, but they are also more rare. I might add that reverie is a tremendous prop to the senses.

Another thing. As I've told you, Roberti was strengthened in his self-deception by the fact that he dreamed far less of Solange when his desires were appeased. You could have drawn a graph of his reveries, which increased in intensity as the day appointed for the next meeting drew near until they reached a pitch which left him sick and trembling, so sensitive was his nervous system. He never failed to observe these fluctuations and, with his preconceived ideas of a man of letters, they led him to conclude that the feelings which inspired him as to Solange were anything but love. What was in my view also highly revealing was his excitement as he made his way to the Square Saint-Lambert and his frigidity as he left it. And that's not all. Long before he even left the place he was already sober and his one idea was to get away, to be alone again, rid of the being his body needed so badly in order to be happy. Once desire was appeased he saw Solange as she really was: her defects, which only an hour before had served as so many aphrodisiac fetishes, appeared to him in their true light and caused him something akin to shame. She was after all a very ordinary young woman with skinny legs and an overdeveloped bust. And with a very limited intelligence to boot. How could he, Roberti, possibly be in love with anything so mediocre, how could he be tied to anyone so imperfect? And oh, how trying women can be! They are never so tender and clinging as when they are no longer wanted, when the satisfied male is longing to escape! However much he forced himself to put on an act, he could never conceal his impatience, which pierced Solange's heart. Sometimes it made her feel so sad and humiliated that, burying herself in her lover's arms, she would burst into tears. These tears flowed silently, like two rivulets down her cheeks. Because the studio was in darkness Roberti couldn't see them, but his hand brushed against this dew. He felt a wave of infinite boredom and disgust, as if he had touched a snake.

I: Admittedly, women who weep are quite exasperating.

HE: Yes. Deadly! So Roberti was sickened when Solange gave him the unpleasant shock of weeping. He questioned her as to the cause of her unhappiness, he wanted to make her say something so that he could ensnare her in the web of his brilliant reasoning, persuade her that she was wrong to shed tears and that he, Edouard, was not to blame. But on these occasions she remained mute. She felt utterly desperate: never would she be able to overcome her lover's indifference. She compared this with her own love; between her stifled sobs she wondered when this love would cease, so that there should be an end to the humiliation of being treated like a whore, dismissed as soon as she had been made use of. In the street, when Roberti invited her into his car, she said good-by, refusing to go with him. She walked off alone into the night and Edouard watched her go with relief. As a rule, on days following scenes of this kind, her voice over the telephone would be as warm and tender as if nothing had happened. So that he felt no grounds for compunction and was confirmed in his idea that he was loved far more than he himself loved, that in the person of Solange he had a mistress wholly subjected to his wishes and even his moods, with whom he could take every liberty. To manage to convince a woman one loves violently that one doesn't love her is the most miserable triumph conceivable! And what about its philosophical implications! Here is another demonstration of that saying of Plato's you quoted earlier: "Everything that you desire you shall have, *unhappy wretch!*"

I: There's an idea, I may say, which has been forming in my mind for some hours. An idea which daren't show its face but which is very insistent. I have to bring it up now since quite possibly it may affect you and alter some of your views on the Roberti affair. I warn you, it goes dead against your theory, against what the court finally admitted at the trial, against all the facts and even against the meaning Roberti gave his misery and despair in prison.

HE: Hell! Now you're beginning to talk like me. What are you leading up to?

I: Something I hardly like to tell you since it upsets your whole interpretation and possibly your whole story.

HE: You alarm me. What is it?

I: What if Roberti, *in actual fact,* had never loved Solange?

494

HE: Impossible!

I: Why? Don't answer now. Keep this idea at the back of your mind. Perhaps I'm wrong, perhaps not. We shall see later.

HE: Love was proved to him by the acts he committed and which led him to murder.

I: There are other explanations besides love for what are known as "crimes of passion."

HE: No, it's not possible. It's not possible I should have been mistaken all along. Roberti was a man who preferred his reason to his heart and was punished for it. Look, if he hadn't loved Solange, how do you explain the fact that his love for Agnes dwindled until it vanished altogether?

I: A false love can destroy a true love.

HE: Then there's nothing left.

I: No, there's nothing left. At fifty-two, Roberti was perhaps a finished man. I mean finished morally, with no strength left in his soul to feel any emotion other than despair.

HE: Listen, I knew him. Knew him well. He wasn't given to despair.

I: How do you know? To my mind, there was a deep well of indifference in him. Now indifference is one of the surest roads to despair. And then this propensity he had for daydreaming, which you have demonstrated at such length: daydreaming also favors despair, I believe. A man who dreams is like a man who goes on a hunger strike. He exhausts his own substance. I am sure most people who commit suicide have dreamed a great deal before reaching that point.

HE: Frankly, I don't know what to reply. I detected in Roberti all the symptoms of love as it has been known and described since remotest antiquity. At the same time I watched a man who wouldn't acknowledge this love, who denied it almost to the end, inventing a host of arguments against it, but was at the last moment finally convinced of it. Only then did he lapse into despair. And this was a despair of love, not an absolute despair.

I: Let me remind you that his amours began under the sign of inoccupation of the soul. Solange turned up and he took her because she was there, because she was pretty, because she offered herself.

HE: Well? Many great loves begin like that, as a gentle slope, without one's being aware one is sliding down it or how far one will go. A year after he started down this gentle slope the situation was very different. What do you need to convince you? To see him caught in the quicksands of love? He was, at least so far as I could judge. Caught in the quicksands of physical love, which has something treacly about it and acts like a spell on the soul. Physical love pervades the soul by capillary attraction, so to speak. Roberti began by loving Solange physically and she repaid him in good measure. For her, all his defects were so many stimulants on which she focused her desire: aging flesh, sagging stomach and so on. She saw him in the guise of a splendid young man; he was far more handsome and desirable than any Adonis. "Today," she often told him, "you look twenty," and she really believed it; or again, "I loathe gigolos," because this was true and she knew it pleased Edouard. He was delighted by this kind of declaration, though he hardly gave it credence. But she put such conviction and persuasion into her words that he was finally forced to believe it. He would laughingly protest at these fond exaggerations. He was sincerely modest as to his body, apart from the fact that it is ill-bred to be anything else: one should always denigrate oneself and above all deny one's most obvious qualities. Until the day came when he evolved the following argument: "In love one has to advertise oneself intensively. People tend to believe what one tells them. If I keep on saying I am old and ugly, Solange will end by thinking it in spite of her illusions. At all costs I must keep on saying that I'm young and handsome. Always retain the advantage. Always keep your opponent handicapped. Drug her. It is all the easier when she is already three quarters drugged by herself." One curious outcome, in marked contradiction to this cynical monologue, was that he began to regard his own body with affection: this protruding belly was loved, this body was the instrument of pleasure and cause of another's delight. He was filled with wonder; he developed a respect for his own flesh. He had never imagined it would one day become precious to him like this.

When he went to meet Solange at the Square Saint-Lambert, it was always in a state of extreme desire and excitement. His heart was pounding. Each time he arrived early. Fretfully he would hang around in the studio for ten or fifteen minutes moodily staring at the hideous picture of the Sacré Coeur. His agitation increased as the minutes passed. Perhaps she wasn't going to come? Something had detained her or else, tired of her lover's coldness, she had decided to drop him? But all at once, just as he had worked himself into a state of utter dejection, the bell would ring. He would open the door. There she stood in the doorway, pretty and trim, with a smile which to Roberti seemed celestial. The smile of the woman you love, for whom you have been waiting and who is there, at last, with whom you are going to rediscover pleasures half forgotten yet quite distinct in your mind, is something wonderful, one of the greatest joys a man can savor on earth. With the door closed,

Solange removing her hat, sitting on the divan and Edouard taking her in his arms, a great feeling of peace would descend on him. The world was going to stop for an hour; infinity was within his grasp. In his arms she was truly melting. A unique sensation. Such softness, such sweetness, this warm sea in which he was drowning—it was femininity in its immemorial splendor.

I: Forgive me for interrupting this lyrical outburst but just now you said something which made me prick up my ears.

HE: Really? What?

I: That Solange rang the bell. Didn't she have a key to the studio?

HE: No. Odd, isn't it?

I: It's more than odd, it's staggering. Left to myself it would never have occurred to me that Roberti didn't give her a key to the place he had especially rented for her. How do you justify that?

HE: I don't. I just mention it, that's all. When he rented the studio, I suppose they only gave him one set of keys. Out of discretion Solange never asked him to have another set made. He never thought of it himself or, if he did, he decided against it.

I: That's more like it.

HE: I'm afraid so.

I: Why?

HE: You know the man well enough to spare me the need for a detailed explanation. He was cautious, jealous of his independence, anxious to keep all the trumps in his hand including the small one consisting of a set of keys unique of its kind. Finally, and I believe that this is the root of the problem, he wanted the studio to preserve its anonymity, to remain always a place of transit, the arid and sordid place it was. Had Solange possessed a key to the studio she would have gone there on the quiet to prettify it, make it welcoming and gay, give it the stamp of a "feminine presence." I don't know whether Roberti had any such precise thoughts but I'm sure that this man who had a mind to everything must also have more or less feared his mistress might spoil his studio for him through her enterprise.

I said that physical love penetrates to the soul by capillary attraction. Here's an almost tangible example of it. When he left Solange after spending two hours with her at the Square Saint-Lambert, Roberti was impregnated with her scent. So do you know what he did? He didn't wash for twenty-four hours in order to preserve her on his skin, in his pores. This scent provided food for his daydreams; it was a constant reminder that he had a delicious secret; it gave him inordinate self-satisfaction. Sometimes the scent was accompanied by an exquisite lassitude, the whole forming a body of sensations he never wearied of distilling for himself in solitude. Amused at such complacency, he thought: "How perverse!" But was it, objectively, perverse? Carnal intimacy with a woman is a considerable thing. And in this case, by dint of experience, he knew the body of his mistress almost as well as his own. The flesh, my friend, goes a very long way. Much further than we think. Roberti's flesh enjoyed a deep complicity with Solange's and this became for him a source of pride. People are right in a case of adultery to talk of "accomplices," since they share an absolute, uncommunicable secret which they themselves would be incapable of making a third person understand. An athlete knows his own body to the fingertips; he knows its potentialities; he has a complicity impossible to put into words with his arms, his legs, his muscles, his breathing. I suppose an artist has these complicities with his mind during moments of creation. It's the same with lovers who suit each other. Roberti believed one cannot truly love a woman until one has discovered in her the sexual half lacking in oneself, which, if one had it, would make one the preternatural hermaphrodite in which some biologists see the culmination of human evolution. On this he built up a philosophy which consoled him for not having other mistresses besides Solange and helped him to believe that she was nothing to him but an object for experiments: "Since we can't have everything in life, we must create equivalences. All absolutes are alike (just as are all beauties in art). Consequently one only has to capture one to know them all. The absolute of love, for instance. If I know a woman through and through, if I give her all the pleasure she is capable of enjoying, I then know all women and all love."

I: The opposite of Don Juanism.

HE: Exactly. The philosophy of Faust. The philosophy of an old doctor rejuvenated by the stroke of a magic wand, who has nevertheless preserved the habits of thought of an old man. The economical philosophy of a sage who would if necessary be content with the symbol of things, who has no need for the world to reveal itself to him in a manifold and repeated fashion to have a clear idea of it in his mind. Besides, he applied a similar argument where Agnes was concerned: "Perfection is not of this world. It is already a great deal to have a devoted, intelligent wife. As she is, she's worth more than nine tenths of the wives I know. I am lucky, I must own to this and take due account of it." His sin was that of Faust: the sin of avarice. He wanted to keep everything, clutch to his bosom a complete, which is to say contradictory, world and thereby rise above the humble human condition, make himself a god without knowing it. Only a god can embrace and reconcile the contradictions of the universe. In this I see a curious fusion of two cardinal sins, namely avarice and pride, one leading to the other, overlapping it, merging with it, and all this naturally throwing the portals of hell wide open.

Since we're philosophizing, I shall seize the opportunity to explain an observation Roberti had made and which he himself explained to me one day with great satisfaction over his insight and ingenuity. He had in fact noted that the three or four women for whom he had felt some attachment during his life and who had really loved him (including Agnes) were roughly similar in character, type, moral outlook and the delicacy of their sentiments. From which he deduced that women are chameleons, mirrors for the men they love. These three or four women no doubt differed widely among themselves but they all had one point in common: their love for him. This love gave them the faculty of resembling their lover, of saying what he wanted to hear, acting as he wanted them to act. Through his women it was himself that Roberti had loved. It was himself he continued to love through Solange. Himself or, rather, his transposed, embellished, idealized self-portrait. In a sense he was possessor of a method for detecting love. "Everything that resembles me is love. Every woman who resembles me loves me, because she wants to resemble me or my conception of a woman worthy of being loved, which is the same thing." There! He was the first man to have trapped Eros, to have pinned a label on his back. In short he was sure that he alone held all the threads in his hand, that he alone was the provider of every thought and feeling. Solange was just a pretext, an interchangeable instrument. No one on earth is indispensable. A person's worth depends solely on the feelings or desires we bring to bear on him. And what is to prevent us from withdrawing these sentiments, snatching away these desires and bringing them to bear on someone else? It is purely up to us. Roberti had been in love before; he was in love now with Solange; but had he not met Solange he would be in love with another woman for whom he would feel the same attraction. He was convinced that he could have broken with her without the slightest difficulty at any given moment. He only kept her on because she was *convenient* and he no longer had to conquer her: she was completely subjugated, he relied on her as he did on his watch or his cigarette case. With her he need waste no time.

He often felt inclined to break with her, moreover. His reason whispered excellent arguments, in the main that she was unworthy of him, that she was a fool, that her legs were too skinny, that she came from too inferior a class. All the same, a certain softness, possibly a certain cowardice, prevented him from thoughtlessly facing her with a break point-blank. Solange was really too much in love with him: so much love holds one to ransom! So he tried in an underhand way to turn her against him, seeing little of her, scarcely ever telephoning, until the day came when desire once again swept over him. During these intervals he was completely sure of not loving her. "How is it she doesn't notice?" he would wonder. "She has no pride. She's like a bitch in heat!" In fact poor Solange had no inkling of the complexities of her lover's soul nor of the perpetual battle within him between his beloved Reason and his heart. She suffered in all simplicity. She forgave in all simplicity. This "bitch in heat" side of her (which also came out in bed) did much to promote Roberti's attachment.

Once, "just to see," he made a more persistent attempt to break it off. For two whole weeks he gave her no sign of life, which was really going a bit far. Even though he knew he had neither the time nor the inclination to be a Casanova, he resented Solange on account of all the women she was causing him to miss. He would have liked to be *available* and was prevented from this by his liaison with her. Faust again, you see, always "having his cake and eating it," always winning on the two conflicting tables of life. But events were against him. During this fortnight of amorous liberty he made advances to two women who both repulsed him. And yet, according to gossip, they were by no means prudish defenders of their virtue; probably he didn't apply himself to their downfall with the requisite conviction. Women are wonderfully quick to sense these subtle distinctions. From the very first word, or almost, they scent out a man whose heart is otherwise engaged and who only pursues them out of sexual dilettantism; to this even the most easygoing put up the resistance of a virgin.

Nothing throws one back on old habits so much as rebuffs of this nature. Vexed and discouraged, Roberti's thoughts took a new twist. He told himself what dismissed suitors tell themselves: that in any adventure the idiotic overtures to which a lady has to be treated are really intolerably boring. Solange immediately resumed possession of his mind; he remembered their secret complicity and how, with her, everything was simple, joyful and triumphant. He was moved to tenderness. "It's she I need," he thought. To this cry of his heart and senses his reason cynically added: "She's better than nothing!" And then, as always, that captivating sensation when he called her up; the little bitch whimpered with joy, yapped with delight at the other end of the line.

I: You amaze me. How the hell do you know all these details? They could hardly be more intimate.

HE: In the first place, I saw a lot and guessed a lot. Second, Roberti confided in me to a considerable degree. I was surprised myself. The more so because he made these confidences in an anxious sort of way, as when one makes one's will, as if he had a foreboding that he would shortly die and that someone must know exactly what had been the real mainspring of his heart. For him I was like the confidant in a tragedy: I was the notary of his feelings, the safe in which he deposited his more precious possessions in case of accident, so that these might survive him.

I: You know, since we first started I have several times asked myself: "Why is he telling me that?" Don't you have the feeling, while you are talking to me, that in a way you are betraying Roberti? And Agnes? Supposing I write the novel of Roberti's and Solange's amours, putting into it everything you have told me. The book gets published. It is in all the shops. The press will certainly pay it some slight attention. Agnes will buy and read it, Roberti's sons will read it too. Don't you think it might hurt them? I wouldn't wish for anything in the world to revive a pain which has perhaps begun to subside, reopen wounds which may no longer be bleeding. Agnes and the Roberti boys have probably only one desire today: to be forgotten.

HE: I have never thought that silence and oblivion were good aids to recovery. In talking to you as I have done since lunch I have never once had the feeling of betraying Edouard or doing Agnes a bad turn. Had you followed Roberti's trial you would know what a stream of filth was poured over him. Agnes and the boys heard or read every bit of this in the papers until they became immune to it. Whenever there's a crime, police, a trial, everything takes on an ignoble hue (and a false one as well, because the police don't understand the true motives, because the judges sum up according to a conventional morality, because the lawyers lie in order to exculpate their client so far as this eternally false morality is concerned). And so at his trial Roberti's true soul never appeared. Only the *material facts* were evoked and by induction a crude portrait was drawn of the accused bearing no relation to the truth, endowing him with coarse and vulgar features which had never been his. Such was the final image he left of himself on earth and Agnes, although she knew him inside out, in part accepted it.

Right. Since all that, I have talked often and at length with Agnes. But you must see how I could never speak to her as freely as I have done to you. I couldn't reveal to her all the details relating to Solange, for instance. She would never have stood it. Yet I should have liked to. The truth—I mean the real truth as it emerges from a mass of precise details—is the one thing capable of appeasing a great sorrow unless, of course, one is addressing a fool. And Agnes is no fool. She's an intelligent, sensitive woman fully equipped to ponder over and draw conclusions and solace from revelations which may be painful on first hearing. In actual fact I should have had with her this tremendous talk I am having with you. I'll go further. If from what I say you make a novel, I want her to read it, think about it, shed copious tears over it. After sufficient tears and meditation I am sure she will feel better. It will be a red-hot iron that has passed over her wounds and cauterized them. By the end of the novel she will no longer hate Roberti. She will pity him, she will feel compassion for him, she will be released. She will have seen a man caught up in a tragedy. The infinite sweetness of forgiving injuries will descend on her, since it is impossible not to forgive a man once all his motives have been made clear; one sees all too plainly his smallness and impotence in face of the terrible ferocity of the world. In essence this novel, if you write it, will be a letter I am sending through you to Agnes; a harsh, implacable letter such as only true friends can venture to send. It will be just too bad if, having received it, she turns against me. I shall feel I have done my duty. As for you, if the role of public scribe embarrasses you, you only have to change the names and a few of the circumstances. Call Roberti Dupont and Solange Suzanne. Set the trip to Italy in Denmark or Holland. Or, better still, invent different but analogous motives (if you see what I mean) for Edouard's actions. Make him a doctor instead of a deputy and so forth. That is the least thing one can ask of a professional novelist. Confuse the trail. I have every confidence in your skill and I know that you alone are capable of not falsifying my words. You are also the only man capable of writing this letter to Agnes which I don't know how to write myself.

I: It would rather appeal to me to write a whole novel for one person alone. But—who knows?—it may possibly have a hundred thousand readers. It would be violating the privacy of correspondence, reading confidential letters in public.

HE: I've thought of that too. In the novel I stand up for, I rehabilitate Roberti, not only in the eyes of Agnes but also in the eyes of the world, which has accepted a shameful and inaccurate image of him. Since Justice never hesitated to turn this poor man inside out like a rabbitskin, to expose his soul (or the idea it conceived of his soul) in the witness box, I don't see why friendship shouldn't do the same thing. But it isn't a matter of setting up one lie against another, of systematically saying "white" every time we find black. No. In every instance, without exception, the opposite of falsehood is always the truth, even if this too is deeply tinged with black. The black is not in the same places and that makes all the difference: what was hateful becomes explicable (and curious), hence pardonable. Finally, I rely on you to make a work of art out of my prattling, that is to say something which in the first place is beautiful and in the second universally instructive, something which can be of use to all men.

I: Very well. I accept. If that's how you see it I regard myself free to carry on. Being an artist I always tend to think that art and truth can never harm anyone, even if experience has sometimes shown me the contrary. There are many people for whom art and truth are merely indiscretion and cruelty. But I should like to ask two further questions.

HE: Ask away.

I: First, how was it that so discreet a man as Roberti confided in you to such an extent? Were you that close to him?

HE: Yes, I was. Rather as I am with you. That is to say he knew me for one of those men to whom one can say anything because they are never surprised and will never repeat it. Roberti had a secret life but he himself was not secretive. A wholly secretive man is a strong man, but Roberti was not a strong man. Sometimes his soul bent under the weight of his secret; then he would talk to me. He found support in me. I listened to him like a doctor. We discussed his case *ad infinitum*. These talks brought him relief, I think; not that any resolutions or plans of conduct emerged from them, but he took comfort in the mere fact of talking about himself, analyzing the psychology of love. After we had talked for an hour or two he would feel quite light and gay.

I: But weren't you embarrassed, listening to these shameless admissions? As a friend of Agnes, weren't you disgusted? Didn't you advise him to consign Solange to the Devil and revert to the straight and narrow?

HE: Embarrassed? No, I wasn't. Vexed, rather. Saddened. Naturally I thought of poor trusting Agnes, who had no idea of what was going on, who continued to love Edouard as the truest of husbands while he wallowed in debauchery. But I learned long ago never to give people advice incompatible with their temperaments. It would have served no purpose for me to preach or nag at Edouard to break with Solange. He would simply have ceased to confide in me. I told myself I could be of some use to this unhappy pair in a different way. By closely following daily events I could keep my eye on things and should disaster fall (that

is should Agnes somehow discover he was unfaithful) I could limit the extent of the damage. Whenever, in a domestic upheaval, a third party —a friend—is in the know, and provided this friend is shrewd, devoted and diplomatic, a few heartaches can be avoided. I merely confined myself to urging Edouard to redouble his prudence and circumspection. At the risk of his own discomfiture, Agnes must never on any account know anything about it. Besides, I was sure that one day his affair with Solange would break up, just as so many of his previous ones had done. Right up to the end, in fact up to the very last moment this could well have happened. The tragedy was unleashed by a misunderstanding, a piece of stupidity I shall tell you about in good time, and this makes it all the more agonizing. Advice to take care, advice to be circumspect— you can imagine how this was welcomed by Roberti! With open arms, if I may say so. Perhaps I contributed to some extent to the way things continued more or less decorously up to the end. I was like a diplomat for whom peace is a game of jackstraws: in approaching to play it he makes his hand as light as possible. But however great his precautions, the diplomat cannot foresee how some small nation on the fringe will suddenly be seized with a fit of passion and plunge the whole world into war. He cannot foresee Sarajevo. Today, when all is laid waste, when the game of jackstraws is scattered, I am no longer a diplomat. I am an historian, pre-eminently for Agnes' sake. So long as she was happy she had a certain image of Edouard which, after she became unhappy, was replaced by a different image of him; without transition the man she had looked up to appeared to her in the low guise of a seducer and murderer, reduced by police and press to the pathetic dimensions of those poor wretches whose lamentable stories we read every day in the newspapers. I cannot allow her to go on laboring under such a delusion, it is really too dreadful. Reading our novel, she will find a third image resembling neither the first nor the second, which were clichés—either too rosy or too morbid. She will see the image of a man she doubtless misunderstood but with whom, beyond the grave, she will find affinities in her heart. I believe that all the fury, bitterness, scorn and hatred she still nurses and suffers from will then fall away and give place to a more tranquil sorrow.

ɪ: What you have just said reminds me of my second question.

ʜᴇ: What's that?

ɪ: This afternoon you talked a great deal about hell and incidentally I gaily followed you down that path. Together we damned poor Roberti. But now, to my way of thinking, the deeper we explore him, the less certain does his damnation appear. And here you are explaining that once Agnes learns the whole truth she will forgive him.

HE: Following which?

I: Following which, if Agnes forgives Roberti, God will forgive him too. He will forgive him his cowardice, his meanness, his abominable selfishness. It seems to me that God cannot do less than a human being, especially when this human being was the principal victim.

HE: I know many things, but I don't know what goes on in God's mind. Turn back to the story of Faust, to which in my opinion Roberti's is a parallel. Marguerite forgave Faust but the latter signed his pact with the Devil nonetheless. Roberti signed his pact the way we all sign things nowadays, without reading it, without even noticing the movements of his hand tracing the letters of his name in his thumb's blood, but he well and truly signed it. Look, I'll give you terrifying proof. When he was in prison or, rather, in the infirmary, and saw Death striding toward him, he had moments of panic. That is to say his despair ceased now and then and he began to think of his immortal soul. How did he think of it? With pain. Memories of his Christian upbringing then took violent hold of him. He had been baptized; he had taken his first Communion; alone and face to face with himself he thought how sweet it would be to turn *in extremis* to the religion he had abandoned since he was sixteen. As there was no other human being at hand to help him bear his burden, God might possibly come to his aid. But each time he forced himself to banish this overwhelming nostalgia from his mind. You will never guess what held him back on the road to a confession which would have brought him so much solace: fear of ridicule! Yes, fear of ridicule, and him in prison! "No," he told himself, "never this final act of cowardice. Let me die like a Roman, or at least like an old Radical!" What a pitiful piece of sophistry, eh? How pitiful to be still thinking of the world's opinion when one is about to appear before God! Perhaps I have too delicate a sensibility, but I can't help seeing the Devil's hand in this crazy obstinacy of a man doomed from every point of view yet still turning away from the last path to salvation left open to him. He rejected it outright. The prison priest came to see him once or twice but he was incorruptible: he affected to discuss literature with the man. The poor priest was quite dismayed. To support him in his final impenitence, he sent to me for Voltaire's *Philosophical Dictionary* and Renan's *Origins of Christianism*. For once I disobeyed him. Instead I sent him Pascal's *Pensées* and Claudel's *Collected Plays*. Being such a devotee of good style, I told myself that with those two authors at least he wouldn't lose by the exchange and that perhaps they would soften his heart. He died a few days later. It is my most fervent hope that Pascal and Claudel shook some sense into him.

I: You know, with your haphazard way of storytelling, which consists of mixing up periods, giving away the end in the middle and then working backward, I find it hard to follow you. I should like to go back to the beginning of 1957, when Roberti had begun to change, to cultivate idleness and daydreaming. When a family man is overcome by inertia and reverie it must end by attracting attention, if only because his business is doing badly. Didn't Agnes notice anything?

HE: No, nothing at all. As I've told you, his position declined very slowly. For a long time this decline remained invisible. All his troubles descended on him at once, within the space of two weeks, at the beginning of 1958. Moreover that is how catastrophes occur. They have several independent causes but it is as if some supernatural engineer adjusted these in such a way that they all converge to produce one single and terrifying impact. Up to the beginning of 1958 nothing outwardly had changed. The causes of the catastrophe were developing below ground, waiting for the moment to break through. As for Agnes, when by chance she found her husband melancholic or taciturn, she told herself that fiftyish is a critical age with men, when they have to surmount a minor physiological and moral crisis. She thought the wisest attitude for her to adopt was her normal one, in other words that of an affectionate and attentive wife; it mustn't appear as if anything was wrong. Since their marriage Edouard had passed through other crises which he had overcome. Finally she attributed his absorbed manner to politics. She knew his deep devotion to the State and its institutions; she knew his patriotism, which was profound although, like all deputies, he expressed it in exaggerated clichés. Doubtless he was worried about the present situation: the Suez expedition which had failed so lamentably at the last moment, just when victory was in our hands; the war in Algeria dragging on interminably; the convulsions in the Assembly; the governments which kept falling after three weeks of tottering existence. All this, she thought, was quite enough to explain the absent air Edouard sometimes had. What encouraged this misapprehension on her part was the fact that every time she discussed politics with her husband he became quite voluble. He gave her a very pertinent analysis of the "predicament," he saw the State disintegrating and Parliament falling into disrepute, but being an expert he didn't draw the commonsense conclusion from it all, namely that things couldn't go on like that for very long, that sooner or later the government would be so weakened and disrupted that it would collapse without any call for a revolution or even a *coup d'état*. Such is the habitual blindness of the specialist: he knows his subject too intimately in detail to see its broad outlines; he follows its daily progress with too close an attention to grasp the general curve of its flight and foresee how it will end. Roberti never imagined that the Fourth Republic could cease to function. Given time, patience and exhaustive finessing it would finally overcome the present chaos, which, incidentally, was partly artificial and due in the main to the painful war in Algeria which looked as if it would never end.

i: By the way, you've never told me what his stand was over the war in Algeria. Perhaps this is the right moment.

HE: Basically, I think, he took no stand over it. He confined himself to following wherever the wind blew. He regarded this war as an unknown equation, no more. No prime minister had as yet solved this equation, but inevitably one must come who could do so. Not once did I ever hear him air high-flown principles regarding this war, bewail "this fratricidal conflict" or contrariwise invoke reasons of State. No. For him it was never more than an extra difficulty to be overcome dispassionately and as rationally as possible, taking into consideration all the circumstances of the modern world which in no way resembles the world of fifty years ago, either in ingenuity or moral outlook.

i: I say, that's not bad.

HE: Yes. Roberti did possess certain statesmanlike qualities, to be sure. Never (save in electioneering or official speeches) did he ever give vent to the humanitarian claptrap or reactionary jingoism with which the press, political thinkers, generals, left-wing intellectuals and extremists regaled us for seven and a half years.

What with all this I've lost my thread. What was I about to tell you? Oh yes, that if Agnes noticed nothing, there was nonetheless one person who judged that Edouard was not the same. Germaine, their maid. This obtuse creature, totally without sensitivity, had a curious form of intuition, doubtless fostered by her propensity for interpreting the majority of human actions in a bad light. For her, "Monsieur was changing." You have probably noticed how when a fool says of someone that he has changed, it is always for the bad. In the eyes of fools any change is disturbing. They would like the world to stand still and its inhabitants to be immutable. Because every change entails a revision of values—a difficult, hateful and immoral undertaking. Germaine's mind functioned like this: What could be *making* Monsieur change? What makes most men change? Alcohol or a woman. Monsieur wasn't a drunkard. Therefore, at his ripe age, he was starting to run around. It was obvious, it was mathematical. Germaine got this idea lodged in her head after the Easter vacation of 1956. This ten days' vacation alone was suspicious in itself. Perhaps Monsieur had gone off to make whoopee with some giddy young thing (Germaine's vocabulary). On his return she examined his linen with the meticulous care of a jealous wife. She would have given a great deal to find some traces of sin among it. She found nothing, but she fancied she sniffed a scent of jasmine which was not wholly unfamiliar, which stirred a memory at the back of her thick skull. Alas, this wasn't enough to justify a formal accusation. She would have to bide her time before she could say to Agnes: "If I was you, my pigeon, I'd keep my eye on Monsieur. He's still a good-looker and he may have got ideas in his head."

I: What an odious woman! Did she manage to identify Solange's scent in the end, did she manage to find evidence to convict Monsieur?

HE: No, but it wasn't for want of trying, I can assure you. "I've got my eye on you, my man!" she told herself in the best style of popular romantic fiction. Roberti didn't distrust her, he thought she was fond of him the way a vassal is fond of his overlord, but on principle he was cunning as a snake. The only indication Germaine could ever lay her hands on was the scent of jasmine which sometimes faintly impregnated her master's shirts. Sniffing at this, she would spitefully prophesy for herself. "All this will come to a bad end," she predicted. She was certain that Edouard was deceiving Agnes. It couldn't be otherwise, for everything in the world begins in the same way. A man who changes is a man who deceives. She thought hungrily of the moment when the scandal broke, when *Madame knew*, for inevitably truth will out. She would then watch some splendid scenes, highly diverting for a poor woman like Germaine who never went to the movies. As for herself, she was blameless. No one could say she had committed any indiscretion; she wasn't one of those loose-tongued gossips who "make bricks without straw." Thus she consoled herself for returning empty-handed from her hunt for signs of love through Edouard's dirty-linen basket and jacket pockets.

I: This Germaine appalls me. She's the stupidest character in your story and she sees all, understands all, foresees all. There must be some profound philosophy underlying it but I can't manage to fathom it. Why, in the great dramas of life, do events always prove the fools to be right in the long run?

HE: Yes, why? I've often wondered myself. I have ten possible answers but none of them satisfies me. Because life is simple when it applies its hand to tragedy; there are few really great passions or interests and fools know them. Because fools are closer to nature than intelligent people; perhaps they have the same obscure complicity with it that animals or plants have. What else? Because fools are nurtured on prejudice and clichés. Now prejudices and clichés derive from careful observations made in the remote past. Generally speaking the march of the world nearly always corroborates the cliché and the prejudice. Lastly—this is an idea I read in one of your books—there are several ways whereby we can attain the truth. Fools reach it down their own special path—the path of error. If fools were never right, I suppose the world would be too simple, too orderly and too easy to understand; intelligence and stupidity would stand face to face like God and the Devil.

ı: God and the Devil don't stand face to face any more than good and evil do. It isn't easy in everyday life to distinguish God from the Devil and make a clear-cut choice. The Devil weighs pretty heavily on the world so far as one can judge from the past ten or twelve thousand years.

HE: You're right. I would add that when a fool arrives at the truth down the path of error, it is a small triumph for the Devil. Fools are the prophets of evil.

ı: Oh, oh! No generalizations, please. Let's say that sometimes fools are the prophets of the Devil. Germaine, for one, and we'll leave it at that. Otherwise I shall make you contradict yourself. My mind is still full of the brilliant exposition you treated me to this afternoon about certain old bores in the Bible who were no sages but were nevertheless filled with the spirit of God, which made just as good use of their stupidity as the Devil, steering it down the selfsame paths of error to arrive at the same goal called Truth. One final thing regarding Germaine: you can't seriously tell me that in two years of persevering search she never came across a trace of lipstick on the corner of a handkerchief or a shirt collar?

HE: She would have loved to and God knows she hunted for such a trace! She had her plan all ready: she would leave the handkerchief lying about in some carefully chosen spot where Agnes couldn't fail to see it. But she never found a thing. For one good reason: Solange made herself up in the "Italian" style, leaving her lips their natural color. This made her look even younger and gave great pleasure to Edouard, who told her so on several occasions. She took up using lipstick again only at the beginning of 1958. A minor detail, a tiny one you may say, but worth noting, since it indicates that at this time she had ceased to conform to Edouard's tastes, bowing no longer to her lover's whims, as women delight in doing with an almost religious zeal so long as they are in love.

Now here's something to please you with your passion for chronology. We are going to jump to January 1957. To be exact, the tenth of January, 1957.

I: Aha! What happened on that date?

HE: That was the date of a first night at the Comédie Française. A rather brilliant affair which caused quite a stir. I was there.

I: What were they giving?

HE: Victor Hugo's *Les Misérables* in a new adaptation by Paul Achard.

I: And was it good?

HE: No, it was very second-rate and something of a bore, given that anything taken from Victor Hugo, even *Les Misérables*, can be a bore. At any rate the play was bad. I mean it didn't compel the spectator's full attention. One lost nothing by looking around and thinking of other things. I don't know if you're like me but I've a great weakness for the Comédie, all that red and gold, all that Republican splendor! First nights are more glamorous there than anywhere else.

I: Skip it. We're not here to boost the national theaters. Stick to the point.

HE: Damn it all, I told you that to give you a general picture: the bare-shouldered women in the foyer, the critics and academicians in the two front rows of the stalls, the smell of the theater, the buzz of excitement—it's fun to evoke it all. At least *I* enjoy it. When I go to a first night at the Comédie I have a feeling that society hasn't altered one scrap for a hundred years. Do you know a painting of 1880 or '90 depicting an interval at the Comédie? It shows stout, bearded gentlemen of the day chatting across the rows of stalls, sitting round with their arms propped on the backs of their seats, Francisque Sarcey, Henri Bauër, Catulle Mendès, Daudet, Lemâitre and so on, interlarded with beplumed and hothouse women. Almost none of this is any different today except for the clothes, if that. In 1957 poor Robert Kemp was still in this world. He had a piercing voice like a duck's and his quacking carried to the back of the house.

I: I find your genre picture a bore. I know it myself. I can paint it just as well as you. I could show you François Mauriac, tall, thin and bald like a stork, with his beady black eyes and wrinkled lids; Julien Cain gossiping with André Maurois, Aragon tenderly watching over Elsa, Gérard Bauër in the same seat as Henri, his father, and so forth. You are right, the picture hasn't changed since 1875. Unfortunately we no longer have the artists capable of reproducing it. The bastards all think they're geniuses nowadays. We're reaching the point of regretting Jean Béraud. So what happened at this first night, apart from the fact that you went to it?

HE: Several things that determined the future sequence of events with which we are concerned. I am one of those people who, in spite of every effort, can never manage to be late anywhere. The theater was still three quarters empty when I went to take my seat with my guest.

I: Oho, who was that?

HE: Someone of no interest and you don't know her. A girl I was seeing around that time.

I: It's really funny! I am always amazed at the idea that a man like you can have a private life, adventures, mistresses, pleasures and pains.

HE: Thanks very much. I am not made any differently from you, after all!

I: Forgive me, but you're a monster. A monster with a hundred eyes like Argus, and two hundred ears. You see all, you hear all, and what you don't see or hear you divine. How can there be any time left for you to live? Time! What am I saying? How can you even have any inclination for living a life of your own? I tell you, you deserve to be an artist. I only know a few great artists like Proust and Balzac who could transform themselves like you into sounding boards of the world.

HE: I sometimes tell myself that God overlooked me. He only gave me one half of genius. I do believe, in fact, that I have a Proustian eye, a Balzacian ear, I see everything without looking, I hear everything without listening but alas, my faculties stop short at that. I have the eyes and the ears but not the hand.

I: What is unique about you is this very fact that you have the ears and eyes without having the hand. As a general rule they all go together. I would even say that everything is conditional on having the hand. One learns to see and hear by dint of writing. It's with the hand that one digs. Deprived of the hand, it isn't a half genius you have but, to my mind, a double genius. This being so—I apologize for the digression—you are a complete mystery to me. You say that a secretive man is a strong man; you, then, are strength made man. Even to me you say nothing.

HE: What do you mean, nothing? I'm telling you everything, I simply don't want to talk about my love life. And do you know why? First, because it is happy; second, because it's vulgar to discuss one's love life; third, even a friend's love affairs are a deadly bore; fourth, because my affairs change pretty frequently and these changes are only fun for me.

But rest assured, I am neither sectarian nor stubborn. One day, maybe, one of my mistresses will appeal to me more than the rest, I shall marry her, you will act as my witness and the happy young couple will invite you to dinner every Tuesday!

I: All the same I'd rather appreciate it, you know, if once in a while you said to me: "I'm crazy about Madame de la Pommeraye, who has a peachy complexion, velvety eyes, hair like silk and the body of the Medici Venus; she adores me, she compromises herself ten times a day for me."

HE: My poor friend, women no longer compromise themselves. Or rather, nothing can any longer compromise them. It's heartbreaking. In 1830 a man had some merit in shouting his conquests from the roof tops: it stood out against the prevailing atmosphere of discretion. Today it is discretion that stands out. Don't you think we've talked long enough about myself? Let's get back to the Comédie. I was, then, sitting in about the tenth row of the stalls. . . .

I: I'll let you off if you describe the girl who was with you.

HE: A peachy complexion, velvety eyes, hair like silk and the body of the Medici Venus.

I: No fooling? How old?

HE: Twenty-six. A dress by Dior of a purplish color, rather extravagant, the way I like them. A stupid but highly affectionate angel. Nothing to write home about, you see. We could have done without this digression.

I: Not at all. It's most amusing, this picture of you as a ladies' man. It makes you human. Very well, so you were in the tenth row.

HE: Tenth or eleventh, I forget which. My companion was studying her program as if it were a legal textbook. Suddenly who should I see appear? Mlle. Solange Mignot accompanied by an extremely good-looking young man adorned with a very small nose.

I: Legay?

HE: Yes, Legay of course. Solange had Dietz's seats; he had a dinner party that night (or else perhaps he didn't much fancy the idea of seeing Les Misérables) and he had given her the tickets. She had summoned Legay and there they suddenly were before my eyes, young, charming and got up to kill. Solange had a pretty pink sequined dress, rather short, with costume jewelry and a chignon. Believe me, she looked fit to eat! Enchanting! Ravishing! And the air of a duchess without knowing it, as sometimes happened with her. As for Legay, he was more of the cicisbeo, the page, but a well-set-up sort of page with enough natural elegance to compensate for his badly cut suit. Together they made a highly successful entrance behind the usherette, who looked like Fairy Carabosse conducting Cinderella and Prince Charming and placed them you'll never guess where. In the row just in front of the one in which I was! As she sat down Solange turned round. She saw me and gave me a shy smile; then she began to chat to Legay, whose voice I heard as he replied to her. It was a nice, warm voice with meditative undertones. I was surprised at their intimacy, at the understanding that prevailed between them. It was self-evident, to me at least: their talk was animated and familiar, like that of two very trusting friends who have countless things in common without actually being lovers. One can accurately sense subtle distinctions of this kind. But, sitting behind them, I could also see Legay's devotion very clearly. It evinced itself in a certain way he had of bending toward his companion, surrounding her with little attentions, helping her to arrange her scarf round her shoulders. There was in his whole attitude an air of shy possessiveness which was wholly revealing. He dared not openly show he knew Solange would one day be his and that he was savoring this happiness in anticipation. A timid fiancé—that's what he suggested. A fiancé who is not yet loved but who feels that he will be, given enough submission, discretion and patience. A fiancé relying on time, habit, the respect and affection he will eventually came to inspire. I've known other men who have waited like this for a woman and who have not done so in vain, as if their humility and self-abnegation pleased destiny or as if by dint of persevering they finally succeeded in softening the cruel one's heart. There comes a moment, in fact, when the latter, after sowing all her wild oats, finds herself alone and despondent with an empty heart. This is her aspiring lover's opportunity: he is there; it is to him she turns, it is on him that she confers the sentiments that must be conferred on someone.

ɪ: Well, you do manage to see a lot of things from the back! And what else did you see? What did Solange's back tell you?

ʜᴇ: As I admired it, that pretty bare back also told me a story. The charming Solange was by no means sitting stiffly in her seat but was leaning slightly toward Legay, not the way one leans against a lover but rather as one inclines toward a friend whose presence one finds comforting and relaxing. What particularly struck me was the naturalness with which she and Legay behaved toward each other. They were neither tongue-tied nor self-conscious nor overtalkative. When their conversation flagged their silence carried no feeling of constraint. It was a "busy" silence during which the thoughts of each peacefully mulled over what the other had just been saying. It even struck me that in her behavior Solange was showing a certain superiority. Legay neither embarrassed nor intimidated her. With him she was the young queen who speaks first, who takes the initiative, gives the lead, directs whatever is said or done. I don't think it was due to skill that he permitted her to adopt this role (although it would indeed have been extremely skillful of him). No, he admired and loved her so sincerely and so desperately that he had no alternative. For an old hand like me, who knows all the answers, you can imagine how easy it was to foretell the future from the sight of those two backs in front of me. It was as clear as if I had seen it printed in a book. I was astonished at the place Legay had come to fill in Solange's life within so short a space of time. I immediately felt that the affair with Roberti was condemned to more or less short shrift. Roberti fatigued Solange; Legay represented a much-needed calm after this storm which had lasted for over a year and a half and was still to last for another year and more. He was the haven long prepared in advance, the dovecote waiting for the dove's exhausted return after a long and ill-considered flight. The dove was not yet quite ready to return to the dovecote but I, as I sat behind her, could sense that she was casting furtive glances at it while as yet unaware of the nostalgia underlying them.

What with all this, time had passed. It was nearly nine o'clock. The warning bell had begun to ring outside. While I was studying the backs of Legay and Solange the theater had filled up. Two seats beside them still remained empty.

I: Waiting for Roberti and Agnes, inevitably.

HE: Exactly. One of fate's unfailing little tricks. One of those encounters we can never believe in when we come across them in novels. And yet life frequently arranges them for us. Even so my heart lurched when I saw Edouard and Agnes appear and, after disturbing several members of the audience who were already seated, squeeze past Solange and Legay and sit down in their seats. Roberti knew at least fifty people in the theater.

I: Glory! The plot thickens. This is fascinating. What sort of a face did he put on it?

HE: Perfectly ghastly! I distinctly saw him go scarlet to the roots of his hair. From where I sat I could almost hear the pounding of his heart in his chest. He pushed past Solange without a word, without even a glance. By another malicious trick of fate Agnes was in front of him, so that he was obliged to sit next to Solange. Take my word for it, it was an incredible sight. He was petrified. Solange had risen to allow him room to pass, turning slightly so that I could see three quarters of her face. She hadn't been expecting this apparition either. But you know the self-control possessed by even the most vapid, most ingenuous of women. You can imagine how I kept my eyes riveted on her! She remained cool as marble. I could see the corner of her eye: it didn't even twitch. Her lover's scarlet face had instantly told her all she needed to know. What a lesson for me to see this artless young woman and this wily old parliamentarian side by side! The attitude of the former was inscrutable. Her heart may well have been beating as wildly as Edouard's but it was impossible to tell. No trace of a blush; she was the perfect image of indifference. Conversely the latter was flabbergasted, scared out of his wits; so much so that when he trod on Solange's foot he didn't even think to say "Excuse me!" It was this, I learned later on, which hurt her most. She imagined that he had stepped on her foot deliberately, out of spite, in revenge for the untoward chance which had set him down beside her in the theater. When Roberti was seated, I looked at his hand on the arm of his stall: it was shaking. He was so ill at ease that Agnes inquired with a touch of anxiety whether he was feeling all right. Instinctively he shifted his whole body toward his right, toward Agnes, as if the slightest contact with his mistress in this public place threatened to brand him. After a couple of minutes he turned round in order to give himself time to compose himself while pretending to scan the audience. But he was still so panic-stricken that he stared me full in the face for twenty or thirty seconds without recognizing me. Since I understood this maneuver, not one of these details having escaped me, I waited for him to recover and calmly, placidly stared back at him with a reassuring smile. He finally became aware of my presence and greeted me with a forced, artificial volubility akin to that of cowards when they have just eluded some danger. He was particularly handsome that night, I must admit, and not so deeply upset that he didn't run his eye over the girl beside me, who, though I say it myself, was also extremely good-looking. There followed a rather curious interlude. The sight of this pretty girl calmed him more effectively and rapidly than anything else could have done; she caught his fancy straightaway and he immediately put on his act: he emphasized the beguiling tilt of his head toward his right shoulder; he smiled; his whole face, which a moment before had been abject with fear, became as if by magic smooth, fresh and kindly. He asked me to introduce him; Agnes looked round in turn and greeted me. I could follow Roberti's thoughts step by step, as it were, and was highly amused. My young friend was claiming his full attention, he had almost forgotten Solange, he was purring. He mentally compared Solange with this young lady and the result was certainly not in Solange's favor. He envied me for being a bachelor and able to choose at leisure from among the most ravishing girls in Paris.

I: And Solange, what was she doing all this time? She could hear Roberti lavishing compliments on your conquest, she could see him flirting under her nose. She must have been foaming at the mouth, wasn't she?

HE: You can imagine how I was watching her as well. But she never stirred. She wasn't talking either, however. Her conversation with Legay, lively enough before Roberti's arrival, had suddenly lapsed. This was the only sign I could gather of her feelings. Apart from that she was motionless. Not the slightest tremor ran down her shoulders. As I said, women's powers of dissimulation are monstrous! She simply turned her head at one moment to give Agnes a long look. I intercepted this look. I tried to interpret it in all kinds of ways, to see in it hatred or sympathy, but so far as I know it expressed nothing but curiosity. Alas, that night poor Agnes was not at her best. Her face looked tired and, as she had doubtless gone to the hairdresser that afternoon, her ringlets were particularly absurd. Turned out elegantly enough as to the rest, but with a drab, a deliberately drab elegance, as befits the wife of a public figure.

I: If I remember correctly, Agnes had seen Solange during the January '56 election. Didn't she recognize her?

HE: Now that you mention it, it's odd, these two women meeting face to face one year later to the very day! I hadn't thought of that. Your question raises an interesting point, you know. Yes, she did recognize her, but only vaguely. The face was not wholly unfamiliar. But she couldn't any longer remember where she might have seen it. The stare Solange gave her must have been loaded with pregnant questions since Agnes, who just then was leaning over the back of her seat to speak to me, suddenly turned round as if in response to a summons. She saw Solange and obeyed the reaction of fashionable women who, if someone stares at them, smile and bow so as to avoid giving any chance offense.

I: So she greeted Solange whereas Roberti had pretended to ignore her? That's really magnificent!

HE: "Greeted" is going too far. She merely nodded and sketched a smile.

I: And Solange?

HE: Well, she gave a slight nod too, but without smiling. A grave, distant, pensive nod which made a rather disagreeable impression on

Agnes. It was the greeting of an enemy. But as Agnes had no reason to think that this pretty, almost totally unknown blonde could be her enemy, she soon put it out of her mind.

I: I must say, I find this encounter between the two rivals at the Comédie superb. What a scene! It must have been a great moment for you, knowing all the cards as you did.

HE: After a suitable amount of blarney and beaming at my young friend, Roberti settled back in his seat; he felt sufficiently cooled down to dare turn his head to the left. He even had an intention, I believe, of giving Solange some sign of complicity. It was at this precise moment that he at last saw who her companion was and his heart received that almighty shock I mentioned earlier. Solange had never described Legay to him. I suppose he had formed a reassuring image of him, imagining him to be sickly-looking, dark, greasy, pimply and wearing glasses. Instead of which he saw before him a tall, handsome young man with a face illuminated by a warm smile, who was fussing about his, Roberti's, mistress as if she were a cherished wife to be protected and pampered. He was at once stupefied, filled with black rage and made indescribably unhappy. Note that he never for one second doubted that the young man was Legay. Most horrible of all, he was powerless to do or say anything. He could only suffer in silence. And I mean suffer, for jealousy, that to him unknown emotion, had now invaded him. He jealous! He was astounded. He tried to reason with himself, told himself it was quite a common reaction, nothing more than resentment, but to no avail. He didn't have much leisure to study Legay, since thirty seconds or a minute later the lights went down and the curtain rose. But this brief look had been worse than a prolonged inspection. Legay's youth and charm, his kindly air and attentive manner had stabbed him to the heart. It was a rude blow to discover so abruptly that Solange had such a good-looking young man for her confidant, consoler and comrade. I don't think he heard much of the first act of Les Misérables. Deep inside he was spluttering incoherently. He was cursing Solange, blaspheming, mentally yelling: "This is the end! Finished and done with. And good riddance! She's betrayed me!" He had been struck by Legay's protective gestures and Solange's surrender to them. He kept on harking back to these like a man who, in an evil-smelling place, can't stop sniffing the whole time.

Poor Edouard now endured a really cruel hour. It is a severe ordeal to experience the torments of jealousy over someone one regards as one's property, trusting in her completely and confident that one has a strong hold over her owing to the pleasures one alone can give her.

Roberti believed Solange lost to him forever and of course suffered unbearable agonies throughout the length and breadth of his soul. Will you allow me a comparison? I see jealousy like this: a man is tied to a woman by hundreds of bonds, sentimental or otherwise. Normally he is unaware of them because she is very close to him. But the woman only has to withdraw slightly for all these bonds to tighten, each of them biting into the flesh of the man who loves her. This can form a pretty good torture. And this is how Roberti suffered during the first act of *Les Misérables*. All the sentimental and physical bonds uniting him with his mistress, normally so slack, had suddenly pulled taut. Jealousy in itself is a terrible thing. But what of helpless jealousy, which one cannot express either by a gesture or a groan, nor even by a sigh? Given his character, given the public place where he was, given Agnes, Roberti was condemned to sit still in his seat, rigid and impassive as a blind-drunk Englishman, while the vulture tore at his heart. Poor man!

During the intermission he took his time studying Legay and then, turning to me, suggested a stroll in the foyer. What showed me that he had been suffering badly was the fact that he no longer had any eyes for my fair companion. The first effect of jealousy is to make its victim faithful. The most ravishing creature in the world appears a toad, a nonentity, compared with the cause of one's jealousy. Everybody knows or senses this, since love's most elementary ruse consists of inspiring jealousy in the person one is out to win. The soul's pain can paralyze like physical pain, that is to say it is all-absorbing, it hangs a curtain between you and the world, it kills every desire other than that your suffering should cease. Roberti's changed attitude was so marked that even my companion noticed it. "What a shame!" she murmured in my ear. "Such a charming man and he doesn't like me any more. He's fickle: during the play he glanced at least thirty times at the blonde on his left. And yet I think I'm better-looking."

I: She really said "Such a charming man"?

HE: Yes, and I even think she found him more charming still during the interval, inattentive as he was, than during those few minutes an hour before when he had chatted to us over the back of his seat. This is sufficiently unusual to be worth noting, for there can be few middle-aged men whose appeal is enhanced by anxiety. As a rule only happiness and good humor can make a man of fifty-two attractive. The slightest worry adds ten years to his looks. Not so Roberti. Under the weight of his unhappiness he was Byronic, he looked like an elderly Manfred, but perhaps that is a quality only possessed by the pangs of love: the pains they cause are so searing that they whip up one's blood, stimulate

one's vitality; they rejuvenate since they are never entirely painful. One cannot help softening toward the creature who inflicts them on one and who, if she wished, could in a flash replace them with utter bliss.

During the second half of the play I believe Roberti spent most of his time *reasoning things out*, that is to say providing himself in the circumstances with a few grounds for optimism. He summoned to the rescue the scenes which normally took place in the Square Saint-Lambert and the last of which dated only two days back. "She can't have forgotten that," he thought. "She never would or could do what we do with anyone else. *She wouldn't dare*: her modesty would prevent her. No other man knows her the way I do, no other man could be as inventive and daring with her as I am. I am as familiar with her body as with my own and she knows it. She knows that the smallest caress from me is already an indescribable ecstasy for her. Therefore I am the only man she loves." In spite of everything he was in a state of such anguish that he felt an urge for some contact with her, however slight, however imperceptible. Very gently, almost without moving, so slowly that it was barely noticeable, he edged toward his left until his shoulder touched that of his mistress. He was hoping Solange wouldn't move, that she would accept this faint pressure as an admission of love and repentance.

I: The poor little goose was quite capable of it.

HE: Yes, of course she was. In January 1957 her love and devotion were still very deep, but directly she felt Edouard's arm against her own and understood his purpose, she leaned away toward Legay. She hadn't yet swallowed the latest insult; Agnes' greeting had equally upset her: finally she didn't want to have the slightest contact with Roberti in front of Legay.

I: Really? Why? As a rule that sort of thing doesn't trouble women at all. I've often noticed them happily kissing yesterday's lover under the nose of tomorrow's. Logically, she should have pointed Roberti out to Legay and told him: "That is the man I love. See how handsome, how intelligent, how smart he is." A woman is always proud of her lover, especially before a friend whom she knows adores her hopelessly. It's just the sort of sadistic little trick women like to indulge in.

HE: Well, so far as I know she said nothing of the kind to Legay. In the first place she wasn't sadistic and would have hated to hurt him. Second (and this is not without importance) Legay was too good-looking himself to be crushed by any comparison with Roberti. Third, she didn't want him to know she had a man of that age for her lover. This too is not without importance. It is the first time we can detect a

hint of shame in Solange. She told herself Legay might well be disgusted to learn she was the mistress of a man old enough to be his father. Last, given that she overruled these three objections, her instinct restrained her from making such a confidence. Legay represented the pure side of her life. This refuge must be preserved at all costs.

Throughout the length of the play Solange kept her distance from Roberti. Her attitude was as plain as if she had said: "Don't touch me, I loathe and despise you." This was how he interpreted it, at any rate. He peered through the darkness to see whether Legay had his arm round her shoulders or was holding her hand. But honest Legay would never have permitted himself such liberties. It was Solange herself who was pressing against him, without the slightest amorous intention, by the way. She had drawn her right arm close into her side and was leaning heavily to her left toward Legay, who dared not move, thrilled as he was by his good fortune and voluptuously letting his companion's warmth and perfume waft over him. Roberti stormed. "Little slut, whore," he thought, "I'll make you pay for this, just wait and see!" He was literally beside himself with fury and chagrin. "But maybe," he thought further, "it's no longer in my power to make her suffer?" Deep in his nerves and muscles jealousy revealed itself in a weird agony of *impatience*. He would have given anything to be able to pound his fist on a table, to say frightful, unspeakable, irreparable things to Solange. Momentarily he lost control of his thoughts, as madmen do. Actually the most painful part of it all was this physical *impatience*, of which I can give you no better description than the word itself. Like anger, it lodged in well-defined places: behind his knees and in the pits of his elbows, his calves, his ankles, his biceps, his chest. You know how highstrung he was: his diaphragm had contracted and was causing him pain. He felt as if his brain were filled with a heavy red cloud. I imagine that for a man of action like him, that is to say a man for whom thought is only the first step toward bringing some pressure to bear on events, such a state must be intolerable. Indeed, he was reduced to one thought alone, and this thought was like a chained beast. At the end of the last act, after the curtain calls, Solange slipped out as quickly as she could with Legay, keeping her eyes lowered and her head averted from Roberti. In this she did the right thing, as he would have filled her with fear. His mouth was so twisted that it was hideous.

He spent a very bad night. Impossible to sleep. At three A.M. he took a sedative which procured him a few hours' fitful dozing. Every hour or so he would wake up and listen to his heart beating against the sheet, which is the sad music of insomnia. He seized these opportunities to *rationalize.* By morning this intermittent rationalizing in the night had certainly not killed jealousy but had at least contrived to mask it. Roberti was convinced he had drawn up his balance sheet with complete honesty and that through it he could now see clearly into his soul. I will try to sum this up for you in one coherent soliloquy. "I don't love Solange," he told himself, "but I want to keep her because she is very *convenient.* I shall never find another mistress whose body has such close affinities with mine. I have always treated her too casually. That young man who was with her at the theater is a timely warning. I must make allowances. I will see her more often, take her to restaurants or for drives in the Bois de Meudon. I don't think she asks for more. Besides she loves me, there's no doubt of that. I behaved pretty shabbily last night at the theater, when I stepped on her foot. I will cover my head with ashes and she will forgive me. Women need a little drama and emotionalism now and then."

ı: Ugh! What a terrifying argument!

ʜᴇ: Yes, it's not very pretty, but what excuses poor Roberti in my eyes is that this argument was a lie from beginning to end, it was the cheap and misconceived explanation of a feeling whose violence he had never suspected. Anyhow, even if it soothed his mind up to a point, it didn't soothe his body, where the same impatience still lodged in the aforementioned places (calves, elbows, etc.). His body was sick from inactivity. To use the old phrase, he couldn't sit still. He would have liked to rush from one end of Paris to the other, grab at events with both hands, get busy, talk, bring his casuistry into play. He was haunted by Solange's anger, so eloquently expressed in the theater by her gesture of recoil from any contact with him; this preoccupation had rooted itself in his mind and he couldn't shake it off. He dared not telephone her. "I mustn't do anything hasty," he told himself. "I'll call her in a day or two. Or perhaps she'll get in touch with me, in which case I shall have regained the upper hand." But he couldn't work or even keep his mind on anything. His heart was beating in an unaccustomed fashion like that of a coward anticipating some danger and curling up within himself, powerless to act, unable to prepare the slightest defense, paralyzed by fear and horror. As the day advanced, the impatience in his muscles diminished, changed its nature. It spread right through him and at the same time was diluted. It became an at once vague and powerful state of being. For the first time in his life he felt what subsequently, when he tried to describe it to me, he called "the bleak impatience of the soul." What is it exactly? A general disposition, not painful but unpleasant. One has the impression of not fully inhabiting

one's body. One is slightly above oneself, as when one has a temperature of ninety-nine or a hundred degrees. One feels out of sorts, one's
heart beats faster and louder than usual. One has no specific desire but
a vague and flabby purpose. One's mind is prey to a mirage, so that
the weirdest measures one contemplates to release one from one's
"bleak impatience" seem completely natural. This bleak impatience is
basically a sort of soul sickness, a languor, an anemia induced by the
destructive action of an exaggerated emotion on an overdelicate or neurotic constitution.

ɪ: Couldn't one possibly call it madness?

ʜᴇ: Yes, possibly. It's a kind of madness. Roberti experienced it
anyway, on the eleventh of January, 1957. On that day he indeed behaved like a lunatic. His delusion lay in that he believed all along he
had the situation well in hand and at worst was only play-acting. Toward four or five in the afternoon, impelled by a really weird notion, he
took his revolver from the drawer in his desk. It was to form one of the
"props" in the pretty scene busily evolving in his mind. As he put the
revolver in his pocket he smiled, he felt almost jubilant. Like someone
thinking up a splendid joke. Whereupon he got into his car and drove
off in the direction of the Square Saint-Lambert. Near the apartment
building was a café which he entered. He asked for the telephone and
dialed the number of Dietz's office. When he heard Solange's voice at
the other end of the line, he was seized with an extraordinary frenzy
as if his nerves, stretched to the breaking point, had suddenly gone
slack. He began sniveling and sobbing and babbling almost incoherently.

ɪ: Babbling what, for example?

ʜᴇ: "Solange, is that you? I love you. I am going to die. I can't go on
any longer. Life is too stupid. I'm a fool and a failure. Good-by. I've got
my revolver. It's odd but it isn't raining today, although it's January.
Don't forget to bring me back the Huxley novel I lent you three months
ago, you must have read it by now. It's not one of his best. I'm such a
fool, darling, such a fool; I never understood what was going on in your
heart. You'll never be loved the way I love you." Solange was panic-
stricken. She was scared out of her wits to hear her beloved, normally
so sarcastic and poised, jabbering such nonsense. The little goose wasn't
deceived for a minute as to the reasons for Edouard's broken stammering. She immediately realized he was asking her to forgive him for his
behavior and she felt such a wave of tenderness that the tears welled
into her eyes—*dixit* Mlle. Angioletti, who was standing beside her and
not missing one scrap of this enthralling episode. In a voice as tremulous
as Roberti's she asked where he was. "I shall be at our place in a min-

ute," said Edouard. "Don't do anything," cried Solange. "I'll be round right away. I love you."—"That's not true," gulped Edouard, "you don't love me. You can't love me. Why should you? You've no reason to. I shall disappear from your life. That will be the last proof of love I can give you." He was stupefied to hear himself saying these things. "Why the hell am I telling her all this?" he wondered. "Is this me talking?" In the telephone booth, search his heart as he would, he could detect no particular pain, no passion in it. It was as if it were all taking place outside him. He was stammering, his voice was choked with tears and it bore no relation to the facts. What a strange phenomenon! "It's my nerves," he thought. He who normally had such command over his words and attitudes couldn't manage to control his voice nor to stem this flood of passionate declarations pouring from his mouth. All he could do was regard it as a physical discharge and marvel at it. "It's not possible," he told himself, "I'm having some kind of fit!" It was in fact rather like a nervous fit, when the subject remains perfectly lucid while his body is reduced to helpless twitching. And this completely altered voice, this voice which was not his own, whispering and moaning, pitiful, wracked with sobs! Impossible to recapture its normal pitch. He couldn't tear himself away from the telephone. It was Solange who hung up first in her anxiety to rush to him. He left the café mentally repeating to himself: "What's going on, but what is going on?" He went up to the studio, taking care to leave the door ajar so that Solange could walk straight in. He sat down on the divan. He was shaking all over but his mind was clear and alert as usual. Out loud he said: "All the same, I'm a damned good actor! I laid it on pretty thick! Poor sweet, she was knocked sideways! Did I overdo it perhaps? She'll end by believing I really love her. That would be a laugh!"

ı: For heaven's sake give me a moment to get my breath back!

HE: You'll get it back presently. He was no sooner seated on the divan than his bleak impatience descended on him again. Solange would be arriving at any moment. He must round off the telephone scene with a really impressive tableau. I hardly like to tell you that "something" outside him drove him to perform all these crazy actions, that would be too easy a way of explaining the inexplicable; and yet that is exactly what it was. Inwardly he was calm, sensible and even cool. With the utmost composure he took off his tie, unbuttoned his collar, removed his shoes, ruffled his hair, undid his trousers and stretched out on the divan. By an incredible effort of will, one of those *tours de force* of nature which doctors can never comprehend, he contrived to drain his face of blood and *turn pale*. He then took his revolver from his pocket and laid it on his chest. "While I'm about it," he thought, "let's carry it right through. When she comes in she'll see me lying white-faced on the bed, she'll think I'm dead and get one hell of a shock." His mind, as I said, was clear and alert, but strangely enough he never noticed that he had lost all critical sense. It never for one moment crossed his mind that he was turning the whole business into a farce. No, he was so deeply caught up in his performance that he was overcome by a feeling that he was really dying, that he was already virtually a corpse and how infinitely sweet it was to be dead. A bit sad but infinitely delicious and consoling. The "I" no longer existed; it was abolished by all this strange behavior.

ı: Forgive me but I'm getting totally out of my depth. Was he mad or wasn't he?

HE: It depends what you mean by "mad." We constantly see completely normal people act as if they were possessed or anyway sick. They begin by putting on an act and then get swept away by their performance. It's something often to be observed in children: they start to play quietly enough and then the game ends in fits of hysterics. In an affair of this kind I believe we should always bear in mind the sort of split which takes place in its subject. The body is seized with frenzy but the mind remains calm and contemplates the body's frenzies more or less with amazement. As a rule it condones them, since it places these frenzies very firmly in their context. They are never gratuitous. A man of fifty-two can develop these childish frenzies when overwhelmed by an emotion like love which he has constantly denied, thwarted, curbed and throttled. I believe that on this occasion Roberti's love for Solange finally spoke or, if you prefer, cried out, and took the form of this present masquerade which was somehow farcical but also touching.

ı: Touching? I should like to know what is so touching about these antics.

HE: This: that Roberti was in a tragic trance. We say "a fit of madness," but tragedy is also a fit. Moreover shortly before on the telephone, it was a tragedian's voice he had, not at all the tones of everyday life but a sort of chanting singsong. This tone of voice was not altogether unfamiliar to him: he had already had it before on two or three crucial occasions in his life. It came from some obscure part of himself; it was not born in his throat but, so it seemed, in his eyes or his brain, whence it descended into his mouth. He was at once deeply unhappy and deeply happy, like a man passing through some inevitable ordeal and upborne by hope. But tragedy has its own inner logic and there are times when it drags you further than you had meant to go. Roberti had laid his hand on his revolver. He raised it and gave it a slow stare, then opened the breech and slipped a bullet into the barrel. He held the barrel to his temple, to his heart, to his stomach, and sank into a little reverie on suicide. A childish reverie, I hasten to add, the principal scene of which was: "Solange arrives, she finds me lying dead and bathed in blood. Her grief. She weeps over my body." He took the greatest delight in the notion of her weeping over his body. It was delicious to picture himself being mourned by his mistress, by this beautiful young woman.

I: Do you know what I think? Your friend Roberti was driven by a constant desire to appear in a good light. In a drama of passion it is always the corpse which appears in a good light.

HE: Aren't you being unduly harsh? So far as I am concerned, I interpret it quite differently. I think that here, alone in the studio waiting for Solange and certain of her imminent arrival, he abandoned himself completely and for the first time to his love. He at last told himself the truth or, rather, his body forced the truth on his mind. The proofs of love are always external, are actions; and here at last love was proved from outside, proved by real acts of madness, by this ludicrous behavior. If you can't see the features of love itself in Roberti lying on the divan in the Square Saint-Lambert and toying with his revolver, you'll never see it anywhere. On the one hand this cool mind and empty heart; on the other this body shaken by a veritable cataclysm—to my mind these are as revealing as an anatomical dissection. I can see love as clearly as through a microscope, I can trace its course with my finger. And what confirms me in this idea is the kind of joy Roberti took in playing the fool like this. He was no longer self-impelled; his soul was pouring out through his body; he felt utterly at peace, he was reconciled with himself.

I: I'm terribly sorry but I don't agree with you at all. I can't see any love in these antics. I see a far less noble sentiment: self-pity, in other words selfishness. He was behaving like a spoiled child anxious to punish its mother for taking away its sweets. He was indulging in emotional blackmail of the worst possible kind; the blackmail of suicide. Besides, you have implied as much yourself in the way you've described the incident. You have several times used the words "performance" and "act." That's what it was—a performance, a comedy.

HE: If you look at it that way, the whole of life is just a performance, just a comedy. One is forced to take men's actions at face value, if only because they perform them. There are some people who carry their play-acting to the point of suicide.

I: Listen! On the one hand you give me a certain number of facts; on the other you give me your interpretation of these facts. Your interpretation is not the same as mine, that's all. I simply said that I could see no love in Roberti's antics, only self-pity. Added to which I see despair. Such tomfoolery, to my mind, marks the beginning of despair, which always expresses itself in the first instance through boredom. Roberti was a man who was bored and seeking some diversion, whence all this mockery. He was out for new sensations like an old tyrant, like Tiberius or Dionysius of Syracuse. As he hadn't the same means as Tiberius at his disposal, no Christians handy to throw to the lions or little boys to bathe with in the rock pools of Capri, he fell back on clowning; it was his way of enjoying a thrill of horror, so dear to the blasé of this world. Solange's absolute love had corrupted him in the same way as absolute power corrupts. She had refused him nothing, complied with all his sexual fantasies, made herself his slave. That wasn't enough. He wanted still more. He wanted to stun her as never before with a scene of mock heroics. I already had a suspicion of this earlier, with regard to the Amouroux episode in Florence.

HE: That can also be a way of loving.

I: Oh no! You can't get away with twisting the point like that. The love of the executioner for his victim, of the pimp for his whore, of the bully for his whipping boy, has nothing in common with the love you've been describing since lunchtime. It's something quite different.

HE: Nonsense. Love is made of thirty-six thousand ingredients. In the long run it is only actions which count, at least in men's eyes. It is by his actions that we finally judge a man. As to his intentions, they are nothing. Hot air. As if they never existed.

I: How do you dare, and I mean *dare*, employ such an argument—you who are always searching for what is behind every action, who regard actions as so many lies nearly always contradicting the inner truth?

HE: Look here, I'll tell you a story. I know a very united couple, married for forty years, a paragon of conjugal love. A painter of allegories or mythological scenes could use them as models for Philemon and Baucis. The husband can never shower enough attentions on his wife. Even old age and habit have failed to damp his enthusiasm, which is that of a young man, a fervent lover still "under the spell." The wife is a capricious and despotic character. They are called Charles and Lucie. Lucie has bad moods which plunge Charles into an agony of despair.

"What can have happened to upset her?" he asks. "She's such a sensitive soul. Any little bit of vulgarity makes her wretched for two days." During these two days when Lucie is mute and taciturn, Charles clearly suffers torments. So he redoubles in tact and submissiveness. It's pathetic to see this man nearing seventy so perplexed and fearful as to what can have ruffled his spouse. Nobody knows any instance of one being seen without the other in public. He still dances attendance on her like a young man: he puts his arm round her shoulders and kisses her hands ten times a day. She accepts this homage unemotionally but also tolerantly. She conveys the impression of being a queen receiving her just due and condescending to love the vassal who so honors her. Charles watches over her happily, gently, anxiously, devotedly. He is so familiar with Lucie's feelings that one can read on his face, according to whether it is lit up or downcast, the gay or sad thoughts passing through her mind. No one has ever heard them quarrel. Never anything but solicitous inquiries, little gifts and artful flattery. It's as if, with the years, Lucie has been infected by such devotion. She too is wrapped up in Charles, worries about his idiosyncrasies, fusses about his health and his peace of mind. Sometimes it is she who takes his hand and gives it a friendly squeeze. Her arid and vindictive nature has greatly softened; her susceptibilities are less acute; her selfishness less pronounced. On occasion she will even subject her own whims to the desires of her husband, when by chance he has any. She has at length been touched and mellowed by the grace of conjugal love. This rather sad woman often smiles these days. Forty years of a man's exclusive adoration have reconciled her to herself.

Now I am practically convinced that Charles doesn't love Lucie and never has. He doesn't hate her; she means as little to him as a stone. For forty years he has been play-acting at conjugal love. Why? For a long time it puzzled me. Finally I came to believe it is out of a taste for glory and self-sacrifice. He wants to bequeath the example of a great love to the world and finds a certain voluptuousness, too, in driving himself on the way he does. This love, though in his heart of hearts he knows exactly what it's worth, is his work of art, his masterpiece. This rare and singular passion he has built up out of nothing is an object of his own creation, of which he alone is the author and to which he is desperately attached, the way all creators are attached to their creations.

I ask you, now, where lies the truth of this man? Which is most real in him: what he shows, that is to say his love, or what he hides, that is to say his indifference? If he dies first, Lucie will cherish a memory of the most delightful husband there has ever been. If she dies first, it is possible that Charles will extend the comedy way beyond widowerhood and give every appearance of dying of grief. I mean that, to be true to his character right through, he will die of a false grief just as he has lived of a false love. Where does Charles's truth lie, I ask you? Don't answer me: I'll tell you. It lies neither in his soul nor in his outward attitude, neither entirely in his thoughts nor entirely in his actions. It lies elsewhere. Halfway between. At a meeting point, a geometrical intersection of his thoughts and actions. Rather closer to his actions than his thoughts, since a man isn't only what he is but also what he wants to be.

I: Why are you telling me all this? What are you getting at? I'm in a complete muddle now.

HE: I'm telling you all this to show that I'm taking your objection into account. Apart from three or four incidents and the final drama, during the whole duration of the affair between Solange and Roberti the latter played at nonlove, whereas I'd bet anything you like that in his heart he was seething with passion. As with my friend Charles, his truth was neither inside nor outside him; it was made up of the blend of outward indifference and inward passion, boredom, laziness, reverie, lust, possessiveness and the fit of jealousy I have described.

I: Your subtleties are quite beyond me. I see Roberti in his studio in the Square Saint-Lambert behaving like a lunatic. *You* say this was love breaking out and revealing itself at last. *I* say that love was never more absent. In other words I am registering a difference of opinion. We shall see at the end of the story who was right—I who never knew him or you who are still too close to him. Let me add one final point: you always like to compare him to Faust. I don't believe Faust felt much love for his Gretchen. His soul was far too blackened, far too scorched by despair. At best he simply wanted to sleep with somebody young. All right. Tuck that away in your pocket and let us have done with this false suicide, which is a really nauseating scene. Solange arrives, pushes back the half-open door and sees Roberti lying white as a sheet with his revolver on his chest.

HE: He had heard her come up the stairs. He had stretched his arms along his body like an effigy and closed his eyes, telling himself that this was a pretty pose, impressive as one could wish for, and that such macabre childishness was most unexpected coming from him. He never opened his eyes, never stirred an inch when she entered the room. She knelt down beside him without a word either. She took the revolver and threw it as far as she could across the floor. Then she murmured: "You're crazy to work yourself up into such a state! You shouldn't do it.

Is it true that you wanted to kill yourself over me?"—"Yes," quavered Roberti, thinking: "She's completely mad. I commit suicide for *her*? We're both raving." Solange had taken his hands and was kissing them. She was deeply moved but in no way surprised. Her love was such that she found the most incongruous scenes quite normal. Joyfully she told herself how "men are like this when they're in love."

I: Enough! I can't stand any more of it. I'm on the verge of being sick.

HE: I don't see why. Far more ghastly things happen in life. There are ludicrous scenes in every love affair. Besides, I believe love thrives on such madness.

I: What makes me feel sick is the mockery of it all. I feel nauseated by Roberti, nauseated by this clown.

HE: We are surgeons; we have no right to be nauseated. What would you say of a surgeon who, after opening up a patient's stomach, suddenly feels disgusted because he finds a cancerous growth there and primly stitches it up again without more ado? Roberti would be nauseating if his performance had been a studied one. But what is so interesting is that it wasn't. He was giving it against his will, poor man. He was undergoing a strange experience reminiscent of the one described by Nerval in his story called *The Bewitched Hand*. A man, if you remember, makes a pact with the Devil, who bestows on him a skillful, powerful, invincible right hand thanks to which he kills everyone in duels, writes sublime poetry, plays the piano like Paderewski and so on. Gradually, however, this hand begins to lead a life of its own. One day, for instance, it deals a senator a series of slaps in the face. The wretched man tries desperately to hold it back with his left hand but can't manage it: the right hand is the stronger. It continues to slap the senator while, with each well-aimed blow, its owner cries: "Oh forgive me, oh a thousand pardons, my dear senator, oh this is too terrible!" The story ends lamentably in the ignominious death of the man so possessed. It's a long time since I read this story of Nerval's and no doubt I've described it very badly. . . .

I: Very. Your summary is full of mistakes. It sheds a disturbing light on the way your memory retains things! How am I to know you haven't transformed Roberti's story in the same fashion?

HE: Have no fear of that! I lived through a part of his story myself, and far more recently than I read Nerval! To go back to *The Bewitched Hand*, the point that particularly struck me about it and which was admirably put across was the man's astonishment at the crazy things his hand got up to. Nothing inside him had changed, he was still the same rather meek, rather timid young man, nice enough, easygoing and on the whole simple. His pact with the Devil hadn't seemed to him a very grave matter—at any rate it hadn't altered his soul. He told himself how this pact wasn't really binding, how he could always denounce it sooner or later with a sign of the cross and a couple of paternosters. And then he found it was too late. His hand no longer obeyed his soul and all was lost. His hand was not himself, it was something external; yet it was this hand which determined his fate.

What more can I say? By summarizing Nerval's story (even if I went astray over details, I at least gave you its basic meaning) I have explained and justified what you call Roberti's clowning. Throughout this scene in the Square Saint-Lambert his body was *bewitched*. It no longer obeyed him. Here psychology merges with metaphysics. I can imagine a doctor explaining how there was no mystery about it, how it stemmed from some neurosis or "syndrome," and talking of hysteria or a split personality; but those are only long words used to cover behavior of which the cause remains unknown. Roberti was not sick; his mind was perfectly clear; his ego was still the old familiar ego he knew inside out; yet he was behaving like a man who was a total stranger to him. He watched his body acting in a play of which he himself was a spectator. He heard a voice which was not his own speaking through his mouth and saying things which in no way expressed what he was thinking or feeling without for all that being deliberate lies. I see no reason not to believe that he was at that moment possessed by the Devil. What was good enough for Nerval is good enough for me. I have said over and over again that Roberti's story, right from the start, was marked by the sign of Satan. In the folklore of Europe and the East, whether minstrels' tales or *A Thousand And One Nights*, we find many cases of the Devil manifesting himself by paralyzing a man or forcing him to do things of which the man himself disapproves. The Devil crashes down on his chosen victim like a bundle of chains. Today the Devil is more civilized, he worms his way into the nerve cells and neurologists give his manifestations names taken from the Greek, but the result is the same. Four times, during his affair with Solange, Roberti was *bewitched* in this way, that is to say on four occasions he did things of which he had had not the faintest inkling the day before and which were as alien to his nature as slapping the senator's face was alien to Nerval's hero. I have just described the first of these fatal acts. It was the least serious. The next one occurred about eleven months later. Before coming to it, we must however linger briefly over the scene in the Square

Saint-Lambert and its sequel. Forgive me for riding so roughshod over your delicate heart but it's indispensable.

After Roberti had been soothed, after his mistress's loving care had brought him back to normal, that is to say helped him to recover his normal voice, wits and natural color, he spoke of Legay, thinking at the same time how stupid this was, how one should never betray signs of jealousy and how he wasn't jealous anyway. But no doubt his fit wasn't yet quite over since, in spite of his better judgment, he was *unable to do otherwise* than talk of Legay. To save face he adopted a casual, almost bantering tone. "Who was he," he said, "that young man with you? He seemed a nice sort of fellow. I thought it was your friend Legay. He's far better-looking than I am. You never told me he was so attractive. I never suspected I had such a rival!"

I: And Solange's reply?

HE: Solange's reply—nothing. She didn't answer, not a word. She lowered her eyes and poor Edouard felt a stab of pain which is physically translated as "a hollow in the chest." He took her hands. Why was she suddenly so silent?

I: Yes, why?

HE: Ah, my friend, you may well ask! Women's souls change from one second to another without our knowing why, without their knowing why themselves. So long as he hadn't seen Legay, Solange was quite happy for Roberti to evoke an image of him; now he had seen him it was different; she was embarrassed. Embarrassed as, for instance, an honest woman can be when caught red-handed by her husband with a handsome young man to whom she has certainly granted no favors but whom she has not expressly discouraged. In a tone no longer bantering but arrogant and stilted, Roberti demanded: "Tell me, you're not by any chance about to brush me off, are you? I'm not in the habit of forcing myself on people, you know. The day you've had enough of me, you've only got to say so and you'll never see me again in your life."

I: He said that? Given the circumstances and the revolver, it was rather steep.

HE: No, it wasn't. It simply meant that the fit was over; his reason had resumed control of events; moreover Solange interpreted it that way. This *volte-face* aroused no sense of irony in her. "I know," she said sadly. Roberti was making giant strides back into his everyday skin. Nimbly as a young man he jumped down from the divan and went to comb his hair before the mirror. He no longer felt the slightest affection for Solange who, only five minutes before, had been rocking and comforting him with a truly maternal love and devotion. "What is she going to do?" he wondered as he combed away. "Is our affair over or not?" He turned to look at her. His body again took the initiative for the last time: despite the irritation which had replaced the madness in his heart, he smiled. It was a good and kind smile. It bore no relation to the situation but probably conveyed fairly accurately the enduring love with which he was imbued. At any rate it pierced Solange like a blessed arrow. She was still crouching by the divan: she jumped up and, flinging herself into her lover's arms, burst into tears. In a passionate and incoherent stream of words she told him that she loved him and him alone, that any other man filled her with hopeless disgust, that Legay meant nothing to her, less than nothing. As for Roberti, he was relaxed at last, happy at last. He held Solange close, stroked her hair, kissed her tears, kissed her mouth, though none of this dammed her stammering flood of words; in short it was a rapturous moment, one of those privileged moments which sometimes befall lovers when, without their knowing exactly how, emotion changes into desire.

Solange had been so stirred by all these goings-on that an old hope which had never been completely extinguished rose, so to speak, quite naturally to her lips. She was not weeping like a woman but like a little girl, hiccuping and sniffling, emitting a sort of lamentation, a watery wailing interspersed with half-intelligible words which touched Roberti more than he cared to admit. The hiccups became less frequent, the lamentation assumed some shape, the wailing acquired an increasingly clear meaning. Edouard finally gathered what she was asking him and, for the second time, the temptation came over him to satisfy her. "I want a child from you, darling," she kept repeating. "I must have one. I feel it. I need it. Do you understand? A child. A little baby. You wouldn't have to recognize it. It would be mine. Yours too, of course: you could see it whenever you liked. I could move in here with it, in the Square Saint-Lambert. You would come to see us twice a week or even less if you found it a nuisance. We wouldn't be any burden on you. I must have a child, my darling, I swear it on my life, I must, I must. I suppose you think I'm being stupid? Women get such funny ideas. Forgive me. But you can't know how a woman feels when she wants a child from the man she loves. And I've had this feeling for months. You've no idea how miserable it makes me sometimes to think how I might be carrying your child if only you'd let me. It's terrible. I'm twenty-six, I'll soon be twenty-seven. Am I never to have a child? What would it matter to you to give me a baby? It wouldn't alter your life in any way. Everything would be just the same and I should be so happy. I'm asking you to give me this baby. I won't ever blame you for it. I'll take full responsibility. I'll never say how you put me in this position and now you must pay for it. Far from it, I don't care if the child's illegitimate. You needn't feel any obligation toward me. If you leave me when I'm pregnant, I promise I shall never complain. I shall understand if you're sick of me or suddenly feel scared by this situation into which I've pushed you, my poor lamb."

Listening to this passionate speech and also (one must admit) these repeated and generous assurances, Roberti was, I say, tempted a second time. But with him temptation made only a halting progress; it was constantly held back by his reason. His heart leaped at Solange's yearning for procreation, which found echoes in the deepest part of his being. His head struggled valiantly against it. To himself he replied to his mistress's arguments: "Don't give in to a moment's enthusiasm. When she's pregnant she'll sing quite a different tune. At any rate I am a man of honor and would never desert a woman to whom I had given a child. Everything she is saying indicates a generous nature, certainly, but I already know darned well she has a generous nature. This generous soul will be an extra chain, an added reason for me to behave irreproachably. Besides, a child at my age! Lunacy! I am not going to turn my life upside down just to please Mlle. Mignot when I've got it so well organized. She wants a child today; by tomorrow she'll have forgotten about it. She'd be bitter as hell if I gave her one. She's just a child herself. At fifty-two it's up to me to be sensible for both of us." Kindly, patiently and very gently he explained to her every good reason there could be—and there were plenty—for not having a child. As she listened her face clouded over. Although her tears had ceased to flow, she was far sadder now than when she had been sobbing on his chest a few moments before. Faced with this genuine grief he pretended to compromise, like parents who don't want their children to despair. "Listen," he said, "what you're asking is a very serious matter. I'd be thrilled too if you presented me with a son or a daughter"—a pious lie—"but I think we ought to consider it more carefully. Look, let's give ourselves six months to think it over. If after six months you still want it, well . . ."

ɪ: How chilling! A lover who talks like a father is not very enthralling.

ʜᴇ: No. And accordingly Solange wasn't very enthralled. She understood perfectly that Roberti was just humoring her. But for once she was carried away, for once "it was her turn to speak." After he had reasoned it all out, marshaled all the arguments, totally defeated her on the grounds of logic, she said: "Forgive me. I'm a fool. Obviously we can't have a child, you and I. I've known for a long time it was impossible. I'm like a cat which longs for a kitten to lick, love and protect. But there, the cat is kept locked in; her master doesn't want her to have any kittens because that would cause him a frightful headache. You have your life and I have no part in it. I am outside it. You're not very brave, my poor darling, and that's a fact. I don't hold it against you. You just aren't. My God, how I would have loved you to be something more for me than what you are merely prepared to be! At the same time as your mistress, I should have liked to be your daughter, I should have liked to be guided by you. You don't know where I wouldn't have followed you. I'd have done anything you asked me, however reckless, but you never ask me to do anything reckless. Only sensible things, when I'd go through fire for you if necessary. Why do you always avoid taking decisions? You have made a woman of me, you have opened my mind to beautiful things, but I can never count on you. You're like quicksand. There's not a single situation in my life in which I can rely on you. Oh, well. I suppose things just have to be that way and that it's all right, since it's you I love. But you mustn't be surprised if sometimes your little cat is sad."

I: I must say she was being damned intelligent that day, Solange was! She had got it all pat. There was Roberti exposed, judged, X-rayed. Quite magnificent and unexpected.

HE: Women are like that, Jean. From time to time they are inspired. They see all and say all. The man in question is abashed by so much perspicacity. It has nothing to do with intelligence. It isn't their minds speaking.

I: At any rate, Roberti must have felt thoroughly cut down to size.

HE: How right you are! Every one of Solange's words went home. But he found grounds for comfort in the fact that she seemed to be yielding to reason. He had convinced his opponent. A victory was well worth a few moral scratches. Moreover through an illusion current among intelligent men, he thought that Solange's remarks, however just, didn't mean anything; she wasn't subtle enough to have found all this out for herself; she had said what she had under the weight of her disappointment; her words had *chanced* to correspond with the truth, just as bad marksmen sometimes unintentionally hit the bull's-eye. Now in this he was wrong; in love there is no bad marksmanship. Every shot is carefully aimed and every bullet hits the target.

He put on an agonized expression for form's sake. In two or three days' time she would have *thought better of it*. Not only did he believe in the sovereign powers of reason and logic but he wouldn't admit that there can exist minds which are impervious to them, vegetable minds, so to speak, like trees whose leaves change direction following the unpredictable whims of the wind and turn yellow in autumn, trees whose branches wither and die if they aren't watered by the rain. What pressure, I ask you, can reason and logic bring to bear on a woman who longs for motherhood, whose body cries out for this suffering and fulfillment, whose heart yearns for this complement to love? One might as well expound Kant's philosophy to a goldfish.

I am always fascinated to see a man apply the tricks of his trade to his private affairs. Roberti here conducted himself like a parliamentarian, for whom talk and action are nearly always one and the same thing and who knows it's by putting forward arguments that one wins a vote. What's more, he conducted himself with his mistress like a French parliamentarian of the Fourth Republic. The way of the old bourgeois democracies doesn't reflect any keen desire for progress; the tendency is more to resist the onward rush of events. It is trench warfare, in which one clings to the ground one holds, as opposed to mobile warfare in the Napoleonic style, in which armies sweep from nation to nation and conquer Europe in a month. This aspect of the politics of his time and country had left a deep mark on Roberti; his character had gradually been altered by it. The drawback to this defensive approach is that any success one achieves is a local, precarious success constantly put in doubt. Sometimes it is purely formal and hence illusory. The success Edouard achieved over Solange was one of these. It wasn't difficult to triumph in argument over this poor girl. The battle lay elsewhere.

I: Where?

HE: Nowhere. There was no possible battle and hence no possible victory. Since I am drawing political comparisons I would add that Solange was in the same confused state of mind as a nation preparing to stage a revolution. She was beginning to feel the injustice of her condition; she was aspiring to reforms. Revolutions are avoided by introducing reforms in time. But the group in power always wants to retain all its privileges, so it keeps them a moment too long and the result is catastrophe. Rivarol has an admirable comment on this: "To bring about a revolution a certain amount of stupidity on the one hand is more necessary than a certain measure of enlightenment on the other." The stupidity of intelligent men when they are in power sometimes passes understanding. With regard to Solange, Roberti was in the position of a conservative government ("immobilist," as they used to say in 1957, if you remember) well content with the order of things, with affairs idling, the stagnation of the regime, thanks to which it can govern in perfect peace without the slightest call for initiative or energy. Women and nations resemble each other in so far as "immobilism" irritates them both; when they become aware of this irritation they will stop at nothing to have done with it. Nations take arms and women take a lover.

1: You'd do better to cut out these high-flown phrases. Put things simply and trust in me as far as style goes. "Nations take arms and women take a lover." Grotesque! I can't stand such fireworks. Besides, you've flown high enough. Come back to earth.

HE: Well, the first thing to point out is that the crazy scene of January the eleventh achieved its aim. Solange had a renewed "crystallization" over Edouard in spite of the disillusioned little speech to which she had treated him and which left her with a bad taste in her mouth. But the bad taste dispersed in the next few hours. At heart she was touched; she was grateful to discover she was more loved than she had dared to believe. This shows how one should never be afraid to "lay it on thick" with women. They are impervious to ridicule; the most ghastly melodrama moves them to tears if it's they who have provoked it: it permits them to measure the extent of their power over their lovers. Solange wasn't in the least shocked by the scene Roberti had just played. In it she recognized the traditional marks of passion, such as one sees in the movies or finds described in heart-throb magazines. "So he really cares for me!" she complacently repeated to herself. After such an outburst "things would be different." She had a simple sort of logic which I translate as follows: "Since he loves me he'll want to keep me. In order to keep me he may not possibly do everything I want but he'll do what he can and that in itself will be wonderful." When one longs for something one easily persuades oneself that it's not impossible to obtain it. Roberti had demanded six months' reflection before they made up their minds about having a child. It was by no means certain that this was just a thinly disguised refusal: why always despair? Perhaps Edouard needed this delay to make the necessary dispositions, to put certain affairs in order. Perhaps she was going to have a "status" at last.

1: What status? What did she want exactly? You ought to try and explain this just once.

HE: I've already told you. She would above all have liked Edouard to install her in the Square Saint-Lambert. This idea, which she had more or less abandoned, took fresh hold of her after the scene of January the eleventh. She would continue to work, since she didn't want to be a kept woman, but she would have what meant so much to her: freedom and love. Setting up house in the Square Saint-Lambert was just a first step; next would come the baby, *Back Street*, what a dream when one is a young mama! Do you remember a novel by Balzac called *A Double*

Family, in which M. de Granville provides his mistress Caroline with a charming apartment in the Rue Taitbout, has two children by her and basks in felicity? Obviously Solange hadn't read it but she pictured her potential life in the Square Saint-Lambert in the same rosy hues.

In January '57 she entertained no thoughts of a rupture, either in the near or distant future. Her mind wasn't working along those lines. She believed she would always love Edouard or at least for a very long time, that she would give him "the best years of her life," the years during which a woman can expect to be loved. She couldn't imagine herself other than *loving Edouard*. One can sometimes be dissatisfied with one's eyes because one is shortsighted; one can sometimes regret having legs too skinny or too plump, but what can one do about them? One has to put up with oneself as the Creator made one, make the best of one's good and bad qualities for all the time one spends on earth. Similarly Solange made the best of her love, while deploring the fact that fate had reserved this particular love for her—this love so painful, so contrary to her nature—instead of a simple and harmonious love with a young man of her own age and background, neither intelligent nor complicated, neither mysterious nor unkind, neither married nor a coward. She was twenty-seven; how much longer would she remain pretty and desirable? Ten or twelve years, after which everything is over for a woman. She was convinced that during these ten or twelve years her life would remain just the same as it was now; she would work, she would see her lover on the sly, she would be bored. This is where the child she so greatly longed for came in; it would be a wonderful way of filling the dead periods between meetings. With the child, these hours of endless boredom would be over, this waste of loneliness would be abolished, this hideous void in her soul and mind would be filled. She would be absorbed in looking after him, coddling him, loving him, washing his diapers, listening to his babbling, teaching him to say "Mama," introducing him to the world. She would devour his soft cheeks with kisses, she would breathe in the good eau de cologne smell of well cared-for babies, she would buy him toys, she would knit vests and socks for him, she would watch him growing month by month, she would have an ivory-handled brush to brush his silky hair. He would be exceptionally intelligent, of course, with such a father! It was still Edouard whom she would love through the child; he would be a little ambassador permanently at her side, a tiny replica without strength and without malice, a miniature of her lover, a delightful companion, a continuous presence thanks to which she wouldn't have a moment's leisure to bewail the unhappy lot of Solange Mignot. A year before, as she fell asleep in her young girl's bed in the Avenue Daumesnil, she would murmur "Darling, darling" ten times, a hundred times over, thinking of Edouard. Now it was the child she would evoke to bring her sleep. "My little boy," she would murmur into her pillow, "my little pet, my little treasure, my little darling, my sunbeam, mother's little precious . . ."

I: Did she never think that it might just as easily be a girl?

HE: Never. Her dreams had been woven round a boy. Edouard's child could only be a boy, in the likeness of this splendid man who anyway (he had already demonstrated it) only ever had sons. Furthermore, you know as well as I do that young women nearly always want their first-born to be a boy. There are a number of reasons for this, the first being that when they are in love they want a second edition of the father. Solange wanted among other things a little Roberti all to herself, defenseless, whom she could love to distraction because children, at least in their early years, are bottomless wells of love into which one can pour a constant flood of adoration without their hearts ever being filled to overflowing. Her dreams did not stop there: one day this little boy would be twenty, he would be at the university and his old mother would be proud to walk down the street on his arm. I could go on elaborating this till tomorrow but I fear it might end by becoming tedious. What I chiefly wanted to show you was this peculiarly feminine notion which had taken hold of Solange, namely that a baby is a delightful source of occupation, an endless diversion. This is, in fact, the philosophy by which the urge for motherhood normally expresses itself.

I: Six months to think it over starting from the eleventh of January takes us to the eleventh of July. Did Solange, on the morning of the eleventh of July, 1957 say to Roberti: "Are you going to give me a child today?"

HE: Don't be absurd! No. It didn't happen like that.

I: Oh, I knew as much. But it's a pity. It wouldn't have been without a certain charm. Tell me how Roberti arranged not to be a father. A woman who wants a child is the very devil.

HE: He arranged it in the same way as parliamentarians do when they don't want to launch a frontal attack on some new bill to which they are opposed. They have a verb to describe these tactics—"to torpedo." To torpedo is to intrigue behind the scenes, start red herrings, employ delaying tactics, discuss other matters and so on, until the abhorred bill dies a natural death without ever having been brought before the house for a full-fledged debate. In the same way Edouard *torpedoed* Solange's child and did it so well that, after the six months' of so-called reflection were up, she had no hope left.

In fact, following the scene in the Square Saint-Lambert, things resumed their habitual course. She saw no more of Roberti than she had done in the past and when she did see him he was careful to skirt round such delicate topics. She kept expecting him to talk over their future and share her dreams but nothing happened. She would have so loved to have had long discussions with him about her "status" as his official mistress, endless talks about the baby and plans for the future! Women adore making plans, even if nothing ever comes of them. Men, alas, who feel ill at ease with unreality and idle speculations, seldom go in for this (whence so many Bovarys and betrayed husbands: because men instead of quite simply playing up to their wives' fantasies, barricade themselves behind common sense and arm themselves with wisdom). It is infinitely sweet to make plans with the man one loves, even if in one's heart one knows them to be only castles in the air. Besides, are they really castles in the air? To experience something in anticipation is almost to experience it in reality and gives just as much pleasure. The rare men who understand this deep-seated characteristic of the feminine mind are extraordinarily beloved. Beloved as only charlatans can be, who make every promise and keep none of them. The plans women make are their poetry.

ı: Forgive me for interrupting, but you seem to forget the chief reason why men are so recalcitrant. It's because they know that it's they, the men, who will have to carry out their women's plans with their own hard work or money. So they pull long faces. Poor things, it's quite understandable. They immediately try to stem this terrifying flood of plans. One only has to make the mere semblance of a promise to a woman and one is done for. She instantly transforms this semblance of a promise into a sacred oath. She reminds you of it every day, pesters you, life becomes intolerable until the moment when, worn out, you give in.

ʜᴇ: You're exaggerating. Generalizing. You talk about women like Courteline. They aren't all so ruthless. At any rate, what you say didn't apply to Solange Mignot. For her gentle spirit, love was not a war in which one allows one's adversary no respite, pitilessly exploiting every advantage gained; on the contrary it was a trusting peace without stratagems or ulterior motives. She was so good-natured that words and words alone would have contented her for a long while: they would have provided sufficient nourishment for her dreams. It would have already made her extremely happy to be assured, each time she saw

Roberti, that he understood her feelings and sympathized with them. Instead of which he behaved like the most obtuse of husbands. Whenever she tried (timidly) to steer the conversation toward the future, he barely responded and then only with a bad grace. It was all very disheartening. So the poor girl was fairly quickly disheartened. And that is how abysses are dug. What would have filled her with joy depressed her lover; what made her talkative and gay made him silent and morose. The most she ever got out of him was a fleeting and rather patronizing airiness, whereby he intimated that she was just the usual sort of nitwit whose foolish ideas are best countered by an indulgent smile. Just once, at least, she would have liked him to raise the question of the baby of his own accord but he kept his lips sealed on that score. It was she, always she, who brought the matter up. Toward April 1957 she finally took a decision which shows that her love had begun to decline. She swore to herself that from now on not one word about the baby would cross her lips. Roberti knew how things stood: it was "his turn" now. It was humiliating to be ceaselessly asking for something he manifestly didn't want to grant her. Instead of being concerned about this sudden silence, Roberti felt a profound relief. He told himself Solange had in due course recognized the absurdity of her mania and dropped it. Now in this he was wrong. It was in about April that the maternal urge in her began to come into conflict with love. This conflict lasted for almost a year and ended in love's defeat.

I: I'm not surprised. There is something desperate about this static and cramped love which never changed, which was established once and for all. To think that it lasted for three whole years! I wonder how Solange could have held out so long.

HE: It was beginning to crack. Between April and November 1957 a secret and steady withdrawal from Roberti took place in her heart, the true cause of which was precisely the sensible, overperfect way in which he had organized his adultery. It was as dull as marriage without the advantage of marriage, namely the constant presence of the loved one. It was only held together by the brief ecstasies the lovers shared in the Square Saint-Lambert, the price of which they both knew well. But this ecstasy itself contributed to Solange's "decrystallization," for once such a process sets in everything helps to hasten it on.

She would join Roberti at about six P.M. (she left her office shortly before, sometimes with the connivance of Mlle. Angioletti, sometimes with the consent of Dietz, who was very tolerant about little things like that). They would spend two hours together in their haven, sometimes an hour only, since Edouard was in a hurry to get home to dinner.

So that at a time when women are at their most languid, when they have the greatest need for their lovers' presences, she would find herself alone in the street. As the weeks went by she had the impression that the adultery she was committing with Edouard was being drained of all love. It was becoming reduced to the pure mechanics of sex, which was certainly marvelously well adjusted but only made all the rest of it sadder still. Despite the tenderness she still felt for him she was beginning to find something dirty and degrading about her relations with Roberti. She could spot within a matter of seconds the moment when the desire to escape generated in her lover's mind. Anxiously she would watch out for this moment; Edouard would be smoking a cigarette, telling amusing stories, exerting himself to make her laugh, discussing this and that, when all at once he would make a certain gesture such as propping himself up on the divan cushions or putting his arms round his knees. In an artificial voice he would say: "I wonder what the time is. It must certainly be very late. When I'm with you I completely lose all sense of time." These words would fall like lead on Solange's heart. For her they meant that half an hour later she would be sent back to solitude. It was then that the idea of the baby stabbed her and caused the acutest pain. Leaving her lover to rejoin her child would have meant leaving one happiness for another. It was then, too, that her resentment was most bitter; how cruel of Edouard stubbornly to deny her so elementary a happiness! It would have cost so little and would have solved all problems. The need for motherhood can lead to genuine aberrations. Solange was so preoccupied by this need that the state of unmarried mother seemed to her enviable. She had built up for her own private use a sort of social hierarchy in which the unmarried mother filled the gap between the young girl and the married woman, forming a kind of intermediate grade. She thought that, having a child, she would suffer far less should Roberti one day desert her.

I: You know, what I just can't bring myself to understand is that he saw nothing, felt nothing, sensed nothing of this tremendous longing in a woman to whom he was after all so close. You can say what you like but it's still very hard for me to swallow.

HE: A stupid objection. It was just because he *was* so close to her that he saw nothing. History is full of parents who treat their children's vocations as idle whims and ruin their lives with the best intentions in the world. In the second place, he was a man without imagination. When Solange wasn't with him, when he didn't have her before his eyes, didn't hear the sound of her voice, he never imagined what she might be thinking. Not only that, but he didn't want to imagine it either. He refused to. I've told you he wasn't jealous by temperament. Now jealousy (I mean suspicious jealousy always on the alert) is a question of imagination. When the object of his love isn't there the jealous man thinks anxiously about her soul and what she is doing, that is to say he thinks about her unselfishly, even if his possessive nature suffers from her imagined infidelities. Roberti, now, only ever thought of Solange in connection with himself, as a nonjealous man and a complete egoist. He would think of the endless source of pleasure she represented for him. He would draw himself a static picture of her; he delighted in contemplating her as an "object" (and here the word assumes its full meaning), something belonging to him, something he had acquired which didn't have to be called in question. Whenever he went for three days without seeing her he never wondered what she was up to, whether she was cheerful or sad. It was of no interest to him. Worse, if such a supposition crossed his mind at all, he found it a bore and instantly brushed it aside.

I: I can tell you why: because we don't like thinking about people we treat badly.

HE: Yes, you're right. But we finally become so bored by the people we treat badly that we stop seeing them altogether. With a mistress one desires with a longing constantly renewed, matters are more complicated. There was a permanent conflict in Roberti's heart; this expressed itself by his reluctance to think of Solange in one respect and his delight in evoking her in another. As he was never short of grounds for self-deception, he acknowledged that he certainly didn't make his mistress very happy but pooh, there was nothing very serious in that. So long as she loved him she needed nothing more. Love takes the place of everything else and it's a hundred times better to be unhappy in love than happy out of love. The mere fact that she loved him was a priceless gift he was bestowing on her, which amply compensated for her small daily disappointments.

Sometimes he peered into the future. Would this affair be over in six months or would Solange still be his mistress in five, ten, fifteen years? What did he really want? To wear her down by his feigned indifference, his neglect, his scenes, until she was led to break with him, or on the contrary keep her forever? He didn't know. He found both possibilities equally alarming. He wasn't ready for either. Indecision is painful, even in daydreams, so he didn't dwell overlong on daydreams of this kind. Deep down he must have felt that his love was doomed, that he himself had doomed it from the start by a decree which his reason had mercilessly upheld against the dictates of his heart. Here the work-

542

ings of self-deception functioned with equal efficiency. Roberti extricated himself from his contradictions by mental somersaults: "In love the past and future are meaningless. Only the present counts, that is to say one's desire and the more or less immediate appeasement of this desire. How am I to know whether I shall still want Solange next week? If desire dies, so does love."

But the following week the desire was still there, and the week after, and the week after that. Roberti was plunging into love as into a forest. He pushed on, thinking with every step he took that he would soon reach a clearing; when he did perceive a clearing in the distance, he thought this was where the forest ended. We often see people who are past praying for but don't realize it. They organize and plan their lives just as if they still had a long time to live; they are prudent, they look far ahead, they don't want to commit themselves to things they might repent of later on. The outside observer, knowing they have barely three months left to live, pityingly watches them as they struggle on in the game of life. He cannot warn them: it would be too cruel. In this way I watched poor Roberti. He had no idea that he was hopelessly lost in the forest of love, that he would never get out of it and would be much wiser to settle down in it like Robinson Crusoe, without hope, renouncing his past life and most cherished memories, rather than plod on like this until he fell from exhaustion.

One of his most persistent illusions was that his desire for Solange was merely the fruit of circumstances. She had chanced to cross his path and he had taken her as a matter of principle, because no prey should ever be allowed to escape. Things would have followed the same course with any other pretty girl. He was convinced that Solange was interchangeable, that any other young and beautiful woman he might meet tomorrow, take a fancy to and seduce, would suit him just as well. But as if it had been purposely ordained, he had never had the occasion to find a substitute. For instance, if a girl gave him a lingering look in the street, he didn't accost her because he had an appointment ten minutes later with the chairman of the Radical Party. At dinner parties there was an obstacle of a different kind: the presence of Agnes prevented him from exploiting the interest he visibly inspired in some female guest athirst for adventure. In short, he was maliciously thwarted by fate every time. These setbacks implanted in him the idea that the world is full of desirable women, that he himself was highly attractive to them and that any day he really felt like taking the trouble he could exchange Solange in twenty-four hours for another more flattering mistress, who would have all the attraction of novelty as well.

Do you believe in chance, in such cases? I don't. In these repeated setbacks I see Roberti's secret will. Deep down and without his knowing it, he wanted no other mistress than Solange. Every time another woman capable of replacing her in his heart or bed crossed his path, he raised obstacles. For instance nothing would have been simpler than to arrive half an hour late for his appointment with the chairman. Nothing easier either, after dinner, than to sit on some secluded sofa with the woman athirst for adventure and surreptitiously procure her telephone number. There is no man seeking a mistress who cannot find one within forty-eight hours if he sets about it with the necessary industry. But Roberti didn't set about it with the necessary industry. He never proffered that faint gesture of encouragement or complicity which even the most brazen women expect from a man who attracts them. His lethargy naturally played a certain part in this. When by chance nothing stood between him and some woman he was filled with an insurmountable boredom at the thought of all the fatuous compliments he was going to have to pay her. "Oh Lord," he thought, "not today. I'm not in the mood. She's a sweet thing, but not sweet enough to make it worth my while. I can't face the idiotic replies she'll probably make." Two years before, he would never have put forward such an argument; then, any opportunity which knocked was fit for the taking. But he had forgotten this or else thought he had grown older; lovemaking no longer seemed so rare and precious a thing. In the old days he had belonged to that category of men who enjoy women's company, love to listen to their chatter and take an almost sensual delight in the interminable exchange of idle gossip with them. But now he had crossed over into the other category of men who find women tedious, who can't put up with their tittle-tattle, who intimidate and paralyze them because they cannot conceal on their faces the boredom women inspire.

So you see, nothing was lacking in Roberti's love for Solange, not even fidelity. This fidelity was deeper than any other, since his secret morality (or immorality) waged a relentless war against it. Not only did he expose himself to temptation but he actually sought it out in the hope of succumbing to it. And against all his expectations he resisted it. He was protected by his love which held him back, which paralyzed him. His mind lasciviously dwelt on all the delights to be discovered with some woman but his tongue would refuse to speak the words needed to set the correct flirtatious tone and his body would refuse to perform the elementary actions (kissing her hand, taking a stroll with her, etc.) which form the prelude to an adventure. Take two men. One says: "I want to be faithful but I can't manage it." The other says: "I should like to be unfaithful but it's not possible." Which of the two, in your opinion, feels the greater love? For me it's the second. He sins only by intention. The grace of love never fails to rescue him at the last moment. After both these men are dead and their intentions have died with them, when only their stories, that is to say their actions, remain in men's memories, people may conclude it was the latter who truly loved. Besides, every time Roberti escaped some adventure his thoughts impetuously surged back to Solange and he was overcome with thankfulness. With her he had no need to talk, no need to organize, make plans, surprise and amuse, no need to fear a failure. This dear creature existed and the mere thought of it gladdened his heart. Somewhere in the world was someone who lived through him, who was always ready to grant him the pleasure he asked for. Given such a mistress he would be crazy to plunge into the uncertainties, difficulties and complications of a new adventure. Limited as she was, Solange nevertheless had one tremendous quality in Roberti's eyes: familiarity. *She knew him*, that is she had a fairly accurate notion of his character, she was used to his ways, she understood his language and even repeated his tricks of speech. He loved being known in this way. In short for three years he was never once unfaithful to Solange although on fifty or sixty occasions he had the firmest intention of being so.

ɪ: Right. So be it. Excellent. But where does Agnes fit in? How do you bring her into this touching picture of fidelity in adultery?

ʜᴇ: I don't, because she never came into it. She belonged to another picture of Roberti's life. In the first place, he was deceiving her with Solange. Agnes had the priority, so to speak. I imagine you want to know whether, despite his increasing love for Solange, he continued to perform his duties as a husband? Well, he did. There was even a period (the spring of '57, to be exact) when he performed them with a veritable frenzy, like a scientist making an experiment. Desire is just a physical need, he thought. Do away with the need and there will be no more desire. But despite all his efforts there always lingered in him a vague desire which, in the final analysis, was focused on Solange. Thus in a way it was indirectly due to Agnes that in that same spring of 1957 he found himself face to face with love. Seeking for one proof he found another, namely that his desire had need of Solange and of her alone. But that isn't the kind of revelation one accepts lying down when one is a man like Roberti. It took months to convince him. During these months, concomitantly, he gradually became aware that he no longer loved Agnes.

ı: At last! Not a moment too soon.

ʜᴇ: One moment, please! There's a wide difference between "becoming aware" and "admitting." Roberti's reason, which ruled so harshly over his relations with Solange, was just as assiduous in this respect as well. He had built up a certain conception of Agnes which resisted all the evidence. It was impossible that she should cease to be what she had always been for him, to wit a confederate, a woman he had molded in his own likeness, the love and creation of his life. It was beyond his power to imagine that this central pillar of his existence could crumble. Agnes was something certain in his life. She would never fail him, he knew. She helped him never to feel much affection for his chance mistresses, she was permanence as opposed to transience. He was always overjoyed to return to her. He had deceived her time and again, certainly, but these infidelities were nothing, they hadn't made the slightest dent in his love for his wife, they were on a different plane altogether. His mistresses had flitted through his life like shadows, leaving no trace in his soul; even the graceful wake they left behind them had vanished forever. It was inadmissible that one of them—neither the prettiest nor the wittiest—should fail to behave with the same discretion, inadmissible that, by the mere fact of his desiring her with greater constancy than the rest, he should have become so infatuated with this doll that he had ceased to love his dear Agnes. That could never be. It was an affront to his mind.

Anyway, how did the decline of his love for Agnes express itself? It is just this that makes the whole thing so odd: it didn't. Roberti out of love was exactly the same as when he had loved. Right to the end he acknowledged nothing, telling himself it was just a difficult time which would soon pass and that above all he mustn't show the slightest coolness. This explains the long blindness of Agnes, who, right up to February '58, suspected nothing, so that the drama burst on her like a thunderclap. The more so since, even if love had died, tenderness or, if this word seems to you equivocal, friendship had remained. Roberti had preserved all his friendship for his wife unimpaired; this was old and deep-rooted, expressing itself in their talk, their implicit understanding, little attentions and gifts. More than that: he made up with friendship for the absence of love; he felt called on to be more assiduous than ever. It was up to him to get through this awkward period without causing any upset. He was convinced that in six months or a year at the outside "something would have happened" and he would have returned to Agnes as he had always done in the past. Something, but what? His reveries failed to offer any precise idea. This hapless dupe's thoughts ran roughly on these lines: "I've had other flutters which temporarily alienated me from Agnes as I am alienated right now. They never lasted. They were just little sexual diversions. So it won't last this time either. One morning I'll turn over a new leaf, that is to say revert to my old self. Let's hope it doesn't happen too soon, however! After all, it's rather fun having an adventure, surreptitious meetings and secrets, even with Mlle. Mignot." What is odd in the circumstances is that it never occurred to him that he was fifty-two, a dangerous age when, ordinarily, the biter gets bitten. He was living on his memories of himself as a young man. He was, in fact, behaving like a young man or a man of thirty-five who has many years ahead of him to devote to women and who can look forward to being loved by them for a long time to come. It never entered his head that Solange might be his last love and that was why this affair was so unlike his previous ones.

Nothing irritates me more than those novelists or songwriters who get worked up about "first love." What is first love? It is like the first time one eats *foie gras* or caviar: one is thrilled by its taste; one never knew the world contained anything so delicious. First love is a matter of the taste buds. But last love! That, now, is interesting and full of pathos! Especially a man's last love, for with women it is different: all women know that round about forty-eight they will experience one final and devouring passion. They prepare themselves for this, they wait for it; for them, their last love is like a last journey before old age sets in. As soon as they have embarked on it, they treasure up every detail so as to provide themselves with *a store of memories*. While living this last love they are already beyond it, thinking only of the moment when it will be over and they find themselves once again alone. They practically never rebel against this; they know they are enjoying a windfall.

It is far more tragic for men. They believe their last love is just another adventure, no different from those they have already had. They treat it just as lightly; they attach no particular value to this final outburst of tenderness and youth and when it is all over they are left empty-handed, ruined like the old grasshopper, reduced to despair. Seen *after the event*, from beyond the grave, a man's last love acquires most disturbing colors. "The last time he inspired desire . . . the last kisses he ever received . . . the last rendezvous he ever made which was kept . . . the last young woman he held close . . ." This is how, to my mind, one could describe Roberti's relations with Solange. The latter was in fact the last young woman he ever held close, the last human being who elected to melt in his arms, whom he made suffer and who made him suffer. "The last torment of jealousy he experienced . . . the last pretty

face he held in his hands . . . the last eyes into which he gazed deep
. . . the last desire . . . the last madness . . . the last passion . . ."
In so saying, it is as if I can hear the smiting of God. Imagine a man in
good health or apparently so. One evening you wish him good night.
The next day he is dead and you realize that it wasn't good night you
said to him but good-by; you realize *after the event* that you have seen
him for the last time. You didn't know it, he didn't know it, but it was
written. One's last love is the same.

One day, for the first time in his life, round about September 1957,
Roberti talked to me at some length about Agnes with deep affection
and emotion. That was the day I realized he no longer loved her, that
his last love had triumphed over his old love. I was appalled. Up to
then Agnes had been as it were a part of himself and he would have
found it as incongruous to describe his love for her as to confess to a
predilection for his left leg or his stomach. All at once, and for no
particular reason, he began to tell me how fond he was of her, how devoted she was, how intelligent, how she understood his slightest word,
everything that twenty-three years of marriage—and successful marriage—had built up between them. He stressed all this like someone
anxious to convince not only his listener but above all himself. He
painted me an idealized portrait of his wife which made me shiver; she
was faultless and charming into the bargain: in her way she was a saint;
the years had left no mark on her; on some mornings her face had an
extraordinary beauty, and so on. Roberti was sensitive and emotional:
two or three times during all this I saw a tear glitter in the corner of his
eye. People who are preparing to hurt someone have two ways of talking
about him: either they slander him, in order to give themselves courage,
or else they deck him with flowers by way of compensation and perhaps
also in one last attempt to hold themselves back for a moment from
plunging down the slope. This latter attitude accorded so well with
Edouard's character that I never had a second's doubt. I saw in a flash
his devouring love for Solange and his indifference toward Agnes. Possibly I reacted to this in a traditional way: I didn't have the courage to
open his eyes. The longer he deluded himself, I thought, the better. I
backed him up. I added my voice to his in praise of Agnes. I went even
further: I told him it was his strictest and most elementary duty always
to behave perfectly toward her. Whatever the circumstances. Because
clearly it was she alone he loved and all the rest was just an ephemeral
fantasy.

To be blunt, in my zeal I only embedded him more deeply in his self-
deception. Besides, this was just what he wanted. Leaving me that day,

he was more certain than ever that the one and only love of his life was called Agnes and not Solange: not only did he have his own will to reassure him on this score but also he had my testimony and word for it, that is to say the pledge of a man in whose perspicacity he professed to have complete faith. Moreover, in my way I was close to sharing his views. I never imagined his affair with Solange could turn to tragedy, and through his own fault. I told myself that this infatuation had temporarily superseded his love for his wife but that it couldn't now last much longer. In six months Solange would grow tired of it and break it off, while Roberti would suffer a nice spell of heartache. He would be only too glad, then, to fall back on Agnes, whose faithful support would help him to ride out this difficult storm. He would feel grateful. Grateful to her for being there, for existing, for being his haven. From gratitude it's but a short step to love, which one is overjoyed to rediscover in one's heart after believing it had deserted it forever. Yes, this is how I saw future events; it seemed to me that in the next eighteen months this was how things should have normally turned out. The essential for the time being was to help Roberti maintain the fiction of marital love. In a word, I acted like a politician, that is a man who knows the truth but prefers to lie for the public good, a man who attempts to establish alongside the true, sterile and disastrous reality a false, promising and fruitful reality, in the hope that thanks to the ambiguity of events, well-kept secrets, occult influences and his own persistence he will have a chance to substitute this false reality for the true one.

I searched long for a roundabout way to put Agnes on her guard and warn her. I could never bring myself to do so, but my conscience reproached me for it. I accused myself of failing to go to the help of someone in danger. After much beating about the bush I took my courage in both hands. I said to her something like: "Don't you find Edouard rather tired, rather depressed these days? It seems to me you ought to keep a careful eye on him. I'm sure he needs you. Men, when they turn fifty, tend to get thrown a bit off balance. It's at that stage that a wife is useful." I said no more than that. It was the extreme limit to which I felt I could go. A more intuitive woman (or one less sure of being loved) would have asked for no more; she would immediately have been alerted. But Agnes replied exactly as I feared she would, namely that on the contrary Edouard needed "breathing space," he must be "given a free hand" and other banalities. It was no good my protesting; she didn't want to listen. She trusted in her sound middle-class prescriptions. As if I were joking I told her how men are weak, how it is particularly unwise to leave them alone when they look sad or absent-minded, how the remedy for any soul sickness they may be feeling is slavery with just a tiny margin of independence, but all she did was laugh. She replied that I was propounding a paradox. This disheartened me; I felt I would never get through to her. In addition to which she regrettably took the line of being noble. "I know Edouard better than you do," she said. "I've seen him like this before, distant, withdrawn, as if his thoughts were elsewhere. It doesn't mean anything. He has spells like that. And anyway what could I do about it? Never in my life would I stoop to questioning him, forcing my presence on him if he wants to be alone, asking him ten times a day whether he is happy, whether he thinks about me, whether he would like to have sweetbreads or ham for lunch, taking an interest in the cases he is working on or the political situation he's worried about. He knows I am there, always ready to talk if he feels like talking, always glad to help find solutions to the problems preoccupying him. Actually it has at times occurred to me that we might go through some sort of crisis when he reached fifty. I'm quite prepared for it. I know that round about fifty men sometimes have a sort of sunstroke, that it may mean two or three difficult years to get through, but we haven't arrived there yet. Edouard is just a bit out of tune. Political events, ghastly as they are, are responsible for a great deal of it. Anyway I'm above all convinced that people must be given all the freedom they want, whatever the consequences: the more freedom one allows them, the less use they make of it. You want me to reduce Edouard to slavery. Let me tell you what will happen: he will acquire the habits of a slave, in other words he'll become a liar, sullen and hypocritical; he'll be unfaithful to me the moment my back is turned, he'll be unhappy and I shall be unhappier still. The mere thought of it fills me with horror!"

I: Roberti strikes me as cutting a pretty sorry figure between Solange and Agnes. He didn't deserve these two women. Each, in her way, is a far better character than he.

HE: Yes. This sort of ill-adjusted relationship occurs fairly frequently. When I look round at the people I know, I can find pretty few men worthy of the women who love them or whom they love. In spite of their traditional reputation, women are much more frank, more loyal, more all of a piece than men. They have *more good will*. Men are only their superiors intellectually. But because they are more nimble-witted and inquisitive they are also the first to be unfaithful. It was difficult, you must admit, to reveal to Agnes that Roberti as a free man was behaving exactly like a slave, that he was a liar and a hypocrite, that he was unfaithful to her whenever her back was turned. It was difficult to tell her he had that well-known characteristic of slaves, a taste for betrayal. How he liked to betray, how this activity was for him a source of secret and real delight. How what possibly bound him more than anything else to his mistress was that with her he had a feeling of betraying everything connected with him: wife, family, background, work and even generation. She'd never have understood. I would have broken her heart to no purpose. It was I who would have filled her with horror.

I knew Roberti no longer loved his wife the day he started to talk to me about her. Conversely, I discovered he no longer loved his children the day I realized that he hadn't spoken to me about them for at least three or four months. This persistent silence on such a topic was unlike him. Indeed, whenever we met he used to describe to me at length the progress the boys were making in their studies, their interests, the books they were reading, the friends they were making, their admiration for him, their little acts of rebellion. Since I knew the boys well, I was never bored by this even though he often overdid his complacency. I couldn't approve of his deliberate indulgence towards his sons' sillier goings-on, but at any rate there was almost as much love as weakness in this indulgence. At first I dared not believe Edouard no longer loved his children. The mere thought of it revolted me. Odd, isn't it? Now and then I suddenly get these conventional reactions. There's no reason why one shouldn't one day cease to love one's progeny, why one shouldn't lose interest in them. I wanted to find out whether his silence was fortuitous or whether there was some reason for it. So I asked him for news of his children. He gave it briefly, with perceptible boredom. I persisted; I asked precise questions: whether the youngest had grown since I last saw him, whether the eldest had studied well for his exams. Edouard replied like a man bored to death by such details and as if they referred to strangers. I returned to the charge two or three times during the next few days: his attitude was always the same. My inquiries failed to command his attention, they aroused no feeling of affection in him. This transformation from a good into an indifferent father was very striking and, I must confess, grieved me. Not on the children's account, for most likely they hadn't noticed anything, but on Roberti's. From this change I measured the extent to which his sex obsession had got a grip of him. The fact that it had also destroyed his paternal love proved the very high degree it had attained—"the breaking point," as the geologists call it. But here again, what could I do? Deep down, I too was blind over the whole business. Right to the end I never ceased to hope that, abandoned sooner or later by Solange, he would be let off with a year's melancholia following which everything would be as it was before.

I: It's rather frightening, this you are telling me now. In the space of a year he has patently withdrawn from everything. He has stopped caring for his wife, stopped caring for his children, stopped caring for his work, stopped caring for anyone and anything. In the next and final stage he will cease to care for himself. He is sinking into despair. The world is deserting him. We are coming to the darkest part of his story. Imagine, it is beginning to make even me feel sad. God, what destruction! Here's a man who will soon be reduced to a heap of rubble. I have never before been given such a murky account of human nature. I can't see the faintest ray of light in it.

HE: There is one, however, a flickering and reddish light: his love for Solange, nurtured on all these other sentiments and now turning into a monster.

I: Is that a light? However closely you point it out, however I screw up my eyes, I can't see a thing. All I can see is the black gloom of passivity, monomania and boredom. Roberti is a man for whom God doesn't exist. Souls in which there is no God are inactive souls. They need some occupation. They need to be continually diverted. Solange wasn't Roberti's last love: she was his last diversion. After which, pouff!

It will doubtless be remembered that we were sitting on our iron seats facing the dark waters of the lake. It will also be remembered that my watch had stopped and that I did not mind in the least. Talking in the dark is not without its charms. "Weren't you feeling sleepy?" one might ask. Not at all. I was torpid, the way one sometimes is at a concert, listening to some long slow symphony by Brahms or Mahler, torpid but not a bit drowsy. I was following the winding melody—rather fascinated, I must confess, by its breadth and myriad motifs, marveling that a man could spin out what was generally speaking a rather trivial little story for fifteen hours and more. Besides, I was listening to my friend's talk the way one listens to music, frequently closing my eyes. I had now had mine closed for over fifteen minutes, yet my mind had remained perfectly alert all the time. I had a big surprise when I reopened them: the sky had changed; it was no longer a night sky. The sun had not yet risen but the darkness was already dispersed. The leaves had recovered a touch of their green; the water of the lake was no longer black. Opposite, a few yards off, I saw a gray swan glide silently by; in an hour's time it would be dazzling white. A duck quacked. I was seized with a brief panic on seeing the world returning to life like this: I was going to have to return to life too, for a whole day, without having had even half an hour's sleep, for there could be no question now of going to bed. I'd be in a sorry state by evening! And how was I going to work without having slept? Farewell for today to my three or four daily pages of writing! I felt a moment's fury: society is permanently plotting to keep artists from their work; it lures them into drawing rooms, night clubs, parties, it parades them, it consumes their time, it says to them: "For once you can give yourself a day off." The poor wretches dare not resist. They go and bore themselves with men who have too much time and waste it accordingly. For an artist, a day during which no work is done is a day lost, cut out of one's life, like a day which hasn't been lived, in short a matter for despair. A glance at my friend's alert and expressive face calmed me. It was the face of a man who has been speaking the truth for fifteen hours, in other words constantly digging deep down inside himself, seeking truth in the caverns where it dwells and is so difficult to reach. I thought that perhaps I hadn't wholly wasted my day and that, failing a novel, I might sometime extract from what I had heard and said—especially from what I had said—some pages that might please me. After all, I wasn't there to enjoy myself: I was there to learn.

The first glimmering of dawn, even in June, is a sad moment. Dawn is only beautiful later on, when the sun is preparing to lift above the horizon and already shedding a diffuse and brilliant light over the landscape. We didn't feel cold; the night had been almost as warm as the day. I told myself how in an hour's time I would be feeling hungry and it would be rather nice to go and have some onion soup in a café at the Halles. But for the next fifteen minutes I felt no desire to move. When one lives in Paris one doesn't so often have the chance to see the sun rise over the Bois de Boulogne.

HE: The incident at Neuilly-sur-Marne took place, as I said, in November, but the way for it had been paved as far back as September. When Roberti returned from his vacation he was agog to see Solange, of whom he had been dreaming his fill during six weeks alone with his family. As to love, this vacation had been less successful than those of 1955. Solange wrote less: one letter a week at the outside, and neither very long nor very affectionate. Her letters began with "My love" but no longer revealed the inexhaustible inspiration of women passionately in love, capable of covering dozens of pages with sweet nothings. Roberti's heart nonetheless pounded fit to burst on his visits to the post office and he read her brief notes with far greater delight than two years before. It was no longer what she wrote that mattered but the fact that she had written at all. He scarcely read these letters; he was in touch with her and this filled him with bliss for several days. Now it was his turn to hope and tremble. He visited the post office more often than was necessary—every three or four days—knowing full well that half the time he would find nothing. But it was a sort of pilgrimage which he found poignantly sweet, a rite of love he needed to perform. His daydreams were all the more exquisite for the doubt that had crept into them. He was too subtle to believe Solange had the same blind and inordinate love for him that she had had in the past, but also too self-confident ever to suspect that his mistress was worn out by the life he was leading her. As a result his reveries were tinged with a vague hint of sadness, of fear, uncertainty and anxiety. This was something new and not unpleasant. He wondered in what mood he would find her on his return.

For the first time in his life he felt unhappy and discontented in the bosom of his family. For six weeks his life depended on Solange's letters. He was in exile. Around him his children were enjoying themselves. Agnes was busy, the sun was shining, the sea was blue. He himself trailed moodily round like a ghost. He spent endless hours on the beach to work up a tan, in order that Solange should find him more seductive. His family, his friends, I myself who went to spend a week with them, the pleasures of the Riviera, nothing could take him out of himself. He made every effort to pull himself together, but I could see he was a prey to a deep uneasiness and the only medicine capable of curing him was six hundred miles away. One evening we went for a walk together. He had been disgruntled and sullen all day, ever since breakfast. I felt sad, both for him and for Agnes. I asked what was wrong. He made no reply but, after a few minutes, in a pensive and rather remote voice as if speaking more to himself than to me, he said: "You know, what is dreadful at my age, what is worst of all, is the notion of generation. Telling oneself the world will never change, that we shall go on seeing the same things in it so long as we're here. Those faces one has known for such ages will keep one company to the end! Just imagine, there are men I met for the first time twenty or thirty years ago and I've seen them every week, sometimes every day since. They're the same age as I. They advance at the same pace as I do; some are a bit behind, others a bit ahead. They'll never die. Never, I tell you! Politics preserve one. Particularly the Radical Party. At times it makes me feel like suicide. It's quite simple. Since they won't make up their minds to die I'll blow my brains out. I'll leave them all behind with their little schemes, their little resentments, their quota of malice. I loathe my generation. It blocks my horizon. I want a new one!" After this curtain raiser he lapsed into silence for five or ten minutes. It was one of those southern nights giving the impression that coolness and heat are doing battle. I thought that to speak like this he must be very dissatisfied with himself and I was right. I learned subsequently that it was at about this time (that is July to August 1957) that the various firms by which he was employed were beginning to get restive, writing to remind him in an increasingly pressing manner that he was neglecting his duties, and that several of these letters even contained veiled threats. It only needs some worry or fear to stir up old thoughts in the depths of one's soul and bring them to the surface. I had hardly any choice but to make light of it. I urged him to be patient; I told him he was being unfair, that some of his friends or colleagues had nevertheless done him the pleasure of kicking the bucket during the past ten years. I quoted names. "Bah, those weren't the worst," he retorted. "They never bothered me! Do you want to know," he added, "why I keep up this liaison with the Mignot girl, whom I don't really much care for? I'll tell you: because with her I change generation the way a man changes his country. With a woman twenty-five years younger I am in a completely different world. I have the delicious feeling of betraying my own generation, of going over to the enemy. Just as she betrays her generation by loving me. Her ways are different from mine. She is fresh. At my age one is superstitious about freshness. Sometimes I am surprised she doesn't find me repulsive. Surprised that this body of mine, which I've known for fifty years, should arouse desire in another, particularly in one so young and pretty, who could aspire to something so much better."

ɪ: The answer: youth and freshness have no need of their like. Second, women's sexual pleasure differs from men's. That's what I'd have replied had Roberti confided in me as he did in you.

ʜᴇ: That's more or less what I did reply. But he wasn't in a mood to listen. He wanted to talk. And the talk we had together that night was, I am certain, the one good moment of his vacation. I only feared one thing, that he would bring up Agnes and include her in his general opprobrium. But I was wrong: she was still sacred in his eyes; he hadn't yet held her up to question. "The older I grow," he resumed, "the more I feel a horror of old age. The Mignot girl's youth is my stimulant. Why do we like children? Because they are far from death. Infinitely further than we ourselves. With her I have the same comforting feeling: she has twenty-five more years to live than I." He always said "the Mignot girl" when referring to her. Never "Solange." This enabled him to keep his distance, at least in words and so far as I was concerned.

ɪ: He was certainly very frank with you. It seems odd, coming from someone so secretive and tortuous.

ʜᴇ: No, not very odd. Roberti wasn't secretive; I would rather say he was *dissembling*. Anyway I had known him a long time. Also I've noticed that men of fifty often feel a need to confide in someone about their love life. Sometimes they even do so to people they hardly know. But such confidences are quite different from those made by the young. More brutal, it seems to me; more cynical. More touching, too, for behind them one glimpses the spiritual, emotional, even metaphysical evolution of their maker; one can reconstruct the various stages in his philosophy between twenty and fifty, one can see the hecatomb of illusions and principles wrought by thirty years of life. When a man of fifty or over tells me about his sex life, as happens fairly often, I feel a sort of pity for him: it means as a rule that he has come full circle and that nothing in the world has a value for him any longer beyond the occasional little kick. The confidences of the young reek with boasting and vainglory; they are inoffensive. Those of the middle-aged are bitter. The middle-aged have the egotism of gangsters, souls laid waste and bare; they pounce on young women like wolves.

But I'm digressing. Where was I? Oh yes, our walk in the night. I remember how Roberti, who certainly had a great deal weighing on his heart, also said this: "At my age the worst moment of the day is the morning; getting up after a bad night of fitful sleep, seeing in the mirror a drawn face the color of lead, gray skin, bags under the eyes. . . . But most pitiful of all is the hair. Those limp wisps of mousy hair, pathetic in their wispiness . . . Being thin as a rake you don't know what it is to have a soft, round little paunch: it's revolting. Every morning is a shipwreck. It takes me nearly an hour to pull out of it. An hour during which I wash, prink, powder and shave myself, scour myself clean like an old cooking pot blackened by the fire. Only after all this do I dare show my face. I still have about thirty years left to live, but what years! Thirty years of torment during which I shall watch everything in and around me die inch by inch, save for the fools of my own generation, of course, who are as firm as rocks. I picture myself at seventy, a dirty old man no good for anything but cuddling. Obscene! During the past few months, you know, I've been thinking quite a lot about death, not as in the old days, in a romantic and abstract way, but vividly and realistically. I see death in people, in objects, in nature. It's as if the idea of death had slid into my heart and flesh. All at once everything has changed its aspect, everything has clouded over, everything to my eyes wears a sort of mourning in anticipation and I know that soon I shall no longer be able to count on my body. That is one of the reasons why I am prolonging my affair with the Mignot girl. I am fully aware, I may say, that this affair is unwise and makes no sense; I am fully aware that I'm bad for the poor child, who loves me whereas I don't love her, but I can't help it, she's young! When I caress her I instantly revert to the world of my youth I left behind so long ago. If I'd been told only ten years back that I should one day join the Mafia of men who fancy young girls, I'd have laughed my head off. Well, now I have, my dear fellow. At fifty-two I feel a distaste for mature or even Junoesque women. For me they are no longer objects of desire. I've got the fetishism of youth. Women over thirty remind me too much of death. The Mignot girl is closer to my children than to me. When I was thirty she was five. I lived for twenty-five years in a world in which she not only didn't exist but which didn't even know she would ever exist. Inconceivable! At twenty-five I was a grown man, I had passions, subtle thoughts, I wanted to make my mark on the world. I was calculating, whereas she was nothing, still unborn. When I was thirty-two she was seven; she was a kid from the Avenue Daumesnil going skipping in the Bois de Vincennes, a skinny little brat with straight bobbed hair, big black eyes devouring her little face and scabby knees. Had I walked past her I wouldn't even have noticed her. Today I think about her, long for her letters, desire her, can't wait to see her again. At night I wake up aching all over for this being who arrived on earth twenty-five years after me, who never belonged to the world I knew and which shaped me. Compared with me she's a savage, an Indian squaw, one of those soft brown-skinned Tahitian girls explorers meet on their travels and become deeply attached to although they don't speak three words of their language. You will say there are other girls besides her. Granted. But one has to go out and hunt for them. At my age one is lazy where that sort of thing is concerned. So lazy that I wonder if, when this affair comes to an end, I shall ever have the courage to embark on another. It's stupid, when you come down to it, all these women whom one finds a bore but still sleeps with. That's why I'm hanging on to the Mignot girl. It's selfish, it's shabby of me, but it may very well be my last adventure. It's possibly the last time I shall feed on fresh young flesh. The old ogre is on the verge of retiring! So I'm in no hurry. I'm spinning things out. I'm making the most of what's left to me. It isn't very gay for her but she'll find someone else. She has time ahead of her. Twenty-seven, do you realize? She looks eighteen."

I: Did she really look eighteen?

HE: She looked very young, that's a fact. Even younger than she was.

I: Well, that's rather rare. Generally one finds the reverse. I know several young women married to men older than themselves: they age as fast as they can, equally out of love, convenience and mimicry. Besides, one could almost say nature helps them: by the time they're thirty they have gray hair and a blotchy complexion. They dress in severely cut clothes which conceal their youthful figures; they wear flat-heeled shoes like elderly ladies; they acquire the sharp and rapid voices of people who have lived long and experienced much.

HE: True, but you forget one thing: Solange wasn't married to Roberti. They never appeared together in public. Consequently she didn't have to adapt herself to him. Moreover she knew he loved her precisely because of her air of great youth. A mistress, a kept woman, behaves in the opposite way to a wife. She more or less guesses that, with her, her lover is betraying everything that surrounds and resembles him. As a result she sets out to be as different as possible. The young mistress of an aging man married to a woman who is getting on emphasizes her youth still further, just as the aging mistress of a young married man knows quite well that what appeals to him about her is her soft and wrinkled flesh, her motherly attentions and so on. All this is elementary.

I: Listen, supposing you brought us back to Paris now? I'm anxious to know how the reunion after the 1957 vacation went off. I still have a fresh and vivid memory of their reunion after the 1955 one. It will be interesting to compare the same event with two years in between. First, what had Solange been doing during this time? The vacations form an important item in a young woman's life. She meets new faces and young men in hot pursuit of love. I can't help feeling that if I had a mistress to whom I was in the least bit attached, I should be very alarmed by the vacations. I should imagine her being unfaithful to me every day.

HE: Roberti wasn't at all alarmed. He knew where Solange was: with her parents in some small resort in the mountains where she wasn't enjoying herself and there was hardly anyone to seduce her. She had felt a need for three weeks' rest and seclusion, to "think things out." She had told him so one day, when by chance he had asked where she intended to go. But she had told him in her own at once candid and reserved fashion. He hadn't been alarmed at the prospect of her "thinking things out." He thought that distance would do its usual work— that is to say Solange, as the days went by, would forget her disappointments and remember only her pleasures. This, incidentally, is what happened. Whereas she said good-by to Edouard with a measure of relief, toward the end of her stay she began to recapitulate their common memories.

I: One detail, please. Was Valentin there?

HE: No.

I: What was he doing?

HE: Well, that's an interesting point. You are right to ask. He had arranged a trip to Corsica with Legay. Work and events had, as you know, conspired to set them apart and Valentin suffered from it. So he suggested that Legay should go hitchhiking with him for three weeks. They took the boat at Nice, landed at Bastia and toured Corsica from end to end, sleeping out in a tent in sleeping bags, very happy to be together, making merry and forgetting everything. Legay was full of gaiety: his extra-thin television set was more or less built. At least he had brought off the essential, namely the screen of platinum wires. In addition his heart was entirely taken up with the charming image of Solange. The fact of being with his sweetheart's brother brought him added happiness. As for Valentin, it was marvelous to be with his old pal once again. By tacit agreement, Solange wasn't mentioned once throughout the trip.

I: What! For a whole month neither of them once referred to what was closest to his heart?

HE: Not once. Valentin had abandoned all hope of ever seeing Legay become his brother-in-law and Legay was as faithful and discreet as a medieval knight undergoing the test imposed by his ladylove, however difficult. Joyously they clambered up the mountain roads and paths, cracking silly jokes and giggling like schoolboys. Valentin was almost reconciled with himself and the world. He had recovered all his old familiarity with Legay. They understood each other's slightest word and their talk was full of obscure innuendoes which left them weak with laughter. They had bought a donkey to carry their baggage and christened it Jules, which filled them with delight. They bathed in the beautiful blue waters of the Gulf of Ajaccio and Ile-Rousse. They lived more or less free, occasionally having a meal in a fisherman's bistro and the rest of the time buying tinned food or *coppa*. In fact, this holiday in Corsica was the last happy time for Valentin but as such it was a complete success. He and Legay returned to Paris radiant, as brown as redskins and dirtier than is generally allowed. The one difference marking this return was that Valentin left Corsica in a mood of melancholy —for him his vacation was well and truly over, he was returning to his old worries and afflictions—whereas Legay set sail for home in high spirits: he was leaving one happiness behind but could look forward to the even greater one of seeing Solange again, of resuming his talks and outings with her. He felt slightly ashamed of having guarded their secret so well; he imagined Valentin's delight on learning of this pure and chaste idyll and he hoped it would be soon. At night, stretched out in his sleeping bag beside his dear friend, whom he certainly loved like a brother, he sometimes found it difficult to get to sleep. He would lie dreaming of the future. In a year or two his beautiful invention would have earned him a large sum of money. He would be quite a catch; he would ask for Solange's hand in marriage and life would be rosy. He had complete faith in his star. Everything was going to succeed. Oddly enough, it was the excellent Valentin's constant friendly and warm presence which made him swell so with hope. The friendship of such a fine young man was a sign from heaven. He never suspected the extent of his clear-sightedness, otherwise he'd have been appalled. Appalled to know that heaven had in very fact singled out Valentin to serve as a propitiatory sacrifice for his happiness.

I: Splendid, the two pals' trip to Corsica. You see? I'm right to ask questions. If I hadn't put this one you would simply have forgotten about them exploring Corsica with a donkey. I needed a little fresh air and sunshine. This trip has done me good.

HE: I'm glad to hear it. Because what comes now isn't particularly refreshing or sunny.

I: Oh dear, all this love! One gets sickened by it in the end. Pleasures of love, pains of love, love here, love there, I feel as if I'd been drinking gallons of treacle. Funny, isn't it? Even in its ugliest shapes love leaves a syrupy taste. I wonder why? Probably because it makes hearts soft, dissolves the will and leaves people helpless in the face of their desire and consequently very stupid. I am always struck by this when I read one of Racine's tragedies. They never kiss, they barely touch each other with their fingertips and yet, once the tragedy is over, one is steeped in the warm, moist odors of the bedroom, of languid femininity and stale cigarettes. One's ears are full of lovers' cooing. To me, Racine has always seemed rather repugnant. What about you?

HE: Why can't you leave Racine alone!

I: Now why on earth should I leave him alone, may I ask?

HE: Because he has been dead for almost three hundred years. Show a little magnanimity!

I: He's not dead at all. The French, all and every one of them led by their professors, spring to attention before his mighty shade. He is the eternal poet of love, his poetry is akin to prose, tralali, tralala. No, I say. A plague on Racine! He made love ignoble. For three hundred years he has given it the reek of sweaty sheets and bloodstains.

HE: Very well.

I: And d'you want to know why I'm attacking Racine like this? Because you are one of his disciples.

HE: I?

I: Yes, you. You are describing Roberti's love as if it were that of Phèdre, Roxane, Monime, Mithridate or Pyrrhus. Roberti's is a Racinian love, in other words disgusting, with *Vénus toute entière à sa proie attachée*. Venus clinging to her prey like a leech, a moray eel, a vampire. According to Racine, Venus was not an appetizing blonde with plump white thighs and creased buttocks; she was a sort of fetid and glutinous monster with a dog's snout, a jackal's pointed ears, slobbering and foul-smelling jaws with pointed teeth, a monkey's hairy body and a vagina as voracious as a sea anemone. Take Corneille, take Stendhal! Those are the men to make one long to be in love. Racine rather makes one long to take a vow of chastity.

HE: May I go on now?

562

ɪ: Please do. I've finished. If I understand correctly, we're entering the last phase of the tragedy and things are starting to go from bad to worse.

ʜᴇ: Yes, everything goes from bad to worse. It began the very day of Solange's return to Paris. In the train bringing her back she was suddenly inundated by a flood of sad thoughts. Twenty-four hours earlier she had been thinking affectionately enough of Edouard and now her bad memories, her old bitternesses were regaining possession of her mind. For the first time in her life she painted herself a precise and complete picture of her position. She pretended to be absorbed in reading a magazine so that her parents shouldn't pester her with tedious questions or foolish little attentions. She thought how after tomorrow she would sink back into her old rut. She would again see this man she loved but who scarcely loved her and wouldn't in any way have changed in his attitude toward her. The furtive meetings, the brief car drives, the rapid sessions from five to seven at the Square Saint-Lambert were going to begin again. She felt quite dizzy, so disheartening was the thought of it all. "It's not possible," she told herself. "I can't go on living forever like this. It's too empty and stupid. I am not a machine. I'm wasting my life. Nothing will ever change. At thirty, at forty, I'll still be at the same point as I am today, waiting for *something* to happen, feeling just as lonely and just as sad. But I am young! I want to be happy, have children. I think I even want to get married. Tomorrow I shall see him. He will be there. He'll be waiting for me in his car at the corner of the Rue Gaillon. He'll lean over and open the door. I'll get in. He'll smile. 'What would you like us to do?' he'll ask. 'Why don't we go to the Square Saint-Lambert?' And, poor little fool, I know how I am. I'll be hurt that he should want to go to our place at once but I'll say yes and probably my head will reel with excitement. And everything will go on again as before. Five nights a week I'll go to bed crying. I'll be bored and lonely and ashamed of myself. I'll read piles of books. It will be frightful. It's not books I want. It's a man. A man who will be all mine and not just a little bit mine between five-thirty and six-forty-five on Tuesdays. A man to pamper me, talk to me, listen to me, comfort me when I'm unhappy, protect me, give me children. Oh, if only Edouard had wanted it that way! How lovely it could all have been, whereas it's all in ruins. I don't even know if I love him any more. To think I've come to that!" I'll spare you the rest. She embroidered this theme for two or three hundred miles, with the extraordinary power of rumination women have when cross-examining themselves about their love. Sitting opposite her, Father and Mother Mignot indulged the while in the various occupations of simple folk on a journey: eating cold chicken and cheese, peeling oranges, sucking sweets, lending their neighbors the newspaper, exchanging idle remarks with an old lady on the advantage of having one's slippers handy when one goes by train and so on. Solange was so absorbed in her meditations that she barely noticed these foolish exchanges. Now and then, *to comfort herself*, she would cast her eyes over the landscape outside the window. The trees, the rivers, the fields, the cows grazing in the meadows—all this rural life brought a measure of balm to her soul. She had found out long since that nature soothed her pain and even ended by making her feel happy. Her affair with Roberti was a Parisian affair, enclosed within stones and tarmac, asphyxiated by coal gas, a love singularly lacking in pure air and wide-open spaces, a love confined, nightmarish, Baudelairian . . .

I: A Baudelairian affair, glory! Does that come from her or you?

HE: It was she who thought it and I who am putting it into words. Don't interrupt me over things that go without saying. The next morning she was glad to see Dietz and Mlle. Angioletti again. She was always glad to see them, anyway, for differing reasons. Dietz because he was good-looking, intelligent, warm, kindly and aloof; Mlle. Angioletti because she was a nice girl. She was even glad to see Valentin again, looking superb and still full of the good humor he had brought back from Corsica. The only worry nagging at her heart concerned Roberti. She waited apprehensively for the phone call he would inevitably make and this irked her. She wished he wouldn't make it, hoped he would leave her in peace for another day or two. What tone should she adopt in reply? And what should she reply? It would be very difficult not to agree to see him that same evening, as he would certainly propose. What surprised her most was that she wanted to see Legay far more than her lover. She didn't explain this phenomenon to herself. She had a thousand things to say to Legay and not one to Roberti; she was longing for Legay to tell her all about his trip to Corsica with Valentin and not at all for Edouard to tell her how much he had missed her. She wanted to know what books Legay had been reading, whether he had kept the promised secret, what stage his invention had reached and so on. To put it briefly, Legay represented pleasure, time agreeably wasted, easy conversation, the luxury of an extended vacation, whereas Roberti represented duty. He was "lesson time." She was returning to love the way one returns to school.

I: Well, I think your story is done. Solange's meditations in the train were decisive. The "decrystallization" looks to me as if it were complete. She no longer loved Roberti.

HE: But she did, she still loved him. A little longer. But from now on the roles were reversed. Roberti was so impatient to hear her voice that he called up Dietz's office barely fifteen minutes after it had opened. When the phone rang, Solange instantly guessed who was on the line and her heart began to thud at the same time as a cloud of depression descended on her. She let Mlle. Angioletti take the call. "Mlle. Mignot, please," said Roberti. "Hold on," replied Mlle. Angioletti, clamping her hand over the receiver while she half whispered to Solange with a chuckle: "It's Doudou! You can't say he wastes any time! You're hardly back before he's after you. He's properly in love with you, my girl!"

I: "Doudou"! She called him Doudou? Poor Roberti!

HE: Yes, she called him Doudou. She had long since learned that his first name was Edouard. So it had to be Doudou, don't you see? Solange took offense at it to begin with, but comic diminutives were part of Mlle. Angioletti's style. She bestowed them more out of good nature than malice. And even Solange, when discussing Roberti with her, sometimes said "Doudou" by way of complicity.

I: All the same, Doudou's going a bit far! It reveals a facetious side in Solange which I hadn't suspected and which shows she was maybe less of a slave than you say. It is through comic diminutives that souls fight their way to freedom. We start by giving our king a nickname and end by chopping off his head.

HE: Not always. Nations also give their rulers affectionate nicknames.

I: Hm! It's rare. Capet and Badinguet reek of the guillotine or exile. So Angioletti handed over the telephone. Solange's expression?

HE: Yes, Solange's expression. She raised her eyes to heaven, instinctively, like someone exasperated. Angioletti was astounded; she immediately understood that her serial romance was starting a new chapter and this made her mouth water. On the phone Solange replied in monosyllables and so coldly that Roberti too realized that this was no occasion for tactlessness. "Any chance of meeting this evening?" he inquired. Almost in spite of herself she replied: "No, not this evening. I can't manage it. I promised the family I'd be home. I'm terribly sorry. It's not my fault. Tomorrow if you like." She had suddenly been overcome by an irresistible desire to see Legay and no one else that evening. To see the gentle Legay, who would gaze at her with adoring eyes, who would be so overjoyed to see her, who wouldn't say much himself but with whom she could chatter away like a magpie. Legay so restful,

Legay so calm, always available, never in a hurry to leave her. One more day of vacation!

At the other end of the line Roberti was furious, disappointed and aggrieved. Solange's last two letters had been rather affectionate and he hadn't expected such a chilly reception. He wondered what to do: become even chillier or make a pretense of cheerfulness, of the artless pleasure of renewing contact with someone one is fond of after a long separation? He adopted the latter course. In a light and jaunty tone he said: "Never mind about this evening. But tomorrow won't be possible either, I've got an engagement. That takes us to Wednesday or Thursday. Look here, let's lunch together on Thursday. I'll meet you at the corner of the Rue Gaillon at twelve-fifteen." Trying to convey a sort of impersonal politeness but with a trembling voice he added: "I'm very glad you're back, you know." He was on the point of asking: "Do you still love me?" But discretion or, rather, his sensitivity held him back. He felt Solange was by no means lost but he would have to go to some trouble to win her round. Show himself gentle, thoughtful, kind, treat her to more frequent meetings. He had an idea so out of his normal character that it seemed to him marvelous: at Thursday's lunch he would take her a present. But what? He realized he knew nothing of his mistress's tastes. At most he knew the name of the perfume she used. Well, it was quite simple, he would present her with a big bottle of it. No, on second thought, a medium-sized one.

"So there's a fly in the ointment, is there?" inquired Mlle. Angioletti. "Are you by any chance beginning to have had enough of Doudou? Let me tell you, honey, it's high time! He's not the right man for you. Things were bound to crack sooner or later."—"No, no, you're wrong," said Solange, "but I need to be alone and left in peace just now." Whereupon she phoned Legay, who emitted such whoops of joy on hearing her voice that she couldn't suppress a smile. Her eyes sparkled, her cheeks flushed pink and she prattled on for over ten minutes. Mlle. Angioletti watched and listened with a knowing air which must have been quite infuriating. An imbecile who assumes a knowing air and betrays by her expression that she fully understands what's what is enough to drive anyone to murder. "So," she said, "it's Jacques you're seeing tonight."—"Why not?" demanded Solange aggressively. "Haven't I the right?"—"Oh, as to that, honey," replied Angioletti, "far be it from me to stop you. You're dead right. Hurrah for youth and the joy of living!"

On Thursday at twelve-fifteen Roberti, who had arrived early according to his wont, was waiting at the corner of the Rue Gaillon and the

Avenue de l'Opéra with his car double-parked. Anxiety and desire gave him a buzzing in his ears. It was as if his heart were a fountain, a cascade spouting jets of blood which coursed through his body at lightning speed. At twelve-twenty Solange hadn't yet arrived. He thought how she wouldn't come, how he would never again see that familiar figure, that lovely blonde hair, that smile he could spot thirty yards off, which was the very promise of sensual delights. He was doing his earnest best to be philosophical when she appeared, but she wasn't smiling. She looked grave and troubled. This didn't prevent him from feeling an immense relief. Nothing was lost since she was there, everything was regained or soon would be. He had complete confidence in his ability to coax her round with his arguments and charm. Smilingly he opened the door of the car. She got in and sat stiffly in her seat. "Good morning," said Edouard with studied simplicity. "Hell," he added to himself, "she's going to be harder to thaw than I thought." He took her to a restaurant in the Place de la République. On the way there they exchanged platitudes and trivialities.

I: And the present?

HE: One moment. I'm coming to it. He waited till they were both settled at a table in a quiet corner before he gave it to her.

I: She must have been thrilled.

HE: No, quite the reverse. She said, "Thank you, you're very kind, you shouldn't have done it," and slipped the packet into her bag without even opening it.

I: Brr! A bad beginning!

HE: Yes, but at least a beginning. There was action. There was a woman to be won back. Roberti was consequently in his element. He threw himself into it wholeheartedly. He began by taking a sounding. "Well," he said, "how nice it is to see you again, my little dragonfly!" But instead of replying with some similar pleasantry Solange remained silent, gazing before her into space. "I've the impression," he resumed, "that it's four and a half centuries since I last saw you." He took her hand; she didn't withdraw it. Nevertheless it was a cold, still hand without the faintest tremor.

I: One might say the sounding produced no results. I'd be curious to know how a seducer of fifty proceeds in such a situation.

HE: You'll find out. Still without withdrawing her hand, Solange said in a flat voice something she had thought out in advance which seemed to her a splendid opening line, as dramatic as could be desired, quite as good as a movie or a novel. "Edouard," she said, "I've been doing a lot of thinking. We've got to have a talk."

I: A well-known cliché. Translated, it means: "I've seen enough of you, good-by." It's funny how women who never think but act mainly on impulse love to say they have been "doing a lot of thinking" and that they must "have a talk" when there's nothing left to say.

HE: Rubbish. "I've been doing a lot of thinking" is just the indispensable opening to an unpleasant scene which good manners require one to make. One has to start somehow or other. Besides, it always achieves its purpose. It gives its speaker self-assurance and puts the person it is addressed to in an inferior position. On hearing it Roberti pricked up his ears. It was a familiar tune. Twenty different women had sung it to him before. He planted a swift kiss on Solange's hand and released it, sitting back in his seat with an air at once grave and offhand. "My angel," he said quite softly, almost purring, "maybe you have done a lot of thinking but it's certainly useless for us to have a talk. I can guess at everything you want to say: it's not very gay, it's rather depressing and it risks being a fearful bore for both of us. I didn't do much thinking myself while we were apart. I simply thought about you. Today I'm very happy to see you again. I've been waiting impatiently, frantically at times, for this moment. I love you. But I can see you aren't at all in the same frame of mind. I know you and you know me. Instead of hurting each other and embarking on an endless dispute, let's rather examine the situation the way it seems to be. You are sitting beside me like an iceberg. You haven't looked at me once. You keep your eyes lowered. It's as clear as daylight: you don't love me any more. So be honest. Say 'I don't love you any more, good-by.' It's terse but I think it sums up your thoughts pretty well and leaves no room for ambiguity. You know you can say anything to me without beating about the bush. You needn't be afraid I'll roll sobbing at your feet or turn difficult. Courage, my pet! Six words and it's over: 'I don't love you any more.' After which you can relax. We can none of us help it: we fall in love and then we fall out of it; that's life. Only fools are surprised and indignant about it. Now I'm no fool. What will happen if you leave me? I shall be miserable for three, six months, perhaps a year, and then I'll start thinking of other things. And so, I beg of you, drop that constipated air. It doesn't suit you. Damn it, if you go on being so intense you'll almost make yourself ugly! Forgive me for harking back to a past which probably fills you with horror, but I've seen you at 'our place' not so very long ago looking far prettier than you are right now. If this is the last time we lunch together, let this lunch at least be a success. Come, give me a smile. It won't commit you to anything."

I: Ah, the cunning old devil. Even so, such a speech was a risky one.

HE: Not at all. It's an old rhetorical trick. It consists, when one faces an irresolute and timid opponent, in making the same speech oneself which he would deliver if he dared to pursue his thoughts through to the end. It succeeds eight times out of ten. One's opponent is put out of countenance and immediately beats a retreat. It worked unfailingly with Solange. While Roberti was speaking, the memories and emotions of former times took fresh root in her heart. She recalled their secret pleasures, the museums of Italy, the books which her lover had led her to discover, the music of Bach and Mozart. With dazzling rapidity she summed up their life together. In it she saw a hundred treasures. Not to mention the fact that Roberti had regained the upper hand: he was placing within her reach a rupture for which she hadn't yet prepared herself and which, brought so close, suddenly terrified her. She had thought it was for her to attack; she had anticipated a difficult scene, a miserable fight, and now she found the enemy had eluded her, was unresistingly offering her victory, siding with her against himself. Such elegance, such generosity shook her. At last she raised her eyes to him; she saw a face radiating kindness and simplicity. His eyes were glittering; his fine mouth was faintly quivering. She was deeply touched. Her old love, considerably weakened but not yet dead in her, woke once again. She leaned against him. Gently she laid her head on his shoulder, as if to rest after a costly effort. Roberti didn't misinterpret this gesture: it was a movement of tenderness, of habit or complicity, no more. He must on no account rush matters. He put his arm round her shoulders and gave her a gentle hug. "What a silly little goose," he said, purring louder than ever. "It's bad to get yourself into such a state. You're trembling like a leaf. And all because you don't know how to give me the sack. I'll help you. Say after me: 'Monsieur, I have loved you for two years but everything comes to an end. Your love does me honor but it's beginning to bore me. So let's break it off here and now.' As you can see, he was staking everything on the spirit of contradiction and he wasn't wrong. Solange had come to this lunch without any particular intention of breaking with him, but women are so made that, had she found a fulsome, whining, overattentive, melodramatic Roberti, she would possibly have been led to make a break. "Be quiet," she said. "Phew! I've won," thought Edouard. "Now I've got to arrange things so that we can go and set the seal on it in the Square Saint-Lambert. It's going to be tricky but it's absolutely vital. Besides, I madly want to have the little bitch." In genuinely woebegone tones Solange murmured: "I don't know how I can be so silly!" Roberti perfectly understood this remark as well. "I have no character," it meant. "I can't follow through my ideas; I have let myself get emotional."—"Why no," he said, "you're not silly, one is never silly to give in to love. What is silly, what is unforgivable, is to resist it. I think you still love me a little."—"I don't know," said Solange. "I had promised myself that I would say a certain number of things to you today."—"What things?" said Roberti, feeling he could now be a little more daring. "Oh, that's of no importance now," replied Solange, "it was probably just a lot more silliness." She gave him a forced but nonetheless very gentle, very sweet smile. Roberti told himself it would be better not to insist. He had won her back and that was enough. Suddenly he felt bored at the idea that she might give him a detailed account of the various emotions she had been through. He didn't want to know. It was of no interest and might even be dangerous. He was almost at the point of wondering whether his victory was worth all the trouble he had taken to win it. "So here we are," he thought, "I'm signing up again, re-enlisting. Had I wanted it, this little goose and I could have broken up today. She was quite ready for it. And perhaps it would have been better." This kind of reasoning was typical of him. Following on action, he often had these lapses of vigor; success brought him no pleasure. No sooner was it won than he saw in it misery and emptiness. In the present case, however, besides his spirit cooling off in this way, there was also his body, and this was hot with desire. But perhaps I'm exaggerating. The fact of having won Solange back filled him with a vague, diffuse, *involuntary* feeling of happiness. "Had I wanted it," he thought, but in actual fact he hadn't. He made himself very pressing. He placed his hand on his mistress's knee, he hugged her to him and was quick to sense how she wasn't indifferent to these advances. The old magic was beginning to work again. As they left the restaurant he said in a voice that echoed his beating heart: "Let's go and spend an hour at our place. Please. I beg of you." The monster even hypocritically added: "We won't do anything if you don't want to. I would just like to look at you and kiss you." Alas, it wasn't possible, she had to be back at the office by two-thirty at the latest; but he insisted: "We can be at the Square Saint-Lambert in fifteen minutes." She weakened. She also wanted to go there, and not just to "do nothing." After all, what was so wrong about getting back to the office at three or three-thirty for once? "Nothing wrong at all," said Roberti. "What harm can it possibly do?" In the end he won her round; she only went on arguing to satisfy her conscience. The car swallowed them both up. It must have been one-thirty or one-forty-five; the traffic had slackened off. They arrived shortly after, both in a high state of excitement. The apartment, which nobody had been into for nearly two months, was stuffy and smelled of mothballs. This smell was extraordinarily aphrodisiac.

When they parted, after Roberti had dropped Solange off in the Avenue de l'Opéra, neither of them was feeling happy. Solange reproached herself for the weakness of her character and flesh. Roberti, having slaked his desire, regretted that he hadn't seized such a splendid opportunity to effect a painless break with someone—and this had been proved and proved beyond doubt—whose body alone he loved. That night, as she had anticipated, Solange cried herself to sleep. The worst of it was that she didn't even know why she was crying. She was to have met Legay the next day but she had put him off. She didn't want to see him again so soon after her revels in the Square Saint-Lambert.

I: God, what a mess! How depressing it all is! There's nothing more frightful than an old love that won't lie down and die.

HE: Yes, frightful. And this particular love was to linger on for six more months. Half a year. It was to sink deeper and deeper into gloom, discontent, darkness and suffering. It was to go down slowly, slowly, like an abandoned ship.

I: Don't be too slow, all the same!

HE: I'm sorry but I shall be as slow as necessary. In accounts of this kind one only appears long-winded when one cuts things short. I shall spare you no horror.

I: A charming prospect.

HE: During the two months that elapsed between the scene I've just described and what I have called the incident at Neuilly-sur-Marne, Roberti and Solange saw appreciably less of each other than they were formerly wont to do, though this wasn't his fault. He frequently phoned his mistress, just as in the past. She would reply in an overloud, almost social voice which let it be understood she was not alone. He proposed meetings; she raised objections: some urgent work for Dietz was likely to keep her late at the office, she had arranged to spend the evening with a girl friend, or her parents were expecting her home for dinner. So that sometimes eight or even ten days would go by between one meeting and the next. There had been a time when she would literally cling on to the telephone and gladly spend the next half hour in empty chatter; Roberti never knew how to cut short this prattling, which bored him and prolonged his fear of being overheard. Now these calls had become very brief. "Good morning, how are you?" he would say. "Very well, thanks, and you?" she would reply. After which, silence. A grisly silence. Crackling noises on the line, *frttt . . . frttt . . . frttt . . .* Solange made no attempt to keep the conversation going. Roberti would try to introduce a little warmth between them by calling her "my darling" or "my little buttercup" but she refrained from taking this meager bait and he got no return for his pains.

People are always rather slow to notice that the love they inspire is on the wane. Solange's changed attitude didn't make Roberti particularly gay but it didn't depress him either. He deduced from it that their affair had entered on a new, practical phase, that she had given up trying to take more from him than he was prepared to give. This was a rather satisfactory development on the whole. Moreover it had never crossed his mind that a break might come from her side, since it was an established fact that her love was greater than his. Oddly and remarkably enough, he now no longer felt bored when he picked up the telephone but excited. If by chance Solange gave signs of being more talkative or forthcoming than usual he experienced a thrill of joy. "I'm getting younger," he thought. "I'm giving myself kicks. How amusing!" In other words still blind, you see. With a methodical, organized, stubborn blindness. Solange's coldness, which would have stared anyone else in the face, appeared to him a temporary condition of no importance. There were shoals and reefs in every love affair. An adroit pilot avoided them. It was enough to steer skillfully, and when it came to skill he feared no rival.

From September to November 1957 one could say that Roberti, like Napoleon in 1813, went through his "Battle of France." At each meeting he had to win back his mistress and he did so. She would turn up with a wooden face, taciturn as a child, get into the car and let herself be kissed without displaying the slightest trace of emotion. Between the Avenue de l'Opéra and the Square Saint-Lambert Edouard knew he had twenty to twenty-five minutes in which to capture her attention with words. During the drive he would talk as if nothing was wrong. He would tell stories; he would discuss literature or music. After about fifteen minutes his charm, his soft voice, his knowledge of the secret ways to Solange's susceptibilities and the familiarity they shared would finally take effect. His skill lay in assuming gaiety and a sort of jauntiness. He wasn't welcoming her as a mistress but as a friend he was always glad to see. At this time she hadn't much love left for him but I think she might have had a revival of passion had he stopped taking her to the studio for a month, had he employed the hours he devoted to her in taking her out for drives, long talks in the gardens and visits to museums. She would willingly have gone with him to a movie. On two or three occasions, anxiously watching him with her huge dark eyes, she said: "Don't let's go to the Square Saint-Lambert today." Such a request could hardly have been more explicit, more eloquent. It meant: "If you want to win me back, show you're more interested in my soul than in my body." But this didn't at all suit Roberti, who had to divest himself of eight or ten days' erotic daydreams. Faithful to his torpedoing tactics he would pretend to acquiesce and then launch into specious arguments from which it emerged that the studio was no more than a secluded spot where they could talk in greater comfort than elsewhere. Solange knew this speech by heart. She had long since recognized its hypocrisy but was too simple, too timid, too resigned perhaps, to refute it.

Roberti told himself that his hold over Solange was a sensual one and that she must be reminded of this as often as possible. It mattered little whether she entered the building in the Square Saint-Lambert with the bad grace and mental reservations of someone being forced to act against her will: as soon as she set foot on the stairs he could feel how, in spite of herself, she was set all aflutter by the voluptuous memories the place aroused in her, just as he was all aflutter himself. He would then take her gently by the arm and whisper words of love in her ear. By the time they reached their door they were both nearly always trembling. Closing the door behind him he would hold her tight, kiss her, caress her, and after a few minutes she would melt into his arms. This was followed by dazzling victories, as intoxicating as those won two years earlier but now short-lived. They were to love what the battles of Champaubert and Montmirail were to Napoleon. Solange would momentarily recover all her old fire. Physical exaltation brought her a transient and doubtless artificial exaltation of the spirit. Roberti would ask whether she loved him. "Oh yes," she would sigh. There were all kinds of regrets and reservations in this sigh.

These triumphs concealed from Roberti the inevitable outcome of the war. Each time, in fact, when all was over and the two lovers had parted, Solange would sink back more deeply into her despair. She read herself little lectures interspersed with tears, the main theme of which was: "I'm disgusted at myself. He's turned me into a slut. He doesn't love me. He despises me. He only speaks to me when he desires me." She would make a firm resolve never to see him again. The next day, if he called, she would get Mlle. Angioletti to talk to him and tell him she wasn't there or was "in conference" with M. Dietz. Then she would cheer up a bit; she would forget, she would think of her lover's body which still attracted her, of his shrewd mind, of the smile he sometimes gave her—and consent to another meeting. She would ponder bitterly over love—so wonderful in its beginnings but gradually declining without one's knowing how until it becomes ugly. She didn't know she had ceased to love him; she imagined that were he to throw her over she would feel the same unbearable misery she would have felt a year before. These illusions are common, especially among women, who find it hard to admit that a great love may not last very long. Solange believed in all good faith that her love, which she had once looked on as a blessing, had turned into a curse but hadn't for all that vanished. I suppose she was seeing the two faces of one and the same passion.

Toward mid-October or thereabouts, Roberti began to feel pervaded by sadness and dissatisfaction. In the long run these victories which must be won afresh each week were exhausting. On leaving him Solange no longer asked: "When can we meet again?" Had he not tirelessly fixed dates with her they might never have seen each other again and so their love would have ended, in silence. He suddenly became aware of this unconscionable fact and felt afraid. "Is she as tired of me as all that?" he wondered. He then plunged into a sort of examination of conscience which gave him no pleasure. For once he saw himself as he truly was— mean, lecherous, selfish, cruel, cowardly, niggardly with his time and his emotions. He saw how he had been wanting in generosity toward Solange, how he had shown a singular lack of gratitude and kindness toward this girl who had *given him her heart* and given it elegantly, the way one offers a worthless trinket. He had given nothing in exchange. He had been grudging in all things. Worse: stingy. He had been parsimonious with himself. He who took such pride in having a noble soul had behaved like a shopkeeper thinking only of his own interests, whereas Solange, this featherbrained little idiot, had acted with the prodigality of a princess. What dismayed him most was the fact that for the past two and a half years *he hadn't once appeared in a good light*. He had to admit this and it was intolerable. He had allowed the honors to be snatched from him by someone quite unworthy, given her small mind, limited intellect and lack of education. How on earth could anything so unthinkable have come about? The only possible explanation was that he didn't love her whereas she loved him. When one is not in love one's mind is full of other things and the soul, alas, remains hidden; whereas when in love one thinks of nothing else and the soul is ceaselessly laid bare. Note the following, which is most unusual and has, I think, rarely been shown: it was vexation at appearing in so bad a light and the desire to remedy this that impelled Roberti more than anything else along the road to evil and horror.

ɪ: I'll note it to please you but it isn't so very unusual. Indeed, the desire to appear in a good light at all costs is a form of vanity and we all know that vanity leads to crime. Especially vanity *vis-à-vis* oneself, which is the worst kind. A noble soul naturally appears in a good light whatever the situation it finds itself in, because it behaves nobly and justly, not in order to admire itself but to preserve its self-respect. A base soul in need of reassurance as to its merits never shrinks from the basest act in order to appear in a good light.

HE: It always annoys me when you say or imply that Roberti had a base soul. It isn't true, I assure you. He had a restless, complex, calculating, weak soul but not a base one, no. He had a horror of baseness. He was always trying to surpass himself, to "do better." Setting aside his affair with Solange and the pitiful figure he cut in it, there is barely a trace of pettiness to be found in his life. He never said (or even thought, I'll bet my last penny) those degrading things which betray the dirty little heart of a petty bourgeois busy counting the lumps of sugar or reading his children's letters. He lived on a different level. For instance, he would have been incapable of guessing at and countering the maneuvers of his servant Germaine. This examination of his conscience with regard to Solange genuinely upset him. He felt ashamed of himself. He judged himself harshly. Then he thought lovingly of her and resolved to be nicer to her in future, more affectionate, more attentive. He owed it to her and *it was only right*. For the first time since their affair began he felt a sort of remorse. For the first time he really thought of her and her alone, instead of her in relation to himself. He tried to picture the loneliness and neglect in which he had always left her; he made an effort to understand her emotional starvation and the result astonished him. He couldn't get over the fact that a man like himself, generally kind, delicate, sensitive and well bred, should have behaved so much like a brute. He was filled with extreme zeal: he would take her out for drives since that was what she wanted. They would go and dine one evening soon in the valley of Chevreuse; another time it would be a movie. On Saturday afternoon they would visit the Cognac-Jay Museum, where there is such a wonderful Rembrandt. As for the Square Saint-Lambert, they would wait until she asked before going there again.

Alas, as so often happens, these reflections came too late. Too late as well the good resolutions which went with them. Why hadn't he thought of this a month before? Everything would then have been saved. But Solange had had to wait a few days too long; the last traces of hope had faded from her heart. When Roberti telephoned her, full of his new plans and joyfully eager to tell her about them, she replied that she was tired, that she needed to "think things over" and would be very grateful if he therefore didn't call her again for the next two weeks. She must have at least that long to put her thoughts in order and find her balance. Thunderstruck, he stupidly said: "But we won't go to the Square Saint-Lambert, my sweet. I've made all the arrangements for a little lovers' dinner in the country. It'll be a huge success, you'll see." Solange was adamant. She wasn't angry, just very bleak, like a patient who isn't well enough to feel any desires. Her voice was gentle but colorless. What she said wasn't hostile but imbued with a weariness verging on indifference. Edouard insisted; he made a fine and most persuasive speech. A waste of his time. He was addressing a plant, a stone. When he hung up he was at once aghast and exasperated, filled with grief and fury. Mentally he cursed Solange. There was a lot of love, I think, in those curses. Poor Edouard! "Very well," he thought, "very well. If that's the way you want it. It won't be two weeks, it will be a month before I call again. Or never. We'll see." To console himself he counted over her physical shortcomings, her rather skinny legs, her rather protruding bust, her figure which wasn't ideally slender. He tried to persuade himself that he could never really be in love with a woman whose body wasn't absolutely beautiful, that there was even something degrading in being infatuated with this rather indifferent body; it was quite idiotic to suffer for someone so commonplace. But ten minutes later he had calmed down. Already the spirit of contradiction, that eternal lever of love, had taken hold of him and he was concocting plans to see Solange again before the prescribed time limit. He loved this imperfect body. He loved its imperfections above all. Besides, the face made up for everything else, that bright and lovely face which in certain circumstances known to him alone acquired an unimaginable beauty that was engraved on his heart. Engraved? Not so sure. Now all at once he was trying to reconstruct it in his memory, that familiar face he had covered a thousand times with kisses, whose warmth he could still feel on his cheek, and he couldn't manage to do so. The eyebrows were missing. Where was the mouth? And the chin? Impossible to re-create its line. Roberti was appalled. Out of prudence he hadn't a single photograph of his mistress. He told himself he would never see her again and he hadn't even borne off a complete picture of her in his mind. How stupid beyond words! If only, at their last meeting, he had made a careful study of her features, taking good care to note the roundness of the chin and the curve of the eyebrows! What fatal negligence! The absurd security in which one lulls oneself to sleep! "I simply must see her again, if only for a moment," he thought. He would take his stand in the Avenue de l'Opéra, he would wait till Dietz's office closed. He would go up to her. Dramatically he would say: "Be quiet. Listen to me. This may be the last time we ever meet. I know you don't love me any more. I wanted to see you one last time. Good-by." Clearly she would never resist such a declaration. She would fling herself into his arms. She had loved him so much: she could never bear to see him so unhappy.

I: The poor man's turning into an out-and-out idiot. How sad! But tell me, at this moment was he sincere or putting it on? Was he really unhappy or just enjoying himself?

HE: A bit of both. But in love false is true and true is false. What was certainly false with Roberti was this daydream—the tragic and extravagant twist it had assumed. What was true was the panic into which Solange's chilliness had thrown him, expressing itself in an impatience similar to the one that had come over him eleven months before following the episode at the Comédie Française, but more gradual, more slow. I shall try to describe this impatience once again, to shed light on it from a different angle. It is very rare for a man of fifty-two to be prey to an impatience of this kind. Normally it tends more to afflict the young. It is a terribly painful state during which one has the feeling of not being alive. Things happen and one can do nothing about them. In rage and impotence one watches the indifferent march of the world. One knows one ought to bestir oneself, do something, impress oneself on the world somehow or other, but one has no idea how to set about it. The wretched sufferer fairly rapidly reaches a point where he can no longer tolerate his own soul. It hampers him. Pains him. His need for action drives him mad. So he flings himself on the world and does absolutely *anything*, not so much to procure results or safeguard his interests as to return to life and prove to himself that he is not dead. Another by-product is that when in this state the heart doesn't function as usual. The soul endures a permanent anguish and the body a feeling of nausea.

I: You know, what you're saying is very true. I feel quite giddy listening to you. I remember my own youth. When I was eighteen or twenty and had blinding passions, the state of impatience sometimes seized hold of me. It was horrible, now I think back on it! Doesn't one also look haggard?

HE: Yes. That's it, haggard. One loses all power to control the expression on one's face. The face is no longer protected by the will. It is a perfect reflection of one's ungovernable and pointless impatience. One's eyes have a wild look, one's hands tremble, one's knees give way. Inside one is a void, but an aching void, the emptiness left by extraction of the soul. The curse of it is that the victim has the feeling, through all the time his bout of impatience lasts, that a dentist has extracted his soul and left a gaping wound.

I: Myself at twenty! The dead spit of myself at twenty! It makes me shudder. Why has impatience never been numbered among the deadly sins? It is worse than anger. How long did Roberti resist this abomination?

HE: Two weeks. He was heroic. Solange had asked to be left in peace for two weeks. What helped him to manage it was a blend of submission to his mistress's wishes and wounded self-esteem. Thirty times a day he would look at the telephone, stretch out his hand, pick up the receiver and then replace it without touching the dial. He was like a chain smoker determined to give up cigarettes. Each cigarette unlit is a victory. Going to bed at night he would think: "Another day over. One more day during which I've held out!" But it was an effort of will which used up almost all his strength. What little remained was spent on keeping a cheerful face at home, small talk, smiling at his children's jokes and replying affectionately to Agnes' questions.

By the end of the second week his bleak impatience had reached its peak. He had calculated, I don't know how, that Solange must show up on the eighth of November if not the seventh. You can imagine his state as he waited through those two days. But nothing happened. The phone never rang. No letter. Nothing. By the ninth, Edouard was so "beside himself" (I can find no better expression) that he was incapable of fixing his attention on anything at all. Worse, he had no power of concentration, no critical faculty left; he found it impossible to put two consecutive thoughts together. Spiritual anguish and physical nausea had such a grip on him that he looked quite distraught. He would open a file, read a few pages without understanding a word, put it back in its cabinet and three minutes later would have lost all recollection of having done any of this. One thought alone obsessed his mind and drove out everything else. Why hadn't Solange called him? He returned to this again and again with the obstinacy of an imbecile or a spoiled child. He dared not go out for a second; what if the phone should ring just then? Toward four o'clock he told himself: "She knows I don't like her to call or write to me at home. So it's quite natural that she hasn't done so. She's waiting for me to call her. We should have arranged how to get in touch again the last time we spoke together. How idiotic! I never think of things like that." With a wildly beating heart and shaking hands he picked up the receiver and dialed Dietz's number. But see how fate arranges things! At that moment neither Solange nor Angio-

letti happened to be in their room. Roberti's emotion was so overpowering that he hung up the very second when Solange, hearing the phone,
ran in to reply. He heaved a gigantic sigh and buried his head in his
hands. He could feel his blood throbbing in his temples. He was trembling down to his knees. He thought how perhaps it was better after
all that no one had answered the phone; he would have been incoherent, he would have expressed himself clumsily and this might have given
cause for alarm. Besides, he didn't know what to say to Solange. Two
weeks without seeing her had made her almost a stranger. He would
far rather see her, meet her. Yes, that was it! He must come on her
unawares and have things out. He recalled the women whom in the
old days he had left without a word of explanation, telling himself that
a man's silence is far more eloquent than words and that a person must
be a numbskull not to understand that kind of language. Now that he
was its victim, he could see the cruelty of this procedure. It is an act of
charity to say to someone: "I no longer love you." It may be unpleasant
but it is something one simply has to do, since no torture can compare
with the few days during which the agony of hope lives on, when the
heart hangs on a telephone call which never comes, on a letter the
postman never brings, on a visit awaited till nightfall. Nothing is more
atrocious than the steadily growing certainty that one will never see
one's beloved again, that this is the way he wants it, that he has fled
because your presence is the only one among all human presences
which he can no longer stand.

ɪ: Enough, enough. We know all this. No generalizations please. Stick
to particulars. Particulars are all I'm interested in.

ʜᴇ: Well, here are some particulars. One of the ideas which caused
Edouard the greatest pain was that, were it written that he should
never see Solange again, she would take with her a pretty ugly image
of him. In two weeks of solitude his imagination had turned turtle. It
was indispensable for him to have one last meeting with his mistress,
not so as to try to win her back—he was beyond that—but to show her
that he was a "man of quality." If he had made her unhappy it wasn't
because he had a selfish and cowardly soul but for higher motives.

ɪ: Such as?

ʜᴇ: Hell, those remained to be found. But that didn't worry him unduly. He was sure that, once face to face with Solange, he would know
how to convince her that he had always acted with a certain pureness
of motive, that is to say out of love. "Love" is a magic word with which
one can explain away anything given sufficient eloquence. He would
contrive to show how, throughout this whole affair, he had been more

sinned against than sinning. As proof of this, who was suffering at this moment? Who was in torment? Who was *enduring*? He was. He was the one being dropped. Given his intelligence, he would end by proving that at bottom and without appearing to do so he had committed his heart far more deeply than Solange and in a far more lasting way. She hadn't understood him. She had let herself be blinded by his attitude (which doubtless might have led her to understand that . . .) but what is an attitude? When one is in love one must bear with such minor vexations. In short he concocted a pretty little homily thanks to which he would withdraw, if not with the honors of war, then at least without cutting too poor a figure, and thus regain his self-respect. This plan at any rate had the effect of redoubling his impatience. It is the usual effect such plans have when our souls are so afflicted. The moment they are made we can't wait to put them into action. Roberti decided to go that same evening to wait for Solange in the Avenue de l'Opéra. He intended to play her a most convincing scene. Out loud he said: "I'll take my revolver, just in case. I'll tell her I've kept it by me for the past week, so as to have it to hand during those thirty seconds when I feel I've really had enough of life. It will fit very well into the picture. She'll tell herself she's jilting Lord Byron!" The idea of this made him laugh and he felt almost gay.

At six o'clock he had parked his car in the Rue Louis-le-Grand and was pacing up and down before the doorway through which Solange must emerge. Every two minutes he looked at his watch. By six-fifteen his legs were so weak that he went to lean against the wall; all the same, in the midst of his agitation he found himself able to reflect that for once time was passing very slowly and philosophized briefly on the advantage of heartaches, which prolong the hours for middle-aged men. His right hand was clenched round the revolver in his overcoat pocket. He was squeezing this object convulsively without even being aware of it.

I: What's going to happen when he sees Legay appear?

HE: Legay? Why should he see Legay appear?

I: Because Solange had a date with this nice young man, didn't she? Obviously. It's as plain as day. Legay's going to turn up at six-twenty-five clutching a bunch of violets. Solange is going to come out chattering to Angioletti. Hello Jacques, hello Solange, where are we going tonight? Well, first to have a drink. Then we'll see. There's an excellent movie at the Aubert-Palace. We could have a quick sandwich in a snack bar.

HE: What's all this you're saying?

i: I'm telling you what happens. Roberti comes to surprise Solange as she leaves her office. It's the normal, I'd even say obligatory thing for him to bump into his rival.

HE: Now that you're showing some imagination for once, I can't compliment you on it. Roberti bumped into no one. Solange had no date with Legay. She came out quite sedately at about a quarter to seven with Mlle. Angioletti. Edouard approached her with faltering steps and a vague smile on his lips. Mlle. Angioletti, intimidated, said: "Solange honey, I must fly! I'll say good-by since you've got company." And there you are. That was that. So much for Legay.

i: How did Solange react when she saw Roberti rise up before her like the statue of the Commendatore in *Don Giovanni?*

HE: In the first place he didn't rise up before her like the statue of the Commendatore. There was nothing of the Commendatore about him, poor man. He tottered forward (fully realizing he was tottering). "My goddamn nerves," he thought. "How idiotic to have the shakes like this, when at heart I'm quite indifferent to the whole business!" Solange put on an earnest expression to meet the occasion. She wasn't very surprised to see him; she had been expecting him to turn up sooner or later. Nonetheless she hadn't decided on her attitude.

i: Because naturally she hadn't "thought things over" at all during her two weeks alone.

HE: Of course not. During those two weeks she had given her heart a vacation. Whenever she thought of Roberti she felt depressed. So she tried to think of him as little as possible and succeeded in it very well. From time to time she caught herself hoping that perhaps it would all end like this, that Roberti, tepid as he was, would grow tired of not hearing from her and give no further sign of life. It would be a pity, no doubt, but it would make things so much simpler. When she paused to examine her feelings and her life, everything seemed to be in such a hopeless tangle that she felt an immense fatigue. With all her heart she longed to return to simplicity. No sacrifice would be too great for that, even the winding up of an affair to which she believed she still clung.

At a quarter to seven in Paris, in November, the night is what I can only call reddish, a darkness whose color resembles the dirt of certain houses. Roberti asked Solange (humbly enough) if she could spare him a moment. Yes, she had a few minutes but not very long. "Let's drive round a bit," he suggested. "We can talk in the car. I'll drop you off in the Avenue Daumesnil." With a touch of irony he added: "Don't worry, you won't be late for dinner with the family." And indeed, as if to show he wasn't making an airy promise, he set off in the direction of the Porte Dorée. He drove in silence. He didn't know what to say to this woman sitting beside him, toward whom he felt drawn by a yearning which brought tears to his eyes. After ten minutes he muttered: "What has happened to us, Solange?" It was very rare for him to call her by her first name like this. It gave his words a strange and faintly tragic allure. Solange didn't mistake it. She turned and looked at him. He had the same pale and drawn face he had had at the Square Saint-Lambert eleven months before. She was filled with a great pain, but a selfish one compounded of annoyance and resentment. She suffered a little for him and a great deal for herself. She would have given anything for him to recover his composure. At the idea that he might be about to indulge in some degrading, melodramatic gesture she was seized with pity and vexation. "I don't know what has happened to us," she said. "I loved you so much, you know. So very much! No one else ever loved you the way I did. For two years my whole life depended on your phone calls. You'd call up, you'd see me and I'd be beside myself with joy. Then you'd go three, four days without calling me and I'd be desperate, I'd feel like throwing myself in the Seine. For two years, Edouard, I did nothing but wait for you. And cry! You'll never know how I cried! I think I cried so much that I've no tears left! They were all shed for you. It's all pretty silly when you come to think of it!" As she went on speaking she took courage, as so often happens. At the same time this speech she was improvising was at last clarifying things in her mind, which had been clouded by love for so long. Something strange was happening to her; it was setting her heart free and at the same time leaving her astonished: through what she was saying to her lover she was at last explaining things to herself. Words are a very useful means for tracking down feelings. She felt almost happy. Why almost? She was *completely* happy. With every word she was breaking a bond. If she had enough strength and wit to say everything she would be rid of her love forever. When presently she got out of the car, she would say good-by without looking back to this man she had loved to the point of believing she would never have enough of his presence. Already the two and a half years her affair had lasted seemed to her like a dream. They had almost ceased to be real. She hadn't loved a man but a reflection, a shadow, a character created by her own imagination, an effigy, a statue. What an amazing discovery! Roberti was not a living being. These thoughts, however, were devilishly difficult to translate into French. It had to be done, however; it was the price of her freedom. "I'm not blaming you in any way, Edouard," she continued.

"I swear I'm not. On the contrary, you have been something unique for me. How strange it is. I feel as if there had been a veil over my eyes and now it is suddenly being torn away. Now, right now, I can see masses of things I couldn't see a mere week ago. For heaven's sake don't think I have any regrets. None at all. I gave you everything I had gladly; I wanted you to take everything. But you took nothing, darling. Obviously it wasn't worth much, I know that. I had little to give. What is Solange Mignot, a secretary, compared with a man like you, so superior and intelligent? But one can only give such presents as it's in one's power to give. With you I never knew where I stood. Doubtless I didn't understand you, I'm too stupid. Sometimes you were so sweet to me that I felt like dying of joy in your arms. Sometimes you were like a stone. As if you weren't there at all. I loved a wall, I was offering my devotion to a wall. You can be terribly hard sometimes. I don't mean unkind, but hard like a rock on which one bruises oneself. I bruised myself too badly, Edouard. Too often. I'm aching all over."

Roberti listened in consternation to this outburst. His lips were pinched and inwardly he felt a most disagreeable mixture of rage and shame. Each one of Solange's words struck home. It was most surprising but it had to be put up with. He marveled at the feminine genius speaking through the mouth of his mistress. Decidedly it wasn't going to be easy to appear in a good light! I apologize for using clichés but there are times when they accurately describe certain states: Roberti felt his limbs turn to ice. Indeed his hands were cold. What Solange was saying was causing an upheaval inside him. His blood was rushing to his brain, deserting his arms and legs. He drove automatically. He didn't speak. This indictment filled his mind with despair, since it wasn't composed of arguments which could be refuted with logic and she was developing it without the slightest trace of anger. She wasn't seeking to prove anything: she was confining herself to describing what had happened and what it was impossible to go back on. She was describing the past with an irrefutable exactitude. So this little goose had understood this subtle man; she had judged him and, what was worse, judged him magnanimously. It was humiliating beyond words. I think that at this moment Roberti's soul presented itself as a wild confusion of vices: pride, vanity, lechery, selfishness, hypocrisy and impotence were crawling there like the monsters in a painting by Hieronymus Bosch, but humiliated monsters, enchained, whipped and tormented already by the avengers of hell.

Of course I have considerably abridged what Solange said. I'm only giving you its general substance. As you can imagine, she repeated the same things several times over in similar or different terms. These repetitions, this excess of words helped her to follow her thoughts right through and gave her fresh strength. Moreover she had two people to convince: herself and Edouard. It was necessary for her to hear the same things repeated several times before she could fully absorb them. She was describing her past to herself and this story, all the details and profound meaning of which she could now at last fully comprehend, entranced her. She would never tire of telling it and hearing it. She was feeling a sort of creative joy and, as she had foreseen, setting herself free. She was so absorbed that she never noticed how Roberti had passed the Avenue Daumesnil and was driving straight on. He himself hadn't noticed it for that matter. In this way they crossed the Bois de Vincennes, then a place which must have been Le Perreux, and found themselves in open country on a side road beyond Neuilly-sur-Marne. It was a deserted region. The kind of place one dreams of to take a girl whom one wants to make love to unobserved. Roberti stopped his car and all at once they heard the silence of the fields and smelled the smell of a cold wet autumn. Solange fell silent. In a tight voice he said: "I love you, Solange. There's no woman in the world I desire as much as you. Everything you have said this evening is frightful. And it's true," he added painfully, for it cost him a great deal to admit it. "I haven't always treated you as I should have. I've often reproached myself for it. I can't help it, I've an odd, complicated and often incomprehensible character; but I can swear my love for you over the past two and a half years has been the only thing that has given me constant pleasure. My only joy. All the rest has bored me to tears. I've just put up with it. Whereas you, you have been my haven, my refuge, the only truth in a world of falsehood, the only reality in a world of absurdity." Solange lowered her window and breathed in the cold air without replying. "He's lying," she thought, "he doesn't love me. Don't listen to all these fine words Solange, or you're sunk!"—"You do believe what I've just said, don't you?" he went on. Without turning she replied hesitantly and out of politeness: "Oh yes, of course."—"I promise you everything will be different," said Roberti. "From now on I'll see you every day. You'll never have reason to complain about me. We'll have endless talks. It's good to talk. One *must* talk. I have millions of things to say to you which I've never said before, I don't know why. I can't live without you, Solange. What do you want me to do? Divorce? Right, I will, I'll divorce." At this she was really startled. Sharply she turned her head. His face in the half darkness was white; his eyes were lowered. "A man who lowers his eyes," she thought, "isn't being sincere." For the rest, her mind was closed against anything he might say since she had so brilliantly described the story of her love. She laid her hand over her lover's and gently said: "Divorce, my poor darling? You? And for me? You know very well I'm not worth it. Anyway you would never do it." —"Just ask me," said Roberti. "No," she replied, "I won't. I don't want it."—"I'm going completely off the rails," thought Roberti, "talking like a lunatic. Anyhow it's making a pretty scene. In the normal course of events she ought to fall into my arms. Perhaps the time has come for action." He raised Solange's hand to his lips but she pulled it away. He tried to put his arms round her; he leaned toward her and placed his hand on her knee. Very firmly she said: "No, Edouard. Please! What's the use?" She knew perfectly well what the use was. What an idiotic thing to say! Here was a woman who had been his mistress for two and a half years and who had always given the most unequivocal proof of her ardor and now, all of a sudden, she was resisting him! How ridiculous! Roberti was as furious as a man seeing himself being robbed of some object he has long been used to and must from now on go without. "It's not possible," he thought, "she's just playing hard to get. How silly women are! This side road, where there isn't even a cat, is a perfect spot and Madame doesn't want to." With these thoughts in mind he looked at Solange so spitefully, with eyes so hard and reflecting a desire so abject given the present circumstances that she was scared. With a gasp she said: "Let's take a walk down the road. The fresh air will do us both good," and opened the door. Roberti held her back by the arm. As sometimes occurs during emotional scenes, the expression on his face in no way reflected his feelings. In spite of his hard, fixed stare there was more dismay and sorrow than rage in his soul. In reality he was in a state of complete indecision. Half imploring, half imperious, his eyes brimming with tears and his quivering mouth doing its best to form a reassuring smile, he jerked out: "No! Stay in the car. What's the matter? Are you afraid of me?" He despaired at the thought that she might be afraid of him. Had he then so little self-control that his face should so belie his heart? Had she drawn so far away from him that she believed he might do her an injury? Solange was naturally all the more alarmed. "Let me go," she cried, "you look like a maniac!" He was holding her rather loosely. He dared not tighten his grip. "I'll have to pull myself together," he thought. "The idea of me looking like a maniac! It's inconceivable! She's asking me to let go of her arm. I'll do so. At once. That way she'll see I'm not mad in the least." Immediately she felt him release her Solange opened the door wider and started to get out, but the car was parked alongside a gutter into which her foot slipped; her heel caught on a kind of stump and she fell to her knees on the sopping wet ground. "This is all too silly," thought Roberti, "too silly for words. The purest melodrama. I'm damned if I'm going to be made a fool of by this little goose!" Seeing Solange on her hands and knees trying to free her heel he was suddenly seized with fury; he felt he was being made cheap and ridiculous not only in his own eyes but also in those of the whole world. He got out and walked rapidly round the car. "Just wait and see, I'll make you get in, you little fool," he muttered. "What kind of a performance is this, I ask you!" He reached Solange, who had at last got back onto her feet. She was trying to master her fear and put a brave and provocative face on things. This attitude enraged him. He found it utterly out of place and in the worst possible taste. He was overcome with a fiendish desire to hold it up to ridicule, turn the whole situation into a macabre farce. Solange couldn't imagine why he was groping so feverishly in his overcoat pocket. A steel object appeared in his hand. When she realized it was a revolver she gave a faint scream. Roberti was trembling up against her. He gave a sort of hiccup, due at once to the laughter shaking him and his anger, stimulated by all this frenzied behavior. "Are you going to get back in the car or aren't you? You're to get in the car at once! Christ, I've had enough of all this nonsense!" He pressed the nose of the revolver into her neck and she believed her last hour had come. She thought of her parents. For an instant she saw Father Mignot in his slippers, roaming round the apartment and asking his wife: "When are we going to have dinner? Solange is very late again. She really has no consideration!" Tomorrow, when he learned that his daughter was dead, he would bitterly repent of his irritability. She also had a fleeting thought for poor Valentin, who had been made so unhappy through her own fault. Two tears trickled down her cheeks. She waited for the explosion that would blow her head open. She was terrified out of her wits. At least half a minute went by and then it seemed to her that her breath, which had stopped, was returning. She raised her hand and took hold of the revolver. Roberti's fingers unclenched. She flung the revolver several yards off, over a hedge and into a field, after which a strange phenomenon occurred: Roberti crumpled and fell back in a faint against the car. She straightened him up. He was breathing harshly, like someone in a coma. She longed to burst into huge, wracking sobs. Why? Because he loved her and she no longer loved him.

I: What a ludicrous scene!

HE: Wait. It isn't over and its consequences were disastrous. Solange was badly shaken, badly upset. Unconscious as he was, Roberti still terrified her. She told herself she must get away before he came round. So she climbed the hedge over which she had flung the revolver, not without tearing her stockings and coat and ruining her patent-leather shoes, and stumbled along behind this hedge for about fifty yards. Finally she stopped, out of breath and with a buzzing in her ears. She heard Roberti call: "Solange, hey there, Solange! Come back! I'll take you home. Hey there, hey . . ." but she made no reply. She crouched in the shadow of the hedge like a hare for a quarter of an hour. Roberti walked up and down the road calling anxiously. Fifteen feet away she heard him shout: "Solange, I implore you, forgive me. You'll catch cold. I swear I'll take you home. Don't be afraid." Then, as if to himself: "She must have gone. Someone must have given her a lift." A moment later the engine of the car started up, then the sound of it faded away and she was wrapped in the silence of the countryside. She waited a little longer and then clambered back over the hedge. It was all over. To her relief she realized that her mind was comparatively cool. Back on the road she tidied herself up as best she could. She walked for nearly a mile, twisting her ankle every now and then. One of her heels was broken. At Neuilly-sur-Marne it occurred to her to look at her wrist-watch: it was only nine-thirty. She boarded a bus which took her back to Paris. At the terminus she hailed a taxi, but when about to give her address in the Avenue Daumesnil she changed her mind. The prospect of the way her parents would exclaim on seeing the state of her clothes was too much for her. Besides, she felt a need for a warmer, tenderer presence than the Mignots could provide. It was Legay's address she gave to the driver.

I: Aha! Now we're really getting somewhere. So these young things are going to be brought together at last. Unless Legay happened to be out that evening.

HE: Rest assured, he was there. He was rather a stay-at-home bird, for the dual reason that he was an inventor and in love. He was fiddling with some bit of wiring when suddenly, at about eleven P.M.—*prrrinnng!*—his doorbell rang. "That must be Valentin," he told himself. For indeed Valentin sometimes used to come round in the evenings after dinner for a bit of a chat and a pipe. He opened the door. It was Solange, pale, her hair disheveled and her coat spattered with mud. This apparition rooted him to the spot with astonishment. "Good God," he cried, "what has happened to you? Come in and sit down. I'll get you a glass of brandy to buck you up; I happen to have a bottle." His apartment was marvelously welcoming, all cluttered up with electrical equipment and dominated by that splendid untidiness which goes hand

and hand with creative activity. As for the lord of this place, he looked so kind, so devoted, so pure and simple that Solange suddenly felt all her strength drain out of her. At last she was secure, at last safe, at last protected from the elements and men. She collapsed onto Legay's chest and burst out sobbing, wailing and sniveling like a little girl. She had flung her arms round his neck and he, in amazement and delight, seized this opportunity to hold her close, stroke her cheeks and hair, patting her on the back and murmuring: "There, there, my little one. My dear little girl. My darling. Don't be so silly. You mustn't cry like that. I'm here," and so on.

ɪ: I can't help feeling she weeps rather a lot, the fair Solange. She bursts into tears at the slightest provocation. In the end it gets one down. If I'd been Legay now, I wouldn't have been particularly pleased at this tearful entry.

ʜᴇ: Nonsense. You'd have been as enchanted as he was. Anyone in love takes an extreme delight in consoling his beloved, especially when he isn't the cause of her weeping. What is exasperating is the woman one reduces to tears oneself. Women who come to offer you their woes as if presenting a cake and inviting you to taste it with them are always welcome. At any rate Legay, with Solange's head on his breast and his pullover drenched with tears, was as happy as a king, so happy that he didn't even question to what he owed this windfall. "Why, you're soaking," he exclaimed. "Take your coat off. You're cold. You're shivering. You must put on one of my sweaters. And I'll fetch you a pair of woolly socks."—"No, no," gulped Solange, "don't leave me, Jacques. I'm so miserable!" She clung on to him. They remained like this, holding each other tight, for at least five minutes. As you can imagine, Legay wasted not a second of them; the romance and unexpectedness of it set him on fire. He was a man after all! Such an opportunity wouldn't occur again in a hurry and, since fate was granting him this favor, he must at all costs strengthen his position. With a beating heart he took Solange's face in his left hand and tilted it toward his own. Impetuously he kissed her eyes, their long lashes wet with tears. She offered no resistance but merely closed them. He covered her cold moist cheeks with kisses. Deliriously he breathed in a faint scent of jasmine which almost made him swoon. Her mouth was quite close to his. He summoned up all his courage and two years of timidity came to an end.

ɪ: You have to describe this kiss. It's an event of the primest importance.

ʜᴇ: What on earth do you expect me to describe? It was just a kiss like any other. Legay gave it with the flame of passion. Solange received it without flinching. Her evening's experiences and her tears had no doubt aroused her too. She was stirred. This man holding her so close, this tenderness she inspired, this love declaring itself all reacted on her temperament, which was never particularly frigid as you know. Legay couldn't get over this stroke of luck. Putting his right arm round her waist and his left arm under her knees, he carried her over to the divan, where he continued to shower kisses on her. His shyness, however, restrained him from going any further. Besides, he respected her. It was Solange who, after a few minutes, murmured: "Put out the light."

ɪ: I hope the confounded young man proved up to the mark.

ʜᴇ: If by that you mean that he understood what was expected of him, yes. All the same he was so worked up that for several minutes he didn't know what to do. He dared not touch Solange. He couldn't believe his good fortune. Then he simply had to believe in it. But his excessive desire, impatience and inexperience made the moment of supreme joy extremely brief, and equally brief the several similar moments that followed it. Solange was appeased but not as satisfied as her body had been accustomed to. In truth I believe that, despite his brilliant youth and repeated ardor, Legay hadn't at any moment—how shall I put it?—captured her interest. Curiously enough, the affection she felt for him had only increased. She gave him the sweetest of smiles, filled with a sort of tender indulgence. Possibly she was thinking how this young man would never rob her of her free will, how she would always dominate him through the superiority enjoyed by one who feels no desire over one who desires. With Legay she was going to taste great sweets of the soul. As for him, he was beside himself with joy and babbling like an idiot. He was making plans for the future like an insurance salesman. He told her how he had "waited," how his love had grown in him, how he had hoped, despaired, then hoped once more. She listened to all this with considerable pleasure but also with some slight vexation, since from time to time his remarks took on a mutually comprehensive turn. For example, "You'll see," he cried, "how marvelous it will be, just the two of us together." Love was making him puerile. Toward one in the morning he had more or less exhausted all his joy and lapsed into gloom. Jealousy, anxiety and mistrust had begun to infiltrate his heart. He asked Solange what tribulations had finally led her to his place in such a sorry state two hours before. "Oh, nothing," she replied with a sigh hinting at all sorts of cruel mysteries. "You wouldn't understand." The poor young man felt a stab of pain. He wasn't so stupid as not to know that when a woman says something like that she means in fact that one would understand only

too well. He put on a sulking air which didn't make the slightest impression on Solange. She drew his face down to her and said: "Don't ask me anything. It's much better that way." He was helpless before this bewitching voice. She rocked him gently, kissed him and added: "Now you must let me go." What a reversal of roles! It was she, tonight, who was in a hurry to get away. Legay begged her to stay but she was adamant. As he saw her to the door he asked her almost bashfully: "Shall I see you soon?"—"Perhaps," she replied. "Do you love me Solange?" he asked her. "I don't know," she replied. "Don't press me." She was rather pleased with these two replies; they seemed to her very literary, very poetic and thanks to them she retained the initiative in their dealings. After she had gone he threw himself on his bed, folded his arms behind his head and dreamed open-eyed for a full two hours. He was so happy that at one moment he began to sing.

    I: That's all very charming, but you haven't told me the essential.

    HE: No, but I can see you have guessed it.

    I: When did she realize she was pregnant by Legay?

    HE: She was already almost sure of it when she left him. She had given herself to him like a wife with nothing to fear.

    I: She must have been thrilled, wasn't she? She had been wanting a baby for such a long time. It only remained for her to tell Roberti that she never wanted to see him again. After a scene like the one at Neuilly-sur-Marne, that shouldn't have been difficult.

    HE: No, she wasn't thrilled. She was horrified, rather. She thought how the night of November the ninth, 1957, marked a turning point in her life. Her lover had tried to kill her and she had got herself pregnant by a man she didn't love. Don't you consider that provides ample food for reflection? Solange reflected accordingly and it took her far into the night. Her mind was full of uncertainties. In running to Legay she had had no precise aim save that of seeking consolation in pure friendship. And then things had turned out otherwise. Through a by-no-means-abnormal twist of the emotions she began to feel sorry for Roberti. He really must love her to have indulged in such a demonstration! She had taken a dazzling revenge on him and, as always, the revenge was almost as bitter as the offense. She banished it from her mind by substituting another cause for woe. What horrified her above all was the coldness with which she had received the proofs of Legay's love. This coldness gave her action the semblance of something performed without passion, even with malice aforethought.

As she hobbled down the road to Neuilly-sur-Marne she had been prey to a fear and resentment which had then seemed inextinguishable.

All that had now evaporated, leaving nothing but sorrow. She even felt compassion for Roberti: she recalled his emotional scenes in the past. He was a man governed by his nerves, unbalanced by the exhausting life of Paris; he often took sedatives, which were certainly bad for his health. He was "more to be pitied than censured." Admittedly there was the revolver he had brandished, but even that didn't make much sense. In the first place, was it loaded? Poor Edouard had held it so limply that she had had no trouble in getting it away from him. The scene returned to her mind with startling clarity. Viewed from a distance of five or six hours she interpreted it quite differently. She no longer saw Edouard as a maniac and a murderer but as an unhappy man temporarily blinded by love. She shed a few tears—of pity, of regret, of remorse. She told herself that he would break with her beyond recall when he learned from her that she was pregnant by another man, and that this was a terrible hurt she would be doing him. She thought of the studio in the Square Saint-Lambert. Would she ever return to that place where, she felt all at once, she had "left the best part of herself"? She went back over her affair since the day it first began, when Roberti had kissed her in his study. She recalled his smile, his slightly bowed head, the intelligence behind everything he said, his elegance, his knowledge of the world, his culture and above all the extraordinary attraction he held for her. Never again would she know the full delights of lovemaking since she had alienated the one man on earth with whom she was capable of experiencing them. She almost came to wish she wasn't pregnant. "I've behaved like an idiot," she told herself. She had a feeling of having "messed everything up," or at least of having largely contributed to the general mess.

Roberti, for his part, wasn't enjoying very pleasant thoughts either. He had returned to Paris without quite knowing how, driving in the middle of the road, swerving perilously from side to side like someone drunk. Instead of going home he went and posted himself in the Avenue Daumesnil. It was his intention to waylay Solange when she arrived home and explain how the scene at Neuilly-sur-Marne was nothing but a grotesque misunderstanding. It was impossible that she should have no love left for him at all; there must still be some spark of it left in her heart which he could fan back into a flame. He was in a pitiful state. He too could see the scene with perfect clarity and he had, he concluded, played a rather odd part in it. The insane way in which he had behaved caused him no deep surprise but a certain astonishment. He lived it through again second by second. He saw himself getting out of the car, fumbling in his pocket, brandishing his revolver. The

sound of his own voice uttering threats and a little later crying: "Hey there, Solange, hey, come back, Solange!" still rang in his ears. "Did I really do that?" he wondered incredulously. "It's not a bit like me. It's quite out of character. Or else what hidden depths did it come from?" He peered searchingly into his innermost being, trying to discover there some passion; but there was nothing. Nothing but the old ordinary self he had been accustomed to for nearly fifty-three years, his old faithful and immutable self, calm and reassuring, about which he had long since learned all there was to know. It never crossed his mind that these fits of bleak impatience which sometimes seized and shook him, these kinds of endurance tests he carried out by splitting himself so to speak in two, were precisely the form which, with him, passion assumed.

He waited for over two hours. At midnight he decided at last to quit. He was worried. He hoped nothing untoward had happened to Solange. On the other hand, if she had hitchhiked she had possibly arrived before he did. He had such a blind faith in her that he never for a second suspected she had gone to visit Legay. His bleak impatience had subsided, to be replaced by a dejection equally bleak but harmless. The word used in such cases is "empty." Roberti felt just that. By the time he got home he literally hadn't a single thought in his head and his heart was doubtless so worn out that it was almost beyond feeling. He went to bed and for the first time in a long while fell asleep instantly.

I: I had been hoping we were getting near the end but I see I was deluding myself. Everything's going to start up again between these two. There's no reason why it should ever stop.

HE: Come, a little more courage. You've listened so far. Don't weaken now.

I: But look, it's almost daylight. It isn't human to talk the way we're doing.

HE: Give me half an hour more. Three quarters at the outside. After which we'll take the first taxi to pass and go and treat ourselves to a good onion soup at the Halles, washed down by a bottle of Beaujolais. How do you like that?

I: Do you swear you can polish it off in half an hour?

HE: Let's say three quarters. In three quarters of an hour my story will be done and we'll talk of other things.

I: Ye gods! "Talk of other things?" Are you made of steel then? Your throat at least must be lined with metal!

HE: Nonsense! There's a lot to be said for an occasional little talk between old friends like the one we've been having today. I feel perfectly fresh. Don't you? I feel as if I could go on for another three days. If I hadn't told you Roberti's story in every (or almost every) detail, we wouldn't be here right now and we should be missing a very pretty sight. All these birds waking up, this good smell of trees and water, are well worth seven or eight hours' sleep.

ɪ: Get on with it then. You're making holes in your three quarters of an hour. After their jaunt to Neuilly-sur-Marne Solange and Roberti got together again.

ʜᴇ: Yes. They got together again the very next day. Roberti was even surprised to find Solange so submissive. He had gone to wait for her at midday, fully believing that this time it was really the end. But not a bit of it. With her eyes fixed on the ground she followed him without a word. In the car he took her hand and she flung herself against him. "Forgive me," he said. "I love you."—"Let's go to our place," murmured Solange, "now, at once. Please." He didn't need to hear this twice. At the studio she displayed an ardor and a sort of despair which made him blissful. Love was not dead or, rather, was being reborn from its ashes. Life, so gloomy and sad only the day before, was a most gay and entertaining business!

ɪ: Your Solange is a tramp.

ʜᴇ: Poor girl, it wasn't because she was two-faced. There was nothing thought out or premeditated in her actions. But I don't suppose you need me to explain the reasons for them. They are explicit enough.

ɪ: Oh, quite. And how long did this new honeymoon last?

ʜᴇ: About two months. Roberti was more assiduous than usual. I believe he really wanted to be forgiven. He took her out to lunch in the country. When they met he didn't sweep her off straightaway to the Square Saint-Lambert. First he talked to her, waited for the charm of his presence to have its effect, waited for her to soften and melt, for desire to be born from these conditions. "Why does he have to be so nice to me *now?*" she thought sadly. "It's going to complicate everything."

ɪ: I note that this normally frank and honest creature never breathed a word about her evening with Citizen Legay.

ʜᴇ: No. Not a word. For several reasons. Out of modesty, because she was ashamed of her weakness. Out of bashfulness. But above all because, without its being entirely clear to her, she had worked out the following: she no longer loved Roberti but he was the only man able to give her certain pleasures to which she was still very addicted. She told herself that if she was pregnant the day would inevitably come when she would have to break the news of it to him. On that day everything would end between them. She was giving herself a reprieve. A two months' reprieve. Following which she would go back to Legay, whom she loved dearly, who would be waiting for her and with whom, perhaps, she would "make her life." In short, it was now her turn to use Roberti as an instrument, as an object.

I: Hang it! The pure Solange, too, is beginning to be ignoble. And where did Legay fit into this arrangement?

HE: You know women. They'll make the men who love them swallow anything. He telephoned her nonstop, begging for dates which he obtained in the proportion of one in three. She pitched him a pretty tale from which it emerged that she "still needed to examine her feelings," that she felt a deep affection for him, that "later, perhaps" and so forth. He was unhappy but buoyed up by hope, and naturally his love grew in inverse proportion to the obstacles it encountered from his ladylove. She told him she was sorry now that she had given herself to him: what was he going to think of her? The poor young man nearly went frantic explaining that he thought nothing but good of her and idiotically admired her for her scruples. He would take her hand and she would let him hold it. Indulgently she would let him kiss her. And yet, in the course of the two months with which we are concerned, his submissiveness, devotion and unhappiness were such that on two or three occasions he managed to lure her to his apartment on feeble pretexts by which she pretended to be taken in. Deep down she was very fond of him; she loved him with her heart and mind and in an enduring fashion. She valued him highly. There were times when she even thought how he would make a good husband later.

I: I must confess I am very surprised that she didn't feel more gratitude toward the father of her child, since child there was. God knows she had been longing for it. God knows she has plagued us with it. Legay gave it to her and she could find nothing better to do than betray him with her old lover. Myself, I would have thought she would welcome her pregnancy gravely and piously. Tell me, do I understand nothing at all about women?

HE: Things never come about the way we wish them to. Therein lies the whole explanation. Solange had her child, she was glad to have it. But she hadn't had it the way she would have liked, nor by the man she would have liked. She already loved this child she was carrying but was in no way exultant about it. She was to grow to love it far more as the months went by. She had had it "by a fluke," so to speak. She knew she was pregnant but didn't feel the happiness brought by the fulfillment of a long-felt desire prepared for with due care. Anyway, what do the first two months of pregnancy in a young woman amount to? Nothing has changed. The emotions come only when she begins to grow heavy, when the milk rises to her breasts, when she starts to feel unfamiliar and exciting things taking place in the body she knows so well. It is then, I think that the world alters and becomes imbued with kindliness and tranquillity for a young mother.

She broke the news to Roberti toward the end of January 1958. This gave rise to a particularly frightful scene which I shall describe to you. They were at the studio in the Square Saint-Lambert. She had shown herself as ardent as usual, but with moments of despondency, anxiety and even sadness which had surprised Roberti without however impairing his good mood induced by a triumphant bout of lovemaking. As they walked down the stairs she said: "Edouard, I'm going to have a baby." He was stunned. He felt in his limbs that peculiar kind of shock induced by the announcement of a catastrophe. He paused for a moment before replying. "That really does it!" he thought. "But it's not possible! After all, I should know!" Out loud, trying to give his voice a tone of affectionate interest, he said: "Well, that's a piece of news I wasn't expecting. Are you quite sure?"—"Yes," said Solange. "And yet," he resumed hesitantly, almost diffidently, "we have always been very careful. Always taken the necessary precautions . . ." He dared not imply more. "It's not yours," she added. Roberti, it suddenly seemed to him, had been waiting for this revelation since time began; even so he turned livid. He was shaking all over. He did his best to get a hold of himself. "Whose is it, then," he said, "if it's not an indiscreet question?" Listlessly she told him the whole story: the night following the scene at Neuilly-sur-Marne, her fear, her misery, her visit to Legay. They were walking on down the stairs without noticing what they were doing. They passed through the main entrance to the building and found themselves in the street. They walked for a long time. Solange was holding his hand the way one holds the hand of a sick man in pain. That, at any rate, was the image which presented itself to Roberti, who thought: "She's holding my hand to comfort me during this torture she's inflicting on me. She's apologizing as she slits my throat." Indeed it was a real torture he was enduring, and it was being applied to several parts of his soul. It wasn't properly speaking jealousy he was feeling, but rather a sort of general despair. Solange pregnant by another man was an irrevocable fact, like death. He had the horrible feeling of having been condemned unheard, without even knowing he was on trial. This was something impossible for him to forgive, however much he might have wanted to. It was incumbent on him to break with her on pain of dishonor. At the same time, he couldn't help feeling relieved at the idea that the child was not of his making. This responsibility at least didn't devolve onto him. He was still free. "I won't be obliged to take flowers to the clinic," he thought. "I won't be obliged to go and register the brat's birth. I won't be obliged to buy baby clothes. She'll have to manage on her own. She's really put herself at a disadvantage now. I can again appear in a favorable light since she has betrayed me." He was overcome with horror and despair; he felt helpless in the face of destiny. He began to talk and the sound of his voice surprised him. It was peevish and perfidious. Since all was lost, why should he worry? Why shouldn't he say whatever he liked? For over two hours he gave vent to all his bitterness in the harshest possible terms; he held up his love, his mistress, himself, Legay, everything to mockery. He depicted Solange's future. He described her white wedding with Legay at the Madeleine. He asked to be the child's godfather; the least they could do was to allow him this honor and so on. In short, whatever could be said to hurt a woman who has done one irreparable harm, he said it. He was inspired. Deep down he took a morbid delight in being justifiably brutal. He interspersed his remarks with disillusioned references to his love, which she had "never understood." To show he wasn't blinded by grief and rage he acknowledged certain wrongs he had done her in the past and measured these against the blow she was dealing him now. She was certainly well revenged. With this one blow she had paid him back knowingly and with interest for all the bruises and scratches he had unwittingly inflicted on her.

They walked down endless streets, circling and returning to their starting point and setting out again without even noticing where they were. Solange said nothing or very little. She hadn't been expecting such distress. She felt pity for Roberti. The horrible things he was saying left her unmoved. They didn't mean anything. He was talking under the influence of his pain and it was she who had caused this pain. She never let go of his hand; now and then she squeezed it, as if to make him understand that she was there, that he could say whatever he liked to her, that she would hear him through patiently to the end, that she realized she deserved these insults, reproaches and bitter sarcasm. She felt very sad, but I believe that underlying her sadness was a glint of satisfaction. "To think," she thought with genuine sorrow, "it had to take this for me to fine out how much he really loves me. Why didn't he talk to me like this a year ago? Everything would then have been so different." Out loud she said: "Edouard, I've hurt you very badly. I'm not asking you to forgive me. I didn't know you cared for me so much.

How could I have known? I thought you were fond of me because I was convenient, because I didn't get in your way. But I wanted so terribly to have a baby! To keep me company, so as not to be alone any more. I have been so awfully alone for the past two years. And now we are going to say good-by, darling. You are going to take away a very ugly memory of me, and in the end I believe it's better like that. When you think of me it will be with anger. With disgust. That dirty little bitch, you'll think, who betrayed me, who wasn't worthy of me. You will despise me. You will loathe me. And you'll see, in a very short while you'll be consoled, you'll think of other things as you yourself said. And then you'll forget me. Who knows, in ten years' time we may meet by chance and you won't even recognize me." What shows how deeply Roberti loved Solange is the fact that these words caused him a more agonizing stab of pain than all the rest put together. She herself, as frequently happens, was moved by what she had said. She expressed her emotion by gently laying her head on his shoulder. At this he was overcome by a wave of heartrending tenderness. He put his arm around her waist; he hugged her to him and murmured: "Solange, why have you done this?" After two hours of abuse and lamentation he hadn't much strength left; he saw that, in spite of what his mistress had done, she still loved him and he felt strangely comforted; this old affection for him lingering on in her heart was the last ray of light in the darkness through which he was groping. He suddenly became aware of this. It was the one thing at all sweet to contemplate, the one idea bringing him a little balm. He suddenly felt weary of resisting, of being vindictive, of being implacable, of sneering, of bruising both her and himself. He had a longing to be happy once again at any price. "Be quiet," he said. "I don't know what I'm going to do. The thought that I shall never see you again, that it's all over, is as frightful as knowing you to be the way you are." Note the euphemism in passing. He was reduced to euphemisms after two hours of battle. He had reached the stage of no longer being able to express the reality in crude terms: his soul could no longer bear it, just as it could no longer bear his voice to pronounce the name of Legay. "Have you told him?" he added. "No," she replied. "I haven't told anyone. Nobody knows. You are the first."— "Thanks for such tact and consideration. I'm deeply touched by it," he replied ironically. Wounded by this, Solange jerked herself away from Roberti, who was still holding her by the waist. Resignedly she told him: "Let me go. It would by better if we parted here and now." He grabbed her hand. To his amazement he heard himself say: "Listen. You're not to tell him anything. Nothing. He must never know. You'll never see him again. This baby you're going to have isn't his, it's mine. I'll look after everything. I'll recognize it. It will bear my name. That's what you wanted, isn't it? I'll set you up, you and the child, in a little apartment with someone to look after him, so you can go on working." At the same time, he thought: "But what's happening? Who is this speaking? Not me! It can't be me. I must be utterly mad to be making such a proposal! Pray God she doesn't accept." Anxiously he watched Solange: her head was bowed. "No, Edouard," she murmured, "it's not possible. It wouldn't do. I haven't the right." This reply at once relieved him and made him desperate. In a mere few minutes he had reached the depths of cowardice and self-abasement; he was ready to overlook any offense in order to keep her. His reason came to the rescue. "Come now," he thought, "let's face things squarely, without prejudice. I am lucky in my misfortune. Were she pregnant by me, it would be a pain in the neck. After all, what does it matter to me if she slept with that idiot? I don't love her: so it's my vanity that's hurt and not my love. Calm down, then, old boy. What do I stand to lose from this business? I shall be deprived of her (so far as we know) for four or five months. That isn't the end of the world. They'll pass all too quickly, alas! At the end of the year we'll get together again and our meetings will go on as before. After this trick she's played me, she'll be as supple as a glove." They were walking slowly. Roberti stopped, flung his arms round Solange and kissed her in the middle of the street with a mixture of desire, disgust and shame which, I think, can't have been altogether unpleasant. He had the feeling of committing a sort of sin; he was debasing himself and reveling in it. They weren't far from the Square Saint-Lambert. Roberti was beside himself with despair and desire. It was an almost unbearable state. He begged Solange to go back with him to "our place." She was shocked; he insisted; finally she gave in with a bad enough grace, but up there the spell worked once again.

I: Ugh! What with that old goat and this woman pregnant by someone else, the whole thing is quite repellent! But rather harrowing too, in a sordid sort of way. Do you think I shall be able to create a novel out of it? It seems to me that I've never read anything so dirty and so sad. It's a far cry from my age-old dream of writing the story of a hero full of sublime sentiments and admirable actions! Poor Roberti, poor Solange, what a mess they landed themselves in! I wouldn't like to have been in either's shoes, for they must both have been feeling very uncomfortable in January 1958. Listening to you, you know, I have the strange feeling they were barely responsible for what they were doing, that there was a malignant fate controlling the sequence of their actions and playing with their souls. You see? I've been infected by your philosophy, since basically they were just people without dignity or any code of behavior. All their misfortunes stem from that. They are really too weak. They stink of corruption. The crime of passion is looming close. It's odd, but I don't even feel so sympathetic toward Legay, as if the fact of having become a third party in the Roberti-Solange affair had belittled him. The sulphurous light emanating from Roberti has filtered through onto him and begun to discolor him. He's no longer the pure-hearted young inventor you described yesterday afternoon. He's already just an ordinary young fellow encumbered with a love to which he has offered no resistance and which is dragging him down.

But tell me, I can't understand why Solange confessed her pregnancy to Roberti before confiding it to Legay. It's an odd procedure, a curious scruple. What, in your opinion, was behind it?

HE: I don't rightly know. It surprised me as much as you when I heard about it. I thought to begin with that she had told herself how confessing her pregnancy to Roberti would give rise to an appalling scene and that first and foremost she wanted to get this ordeal over, but as a theory it doesn't stand up to examination. In fact, had she and Legay shared this secret she would have felt much stronger and tackled Edouard with much less misgiving; she would have had Legay's joy to support her in the background. No. The root of the matter is far more subtle. In the first place, although she no longer loved Roberti, Solange was still very close to him; much closer, in a certain sense, than she was to Legay. Second, with people's actions one must always take their private code of honor into account. I believe she felt she *owed* it to Roberti that he should be the first to know of this great upheaval which was going to affect their two lives. Third, it never crossed her mind that he mightn't break with her on learning she was carrying a child he hadn't himself begotten. She had certainly reckoned that he would take to his heels forever; and so she would be free, divested of all ties by having abolished the past, wiped clean and ready for a new life.

I: Ah, I can recognize in this the practical mind of all women, who weigh things up, make plans, organize, look ahead and have infinitely more self-possession than men believe!

HE: Yes. Men are always thunderstruck when they see how women, even when showing the most obvious signs of passion, keep one eye wide open for future developments and always see to it secretly but very efficiently that they have positions to fall back on. All the more so with a woman like Solange in whom passion had died, who was already looking ahead to the future and only held back by sensual habit.

I: Well and good. But Roberti, with his love, his cowardliness, his proposals to recognize the child, his volcanic desires, wrecked it all.

HE: No, he didn't do that. He merely postponed the day of reckoning. For what happened, to my mind, was this: Solange was touched by his misery, which was very acute. I don't say she took a positive pleasure in thus inflicting suffering on a man who had so often made her suffer herself, but willy-nilly she drew a certain strength from it. She realized she had more power over Roberti than she had supposed. Her thoughts ran roughly as follows: "The situation is reversed. Here's a man with whom I won't have to put myself out any more; he will agree to everything I want from now on."

I: Gracious, what cynicism!

HE: Take care. The cynicism is mine. Solange herself was not cynical, that is to say her ideas weren't as clear-cut as I have made them, but that was surely their essence. Since she was warmhearted and the idea of vengeance could hardly have been further from her mind, she equally thought (at least I'd bet my life she did): "He'll calm down in time. He'll have second thoughts. I shall become very fat and ugly; he'll find me repellent. He'll end by realizing how impossible it is for us to go on seeing each other. Gradually he will get used to the idea that it's over. Besides, my time is going to be fully taken up from now on. Everything will sort itself out on its own. I could tell him I've finally decided to leave him, I feel I have the courage to do so, but what would be the point of causing him this additional misery? I know myself that it's finished, that nothing in the world can prevent its being finished."

I: How did Master Legay react on learning he was about to become a father?

HE: Actually, not at all as one might have anticipated. Solange broke it to him gravely, possibly in a somewhat theatrical way. In a small, rather breathless voice she said: "Jacques, I am going to give you a child." She had been dreading an explosion of joy, wild hugs and absurd emotionalism; but Legay behaved admirably. He confined himself to taking her hand and giving it a light kiss. He had in fact been expecting such a revelation. He had his own reasons for this. He was even surprised it hadn't been made sooner. He regarded Solange pensively and asked her: "Does it make you happy?" That's all. Nothing more. She was strangely overcome by this commendable reaction, so different from his usual rather ebullient manner; she dissolved into tears; but these were not tears of bitterness, they were tears such as one may shed on hearing some beautiful piece of music or reading some beautiful poem; they were the tears that all beauty wrings from any heart sensitive to the sublime. Moreover she wasn't now weeping in her usual way, namely whimpering and sniffling: her tears were welling out of her eyes and trickling slowly down her cheeks; her face was calm and smooth and she was even smiling. "Oh yes, Jacques," she cried, "I am happy, I am tremendously happy!" With a strength which, but for one's dread of clichés, one might define as superhuman, Legay suppressed the great surge of joy he felt rising up within him; he forced his face to remain impassive. "Not a word too many," he thought, "not a smile. This is my chance to win my wife. One foolish slip and I shall lose her forever. And I don't want to lose her. I want her for the rest of my life. At this moment my whole life hangs on a smile."

I: Bravo! Splendid!

HE: Almost coldly he said: "What will you decide? I will do whatever you wish. Naturally I don't intend to shirk my responsibilities for a moment. But I don't think that is what's on your mind." It is always a surprise to see how nobly people express themselves in crucial circumstances. Legay had a rather common way of talking, with a slight Parisian accent: this had momentarily disappeared. He was grave and considerate. Solange was struck by this and at the same time astonished by what he was saying. Had he read her thoughts? "I know you like me," he went on. "I believe you are fond of me, even very attached to me. I am your friend, your comrade. One night you took refuge here after something had badly upset you. You had need of protection. You had need of consolation. You turned to me as one turns to a friend, not as one turns to a lover. I realized this afterward. You've got to be honest with yourself: you don't *love* me. I have little experience of this kind of thing, but even so I understood that much. What we did, what circumstances led us to do, is for me something beyond price. It will probably remain my most wonderful memory. But don't for heaven's sake think it puts you under any obligation to me. I don't consider myself as having any rights over you. Everyone can make mistakes. You made a mistake, that's all. I wasn't the right man for you. These things happen!"

I: Well, I take my hat off! Citizen Legay was clearly flying high above his usual level. He couldn't possibly have been deliberately calculating at this moment. Had this been part of a maneuver, he'd have been flat-footed and stupid. But he said all that needed to be said, and even with a certain nobility.

HE: I myself think that what happened to him was what happens to most honest folk when they take it into their heads to be calculating: they get taken in by their own maneuvers and are touching without meaning to be, for it is their hearts speaking instead of their minds. In short Legay, if you see what I mean, was maneuvering sincerely.

I: What particularly impresses me about his approach is that the whole thing seems designed to provoke the spirit of contradiction in Solange. Either it was high art or it was instinct. So he wasn't actually calculating or barely so. In the normal course of events, on hearing all this she should have been seized with a desire to emulate him. She should want to outdo him in generosity, she should want to love him in earnest.

HE: Yes indeed, she must have had such feelings. But Legay didn't give her time to express them. He thought that once he allowed her to speak the mere sound of her beloved voice would put all his ideas to flight and that it was imperative to finish saying what he had to say. "We are not old-fashioned people with prejudices," he went on. "I know you well enough to understand that you would rather have an illegiti-mate baby than marry someone you didn't really care for. That's why I'm not asking anything of you. A girl like you and a young man like me with no money and no family, or hardly any, have no reason for marry-ing if they don't love each other."—"Don't you love me then?" inquired Solange with a sort of anxiety which swamped him with joy. "It's not a question of what *I* feel," he said, "it's a question of what *you* feel. I love you so much, Solange, that I suggest the following. Our baby mustn't go without a father. If you like we'll get married and I'll take a solemn oath, I'll swear on the head of this baby which is mine and which I love above all because it's you who are giving it to me, that in a year I'll apply for a divorce. During this year we'll live however you like best. You wouldn't even need to move in here with me. You could stay with your parents and brother. Nothing in your life would be changed. If one evening you felt too lonely or depressed, you'd just have to ask me over and I'd do my best to distract you. What I want you to be absolutely sure of is that I'll never be the one to throw you over. Never." He was so deeply moved, poor fellow, that he had a lump in his throat and spoke these last words in a strangled voice. Solange was no less moved herself. Such nobility of spirit was having an alarming effect on her. She thought with disgust of her own scheming, her selfishness, the duplicity into which her sensuality and weakness had led her for the past two months. What overwhelmed her most were the few words Legay had spoken about the baby: how he loved this child because it was she who was giving it to him. An abyss of love was opening up before her! Teem-ing thoughts of motherhood, infinitely sweet and exciting, filled her heart; her feelings of a year back when she had so longed to have a child, by now almost forgotten, all at once swept over her again. She suddenly considered what her future was really going to be like: she saw her child, felt its weight on her arms, its mouth on her breast, and she was dazzled. She was bearing within her the seed of this man standing there and confessing to a matchless love, a love set far above desire. This man wanted their joint flesh to be made one, wanted to merge their two souls with a third which would live after them. Smiling through her tears she flung her arms round his neck and said: "You're not to say another word. I can't bear it. I am proud to bear this child of yours. There's only one thing I want—for it to be like you. Handsome like you, good like you, kind like you, unselfish like you. How could you bring yourself to say everything you've just said? Were you so unhappy then? I'll never forgive myself. You'll be the most marvelous of husbands and, if you really want me, I will be the most grateful and adoring of wives. But take a look at yourself, darling: women would be fighting over you if you'd only so much as glance at them. And you are so kind! Why are you so kind? I want so much for you to be happy. I'll do everything I can to make you happy. Stay with my parents? You're crazy. We'll live together, you and I, and the baby when it arrives. Forever. I'll run the house for you. We'll have other children. Three at least. We'll settle down together, you'll see. You'll find out what I'm really like. I'll help you to find out. Already there's no man in the world I enjoy being with as much as you. That counts for a great deal in marriage. When people get married they are together all the time, talking all the time, they have no secrets. The rest is unimportant."

ɪ: Well, what a victory for Legay! But Solange's reply was less successful. Immediately women take a hand in it, things go flat, the temperature comes down a degree or two. And then that way of calling everyone "darling," Roberti, Legay and next year Tiddlypush, it isn't really in the best of taste.

ʜᴇ: What the hell do you expect her to call him, since she loves him?

ɪ: You can't expect me to know. It's up to her to think of something. This "darling" irritates me. It has a 1910 ring about it. Artificial. Sort of demimonde.

ʜᴇ: Don't be so silly. Women say "darling" the way they breathe. They punctuate every conversation with it. For them it's like a comma. When you speak to a general, what do you call him? "General." "Darling" is the same thing. Love has its code of civility, its *outward forms*, just as the army has. Sometimes "darling" means "lieutenant," sometimes "colonel." In this hierarchy Roberti was doubtless a colonel and Legay a lieutenant. But there must also be young generals of twenty-five, as during the revolution! Casanova at seventy-two, at the Château de Dux, with his rusty lace, threadbare clothes, tarnished paste jewelry, wrinkles, powder, moth-eaten wigs and eternal syphilis reminds me irresistibly of an old marshal covered with scars and glory. The great field darling of the eighteenth century.

1: Well, well! It's a long time since you made a digression. I'll overlook this one since it has been short and amusing. Let's get back to Legay.

HE: Back to Legay, then. He was quite dazed by his victory. His heart leaped within him. To prove his strength of character, he forced himself to raise one more objection. With a steady voice he said: "Has it ever occurred to you, Solange, that I am far less intelligent than you and certainly far less educated? You'll be bored with me."—"I shall end by thinking you don't want me any more," she replied. This overcame his last powers of resistance. While maintaining his outward reserve, he allowed the joy he had been stifling for so long to spread through his soul. Despite an acute feeling of responsibility and superiority, he nonetheless retained sufficient caution to show none of it. He felt the battle was won only by a hair, because at the cost of a gigantic effort he had displayed neither eagerness nor enthusiasm. His whole being was yearning toward Solange but it was as if an iron hand were holding him back. He was astonished to find such strength in himself. He didn't know it was there. He was discovering himself to be a strong man capable of resisting his impulses, of concealing his intentions to attain his ends, of employing strategy, and he marveled at this discovery. He thought how this day would be a turning point in his life: at this very moment he was ceasing to be a young man, that is to say scatterbrained and irresponsible, foolishly blurting out his every thought in response to his inward urges. Moreover he had a secret conviction that he wouldn't make the slightest false step until the end of this duel with Solange; that a higher power was guiding him and preventing him from putting a foot wrong. He gazed at her tenderly. "Oh, how I would love to tell you everything that is in my heart," he thought, "but it isn't possible. I must hold my tongue in your own interests as much as mine. I must pretend to be cold and unenthusiastic. If I allow any suspicion that there is no man on the whole surface of the earth happier than I, we are lost. What an idiotic game love is!" All this was quite well thought out, as you can see. With an indifference worthy of a minister plenipotentiary he explained to Solange that, since she didn't find the idea of marrying him too repugnant, it would be wise to fix the date of the ceremony in the fairly near future. This indifference was wasted; she was completely won over. Here was a man who wasn't forcing her into anything, wasn't trying to rush her and who, wonder of wonders, wasn't looking particularly pleased about it all. She made no bones about committing herself. They finally decided to get married toward the end of February or the beginning of March. Solange insisted that it should be kept a secret until the new order came into being. She would have liked for them to slip off to the country and come back one fine day duly married, so that all that remained for them to do would be to present parents and friends with a *fait accompli*. Alas, this was scarcely feasible. "At any rate," she said, "don't let's tell anyone, please. It concerns only the two of us." This plot, this collusion he was being invited to share in, was not unwelcome to Legay. "There's one person," he objected however, "to whom I should like to break the news, someone to whom it would give so much pleasure . . ." But she immediately cut him short. She had perfectly understood that this person was Valentin. Her face became almost hard. In an icy voice which made him shiver she said: "Jacques, if you want me to become your wife do what I ask you." He considered it his duty to press her: "Poor Valentin!" he murmured. "I was hoping we could at last tell him all about it." He felt oppressed by this affectation of secrecy, which had been going on for nearly a year and a half. Worse, it made him uncomfortable and, without knowing why, he couldn't help regarding it as an evil omen. More gently and as enticingly as any Circe, Solange said: "No, darling. Let's not say anything to Valentin. In a month's time he'll have to know about it anyway. He'll have the rest of his life to congratulate himself on his sister's marriage to his best friend. Give me just one more month of peace. A month during which we can be alone, you and I." She needed a good month to get used to the idea that the morose and hostile Valentin was suddenly going to become affectionate and gay again. She was apprehensive about this abrupt change, which seemed to her almost obscene. Something in her heart refused to relent, although she no longer loved Roberti and would no longer have to protect her love from her brother. Rancor not infrequently outlives the cause that first provoked it. And anyway, even the gentlest of hearts can be known to harden. For two years Solange had been *in the habit* of hurting Valentin; this habit had become a component of her nature, as it were, and no doubt she found it painful to think it was coming to an end. It is always difficult to give up tormenting a scapegoat; it seems absurd and faintly humiliating. Naturally Legay bowed to her wishes. At the same time, he pictured his dear old Valentin's delight and felt remorse at denying it to him. It was lovely to share a secret with Solange but it vexed him that this must be accompanied by such a lack of loyalty; a month is a long time. And what if Valentin were to die a week later, run over by a car in the street? Legay chased away this idea, which struck him as childish. All the same, Solange was very inhuman and incomprehensible. He had a fleeting desire to disregard her wishes, go and find Valentin and tell him the news of his engagement while insisting on absolute secrecy; but he immediately reflected that this would hardly be wise in view of the latter's character. Valentin would go round beaming at all and sundry and dropping heavy hints which would exasperate Solange and let her know she had been betrayed. Following which the worst was to be feared: this frail marriage won at swordpoint might easily be imperiled by as little. "Hell! So much the worse for Valentin," he thought. "After all it isn't so important. And I'm certainly not going to risk wrecking my whole life just to please him." It was highly important, on the contrary, as the future revealed, but Legay couldn't know that. He found a further weighty argument which swept aside his last scruples: "What does Valentin want? For me to marry his sister. The essential thing is that this marriage should go through. If I keep quiet I shall be ensuring the happiness of all three of us."

I: Nine times out of ten women demoralize men. Take Solange: here we have a good, honest girl. The first thing she demands of her future husband is something dishonorable. And he gives in. He hasn't enough spirit to show her she is wrong, that what she is demanding is neither just nor charitable. It bodes ill for his married life. For the first five years, love will make him weak. Once love has gone, he will be weak out of habit, so as to avoid scenes. By the time he's forty he'll be a helot, a petty bourgeois without any moral fiber or honesty! A sinister prospect!

HE: I think you're being too harsh. You should make allowances for people who are happy! These two hadn't always been, nor would they always be. Happiness is never without a trace of cowardliness and self-ishness. We make up for this in times of misfortune, when we show courage and think of our neighbors. Legay was all the happier (and hence all the more jealous of his happiness) in that it still remained for him to announce a great piece of news to Solange. While he had purposely kept quiet about it throughout the whole scene I have just described, his extra-thin television set was completed down to the smallest details. Solange, whom Roberti had taught to despise radio and television as vulgar entertainments unfit for the truly cultured, was not unduly impressed. To spend two or three years seeking for means to reduce the thickness of a television set by six inches seemed to her the height of futility and pointlessness. However, wishing to be polite, she exclaimed: "Oh Jacques, why didn't you tell me before? I'm so terribly glad!" Legay thought this showed a great enthusiasm, which after all was the essential. Not without daring, he replied: "I wanted to win you independently of that. I wanted to find out whether you would agree to marry me as you thought I was—with nothing behind me, possibly a failure; whether you would consent to live with a penniless inventor in a one-room studio on the sixth floor without an elevator; whether you weren't afraid of sometimes going hungry with me."—"Don't be such an ass," said Solange. "I know you're not a failure." Finally, and with considerable style, he added: "I am dedicating this television set I've constructed to you, Solange. All the time I was working on it, I was thinking of you. I wanted to bring it off to please you, to win your respect. I told myself that, thanks to it, I would one day have money and be able to offer you the kind of life you deserve. You won't be marrying a nobody but someone who has achieved something, someone whose life won't have been entirely without significance." Don't you think that's splendid?

I: Yes, it's not bad, but I presume Solange missed the whole point of it. She must have told herself it was a lot of fuss to make over a wretched bit of electrical work. If, instead of this, he had delivered a fine lecture on Camus and Saint Exupéry, she would have gone into ecstasies.

HE: You're not altogether wrong and yet, in spite of her literary and artistic pretensions, she was touched. She took hardly any interest in the extra-thin television set but she was interested in Legay. For a year and a half she had followed the development of his masterpiece step by step and she knew how much it meant to him. She was glad for his sake.

I: Had she loved him, she would have been glad for her own sake. She would have felt personally proud.

HE: Well, it can't be helped. That's life. She agreed to marry Legay and she didn't know who he was. She was going to marry a nice young man to whom she felt very attracted, who had given her a child and who was going to relieve her of a painful and miserable affair. She didn't know this young man was a genius because she was incapable of imagining that genius could exist outside of literature and the fine arts.

I: And do you want to know what the future will bring? Since Legay loves her more than she loves him, she will gradually persuade him that science is a lot of nonsense, unfit to occupy the faculties of an intelligent man. She will force him to read the complete works of Gide, Giraudoux, Valery Larbaud, Huxley, Hemingway, Sartre and others of that ilk. He, naturally, will obey his idol; he will progressively abandon his researches. It is she who will make him a failure. Take good note of this.

HE: I take note of it all the less reluctantly in that I fear, alas, that you're right. With Solange and Legay we are once again putting our fingers on a misunderstanding. In order to resist love and happiness, in order to preserve this vocation of his, Legay would need to have more character, more strength and also, I think, that insensitivity peculiar to artists and inventors. But he's far too tenderhearted. With natures like his, love always prevails over the vocation. Ah well, it's just too bad. It takes all sorts to make a world. Besides, at this moment we are still at the stage of conjecture. We may be entirely mistaken. We are forgetting one thing, which is that during the three years he took to construct his TV set, he showed a quite remarkable tenacity and strength of will; he devoted thousands of hours to it without ever losing heart. That is also a sign of character.

I: No. It isn't character. It's tenacity, as you yourself said. And I see more good will than strength of will in it. He was facing his task all alone, without distractions, without money, without friends, without a mistress. He was spurred on by the wish to succeed. He was kept going by the professional conscience of the artisan who never gives up a piece of work before he has perfected it. Character is something quite different. Legay belongs to that category of men who through their perseverance triumph over objects but are defeated by human beings, because they have not enough strength of spirit. Vis-à-vis Solange, he has no character. She will do with him whatever she wants. And what she wants is the complete opposite of his capacities. She will mold him according to her own desires. Do you want to know what I really think? She will never give up until he finally comes to resemble Roberti.

HE: I believe I already told you how he sold his splendid invention.

I: Yes, you did. He sold it to a swindler who paid him a pittance for it.

HE: Not altogether a pittance: ten million in 1958, which makes a hundred thousand francs today. But it wasn't much compared with what the swindler made thanks to Legay's talents. What I didn't tell you was the way this deal came about. The swindler in question had got wind of Legay's work several months earlier and sniffed, as they say in his circles, "a big deal." So every now and then he called on Legay; he had taken a sentimental option on the discovery. "If you're ever short of cash," he told him, "you know you needn't worry, my dear fellow. I shall be delighted to lend you a few hundred thousand francs. You just pay me back when you can." Legay had never taken advantage of this invitation, since he had to the highest possible degree that characteristic of humble folk, a holy horror of debts. But he was touched; he naïvely believed that in this man he had a friend, someone who understood him, a virtual patron. He felt a certain bond with this excellent man.

When he announced to Solange that his set was finished the latter, despite her lack of enthusiasm, had a feminine reaction, that is to say a reaction of wisdom and good sense. "Come and see me tomorrow at the office, at six-thirty," she told her fiancé. "Don't wait downstairs. Come up. At that hour the boss isn't very busy. I'll ask him to see you. You can tell him about your set. I'm sure he'll give you excellent advice as to how to sell it." It would seem that certain people, unfortunately, have an "anti-instinct." It may sound odd but this proposal, instead of pleasing Legay, irritated him. It complicated everything. In his mind he had already more or less concluded an agreement with his precious swindler. Have you noticed how ordinary people, the petty bourgeoisie in every walk of life, are fascinated by crooks? They find an irresistible attraction in them. Doubtless because crooks have smooth tongues and recklessly dole out all that humbug known as compliments. The petty bourgeoisie, who have no imagination, who never think—honest as they are—that anyone might be lying and flattering his way into their good graces, take these compliments at face value. Their souls expand under this balmy dew. For all that they uphold La Fontaine as the greatest thinker of all time, they ceaselessly re-enact the fable of the crow and the fox and regularly drop their cheese.

To cut things short Dietz, in order to oblige his pretty secretary, received Legay. He heard him through, he was struck by the interest of the discovery, but like any well-bred man he didn't launch into rapturous paeans of praise. He congratulated Legay calmly and decently, and truth obliges me to say that Legay was almost vexed by this apparent coldness. He couldn't begin to understand it. After three years of strenuous and obscure labor, vanity had at last blossomed in his heart and was clamoring avidly for its measure of praise. Dietz telephoned then and there to the boor I mentioned yesterday afternoon. He arranged an appointment the next morning for Legay, who went to see the said boor and took an extreme dislike to him because he was churlish, because he paid even fewer compliments than Dietz and doubtless also because he was honest. Fate willed it that the same afternoon, lured by the scent, the swindler called on the young inventor. He hadn't omitted to bring his checkbook. He examined the TV set, he made it work; for the next half hour he went into ecstasies, then took out his pen and, without a word, wrote out a check for ten million francs which he laid on the table together with a fully made-out deed of transfer. Legay was thunderstruck. He had never seen so much money in his life. He took the check and signed the transfer. The swindler was so pleased that he made him a present of his pen into the bargain. And that is how, in forty-eight hours (for only forty-eight hours elapsed between Legay's winning Solange's hand and selling his TV set) one can make the most foolish mistake of one's life. But the poor young man's head was completely turned. So much good fortune coming all at once —love, marriage, wealth—had plunged him into a state of agitation verging on dementia which filled him with a confused and irresistible need for action.

I: And what did he do with his ten million?

HE: What would you expect? He did what all poor people who win a lottery do: flung his fortune out of the window. He was intoxicated by having so much money all at one go, money he hadn't earned penny by penny as usual. He succumbed to the illusion that this was just the beginning of a brilliant career, that he had a treasure in his brain, that he would make a hundred inventions, each one more admirable and lucrative than its predecessor. He looked to his future like a wonder-struck simpleton. He felt full of strength, he was brimming over with optimism. The swindler's extravagant compliments rang in his ears like heavenly music. Success plus wealth was a lot. It was even too much. He began by choosing a beautiful engagement ring for Solange, then a secondhand car, and finally paid out one and a half or two millions for a four-room apartment, I forget where. After which the place had to be furnished, that is to say sheets, napkins, plates, furniture, cooking utensils, etc., had to be bought. At this rate the ten million were frittered away pretty fast. Legay trotted round the big stores with Solange, whom he went to fetch every day at her office, and this activity brought him a joy he had never known before. He felt a different man. He surpassed himself in generosity and mad squandering. Solange, who was rather amazed that the television set should have brought in so much and also pessimistic like all women, tried to restrain him but it was a waste of time: he was having a veritable orgy of spending. He took a childish delight in signing check after check with the swindler's fine Parker pen; its nib was so soft and velvety that he had a constant desire to use it.

I: All this is terrifying. It makes me feel quite giddy. Poor Legay subsiding into materialism! Solange decidedly brought about everybody's downfall. She was an instrument of fate. How long did he take to ruin himself?

HE: Four months.

I: My word! Getting through ten million in four months is on a princely level! It presupposes an income of thirty million a year. This young man was properly living it up.

HE: He thought his little hoard was inexhaustible. He went on firing broadsides into his bank account and never had the courage to examine the wreckage. One day, however, he received the bank's quarterly statement and was staggered to see that he only had about one million eight hundred thousand francs left. This amount bore no relation to the vague calculations he had now and then made in his head. He believed he still had four to five million. He was horror-stricken. The bank, he thought, must have made a mistake. He carefully went over every item. Alas, the stubs in his checkbook told the same story as the statement and arithmetic never lies. He was then thoroughly disheartened and rather panic-stricken. He switched overnight from prodigality to avarice and decided, rather late in the day, that the swindler had cheated him. After endless vacillation he finally went back to see him. In all likelihood, swindler though he was, this one hadn't too bad a character. He offered Legay an engineering job at a hundred and eighty thousand francs a month, that is to say eighteen hundred francs today, which the latter was only too happy and pleased to accept. If my information is correct, he even gave him a five-year contract. Legay, who had allowed himself to be fleeced like a lamb, didn't dare ask for a share in the profits. He was stupid enough to feel grateful for the job at eighteen hundred francs: he hadn't been hoping for as much.

It seems to me that I have considerably anticipated events. We are a long way from Roberti. Let's go back four months. After having fixed the date of her marriage with Legay, Solange took the honorable decision to tell her elderly lover about it at the earliest possible moment, hoping this final blow would suffice to put an end once and for all to an already half-shattered liaison. But when she next saw him, three days later, she was seized with an odd fit of cowardice. She didn't dare tell him. She let herself be led to the Square Saint-Lambert without joy but still with a hint of excitement. The situation had a curious effect on her senses. Roberti was very gloomy, very depressed and rather arrogant. He hadn't yet got over the despair her pregnancy had caused him. He kept looking at her, now with yearning, now with hostility. She realized how unhappy he was and was touched. He was suffering through her. Doubtless to excuse her strange conduct in her own eyes, she told herself that she couldn't abandon him all at once, that for a few days longer she must lead him by the hand until he had got over the worst, that it was her duty to do this. She could measure the extent of Edouard's suffering by the alternate bouts of tenderness and spite through which he was passing. Sometimes he would hug her desperately and kiss her like a madman, sometimes he would turn away from her in horror and become absorbed in sullen silence. He said the most insulting things to which she didn't reply. She was disturbed by the look—pale, tense, stern, drawn with pain—which he couldn't prevent his face from assuming in her presence. This face *took shape*, so to speak, as soon as she appeared. It was a face put on for the occasion, of which Roberti was perfectly aware, a mask which he adopted: that of a man with an incurable wound in his heart, whose forgiveness can only be won by endless acts of submission. He even went so far as to take a secret pleasure in assuming this martyr's air: he had a right to it. What shows how deeply he loved Solange at this time was his naïve idea that she would love him more on seeing how unhappy she had made him. For the rest, still cold in his innermost heart and consequently still deluded. "I'm playing the part of the jilted lover," he thought. "How interesting!" To be brief, fifteen really bizarre days passed in this way. Solange saw Roberti about twice a week. They rushed off to lock themselves into their studio and surrender to each other with a frenzy equaled only by their misery. They were discovering an ecstasy it seemed to them they had never known before, born of the ignominy in which they both felt steeped. When Solange went to these meetings she was careful to remove her engagement ring.

I: Forgive me for interrupting but there's something here I don't quite get. Or else I haven't paid sufficient attention to the sequence of events. Do you mind if we go back over this for a moment?

HE: Of course not. What do you want to know.

I: Solange broke the news of her pregnancy to Roberti toward the end of January. Right?

HE: Right.

I: And to Legay?

HE: The next day or the day after.

I: Very well. Legay sold his TV set two days later and became a millionaire. As a result of which from the second or third of February Solange and he began to buy mattresses, saucepans and chandeliers.

HE: Correct.

I: That's where I find the shoe pinches. What can be the motives of a young woman engaged to a man, pregnant by him, planning to set up house with him and running round all the stores buying furniture for four rooms, who still finds the means at the same time to go twice a week to make love with an old goat? I can only see one explanation: lechery—something extremely rare in our day, especially in a working-class girl. You must admit that such depravity is most unusual.

HE: Unusual but not so very rare either.

I: Wait. I haven't finished. The state of mind of a woman on a spending spree is something altogether special. She is prey to a veritable mania of materialism. Coveting objects, acquiring them, seeing them pile up, caressing them with her eyes and fingers, admiring them, browsing over them so to speak, leaves no room in her heart for other emotions. The white or pink enamel of an ultramodern cooker, the chromium of an electric toaster, a refrigerator as luxurious and silent as an American car, pearly-hued lampshades, induce a wholly exclusive rapture. Incompatible, at any rate, with lechery, which is a vice of the mind. Not to mention the spirit of rivalry which descends on women in shops. Have you ever seen them fighting over a remnant of chintz or marked-down dresses at a sale? It's a revolting spectacle. They screech like magpies, they snatch the goods out of their neighbor's hands, they bawl each other out, they practically come to blows. Their spirits are completely swamped by greed and covetousness for material things. Lechery is as far from their minds as Plato's philosophy or the theology of Thomas Aquinas.

What, at bottom, bothers me is this: you are showing me two Solanges and I can't manage to reconcile them. I don't see how the future Mme. Legay, proprietress of a four-room apartment, a car and all the rest, can go on secretly meeting Roberti. I can see it all the less in that she is engaged and not married. Were she married, it would be quite another matter. A woman will do anything to her husband, but not to her fiancé. The fiancé is sacred because he brings with him a rank, a name, a condition—in the present case affluence.

HE: I shall try to answer you. In the first place it wasn't Solange who was, as you put it, "on a spending spree." It was Legay. It was he who was pervaded with materialism. She merely confined herself to going round the shops with him, choosing objects with him, advising him when necessary. Her heart was actually too full of conflicting and violent emotions to stand aside in favor of refrigerators, washing machines, standard lamps and rustic sideboards. I don't say she was indifferent to it all, but she was interested in it only to the extent that it gave pleasure to Legay; she was touched by the passion he put into his shopping. It was for her that he was spending so wildly. She considered she could hardly do less than accompany him on his ruinous expeditions and pretend to find some fun in them. There was so little materialism in her that at times she regretted it. She reproached herself for not feeling more joy at acquiring useful and pretty objects. She told herself that life is very badly organized and things never happen at the time when one could really enjoy them. Had her heart not been bowed down by Roberti, by the debris of her love, she would have scoured the Galeries Lafayette, the Trois Quartiers and the Bazar de l'Hôtel de Ville with an ardor rivaling Legay's! She had a desolate feeling that, through destiny's fault, she was missing a tremendous treat. This indifference she felt toward everything that normally brings so much excitement to women seemed to her almost scandalous.

As to her concomitant relations with Roberti, I don't share your view. I don't see how lechery, properly speaking, comes into it. Lechery is cold and premeditated. Solange no longer had any love for Edouard but she couldn't manage to disentangle herself from him. She was paralyzed by the physical attraction he still held for her. She thought she must be the victim of some diabolical sorcery and perhaps in this she was right since she was astounded at her actions, her dishonest and equivocal behavior, whenever she chanced to give it a thought. It couldn't possibly be she, Solange, acting in this way—little Solange who was so upright and simple and so hated lies. And yet she was playing this dual role, deceiving Legay with Roberti and Roberti with Legay. She despised herself but couldn't break free of the spell she was under. Roberti was a sort of vampire: he had bitten her and as a result had made her a vampire too. "When is all this going to end?" she wondered in terror and despair.

I have tried to unravel what the first two weeks of February 1958 must have been like for Roberti and now I will try to explain my conclusions. I won't say they formed the darkest moments of his life, for he had worse to come, but they were very hard to live through. He was torn between resentment and desire. The word "resentment" is too feeble. It was in fact a deep-seated rancor such as one might conceive against a person who had done one an unforgivable injury. He thought of Solange with hatred, the way you think of an enemy who seeks your ruin or death and whose ruin and death you seek in return. He loathed the child she was carrying. He actually told her as much on two or three occasions, at moments when he felt so bereft and unhappy that he simply had to speak out, say anything horrible he could think of in order to bring himself some relief. Her resigned expression only increased his fury, grief and cruelty. This last was all the more savage in that in insulting his mistress he was really addressing himself; it was himself he was wounding the most deeply. The fact that Solange was pregnant by another man was unconscionable, humiliating and absurd. It kept him in a perpetual state of fury, but at the same time he found to his surprise that this wasn't enough to turn him against her. On the contrary his desire was more violent than ever, as if all this misery, all this mire, were working him up to a paroxysm. He was devoured with lust, mad with erotic frenzy. Solange merely acquired added value for having been possessed by another. He dared not discuss Legay with her; he was afraid she might confess she was still sleeping with him. This uncertainty only served to inflame him all the more. He called her up every day. These phone calls were dismal affairs, but he needed to hear her voice, that dear voice which used to answer him so gaily two years before; now its modulations caused him an agony of soul he was unable to dispense with.

What is remarkable is that, in the midst of all his insults and recriminations, he would often tell her he loved her, was mad about her and ready to do anything to keep her. He even told her this far more often than in the old days, when she loved him and would have been so overjoyed to hear such declarations. Now she made no reply, since she no longer loved him and found such protests a torment. He would switch without transition from the coldest hatred to the most exquisite devotion. He would go into ecstasies over the ravishing shape of her mouth, wax eloquent as a poet over her eyes. He confided to her that he even cherished the misery she was inflicting on him because it came from her. He never wearied of describing his love, all the while thinking, according to his wont, that he was lying. But these so-called lies gave him infinite joy; they soothed him, "brought balm to his soul." It was to treat himself to some small happiness that he enumerated all the sufferings and delights in his heart. He reveled in this picture he was painting for Solange. It had a poignant sweetness. So poignant that Edouard, who would slip a witticism into even his most pathetic appeals, said: "At bottom it's not so unpleasant after all to suffer through love." Simultaneously he thought: "Suffer through love? Suffer through love? What a way to go on! I'm no more in love than a salt cellar. I'm pretending to despair for purely practical reasons. Given this preposterous act I'm putting on, Mlle. Mignot will never have the courage to throw me over. Thus I shall retain a mistress I don't love but with whom I must admit I make love better than with anyone else. It would be an awful pity to lose her." All the same, Solange's silence acted on him like a curious stimulant. When he was with her he always found himself being led into saying and doing far more than he had intended. He naïvely attributed this to the exaltation of the moment, persistently omitting to take the genuine hatred or happiness he was feeling into account. He was watching himself give a performance, watching himself suffer: this duality only served to confirm his illusion that he wasn't really suffering and that his actions were just part of a game. Even only a few days before his final downfall he was still convinced that, were he but seriously to make up his mind to it, he could at any moment "cut it out," as he put it—that is to say slough off this skin of a frantic betrayed lover and reappear in his old skin of a rational, calm and prosaic family man, a conscientious and respected deputy. His passion for Solange was something external—a wart, a swelling, an abscess which he examined with curiosity and could easily lance when he judged the right moment to have come. He told himself that since he was capable of detaching himself from his grief and contemplating it as an isolated phenomenon, it wasn't therefore genuine grief. Genuine grief does not permit this faculty of abstraction, of standing back and considering it the way one considers some event with which one is unconcerned. Truly a quaint philosophy which, when deciphered, amounts to saying that one ceases to suffer directly one knows one's suffering! But dupes find sustenance in any piece of sophistry.

Apart from the times when he saw Solange he wasn't very gay and this, to my mind, should have revealed such reflections for what they were. At home he was gloomy, silent, absent and remote. His wife and children had to repeat something several times before he would deign to reply, not that he was sullen toward them but he simply didn't hear them. He was lost in his thoughts, as the saying goes. These were not clear-cut but more of a confused hodgepodge of emotions mingled with erotic fantasies which were as a rule very somber in hue. Nothing pleased him, nothing distracted him, nothing even captured his attention. Lovesickness had as it were made his mind soundproof. Even Agnes became worried in the end. Such a persistently black mood wasn't natural. She unburdened herself to me. She was very agitated, very depressed; never before had Roberti been so morose and uncommunicative. She wondered if he wasn't incubating some disease. She questioned me anxiously about him; she wanted to know if he was equally dejected outside his home. I replied evasively. In truth, I told her, Edouard didn't appear to be in very good spirits and this seemed to be his general mood. "Do you think he no longer loves me?" she asked. "That would explain why he looks so depressed. He's bored with us. The children bore him. I bore him. Everything bores him. He can't help showing it. Thinking about it, a horrible idea came to me the other day. Could he possibly be in love with someone else? I didn't dare mention it to him; I was so afraid I might be right." I was very upset by what she said. I reassured her as best I could and determined to have it out with Edouard that same day. So far as I can remember, it must have been the tenth or twelfth of February. All at once things appeared to me in a really serious light. So long as Agnes didn't know what was going on, so long as Edouard maintained his permanent deception, one could at a pinch leave things to take their course. But now it was an urgent question of doing something to prevent the damage from being irreparable. So I telephoned Edouard and arranged to meet him somewhere outside his home, so that we could talk undisturbed. My phone call had alarmed him but even so, when he turned up at our meeting place, he appeared far less agitated than I had expected. Nothing unconnected with Solange touched him. I plunged straight into an account of my talk with Agnes and this did at any rate upset him. I more or less knew the mess he had got himself into. I took advantage of his despondency and confusion to read him a stern lecture. I was emphatic and, I think, pretty tough. I insisted that he should make a break. I drew him a startling picture of what he had become, of the abasement into which he was subsiding and its possibly fatal consequences, of the spiritual disintegration toward which he was heading. He was astounded by my violence. He was embarrassed and looked down his nose. I felt as if I were scolding a child. He was a pitiful sight and I felt terrible about it. I remember, too, that he wasn't looking at all well that day. His skin was gray, his face was haggard, his hair dull and lifeless and he looked extraordinarily tired. Naturally he served up his eternal self-deluded claptrap, to wit that he wasn't in love, that this whole business meant nothing and so on. This made me angry. I retorted that in that case there was no reason why he shouldn't break with Solange immediately. I didn't often interfere in his little affairs. If for once I was doing so, it was because there was an excellent reason for it. At this point the poor man gave me a look I shall never forget. It was the look of the aging Mme. Du Barry at the moment of being guillotined: "Just one more minute, Executioner!" For all my determination, I was moved. He seemed so old and frail that for a fraction of a second I saw myself as a monster. It was late at night; we were walking through the streets. The light of a lamppost caught him obliquely in such a way that I could see a whole network of wrinkles and puffy marks on his face. This light threw his face into relief, like one of those old Amsterdam beggars Rembrandt used to dress up as noblemen in order to paint them, showing above gilded raiment an ancient face eaten away by wind, rain and a blighted life. I felt a wave of pity! I saw him in all his misery. It's a depressing memory! Most frightful of all was the way he was shambling along. I fought back my impulse to compassion. This was no moment to weaken. I told him with all the vigor one has when one wants to save someone, and several innocents along with him, that he absolutely must break it off, break it off, break it off. I repeated these words ten times over, so that they should thoroughly sink into his brain. "Not right away," he said imploringly. "In a week's time. I promise I'll do it then. What is a week?"—"No," I cried, "don't wait a week. Take an oath here and now, in front of me, with me, that you'll never see her again. It will be quite simple. All you need do is refrain from calling her up and, since she won't call you, that will be that. Go away somewhere." But unfortunately he had managed to collect his wits. With that false lightness of manner he used to put on when lying to himself or other people, he said: "Come, come, my dear fellow, you're making mountains out of molehills. I admit I'm a bit below par just now but there's no cause for worry. Good heavens, you should know me well enough! I'm far too sensible a sort of man, alas, to do anything foolish. You seem to believe I'm head over heels in love with the Mignot girl. I'm not: I'm just upset. If I were in love it would be another matter: I would listen to you, I'd break with her instantly, I'd run away to Japan or Tierra del Fuego with Agnes, to whom I am utterly devoted and who is the one person in the world who matters to me. But you know how these things come about: so long as the Mignot girl was making eyes at me, I found her a bore; now she's drifting away I find her more alluring. None of it goes very deep. In a week's time the itch will have worn off. In a week's time, so long Mlle. Mignot!" At this point I must confess I was filled with discouragement. And I did what all discouraged people do: I accepted the compromise Edouard was offering me, hoping that perhaps in a week's time he would in fact have managed to take himself in hand, argue it out sufficiently with himself and finally make up his mind to it. I granted him this week's reprieve with the threat that, if he didn't keep his word, I would tell Agnes everything. That frightened him pretty badly. "No," he exclaimed, "you couldn't do that. It's not possible. You're my friend and Agnes' friend. Don't you see?" Sternly I replied: "It's just because I am a friend of you both that I'll do it, even if it means falling out with the two of you forever. I regard it as my duty and, I might add, I blame myself for not having subjected you to this blackmail six months or a year ago." Once again he lowered his head and I had the illusion of at last having got somewhere with him. "Perhaps you're right," he muttered. "I'll see what I can do." Since then I have bitterly repented of allowing him this week's respite. I should have clinched the matter then and there. I should have taken advantage of his dejected state, his panic and fatigue, to drag him off to a travel agency and book two seats for Agnes and himself on a plane leaving the next day for Venezuela. That's what I should have done, and what fills me with remorse is the fact that for a moment I thought of doing it. But poor Edouard looked so woebegone that I took pity on him. I granted him this last week of love. I was weak. Had I been merciless, had I insisted fifteen minutes longer, he would have given in. That is how one allows people to go to perdition. Through misguided goodness of heart, misconceived charity. Had I myself driven Roberti and his wife the next morning in my car to the airport, had I myself put them on the plane, no catastrophe would have occurred. Do you remember a passage in the *Chartreuse de Parme* when Mosca makes the Prince of Parma sign Fabrizio's pardon extorted from him by La Sanseverina? As he writes out the pardon, the Prince omits one sentence. Mosca notices this but the sentence seems to him really too insulting to the Prince and not so very important. Out of respect, out of good breeding, out of a sort of stupid generosity he says nothing. As a result the drama breaks over everyone's head and poor Mosca forfeits the affection and respect of the one person he loves above all others in the world. Well, in the Roberti affair, on the day I'm telling you about, I behaved like Mosca. I sinned out of good breeding. I never imagined that, three or four days later, Edouard would descend one step deeper into evil. I believed that his passion was in its death throes, that he was only bound to Solange by a last few frayed bonds, painful to rip out but which I could help him to snap by giving them one sharp blow. Above all I didn't foresee the unexpected quarter from which the tragedy that was to bring this story to an end would come. One cannot foresee accidents, one cannot foresee the impulses of those who, by some ordination of fate, fulfill what after the event we call their destiny. It would have been necessary for Roberti and Agnes to be absent from Paris during the second half of February 1958 in order to elude the workings of chance and consequently be spared by destiny.

About the fifteenth of February, Solange finally made up her mind to tell Roberti she had settled to marry Legay and that this event was imminent, since it was to take place in the first days of March. This was a fresh disaster which, contrary to what one might have thought, he hadn't been expecting. In fact he had refused to consider the fact that, being pregnant, Solange had every reason to be preoccupied over her future. He was seeing her, he was thinking about her, and his imagination didn't go beyond that. At bottom I believe he was vaguely hoping that, despite her pregnancy, she would never marry anyone; that she would remain, as they say nowadays, a bachelor mother. It was inconceivable that she should upset the unchanging and unending organization of their adultery. By forgiving the infidelity of which he had been victim had he not shown proof of an unparalleled magnanimity? This was surely not overlooked? Surely she must be feeling very grateful to him? He was like a sick man who has resigned himself to his illness, who has come to accept his pains and concludes that he is going to recover from the fact that these are getting no worse. He was lulling himself with the idea that the rather shameful situation which Solange was bringing on herself wouldn't be a bad thing for their future amours. In spite of declining prejudice, it still isn't much fun these days to be an unmarried mother. Solange would be only too glad, once she was saddled with her brat, to keep a lover who had behaved as elegantly and broadmindedly as he had. In short, as always, he was putting his head in the sand; this man of action declined to see anything that was possible but delighted on the contrary in the impossible; he was living his passion, miserably, from day to day; he was so afraid of tomorrow that he dared not even face it.

This time Solange didn't wait until they left the studio before telling him. As soon as she was settled beside him in the car she informed him of her decision. She had been working herself up to it for several days. She was hoping that this final revelation would be sufficient to provoke the break and that she would have no need to say the irrevocable words she was always promising herself to say; she often rehearsed these to herself when she was alone but they obstinately refused to cross her lips when she was in the presence of her lover. She was devoutly praying that Roberti wouldn't be brave enough to bear the idea that she was going to belong legally to another man, that she would never again be free to run to him like a little bitch in heat every time he whistled, that she would be sharing her life—that is to say her nights—with someone other than he. She had lived through this scene in anticipation. He would turn pale, his mouth would begin to quiver, he would open the door of the car and say: "Get out! This is the end! I'll never see you again." She wouldn't need to be told twice. She would watch the familiar black car drive off forever down the Avenue de l'Opéra and the weight oppressing her heart would be lifted at last. All this moral filth, all this scum with which she was covered and which often sickened her, would instantly vanish. In a flash she would become once again the good little Solange she had always been and always would be. Three years of defilement and unhappiness would abruptly be wiped out of her life. It would be as if those three years had never existed. She would at last be able to love Legay, for she sincerely longed to love this good young man. So long as Roberti had a hold on her, her love for Legay would be as it were hamstrung, paralyzed, dormant. She dared not unleash it, dared not awaken it. Some kind of moral honesty was holding her back. She would have judged herself truly too false and too contemptible if, while continuing to visit the Square Saint-Lambert with Roberti, she had at the same time shown Legay signs of devotion which would have expressed the true and great affection she felt for him.

She got into the car with the bored and implacable air of women who have decided to inflict the deathblow on the man they no longer love. Once again Roberti had that sensation he was beginning to know so well, of his heart sliding slowly down to the pit of his stomach; this is the constant lot of those wretches on whom fresh misfortunes fall each day and who, although they live in a state of perpetual alertness, are too cowardly to guard against the blows, however predictable, which fate is so eager to deliver. Thud, thud, thud! Solange's words fell on his skull like hammerblows. And yet her words were perfectly clear. They were quite simple: "Edouard, I'm going to get married. You must see I've got to. You can't have supposed that Jacques wouldn't insist on it. After all, it's his child." He had turned pale, as she had imagined he would, and his mouth was quivering. He saw how events follow in an inexorable chain, a discovery which always astonished and depressed him. He had exhausted his mistress's patience, she had deceived him, got herself pregnant and now she was marrying the father of her child. There was a truly fatal logic and simplicity about it all. Sometimes, in his political life, he had been disconcerted in the same way by similar chains of events, perfectly simple and logical, which had made a complete mess of his subtle calculations and predictions. Stunned as he was, he was still able to look inside himself and analyze this new mortification. Was Solange's marriage bringing him an increase of pain? All things considered, no. It was just an added nuisance; he was more vexed than distressed. Vexed like a man who learns that he will have to pay twice as much income tax as he thought he would. Such a discovery may make one feel fed up but a financial wound is not a mortal one. After all, what is a mistress who gets married? Nothing much, truth to tell. For a moment, however, a wave of discouragement swept over him. He was on the verge of saying the words Solange was hoping to hear; "Good-by, get out, go to hell, this is more than I can stand, this is the last straw!" But he made the rash mistake of looking at her. She wasn't exactly pretty with her wooden face, her lowered eyes, her hard expression; but she was breathing too quickly, her heart was visibly beating faster than usual. Her mouth, too, was slightly quivering. At the sight of this agitation, at the sight of that pretty, smooth and perfumed mouth he would never kiss again, desire raced through him. It was a desire of such sadness that he couldn't resist but instantly gave in to it. Capitulated without a protest, unconditionally. He was glad to capitulate. At once his heart climbed back into his chest, his diaphragm relaxed, he took a deep breath. Happiness was returning. Happiness in abasement is doubtless the kind to which we are most responsive, since to capture it we have to sacrifice something very precious—our self-respect. "My mistress will be married," he told himself, "and that's that. Free, she was a nuisance; once under a husband's control, I won't find her any trouble at all. She'll have to get home punctually for dinner, she'll always be in a hurry. Let's be clear about it: which is to my best advantage? I shall be surer than ever of her discretion. Everyone has a married mistress. It is well known how much more convenient they are." A facetious idea crossed his mind: he felt an urge to say to Solange: "We must go and celebrate your marriage at once with one of our usual little frolics!" But he didn't dare. Such cynicism might easily have shocked the little fool, who was far from sharing the outlook of a Messalina. On the contrary, he must make himself smooth-tongued and insidious, pretend to be miserable, adopt a desperate and pleading tone. In a muffled voice he asked her to accompany him to the studio as one last favor. She refused, naturally, but he detected a hint of uncertainty in her refusal. It was a weary, an almost supplicating refusal: once again he had won the round. All his powers of seduction had returned. He took her to the Square Saint-Lambert. She was in despair; she despised herself for being so weak, she felt more humiliated and soiled than ever before, but without going so far as to say yes she didn't actually say no. The listlessness of her body silenced her mind. She loathed herself. She longed to weep; she longed to die. For Roberti it was different; this pitiful victory temporarily deadened his pain. The thought that he was going to make a young woman who had just got engaged moan with pleasure, that he was going to cuckold his rival in advance, that he was about to triumph once more on his favorite battlefield, delighted him and even gave him a sense of pride. What a piquant situation! So piquant that for a moment he could almost have been annoyed had she not been engaged.

This scene took place in the evening; they remained together about four hours. Roberti was in an unfamiliar mood: he had no wish to leave his mistress. He was even apprehensive of the moment when she would bid him good-by. He was clinging to her. His misfortunes made him eloquent with the eloquence of despair, like that of men who put all their strength to defending a lost cause in which they scarcely any longer believe. He talked very rapidly, in a light and resigned tone of voice. He recounted the story of their love and took a bitter joy in doing so. Now and then, as he listened to himself, he thought how moving he must be. Solange was sitting half dressed on the divan, gazing at the floor with her chin in her hand, looking at once bored and pensive. In fact she wasn't thinking of anything. She was absorbed by her own torment, which she was ruminating like an animal. Her conduct appeared to her in the form of a glaring moral antithesis: she was acting the little hypocrite with Legay and wallowing in debauchery with Roberti. She couldn't understand how she had got herself involved in such a degrading situation. She was barely listening to Edouard. She was subjecting her innermost self to an intense examination; far away, in the depths of her bitter introspection she could see a small determination forming; it was as yet no bigger than a pea but it was hard as stone: the determination to have done with this man she no longer loved. She was finding to her relief that her heart detested him more than her body desired him. And why did her heart detest him? Because he was leading her down terrifying paths into a frightful abyss, where she felt afraid. In her own way she was making a descent into hell. These were not real flames licking at her flesh: the red-hot coals were inside her. Solange's soul was burning, not like a torch or a funeral pyre but smoldering like peat or a rubbish heap, giving off an intolerable stench. The fires of hell have this peculiarity, that they do not purify but increase the impurity still further. The soul they burn resembles a blackened and evil-smelling ruin. As she brooded over herself Solange, who was scarcely religious and hadn't been to mass since her first Communion, was experiencing the disgust a monk may feel for a lecher. Her own flesh was giving her nausea; this pretty body, this warm and downy flesh was appearing to her like carrion, like a corpse, like a bag of offal. That was what she had been turned into by this man who stood there talking, affecting a refined and poetic melancholy, telling her about his heart. The worst of it was that it was true—he had a heart, and his heart was suffering. This, combined with the difficulty of translating her confused and desolate emotions into words, kept her lips sealed. Occasionally she would glance up and stare at Roberti for a moment. These looks she gave him were unfathomable, like those of an animal.

Pathetically, clumsily, the poor man talked on. After evoking the past at considerable length, he sought to force a few words about the future from his mistress. He described what their life might be like later on. They would continue to meet as before. They would organize their lovemaking meticulously. There were so many ties between them that their affair couldn't just stupidly end like this, with her marrying a man she didn't love. For she didn't love him, that was plain. They would take even greater care to keep it secret. He, Edouard, was the last man ever to compromise a woman. "Oh, I know that," said Solange with a bitterness which momentarily disconcerted him. What shows how completely off the beam he was is that, in the face of her stubborn silence, he asked her two or three times what she was thinking. He wanted to know. Nothing was more important to him than the thoughts locked up in that pretty head. He was furious at not knowing them. These thoughts were his life, his oxygen, and he was being denied them. "Nothing," replied Solange in the tradition of bored lovers. She was thinking fondly, nostalgically of Legay. Her spirit was fleeing from this vile studio, running to take refuge with that pure-hearted young man. She wasn't even regretting Legay's inadequate lovemaking. *He* would never turn her into this wanton, whining animal helpless before its pleasure, this dead dog with a swollen belly. What Roberti was saying about how to organize their twofold adultery in the future seemed to her utterly unreal. She was entering marriage as one enters a convent, to find order after disorder, the strictest and most complete economy of body and soul after having known the wildest prodigality of them. She was thinking of all the tedious occupations of married life and yearning for them, calling out with all her heart to the countless constraints of the married woman. From the depths of her present abasement she was looking forward to a long and humdrum life, filled with little obligations and little duly rationed satisfactions. She was longing for this peace of the spirit like a girl enthusiastically taking her vows. Tomorrow she would write her letter breaking it off. "I must go home," she said. "I'll take you," said Roberti, who couldn't bring himself to part from her that evening.

Contrary to the old saying, chance arranges things badly more often than well. By a truly exceptional mischance, when he deposited Solange outside her house in the Avenue Daumesnil round about ten-thirty that night, Valentin was just coming out of the Métro. From fifty yards off, thanks to the light from a lamppost, he saw his sister getting out of that abhorrent automobile. Just then no sight could have been more hateful. Indeed, he had been spending the evening with his dear

Legay. Together, in one of the numerous dives known only to Valentin, they had celebrated the wonderful sale of the television set. It was Legay's party. They had had a heartwarming and joyous talk. True to the orders Solange had given him, Legay had carefully avoided mentioning his marriage but had been unable to prevent himself from extolling his beloved and giving his comrade to understand—very subtly, according to him—that he still cherished a tender feeling in his heart for Mlle. Mignot. He had even gone so far as to say that, if Solange would agree to it someday, he would gladly marry her for the asking. It was out of charity, of course, that he had made this half confidence, and also to mitigate his remorse. But one could hardly imagine anything more foolhardy, for Valentin's old hopes immediately sprang to life again: he believed Legay was giving him a tremendous opening, that he was officially appointing him to resume negotiations and this time bring them to a head. This was quite unhoped for. He felt himself entrusted with a sacred mission which must be accomplished by every possible means. He was brooding over these means on his way home and, following the normal trend of his character, the more he thought about them the angrier he grew. Simple and violent minds always fret at the complications of the world. Any action which isn't elementary and immediate, but calls for wiliness or patience, makes their blood boil. They never suspect that it is they who are stupid or helpless: they believe themselves to be the only just men in a world incomprehensible in its deviousness.

Coming out of the Métro, he made up his mind to force a showdown, without however knowing precisely what arguments he would use to persuade Solange to marry Legay. But he had faith in his inspiration. He would at last say everything that was weighing on his heart. He would impress upon his sister that she was wrecking her life, that her affair had gone on far too long, that the time had come to be sensible and so forth. After having put her thoroughly to shame he would then evoke Legay, so upright, so loyal, so faithful. She certainly didn't deserve to marry such a man. It was an opportunity not to be missed. Unless she was a supreme idiot, she wouldn't let it pass. This had appeased Valentin's anger, but when he saw Roberti's car all his plans fell in ruins and his heart filled again with rage. He recalled a similar scene three years before. In despair he told himself: "There's definitely nothing to be done about it. She's getting madder and madder. Talking to her won't serve any purpose. I'll have to find some other way." He concealed himself in the shadows of a building and waited until Solange had closed the front door behind her. Roberti's car passed by him, slowly enough for him to see the profile of his sister's friend for several seconds in a spectral light. He spat on the pavement out of disgust and defiance. But this rapid vision had brought him a revelation. At the sight of this elderly and heavy profile, his mind underwent a sort of Copernican revolution. Since he would never bring his sister to give up Roberti, it was the latter he must attack: he would force Roberti to renounce his sister. It was as plain as daylight. Why on earth hadn't he thought of it before? Obviously it would be a bit risky, a bit tricky and not quite the right thing. But the ends justify the means. On this he went to bed and fell asleep with a peace of mind such as he hadn't known for three years. He was highly content at the prospect of provoking a tragic situation. It would put him completely in his element. Have you noticed how widespread a taste for tragedy is among fools? They are gluttons for misfortune and catastrophes; if necessary they provoke them, since this is more or less their only means of achieving importance. They snatch at doom the way burglars snatch at diamonds. As he fell asleep Valentin thought pleasurably how because of him everyone would be made unhappy, including himself. He would have the joy of adopting a grave expression, frowning the whole day long, being as darkly silent as an augur; he would feel bigger than nature, like a judge.

The morning following this painful day, Roberti woke up in such a state of misery that he was surprised. As soon as he opened his eyes and saw the murky February daylight filtering through his shutters, the memory of what his love and his life had become crashed down like a rock on his chest. Throughout the morning this unhappiness only increased. That afternoon he shut himself up in his study on the pretext of having work to do but in reality so that he could dream and fret, and by dint of dreaming and fretting overcome this black depression which seemed to him quite out of proportion with the by-and-large rather banal little adventure he was living through. But left alone, his thoughts so to speak eluded him. Behind his closed eyelids he could see Solange and it was a bitter vision, since he knew he no longer lived in her heart, knew she had grown indifferent to his thoughts and feelings. This creature over whom he had had complete power, who had been an object in his hands, had regained her freedom. She didn't care two pins for him. She was deciding her fate independently. Ceasing to mean anything to someone for whom one was once everything is an agonizing torture. One not only suffers from jealousy but also from wounded self-esteem. I don't use this word in the debilitated sense it has nowadays but in the strong sense it had in the past: self-love. When a woman you love becomes a stranger or an enemy, you begin to doubt yourself. You are cut in half and made up of two separate and fiercely antagonistic parts. Being no longer loved, you no longer love yourself, for self-love had come to you through the other's love. Jealousy is nothing. I would even say that, up to a point, jealousy is agreeable since it is optimistic. One suffers while thinking that one will surely win in the end, whatever torrents of one's own blood have to be shed in the process. But nothing is more horrible than finding one's self-love dwindling, withering away, ceasing to exist. To cease to love oneself is despair; it is the major sin against God. Such was the new feeling taking hold or, rather, which had taken hold of Edouard. In spite of all his self-deception, he knew in his heart of hearts that Solange no longer loved him and by the same token saw that he no longer loved himself. He felt no more curiosity about his soul. It had suddenly ceased to interest him. It remained attached to him like a loathsome beast, like an octopus which was strangling him and which he found hateful.

Toward four that afternoon his despair had become so oppressive that he was unable to remain any longer indoors. He pulled on his overcoat and went out. He felt he couldn't stand his life any longer. He walked up the Rue Oudinot as far as the Boulevard des Invalides. It was freezing hard; the sky was a maroon color, the way it sometimes appears in Paris during winter. The buildings looked leaden and dirty, and formed a setting scarcely designed to bring joy to one so utterly deprived of it. When Roberti found himself on the pavement of the Boulevard des Invalides a rather welcome thought struck him: the thought of dying. It was one of those fleeting notions which must not be allowed to escape when they present themselves, since if one pauses however briefly to consider them one loses the courage to put them into execution. "I'm going to die here and now," he thought. "End it all. Nothingness. Darkness. The end of all this stupidity. What a relief! And not a moment too soon. Everything disgusts me. Love, politics, France, the international situation, the war in Algeria, ugh! It's all so dreary. So threadbare. So tedious! Good-by. Nothing amuses me any more. I'm not fifty-three, I am a thousand, a million years old. I'm as old as the world and perhaps even older. I can see it now. Life is nothing but a monotonous farce without meaning or purpose. Who will really care? That little idiot of a Solange! She'll believe I loved her and killed myself on her account! I rather like the idea of ending on a misunderstanding." He never gave a thought to his wife and children. They were as remote from him as Pandit Nehru or President Eisenhower. With a sort of lugubrious joy he walked out to meet death, which he saw approaching in the shape of an enormous truck. He stepped off the pavement, stopped in the middle of the Boulevard des Invalides and frantically shut his eyes. He heard the roar and rattle of the truck bearing down on him full tilt. He was going to be knocked down, crushed, reduced to pulp. Over what part of his body would the huge wheels pass? Chest, legs, head, stomach? His bones would be crushed to powder. His bag of flesh would burst like a balloon. There would be one ghastly moment, one terrible flash, and all would be over forever. This distinguished member of the Chamber of Deputies would be seen sprawling in the road, sliced in two like a fat white worm. "Hey, pop, are you nuts?" shouted a furious voice amid a hideous screeching of brakes and screaming of tires. Roberti opened his eyes. The hood of the truck was two inches from his face, steaming like the jaws of a dragon. Its driver was gesticulating and bawling through his window. Roberti's heart was pounding in his chest. The instinct of self-preservation again surged through him. He jumped back and ran to the pavement, followed by the delirious insults of the truck driver, giving vent in this way to the scare he had just had. After this exploit Roberti went home, trembling in every limb. Between the moment he left his study and the moment of his return, less than fifteen minutes had gone by.

He threw himself down in an armchair without removing his coat. When the pounding in his chest had subsided, he found his self-hatred again, intact. For all that it had in truth come within two inches of him and he had keenly smelled its breath, death had not restored any inclination in him to live. Far from it: he was disappointed. He regretted not having been run over. What was he to do now? All at once he was in the grip of his bleak impatience and it seemed to him that a spirit not his own was taking possession of his will. A violent, restless, painful, alien, overriding spirit he was unable to resist. This spirit was suggesting strange things; Roberti heard them in the depths of his conscience, which suffered as if it were being violated while at the same time giving infamous signs of assent. "Since you can't manage to kill your body, you are going to kill your soul. You will be a body with a dead soul, and therefore it won't make you suffer any more. There are no two ways to kill a soul. You have to force it to perform a deed wholly contrary to its nature. A deed so vile, so horrible that, once perpetrated, your soul will not have the strength to survive. You are going to make your soul die of shame." At the same time he was consumed with an uncontrollable urge for immediate, instant action. A day of inertia, of despairing inactivity, was resolving into an itching in all his muscles and

irritableness in all his nerves. Without removing his overcoat he went
to sit at his desk. He drew out a sheet of paper, unscrewed his pen
and, with a blend of horror and delight, began to write an anonymous
letter.

For once he was inspired. This was no letter he was composing but
a sort of interminable obscene poem, full of lurid details and foul words.
He described Solange in every imaginable posture, he conjured up the
scent of her and the secrets of her body; he reproduced her moans; he
abused her; he evoked an equally shameless picture of himself in the
third person. In this way he covered eight pages in disguised handwriting, without crossing out one word. He then reread this tissue of
corruption, the style of which amazed him. It was totally unlike his
normal style. Although he had never written an anonymous letter in
his life he had unwittingly adopted the sly and suggestive turns of
phrase, the vulgarities and hypocrisies peculiar to this type of epistle.
Here and there he had even exaggerated them, raised them to a level
of caricature, as if he were not writing an anonymous letter but a
pastiche of one, as if he were indulging in an exercise in literary composition.

It always surprises me to see a man premeditate some bad deed and
then carry it through with the full awareness of what he is doing. I
can never understand why, after having made the first move, he doesn't
stop short, aghast at the absurdity and futility of what he has under-
taken. For evil seems to me essentially futile. If those who commit it
did but suspect the inner frailty and ennui which it betrays, they would
be paralyzed by a sense of shame. But doubtless they suspect none of
this and evil flows from them as naturally as rash words or thoughtless
gestures. After giving the matter considerable thought I finally concluded that, while he was composing this letter, Roberti's soul was
mute or, if you like, absent. When the letter was done he felt no relaxation of his muscles and no calming of his nerves. He was in exactly
the same physical and spiritual state as before. To the extent that, after
he read it through, the notion crossed his mind that he wasn't the
author of all this muck but only the copyist; that it had been dictated
to him by some hideous ghoul standing behind his chair. He held the
four sheets of paper between the thumb and forefinger of his right hand
and wondered whether or not he should send them to their destination.
A crucial moment! The die was not yet cast. Roberti was perfectly
balanced on the line dividing exceptional evil from everyday life, the
Devil from men. Nothing was yet final. He had been playing the part
of a man who writes an anonymous letter. He had been occupying his

mind and hands for half an hour. If his story were one which could be told to children and you were a child, I would much enjoy showing you Edouard's guardian angel at this moment, silently crying out to him: "Tear it up and you will find yourself intact again. You will have only sinned by intention, and paradise is paved with bad intentions. An anonymous letter which is never sent is nothing, it doesn't alter the world; it has no more significance than the wicked thoughts that pass twenty times a day through the purest of hearts, only to be immediately dispelled; one is no more responsible for these than for blinking one's eyes. Tear up your letter, Edouard: that is the only way to attain the peace you seek." The temptation to good is just as strong as the temptation to evil, and I think Roberti must have had great difficulty in resisting his angel. But I also think that, when an angel speaks, no one listens more attentively than the Devil. To Edouard's woe, the memory of what was tormenting him returned: Solange pregnant, Solange married, the solitude of the flesh in which he was going to find himself. Fury and misery swept through him again and hardened his heart. Solange belonged to him, Solange was his. She was being stolen from him. Such an injustice was intolerable. Intolerable, too, the thought that others were happy while he was suffering so deeply. The falsity of such considerations never struck him. On the contrary they seemed to him to carry such astonishing force as to justify any act of wickedness. Evil was no longer a choice: it was a necessity. He was being driven to it by events. He took an envelope from the drawer and inscribed it with the name and address of Legay, which he somehow knew. Then, for the second time that day, he went out. Just as he was about to put the letter in the mailbox he again hesitated. He listened anxiously: what was his soul saying at this vital moment? It was saying nothing. Absolute silence reigned over it. The silence of nothingness. *Pfrittt!* The letter dropped into the box. Its fate was sealed. Roberti's heart gave a tremendous lurch, such as one feels when one stumbles and falls into a hole. At the same time his soul began to hum again. In his inner confusion he thought: "I, Edouard Roberti, a deputy, a sensitive and cultured man, have written and sent an anonymous letter. Yet I am still the same. I can smile as I did yesterday. I can see the same things. My face has not turned black. I am still moved by Mozart's music. Who am I then? How weird this all is. It isn't I who have done this. Someone I don't know has borrowed my body this afternoon." He felt strangely younger; he recalled to mind several little atrocities he had performed in his childhood. He had stepped back forty or forty-five years in time. He had displayed the viciousness of a weak and amoral child. He stared at himself in stupefaction, but now without hatred. He saw a new man who was not the rational and transparent Roberti to whom he had been accustomed since early youth. He even felt a gust of pride. "I never knew I was capable of doing such a thing," he reflected. "Can there then be dark recesses deep within me, unsuspected reserves of strength? In that case, all ambitions are permissible! I shall be a minister in the next cabinet!" He thought again: "While I always regarded anonymous letters as the height of ignominy, I see now that I was wrong since I myself have sent one. Any act of mine can never be wholly shabby. Why? Because I am not a shabby character. I shall never see Solange again after this. I have buried our love in slime. I have sacrificed myself. I have shown myself in the worst possible light. This was probably the only way to put an end to it. I've burned my boats. Blown up my bridges. What memory will she retain of me, this woman whom I never loved but who has filled such a place in my life? Ah well, never mind. I just don't care!" Over dinner he displayed a more cheerful mood than he had shown for two months. The whole family was delighted. There was laughter round the table, which was not so frequent nowadays. Nobody noticed that, on several occasions, Edouard sank into a little reverie.

It was only at about three o'clock next morning, awakened by insomnia, that anguish settled into him. With the dazzling mental clarity one has in the middle of the night, he once again lived over his fatal day minute by minute and felt sick with horror. Why couldn't he cut this day out of his life, omit it from his history? Alas, what is done can never be undone. Childishly he prayed that his letter would get lost. He was incapable at the same time of taking the slightest decision, were it but to flee to the other end of the world for a year. He was like a rabbit in the sights of a sportsman's gun, waiting in obscure terror for the shot that will rip its flesh. He was waiting in fear and trembling for the catastrophe he had prepared to unleash itself and engulf him. This Radical Socialist felt irredeemably damned, and damned all the more in that, since he didn't believe in God, there was no one of whom he could beg forgiveness. There was no power capable of absolving his sin, of prising loose the horror clamped to his soul. All his life, which might yet perhaps be a long one, he would drag this infamy after him. He would surely know a few more moments of happiness but they would be poisoned. Always the memory of this anonymous letter he had written would rise up between him and the world. This letter would remain embedded in him like a harpoon. He had wanted to strike at Solange and Legay: it was in his own side that he had torn open a wound which would never cease to suppurate. He recalled the various things he had written, had dared to write, and an icy sweat broke out on all his limbs. Where could he flee to, where could he hide? Nowhere. He was tied down by his public position and his marriage. Today he would be going to the Assembly. Agnes lay innocently asleep beside him. He tossed and turned on his mattress like one possessed.

Legay received the letter by the next morning's mail. As he opened it he wondered: "Goodness, who could possibly be addressing me as 'My poor Jacques . . .'? Before reading any further, he glanced at the last page. He was so naïve that, seeing no signature, he thought his correspondent had simply forgotten to sign it. It was not until the end of the second page that he realized he was reading an anonymous letter. I won't describe the feelings of a man who receives an anonymous letter. You must have had more than one yourself, like anyone whose photograph appears occasionally in the papers. So you know exactly the degree of disgust and curiosity one feels. It is rare for anyone to have the courage to tear the letter up after only reading three lines. No, one goes on to the end, in order to find out how much one is hated and whether what one's unknown enemy writes is true or false. The manifestations of evil exert a fascination to which no one is immune. Legay, who had never had an enemy in the world, was staggered to discover one so rabid, so smooth-tongued and—most sickening of all—so close to him. Indeed there was a familiarity, an odiously affectionate tone to the letter which pierced his heart. This unknown man was his brother, a most vile brother but one to whom he was attached by mysterious bonds as strong as those of blood. He was appalled by what he read, and all in all couldn't help feeling a kind of pity for the man who had written it. Behind the disguised handwriting and ironical style he glimpsed a black and unhappy soul writhing in agony at the bottom of an abyss. He realized something else which filled him with astonishment: he wasn't surprised. He felt quite certain that everything he had read was true. Worse, he had been vaguely expecting such revelations. He read the letter to the accompaniment of an inner voice saying: "It wasn't possible for Solange to be what you believed her to be. That would have been too easy and nothing is easy for you in this world. You have to win everything the hard way, with infinite pains, at the price of your blood and sleepless nights. Happiness is further off than you thought. Read this letter right through and try to rise above it. It is a chain of mountains, a desert you have to cross, where you may well die of thirst and exhaustion." He couldn't tear his eyes from the letter. Even so, once he had finished it he didn't dare read it through a second time. He put it back in its envelope with the certain knowledge that he would never look at it again. Besides, this would have served no purpose. It was, as they say, branded on his mind in letters of fire. Doubtless he would forget its details but he would never forget its tone. For five full minutes he paced up and down his room without any idea of what he was doing. Mechanically he folded his pajamas, shifted a few objects, opened his chest of drawers, pushed a chair back to the wall and so on. He was in a daze. I think his face must have reflected the bewilderment of a man who has just had an accident and can't understand how it only took a second for disaster to fall on him. The soul is like the eyes: it needs to *focus*. When Legay's soul had at last *focused* he was astonished for a second time: he had preserved all his aplomb. Very calmly, taking care not to crumple the sheet, he lay down on his bed. Fixing his eyes on the ceiling, he tried to analyze his feelings. First and foremost, shame. The anonymous letter had soiled him. It had spattered him like a jet of slime. But at the same time it had, in one way, brought him relief. Ever since Solange became his mistress he had been prey to an inexplicable unease to which he now held the key: she wasn't the woman he believed her to be. She was someone else whose nature he hadn't even guessed at. The truth, however painful, always brings a kind of peace with it. A world of dark but true colors is always preferable to a world of bright but false ones. Legay now knew exactly who his fiancée was and he was so honest, so full of good will, that he suffered no disappointment. I would even say that his positive and practical engineer's mind felt an obscure satisfaction. At last he knew the cause of Solange's mysteries, her silences, her bouts of melancholy. Instead of hating her for this, as if it had all been directed against himself, he sensed the inner conflict it betrayed. He was seized with so violent a pity for her that he found it hard to breathe. Hitherto he had loved Solange blindly; he had loved what she was not. From now on he would love her in full knowledge of the facts. Then his reflections took another turn. The anonymous letter was horribly crude; it was full of descriptions and evocations. These too were burned into his memory and he found himself unable to keep his mind off them. His imagination was all on fire, the more so in that he could see Solange extremely clearly behind his closed eyelids. This young woman who intimidated him, whom he had believed to be frigid, was a deep well of voluptuousness. Such a discovery might well perturb a humble engineer with a simple heart and an inexperienced body. Legay was filled with pity, horror, disgust, jealousy and desire, which as you know make a delicious combination. In other words, Roberti's letter had redoubled his love; it had also liberated it, since he no longer felt the slightest shyness. He was tempted to burn the letter and never breathe a word of it to anyone. But, strangely, he told himself that this wouldn't be fair to Solange, that she must be made aware of it, so that she could be as strong as he in the time to come and they could live together in truth. Above all he had a devouring longing to see her as soon as possible, to take her in his arms, to touch her. Dare I say it? Deep down, without admitting it to himself, he wanted to verify whether or not the letter had lied.

That day was a Saturday—I remember this well because the banks were closed—and Solange wasn't at the office. She was certainly at home. Legay called her up. Hearing her fresh young voice at the other end of the line, he almost fainted with excitement. "Could you come round here for a moment this morning?" he asked abruptly. There was a silence. "What's the matter?" said Solange, whose instinct had immediately sensed something wrong. Legay, whose heart was pounding furiously, could find nothing better to say than: "I've received a letter." —"I'll be round in ten minutes," said Solange. These ten minutes seemed interminable to Legay, who opened the door four times thinking he heard footsteps on the staircase. Finally she arrived, pretty enough to eat in spite of her anxious air. Legay was smoking a cigarette which she could see trembling at the corner of his mouth. "What is this letter?" she said, knowing well that it could only be a letter from Roberti. "Here," he said, holding out the envelope. She began to read. Legay watched her, thinking: "By now she has reached this bit, by now that one. What effect can all this filth be having on her?" She was visibly turning pale. Her hand was trembling like his lip. She was standing, breathing heavily. After reading to the bottom of the second page she dropped the letter to the floor and slowly raised her eyes to her fiancé. "Is all that true?" he asked. "Yes," she replied. He was expecting this "yes," but for all that took it like a body blow. At the last moment he had hoped she would lie to him. "You must find me repulsive," she added. "If you want to break off our engagement I shall quite understand. I'd even go so far as to suggest it. You won't be obliged to recognize the child." She was dry-eyed. Not a tear. Nothing.

A most unexpected phenomenon then occurred. Legay dropped into a chair and began to sob. He hadn't wept since he was a child. Big, warm, salt tears, the painful tears of a man, squeezed with great difficulty from his eyes and rolled down his cheeks. He chewed at his knuckles and beat himself with his fists. He stammered incoherent words of some unknown origin which was certainly not his mind: "No, no, it's not possible. It's too frightful. You, Solange, no. I can't believe it." In short a real fit of hysterics brought on by the sight of Solange and by her brief comments. He had all at once been rent by the old, primitive despair of the cuckold, resenting the infidelity of his female as a mortal insult to his own flesh. Added to which he was crushed by the idea that Solange was prepared to leave him, that he only had to say the word for him never to see her again. It was terrifying to be thus master of one's fate. He wanted to be immediately consoled by the girl who was making him suffer so deeply. He felt small, weak and childish; he needed to be welcomed into the beautiful arms he loved so much, to be reassured by them, rocked by them. He wanted to hear words of gentleness and compassion. He wanted to be pitied and given fine reasons for happiness to come. At this moment Solange was more than a fiancée; she was the mother who had first caused pain and was then going to bring comfort. Through his tears he half glimpsed an all-powerful mother figure, at once terrible and eager to help, toward whom every part of him yearned. In Solange were peace, warmth, love, self-abnegation. He needed this constant presence to stand between himself and the world. He had never felt so reduced to nothing and, I believe, so happy to be so. "Don't leave me," he gabbled. "I love you. I need you. And you need me too." He was ready to commit any act of cowardice. Had it been necessary he would have groveled at her feet.

This natural reaction to pain, this lack of pride, this love, caused Solange an emotion more intellectual than sentimental, if I may so express it. She was more touched than perturbed. She admired Legay's pain as one does some beautiful vision or noble action; it flattered and saddened her but she didn't share it. Nevertheless she knelt down beside him, took his hand and pressed it to her lips. As if she had guessed the kind of comfort he was seeking, she began talking to him like a mother. She even went so far as to say those foolish things one says to a deeply unhappy child. Legay's weeping soon became more bearable; he laid his cheek against Solange's hair and put his arms round her. Little by little his pain subsided, giving way to gratitude and certainty. He was so preoccupied with himself that he failed to notice that Solange was distant and inattentive. Indeed, she was thinking primarily about Roberti. She was filled with hate. It never occurred to her that his sending an anonymous letter was a disclosure of insane love. All she saw in it was revenge. "God, to think he's come to this!" she thought. "And he claimed to love me!" This cheap and even stupid reasoning led to reflections which immersed her in a great sorrow of the spirit, to the effect that the world is fundamentally base and ignoble, that men are vile and all one can expect from any of them is deceit, humiliation and every kind of heartbreak. Here we lay our finger on what most people call *experience*. They say the world is a terrible place, they play at skepticism, disillusionment and pessimism without ever suspecting that their misfortunes spring entirely from their own cowardice or foolishness. For six months Solange had behaved foolishly and cowardly in her relations with Roberti, but she never thought of it that way; she was just a victim.

"Listen," she said to Legay. "I'll tell you the whole story. It's important for you to know what really happened. I met this man three years ago. I loved him. I don't love him any more. He fills me with horror." She opened her bag and took out a stamped envelope. "Look," she went on, "read this. From now on I don't want to have any more secrets from you." Legay glanced at the sheet of paper she was holding out to him and which began: "Edouard I shall never see you again. . . ." He read no further. It was the letter she had at last decided to write, breaking it off. "Take it," she said. "Go and deliver it yourself to the address on the envelope. We shall never hear of him again. I feel I don't even know any longer who he is. It's as if he had never existed." Legay got up from the chair in which he was still limply sitting. Desire had suddenly swamped every other emotion. He took Solange in his arms, held her close and kissed her fiercely on the mouth; he breathed in her scent, he caressed her, he no longer knew what he was doing. This whole scene had aroused her as well, so that she was soon responding to his advances with equal impetuosity. I suppose it could hardly have turned out otherwise. One might say that destiny is never lacking in irony. Poor Roberti never suspected that by sending Legay this anonymous letter he was at last establishing his rival's happiness on solid foundations. By ten that morning victory was chanting in Legay's heart. He didn't yet feel himself Solange's master but he had no more fear of her. He was her equal. He could read this equality in his fiancée's looks and gestures; he could tell it from the new sound in her voice. For the first time she had lost that faintly superior, faintly indulgent affection which intimidated him and was showing something akin to surprise and love. And he himself, who had believed no one could love more than he did, discovered that this love was prodigiously enriched. Quite calmly, perhaps to prove the power he had just acquired, he said: "We can't keep Valentin in the dark any longer. I'll go and tell him the news of our marriage this afternoon."—"Do you really want to?" asked Solange. "Yes," said Legay. "Then do so," she said with a good-humored smile, "but even so, wait till tomorrow. You don't know him. As soon as he learns we're getting married he'll be unbearable. He'll say 'I told you so' a thousand times. He'll want to come out with us. He'll give us presents. He'll go round singing all day. Give me twenty-four hours to prepare for the hurricane!" Legay was so happy that, forgetting the pain that had been racking him only an hour before, he exclaimed: "Super!" like a true boy scout. To wipe out all traces of the past he proposed that they should burn the anonymous letter. But there were no matches. He had used up the last one in the box to light the cigarette Solange had seen trembling between his lips. She took a little lighter from her bag (one of those little lighters that never work) and flicked it several times unsuccessfully; the flint was worn out. On what little things do great events hang! This anonymous letter which played such a part in Roberti's trial might easily have been destroyed but it wasn't, because the matchbox was empty and the lighter flint worn out. Had his sister not requested twenty-four hours' respite with a good-humored smile, Valentin would have escaped his fate. "I've an idea," said Solange. She picked the pages of the anonymous letter off the floor with her fingertips, put them back in the envelope and slipped this into the envelope containing her own letter to Roberti. After which, since it was Saturday and there was nothing to keep them in Paris, the pair of them decided to go and have lunch at Chartres and admire the cathedral. The weather was more clement than the day before. February sometimes brings us fine days, cold but cloudless, lit by a wintry sun which is by no means unpleasant. Not to mention that Legay was avid for every opportunity to use his car. On their way they made a detour via the Rue Oudinot. It must have been ten-thirty. More through lack of imagination than bravado, Legay stopped his car right outside the building where Solange's lover lived. It was he who handed the letter to the concierge. Solange stayed in the car, keeping her eyes grimly lowered. By eleven they were doing seventy along the motorway to the west, gay and lighthearted as people who have settled all their debts and see a limpid future ahead. They never guessed what would be awaiting them on their return six or seven hours later.

I: This time I've let you talk so long I hardly dare interrupt. I've almost forgotten the sound of my own voice.

HE: Well, that's a triumph! Are you sure you weren't asleep part of the time?

I: No, I was never asleep. On the contrary, while listening my mind was constantly traversed by images, a proof that you were telling your story well. I saw Roberti in his study as if I were there myself. I saw him in the Boulevard des Invalides, standing in the middle of the road, his half-buttoned coat billowing in the wind. I even wondered if he was wearing a hat and, if so, what kind.

HE: Yes, he was wearing one. A pearl-gray hat with an upturned brim. A rather sober, rather outmoded but very smart kind of hat. He wore it tilted back and slightly to one side, to make himself look younger. It suited him very well. On the day he went to the Boulevard des Invalides to get run over by a truck, he had his hat tilted as jauntily as ever. I even believe that, as he left the apartment, he glanced in the hall mirror to make sure that nothing in his appearance was out of place, that he was as good-looking as usual.

I: I also had a very clear vision of Solange and Legay and I thought how by sending them his anonymous letter Roberti had dragged them down into his own hell, into his own private horror. They were now tarnished forever. The contamination of evil is an interesting subject for study. The torturer doesn't corrupt only his accomplices but also his victim. The evil he does forces its way into the latter and remains there. The victim ends by resembling his torturer. The wicked, by tyrannizing the weak, teach them to be wicked in turn. Such is the general way of the world, particularly with the petty bourgeoisie.

HE: True, but there are exceptions. Sometimes the victim is stronger than the torturer and good triumphs over evil. Sometimes he is insensitive. There exist certain natures over which horror flows like water, not because they are very pure or simple but because they are inconsistent. These persons suffer at one moment, then shake themselves, shrug it off and forget. There is a grace of the Devil, I dare say, which is as rare as the grace of God. Evil also has its elect. I don't see Legay and Solange having souls profound enough to be wrecked in any permanent fashion by Roberti. Look how, barely an hour after having swallowed the ignominies of the anonymous letter, they set off singing in their secondhand car to lunch at Chartres. Legay was making adoring eyes at his fiancée. They had already relegated everything to the past; they were thinking only of themselves, of their little happiness, their little future, their little apartment, their little child. I am sure that today, now that all is over, they never even refer to the whole business. Roberti, dead and buried, no longer weighs at all on their hearts. In three years the horror has blurred and faded out of sight. Why do I say three years? After three weeks, after three hours, it had already ceased to exist. Had there been no trial, with all the stir it made, they would have married at the beginning of March 1958 with the carefree hearts of adolescents. If you want my opinion, I find it even more horrible that way. Wretches like Roberti, touched by evil too late in life, so that they have not acquired from childhood the habit of it and ability to guide it to selfish ends, to administer it wisely so to speak—these wretches are doomed to a terrible solitude. The world erects walls around them which they can never surmount and against which they batter in vain. They rarely have the consolation of sharing the evil that inhabits them with others. They do evil, of course, they precipitate disasters, they sow ruin about them; but this evil is as securely locked up inside them as a snake in a box. In their way they are as lonely as the saints. As misunderstood. No one suspects the weight of the burden of doubts, regrets, anguish and fears they bear.

ɪ: Look, I'm going to ask you something that will show how well I've been listening. You say the anonymous letter played a large part in Roberti's trial. How can this be, since Solange returned it to him? Didn't he tear it up when it came back into his possession?

ʜᴇ: No, he didn't. He read Solange's letter with a sort of agonized delight. It was a very brief and terse letter which said in so many words: "This time it's really over." She made no reference to the anonymous letter, since she had written her own note before she knew about it. Roberti was moved to tears to see her handwriting. This sheet of paper addressed to him seemed very precious. It was the last letter he would ever receive from her. He must keep it. He was moved, too, by the fact that his mistress had returned his anonymous letter without a word of condemnation. Into this act he read more magnanimity than contempt. Without a word she was handing him back this weapon he had given her to use against him. He locked the whole thing away in a drawer of his desk, thinking: "I'll keep it for a few days, then I'll burn it."

ɪ: I can understand his keeping Solange's note, but why the anonymous letter? It seems inexplicable.

ʜᴇ: No, it isn't really. He wanted to read it again later on, after a couple of days perhaps, calmly and objectively. You have perhaps noticed that I often use the words "tender" or "tenderness" to define Roberti's thoughts where Solange was concerned. Well, this anonymous letter he had written in order to do her harm moved him to tenderness in so far as it had to do with her. He was giving himself a respite before burning it because he knew that when he came to reread it he would be moved more to tenderness than shame. There is something sad and sweet in the sight of the evil one has done to a person one loves and who has loved one in return; it brings delight to certain dark souls.

ɪ: I myself would say "certain black souls."

ʜᴇ: In short he never took the anonymous letter out of its envelope, which was postmarked. When the examining magistrate went through his papers he came across this envelope, which proved that the letter had been posted. Unfortunately he was a young magistrate who was keen at his job. Instead of suppressing this piece of evidence, which offered no additional proof of Roberti's crime but merely blackened the poor man further and covered Solange with mud, he exhibited it triumphantly at the trial.

Before I go on with my account of this Saturday, which proved such a fatal one in Roberti's life and in which, as you will see, events proceeded as inexorably as in a classical tragedy, not forgetting the unities of time and action, I have to go back a little. About three weeks or a month. Among Edouard's other misfortunes there was one I forgot to mention: two of the companies which employed him as legal adviser had dispensed with his services. This had been done very suavely, since one doesn't fire a deputy like any common employee. The task was allotted to no less than the presidents of the respective companies; these, with a few days between them, had explained in almost the same terms and with identical sighs how business was no longer what it used to be, how they were faced with the regrettable but imperative need to abolish certain posts, how they had hesitated a long time before tackling M. Roberti's but that this was no moment, alas, for half measures. Edouard had faced this blow with resignation and even a certain nobility of bearing, due to the indifference he felt toward everything unconnected with love. Not without a hint of complacency he watched his life crumbling about his ears. "How far will I let things slide?" he wondered curiously. He had no desire to react. He needed more ruins still. Anyway, the situation was by no means critical. There remained his third company and his parliamentary salary, which still amounted to quite a handsome income in spite of all the expenses a deputy has to incur. He had already been through similar stretches of bad luck and inertia in the past, when nothing mattered to him, when he was like a man knocked to the ground, waiting supinely for further blows to fall. Then all at once, after being thoroughly trampled on by fate, he had sprung to his feet again, energy and ambition had surged back into his heart, he had thrown himself into his work, luck had returned and in three months he had achieved a magnificent comeback. In February 1958 he was at a very low ebb but it was of no importance; he must descend several stages further into spiritual poverty and adversity; he must eat his fill of them to the point of nausea, advance to the outer limits of self-disgust. When he reached the uttermost depths of his abasement, everything would suddenly brighten. The Roberti of

yore would be reborn from his ashes. Two companies lost? Ten regained! All he need do was make a few phone calls. He would make
them next week. Or the week after. Just a little more rest! I am only
outlining all this, but you can fill in the details. You can also see the
causes. The price middle-aged men pay for love!

I: Happily it isn't always so costly and, for their salvation, all middle-
aged men are not as rational as Roberti. I know several far more im-
prudent than he, and their follies have been far less grievous.

HE: Well, yes. Not everyone can be Faust. I still wonder why he was
chosen; why, from out of a hundred thousand or a hundred million
middle-aged men it was he who was marked by the grace of Satan. He
was really crushed by this black grace, as unpredictable and heavy to
bear as that other one which is the reverse of Satan's, the positive as
opposed to the negative, so to speak. Why Faust? Why Roberti? Why
those two souls, when at the time of their passage on earth there were
so many others far more deserving of the Devil's attentions? It was
they, these two wise men, whom he wanted. I suppose madmen don't
amuse him. The impressive and frightening thing about it, at any rate,
is to see what a pressing creditor the Devil is, what a hurry he is in to
collect his debts. He gave Faust thirty years of youth, if my memory is
correct. These thirty years were stipulated in the contract but it only
took poor Faust six months before he found himself simmering for all
eternity in the cauldron. To sell one's soul for six months' fun is
scarcely a "proposition," as young businessmen say nowadays. All the
more in that the fun was very relative. During these six months Faust
carried on like an irresponsible young provincial. Instead of offering him
evil in all its splendor and profundity, Mephisto merely gave him the
briefest, most elusive, linear, flat and colorless summary of it. Roberti,
in his way, put up a better defense. He held out for three years. He
even came close to pulling through and doing Mephisto down. Until
that fatal Saturday in February when Mephisto served his writ for non-
payment. Have you noticed how Saturday is an unlucky day?

I: Yes, I have. It's always on Saturdays that disaster descends on me:
the car breaks down and all the garages are shut; one of the children
wakes up with bronchitis and all the doctors are away for the weekend;
and it's unfailingly on Saturdays that my bank writes me that I've over-
drawn my account. All the same, I don't see the Devil's hand in these
little annoyances.

HE: You must admit, however, that there is something odd about this
way fate has of plaguing one on Saturdays in preference to the other
days of the week. On Saturdays the witches go to screech on the

Brocken and fornicate with goats. The Jews, who are a race full of prudence and foresight, didn't just chance to pick Saturday as the day on which to stop life completely and devote themselves to fasting, inactivity and purification: these are the measures they take against the Devil; they leave him nothing into which to hook his claws. A scorched-earth policy, in a way.

I: That's enough. We're back in the realms of imagination. Let's strike a bargain. You describe this *tragic Saturday* to me right through without a break, leaving the Devil in peace, and I won't interrupt you any more. Is it a deal?

HE: It's a deal.

I: After which, we'll go and have our onion soup at the Halles. I'm beginning to be in a state of bodily misery. Will it take long?

HE: Fifteen minutes. It all speeds up.

I: On, then. Haven't you wings? Your long story is nearing its end.

HE: Ah, don't be impatient, I beg of you.

I: *I* impatient? I've never heard the like. Get on with it!

HE: That Saturday Roberti had received in the morning mail an extremely disturbing letter from his third company in which the duly appointed president proposed a meeting for "a friendly discussion." Whereas Edouard went out of his way to be a dupe of his sentiments, he was by no means deceived as to the meaning of these words. He understood perfectly what such a term implied, namely that he was shortly going to lose this third source of income and would then be reduced to his parliamentary salary pure and simple. As I believe I told you, he was due to go to the Assembly. The sitting was to begin at eleven-thirty. Before setting out he had withdrawn into his study. It was in fact his habit to shut himself up there when he had some problem, not so much to brood on his troubles and try to find remedies for them as to digest them, measure their full extent, taste their bitter savor to the full. Savoring a misfortune has the added advantage of giving one a moment's respite before going into battle against it. As a rule, moreover, he found being alone rather helpful in such instances. By flexing his muscles in this way, where no one could watch him, surrounded by his familiar furniture, he would gradually win back his confidence, find his feet. The gloomy forebodings with which he set out would soon blossom into various projects; most of these were chimerical but one or two would be based on sound good sense. Some people, when faced with an anxious problem, lie down. They undress. They get into bed and remain there for twenty-four hours with the curtains drawn. It's not such a bad method, even if it does look a bit absurd to an outsider.

After twenty-four hours they get up, their minds clear and ready to do battle, ready to put up a courageous front against the hostility of the world. Roberti was following rather the same course when he shut himself up in his study to suffer at leisure.

One might think that after the day he had just spent and the painful night following it, this president's letter would have finally laid him low. Quite the reverse. After due consideration this latest trial almost cheered him. It seemed to be bringing back that *hope* which had deserted him for so long. Since about September he had been groping his way down a long dark corridor, like those in which one sometimes loses oneself in nightmares. And now, unexpectedly, a distant glimmer of light was announcing the end of the tunnel. Who could tell? Perhaps this letter in the Saturday mail was a punishment sent him by heaven for having written an anonymous letter the day before. For several minutes he had an illusory impression of redemption. I don't really know how to explain this sudden gust of superstition in a Radical Socialist's soul, but it is a fact that for a brief moment Roberti told himself he was paying for the foul deed he had performed and that he was paying in cash, that his debt was being canceled. This notion suddenly took firm root in his mind shortly after, when he saw his anonymous letter returned by Solange.

Legay had delivered his missive at ten-thirty. Ten minutes later, Germaine handed it to Roberti. The old servant had a particularly ugly look on her face that day. So ugly that Edouard, for all that he was so used to it, couldn't help commenting on it to himself. "The concierge brought this up for Monsieur," she said. "Seems it's urgent." With a hideous leer she added: "Perhaps it's an invite to lunch from the President of the Republic?" As he looked at her Roberti thought: "This woman has such a shifty glint in her eye and so evil a grin that it can't possibly have the slightest significance; otherwise she'd be a monster!" As you see, his reason was misleading him in even the most trivial matters. He was hopelessly weak in the face of this domestic viper and, driven by some strange timidity, never dared not to share in her jokes. With forced good humor he replied: "If this is the President inviting me to lunch, I shall stuff my pockets with cakes on the sly and bring them back to you, my dear Germaine."—"He-he," tittered Germaine. "Monsieur's having fun with me; deputies don't come like that any more. If they were all like Monsieur in the government, things'd be going a bit better, you mark my words!" As she withdrew, Roberti thought: "She's got an ugly mug but at heart she's a good soul. And she's very devoted. One should certainly never go by appearances." Inquisitive and malevolent as she was, Germaine hadn't failed to notice how Edouard had been looking very worried for some time. She kept watch on him from her kitchen, the way a crow perched in a tree watches a soldier in his death throes on the battlefield. Her instinct, her antennae—something, at any rate—told her that her employer was doomed. She was no longer in a hurry. The details of his last agony fascinated her; she was hoping this spectacle would last for several more weeks.

As Roberti read Solange's letter of rupture, trying to suppress the racing of his heart and the trembling of his legs beneath his chair, the hope that the president's letter had brought him grew stronger. Nothing more unpleasant could happen to him now except the loss of his seat in the Chamber, which was impossible. He reviewed the situation as a whole and came to the age-old conclusion that man's place in the world is indeed precarious: one believes oneself secure for life; with mighty efforts one surrounds oneself with ramparts against adversity; one achieves, if not happiness, at least tranquillity; then all at once the walls crumble about one in three weeks and one finds oneself again exposed to the slings and arrows of life, just as when one was twenty and with all the vulnerability of that age. A man can never count on anything; no society or position has such firm foundations that it doesn't quake beneath his feet, perpetually at the mercy of some mishap or rash impulse. Roberti was now without love and without money. He was completely cleaned out. It followed that at this point his misfortunes must cease. He had nothing left to be taken away from him. He was filled with the gaiety and pride of a man who has lost everything. Destiny was being so relentless that it was becoming grotesque. It was unbelievable. It was funny. Some people have fits of depression or joy; he, Roberti, on reviewing his misfortunes, had *a fit of irony*. He rose from his desk, crossed over to a big Venetian mirror hanging over the mantelpiece and stuck out his tongue at himself. This childish gesture made him smile. He shrugged his shoulders and murmured rather fondly (since momentarily he felt a return of his old affection for himself): "Get along with you, you poor old nut!" Following which he paced up and down for five minutes. "Well," he declared to the walls of his study, "I've still got myself. That's quite enough!" He was going to be unhappy and have money problems. So what? Two hundred of his colleagues managed to live well enough on their parliamentary salaries: he would do likewise until he had found other resources, which wouldn't take him long. As for being lovesick, did it even amount to that? Logically, when abandoned by a woman one has never loved, one oughtn't to feel anything more than resentment. "Am I really lovesick?" he wondered quite seriously. Suddenly the thought that he would never see Solange again, never touch her again, never live again in the mind of this woman, swept over him like a physical pain briefly forgotten and now returning. He had a presentiment as to his future but this, as is always the way, appeared to him in an allegorical form. He thought how he was going to be shut up in an inner prison, in a cell where he would be all alone, all alone in the dark, tirelessly trying to fight down a boundless grief. Destiny was condemning him to solitary confinement. Solange was freedom, sunlight, joy, and from this instant he was going to be deprived of joy and sunlight until a new order of release. He was entering a dungeon like the Count of Monte Cristo. He felt the despair of a man of twenty, full of energy and ambition, eager to explore the world and make love to women, who is left in chains in the depths of a prison. This was so painful that he instantly summoned up all his faculties of daydreaming and self-deception. He must at all costs explain and justify this pain out of all proportion with reality, for once a pain is explained, once its causes are made visible, once it is thus isolated like a chemical element, it loses its sharp point and becomes a matter for intellectual speculation. "I love Solange," he thought fervently. "I love her today for the first time in my life. For three years she was my mistress and I didn't love her. Now that she's my mistress no longer, I love her. That's exactly like me! My lucky star is watching over me. I wasn't in love when it could have been dangerous. I am when it ceases to be so." Lovesickness can be organized and savored. He would first wrap himself up in it like a cocoon; he would abandon himself to the joys of daydreaming and woolgathering—they are sweeter than we think—he would cradle his poor heart, he would pamper it like an invalid, he would tell it beautiful improbable stories. He knew what lovesickness was. He had experienced it in the past and he was so intelligent that he had learned how to extract its delicious sweetness. He reckoned that in three months' time he would begin to destroy the image of Solange he carried within him, begin to erase it, abolish it, deprive it of the painful reality with which it was charged. This latter would take a further three months. And the process, too, would not be without charm. It would be like a slow assassination within him; there would be interesting ups and downs; the dying image would often revive at unexpected moments. Ah, his heart had not yet ceased to beat; and he had not yet finished with being young for, be he old as a patriarch, lovesickness brings its sufferer a feeling of perennial youth. In the end, after six months or maybe a year, he would alas no longer be in love. It would be most depressing. Unhappiness in love is almost as poignant when it ends as when it begins. One is left at last alone with oneself, with one's old age, with one's drab selfishness. The world again becomes real and gray. When Roberti had ceased to love Solange he would no longer think of her as a hearth always ablaze with happiness, as the one being capable of diverting his body and soul; she would be just like anyone else, like the hundreds of people he knew who meant nothing to him. He would no longer even feel any desire for her. He would have a clear picture of this nondescript narrow-minded girl with her lack of conversation, her absurd aspirations, just as she had always in fact been, and he would be astonished to think he had been unhappy on account of *this*, that he had loved *this* to the point of wanting to kill himself and writing an anonymous letter. Meanwhile there was nothing else to be done but bury his feelings in the deepest part of himself, confine them closely inside him where they would wilt for lack of that dangerous sustenance known as confidences. In any case, everything connected with love, including unhappiness, only really overwhelms the heart when buried in the deepest secrecy. "In the long run," thought Edouard, "it's better this way. I've lost a few feathers. But feathers grow again. The end of another adventure no one will ever know about. I shall become a minister. Everyone will be properly had!"

1: You know, if you were kind you would stop the lamentable story of poor Roberti and the fair Solange here. We'd get up off this iron seat, which incidentally is beginning to make my behind ache, take a taxi and be off. After all, why shouldn't Roberti's story end relatively well, that is to say without a major drama, like most human stories? Be generous! Give me a happy ending. He isn't mad; he wraps himself up in his unhappiness for six months, he breathes no word of it to anybody, Solange burns all his letters (a great loss for the literature of letter writing) and marries Legay, Valentin eats like a pig at the wedding and gives himself the worst indigestion of his life. He'll be the child's godfather. The Mignot parents buy a stuccoed house at Viroflay or Gournay-sur-Marne with their savings. Why, I'll take it further than that; Roberti becomes Under-Secretary of State without portfolio in Tiddlypush's cabinet which lasts one week, as a result of which he can be addressed as "Monsieur le Ministre" for the rest of his life. On the thirteenth of May, 1958, on the collapse of the regime, he backs the wrong horse, that is to say he parades outside the Bastille with Mendès and the simpletons of the progressive left wing, so that at the November elections he is blackballed. But this isn't serious: his three companies have signed him on again and he lands a seat in the Senate. At

Easter 1959 he organizes a cruise to Greece with Agnes, who spends the happiest month of her life there. His eldest son passes his exams with merit. Three years later he meets Solange by chance in the street. She is no longer so elegant, nor quite so pretty. She comes up to him with a beaming smile. He is touched. He invites her out to tea. She refuses because she has promised the children (she has two now, a boy and a girl) that she will be home early. They walk along together for a few minutes. With a sigh she says: "How far away it all seems." He lets his gaze slide toward her neck. He sees there a tiny wrinkle and a rather stiff curl of hair. He is moved to tenderness. They part. Roberti has vague yearnings. He allows himself fifteen minutes' daydreaming. He ends by telling himself: "She's become very commonplace." Whereupon he goes into Hermès and buys his wife a new handbag.

HE: I wouldn't call that a happy ending but I'd have been quite content with it. Unfortunately events didn't turn out that way. When Roberti left for the Assembly at eleven, fate had already been advancing to meet him for the past half hour. At five past eleven—do you hear?—at five past eleven, that is to say five minutes after his departure, it rang his doorbell. Germaine had gone out shopping. Agnes was alone in the apartment. It was she who opened the door. She found herself face to face with a burly, red-complexioned young man who looked at once embarrassed and furious.

I: Valentin?

HE: Of course. He had concocted the following plan: he would turn up unexpectedly at Roberti's apartment, catch him unawares and fell him at one blow with: "I am the brother of Mlle. Mignot, on whom you have been bringing dishonor for the past three years; you a married man, a father, a deputy who ought to set a good example. It's disgraceful. It has got to stop. If you haven't broken with my sister within forty-eight hours, I will inform your wife and tell the whole story to the newspapers. There'll be a scandal and you'll have brought it on your own head." He had worked out this speech at leisure, polished it, learned it by heart and repeated it to himself several times over in the Métro. It seemed to him a bit abrupt but it covered all the facts and was unanswerable. He would deliver it with the impressive and saturnine air of a man with responsibilities. To reinforce his blackmail he had even stolen two of Roberti's letters from Solange's cupboard and had these tucked away in his wallet. What is remarkable is that this little man without social substance, moral strength, tact or even experience never had a moment's doubt or misgiving once his plan was made. He was not a bit afraid of attacking a high and mighty member of the administration. He had taken up the cross in a righteous cause. He was in the mood of a Roman gentleman four hundred years ago, going out to fight a duel. He hated his enemy. He never wished to meet him in his path again.

He had set out at ten-thirty. He had taken the Métro at the Michel-Bizot station a hundred yards from his home. On Saturday mornings the trains are less frequent than usual. As he reached the platform the last one had just left; he had to wait several minutes for the next. The same thing happened at the Daumesnil station, where he had to change, and the same at Montparnasse. If he hadn't wasted a total of ten minutes in these various stations he would have arrived at the Rue Oudinot at ten fifty-five and seen Roberti himself, who would have replied to him: "My good sir, your sister has given me the boot and is preparing to marry a certain M. Legay, who has put her in the family way."

Agnes assumed that this was one of Edouard's constituents, who not infrequently called in this way, so she adopted a cordial expression, for constituents are sacred. "I've come to see M. Roberti," said Valentin in menacing tones. "He's at the Assembly," said Agnes. "Can I give him a message?"—"It's personal," said Valentin. "I have to see M. Roberti on a matter of great urgency. In his own interests and in those of someone else." He was so agitated and frowning in such a forbidding way that Agnes felt quite alarmed. She debated whether to shut the door in his face but had an intuition that this man was threatening to harm her husband and thought it would be useful to discover what his grievance against Edouard could be. Bravely she bade him come in. I say bravely, for instinctively she felt that her visitor's heart was full of hatred and this made her falter. "You can talk to me in complete confidence," she told him. "I am Mme. Roberti." Valentin was disconcerted. He hadn't anticipated such an eventuality. He had nothing to say to Roberti's wife. Quite the reverse: for her he felt something more akin to pity and he found her sympathetic. He remained silent and morose, his arms dangling. He was a good fellow at heart; he had never really thought of putting Agnes wise except as a last resort, if there should be no other alternative.

Confronted with Valentin's embarrassment, Agnes recovered her poise and felt an avid curiosity. Valentin stood up for himself as best he could. Awkwardly he declared: "I don't want to disturb you. I'll call again. I'll see M. Roberti another day. After all it can wait twenty-four hours. I'll telephone him to fix an appointment. Excuse me, I have to be going now." He had come as an outraged brother, as a judge, as a protector; he had sharpened his weapons in order to cleave a formidable adversary and now all he found facing him was a weak woman, even more to be pitied than he, and a woman who was moreover on his side although she didn't know it. But these evasions didn't suit Agnes at all, now she saw that she had the upper hand. She came from Bordeaux, as you know; she had Gascon blood. She was at once sensitive, prudent and courageous. Valentin's awkward and clumsy attempts to beat a retreat goaded her into a warlike mood. She wanted to harry him and emerge victorious by extorting his secret. They were both standing in the hall, since Valentin refused to penetrate farther into the apartment or sit down, while Agnes plied him with questions in a social tone of voice: "You are one of my husband's constituents, aren't you?" No, Valentin wasn't a constituent properly speaking: he lived in the Twelfth Arrondissement, at the far end of the Avenue Daumesnil. What was his name? M. Mignot. It would be enough to mention this name to M. Roberti, who would understand. But if M. Mignot wasn't a constituent, perhaps he hadn't called about political matters? No he hadn't: M. Mignot had strictly personal matters to discuss with M. Roberti. M. Roberti has no secrets from his wife, Monsieur: everything that concerns him concerns her as well, and so on. This exchange of skillful questions and embarrassed answers lasted five minutes. Pitted against a woman like Agnes, alert, tenacious, more intelligent and experienced than he, Valentin was helpless. His only salvation would have been in ill-mannered flight. But intimidated as he was, vexed, feeling guilty and lacking in any social graces, he dared not flee. Four minutes of this torture led to the inevitable result with a character like his: his smoldering anger burst out afresh and he began to answer back bluntly. The pity and sympathy Agnes had at first inspired in him evaporated. What was she in fact to him—this woman questioning him so recklessly, needling him with her superior smile and making sport with his pain? An indifferent stranger, someone for whom he wasn't *responsible*. For all her quick temper she would certainly side with her husband against the poor Mignots in the event of a showdown. All of a sudden it seemed to Valentin that he was coming out of a trance: he had allowed himself to weaken; he had almost betrayed his cause and, if not gone over to the enemy, at least fraternized with its advance guard. His sixteenth-century outlook returned in full strength. In a final effort to save Agnes he said in a voice so cutting that this unhappy woman's heart stopped beating for three seconds: "You're making a grave mistake interrogating me like this, Madame; I could tell you things you would spend the rest of your life wishing you had never heard."—"I have nothing to fear," retorted Agnes. "If you have some complaint against my husband, you can tell it to me. It can only be a misunderstanding or a mistake. My husband is a very good and generous man, Monsieur, who has never wronged anyone. If he has wronged you, it was certainly unintentional." Almost anyone would have been touched by these words. Not so Valentin. He was tingling with rage down to his fingertips. I don't know what idiotic ideas didn't possess his mind: how no member of his enemy's clan was to be trusted, how this was not the moment for tact, how this woman was false and devious like all her kind. Who could tell? Perhaps she was "in cahoots" and was trying to get round him. Coldly he declared: "Do you really want me to tell you what I have against M. Roberti? Think carefully. Are you quite sure? I warn you, it's no joke. Especially not for you." Agnes was tempted to cry out: "No, I don't want to know anything, go away!" Then curiosity got the better of her, as in the story of Bluebeard. She no longer felt in any way superior to this lout. She was gripped in a vise. She was fascinated. She had a foreboding of the horrors she was about to hear. Valentin's fat, furious and crimson face appeared to her like a harbinger of disaster. She realized that twenty-four years of happiness were coming to an end at this moment and that she had been waiting for this unknown visitor all her life.

Like most narrow-minded people, Valentin saw none of this. When in the grip of a passion he never looked either inside or around him. He was wholly taken up with the successive emotions racing through him: desire, rage, relief, etc. Agnes' agitation completely escaped him. "Since she wants it," he thought, "I'll let her have it. She won't be able to say I didn't warn her. I'll tell her the lot. After all, what do I care about this woman? She's not one of my family. It's not for me to worry. She should've known how to keep her dear husband. Why, that's true! What has happened is all her fault. It'll teach her to be more careful next time." I am giving you his reasoning in some detail since it perfectly illustrates the *weak* moral outlook of fools, who believe in all good faith that in certain circumstances *one has the right* to behave badly. Moreover Valentin was filled with family patriotism, that is to say he didn't feel called on to show any consideration for people who didn't share his blood or, to use an old-fashioned term, were "not of his tribe." The attitude of a man of the past, perhaps, from the days when each family formed a little world of its own entrenched in a Roman palace, at war or in league with other families; but also the attitude of a poor young man with a narrow mind, a primitive heart and no knowledge of the world. Family patriotism, like all patriotism, makes people pitiless and blind. In a few furious sentences Valentin described the affair between Edouard and Solange. He never noticed Agnes turn deathly pale or that she was on the verge of fainting. His expression was so sincere and above all so incongruous that she never for a moment doubted what he was saying. As he spoke she had the impression of watching a play she had already seen, but this didn't prevent her from suffering horribly and in a number of ways, compounded of betrayed love, misplaced trust, disgust, disappointment and fury. Nothing in the world from now on could prevent her knowing that her husband had miserably deceived her with a typist; this would exist for all eternity. She also told herself: "At this moment I am being dealt a series of blows. Presently I shall begin really to suffer and it will be atrocious. My whole life is collapsing. I have lived twenty-four years for nothing." Valentin's account doubtless didn't take more than a few minutes. Agnes heard him through without a single interruption. When he had finished, she closed her eyes for a moment and murmured: "I won't keep you, Monsieur. You should never have told me what you have just done. I hope that one day you will forgive yourself for it." Valentin was stunned; idiotically he cried: "But you wouldn't stop pestering me to tell you. This is really the limit! The way you talk, anyone would think I was the guilty one."—"That's enough," said Agnes. "Go. I can't stand the sight of you." Her features were so convulsed that, in spite of his thick skin, Valentin was impressed. He didn't feel so much ashamed as abashed. Nevertheless his lingering anger prevented him from feeling any remorse. Hell! One can't wage war without bombarding a number of innocent people. He had at any rate fulfilled his mission and M. Roberti would from now on be kept busy enough at home to prevent him from any further dealings with Solange. Incidentally, where could she be? Out philandering with her old man, no doubt, who had told his wife he was at the Assembly. Saturday is the day for lovers. When she came home that evening she would receive a rather nasty surprise! Valentin had a pang of misgiving at the thought of confronting his sister. When she learned what he had done she would fly at him like a tigress. At the thought of this his anger blazed up afresh, the more so in that he wasn't feeling any too proud of himself. It is through anger and violence that fools try to compensate for the inadequacy of their principles and to justify their evil deeds after the event. And why not? There are occasions when one has to force destiny's hand. He couldn't be on worse terms with Solange than he was already. He told himself that he had at least "cleared the ground." Now he was going to be able quietly to set about the major problem of his sister's marriage to his friend. Later she'd "thank him for it." On leaving the Rue Oudinot he felt a need to see Legay, for whom he had just done such determined battle. He went round to his studio but there was nobody at home. Legay was gaily speeding over the wide plain of Beauce. He was happy because Solange had laid her head on his shoulder: for him this gesture was the symbol of intimacy. Disappointed, Valentin returned to the Avenue Daumesnil, where his parents were waiting for him to start lunch. I can even add that Mother Mignot was serving roast veal.

I: How do you know that? You're making it up. You've this minute invented the roast veal to make fun of these poor folk. I know how you are!

HE: I haven't invented a thing. At the trial Mother Mignot herself said in the witness box how she had roasted some veal for lunch that day. Moreover the way she said it was rather touching. There was something extraordinarily naïve about it. Such a domestic detail, coming in the middle of her clumsy and terrible testimony, raised not a single laugh.

After Valentin's departure, Agnes began to tremble. She told me this herself. Not in the way one trembles after some emotional upset, that is lightly, with occasional starts which soon subside, but like someone with locomotor ataxia. Her whole body twitched convulsively. She was forty-six years old. At that age women have a far more brittle sensibility than when they are young. Even the sturdiest, the staidest of them give the impression of being at the mercy of a harsh word. It is as if they were never completely tranquil, as if their instinct slept with one eye open like a cat or a hare, quivering at the slightest and most distant sound of doom. Moreover their faces are extraordinarily revealing. All their sensations are reflected there, even when they conflict with each other. They turn pale over nothing. Their eyes widen, their lips tighten; they have no control over themselves. I suppose that Agnes, alone in the empty apartment, threw a fit of hysterics. Instead of going to her room she made for Edouard's study and collapsed into an armchair. Every now and then she gave vent to a sort of scream which she tried to stifle by cramming her hand into her mouth. For a quarter of an hour she was incapable of thinking of anything, that is to say of analyzing her pain. This was like a solid block which made her suffer in every fiber of her being, dwelling in every part of her.

She was half hanging over the arm of the chair, feeling as if she were about to choke. She was pressing her hand into her ribs below her left breast, so great was the physical pain down this whole side of her body.

She was panting hoarsely like a lumberjack. From time to time she emitted a moan like a woman in labor. It was like a long low howl, as much of hatred as of despair. She bit her fingers, she chewed at her little handkerchief. Suddenly she was seized with an attack of pins and needles; jumping up, she began to walk or, to be more precise, flounder round the room. She went from wall to wall, from corner to corner, without knowing what she was doing, driven only by the need for movement; she longed to escape from her body as from a prison. She even hammered her small fists and her forehead against the wall, seeking through physical pain to deaden the spiritual pain possessing her. She opened the window with the intention of climbing over the balcony and jumping. I think that what held her back was the thought of her three children—a thought so constantly uppermost in this mother's mind that it immediately rose up before her. "I've got to calm down," she kept repeating out loud without hearing what she was saying. "I've simply got to calm down." But before this could happen she had to commit some act of violence. Viciously she snatched up off Edouard's desk an antique crystal goblet in which he kept his pencils and to which he was very attached, and smashed it against the marble mantelpiece. Then she flung the lamp (Louis XVI style) on the floor and stamped on it. This wave of fury was succeeded by a wave of grief, but less acute. A few tears came—only a few, for Agnes was not the type to weep—but enough to bring her release and restore her powers of reasoning. Little by little she traced channels in her grief, so to speak; she tried to tune in to its various wavelengths. In flashes of clear, hard, decisive thought she began to make her way through her suffering soul. What plunged her into such despair was not the fact of having been deceived, but of having been deceived by Edouard. This did not accord with the image of him which filled her heart—an image of benevolence, gentleness, sincerity and fidelity. Was this image false then? For twenty-four years she had lived alongside a man she didn't know. She had believed that with Edouard she formed one single mind and flesh, but this was not true. It had been a long illusion. Two or three times she said: "There was him and there was me: there were the two of us." With this phrase she summed up everything that had been her conviction and her life since she married, and which was now ceasing to be. "I gave him everything," she added, "I shared everything. He didn't. Now I am going to have to learn to give him nothing any more, to keep everything for myself." She was so accustomed to regarding Edouard as she regarded herself that she couldn't bring herself to conceive that he had become *someone else*. "It's as if he were dead," she thought. Well, no, it wasn't as if he were dead but something was in reality dead or withered, a flower, a connubial purity which Agnes had flattered herself that she, among all women, would possess to her dying day.

Like Edouard an hour before, she went to stand before the big Venetian mirror. A bitter spectacle! She saw a white and crumpled face, aged by grief, made ugly by rage, with big red-rimmed eyes and frizzy hair. She hated herself. What a face! Pain didn't even give it nobility but only made it ridiculous. Insultingly she declared to her reflection: "You are old. You are dowdy. How could you have believed for twenty-four years that a man like him would be content with a dreary little woman like you? Old, dowdy and presumptuous! The love one gives doesn't make up for one's dowdiness. Understanding is no substitute for beauty. We were not a unique couple. Poor fool! We are a couple like any other: Monsieur has tarts and Madame is the last to know about it." In brief, she spent two very savage hours in Edouard's study, besieged as she was on two fronts by despair and rage which swept over her in waves, sometimes alternately, sometimes together. In this storm there were moments of lucidity during which she tried to revise her feelings and principles, like a woman preparing to change her way of life because she has been ruined or left a widow. Of all the tales of mythology, that of the poor satyr Marsyas flayed alive by Apollo has always made me shudder. Well, Agnes spiritually underwent a similar torture. A ferocious god against whom she had committed no offense ripped the skin off her soul, that is to say that protective membrane, that tissue of sentiments, habits, illusions and beliefs which covers and is incorporated in the soul of every one of us.

Do you remember something I said when I was describing the first blows Solange dealt Roberti, namely that what is so frightful about the pains of love is that they are inflicted by the one person to whom one would like to run for protection and comfort? This observation is all the more true with regard to Agnes who, for twenty-four years, whenever she had the slightest worry, would unburden herself to her husband, who immediately relieved her of it. It is correct to say that in love he who deceives betrays, since what his victim feels is truly the effect of a betrayal: the latter had a friend, an ally whom he believed to be incorruptible but who suddenly crosses over to the enemy and by this defection deprives him of almost all his strength. Don't, however, misunderstand me: Agnes was no broken reed: she had brought up three boys; as a mother, she had had plenty of leisure to learn that one must love people for themselves, for their own salvation, and that the wounds they inflict can be healed only by being cauterized. In short she knew that faults have to be punished, not in compliance with some vague and abstract notion of justice but for the peace of mind of the culprit. She wasn't as a rule given to self-restraint. She didn't even ask herself what she would say to Edouard presently, when he came back from the Assembly. She was seething with violent words which she knew she wouldn't be able to hold back, a thousand furious, exaggerated, almost demented things which would be so many cartridges loosed off against the powers of evil. She was going to fight with Edouard, fight with her own pain and perhaps, given enough anger, hardness and inflexibility, salvage something from the disaster. What? She did not as yet know, but surely something. If she could manage not to weaken, that is to say prevent grief from encroaching upon her anger, prevent her anger from cooling down for a day, two days or more, she would get the better of fate, she would triumph over it, over Edouard, over events, by strength of spirit alone. Such was Agnes. Like all truly brave people, she didn't summon up her courage all at once, but only after a more or less prolonged, exhausting crisis and after having descended into the depths of her weakness.

Toward one o'clock that afternoon she looked at her watch and reflected how Edouard, who had said he would be home for lunch, ought to be back by now. Suddenly she couldn't bear to wait any longer. She felt an urge for action. At this moment there was a knock on the study door and Germaine's head appeared round it. "Ah, so Madame is here!" she said. "I was wondering where you were. I've been back from the market for over an hour." Lunch was ready. The boys were hungry. "Let them have it," said Agnes. "Monsieur and I will lunch later." Germaine didn't fail to note her mistress's distraught expression and hollow voice. She gave Agnes the piercing look of a vulture which has spotted an animal's carcass. She saw her chalk-white face and red eyes. Moreover Agnes was still clutching her handkerchief, which she had reduced to the state of a little wet, tattered ball. "What's the matter?" asked Germaine in a honeyed and commiserating voice. "Isn't Madame feeling well? Is there anything I can do?"—"No, thank you, Germaine," replied Agnes. "Give the boys their lunch." Germaine was so intrigued that curiosity got the better of caution. With mock artlessness she inquired: "Has Monsieur done something to upset Madame? He'd better watch out for Germaine. Germaine won't have anyone harming her precious lamb." Far from provoking confidences, this inquiry wounded Agnes. She gave her servant a cold look full of Gascon pride and, following the best bourgeois tradition, told her in the commanding voice used by housewives in 1910: "Go back to your kitchen. I don't need you." On her way back to her kitchen, Germaine told herself jubilantly: "This is it! At last! The fat's in the fire." Her jubilation didn't prevent her from being extremely annoyed by the tone Agnes had adopted to send her back to her stove. "These women are all the same," she thought. "They despise ordinary people and make sure you know it. I've only to be nice to her and she blows up at me. She's getting what she deserves. I'd be a fool to fret over her."

There's one curious detail I don't know how to explain, though it seems to me important and I wouldn't like to leave it out: nothing in the world would have led Agnes to leave Roberti's study. She had taken shelter in it as in a fortress. This place so full of her husband's presence, of his habits, his tastes, even his scent, should have filled her with aversion. But no. It was here that instinct had directed her steps, here that she was held spellbound. Almost immediately after Germaine's departure, the telephone rang. It was Edouard announcing that he wouldn't be home for lunch, that they should sit down without him, that he would eat a sandwich at the refreshment room in the Assembly. He had his everyday tone of voice. He said perfectly simple and everyday things. Agnes listened to this in a daze. Her heart was pounding; rage was buzzing in her ears. For three years Edouard had lied to her. He was still lying. He wasn't telephoning from the Assembly. How did one recognize the presence of a lie in a voice which had always had the ring of truth? She made a great effort to master herself but her tone gave her away. It was so cold, so icy that Edouard was quite frightened. "What's the matter?" he demanded. "Aren't you well? Is anything wrong?"—"Nothing," replied Agnes. "Everything's fine. Thanks for showing such an interest." At this he was panic-stricken. He instantly jumped to all the possible and most pessimistic conclusions. He begged Agnes to tell him over the telephone what was on her mind. But she remained mute. She refused to speak. His agonized questions fell into a void. "Speak!" he cried. "Say something! What have I done?" No reply. "Are you there?"—"Yes," said Agnes, "I'm here." It was at once crazy and unbearable, this conversation without rhyme or reason and yet so tragic for these two. Roberti frantically wondered how Agnes could have learned of his affair with Solange, for he never doubted for a moment what the trouble was and wondered how to stave off this new disaster. There could be no question of admitting it. On the contrary he must lie, find splendid, brand-new convincing lies. The tenderness he felt for his wife reawakened, not from a long sleep since it had never entirely gone to sleep, but from a torpor in which it had been sunk for over a year. The idea that his wife was suffering drove every other worry out of his head. His past conduct flashed through his mind and he told himself fervently that he must preserve his union with Agnes at any price, that this must not be allowed to perish, that it was the last thing left to him. Agnes was the only being in whose mind his image had not been soiled, corrupted, destroyed. After he had lost everything else, it would be too great a blow to lose her love and esteem as well. He couldn't bear that. It would kill him. This business had to be settled then and there. "I'm coming right away," he told her.

Unfortunately I only know fragments of the dispute they had in the study, brief snatches of which one or other of them repeated to me. Doubtless such a dispute proceeds without order or logic. A woman mad with grief and rage can hurl invective for a long time without saying anything very precise or conclusive. An unhappy and guilty man, constantly placed on the defensive and unable to exonerate himself on the general issue, can only answer back over points of detail. He seeks to justify himself over petty side issues. What I can affirm, at any rate, is that for most of the time this scene was a pretty frenzied affair. Confronting Edouard, Agnes found no difficulty in giving vent to her grief through rage. She screamed at him. She gave her own version of her husband's affair, that is to say she travestied it, painted it in even more sordid colors than its true ones had been. Who was this Mignot girl? A typist. Might as well say a housemaid. So this was what Edouard had found! Really, he might have picked on something better. Some beauty. Some woman of his own set. One more in keeping with his position. That, at a pinch, she might have understood. The fact remains that Agnes came from the bourgeoisie and, even in the midst of the most genuine grief, couldn't help now and then having bourgeois, hence preposterous, ideas. The social rank of Edouard's mistress humiliated her and she expressed this humiliation forcefully; it brought her the same relief as when she had smashed and stamped on the desk lamp. And how did she look, this creature? A flower of the Paris streets, skinny, thin-blooded, with the air of a whipped dog. Pouah! Oddly enough Edouard, normally so given to lying, felt strangely eager to re-establish the truth. In this way, by showing his wife that his affair hadn't been as wholly ugly as she affected to think, it seemed to him he was bringing her some slight consolation, redeeming himself in her sight. This, I believe, is a fairly frequent reaction with people who cannot deny their guilt when accused. Granted that they are guilty and recognized as such, they at least want to convey their true motives, their true circumstances, imagining that thereby they will extenuate their baseness. But the minor corrections which Edouard made in a quavering, almost timid voice only served further to exasperate Agnes, who knew that she was in a rage and out for blood: she saw in his reaction an undercurrent of pride. "You've seen her," said Edouard, "you know her." He reminded her of the last day of 1956 elections and the first night of *Les Misérables* at the Comédie Française. Agnes then recalled the pretty blonde and the forebodings the sight of her had inspired, and the tears sprang to her eyes. Stricken, Roberti stepped forward to take her in his arms and I would swear that, for once, there was no calculation behind this move. But she recoiled with flashing eyes and cried out with a sort of terror: "Don't touch me! Don't ever touch me again!" These were just words, and not very original ones, the sort of words spoken by jealous, furious and unhappy women, but Edouard was in such a heightened state of sensibility that he was cut to the quick. He took this behest literally. Completely stunned, he fell limply into an armchair, drooping with his head bowed, his arms dangling between his legs and a glazed expression. Agnes, across the room, closed her eyes to prevent a shudder at the sight of this broken man. She then spoke eloquently and at length of their marriage, of the twenty-four years they had lived side by side, of her past love and devotion, of her blind faith and present confusion. She was finding herself all alone at an age when women have so great a need of support. Something between them was shattered for good and all and so on. Occasionally Roberti said in a pitiful, pleading voice: "But I love you, Agnes. I've never stopped loving you. You're the dearest thing in the world to me. This whole business is nothing. It has never meant a thing." He took advantage of a lull in the storm to try to explain how everything was over between him and Solange. "It may be over for you," said Agnes. "For me it's just beginning." His despair was the greater of the two. Agnes at least was upborne by her passion; she was fighting the world, she was visibly scorched by suffering, whereas he was like Priam on the ruins of Troy. He could see nothing around him but destruction. Agnes, who was part of him, one with him, was in turn drawing away; he had cut her off from himself. He was engulfed in a black, hostile world in which there was no longer a trace of love for him anywhere. The last light had gone out.

I don't know how long this scene in Roberti's study lasted. Possibly two hours, possibly three, possibly longer. In certain circumstances time ceases to exist and the minutes are at once long and brief, interminable and dazzling in their rapidity. One wishes it were all over and at the same time longs passionately for the situation to last forever, for the torture never to end, because one knows that at the end is death. However miserable Roberti may have felt, he found the courage to ask Agnes how she had learned of his affair. With sobs of humiliation she told him of Valentin's visit and what he had said. "My God, how stupid!" thought Edouard. "The fool chooses to come on the very day when Solange breaks with me. How stupid! How hopelessly stupid!" He was so disheartened that he couldn't even feel hatred. "What are you going to do now?" he asked. "I don't know," replied Agnes. "I'll see. I'll let you know what I decide." On this I think they parted company. Agnes at last left the study. She went to lock herself into her bedroom. Throughout the whole scene Germaine had prowled around the apartment, trying from their upraised voices to catch the gist of the quarrel. She wheeled round the study in concentric circles like a vulture and raged at being unable to hear anything but a jumble of voices, moans, meaningless cries and hiccups which taught her nothing save that they were in the middle of a violent scene. This at least was entertaining. Sniggering, she said to herself: "What can be up? He hasn't kicked her out. A good thing the kids are at school, poor little things. It's not for their ears."

After Agnes' withdrawal Edouard, still sagging in his chair, discovered two things: first that he was trembling, second that he had no heart left. It was a weird sensation: he felt as if this organ had been surgically removed or, rather, anesthetized with cocaine, since it was still beating though he couldn't feel it. He was filled with confused thoughts, the common theme of which was death. Had he preserved the slightest critical sense I think he would have realized that Agnes' fury was a fury of love, that nothing was lost between him and his wife and that, in spite of her invective, she was in fact very close to forgiving him. But he was bereft of any critical sense. He was wholly taken up with what he had just seen and heard and incapable of interpreting it in any way whatsoever. He never for a moment doubted the immensity of his wife's despair. You will say that I see the Devil everywhere but I think that just then the Devil was close by, whispering with his persuasive voice in Roberti's ear: "Your wife loves you as no man has ever been loved. You have gambled with this prodigious love which you, alone among men, have known how to inspire. You have gambled and lost. You are surely going to cause this being, who loved you above all else in all the world, to die of grief." Roberti listened in terror to this voice without perceiving that it was the voice of vanity. "I must get ahead of Agnes," he thought. "I must get ahead of the whole world. I must be the first to die." The idea that he was going to die immediately filled him with sorrow and sweet consolation. It is a comforting thing to die when one has failed in every respect. One cannot struggle on forever in a lost cause. One has to turn a new page. "Well," he told himself, "now I'm going to turn the last page. The book is ended. Or at least I have no wish to know the rest of it. It's too sinister!" He even felt no interest in future political events, curiosity over which is so great that it would restrain many a man on the brink of suicide. The government was as rotten and insecure as he was. One of these days it would collapse, and what would be put in its place? A camarilla of generals living like satraps at Algiers, who would come one morning by plane to take over power in Paris. Their first care would be to dissolve the Assembly. The France of tomorrow wore a face hardly welcoming for Radical deputies. It would be better to be done with it right away. The Republic, France, the world which would be slaughtering itself within two years, Roberti himself who within six months would be reduced to penury or prison—all these lost causes sickened him beyond words. He didn't even have a thought for his three sons: they had completely escaped his mind. On the other hand he tenderly evoked Solange, who had made him so unhappy after having loved him so well. He would die thinking of her. Her pretty face would be the last image he would take out of this life. He would have given everything he had to be able just then to rest his head on Solange's bosom and close his eyes. Everything he had to feel her gentle hand stroking his hair. He couldn't die without seeing her once more. Besides, his death would only have meaning if it took place before the eyes of her who was at bottom responsible for it. By killing himself in front of Solange he would bring her one final tragic gift, he would procure her one last thrill. Who could tell? She might possibly realize that she loved him alone and spend the rest of her days mourning for this man she had failed to understand.

Among his various ornaments Roberti possessed a little eighteenth-century dagger, very bright and sharp, with a carved ivory handle; he kept this on his table and sometimes toyed with it. He now drew it from its sheath and pressed its point against his thumb, where a drop of blood immediately appeared. In his mind there blended the two images of Agnes and Solange, who were the two poles of his emotions and who, each in her way, were making him suffer beyond all enduring. He pulled on his overcoat. He put the little dagger in his breast pocket. It must have been five P.M. It had been a beautiful day. The falling twilight was pellucid. Roberti was convinced that he was preparing to do the only, most logical, most inevitable thing it remained in his power

to do. Everything he had experienced during the past year was leading
him to this final step: to ring at Solange's front door and, when she
opened it, give her one last long look and plunge the dagger into his
heart. A feeling of insurmountable doom is common to every type of
act of folly. With immense sorrow he set out for the Avenue Daumesnil.

I don't know if you realize it, but we have now reached the end, or
almost the end, of our story. We are not embarking on the last act but
on the last scene, the last gesture. And, like all those which have gone
before, this last gesture was fortuitous. It wasn't written in advance,
unless it were in the great book of good and evil which unfolds a vast
novel, full of incoherence and chance. Poor Roberti! It was written that
down to his very last moment he would stand apart from life and nothing he did would have any meaning. He had never been to Solange's
place, but he knew what floor her apartment was on. He arrived panting
outside her door, for there was no elevator and climbing the stairs had
increased still further the excited pounding of his heart. After vainly
waiting two minutes for this to subside he rang the bell. He heard a
shuffling of rather heavy footsteps, then the latch gave a fateful click.
The door was opened. Valentin stood there in his shirtsleeves with his
tie unknotted. Roberti was stupefied. It had never occurred to him
that he might be greeted by someone other than Solange. At least
thirty seconds ticked by during which the brother and lover of Mlle.
Mignot stood silent with the shock of finding themselves at last face
to face. Then both began to speak at once. "Let me in," said Roberti, "I
want to see Mlle. Mignot."—"Christ," cried Valentin, "I've never seen
such nerve. You here! Get the hell out of it, you dirty bastard! How can
you possibly expect to see Mlle. Mignot? Don't you think you've done
her enough harm already? I'll smash your face in first!" Roberti was as
pale as Valentin was scarlet. Confronting this man who out of stupidity
and misplaced zeal had provoked the catastrophe, he felt rage lick round
him like a flame, flashing up from his feet to his brain. It was a rage
such as he had never experienced before, a seismic, convulsive rage
obliterating every human feeling and making all his limbs tremble as if
he were afraid. And indeed I believe he was afraid of this rage which
suddenly raced through him like a monster. I believe he tried to resist
it, made immense efforts to remain cool, say nothing, prevent his teeth
from grinding, his muscles from contracting, his eyes from flashing. In
order to stay calm he forced himself to keep his eyes lowered. Observing
his chalk-white and ravaged face, Valentin misconstrued the reason for
this agitation. He told himself that now was his chance to finish off
the morning's work. An extremely simple plan immediately formed in

his head. Since he had his hands on his sister's lover, he would take this opportunity to shatter her hateful liaison forever. In far less violent tones he said: "If you want to talk, you'd better come in then. There's no point in the neighbors overhearing what I have to say to you." He closed the door and led Roberti to his room. Father and Mother Mignot, who were in the dining room, wondered who had rung. But the brief altercation on the landing had rather dampened their curiosity. They looked at each other. "It's some business of Valentin's," declared Father Mignot. "I'm steering clear of it. He's big enough to look after himself."—"Too true," said Mother Mignot. "Valentin has his own life; he has his friends and his enemies. We're too old for that sort of thing." Father Mignot settled back in his chair and picked up his paper. Mother Mignot went on with her knitting.

Roberti was concentrating so hard on mastering his rage that he noticed nothing of the place to which he had been led, which was an ordinary bedroom furnished with a brass bedstead and a cupboard with a mirror. He was standing with his fists clenched behind his back. Valentin stood facing him, seething with agitation, glowering, with his eyes starting from his head. "If you've come to tell me I did wrong in speaking to your wife," he said, "I warn you I have no intention of putting up with any reproaches from a fellow like you."—"I came to see Solange," said Roberti in an exaggeratedly gentle voice. This was all it required to needle Valentin, who began to shout that Roberti had "dishonored his sister enough," that he had turned her into a whore, that it was a disgrace on the part of a married man and a father, etc. This hysterical diatribe lasted five good minutes during which Valentin became progressively more and more worked up. Toward the end he raised his voice so high that his vociferations penetrated the partition and the old Mignots in the dining room eyed each other anxiously. With a cowardly snigger Father Mignot said: "My, they're having a real row next door."—"Don't you think we ought to go and see, all the same?" queried the mother. Finally they decided not to budge, in pursuance of the principle cherished by humble folk that one must always be *discreet*, that it is better to die rather than interfere. During his diatribe Valentin had advanced until he was standing right up against Roberti and shouting into his face. Roberti was overcome by the revolting smell of his adversary's sweat. "I must get out of here right away," he thought, "or God knows what rage will lead me to do. But if I go, this fool will think I'm scared of him." Now he wasn't scared. This even momentarily astonished him. He failed to appreciate that, like all excessively unhappy people whose misfortunes have deadened their sensibilities, he was beyond all fear. All at once he had a disastrous idea: he must speak up at all costs. It was really intolerable—being insulted by a cretin who didn't even know Solange had broken with him and was engaged to someone else, who didn't know the cards and wanted to play all the same. But how to get a word in between this flood of foul and absurd insults? There was only one way possible: to shout even louder. He had an inspiration and veritably yelled: "Will you shut up!" A fatal step: it unleashed all the pent-up fury which for the past ten minutes he had been controlling with such difficulty. It broke all the barriers of his will, unknotted all the cords whereby the poor man had sought to bind his soul. Rage flooded through him like a sea of fire. It seared his legs, exploded his chest, blinded his eyes, swelled his muscles, transformed his brain into bubbling lead, deafened his ears; it projected him out of his soul and body. With his left hand, without knowing what he was doing, he grabbed Valentin by the tie. It seemed to him that this big man, purple with rage, was shriveling up before him, becoming tiny, losing all semblance of reality. With his right hand he seized the dagger in his pocket, pulled off its sheath with his teeth and brandished it like an assassin. "Will you be quiet, you fool! Will you be quiet!" he jabbered. "I don't want to hear another word from you. Never!" His hands were like steel. Their gestures precise and economical. They were bewitched; the strength in them belonged as little to this world as the will driving them. Half throttled, Valentin helplessly flailed his arms. "He's going to kill me!" he thought. He tried to cry out but managed nothing more than a choking gurgle. His last words were: "Papa, Mama, Solange!" Then he fell with a thud to the floor in a great welter of blood, dead. Unhesitatingly, unflinchingly, Roberti had with one blow plunged his dagger into Valentin's heart.

i: My God!

he: And there you are. Roberti's story is over. As in Faust, Valentin died for seeking to avenge his sister's honor. Covered in blood, Roberti fled from the Mignots' apartment like one damned. He was arrested that same night. The rest is familiar. All you have to do is consult the newspapers of the time.

i: So Valentin died without knowing that his sister was going to marry Legay, without suspecting that in the long run he had won, that all his sufferings had borne fruit.

he: Yes. He died a few feet from his parents, who let him be killed because they didn't want to "interfere."

i: It's all quite revolting.

HE: Yes, you're right. Murders become truly revolting when one is reduced to feeling sorry for the murderer.

I: Well, you have achieved your ends. I'm sorry for him now. But do you remember one little thing I told you earlier?

HE: What little thing? You told me a great many.

I: This: that Roberti was possibly not so much the dupe of his sentiments as you have all along maintained. This murder brings me proof of it. It wasn't for Solange that he killed Valentin. It was for Agnes. At heart he never loved Solange. But no, he didn't even kill for Agnes. He no longer loved her either. He no longer loved anyone. Do you want me to tell you why he killed? Out of boredom. Boredom is at the root of most crimes. Boredom or despair. Anyway, they're the same thing. And it is at this juncture that we catch sight of the Devil.

HE: I really no longer know what to say. I myself have believed and still believe that he was a dupe, that he loved madly with his heart and against his reason. But naturally one is never sure of love.

I: In every tale of damnation there is one character who is saved. Who was saved in the damnation of Roberti?

HE: Agnes, of course. Saved completely. I would almost say sanctified. The last time we saw her she was in a rage. But I hope you have understood that this was quite different in essence from the rage that seized hold of her husband in Valentin's bedroom and drove him to murder. It wasn't the rage of a weak man but of a strong woman, a rage she had no call to resist but, on the contrary, tried constantly to feed. Not a vengeful rage but a creative, educative rage such as angels may sometimes feel when they seek to aid sinners in spite of themselves. The unselfish rage of a mother even more than of a wife. When all was over, when the scandal and horror burst upon her, Agnes' rage subsided. She had expected despair to take possession of her soul but she misjudged herself, underestimated herself. Her rage was immediately replaced by a sort of transfigured hope, a profound gentleness and an invincible strength. She saw herself deprived of everything and it came to her as a revelation that she was richer than ever, that she had inexhaustible gifts to bestow, that during twenty-four years of quietude she had possibly amassed a store of happiness sufficient to illumine the lives of those around her to the end of their days, till the final accomplishment of the centuries. In a word, *she ceased to think about herself.* I am not saying she suddenly felt happier than she had ever been before, for that would be silly or at least wouldn't mean very much; it was more that her conception of happiness changed. She realized that it doesn't consist of being happy but of forgetting—forgetting without regret, forgetting unremittingly once and for all, flinging into a bottom-less abyss everything that personally concerns one. Not forgetting one's soul, of course, but reinstating it, occupying its full extent, filling every corner of it thanks to this prodigious discovery of charity. Yes, my friend, Agnes—this rather plain woman with her blotchy complexion, tiny nose and ringlets, this little woman who had been flattened into insignificance by twenty-four years of tranquillity—realized all of this. At least, I don't know whether she understood it or whether it was I (for I was seeing her every day at this time) who understood it for her, but I can certainly promise that she sensed it in the uttermost depths of her being. And I, the onlooker, distinctly saw day by day, hour by hour, the grace of God descending on her head, opening her heart as with a knife and, if you permit this physiological monstrosity, bringing forth from it a gush of milk.

I: When did Roberti die?

HE: By a strange coincidence he died on the tenth of November, 1958. It was a Monday. That same Monday was the opening day of the first election campaign of the Fifth Republic. Do you believe in palmistry? I rather incline to. At any rate I'll tell you something odd. A few days before he died, on the third or fourth of November, Edouard was very weak and very much thinner, looking quite yellow. A mere shadow of his former self. He happened to glance at the palm of his left hand and failed to recognize his life line; it had shortened by a good third. It had altered. I didn't know such things could happen. And then he died. He had fallen ill on the day he went to prison. This is a normal occurrence; we often see it. It's as if the body were hastening to join the spirit.

I: Poor Agnes. Does she still have her ringlets?

HE: No. She has aged a great deal. Her hair is quite white. Fate hasn't treated her kindly. After the trial her eldest son joined up. A year later he was killed in Algeria.

I: How does she live now?

HE: With difficulty. But she has a deputy's widow's pension. Her other two sons are grown up. They'll soon be earning their own livings. And she has friends. Dietz and me among others. I didn't tell you Roberti had been condemned to twenty years' hard labor. But doubtless you knew that.

I: Yes, I did.

HE: One thing puzzles me, you know. How did this man who loved beautiful things—Titian, Mozart, Stendhal, Bach—go so far as murder?

To my mind the keen pursuit of works of art ought to prevent one from falling into certain extremes of horror.

1: My dear man, loving beautiful things doesn't mean one has a beautiful soul but that one has a taste for luxury. The supreme luxury, which is the prerogative of artists of genius, doesn't presuppose that one possesses the supreme virtue, which is charity.

HE: Up, comrade, we're off! My tale is done, I apologize for any author's errors! I'm famished.

1: I too!

The Bois de Boulogne was as beautiful as a real stretch of country-side. An imperceptible breeze ruffled the trees round the lake. The ducks were sporting in the water and the swans were nuzzling in their feathers like dogs. An angler came to take up his place close by. "It's nice, eh, the Bois like this in the early morning?" he said. The sky was of so pale a blue that it was almost silver. There was already considerable warmth in the sun. Workmen on bicycles were riding silently off to work behind the trees. We rose to our feet. I whistled the first bars of the Pastoral Symphony. We went and stood at the edge of the pavement. A taxi passed. We hailed it. "I'm just starting my day," said its driver with a smile; "you're my first customers. Where can I take you, gentlemen?"